Steamboat Gothic

BY

FRANCES PARKINSON KEYES

JULIAN MESSNER, INC. NEW YORK

To the memory of
HERMINE BACHER DEUTSCH
Who, when I was a stranger,
Received me with kindness
Acknowledged me as her neighbor
Cheered me with her hospitality
Shared with me her culture
And honored me with her affection

AMERICAN   STEAMBOATS

Theirs was no beauty of sharp prows and spars
Or bowsprits slanting upward towards the stars,
Porthole, or squat huge funnel, rakish mast
Sky-scraping to catch clouds that linger past;
Nor theirs the beauty of the deep keels that go
Cutting far down beneath the ocean's flow,
Cleaving the gusty rollers right and left,
Mounting each green hill as its crest is cleft
To settle troughward with each passing swell! . . .
Ships of the sea I loved not half so well
As these:—who wore strange beauty all their own—
The mighty river boats that I have known
And have long lost, save that I still may find
Their mirrored likenesses within my mind.

Can you not hear them now—their blended notes
Fluting at dawn from steam-stained copper throats
Over the water, up the shelving bank,
By forest ways and fields yet dewy dank,
Through the hushed town and yet unpeopled street,
In at your window? Music mellow and sweet!
Where shall I find it—that strange music, gone,
Of steamboat whistles blowing in the dawn?

Can you not see them still, airy and white,
Tall-chimneyed, surface-gliding, moving light
As shallops on ten thousand miles of river?
Scarcely their passing made the surface quiver
In lessening bright waves. Now they are gone!
Each to its destined fate—a proud white swan.
And we who loved them look for them in vain
On now unburdened rivers. . . . Ah, not again
Shall tawny streams, once crowded with their weight,
Bear gulfward river argosies of freight
In the great packets! No, nor shall there be
That flounced, side-whiskered aristocracy
Of ladies, captains, judges, gentlemen—
A gay proud people, on their decks—as when
Those swift white steamboats yet supplied their need
And twenty miles an hour was reckoned speed!

Yet here on silent nights I think there floats
A ghostly company of lovely boats
(Dark shapes, against a dark like amethyst!
Still misty hulls, yet whiter than the mist!)
And moving on the channels without sound
Great wheels ply endlessly around, around,
While neither waves nor ripples rise and die
To show the mystery of their passing by!

—By Garnett Laidlaw Eskew, from *The Pageant of the Packets,*
New York, 1929: Henry Holt & Co.

I have observed several times before—and shall probably have occasion to observe several times again—that sometimes titles are written to stories and sometimes stories are written to titles. In my case, the latter has been true in two outstanding instances—*Queen Anne's Lace* and *The River Road*. It is even truer in the present instance.

It is now nearly ten years since I first heard the term Steamboat Gothic applied to that type of architecture which was inspired by the style of the floating palaces that plied the Mississippi River during its Golden Age, and which was developed by the retired captains and wealthy planters who wished their permanent homes to resemble, as closely as possible, the sumptuous vessels they were accustomed to command or on which they habitually traveled. I was instantly struck by the originality and cogency of the designation; in two words, it enabled me to envision a period and a mode of life more vividly than I ever had before. Shortly thereafter, while driving along the river road between New Orleans and Baton Rouge late one afternoon, an abrupt turn in the highway suddenly revealed a magnificent mansion which was the embodiment of the term I had found so striking. Almost as suddenly, I knew that someday I should have to write a novel entitled *Steamboat Gothic*.

The force of that conviction never lessened; but as time went on, the character of my work and my general mode of life took me farther and farther away from this special source of inspiration; it looked as if that particular project should be relegated to the dim and distant future. Then an unwelcome period of enforced physical inactivity, following a severe siege of illness, confined me, for nearly four months, to my bedroom and its adjacent study in the slave quarters of Beauregard House. I could not set out from New Orleans in search of the source material which I had meant to make the basis of my next book; on the other hand, it was clear to me that a protracted convalescence would be doubly tedious if I passed it in idleness. The opportune moment had arrived—sooner than I expected—to work on *Steamboat Gothic*. My acquaintance with the river road was by this time long and intimate, and I had already secured the kind permission of the magnificent mansion's present owners to use it as the setting for a story peopled with imaginary characters. They came to life as quickly as if they had been awaiting such summons. For days on end I wrote more rapidly than I had ever

---

* N.B. To be skipped by reviewers who admittedly find such forewords tedious. This one is not written in defiance of their respected opinions, but in an effort to placate the readers who have clamored for a resumption and expansion of the explanations as to why, how and with whose assistance such a story happened to be written, after observations of this character had been omitted or abbreviated in previous volumes, through deference to the critics' viewpoint. There is a good old German proverb to the effect that *Allen zu gefallen ist unmöglich*. Since it is indeed impossible to please everyone, and since there are, fortunately, more readers than reviewers, it seems best, in this instance, as in many others, to heed the mandate of the majority.

written before—sometimes as much as sixty pages without a break. I flattered myself that for once in my life I was going to produce a novel without much effort and without stirring from my own hearthstone. I could not possibly have been more mistaken.

I was first brought to a halt by the realization that however much I knew about the river road, I knew comparatively little about the allied subject of steamboating. Conscientious and omnivorous reading failed to bring it alive in the same way that my imaginary characters had come alive. The beautiful poem entitled "American Steamboats," by Garnett Laidlaw Eskew, which appears on a flyleaf of his fine book *The Pageant of the Packets,* and which he has kindly permitted me to have reprinted on a flyleaf of *Steamboat Gothic,* conjured up a vision of splendor. A passage from *Mississippi Steamboatin',* by Herbert and Edward Quick, gave me the following vivid generalization: "Cotton was king, and though the steamboat business extended over the Mississippi, the Missouri, the Ohio and practically all their navigable tributaries, it is the lower Mississippi that is remembered as the river of steamboats; the river where every boat had a nigger on the safety valve, a gambler on the hurricane deck and romance in the cabin." Louis C. Hunter, in *Steamboats on the Western Rivers,* supplied me with information on that phase of steamboat adornment of the most immediate interest to me by stating that "To the predominantly backwoods population of the west 'steamboat gothic' was an esthetic experience. The decorator . . . laid out the whole surface [of the ceiling] in arches and pendants, fretwork and scrolls, covering it with paint, gilt, and gold leaf; letting it be tinted by sunlight falling through stained glass. At night the ceiling was brightened by soft light from candelabra or later by the brilliant blaze from gilt and crystal chandeliers. . . . It was the handling of the ceiling and supporting members . . . that gave rise to the term 'steamboat gothic.' " And finally, George Dangerfield, in *The Era of Good Feelings,* summed up the subject for me by saying, "The river steamboat went against the current; it was always in danger from its own mechanism; it was threatened by snags and the weird shiftings of the river bed: *but it has survived in memory as the greatest and most loved adventure that America has produced."*

And still I was not satisfied; in spite of my ever-quickening enthusiasm, I felt I was not learning enough. I wanted to see plans and models of steamboats, so that I would know exactly where the staterooms were placed in relation to the saloons, whether they were large or small and how they were furnished. I wanted to see old steamboat menus, so that I would know what the passengers ate and, in this connection, at what hours they were served and in what manner. I wanted to see copies of old steamboat newspapers, so I would know what the passengers read, in the intervals between drinking and dancing, gaming and gossiping. I wanted to know something about the personalities and peculiarities of outstanding steamboat captains, something about the songs which the roustabouts sang, something about the ways of speech among the men, from the highest degree to the lowest, who "followed the river." In short, my curiosity, once roused, became almost insatiable; an extensive correspondence with one of the greatest living authorities on steamboating—Captain Frederick Way, Jr., of Sewickley, Pennsylvania—soon convinced me that I needed to confer with him personally, and not only with him but with various other authorities who could supplement his knowledge and experience. This conviction took me to Newport News, to Pittsburgh, to Marietta and—through the courtesy of the Ashland Oil and Refinery Company—down the Mississippi River from Ashland to New Orleans, on the maiden voyage of the towboat *Aetna-Louisville*. It also led to a series of later conferences in New Orleans, whither Captain and Mrs. Way and their friend Mr. John Zenn—who had already given me the benefit of his familiarity with iron foundries while I was in Pittsburgh—opportunely came on the annual spring voyage of the *Delta Queen*. In these conferences, Mr. Leonard Huber—another outstanding authority on the subject of steamboating, whose "home port" is the Crescent City—and Hermann B. Deutsch, associate editor of the New Orleans *Item*—always my best and most faithful editorial adviser—joined the Ways, Mr. Zenn and myself. Later, through the good offices of Mr. Deutsch, his friend Mr. Michael McDougall, still another outstanding authority, checked and rechecked the references to gambling. Internationally renowned as a detector of crooked gambling practices, which he has consistently exposed, it was he who suggested one of the gambling artifices which figures in the development of the story of Cindy Lou.

Before all this happened, however, I had come to the realization that Newport News was by no means the only place to which I needed to return in Virginia, or its director and librarian Dr. Frederick Floyd Hill and Mr. John L. Lochhead, the only persons in my native state whom I needed to consult. The never-failing courtesy and co-operation of the great historian Douglas S. Freeman, who is always ready to share his vast knowledge with writers less gifted and less learned than himself; the further helpfulness of his accomplished secretary Mrs. O. O. Ashworth; and the gracious hospitality of his lovely wife all contributed to make a stay in Richmond one of memorable personal delight, as well as one of immeasurable professional benefit. Clifford Dowdey, the author of one of the finest novels ever written on the War Between the States—*Bugles Blow No More*—and other works of comparable excellence, was a further contributor to the pleasure and profit of my Richmond visit. I am very proud to number him among my helpers and both him and his wife among my friends.

Other Virginians who have assisted me in one way or another with my research, and to whom I wish to acknowledge my indebtedness, are Dr. Lewis M. Hammond, dean of the Department of Graduate Studies at the University of Virginia, and Archer Jones and James E. Kinard, also of the University; August Dietz, Jr., of Richmond; and J. Randall Caton, Coleman Gray and Meredith Johnson of Alexandria.

Pennsylvania, Ohio, Kentucky and Virginia by no means brought me to the end of my wanderings: a Christmas present from my friend Colonel Jules Amiot of Saumur, which took the form of a beautiful book about certain chateaux in the west of France, led to the conviction that one of these should form the *mise en scène* for part of that portion of the new novel which would logically be laid in France. It happened, I think almost providentially, to be one I had never seen—La Roche-Courbon—situated in a region—Charente-Maritime—with which I was wholly unfamiliar. Through correspondence, both Colonel Amiot and his friend M. Garneaud of Cognac helped to make these less unfamiliar—and very enticing. The next step seemed equally logical: as soon as I was well enough I embarked, accompanied by my faithful secretary Deanie Bullock on a small French cargo the *Cavelier de la Salle,* which landed us at La Pallice, the new port of La Rochelle, within half a day's easy motoring distance of La Roche-Courbon. There we were most kindly received by the present proprietor M. Paul Chenereau and his sister Mme Chenet. Far from putting any obstacles in my path, when I explained my mission they took me from attic—which is a chapel—to cellar—which is a dungeon—of their chateau, and guided me through their enchanted forest to its secret bowers, its prehistoric grottoes, its rippling river and its perfidiously placid pool.* Meanwhile, they shared with me the legends which have sprung, inevitably, from such magic settings. Many of these have simply been handed down verbally from one generation to another; but I am by no means the only author to whom the charm of this place has been irresistible. In *La Roche-Courbon Beau Manoir de Saintonge,* Pesmé sketches its history from its foundation in the fifteenth century to the present day, and I am indebted to this slim but charming volume not only for much solid information, but for the lighter stories about the gypsies who once frequented the estate, which I have adapted to my own uses. Moreover, that great genius Pierre Loti made La Roche-Courbon the subject of the classic appeal which he called *La Belle-au-Bois-Dormant,* and which undoubtedly saved this splendid property from the devastation of its forest. It had been bought, after passing from the possession of the family which had owned it for centuries, by a ruthless industrialist who visualized its matchless trees merely as so much lumber. Probably today nothing would remain of the forest—the most beautiful one, I think, that I have ever seen —if Loti had not so magnificently protested against its destruction and if M. Chenereau had not rescued it through his purchase. Now, thanks to these two, it has been preserved for posterity.

A degree of helpfulness, similar to that with which I have been favored by M. Chenereau and Mme Chenet at La Roche-Courbon,** has been shown me by Mr. Leslie Levet at San Francisco—that perfect example of the Steamboat Gothic, whose architecture so swiftly captured my imagination the first time I beheld it and whose charm for me, after all these years, has in no way diminished. Mr. Levet, himself an important planter, represents his near kinswoman Miss Orley, the owner of San Francisco, who is not in robust health; and it is due to his good offices that I have been able to visit the house and grounds freely, find and study their history and—best of all— secure permission to fictionize them under the name of Cindy Lou. It is, of course, superfluous to add that none of my imaginary characters at Monteregard and Cindy Lou bear the slightest resemblance to anyone now living at or near La Roche-Courbon and San Francisco or to any relative of theirs who has lived in these places during the past. The first white settler who

---

* On the occasion of my second visit, a year after my first, M. Chenereau's head gardener M. Louis Penot accompanied Mme Chenet and myself to the grotto called the Cathedral and built a fire there, so that I could see the effect of its light upon the encircling stone and hence describe it accurately. This will give some idea of the lengths to which my kindly hosts went in their helpfulness.

** In my story, I have called La Roche-Courbon Monteregard.

helped the Indians in the culture of the unique tobacco—perique—which grows only on one small triangle of land near Convent, Louisiana, was indeed named Pierre Chanet, and the tobacco derives its name from an affectionate corruption of his by the Indians; but, as far as I have been able to discover, he did not leave any descendants—certainly none who had the names and traits that I have given to characters in this book. The erection and embellishment of San Francisco took place under circumstances similar —though not identical—to those I have described; but any resemblance which may be imagined between its actual builder and the fictional Marchand Labouisse is entirely accidental; and the characteristics of Dorothée Labouisse are based, not on those of anyone who has lived at San Francisco, but on those of a lovely but erring lady who lived at La Roche-Courbon several centuries ago and who, to the best of my knowledge and belief, left no descendants.

The idea of finally transforming the Big House at Cindy Lou into a community center was suggested to my mind by the fact that this is exactly what was done at Destrehan, a fine old plantation house, now owned by the Pan-Am Oil Company, which is situated on the river road somewhat closer to New Orleans than San Francisco. A vice-president of this company Mr. R. T. Colquette, and Mr. Rogers and Mr. Heiss of his Public Relations Department, have been extremely helpful to me in the correlation of material applying equally well to both places, and in supplementing Mr. Levet's information—with the premises as factual examples—as to how, when and why the ground-floor rooms in plantation houses have been frequently adapted to business purposes, both in the past and in the present.

I myself have a modest collection of *veilleuses* to which I am slowly but steadily adding; some of those described in *Steamboat Gothic* have their counterparts at Compensation, my house in Crowley, Louisiana. However, the far finer and larger collection belonging to Mme Pierre Poirier of Paris and Dr. Frederick D. Freed of New York have furnished me with even more extensive source material on which to base my descriptions of these uniquely charming old night lamps.

I observed, somewhat earlier in this Foreword, that when I began to write *Steamboat Gothic* I did so with a certain amount of confidence because of the familiarity, based on ten years' acquaintance with the region where the style of architecture so designated came to its finest flower. But of course the further the story progressed, the more knowledge I sought, not only about local architecture but about local laws, local products, local institutions of learning, local customs, local celebrations—in fact, about everything that goes into the life of a community. For information along all these various lines, I am indebted, most of all, to Hermann B. Deutsch, whose vast store of knowledge about everything connected with Louisiana is comparable in extent to his great love of the state and whose kind helpfulness to me has been equally inexhaustible. But I am also greatly indebted to Mr. C. Cecil Bird, Jr., Mr. Lewis Gottlieb and Mr. Elemore Morgan of Baton Rouge; Mother Alice Kock of Grand Coteau; the Reverend Eugene Bleakley of Convent; Mr. Edward P. Munson of Napoleonville; Mr. and Mrs. Warren Roussel of La Place; Mr. and Mrs. Conner Randolph of Romeville; and Mrs. John St. Paul, Jr., Mr. Eberhard P. Deutsch, Mr. Samuel

Wilson, Jr., Mr. and Mrs. Robert Crager, Dr. Robert C. Kelleher and Mrs. M. L. Clark, all of New Orleans.

My own household, as well as those friends who are close to it, should have its meed of praise. If Deanie Bullock had not been as ready to work endless hours in the office leading from the patio at Beauregard House as she is to board a ship with very little advance notice, the typescript of *Steamboat Gothic* would never have been done on time. If Clara Wilson had not been willing to give me a cup of soup and a sandwich at ten or eleven o'clock at night, instead of a normal supper at a normal hour, I could not have worked on and on myself, when the words were coming almost of themselves—or when they would hardly come at all and I knew that somehow I must get them on paper before I stopped. If Carroll Fuller had not kept the garden growing in the summer and the fires going in the winter, at the Oxbow and Pine Grove Farm, I could not have ranged the world in the interests of my writing with an easy mind, knowing that the places dearest of all to me were safe in his keeping. And if Creacy and Beverly King had not given the same faithful care to Lucky and her progeny at Compensation, I could not have looked forward to that chorus of joyous barks and that trustful and undemanding canine companionship which are always among the most important parts of my welcome.

Going farther afield, I must include in the record the statement that Miss Jacqueline Parsons, Miss Marilyn Moral and Mrs. Doris Flowers, all of New York City, were of great assistance in establishing the authenticity of details regarding the Fifth Avenue Hotel, as it appeared in 1869, and the general picture, as far as theatrical entertainment, dressmaking establishments and department stores and sailing schedules of the same period were concerned.* Miss Edna G. Grauman of the Louisville Free Public Library and Miss Audrey Sturgeon, also of Louisville, Kentucky, made available to me copies of contemporary press descriptions of the *Richmond*.** Mrs. B. F. Reiter, director of the Campus Martius Museum at Marietta, Ohio, was equally helpful in regard to contemporary press accounts of other steamboats and in many supplementary ways. The Hon. James G. Fulton, member of Congress from the Thirty-first Congressional District of Pennsylvania, Mr. Philip H. Lantz, director of the Historical Society of Western Pennsylvania. Captain Walter C. Booth,*** Mr. David C. Chaplin, Mr. Herbert A. May, Mrs. Clifford Heinz, Mr. and Mrs. Clifford

* M. Sven Nielsen, Director of Les Presses de la Cité, performed a similar service in regard to Paris.

** In order to achieve the best results, fictionally speaking, the *Richmond* is presented, in *Steamboat Gothic*, as plying between St. Louis and New Orleans. Actually, she plied between Louisville and New Orleans. With the same results in mind, her destruction by fire, which actually took place in 1869, has been postponed, fictionally, for a few months. Similar liberties have been taken in regard to the gravel pit at Cindy Lou and the change in the position of the levee in that locality. Actually, there is no gravel pit within thirty miles of this region and, though the levee was moved back slightly in 1892, its position was not radically changed until 1930.

*** Captain Booth, like his father and grandfather before him, followed the river and now his son is worthily carrying on the great tradition. His untimely death, which occurred shortly after my stay in Pittsburgh, represents a tremendous loss to the lore of steamboating and, consequently, to all those who hold this important and precious, as well as to his innumerable personal friends. He first became interested in my under-

x

Hood, Mr. and Mrs. Roy Arthur Hunt, Mr. Russell Steele, Mr. John T. Shillingford, Mrs. Thomas M. Jones, Mr. and Mrs. Jonathan Raymond, all of Pittsburgh, contributed in different ways to the pleasure and profit of my stay there.

Many details of the revival of barge-and-towboat activity on the river just prior to the first World War were given me by Captain Joseph Chotin and by his son, Captain Scott Chotin. In an era of demands for "assistance," it is worth noting that the senior member of this family partnership factually founded a transportation dynasty by raising and rehabilitating the hull of a sunken steamboat from the waters of Lake Verret.

The Spanish-American War was the first of which I have a definite memory and it inspired my first crude but impassioned attempts at verse * and the collection of other war verses which I painstakingly copied, under the general caption "Gems of Poetry," in a ruled copybook similar to those I still use for all my penciled drafts. Last summer, while going through old trunks in our spacious New England attic, I found this long-forgotten copybook and succumbed to the temptation of reading it through. Among the "gems" which I thus rediscovered was one entitled "The Yankee Dude'll Do," published in the old *Life*, of which Tom Masson was editor. I feared that my younger readers would be confused if I mentioned *Life* in the text of the novel as the source of the verses which Mabel shows to Miss Sophie. Naturally, the oncoming generation thinks of *Life* in different terms. (No intention of a bad pun, but an explanation of my reason for my reference to the former *Life* only as "a prominent weekly"; to which I should like to add a glad tribute to the present superb publication whose name is the only thing it has in common with the periodical of my childhood.)

My enthusiasms at this time were by no means confined to literary (?) efforts, either my own or those published by Tom Masson. Joseph Wheeler —"Fightin' Joe"—was my great hero, and I insistently claimed relationship with him on the strength of our common surname; a chance meeting with him, in a corridor of the Capitol, represented the highlight of a spring trip to Washington. Years later, when I went to live in Washington as a senator's wife, his daughter Julia—Mrs. William J. Harris, wife of the late Senator Harris of Georgia—became one of my most valued friends, and once a year we received together. So my acquaintance with his remarkable career, though certain details of it have been refreshed by Mr. Dyer's excellent biography, goes back a long, long way. I hope no one will feel that I

---

taking through the intermediary of Captain Way, and entered into extensive correspondence with me. Afterward, I had the benefit of several personal conferences with him; and it was he who first suggested—not only to me but to the Ashland Oil and Refinery Company—that it would be a good plan for me to travel by towboat down the Mississippi River. Mr. Paul Blazer, the president of this organization, and his associates Mr. John Fox and Mr. James Wallen made the arrangements for this delightful trip, in the course of which I did a tremendous amount of writing, under conditions far more restful than those I am usually able to achieve.

* These were printed in a local weekly, the *Bradford Opinion,* and, as far as I can recall, were the first product of my pen to be published, though five years earlier still, at the age of seven, I had "collaborated" with a contemporary in the writing of a "pageant," which was enacted by the authors and other contemporaries in my mother's drawing room.

should apologize for giving so important a general—who was actually a far greater hero than my childish fancy could envision—such an unworthy fictional lieutenant as Bushrod Page. It was only through the medium of Bushrod, as the story developed, that I could bring Wheeler into the book, and I wanted very much to pay this tribute to his memory.

The verses which World War I evoked differed as much in feeling as they did in form from those obligingly printed in the *Bradford Opinion*. The sobering—and sometimes shattering—awareness of the real meaning of the prayer for deliverance from battle, murder and sudden death had long since supplanted earlier dreams of glory; neither did any one military figure emerge from afar as the hero of the day. This was probably because I was too much concerned about the men I knew personally, who would have been either amused or annoyed if I had thought of them as heroes, much less spoken of them in that manner, but who were, nevertheless, contributing in many different, difficult and dangerous ways to the winning of the war. I could not have written about any of Larry Vincent's experiences, from the time he wanted to enlist to the time he came home on the transport *St. Mihiel*, if that war had not touched me closely from various angles; but I am especially indebted to Richard Bayley Cobb—a very old friend, as well as a distant cousin—for permission to use the letters he wrote his family, from the time he left Camp Merritt in 1918 until shortly before he returned to the United States in 1919, as the basis for those attributed in this novel to my imaginary character Larry Vincent. The references to news received from home during this interval have, of course, been changed, since those in the original letters dwelt on happenings in a New England village, not on a Southern plantation; and a few corresponding fictional touches have been added, to make the character fit a Louisianian instead of a Vermonter. There have also been occasional editing, abbreviation, etc., and the final letter—the one appearing under date of April 30, 1919—is fictitious, as Richard Cobb did not join the Army of Occupation or visit at Chateau Monteregard. But, aside from this one, all the letters are genuine; they were written in the places and under the circumstances described, and voice the opinions and impressions here given; moreover, no detail of military training or service has been changed in any way.*

In this general connection, it may interest those faithful followers of my work, who were good enough to say they enjoyed *Came A Cavalier* and who are now reading *Steamboat Gothic*, to know that my own interest in Saumur was first roused by the letters Richard Cobb wrote me from there and that these laid the foundations for my visits to that pleasant place, which began in 1946 and have continued at frequent intervals ever since, and for my own happy association with the famous cavalry school.

Indeed, it seems to me rather a happy accident that the book—begun in the slave quarters of Beauregard House, because I was too ill to leave New Orleans, and could therefore write only about a region with which I was

* For their help in military research, I am indebted to Brigadier General Frank Dorn, Lieutenant Colonel E. Pendleton Hogan, Major Vernon Pizer, Captain Irwin Forman and Lieutenant Bernard Glaser, all of the Office of the Chief of Information, Department of the Army, Washington 25, D. C., and to Miss Katharine L. McKiever of the N.C.W.C. News Service.

familiar—should be finished in Saumur—whither I had come, for once, not to write about it, but to attend the famous Carrousel which marks the greatest annual celebration of its cavalry school. I am not ill any longer; there has been nothing to interfere with my pleasure in the company of my many friends, among them Colonel Amiot, who is, indirectly, so largely responsible for many portions of this book and others. I have enjoyed it all: the festivities I have shared with these friends; the beautiful countryside blooming with flowers and rich in the vineyards which produce that incomparable drink—Sparkling Saumur; the superb sunsets over the river Loire; the nightly illumination of the chateaux and churches along its shores; the ringing of its carillons on Sundays. . . . Yes, I have enjoyed it all very greatly; but I should not have said there was nothing to interfere with this enjoyment. For there has been the ever-present consciousness that *Steamboat Gothic* must go to press and that a patient publisher was waiting for its Foreword.

Logically, this consciousness brings the Foreword to an end!

FRANCES PARKINSON KEYES

Steamboat Gothic was begun on January 11, 1951, and finished on August 1, 1952. Work was done on it in all the places mentioned in the Foreword, and also at the Oxbow, Newbury, Vermont, in the early summer and late fall of 1951 before and after my first visit to La Roche-Courbon.

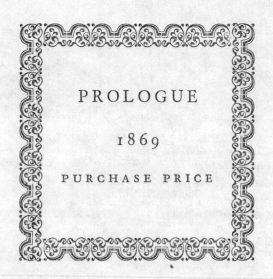

PROLOGUE

1869

PURCHASE PRICE

THE DAY was warm for March, and the stranger, who had been walking for nearly half an hour along the river road, took a fine embroidered handkerchief from the tail pocket of his burgundy-colored frock coat and mopped his face with it. Then he flicked the handkerchief lightly over his tight-fitting mouse-gray trousers and his shining congress boots. He had no mind to reach his destination dripping with sweat or powdered with dust.

He had been reasonably well pleased with his appearance when he had surveyed this, before starting out, in the blurred mirror of his room at the dirty little hostelry with the pretentious name of Grand Hotel Pierre Chanet. To be sure, he had fiddled for some moments with the long bow of his black silk tie before it suited him; but there had been no doubt whatsoever that his plain gold studs gave the finishing touch of refinement to the starched shirt bosom which the large—and undeniably flawed—diamonds, worn for so long, had failed to impart. Lucy had never made any comment on those flawed diamonds, or on the still larger—and still more imperfect—one which had formerly adorned the third finger of his left hand. But he had caught her glancing at them several times, and he had noticed the change in her expression when he substituted the gold studs and the heavy gold ring whose seal duplicated the one on the charm which dangled from the chain spanning the figured white waistcoat.

Well, it had taken him time to learn how to dress like a gentleman, but by slow degrees he had done it; and he could be thankful—and was—that he possessed the natural attributes of a fine person to set off his good clothes. If his stomach had not still been as flat as a sixteen-year-old boy's, he could have ill afforded to call attention to it by that gold chain. The mouse-gray trousers could be worn to good advantage only if they fitted closely over narrow hips and the burgundy broadcloth would have lost its effect if it had not been cut to fit wide shoulders. Moreover, there was satisfaction in the knowledge that, in addition to the advantages which his figure gave him, his fresh color belied the belief that a man must live an active outdoor life in order to have an appearance of ruddy health, and that no amount of care would have given his reddish-blond hair its burnished look if it had not been abundant and glossy to start with.

He had run a small ivory comb along its low side parting and the wavy locks above his temples before the final adjustment of a shining gray beaver "stovepipe" and, the last thing before leaving his hotel room, had passed his hand over his cheek and chin below his sideburns.

It was less than an hour since he had shaved with a fine Swedish razor, but still he wanted to be sure. . . . And, though the surface was smooth enough to suit him, he had frowned a little at the sight of his hand, as he saw this reflected in the mirror before which he was still standing. It was blunt fingered, and the back of it was haired with down, the same color as the locks he had just combed with such care. But it was softer and whiter than the hand of a vigorous man ought to be. It detracted from the fresh ruddiness of his face. He must do something about his hands. Perhaps riding about a plantation would help, getting out into the sun, handling the reins. . . . Well, the thing to do now was to reach his destination as soon as possible and find out what the prospects were. He had already told the slatternly little Negress, who brought early morning coffee and a noon breakfast to his untidy room, that he wanted her to send up one of the boys from the livery stable attached to the Grand Hotel Pierre Chanet. The awaited knock came while he was adjusting the beaver hat.

"Get the best rig you can turn out for me, and straight off, you hear?" he had directed the grinning darky who answered his summons. "I've been waiting for you the better part of the morning already. So slope right along now."

"Ah sho' is too sorry, Cap'n, me, but us got no rig for you dis day, suh, no," the boy replied, chuckling as though this were a jest of rare proportions. "All both of us buggies is took out, suh, dey is and dat's for true. Ki-yi-yi-yah!"

The boy had suddenly burst into high-pitched, cackling laughter, as if the humor of the situation had now completely overcome him.

The stranger made a gesture of impatience. "Try another livery stable then," he ordered. "Surely someone in this pocky—" He caught himself up short. If all went well, he would be part and parcel of the local scene himself in the not too distant future. Best to get off on the right foot. In a milder tone, he continued, "Surely someone hereabouts still has a horse and buggy for cash hire!"

"Ah tells you frankly, me, Cap'n-suh, it ain' ere other rig, no," the little darky chuckled. "Anyways, us rigs is too pitiful, Ah specks, me, for a quality gennelmun to drive."

"Well then, as I cipher it, I'll have to ride shanks' mare. As for you, I've told you once already not to stand there grinning at me. Now cut stick!"

The small stableboy scuttled away, without waiting for a second bidding, and the disgruntled guest, shrugging his broad shoulders, selected a cigar from a yellow leather case and lighted it with a sulphur match. Then, with a final glance of distaste at the rumpled bed and the dingy mosquito bar hanging limp and awry from its tester, he left the room, went quickly down the rickety stairs, through the open space which served as a lobby and across the unpainted gallery of the hotel.

4

In front of this, a weedy, crescent-shaped driveway, bordered along its outer arc by a hitch rack, curved away from a sawed butt of cypress which, apparently, served as a carriage block. Also within the range of vision were a general store whose canopied front extended over a loading platform, a small weather-beaten church with a squat spire, and a long brick shed which was obviously a warehouse of sorts. Beyond lay the open road, fringed on one side by the levee and on the other by open fields spreading back toward swamp forests.

"Of course I never expected any of it would look the same from the land as it did from the river," the stranger muttered to himself. "But I didn't expect it would be so *damned* different, either!"

No one spoke to him as he went through the lobby and crossed the gallery. The night before, when he stepped off the gangplank, there had been only three white men at the steamboat landing—obviously a storekeeper and his assistants. They had glanced up from the bales and crates whose tally they were checking, and even in the smoky, fitful glare of ironwork torch baskets, the stranger had been able to recognize as a sneer the glance directed at his gaily patterned carpetbag. Then, almost immediately, the three men had turned their backs on him with elaborate and calculated ostentation. Now the wispy little clerk at the hotel and the drab loungers on the front gallery, after one equally eloquent glance, looked away just as pointedly. Well, this was by no means the first time the newcomer had been treated like a pariah, and it probably would not be the last. If he had not instantly been appraised as a carpetbagger. . . . But what did it matter, as long as Lucy, far from misprizing him, had trusted him from the beginning, and had finally given complete proof of this by confiding her future into his safekeeping?

The thought of Lucy, of her trustfulness and her steadfastness, was what he needed to restore his self-confidence. At the bottom of the gallery steps, he paused before the demilune of patchy turf enclosed by the arc of the driveway, to which a cluster of azaleas in full bloom gave the only touch of beauty in sight. Aware that the eyes of the loungers were still on him, even though they seemed averted, he broke off a spray, fastened it into the buttonhole of his burgundy-colored coat and, humming the tune of "Green Grow the Rashes, Oh," set off down the river road.

However, he did not continue to hum after he was beyond earshot of the loungers. No matter how much he tried to pretend, no matter how often he told himself that Lucy's love was all that counted, he wanted the good will of men, too—wanted it and needed it, if he were to live as he hoped and expected in the future. The obvious lack of it rankled; and now there was also that disturbing consciousness of change.

"Different—all so damned different," he repeated, half aloud this time. The river looked different, seen from the land; and the land itself

5

was unrecognizable as the same he had so often regarded with absorbed attention from the texas of a passing steamboat. Even in seasons of high water, when the boats were elevated far above their normal level, so that spires and belvederes were plainly discernible above an arched screen of live oaks, magnolias and pecans, the countryside had not looked like this from the river.

For one thing, as a voyager he had always been conscious of continuing motion, and not merely of the vessel's throbbing drive, or of the tormented current whose ageless sweep was carrying a continent, grain by grain, into the sea. The riverbanks seemed to be in motion, too, passing sedately, without haste yet without halt, in and out of sight, or approaching and receding with every landing, whether this were at a plantation, a village, a woodyard or the wharves of a city. Here on shore, however, the prevailing impression was one of stillness. Metallic beyond the *batture,* the river itself seemed bereft of movement. Even time had become static. Dust motes, inertly suspended above the shimmering road, had apparently been left there by the creaking passage of yesterday's carts. Was it possible that a steamboat had brought him to this place of immobility only the night before? . . .

His train of thought was interrupted by the appearance of a wizened Negress, hobbling toward him up the river road along which he had now been trudging for more than half an hour. She wore a shapeless calico garment and three wide-brimmed hats, one perched atop the other and all made of coarsely plaited palmetto strips. He remembered now that he had seen her from the upper gallery, earlier in the day, hitching along across the path of two men who were proceeding at a leisurely pace toward the warehouse, engrossed in conversation. As her course intersected theirs, she had snatched off the top two hats, extending one, upturned, to each of the men with the single wheedling word, "Mishay!" and each had dropped a small coin into the hat nearest him. The third hat had remained on her head, shading her woolly pate from the burning sun. She was now approaching the wayfarer in much the same manner, except that she removed only one hat. He felt in his pocket, extracted three silver dollars and tossed them to her.

"Here's a coin for every one of your hats, Auntie!" he said. "Wish me luck!"

"Praise de Great I-Am, mishay!" the Negress exclaimed. "Praise de holy angels in he'm what bring Moppy to dis day o' glory. Wish you luck, mishay? Shuh, you don' need no mo' luck dan you already is got. Moppy tellin' you what Gawd love, mishay, you gwy' git yo' wish dis day, same as you taken keer o' me. Hallelujah! Bless you to de bones an' de heart an' de soul, mishay. Moppy gwy' cast her spell fo' you fo' true. Go git yo' wish, mishay. Go git it now."

She hobbled off and, almost immediately, he saw, beyond an abrupt bend in the road, the house toward which he had so persistently been

6

heading. In fact, it came into view so suddenly as to give him the triumphant feeling that, leaving aside all question of "spells," luck was with him at last; for here before him, gloriously unaltered in the midst of the prevailing change, was the object of his heart's desire.

He stood back to look at it, in the glowing light of the afternoon sun. Yes, this was as he remembered it; only, now that he was closer to the mansion of his covetous recollection, it was even more impressive, even more splendid and desirable than he had been able to discern from afar. It was not long and low and rambling, like so many of the early examples of Louisiana architecture; its Corinthian columns surrounded a massive structure which stood foursquare and which rose to the soaring height of three full stories, without even counting the belvedere which surmounted these. Neither did it have the much-vaunted simplicity—which, to his way of thinking, was mere severity—of the neoclassic ante bellum mansions; the columns, superb as these were in themselves, formed only one feature of adornment. Their iron entablature was studded with stars and wreathed with acanthus leaves; and the railings of both galleries—a lesser located above a greater—were elaborately wrought. But it was not only this variety of embellishment that made the house before which he stood a marvel in his eyes; it was likewise the almost uncanny resemblance which it bore to the most magnificent of those floating palaces where he had founded his fortunes. The broad galleries were like spacious double decks; the twin stairways, widely separated on the ground, met, high above it, at the front door, exactly as similar stairways approached the grand entrance to the main saloon on a luxurious river steamer; even the belvedere, with its glitter of glass, suggested a pilothouse. This, too, was a palace, all the more to his taste because it stood on solid ground instead of moving over the water. His wander years, or so he hoped, were behind him. He wanted a place where he could strike roots. Since this palace could not float, neither would it glide away from him, leaving him stranded. -

He was still standing, his eyes fixed in fascination on the sight before him, when the front door opened slowly and a lady came out on the gallery. He felt quite sure that she must be aware of his presence; however, she did not immediately glance in his direction, but turned a little to the right and, leaning lightly on the railing, looked down toward a near-by fountain in the garden as if there were something about it which required her attention or arrested her interest. He had almost completely overlooked the grounds, because of his absorption in the house; after all, gardens did not loom large in the consciousness of a man whose best years had been spent on river steamers. But he was glad of the opportunity afforded by the lady's apparent abstraction to observe her carefully while still not seeming to stare at her.

She was wearing black and her dress was distinctly outmoded; it had

7

all the amplitude of the prewar days, instead of the more restrained fullness currently in vogue. Nevertheless, she wore it well, even with a certain dash. Her face was oval and properly pale, bespeaking care not to risk her complexion to the sun; since she had half turned away, he could not see her eyes and quickly regretted this; on the other hand, her position gave him an advantageous view of her profile, which was piquant rather than pure, and further stimulated the admiration aroused by her sloping shoulders, swelling bosom and small waist. Her hair was as black as her gown and had far more sheen; there were quantities of it and it was elaborately arranged in a profusion of ringlets and plaits, ending in a "waterfall." Shrewdly, he guessed that she lacked the wherewithal to buy new clothes and either the skill or the incentive to remodel old ones, but that she took pleasure in following the fashions of hairdressing as displayed in *Godey's Lady's Book*. The large locket which hung from a velvet ribbon at her throat, the still larger brooch which clasped without confining the laces at her breast, and the wide bracelets which encircled her wrists were evidently all parts of a ponderous parure that had no great intrinsic value. But somehow they seemed peculiarly suited to her apparel; they became her and she wore them with an air, just as she did the overfull, rusty black dress. All in all, her appearance was intriguing. He was conscious of no disloyalty to his treasured Lucy in appreciating its charm, and its harmony with the house of which this more provocative lady was obviously the chatelaine.

She turned away from the fountain, slowly, as she had emerged from the portal, and allowed her gaze to linger on a flower bed, before glancing in his direction. Then she drew back hastily, with a slight, smothered cry, while grasping the railing with one ringed hand and raising the other, in fluttering fashion, to her lace-veiled bosom. She so plainly wished to give the impression of having been startled that he tactfully forestalled a confused greeting. He was already bareheaded, but, holding his hat in his hand, he made a low, sweeping bow and then looked up toward the gallery with an ingratiating smile.

"Good evening," he said, without stepping forward and speaking in a way which was somehow both respectful and flattering. "I must ask you to forgive this intrusion, which was really involuntary. In passing along the road, I was so struck by the beauty of your house that I could not help coming closer to it and pausing to admire it. . . . And the longer I lingered," he continued, the flattery now slightly outweighing the respect, "the more I found to admire."

He bowed again, less deeply, and again looked up toward the gallery, with a still more ingratiating smile. The lady found it increasingly difficult to assume a displeasure she did not feel.

"I confess that you did frighten me, monsieur, for a moment," she said. She spoke with a decided accent, but like everything else about

8

her, this accent was exceptionally attractive. "I live such an isolated life that I have ceased to expect visitors."

"If your life is isolated, madame, it must be through your own choice. And it must leave many unfortunate persons—perhaps you will permit me to say many unfortunate men—quite disconsolate."

The lady extracted a handkerchief with a wide black border from the hollow between her breasts and raised it to her eyes. However, she did not conceal her face with it very long.

"I am the disconsolate person, monsieur," she said. "My dear husband—the best, the kindest, the most adorable creature who ever lived —died eight years ago—before this house, which you have been good enough to admire, and in which we expected to have many years of happiness together, was entirely completed. Since then, I have lived here alone—all through the terrible war—all through the desolation which has followed. There is no visiting back and forth any more, as there used to be among the old river families; most of them are in mourning, as I am. They lack the spirit for society; in fact, they are utterly crushed. As for strangers, why should they seek us out? There is nothing left to bring them to the great plantation houses now."

"I am in no position to judge about the old river families. But you can see for yourself that one stranger, at least, has been irresistibly drawn to a great plantation house."

She did not answer immediately; instead she stood toying with the black-bordered handkerchief. Again he came to her rescue, this time by asking for the invitation which he knew she was longing, but not quite daring, to extend.

"And he is lingering, madame, with the hope that you will not think him overbold if he says that he most earnestly desires to see more of it. In short, with the hope that you will permit him to enter it, not only in order that he may study its marvels, but in order that he may be in a more advantageous position than his present one, while offering his homage to its charming mistress."

The lady met his eyes at last and he saw, as he had expected, that hers were almost as dark as her hair, and lighted with a sparkle which more than matched its sheen. However, she still hesitated to speak, although it was obvious by this time that the words of welcome were fairly trembling on her lips.

"Perhaps I should have identified myself more promptly," her visitor went on, with increasing suavity. "My name is Clyde Batchelor. Yes, I realize that would mean nothing to you. But, unless I am much mistaken, I had the privilege of a slight acquaintance with your late-lamented husband. Was he not a frequent traveler on the great river boats? And am I not addressing Mme Labouisse, the widow of Marchand Labouisse, who was known to everyone as a great planter and an even greater gentleman?"

9

"Yes!" she said quickly. "Yes, monsieur, you are right! And to think that I have kept you standing outside all this time, like some intruder —a friend of my dear dead husband's!" Again the handkerchief came into play, but even more briefly this time. "I beseech you to ascend," she went on. "Why, I have probably met you before myself—how could I have forgotten it? Most of my husband's trips were taken before our marriage—after it, he was preoccupied with the building of our home. But now and then he was still obliged to travel, and on these occasions I accompanied him, for he never consented to any separation from me, however brief."

While she was speaking, she had moved from the railing to the top of the stairway and stood, her hand already extended in welcome, while Clyde obeyed her injunction to "ascend." When he came close to her, he took her extended hand and raised it to his lips, the gesture, like his earlier speech, one in which respect merged gradually into a less impersonal form of tribute. He gave no direct answer to her statement that probably they had met before; instead he made a remark which was even more pleasing to her.

"I can well understand the reluctance of M. Labouisse to be separated from his wife for a single day," he said. "Or a single. . . ." He did not actually pronounce the word "night." But it hovered on his lips, as her invitation had hovered on hers a few minutes before, and she knew, as surely as he had, that it was there, and that only regard for the conventions kept it unuttered—conventions which did not affect his thoughts, or hers, however much these might curb their speech. She withdrew her hand, not abruptly, but in such a way as to imply a slight reproof.

"You confuse me, monsieur, with your compliments," she said. "Come, let me lead the way into the drawing room. Then I will leave you and order some light refreshment. I am afraid it will be most inadequate. When my dear husband was alive, we dined royally every day. But since his untimely death, I have had no reason to keep the larder stocked. As I told you, I now lead a very solitary life, and I have no appetite, myself. . . . Enter, monsieur, I beg of you."

She threw open the great portal under the spreading fanlight. Inside, a hall, which failed to appear wide only because of its still greater length, bisected the entire house. In this respect, it followed the general plan of plantation houses in the Deep South; but the double drawing room, into which Mme Labouisse next ushered her guest, was far from doing so. Like the hall, it ran the length of the house; to be sure, an arcade of pillars separated the front parlor from the back parlor; but this added rather than detracted from the whole effect of spaciousness. Nothing in the shape or size of this drawing room was suggestive of the usual square style and its type of decoration was even more extraordinary. Walls and ceiling were alike lavishly covered with frescoes;

and though the light in the room was dim, because the shutters were closed against the brightness of the afternoon sun, Clyde could follow, in a general way, the design of these paintings: on the walls, a high trellis entwined with flowers and overhung with vines and, above the trellis, birds of bright plumage darting back and forth against a brilliant sky; on the ceiling, a correlative trellis, enclosing the twin cherubs who appeared to support the crystal chandeliers.

"I see that you appreciate beautiful frescoes," Mme Labouisse said softly. She had not failed to notice the searching glances which her guest cast about him, or to hear his exclamation of delight at what he saw. "I will leave you to study them while I give orders for such poor entertainment as I can offer you. They are the work of Dominique Canova, the famous artist who also painted the dome of the St. Louis Hotel. I am sure you are familiar with that?"

"Of course. I have frequently made it my headquarters when I went to New Orleans; and I have always thought the rotunda a work of art. But, to my way of thinking, madame, it cannot compare with this drawing room."

"It was our idea that the whole house should be a bower of beauty. Alas, for all our dreams of happiness! However, if it interests you, in its present sad state, I shall be glad to show you more of it after you have had some coffee. Meanwhile, perhaps you will find the *etagères* amusing if you tire of looking at the paintings. My poor husband's collection of Parian figurines was considered very fine by some authorities, even though he had hardly begun it when he died. And, needless to say, I have never had the heart to add to it."

She left the room with gliding grace, her immense skirt billowing about her; evidently the vogue of the "Grecian Bend" had not reached the river road. Clyde's eyes were no longer turned on her unfashionably large hoops; instead they were fixed on her almost unbelievably small waist. The ideal of feminine beauty, in this respect, was still traditionally one which could be encircled by a man's hands; but he had seldom seen a waist which could actually meet this test. Lucy's could not, he remembered rather ruefully. He had been so sure it could that, one day, when she was in a rather melting mood, instead of putting his arm casually around her, he had deliberately pressed both outstretched palms against her middle, with his fingers meeting in the back. But his thumbs failed to meet in front, as he had so confidently expected, for he had always considered Lucy's figure faultless. And Lucy had drawn away from him, flushing, whether with chagrin—since she had of course divined his expectation—or offended modesty, he could not tell. Lucy was extremely sensitive, when it came to love-making. In spite of the fact that she had borne two children, it was hard, sometimes, to realize that she was a young widow and not a young virgin. . . .

Well, this woman had been married, too, and she certainly did not require a widow's weeds to reveal that she had been acquainted with matrimony. Her behavior was wholly correct, but there was nothing virginal in her looks or bearing. Clyde found himself wondering how she would react if he tried to span her waist. Of course he had no idea of making the attempt—just then. But if he should happen to do so on the occasion of some future meeting. . . . Somehow, he felt that there might be future meetings and that possibly, just possibly, on one of these he might be tempted to find out. . . . Naturally, she would begin by repulsing him with indignation; she might even try to slap his face. But, when he had succeeded in doing what he wanted to do, she would certainly feel no chagrin. On the contrary, she would be filled with joy, because she had met the test when so many women—including Lucy —could not do so. If she flushed, it would be with pride. And her pride might very well contribute to a mood more melting than any in which he had so far found Lucy. Not that he had lost his desire for Lucy, who was so sweet and so lovely and so completely representative of everything that a southern gentlewoman should be. But, after all, Lucy was in Virginia and he was in Louisiana; and this hostess of his, this charmer with the small waist, was not, he believed, a southern gentlewoman in the generally accepted sense of the word. According to rumor, Marchand Labouisse, in the course of his European travels, had met a French girl, Dorothée Somebody-or-Other, with whom he had fallen violently in love, almost at first sight. Well, Clyde could understand that, now that he had seen this girl, or rather the *grande amoureuse* of her later development. For there was no doubt in his mind, by this time, that she was a *grande amoureuse,* or at least that she had the makings of one. The miracle was that she had remained a widow all this time. . . .

He tried to stop thinking about Dorothée Labouisse and her small waist and to fix his attention on the Parians which, being snow-white themselves and set out on black lacquered whatnots, were easier to see in the dim light than the multicolored paintings. He picked up several of the figurines and examined them closely; but they seemed cold to him, figuratively as well as literally. For the most part, they were reproductions, in miniature, of famous statues. A few of them were nude, or near nude; but the majority were discreetly draped or were modeled to show only a head and shoulders. They were remarkable only for their number—Clyde had never seen so many of them gathered together in one place—and since, according to his hostess, they represented only the beginning of an interrupted collection, he idly wondered to what dimensions this would have run, if death had not put a stop to it. Nothing else in the room interested him much, either, except the frescoes; and he was considering whether he would be inexcusably presumptuous if he opened the shutters a little, in order to see the design more clearly, when Mme Labouisse re-entered the room.

She was now followed by a massive and rather untidy Negress, bearing a handsomely set silver tray.

"Put that down here, Belle," Mme Labouisse ordered, indicating a small carved table in front of a brocaded sofa. "You needn't stay." And when the Negress had taken her apparently reluctant departure, after staring for a moment, with frank curiosity, at the unexpected visitor, the lady of the house went on, in a low voice, "These modern Negroes know nothing about civilized service and it's impossible to teach them anything they don't want to learn. I don't know whether it's because they're too stupid or too lazy. Now, when we still had slaves. . . ."

She left the sentence unfinished and shrugged her shoulders prettily. Then she began pouring from a delicate Sèvres pot into an equally delicate cup. Yes, she was the sort of woman who would have enjoyed having slaves, Clyde reflected, as he stirred sugar into the coffee she handed him; but she was also the sort of a woman who enjoyed a tête-à-tête and was not above fabricating an excuse for one. However, he suspected that Belle might be eavesdropping from the hall and guessed that Mme Labouisse shared his suspicions, for she invited no further compliments, but kept up an agreeably impersonal flow of chit-chat, while he drank three cups of the coffee, which he found excellent, and ate two of the small sweet cakes, which were served with it, and which were very much less to his liking. She did not ask him what had brought him to the plantation, or even how he happened to approach it on foot, though both would have been natural questions. But eventually she asked a rather surprising one.

"Would you care for a cigar? My dear husband always liked to smoke one after finishing his coffee."

"I should like one very much. But I've always thought ladies found it most distasteful to have men smoke in their presence—indeed, that they did not consider any man who would do so really a gentleman."

"I appreciate your delicacy, monsieur. But in this locality most ladies are somewhat more lenient."

"You say *in this locality*. What is there about it that causes this agreeable leniency?"

"You betray the fact that you are not a Louisianian. Did you never hear of perique tobacco?"

For the second time he made no reply to an indirect question which called for one. But he answered the direct question instantly and eagerly.

"Now that you speak of it, it seems to me that I have. But I know very little about it. Is this where it is grown? On your plantation?"

"Yes, and on those directly to the north of it. And strangely enough, nowhere else in the world. Perique has never flourished except in a small triangular area in this immediate vicinity."

"Perique. . . . That seems an odd name for a type of tobacco. Wouldn't you say so?"

"It is a nickname for Pierre. The first settler who grew it was a certain Pierre Chanet. When he and other Acadians came here from Nova Scotia, they found the Indians raising this so special tobacco. Pierre Chanet showed them how to make it better, so they named it after him. It made him rich, too. Some of his descendants still carry on its cultivation—the Vincents, for instance, who live on Victoria, the plantation just above here. . . . But I should not be boring you with all this ancient history, especially as you are not smoking while you listen. I rather took it for granted that you would have cigars with you. I hope I was not mistaken, for I have none to offer you."

"Not even some made from tobacco grown on your own plantation?"

"No. I sell the cane crop, standing, to the Vincents, and the tobacco to Auguste Roussel, as many others do. And, in any case, I doubt whether you would care for perique; it is very strong in its natural form. Generally, it is mixed with milder types."

She had begun to speak a trifle impatiently. Obviously, she did not consider the subject one of sufficient interest to discuss at greater length. Clyde again drew a cigar from the case he carried in the pocket of his burgundy coat, removed the red band which bore its trade-mark and started to light it. Then, with a match already in his hand, he paused.

"I appreciate your graciousness in permitting me to indulge my bad habits," he said. "But I still hesitate to do so in this elegant drawing room. Perhaps you have forgotten how the odor of smoke—even the smoke from a mild cigar—clings to draperies and upholstery, especially in a place where the windows are closed. Possibly we could go somewhere else?"

"You are most considerate. If you like, I could take you to the gaming room."

"The gaming room!"

"Yes. It is directly across the hall, in front of the dining room. Probably you expected to find a library there. I think myself that it would have been much more appropriate—that was the one point on which my dear husband and I differed. I insisted that the gaming room might equally well be placed on the ground floor, along with the wine cellar, the store closets and the rooms for business visitors. The location is, of course, unsuitable for books, because of the occasional dampness. And it is my opinion that every house should have a library—it imparts an air of culture which is otherwise lacking. All the other plantations of any importance have their libraries. Perhaps that was one reason why my husband stood out so stubbornly against one. He was determined that this house should be different, in every way, from the others. He said he did not wish it to have an air of culture; he wished it to have

14

an air of gaiety. He intended it to be a center of enjoyment, even of revelry, not only for us but for all our friends. Above all, he wished it to be a constant reminder of past delights which he had experienced— the delights of the great river steamers—in its atmosphere as well as its architecture. That is why he insisted on giving a place of such prominence to the gaming room."

She stopped, a little breathlessly. Then she rose and looked at Clyde, as if awaiting some comment from him before he followed her into the gaming room. This comment was not instantly forthcoming. Clyde had lighted his cigar, after all, but his countenance had now lost its eager and alert expression; as far as it had any at all, this was one of patient politeness. But it did not have very much; it was curiously blank. Fleetingly, Mme Labouisse recalled that she had heard such blankness described as "poker faced." But the expression had never meant much to her. Americans had many strange ways of saying things, and most of these had no meaning to her, even now. She had never tried to understand them. They bored her even more than they puzzled her. . . .

She did not guess that Clyde's mind had been much less blank than his face while she had been talking to him. In fact, his thoughts had raced ahead so fast that only his exceptional mental quickness had enabled him to keep abreast of them. First, about that missing library. . . . Of course Lucy would consider any house ill equipped which did not have a library; in this respect, if in no other, she and Dorothée Labouisse would have been in one accord. Her grandfather's library had been famous throughout Virginia, where there were many fine libraries; and fortunately, nothing had happened to it during the war, though afterward Lucy had been on the point of regretfully selling some of the rarer books, when he, Clyde, had succeeded in dissuading her, by convincing her that the need for such sacrifices was past. . . . But that idea of demoting the gaming room from the main floor to the ground level was a good one, and there was still no reason why it could not be carried into effect. Possibly, it would be best to make this change without consulting Lucy beforehand, though of course he would explain to her that in this part of Louisiana there were no basements, as the term was understood in Virginia, and that the dining room and drawing room were on the "main floor" and not on the ground floor of the house which was to be theirs. But there were all kinds of advantages to the latter location for a gaming room—quiet, privacy, an opportunity for detachment and freedom. Besides, chips and cards and felt-covered tables would not suffer, like books, from dampness. . . . Probably it would also be possible to provide for a small office, which would connect with the gaming room. It would be more convenient than one in a separate building, such as most planters used. But, if so placed, it would not affect the general tone of the estab-

15

lishment. Personally, though Clyde knew Lucy would agree with Dorothée about the library, he himself agreed with the late Marchand Labouisse about the atmosphere that the house should have; most of all, about the memories it should evoke of the great river steamers in all their pleasurable and exciting aspects. . . .

"If you are not interested in the gaming room, we could go outdoors. We could walk in the garden while you smoke your cigar," Mme Labouisse suggested. Although she did not bother her head about the way Americans expressed themselves, when they called blankness "poker faced," it bothered her very much if any man, whatever his nationality, appeared to lose interest in what she was saying to him. And, up to the very moment when she had mentioned the gaming room, this engaging stranger had been all attention. She desired to have this attention continue and, if possible, intensify.

"Of course, it never became what we planned and hoped," she went on. "It was our idea that it should be, in miniature, something like the garden at St. Cloud. It was there that my dear husband and I met. . . . Possibly you have already guessed that. You would have easily divined that I am French, with your delicate perceptions, monsieur, even if no one had told you so. And then, the name of this plantation—"

"But it is called Cindy Lou, is it not?"

"Yes. But of course that is a corruption, like perique." She was patient and polite now; after all, two could play at such a game. "We named it St. Cloud after—after our first trysting place in my own beloved country; and then we went through more trouble than you can believe, because almost everyone who saw it written insisted on calling it Saint Cloud instead of San Cloo. You would think in a locality where there are so many persons who, if not French, are at least of French extraction or who claim it. . . ." Again, she shrugged her shoulders prettily, leaving a sentence unfinished. "Of course, I suspect there were few Parisians among them. I believe they were provincial before they ever left France, and their sojourns in such places as Nova Scotia and Santo Domingo certainly did nothing to improve their culture. But let that pass. . . . We finally convinced our neighbors and my husband's business associates that they must say San Cloo; and then, as usual, the slaves promptly corrupted the name. It became Cindy Lou to them and presently everyone was calling it that—a sad ending to a proud title. But this is a place of sad endings."

He was smiling persuasively again. He still cared nothing about seeing the garden. Among other reports that had reached him concerning the house was one to the effect that the entire third floor was designed to be a great ballroom, that its ceiling was formed from panes of multicolored glass which had been set in lattices beneath the raised floor of the belvedere. Through the use of a complicated arrangement of powerful carbide lights and raised reflectors, this multicolored glass was intended to give a kaleidoscopic effect to the dress of the dancers, as they swung and swayed to the lilting sound of music—or so it was rumored; and Clyde would have vastly preferred to gauge the possibilities of this ballroom for himself, rather than to wander along the unkempt path of a garden which had failed of fulfillment. But he decided this was not the time to express a preference; to reach the ballroom, it would be necessary to go through the upper hall, where the doors doubtless stood open into the bedchambers; so if he said, on his own initiative, that he would like to do this now, he might seem lacking in that delicacy on which his hostess had just complimented him. Moreover, though he himself knew nothing about gardens and cared less, Lucy knew a good deal about them and cared for them greatly, like most Virginians. In her interests, he could not afford to miss the opportunity offered.

"By all means, let us wander in the garden," he continued, with this in mind. "And while we do, tell me more about the plans you made for it. Unfortunately, I never saw the original St. Cloud." He was careful to give it the proper pronunciation. "But I cannot believe that it is half so beautiful as its namesake."

"As its namesake might have been, you mean," Mme Labouisse corrected. But though she managed to tinge her tone with sadness, she did not speak severely; she was already mollified. Again she glided from the room, and again Clyde, following in her wake, was aware of her waist's tempting smallness and not of her skirt's unfashionable fullness. He thought he saw the immense, untidy Negress lurking in a corner of the dim hall, and realized that if he were not mistaken, she had been eavesdropping, as he had expected she would. But the suspicion neither angered nor disturbed him; instead it gave him a fleeting sensation of amusement, mingled with scorn. How speedily and effectively Lucy would have dealt with such a creature! Inside of a week, the Negress would have been neat in person, respectful in manner and capable in service—or she would have been turned out of the house. And Lucy would have accomplished the transformation—or, if necessary, brought about the dismissal—without once raising her voice or losing her air of detached serenity.

His admiration for Lucy increased every time he appraised her attributes; but this did not keep him from making other appraisals. He hardly took his eyes off the revealing black bodice as he and Dorothée Labouisse went out on the gallery and down the branching staircase. Once on the ground, however, it was clearly indicated that he must walk beside and not behind her. Regretfully, he fell into step with her and paced slowly along, smoking his cigar, while she talked to him about the garden.

"You see we have only one fountain. We had planned for a series of these, on terraces. I am sure you know that most plantation houses in Louisiana are approached directly through an *allée* of live oaks. But at Ashland, for instance, a terraced garden goes straight to the river road, and the carriage entrance is through a beautiful grove of trees located at the side."

"Yes. I have observed all that many times from the river, and admired it."

"My husband and I observed it at close range, when we were invited to Ashland," Mme Labouisse replied. She was not averse to letting this outsider know that she had formerly enjoyed an entree at the home of Duncan Kenner, who had been Jefferson Davis' minister to Europe during the days of the Confederacy; it was the war and its aftermath which had isolated her, not lack of social standing. Perhaps she should drive this point home. "As I told you, my dear husband did not wish this house to be like any other; he wished it to be unique—"

"As indeed it is!" Clyde interrupted her.

"But he felt differently about the grounds—after all, he could not re-create steamboat days in those! Rich and resourceful as he was, he could find no way of imitating waves and currents in flower beds!"

She tossed back her head and, for the first time, permitted herself a little laugh. The tinkle of her earrings mingled with the tinkle of this laugh and the sound was very pleasant. Her quick movement had slightly disarranged some of her glossy ringlets, and she raised both jeweled hands to pat them back into place; the gesture was close to coquettish.

"So it was his decision and mine that we should adapt the models that pleased us both to our own uses," she went on. "We wished to remind ourselves of our happy days in France, to have our own St. Cloud here on the Mississippi; and, at the same time, we did not mean to copy the original garden slavishly. We were also guided by successful local patterns like Ashland's. But we intended to surpass these. We meant to have a maze. We meant to have every rare tree which will thrive in this region, and such a variety and profusion of exotic flowers that they would be almost bewildering. We meant to have peacocks strutting pridefully from terrace to terrace!"

At last she had spoken of something which he could visualize. He had never been to France, as he had confessed, and he had never seen Ashland from the viewpoint of a privileged guest, as she had inferred. He knew nothing of landscaping, of mazes and terraces and fountains, of rare trees and exotic flowers. To be sure, he knew nothing about peacocks, either. But he could see that they belonged. In fact, their iridescent feathers would seem a fitting complement to the multicolored frescoes and the kaleidoscopic lights. He looked out over the neglected expanse of grass before him, gilded by the setting sun, and suddenly it came alive with regal birds, strutting for the delight of Lucy's children, who were so soon to be his.

"Are you never homesick for France?" he asked abruptly.

"Am I never homesick for France! Monsieur, how can you ask such a question? You must know there are days—and nights—when I think I shall die of longing for it!"

Here at last was a cry straight from the soul. She was no longer posturing and pretending, she was no longer seeking to impress him with her broken heart and her undiminished charms. She was confessing, without elaboration or artifice, her desolation amidst the alien corn.

"Then why not go back there?" he asked, still more abruptly.

"Why not go back there? Again, I demand why you ask such a question. Do you suppose, if I could have found a purchaser for this place, that I would not have gone long ago? I lied to you when I told you I loved it. I loathe it! But I cannot abandon it. It is not a rich plantation any more—you have been deceived, monsieur, if you thought it was. But it provides me with a livelihood, such as it is. And I have no other. I—I was not a wealthy girl. My family could do nothing for me. I did not even have a proper dowry. My husband took me without one— for love. The home that he provided is all the shelter I have left. And sometimes, I have been so hard pressed for ready cash that I have tried to think of some way I could retrieve the gold pieces which were buried in the cornerstone when the house was started, in accordance with local custom."

"Well, in that case—" Clyde began. Then he started over again. "If you want to stay here, out of sentiment, that's your affair. But if you don't, if you really meant what you said about loathing the plantation and longing for France, there's no reason why you shouldn't take the next boat."

"I—I do not quite follow you, monsieur."

"I'm telling you that you've got a purchaser for the place and everything on it. I'll buy it from you, today, with all its equipment, if you'll sell it to me."

She had continued to toy with her curls while she talked of peacocks, but she had swiftly lowered her arms when he asked his first question about France. Now, she raised her hands to her face and looked at him wide eyed above the fingers digging into her cheeks.

"You're joking," she faltered. "You're making fun of me, monsieur. The jest is unworthy of you."

"I'm not joking. I'm not making fun of you. What do you consider the place worth? I mean land, livestock, buildings, equipment, furniture, everything. Thirty thousand dollars? Fifty thousand? I'll pay you for them, in cash, as soon as we can pass papers. If you like, I'll give you five thousand to bind the bargain here and now."

She screamed, without smothering the sound this time, and swayed toward him. He caught her around the shoulders to steady her. Then, still holding her firmly, his hands slid down over her arms to the elbows. After that, it seemed so inevitable they should encircle her waist that he did not even stop to consider whether the great cistern which towered above the garden walk would conceal them from the road, or whether some servant might not observe them from a rear window.

He planted his fingers in the small of her back and curved his outstretched palms around her. His thumbs not only met in front; they overlapped. He could feel the whalebone with which her corset was mercilessly stiffened; but though its lacings were tightly drawn, there was a tiny space where the two sides of the corset did not quite meet. Here the lacings merely formed a latticework over the thin cambric chemise beneath them, and under the cambric was warm, yielding flesh. As Clyde became increasingly aware of this hidden softness, his grip tightened and he drew Dorothée closer to him.

He had been only partly right in his guess. She did not repulse him with indignation, she did not try to slap his face. To be sure, she did flush; but he knew this was with triumph even more than with pride. Her joy was so great that it swallowed up all semblance of resistance. He had hoped only for a melting mood and he had got, or could get, everything from her that he could possibly desire.

He did not deceive himself. He knew that, though she had been attracted to him, as he had to her, she would not have found him irresistible as a man if he had not been able to free her from the plantation and send her back to France. Indeed, it was quite possible that she considered her acquiescence a part of the purchase price. Well, he had not thought of it that way, but what difference did it make, since she had? He had never been one to lose sight of an unexpected advantage and he thought none the less of Dorothée Labouisse because she was prepared to give him one.

Of course, it would have been entirely different in the case of Lucy.

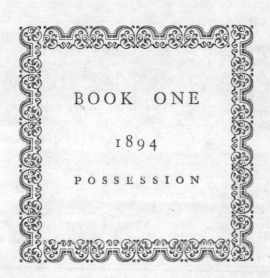

BOOK ONE

1894

POSSESSION

As usual, dinner at Cindy Lou had been a rich repast, and conducive to pleasant somnolence. It had begun with a dish of butter beans and fresh river shrimp—actually a stew rather than a soup—in the concoction of which Belle eclipsed every cook within a day's journey. Next had come a grillade—thin, tender slices of veal, browned in a rich sauce; and with this, flaky rice, crowder peas and corn on the cob were served. A cheese platter had accompanied the green salad; and finally, one of Lucy's famous Spanish creams had been proudly brought into the dining room. This was unlike all ordinary Spanish creams, partly because the blending of its ingredients was timed in such a way as to leave half of the main mold clear and half opaque, giving it a striped effect; and partly because this main mold was surrounded by a galaxy of small ones, made of jewel-colored sherry jelly which, in turn, were ornamented with whipped cream and candied fruits. Like many Virginians of her time and class, Lucy always made the daily desserts for her family, unless she were ill; if there were sickness among their friends in the neighborhood, or among the servants, she made a double quantity of sherry jelly, so that there would be plenty for general distribution; and she also made broth, gruels and shrubs which were highly prized as gifts. But the Spanish cream was her chef-d'œuvre.

Clyde had done full justice to this and, indeed, to the entire dinner; but, after rising, with a sigh of satisfied repletion, and kissing his wife as they reached the threshold of the dining room, he had gone direct to his favorite wicker armchair, under the great oak between the house and the first fountain. He had not meant to make a practice of taking a daily nap, any more than he had meant to permit himself a preference for any certain chair; both the practice and the preference were telltale signs of advancing years and, as such, distasteful to him. But the chair was so comfortable, the drowsiness so agreeable! Why forgo the one and fight off the other?

No reason at all, he told himself, sinking back luxuriously and closing his eyes. After all, advancing years were different from declining ones. Indeed, advance of any kind usually carried with it the connotation of progress. And the man he now was—the happy husband, the fond foster father, the landed proprietor, the substantial citizen—had progressed a long way from the street Arab who was better at crap-shooting than any of his lawless cronies—not to mention the card-sharper who had made his way from the lowest dives of St. Louis to the shanty boats, swarming with peddlers, medicine men, prostitutes and lottery operators and, thence, to the gaming rooms of the great river steamers; the professional gambler who had turned purveyor to sutlers when the river steamers made way for gunboats; and the speculator in tobacco and cotton whose first Southern associates had been hoarders and profiteers eager to welcome the outsider possessed of ready gold.

It often seemed to Clyde Batchelor that the third step had marked his greatest stride forward; and this was less because he had so materially furthered his fortunes by following a victorious Union Army into the stricken South, than because he had found an even richer reward in another way. It was in Virginia that he had met Lucy Page and persuaded her to marry him; and that was no mean achievement for a man whom she could not possibly classify as a gentleman and whom she did logically classify as an enemy. When he thought of the loathing which the feminine members of Richmond's first families almost universally felt for the invaders, the scorn these ladies did not hesitate to show even high-ranking officers of impeccable conduct, he realized that his wooing and winning of Lucy was the supreme triumph of his life, and the one which had called for the greatest patience, adroitness and suavity.

He had heard her speak before he saw her, and it amused him to tell her—after he knew her well enough to risk a mild jest in her presence —that he fell in love with a voice and not with a woman. Since the voice was characteristic of the woman, the statement was not as extravagant as it might otherwise have been. He was passing along Franklin Street when he was arrested by the sound of sobbing beyond a garden wall and of soothing words spoken in comfort.

"Don't cry, honey. There'll be something to eat tomorrow."

"You told me that yesterday."

"I know, and there was, wasn't there? Not much, but something. And I'm almost sure there'll be more tomorrow."

"But I'm hungry *now*."

"If you'll come to bed, like a good boy, you'll forget that you're hungry. I'll read to you out of *Susie's Six Birthdays* until you get sleepy."

"That's a *girl's* book! A *Yankee* book! Father said so. I don't want you to read to me out of that book. Father doesn't want you to, either!"

"I'm sorry, honey. Then I'll read to you out of *Dick and His Cat*."

"But I'm h-u-n-g-r-y!"

Clyde could stand it no longer. He went up to the garden gate and rapped boldly on it. When it was not instantly opened, he rapped again, harder and more loudly.

The second time, his knock produced results. The sound of sobbing ceased abruptly, to be followed by the sound of soft, swift steps, accompanied by small, pattering feet; then by that of a drawn bolt and a turned key. The gate opened to disclose a fair-haired girl, framed against a background of brilliant box and cascading wisteria, with a pale, peevish-looking little boy dragging at her mauve muslin skirts.

Clyde's spontaneous sympathy for the little boy subsided almost as quickly as it had been aroused. This was the sort of child who would whine whether he were really hungry or not. Clyde had seen dozens of disagreeable, pampered children in the course of his travels up and down the Mississippi; he recognized—and despised—the type at a glance. But the feelings awakened by the girl were vastly different. Everything about her was as lovely as her voice—her fair hair, her gray eyes, her clear skin, the expression of her face, her general bearing. Yet this loveliness in no way suggested a lack of stanchness. This girl would never whimper because she was hungry; she was made of the stuff which faced privation with serene and smiling fortitude.

"Good evening," she said pleasantly, and without the slightest indication that she was surprised by the presence of a stranger at her door.

"Good evening," Clyde responded mechanically. Then he suddenly found that it was hard to say anything further. The girl stood, with no visible sign of impatience, waiting for him to do so. But the disagreeable child tugged again at her delicately tinted skirt and whined, "What does the man want? What has he come here for?"

"Hush, Bushrod. The gentleman will tell us in a minute," the girl said softly, stroking the little boy's tumbled hair.

"Is he a Yankee?"

"Of course not, honey. The Yankees all wear uniforms—*blue* uniforms."

Her artlessness was disarming; in the face of it, Clyde decided there was nothing to do but plunge straight into the truth. "I am afraid I must undeceive you," he said. "I'm from St. Louis and I'm at present—er—connected with the Union Army, though not in a military capacity. So I suppose you would call me a Yankee. But I happened to overhear this little boy crying and I thought he said he was hungry. It so happens that I have—well, access to plentiful provisions. So I hope that, perhaps—"

"He *is* a Yankee!" the child said shrilly. It was evident that the words "access" and "plentiful provisions" were beyond the range of his comprehension. "Why don't you send him away? Father'll be very angry."

"The suggestion wasn't meant to be presumptuous," Clyde hastened to say. To his annoyance, he feared that he was flushing. "It was just that—"

"I am sure it was not," the girl said quietly. "You are very kind. I shall be thankful to accept anything you can conveniently spare. My little boy *is* hungry. And my husband is very ill. He has been wounded four times, each time more severely than before, but each time he has

25

returned to the battle line. Now he has been brought home to—to rest."

Her husband! Well, Clyde might have known! Any man would be tempted to do some swift cradle snatching, if he found someone like this, and what was more, any man should be forgiven if he yielded to the temptation, provided he could get away with it. But the girl in mauve did not look a day over eighteen, in spite of the telltale signs of fatigue in her face; and if that horrid little boy was her son, instead of her brother, as Clyde had at first supposed, she must be at least five years older than that. But after all, this was beyond the point and he did not see why he wasted a moment's thought on it. The point was that, if her child was hungry, she was undoubtedly a good deal hungrier, since she herself would certainly have gone without in order to feed him; and when she said her husband had been brought home to rest, that meant, of course, that he had been brought home to die. Why, if he did, this girl would be a widow, a charming young widow— hang it all, that was not the point, either!

"I know this is Franklin Street," he said hurriedly. "But I did not happen to notice the number of your house. And the name is? . . ."

"The number is twenty-one. Twenty-one West. And the name is Page. I am Lucy Page and this is my little son Bushrod. My husband Forrest Page is a colonel on Lee's staff—that is, he was."

Clyde took a small notebook, to which a tiny pencil was attached, from his waistcoat pocket and wrote rapidly. "Thank you, Mrs. Page," he said, replacing the memorandum. "I will send you a few—ah— delicacies immediately. I hope they will serve to tempt an invalid's appetite."

"They will probably save his life," Lucy said, speaking more quietly than ever. (How typical that had been! Never to lose her serenity, but never to dissemble, either!) "You reveal your own delicacy, sir, in so referring to nourishment that is more sorely needed than you can know."

An unaccountable feeling of happiness permeated Clyde's senses as he listened to her. He had performed many similar kindnesses before, especially to children, for he had never forgotten what it had meant to be hungry as a child; but none had ever given him this sensation of warmth and well-being. It was as though he were receiving a benison, rather than bestowing a favor. He would have loved to linger, to enter that walled garden filled with the fresh fragrance of box and shaded with purple wisteria. So many doors had been closed to him that the half-opened gate seemed to offer a glimpse of Paradise. And its guardian angel was this girl, whose hair and eyes and manner and speech were all the acme of loveliness.

"I will return tomorrow, if you will permit me, to make sure my little offering has arrived safely and to inquire for the colonel's health,"

Clyde said. After all, this was no time to linger. The provisions were badly needed, there was not the slightest doubt of that; it would be no indication of "delicacy" to retard their delivery. But to make sure they had arrived and that they filled a cruel want—why, that would be only taking a proper precaution, only showing common courtesy!

"Thank you. I shall expect you," Lucy replied. She did not shut the garden gate, but stood still, holding it open, as long as he could see her —as long, or so he believed, as she could hear his rapidly retreating footsteps. She had given him no sense of dismissal. Quite the contrary —so much the contrary that, had the idea not been fantastic, it would have seemed as if she were watching him until he was out of sight and hearing because she wanted to prolong the time when she was conscious of his presence, as a woman will do only when a man means much to her. . . .

So that was the way it had begun, soon after the fall of Richmond. Later, Clyde Batchelor, perforce, frequently went north, in connection with his manipulations; but meanwhile the big gray house on West Franklin Street lacked nothing that he could send it; and every few days, when he was in town, he called there "to make sure his offering had arrived safely and to inquire after the colonel's health." He never saw the colonel, who, though reported as "miraculously improved," was still reputedly unable to stand the strain of receiving visitors; but Clyde did meet Lucy's mother Mrs. Virginius Cary, who had lost her husband and all four of her sons in the war. Their plantation home had been burned during Dahlgren's Raid, and she lived with her only surviving child Lucy, and Lucy's husband Forrest Page, at their Richmond residence. Clyde guessed that the colonel resented the largesse he was receiving, that he would have declined to accept it had it not been for his little son, and that Mrs. Cary was hardly less resentful. Doubtless she consented to see the Yankee interloper only because, otherwise, Lucy would have seen him alone, except for Bushrod who, now that he had enough to eat, rushed noisily around, banging doors and bursting in on orderly conversations. Mrs. Cary probably thought that such interruptions did not contribute enough of a safeguard, that at any advantageous moment the obnoxious creature, who had added to the insult of his mere presence in Richmond by making them his debtors, might "attempt liberties." She need not have worried, and Clyde would have liked to tell her so, angrily; he would no more have made improper advances to Lucy than he would have desecrated a shrine.

As time went on, his profitable business ventures required longer and longer absences from Richmond; and, after one that was unusually protracted, he saw, as he hastened along Franklin Street from the Exchange and Ballard House, that workmen were swarming over the big gray mansion which now meant so much to him, painting it in gaudy colors, and that other workmen were passing in and out of the garden gate, which stood wide open. He quickened his pace and went rapidly up the front steps.

Beyond the gaping entrance, leading to the denuded hall which had once afforded so seemly and gracious an approach to the double parlors, in the rear, a burly and begrimed individual, evidently a foreman of sorts, confronted him with a belligerent stare.

"Well, what's your business here?" this hostile artisan inquired abruptly.

"I am calling on Mrs. Cary and Mrs. Page," Clyde informed him coldly. The coldness was meant to be cutting, but it was uncomfortably akin to the chill of foreboding which was creeping through his being. The foreman laughed, disagreeably.

"Then you're in the wrong pew. This place is the property of Ross Judson."

"Ross Judson!"

In his horror, Clyde had echoed the name before he could stop himself. Unscrupulous as he had been himself, he had never stooped to the level of this wily and notorious trafficker with the enemy of his own people. The foreman's stare became increasingly belligerent.

"That's what I said. And now you know the Cary tribe ain't here any more, maybe you'll shove along and let me get on with my work. This old ark was just about falling to pieces when Mr. Judson took it over. I aim to put it in good shape for him."

Clyde went down the front steps as rapidly as he had mounted them. He was not only seething with rage; he was consumed with anxiety. Almost the only acquaintances he had in Richmond were his business associates and he shrank from questioning them about Lucy. The boon companions with whom he had formerly spent such convivial evenings at Johnny Worsham's elegant gambling parlors were now scattered to the four winds; and, even if this were not the case, he would have been still more loath to mention Lucy in their hearing. However, he overcame his reluctance sufficiently to make discreet inquiries at the Exchange and Ballard House and there, information was readily forthcoming: Colonel Forrest Page had died, leaving his widow almost penniless. The mortgage on their house had been foreclosed, and it had been sold at auction. Mrs. Page and her mother had gone back to the plantation. The Carys had always been country people; it was the Pages who were city folk. So perhaps, in a way, the ladies were not taking the loss of the Franklin Street house as hard as they might have.

But how could they live in the country? Clyde wanted to know. The plantation home had been burned, hadn't it? Yes, the Cary plantation home, Amalfi. But Mrs. Cary, before her marriage, had been Sophia

28

Peyton and the Peyton plantation home, Sorrento, located on the next "curl" of the James to Amalfi, was still habitable—that is, more or less. It had run down after the death of Alexander Peyton, who took more pride in his library than he did in his crops; and it had been damaged, though not destroyed, during the war. Rumor had it that, when Dahlgren's Raiders went there, old Mrs. Peyton—that is, Mrs. Cary's mother, who had afterward died as a result of the shock—had stood her ground with great bravado. She had actually invited the Union officers to help themselves to the contents of her fine cellar. Sometimes, when the Union officers drank too much, they became doubly destructive; then again, sometimes it worked just the other way. It did that time. So, Sorrento was spared and that was where Mrs. Cary and Mrs. Page were living now. It would be hard for two lone ladies. There was a lot of land, now that Amalfi and Sorrento were thrown together. And there were no slaves left to work it. Besides, it would be bitter cold down there, with winter coming on and no house servants, or hardly any, to tend the fires. . . .

Clyde hired a horse and buggy and set off down the rough road where the thick red mud was already freezing in deep ruts. He started early in the morning, but though the distance from Richmond to Sorrento was allegedly only ten miles or so, it was well past noon before he turned in at the driveway which answered to the rather vague description that had been given him of the one leading to the plantation house. There were no signposts left anywhere and he met almost no one as he jogged and hitched along. The stray Negroes whom he saw, at lengthy intervals, for the most part merely stared at him stupidly when he questioned them; and those who answered did so in a disjointed and contradictory fashion. After he had turned in at the driveway, he still went on and on, through fields that must once have been fabulously fertile, but which were now bleak and barren; then through shadowy woods, where the branches of the trees, to which only the bronzed and brittle oak leaves still clung, seemed to close in upon him, shutting off both progress and escape; and still he saw no sign of a house or anything that suggested the approach to one. Finally, when he had almost decided that he must be hopelessly lost, the branches parted and he beheld a great unkempt lawn, edged in by shaggy bushes, and beyond it, the noble façade of a mansion that was still stately and symmetrical, despite the state of decadence into which it had sunk.

He hitched his tired horse and went up the broad grassy path leading to the front door. The bellpull hung loosely against the wide paneling, but it worked; he could hear the bell pealing sharply and then echoing, as if its sound had traveled a long distance. But there was no response until he had rung three times. Then he heard doors opening and shutting and shuffling footsteps, approaching slowly and uncertainly. At last a bolt was drawn back, to the accompaniment of much muttering and mumbling, and the door opened to disclose a very shabby, very aged, very decrepit Negro.

"Are Mrs. Cary and Mrs. Page at home?" Clyde inquired. The Negro cupped his ear with his hand.

"Scuse me, suh, Ah don' heah so good no mo'."

"Are Mrs. Cary and Mrs. Page at home?" Clyde repeated, shouting now.

"Oh, yessuh, yessuh. Would you kindly step into the parlor? Ah knows Ah ought to reckernize you, but Ah don' see so good no mo', neithuh. Who shall Ah tell Miss Sophie done come to see her?"

"Tell her Mr. Clyde Batchelor."

"Mistuh Hyde, yessuh, yessuh. Miss Sophie sure will be mighty pleased to see you."

Of course, she was not. She was perfectly polite—her code would have permitted nothing else. But she acknowledged his expressions of sympathy on the death of her son-in-law as briefly as was consistent with courtesy. Yes, it was all very sad. The colonel had seemed so much better—in fact, so much like his old self—that they had been greatly encouraged. But an old wound had broken open and infection had set in. It was just six months now. . . . She and her daughter had retired to the plantation for the period of their mourning.

As Clyde had never yet seen Mrs. Cary when she was not swathed in crape, he feared that Lucy must now be practically smothered by it. He remembered how fresh she had always looked, in her cool grays and lavenders, and hated to think of her as loaded down with widow's weeds. She had once explained to him, almost apologetically, that her husband found it depressing to be surrounded by black on his sickbed, and that therefore she had not worn it, as long as was customary, for her father and brothers. Clyde could almost hear the colonel telling her, in one of his more irritable moments, that there would be time enough for that after he was dead. Clyde knew that very possibly he was unjust; but since Bushrod in no way resembled his mother, it was not too illogical to assume that the obnoxious child might be a second edition of his father. Well, inevitably, Lucy would be wearing deep mourning now, but Clyde's distaste at the thought of this was mitigated by the realization of its underlying meaning: Lucy was no longer another man's wife and he himself could make her an honorable proposal of marriage at last, after wanting her ever since he had first heard her voice beyond a garden wall. . . .

"I do not wish you to feel that I am intruding on your solitude or hers," he eventually told Mrs. Cary. "But, before I leave, I should like to pay my respects to Mrs. Page, also."

"I am very sorry. My daughter is not able to see anyone at present."

"She is ill?" Clyde asked in alarm.

30

"No, not exactly. But she is of course completely crushed by sorrow and—"

Clyde interrupted her. "I shall be very careful not to say anything which could possibly add to her grief," he said hurriedly.

"I had not quite finished, Mr. Batchelor. My daughter is completely crushed by sorrow *and* in addition to this, she has been called upon to undergo the greatest ordeal of womanhood. Less than a fortnight ago, after prolonged travail—lengthened no doubt by the strain she had already suffered in her husband's death—she gave birth to a little girl. She is still prostrated, as I said."

Clyde's first reaction to this statement was one of rage that he could hardly conceal. So this hero of a hundred battles, despite his weakness and his wounds, had still been able to beget a child! Lucy would never have failed in her wifely duty, he felt certain of that; but the fact that she fulfilled it unflinchingly could not have meant that she had accepted willingly, much less gladly, the embraces of a moribund man! It was sickening to feel sure that a child conceived as a result of such submission would be even more obnoxious than the one who was presumably the offspring of bridal rapture.

Clyde was almost instantly ashamed of the resentment which caused his anger and which, he ruefully admitted to himself, was not untinged with jealousy. Momentarily, he had forgotten that Lucy, now more than ever, should be the object of his deepest sympathy. She was bereft, and certainly she must once have loved her husband, or she would not have married the man in the first place; now that he was dead, and dead of wounds suffered for the Lost Cause, his every pleasing attribute and daring deed would have taken on new glamour and glory in her eyes. There was no doubt that her sorrow was not only sincere but profound. And she had given birth to her child "after prolonged travail" on this lonely plantation, probably with only some ignorant colored midwife in attendance; unquestionably, Mrs. Cary had not exaggerated in saying that her daughter was still "completely prostrated." Moreover, there were no signs of circumstances less straitened than those with which the family had been obliged to cope in Richmond. The frayed furniture in the cold drawing room was bursting at the seams, and Mrs. Cary had not offered her visitor any refreshment; this would never have happened, he knew, no matter how unwelcome he had been, if there were anything available to eat and drink and anyone on hand to serve it. In fact, everything about the once proud plantation bespoke bitter poverty. This time, he did not dare suggest help; but he had brought a basket of wine with him, as a courtesy gift, thinking that he could present it on the grounds that such imports were still not coming freely across the Atlantic and that he had happened on some good vintages by a fortunate chance. Mrs. Cary did not decline the gift and, after a barely perceptible pause, she

31

even asked Clyde if he would not open one of the bottles so that they might share the savor of its vintage. He declined, saying that it was getting late and that he would rather not attempt the trip back to Richmond, over unfamiliar roads, after dark. Since he could not see Lucy, much less propose to her, since he could not even immediately help her, his visit had failed of its purpose.

But he had never been one to accept defeat for long. He felt certain that Mrs. Cary would not stoop to intercept—or read—her daughter's mail; and the next day he wrote to Lucy, expressing his disappointment at not having seen her and his hope that her health would permit her to receive him the next time he came to Richmond. Her answer was delayed in reaching him, because several forwardings were required before it could do so; but when it came, it brought him back, posthaste, to Sorrento. She had been very sorry to miss him, Lucy wrote. Indeed, if she had known he was calling, she would have insisted on seeing him, so that she could show him her beautiful baby. She had named the baby Cary, since there was no one else, in the direct line, to carry on the family name. Mr. Batchelor probably knew that this was not at all an unusual custom in Virginia. Lucy was disappointed because Bushrod did not seem to be much interested in Cary; however, that was not surprising; very often boys were not interested in their little sisters. But everyone else adored Cary. Lucy was sure Mr. Batchelor would find her enchanting and hoped that he would not postpone his next visit until she had outgrown her sweet baby ways. Besides, Lucy herself would be extremely glad to see him, to thank him in person for the wonderful wine, which had proved such a valuable tonic during her convalescence, and to take him around the plantation, which was still worth seeing, though not, of course, comparable to what it had been before the war. And she was, very sincerely and gratefully, his friend, Lucy Page.

The final lines of the letter were the ones which had brought Clyde posthaste back to Sorrento. He was not at all interested in the baby girl; in fact, he was inclined to believe that her charms, like those of every other infant, existed largely in the imagination of her doting mother. But when he was ushered into the drawing room, he found Cary in her cradle, beside her mother's chair. She had a pillow behind her, but she sat up sturdily enough without it, and she swayed slightly back and forth, singing to herself. Her shapely little head was covered with soft ringlets, bright as spun gold, and her blue eyes danced, as if with some secret infantile joy. The child whom he had expected to find detestable was adorable instead. When she caught sight of Clyde, she laughed, and held out her chubby little arms for him to take her. From that moment, he was her willing slave. . . .

He proposed to Lucy the same day. It was too soon, he knew, by all conventional standards, and he also knew that by some of them his suit

32

would smack of presumption at any time. But she had not thought him presumptuous when he offered her food; there was just a chance that she would not do so when he offered her lifelong security for herself and her children, and with it lifelong devotion.

She heard him through, gravely, according him the same courtesy and consideration that she would have shown had he been pleading some other cause. Cary had been in the room with them all the time and, when she began to show signs of restlessness, Lucy had picked her up and quieted her. Then the baby had been put back in her cradle, where she had drowsily nestled down, and the young mother had looked at her suitor across the cradle of her sleeping child.

"I thought you would ask me to marry you," she said in that serene voice which was music to his ears. "I am very much honored by your proposal."

"Very much *honored*!"

"Yes, of course. Any woman is honored when a decent man asks her to become his wife, to be the mistress of his house, to take his name and—"

She stopped, flushing for the first time.

"You don't know that I'm a decent man," he said impetuously. "And I haven't a name like Cary or Page to offer you. I haven't told you much about myself yet. I ought to. You have a right to know."

"I will have, if we both decide, later on, that it is best for us to be married," she said. "But you interrupted me—or rather, I interrupted myself. I was about to say, any woman is honored when a decent man asks her to become his wife and the mistress of his house, to bear his name and—to be the mother of his children. Then I stopped, because there is something I ought to add to that and it is not an easy thing to say. I do not mean merely because it brings up a subject which is not usually discussed between men and women, unless they are intimately connected. I would not want you to think I was immodest—"

"As if I could ever think that!"

"Thank you. But it is also hard for a young woman to confess that she may never be able to have any more children and, in justice to you, I must do that. I—I had miscarried twice before Cary was born and I did not have much care either time. It seems nothing short of a miracle that I was able to carry her to full term. I think it must have been partly because I wanted her so much that I was determined not to lose her. But there was no one here with me when she was born except my mother and an old, old Negress who is half blind like her brother Simeon, whom you have seen. She did the best she could for me, but—a good many things went wrong. Since then, I have managed to consult a doctor and he has told me what I have told you. You will want children of your own, like any normal man. And I probably could not give them to you."

33

"Lucy, darling, it's you I want."

"You feel that way now because you're in love."

She was speaking with exceptional candor for a woman of her kind and her class, and every word she said seemed to endear her to him the more. In his eagerness, he leaned forward and took her hand.

"Why should I care whether I could have any children of my own if I could have Cary? She's never seen her own father—she'd always think of me as one. Why, we're friends already! You saw how she held out her arms to me the minute I came into the room! I'd make her my heir. I'd ask you to let me give her my name, too, only, as I've tried to tell you, it's a name that doesn't stand for anything great or even good. I can't rob her of her father's, when that stands for so much."

"Would you make Bushrod your heir, too?"

Momentarily, Clyde hesitated. He had never overcome his first dislike for Bushrod; instead, it seemed to grow greater with time. But he knew that if his answer were no, he would lose all chance of getting Lucy; she would not, indeed she should not, permit discrimination between her children.

"Of course," he said, speaking hastily, as if to make up for his first hesitation. "Of course I'd do everything I could for the boy. And I can afford to give him a good education, a good start in whatever profession he chooses. I want to."

"Thank you," Lucy said again. Then she rose. "I think perhaps we'd better not talk about this any more today," she went on. "You will not consider me unreasonable, will you, if I ask for a little more time to think it over? Perhaps you ought to think it over, too. It would represent a very important step for both of us, you know."

"I don't need to think it over any longer. It's a step I want to take just as soon as I possibly can. But of course I won't try to hurry you against your will."

"Thank you," she said the third time. "I will try to answer you more definitely in the course of your next visit—if you do not come too soon. . . . Would you care to take the walk around the plantation which I suggested in my letter? If you would, I will ask my mother to sit with Cary while we are out."

He gave her six months, meanwhile writing her restrained but affectionate letters, which she answered in a friendly way, without making any reference to the few loverlike passages which they contained. He also sent her such conventional gifts as sheet music, classical novels in cloth bindings and bonbons in hand-painted satin boxes. These she accepted without demur; but when he slipped a brooch in among the bonbons, she returned it to him, without any word of explanation, obviously considering that he should need none. However, he brought the brooch with him on his return and boldly handed it to

34

her, though without much hope that she would accept it. The reason she gave for doing so surprised him as much as the fact itself.

"I wasn't pleased when I found it hidden in the candy, as if it were shameful for you to offer it to me or for me to accept it," she said. "But now that you've brought it openly, that's different."

"May I put it on for you? I'm afraid the fastening is a little complicated."

"I'm not ready to wear it yet. When I am, I'll be glad to have you put it on. Not because of the fastening though. I think I could manage that."

"You said *when*! Does that really mean? . . ."

"May I ask you a few more questions?"

He had an instant of panic. *Now I've got to tell her everything*, he thought. *I suppose I'd have to tell her sometime. But if I could only wait until after we were married.* "Of course," was all he said aloud; and the questions proved undisturbing, after all.

"Where would we live after we were married?" she asked. "You haven't told me much about your business interests—naturally, there's no reason why you should have. But a good many of them seem to be in Virginia. There are reasons why I'd rather live somewhere else, if we could. You see, I'm afraid there's bound to be a good deal of opposition to our marriage, from the Carys and the Pages both. I hope it doesn't hurt your feelings to have me say that. But I think we'd have a better chance of happiness if we went somewhere else. Of course, that would leave my mother very much alone, unless I could find some relative who would be willing to come here and live with her, someone who would be congenial to her. A good many of our kinfolk have died or moved away, but still I think. . . . And if I could, that might be a solution."

"I hope it would. Because you haven't hurt my feelings and I agree with you that it would be better for us to live elsewhere. I do have business interests in Virginia, but there's no reason why they shouldn't be very quickly liquidated. How would you like to live in Louisiana?"

"Why—I don't know! I've never thought of doing so. How did you happen to think of it?"

"I've thought of it for years. I've wanted to do it for years. Not just in Louisiana, either. On a certain plantation, beside the Mississippi River. In a certain house."

"I've heard about those houses, along the river road. I've been told they're just as beautiful as any we have in Virginia, that they're truly classic in style. Why, some kinfolk of ours, named Conrad, live in one of them! They're connected with us, distantly, through the Washingtons. Did you know that the earlier Conrads are the only persons, besides the Washingtons, who are buried at Mount Vernon?"

"I didn't know about the burial at Mount Vernon, but I do know the house you mean. It's called The Cottage, because it has only twenty rooms in it." For a moment his eyes twinkled and his lips curved in a rather mocking smile. "The house I want isn't classical in style. It looks like a river steamer."

"*Like a river steamer!*"

"Yes. Some of the men who'd traveled up and down the Mississippi, in the golden days of steamboating, thought there was nothing to equal those floating palaces, as they were called. So these men built houses that would resemble them as much as possible. The type isn't called ante bellum, like the one you've been talking about. It's called Steamboat Gothic."

"*Steamboat Gothic!*"

"Yes. I think that's rather intriguing, don't you?"

"Yes, it is intriguing," she said slowly. If she felt any disappointment, if his first words about a mansion on the Mississippi had conjured up a vision which was now dispelled, she did not say so. "Who built these houses? Retired captains?"

"Sometimes; and sometimes, steamboat owners. As a matter of fact, the captain and the owner were very often one and the same man. Captains frequently drew the plans and supervised the construction of the boats they commanded, and were already aboard when these slid down the ways for the first time. But the Steamboat Gothic houses were generally built by wealthy planters whose business took them up and down the river. The one I want was built by a planter named Labouisse. But I've heard he never lived there. I believe he died before it was finished."

"Then it's unoccupied? It's for sale?"

"I don't know. But I can easily find out. It wouldn't take long to run down to Louisiana. Besides, I'd enjoy doing so. I told you I've always wanted to live there."

"You've spent a good deal of time there already?"

"I've spent a good deal of time on the river steamers—most of my time, before the war. I've been past the house I'm talking about over and over again. I saw it when it was being built. In fact, I noticed the preparations for the building before they actually started. The location's unusually fine—there's more of a rise to the ground sloping back from the river right there than there is on most of the land so far south. That makes it outstanding." He checked himself suddenly. The fact that the place he coveted was so pleasantly situated, geographically speaking, was not the only reason it had arrested his attention. It was just below a meander in the Mississippi which the rivermen had nicknamed Aces and Eights Bend, to commemorate the bloody killings of an epochal poker game aboard the *Winged Victory*—a game in which he had played a rather conspicuous part. It had been on the tip of his tongue to mention this meander, and its nickname would certainly have roused Lucy's attention. "I saw the thick, bristly willow scrub cleared away from the site," he went on hurriedly. "Then I saw something that looked like a magnified molehill on the clearing—and another and another. Those were the kilns where the bricks for the walls were fired. Presently, I saw slaves digging pits among the molehills and I knew that lime putty for the mortar and the plaster was being slaked. After that, the walls began to rise and I saw them getting higher and higher."

The haste with which he spoke gave the impression of excitement so enthusiastic that it was contagious. Lucy leaned forward, catching her breath a little, and fresh color came into her pale cheeks.

"You make me see it all, too, Clyde, while you're telling me about it," she said, speaking excitely in her turn.

"Can I really? Can I make you see the roustabouts unloading the trappings for the house that were sent over from France—the marble bathtub, the marble mantels? Can I make you hear them singing at the landing while they do it? Songs that go something like this:

> *'They ain't but a thousand mo'—*
> *My knee bones is achin',*
> *My shoulder is so'—*
> *When I make this trip*
> *Ain't gonna make no mo'.*
> *Coonjine, nigger, coonjine.'"*

"Why, Clyde, you never told me you could sing! You've got a good tenor voice! We could sing duets together!"

"I'm afraid you wouldn't care to join in the only kind of songs I know."

"You could learn others, couldn't you? And anyway, I enjoyed that one. Do you know more like it?"

"Of course. I know any number of rivermen's songs. And a few Negro spirituals. The slaves who built the garden terraces, shovelful by shovelful, at this place I've been telling you about, sang songs like this:

> *'Oh Je-sus nev-uh come in the morn-in',*
> *Nei-ther in the heat uv the day, But come in the cool*
> *uv the eve-nin' An' wash my sins a-way.'"*

"That sounds almost like a jungle chant."

"You're right, it does, almost. No wonder. That's what it is, almost. . . . Well, when this house I've been talking about was finally finished, it was the most magnificent mansion I ever saw."

"And that's the house you'd like for yours? That's where you'd like to take me as a bride?"

"What I'd *like*! What would mean more to me than anything else in the world!"

For the first time, he tried to take her in his arms. She slipped from his embrace, shaking her head.

"Not yet, please, Clyde. Give me another six months."

"Good Lord, Lucy! I've waited for years already."

"Then couldn't you wait a little longer?"

"I suppose I could. But I certainly don't want to."

"It's so important for me to be certain. I'm afraid if you can't wait the answer will have to be no."

"Well, of course, in that case. . . ."

In some ways, the next six months were easier than those that had just passed. Despite Mrs. Cary's tacit disapproval, Clyde came to Sorrento as an acknowledged, if not an accepted, suitor. When Lucy played for him, at dusk, on the old square piano, he turned the sheet music he had given her. When she bent over her embroidery frame, by lamplight, he read aloud to her from the classical novels he had sent her, skipping lightly over the passages which he thought might offend her. And, on the "pretty days," as she called them, of early spring, they wandered down to the riverbank and sat on the sandy beach, talking or keeping silent, as suited their mood. While this left him unsatisfied, he found it extremely pleasant. Besides, he realized that it was a privilege for a man like him to be received as a guest at such a plantation, even though this hospitality brought with it no special perquisites; he understood now how logically he might have thought himself lost, the first day he came there, even if the way he took had not been so strange and forbidding. The plantation drive, which traversed the once fertile fields and the still shadowy woods, extended five miles from the gateposts to the high cliff overlooking the James, where the house and gardens were located; even without the addition of Amalfi, the domain was one of princely proportions. The great brick house had been built from plans drawn by Thomas Jefferson shortly after his return from France; its central portion was connected by covered passages to the wide-spreading wings on either side; the whole effect was one of dignity and grandeur; and the extensive gardens, where every flower bed was outlined in dwarf box and every walk shaded by ancient elms and yews, enhanced the general effect of spaciousness and elegance, none of which was lost on the visitor. Moreover, he marveled at the wonders Lucy had already wrought. Somehow, she had found and gathered together a few scattered and bewildered Negroes and brought them "home." That was the way she referred to it; they did, too. Plowing and planting had begun, grass had been cut, flower beds weeded, brick walks repaired. Indoors, the change was equally great. The house had been swept and garnished and, in the process, it had lost much of its air of shabbiness and gloom though, as far as Clyde could see, its furnishings remained much the same, except that the worn places in the draperies and upholstery had been neatly darned and broken chairs and tables skillfully mended. He missed no important feature of equipment or adornment in any room, and would probably not have done so had it not been for overhearing a conversation between Lucy and her mother, one morning as he was coming down the stairs, when they supposed him to be still asleep.

"You had no right to sell that highboy, Lucy. It was an heirloom."

"In Cousin Tom Carter's family. But Cousin Tom gave it to *me* when he joined Stuart's Cavalry and told me to do whatever I wanted with it."

"He meant, of course, that you could keep it at Sorrento or at Richmond, whichever you preferred. He never dreamed that you would dispose of it."

"I've acted on what he *said*, believing that was what he meant. And I intend to sell other things, if necessary. Even Forrest's things. It's better to keep some in decent order than to let them all go to rack and ruin. And it's infinitely better to make this plantation productive again than it is to have a child go hungry again. In fact, I don't want to go hungry again myself. I don't intend to."

"I should never have believed that you would show so little sentiment, Lucy."

"Or so much sense? I'm sorry, Mother, that you don't approve. I hate to hurt your feelings. But it shows more delicacy, doesn't it, to sell a highboy, or even several highboys, than to make a mercenary marriage?"

"I think you will have other chances to marry, Lucy, if you'll wait a little. In fact, I have certain knowledge that you will. Only a man lacking in fine feeling would have addressed you so early in your widowhood. A man of your own class would have shown proper respect for the dead."

Clyde did not hear Lucy's answer, for he turned on the stairway and went, as quietly as possible, back to his room. He was not especially ashamed of his involuntary eavesdropping. But he knew he ran the risk of discovery where he was, and that Lucy would be deeply chagrined and her mother furiously angry, if they found out he had overheard. On the whole, however, he was pleased that he had. He did not like to think of Lucy selling her furniture, or anything else she possessed, and he wished he had the authority to put an instant stop to such sacrifices. On the other hand, he knew now that if Lucy did accept him, it would not be on account of his money; it would be because she cared for him—not as much as he wished she could, but that was too much to hope; at least enough to prefer him to those laggard suitors who had still not had the gumption to approach her. He sat down by the open window of his bedroom and looked out toward the fields, where two Negroes were singing as they sowed, and toward the woods beyond, where the redbud was just bursting into bloom beyond the fringe of feathery weeping willows, and suddenly he felt at peace with the world. And when he started down to breakfast the second time, Cary, who was walking quite steadily by herself now, came toddling out to meet him with cries of joy. And in the dining room he found a bright fire burning behind the polished andirons—for the early morning air was still crisp—and Lucy waiting for him at a table set with a shining silver service. He lifted Cary into her high chair and helped her spoon oatmeal from her porringer, while he and Lucy drank their coffee and ate homemade sausage and eggs which had been gathered that morning and hot biscuits dripping with freshly churned butter and preserves made from the figs for which Sorrento had been famous before the war.

The day marked a turning point. In the state of contentment and well-being which it engendered, he could afford to overlook even Bushrod's behavior, which had hitherto been a thorn in Clyde's flesh. The boy was less noisy and obstreperous than when he was younger; but he had turned sullen and would hardly speak to the visitor. This attitude, like his grandmother's, created a strain in the atmosphere. However, Clyde managed to ignore this now and Lucy's detachment troubled him less and less; though she continued to be elusive, Clyde knew this was not from coquetry, but from caution. She was trying hard to be fair to everyone—to her mother and her dead husband's family and her own children; most of all to Clyde himself. She was honest in her claim that he could offer more than she could give in return. And at last she capitulated: she would marry him, she said, the following autumn. If he wished, he might go to Louisiana at any time convenient for him and find out whether the house he wanted was for sale. If it was, she would go there with him to live. . . .

He returned from his trip, flushed with triumph, and proudly displayed his deed to Cindy Lou Plantation. She laid it down on the table beside them, as if it were of minor importance and, for the first time, on her own initiative, threw her arms around his neck.

"Oh, I'm so glad you're back!" she exclaimed. "I've missed you terribly!" and raised her face to his.

He never knew how long they remained, locked in that fond embrace. But it was he who finally released her, not she who sought release.

"Lucy," he said, wondering why his voice sounded so strange to him. "Lucy—I haven't asked you this before, but . . . I know you're fond of me in a way, I've known it for a long time. I know you have confidence in me, too. You're sure I'll always be a good husband to you and a good father to your children. You're not marrying me just for my money. I wouldn't insult you by such a suggestion. And not out of gratitude because of the little I've done for you, either. That would be hard for me to take, too. I know you've got—well, it's a queer thing for me to say, but I believe you actually have a certain amount of respect for me, though Lord knows I don't deserve it. But I've never dreamed that you loved me—at least, that you were in love with me, the way I am with you—never, that is, until just now."

"Why, of course I am!" Lucy exclaimed, and put her arms around his neck again.

It was a great moment, the greatest in his life. But it might have been so much greater if it had only come before he went to Louisiana.

 CHAPTER II

IT WAS years now since that regret had risen from the past to trouble him. Lucy did not suggest a further postponement of their marriage, as he had half feared she might; on the contrary, she consented willingly when he asked to have the date slightly advanced. The thought crossed his mind that she felt the first embrace she had so spontaneously given him was more appropriate for a wife than for a sweetheart, and that since she had inadvertently revealed she was capable of passion, she should not risk further betrayals of her feelings until she had crossed the threshold of the conjugal chamber. He was faintly amused by this suspicion, but at the same time it raised his admiration of Lucy to still greater heights. What a lady she was! What a lovely, refined, cultured lady! In his highest hopes for success, he had not dreamed that anyone like Lucy would become a part of it. He would never quite believe in his good fortune until they were actually married.

The wedding took place in the parlor at Sorrento in the presence of a mere handful of guests. Lucy had asked Clyde if he had relatives or intimate friends whom he would like to invite; and when he told her he had not, she murmured sympathetically that she was only beginning to realize how lonely his life had been and that she hoped it would be very different in the future. Apparently it did not occur to her that a waif might not even be certain of his parentage, or that it was the caliber and not the lack of later associates which made him loath to introduce them to her presence. As far as her relatives were concerned, most of the Peyton and Cary kinfolk and all the Pages disapproved of the match and found pretexts for absence; Clyde was not deceived by this, but neither did it disturb him, and he made himself so agreeable to the few who did come that they went home to spread the tidings that Cousin Sophia Cary must have been mistaken in her estimate of Mr. Batchelor or that they must have misunderstood her: he was entirely presentable, indeed very good looking, his manners quite polished, his conversation that of a cultivated gentleman. After all, it was not quite fair to condemn him as a Yankee, because he came from St. Louis. Everyone knew, or should know, by this time, that Missouri, like Maryland, had been largely southern in its sympathies, even if the baser elements in its borders had kept it in the Union. And it was sad to think that his family had been decimated, exactly like so many in Virginia. . . .

Among the relatives who voiced this opinion most persistently was Mrs. Cary's elderly cousin Miss Mildred Caskie, who had needed very little persuasion to attend the wedding and to stay on at Sorrento indefinitely. Her brother Edmond Caskie had been one of the small but notable group of former Confederate officers who had emigrated to Mexico, rather than take the oath of allegiance to the United States government; and since he and she were the only members of the immediate family left, Mildred had loyally accompanied him. Now Edmond, like his revered leader Kirby-Smith, had married a Mexican and settled down to comfortable and contented domesticity. But no suitor had mitigated Mildred's exile; and though her brother and his young bride had been kind to her, and assured her that their home would always be hers, she had known she was not needed there, and that, sooner or later, her presence would seem superfluous, if not actually irksome. She had welcomed the pretext of returning to her native heath so providentially indicated by Lucy's marriage and Cousin Sophia's consequent need of companionship. The least she could do was to express approbation of the bridegroom who had put an end to her banishment; and, as a matter of fact, she found to her relief that she could do this without perjuring herself.

Clyde was conscious of the good impression he had made on the relatives present at his marriage, especially Cousin Mildred, just as he was conscious of the reasons which had kept the others away; but he was no more gratified by one attitude than he was upset by the other, for all his thoughts were centered on Lucy. She was beautiful as a bride, in a gown of rich garnet-colored silk and garnet jewelry. The dress was not new, she told him blushingly, when he complimented her on her appearance; it was her mother's second-day dress, which had been carefully kept in a trunk under the eaves, and she had made it over herself. Clyde had never heard of a second-day dress before, so Lucy was obliged to explain to him, blushing still more deeply, that a second-day dress was always included in the trousseau of every well-equipped Virginia bride; that is, every bride who was a—every bride who was marrying for the first time. Such a bride wore a white dress, of course, for her wedding, and a veil; but she was also supplied with an equally handsome colored dress to wear after—well, the next day. Of course,

Mrs. Cary's wedding dress was in that attic trunk, too; it was very beautiful, as everything in her trousseau had been, because at the time she was married, in the thirties, there was plenty of money in the family. Perhaps little Cary would wear that bridal dress someday. Lucy hoped so. But she herself could not wear it because. . . . She stopped, entirely suffused with blushes. Candid as she was in all other respects, there was one subject on which she could not touch without self-consciousness.

"Well, I think the garnet silk is superb," Clyde assured her. "In fact, I believe it's more becoming to you than the white outfit would have been." He did not say he really preferred seeing her in garnet; it was impossible to lie to Lucy, and of course, like any other man, he would have preferred to have his bride a virgin, rather than a widow. But, as he had often observed before, many of Lucy's attributes were singularly virginal. Among these were her inability to speak naturally of anything connected with sex, her conviction that ardent caresses and the feelings which inspired them should be restrained—attributes in which Dorothée Labouisse had been so singularly lacking. Sometimes Clyde had moments of fearing that even after marriage Lucy might feel joy in self-abandonment was slightly shameful on the part of a gentlewoman, though she would expect a man to demand and desire complete submission. She would never forget it was ordained by scriptures that a woman's husband should rule over her and she would conduct herself accordingly; but compliance would not be enough for Clyde—Lucy had shown that to her first husband. He wanted her to stop thinking about love as a sentiment and recognize it as a vital force which could not attain its full power and majesty unless passion were reciprocal. And then he would reproach himself for this yearning and remind himself again how overwhelmingly fortunate he was to have her at all.

The wedding ceremony was deeply impressive. The parlor where it took place, decorated with autumn foliage, gave a far greater effect of spaciousness than it would have if it had been overcrowded with disapproving relatives. The colored servants gathered around the doorway, their black faces beaming. They had favored Clyde's suit from the beginning, and not merely because of the generous tips he gave them, either; now they were delighted that he had won through and they showed it. The elderly clergyman who performed the marriage service was a benign figure, his still abundant hair as snowy as his robes. Cary was a bewitching flower girl, and even Bushrod's sullenness was in abeyance, and he acted the part of a page boy to perfection. Mrs. Cary gave the bride away, since there was no close male relative still living, and this gave an added touch of solemnity to the occasion; and after the benign clergyman had pronounced Lucy and Clyde man and wife, he kissed her gravely on the brow and told her he hoped she would be very happy with her husband in her new home. Then Clyde kissed her

43

himself, rather gravely, too, because he was greatly moved; and after that her mother and her children and her other relatives came up to kiss her and a few of the kinfolk kissed Clyde, too, telling him he was now one of the family and that this was a cousin's privilege. Gradually, the solemnity gave way to festivity. Everyone went out into the dining room to drink the champagne which Clyde had insisted on providing and to cluster around the bride while she cut the cake she had made herself. Finally, someone suggested that there should be dancing in the hall, and a pickaninny was sent running to fetch old Blind Simeon's fiddle, and he played for reels and lancers and waltzes until everyone sank back breathlessly, admitting that it was impossible to dance any more, and that perhaps it was time to permit the bride and groom to slip away.

Clyde had suggested a grand tour in Europe for a wedding trip, but Lucy objected that Cary was too young to leave for so long or to take on such a journey; it would be better to wait for the grand tour until she was a little older. However, Lucy made no objections to leaving both children, temporarily, at Sorrento, with their grandmother and their cousin Mildred, with the understanding that Cousin Mildred should bring them to Louisiana later on; and she also agreed to Clyde's second suggestion in favor of New York for their honeymoon. The journey was a tedious one, since it involved a jolting carriage ride from Sorrento to Richmond; a trip from Richmond to Aquia on a train with only antiquated equipment; a river trip in a small side-wheeler from Aquia to Washington; a second train trip from Washington to Jersey City; and finally, a ferry crossing to New York. Lucy slept a little on the way to Richmond, supported by Clyde's arm around her waist and resting her head against his shoulder, as the carriage went jerking along in the darkness of the November night after the wedding dance; and she had a really good nap in one of the little cabins on the side-wheeler. But she had vetoed Clyde's recommendation that they should break their journey by a stopover in Richmond, and he had not insisted, rightly divining that the memories of her later years there were still so painful that she did not wish to associate that scene, in any way, with her honeymoon. The idea of a stopover in Washington was equally distasteful to her; she still visualized this only as the place where the downfall of the South had been plotted and been brought about and Clyde could understand that viewpoint, too. But the unbroken trip taxed her strength to the utmost and despite her efforts to conceal her weariness, Clyde realized that Lucy was very tired by the time they reached the Fifth Avenue Hotel; before they escaped from the reception hall, her exhaustion was still more obvious. The marble-tiled, brightly frescoed foyer was filled to overflowing with fashionably dressed people; the air heavy with cigar smoke, the confusion of sounds bewildering. The office bell, ringing incessantly, sent servants scurrying in a dozen different directions at once, to execute peremptory orders; and porters, bearing huge trunks on their shoulders, pushed their way through the crowds with shouts of warning. One vociferous group was discussing a burning political issue; another, almost equally excited, the latest developments of the stock market; and above the babel of voices came the clink of glasses and the echo of laughter from the bar-room beyond. Lucy clung to Clyde and the look she turned on him was one of mute and involuntary appeal. He guided her expertly toward the marble counter enclosing the offices at the rear and wrote their names on the visitors' register, where other newcomers had already filled several pages that day. The reception clerk glanced at the signature and inclined his head respectfully.

"Good evening, sir. Good evening, madam. I hope that you will be pleased with the suite that has been reserved for you. We have tried to follow all your instructions meticulously, Mr. Batchelor."

"What instructions did you give them?" Lucy whispered, as the clerk reached for a big key and rang for a bellboy.

"I said I'd expect them to make us comfortable and I think you'll find they have. This way, dear. No, you don't have to climb up that mammoth staircase. There's an elevator right here on your left."

"I—I don't think I know just what you mean."

"An elevator is a sort of enclosed cage that's hoisted by pulleys from one story to another—the Fifth Avenue Hotel installed the first one in this country. Don't be afraid. It's perfectly safe and a great saving of time and effort. I know you're tired to death. But we'll be out of this hubbub in a moment now and then you can rest."

He realized that she was experiencing fresh qualms as they entered "the cage," but she suppressed her fears as she had suppressed her weariness. They had now been joined by an elegant functionary of the hotel who introduced himself as Mr. Puthammer, one of the managers, and who had taken charge of their key, informing them that he was giving himself the pleasure of seeing them to their suite; he wanted to make sure, for himself, that everything was satisfactory. He continued to give directions to the laden bellboys as he and his charges alighted from the elevator, and steered them down a long hall, flooded with brilliant gaslight and so deeply carpeted that their feet sank noiselessly into the rich pile. Then he paused, glancing at the number on a panel of black walnut and, having inserted the key in its ornamented lock, threw open a double door and stood back, bowing, to permit the entrance of the bridal pair.

Beyond the vestibule, a second door opened into a large parlor, furnished with the utmost opulence and decorated with a profusion of flowers. A fire burned brightly under its marble mantel; its center table was already set for dinner with spotless linen and sparkling silver, and near by the gold-wrapped neck of a champagne bottle emerged from the shining ice bucket in which it was immersed. On either side of the parlor, still other doors opened out, revealing glimpses of a chamber dominated by a huge black walnut bed and a dressing room with a tall-mirrored shaving stand. Clyde went rapidly from one to the other, assuring himself that there were fires and flowers everywhere, and that there was a private bath beyond the dressing room. But Lucy stood as if transfixed, just beyond the threshold, and when Clyde rejoined her she reached suddenly for his hand, with an exclamation so expressive of amazement and delight that he knew her weariness and her qualms were all forgotten.

"Why, Clyde, it's—it's like a vision of fairyland!" she exclaimed. "Are you sure it's real? Are you sure *we* are?" Clyde returned the pressure of her hand and glanced at Mr. Puthammer.

"The suite is entirely satisfactory," Clyde informed him. "We will ring when we desire service. I wish you good night."

"That dummy cheated me out of lifting you over the threshold," Clyde told her when he released her from the embrace in which he had enfolded her as soon as the door closed behind the obsequious manager and the grinning bellboys. "Never mind, I'll do it at Cindy Lou. After all, that's going to be our real home—this is just a way station."

"I tell you, I believe it's fairyland," Lucy insisted. She went readily enough now, under Clyde's guidance, from one part to another, still giving little unsmothered cries of delighted amazement. However, when he suggested ringing for a maid to unpack their bags, she shook her head.

"It won't take me any time at all to do that."

"But you're tired. And of course I can't let you unpack my things."

"But of course you can. I'm your wife now."

"Yes, you're my wife now. And that means you're never going to lift your finger again, unless you feel like it."

"But I *do* feel like it. I suppose we'll have to let a waiter bring us our dinner. But don't you think, except for that, it would be pleasanter not to have any—any intruders?"

He was obliged to admit that it would be; and eventually, they agreed that he should unpack his bag in the dressing room while she unpacked hers in the bedroom and that, when she had changed her traveling costume for a *robe d'intérieur,* they should meet again in the parlor and Clyde should ring for dinner. She pronounced all the dishes which were brought to them delicious and praised the service highly, both in the hearing of the deft waiter and after he had withdrawn. But Clyde noticed that she was eating very little of the rich viands which he consumed with lusty relish and merely sipping the champagne which he was quaffing in deep draughts. The pinched look of fatigue was coming back into her lovely face, too; it was not rapturous any longer;

46

and suddenly Clyde realized that returning exhaustion was not alone responsible for her expression. When the waiter had noiselessly withdrawn for the last time, Clyde rose and held out his arms.

He could not honestly have said that Lucy was slow in rising to her feet or that she came to him with any sign of hesitation. She was sweet, she was smiling, she was utterly compliant; but the spontaneity which had meant so much to him on the rare occasions when she had shown it was lacking.

"Lucy," he said tenderly, "Lucy, darling! A little while ago you reminded me that you're my wife now—as if I needed any reminder! As if this hadn't been the greatest day of my life! But you said it as if it meant that I would expect you to wait on me. I tried to tell you that I don't, that I not only don't expect it, I don't want it, I won't allow it. I think I ought to tell you something else. I don't want a 'dutiful' wife, much less a 'submissive' one. I think the word 'obey' ought to come out of the marriage service. You're terribly tired. You've had a hard journey on top of all the strain of getting ready for the wedding and of the wedding itself. If it would be a relief to you to go into the bedroom and shut the door, and lie down to sleep, knowing you wouldn't be disturbed, that's what I want you to do. I'd never reproach you for it in my mind and I'd never refer to it again."

"But—" Lucy began falteringly.

"Please let me finish, darling. I'm terribly serious about this and I'm trying to be completely sincere, too. That *is* what I want you to do if it would be a relief to you. But I'm not sure that it would. I'm afraid you wouldn't go quietly to sleep. I'm afraid you'd be disquieted, not just by the feeling that you'd been unfair to me, either—I've told you to stop thinking about that, once and for all—but by the vague consciousness that you weren't fulfilling your own destiny as a woman. Because you wouldn't be. You won't be until—well, until I've helped you to do it. It's just as instinctive for a woman—a woman like you, I mean—to resist physical union as it is for a man to seek it. At least, that's the primary instinct. Once it's overcome—once you've given me a chance to overcome it—you'll want it as much as I will."

"But—" Lucy said again.

"I haven't quite finished even yet, darling. There's something else I want to make clear to you, if I can. In fact, it's even more important for me to tell you what I do want than it was to tell you what I don't want. I want you to get over the idea that it's shameful for a woman—and again, I mean a woman like you—to feel passion and to show that she does. It's normal for men and women to share the full experience of love, and they can't do it, if the desire for it is one sided. *It's got to be mutual.* And it will be for us, if you'll just believe me, if you'll just trust yourself to me."

"I do believe you, I do trust myself to you. Oh, Clyde, I'm so—so

47

grateful to you for talking to me like this! No one ever did before. No one ever explained—no one ever revealed. . . . I'm not tired any more, truly I'm not. I'm not afraid, I'm not ashamed. I want you to come to me and stay with me, I want you to overcome that instinctive resistance. I want our desire to be mutual and I know it is going to be. *It is already.*"

So the opulent bridal suite had become the scene of repeated raptures, for, as Clyde had promised Lucy, their marriage quickly became one of shared desires and shared delights; but he was also insistent on her need for repose and refreshment and, because of his loving solicitude, the fatigue of travel was quickly overcome and Lucy swiftly embarked on a round of shopping and sight-seeing and theatergoing which Clyde mapped out for them. The garnet silk dress was beautiful, Clyde told her again. (She had brought it with her, for it was the best one she had.) But there were to be no more made-over dresses in her life. They would find out immediately who were considered the very best dressmakers, and then Lucy must order a complete outfit of new clothes, including a quilted skirt, to wear over her hoops, and a full-length sealskin coat; also a tippet and muff of chinchilla which, Clyde had been told, should be worn with a velvet casque. And of course she must get several evening gowns—she would find that everyone in the hotel dining room was in full dress, the ladies' toilettes magnificent; he wanted her to outshine all the others. The garnet jewelry became her and he knew she valued it as an heirloom; but she must also have diamonds and other sparkling gems, which he and she would select together at the great silver and jewelry house of Tiffany, Young and Ellis. And she must not neglect to get household linens and all such supplies for Cindy Lou; he knew she had not felt free to draw on the depleted stock at Sorrento, and that it was still impossible to buy such things in any quantity or of any quality at the Richmond stores. Nonsense, what was she talking about? It was the bride's place to supply such things as linen? Well, that was just what he was asking her to do! Why, of course she was spending her own money! Didn't she understand, even yet, that the money he had given her at the time of their marriage *was* her own, that he would never consent to an accounting of it!

The shopping excursions alone would have left Lucy breathless with delight. She could well understand why the establishment of Lord and Taylor, at the corner of Grand and Chrystie streets, should be called "one of the architectural wonders of Manhattan." It had a large central rotunda, surmounted by a dome, and the windows were as handsome as those at St. Patrick's Cathedral. Lucy was prejudiced against Lord and Taylor's at first, because it made so much of the fact that Mrs. Abraham Lincoln had been one of its most prodigal customers; she said she would prefer to purchase from Arnold Constable, which had a really exclusive clientele and did not need to publicize this or seek to enlarge it—indeed, its window displays consisted of nothing more elaborate than a half dozen umbrellas, arranged fan-shaped, or a few lengths of dress goods. But she was drawn back to Lord and Taylor's in spite of herself and she also went to Stewarts' and McCreery's and Hearns', finding at each some special attraction which would have satisfied her completely if she had seen nothing else.

However, Clyde insisted that the magnificent stores were only one of New York's great sights; they could not see them all, and they must not try to see so many that Lucy would be tired and not feel like going to a play in the evening. How could she get tired, she asked, when everything was made so easy for her? She was getting disgracefully lazy, breakfasting in bed, bathing and dressing at her leisure, sitting down to perfect meals without a thought as to their preparation, their service or their cost, and then getting into a carriage every time she and Clyde covered more than a few blocks. The only exercise she had was in walking around their suite. To be sure, that was enormous—almost as large as the second story at Sorrento. But in the Fifth Avenue Hotel she did not even walk up and down stairs—not that it would have been any effort to do so, but she had become fascinated by that strange contraption called an elevator and readily consented to Clyde's insistence that she should always take it. She really wondered that he would permit her to walk as far as the Fifth Avenue Theater, though that was directly back of their hotel!

They joked about this, and Clyde offered to carry her; he might even have made a show of doing this, if he had not known that Lucy hated to be made conspicuous. But he could not refrain from pressing close to her as she took his arm to cross the street, or from holding her hand when the lights had been dimmed in the rose-walled, mirror-lined parquet; and throughout the performances of *She Would and She Would Not* and *Much Ado About Nothing,* he was far more conscious of her intoxicating nearness than he was of Fanny Davenport's fascination as Viletta and Mary Scott-Siddons' charm as Beatrice. Lucy, divining this, chided him gently, reminding him that Fanny Davenport was the most photographed young actress of the day, and Mary Scott-Siddons a direct descendant of the greatest actress of all time. But Clyde only retorted that the reason Fanny had such a clear field was because far more beautiful women declined to be photographed, and that all the critics were saying Mary was "no real successor" to "the Magnificent Sarah," her great-grandmother.

How could those critics tell, Lucy inquired, with mock haughtiness, disregarding the comment on photography, which, she knew, was aimed at herself. Had any of them seen the Magnificent Sarah in the flesh? Of course not! Well then! As far as she was concerned, she thought the current Beatrice could not have been better and she wanted to see Mary's Viola, too, if Clyde did not think they were spending too much time—and too much money—on the theater. Why, they had all the time there was, and all the money, too, Clyde answered. Besides, he added, studying his program, *As You Like It* was a matinee, a special performance at special prices; they could go to that in the afternoon without spending much money and still get to another play in the evening—perhaps something a little lighter than Shakespeare. What would Lucy think of *Little Nell and the Marchioness* at Niblo's Garden?

The Fifth Avenue Theater, like the Fifth Avenue Hotel, laid great stress on refined elegance; but Niblo's Garden was even more glamorous, and proclaimed its presence at the rear of the Metropolitan Hotel by a great illuminated sign, composed of gas jets in red, white and blue glass cups, strung on an iron pipe. Clyde gathered that Lucy did not admire this sign quite as much as he did, and that she preferred Scott-Siddons' interpretation of Viola to Lotta's performance of *Little Nell*. But it was not because of anything she said or did to dampen his enjoyment, only because he was more and more sensitive to her tastes, her moods, her feelings, more and more eager that nothing should mar her pleasure or offend her delicacy.

Following the theater, there was always a midnight supper, at the Metropolitan or the St. Nicholas or Delmonico's. Lucy gasped and remonstrated when she caught sight of a check setting forth a charge of ten dollars a plate for breast of chicken; and after that, Clyde systematically hid the checks from her, teasing her again and saying he had no idea he had married a miser. He would not tell her, either, how much he spent on carriage hire when they drove through Central Park at the smart clip of six miles an hour, or went as far afield as Claremont for a day's outing; so presently, she ceased to ask even casual questions about money. He realized then that she was sensitive to his feelings, too, that she knew he did not want to talk about it, only to spend it; and he tried to tell himself that his prodigality would atone for the devious ways in which he had won his wealth, and that when Lucy found out what these had been, as sooner or later she must do, he would succeed in making her feel that way about it, too.

Finally, they went to grand opera at the Academy of Music—a superb performance of *William Tell,* in which Madame Biol sang Mathilde and the great Le Franc Arnoldo. This was an occasion when Lucy must wear her most striking dress, Clyde told her, and all her most dazzling new jewels. He was ready to agree with her, by this time, that, generally speaking, simplicity became her more than showiness and pearls better than sparkling gems. But there were exceptions to every rule and this time he wanted her to be resplendent. So she put on her parure of rubies and diamonds and a satin dress, striped in shades of magenta and cream and trimmed with black velvet and rose

50

point lace. It had just been delivered from Sophia Diedens and was made in the latest style, with hardly a suggestion of a hoop, but with a hint of a bustle—a dress that accentuated her charms and revealed her figure to a far greater degree than anything she had ever worn, except in private. She tried to draw her great circular cape of white swansdown more closely around her; but it kept parting and when she took her seat in the central box of the grand tier, opera glasses were turned upon her from every part of the house and an audible murmur of admiration rippled through it. Lucy blushed so deeply that Clyde realized she did not wholly share his undiluted pride in this tribute to her beauty; and as they sat at supper, after the spectacle, she asked him a question which revealed afresh her instinctive aversion to attracting public attention, tactfully as she worded her suggestion.

"I'm sure nothing could surpass the splendor of that opera. Don't you think perhaps it would be a mistake if we tried to find something that would?"

"Just what do you mean, honey?"

"Well, I've been wondering—just wondering, of course—if we shouldn't begin to think of leaving New York. You said you wanted to celebrate Christmas at Cindy Lou. I'd like that, too."

"All right, we'll consider that settled. Even so, we don't need to hurry. It isn't as if there'd be a lot for you to do after we got there. The house was left in perfect order when it was vacated."

"You mean by Mme Labouisse?"

"Yes, of course. She was the former owner. You knew that." He realized he had spoken abruptly, almost reprovingly, but he could not help it; and suddenly he feared that his discomfiture might have betrayed him, that he might have grown red in the face, instead of assuming that blank expression which, hitherto, he had always been able to command at will. "She saw that it was thoroughly cleaned," he went on hurriedly. "In fact, I imagine she did a good deal of the cleaning herself—she had only one house servant left, a Negress named Belle, who, incidentally, has great potentialities as a cook." He paused and took a sip of wine. "However, you'll find the house completely staffed now. When Belle got wind of what was happening, she began calling in all her kith and kin and they're pretty numerous. I couldn't stay around long enough to find out whether they were any good or not and Doro—Mme Labouisse was eager to be on her way to France as soon as the sale went through, but—"

"Of course she was," Lucy interrupted sympathetically. Apparently, she had not noticed his slip. "Of course it would have been painful to stay in or near her old home after it belonged to someone else. Remember how I felt about Richmond!"

"Yes," Clyde answered, swallowing hard. "Well, she left—immediately, as I've said. But I spoke about my problem—about wanting to be ou had suitable house servants, I mean—to M. Gilbert Ledoux, notary who handled the sale, and he introduced me to a Mrs. Surget, the widow of a very eminent physician who used to practice in that locality. I'm sure you'll like her very much, Lucy—in fact, I believe you and she will become great friends, though she's considerably older than you are. I could tell, at a glance, that she's your kind. She lives all alone now, very simply and quietly. I'm afraid she's in rather reduced circumstances, but her house is charming—in fact, it's unique. The main part is square, with three front doors—"

"Three front doors! Whatever for?"

"I haven't the least idea. One of them leads into the hall and one into each of the drawing rooms and they're outlined in a rectangular design, almost Egyptian in effect. Back of the drawing rooms are two bedrooms and overhead there's an attic, reached by a tiny winding staircase. Outside, it looks like a belvedere, because it crowns a hipped roof, but actually it fulfills a useful storage purpose."

"The whole thing sounds very intriguing. But where's the dining room?"

"I'm coming to that. Back of the bedrooms there's a breezeway and back of that is a separate building, containing a large dining room which runs all the way across it, and two more bedrooms. At the rear, in still another building, is the kitchen. The doctor's old office is in front, near the main house, and that's even more striking. Its pillars are made of solidified bagasse—Dr. Surget was almost the first person to advance the idea that this could be utilized instead of burned as waste —and the decorations are arabesque rather than Egyptian. So altogether there are four separate units in the establishment and a surprising amount of space, though it looks much smaller than most of those belonging to the country gentry around there. But the effect of the coloring is the most surprising of all—the buildings are chalk white, the shutters bright green and the decorative design bright red—even the glass panels above the three front doors are painted to simulate bricks. But the whole thing's outstanding in every sense of the word. However, I'm afraid the poor lady's had to sell a good many of her treasures, for there isn't much that's especially beautiful or attractive inside the house, except a collection of some rather odd little bedside lamps that Mrs. Surget calls *veilleuses*—and of course it must have had all sorts of fine furnishings, once."

"Of course it must have—an original place like that—" Lucy exclaimed, still more understandingly than she had spoken before. "I never heard of a *veilleuse* before. Can you describe one to me?"

"Yes, I can, because Mrs. Surget showed me the whole collection," Clyde answered, glad of the diversion. "A *veilleur* is a watchman, isn't he? I don't know much French, of course, but I believe that's what Mrs. Surget said and that *veilleuse* would be the feminine form of the noun. Well, anyway, the kind of *veilleuse* she has is a small vessel something like a teapot which fits on a stand large enough to contain a short candle or a little lamp, just big enough to float a wick in oil. I understand that the wick of the lamp serves a dual purpose: it gives enough light to prevent a room from being completely dark and it keeps the contents of the vessel warm. Mrs. Surget says *veilleuses* are not used, currently, quite as much as they used to be, but that, in provincial France and rural Louisiana, they still serve to keep a baby's milk or an invalid's tisane warm through the night. You'd be surprised to see all the shapes the little pots are made in. Elephants carrying howdahs, castles, loving couples, Madonnas complete with angels, jolly friars with baskets of bottles. There was even one shaped like a nun with a little cup in her hand as if she had been preparing a drink for an invalid herself. Mrs. Surget's enormously proud of her collection and it's one prize possession she's kept intact. I think though, from something she said, she plans to give you a choice item from it for a wedding present."

"That would be very, very kind of her," Lucy said warmly. "But I wouldn't like to feel I was taking anything from her that she really valued, when she's lost so much already."

"I think she'd really like to give you a *veilleuse*—that is, if she takes to you, and of course she will. I just told you, she and you are the same kind. And, even if she has had to dispose of some things she valued, everything about her house revealed good taste and good management," Clyde went on, "and she herself struck me as being not only a lady of great culture and refinement, but one of considerable efficiency. I asked her if she would be willing to take charge of training a corps of house servants and otherwise preparing Cindy Lou for your reception and she said she'd be delighted. Naturally, I put the transaction on—well, on a practical basis. I didn't ask her to do it as a favor."

"And I'm sure you did it very tactfully, just as you offered to bring 'delicacies' to the house for me and my family when we were starving," Lucy said, with a glance of grateful affection. "Very likely you kept her from going hungry, too. You're always doing kind things for people, aren't you, Clyde?"

"Not by any means. But I certainly intend, as I've told you before, that you shan't ever lift a finger again, unless you feel like it. You won't need to do anything, when you get to Cindy Lou, but walk into your new house and enjoy it. Someone else will have done all the hard work. We could be ready to celebrate Christmas the day after we arrived, if we wanted to, which means we could stay in New York at least a week longer and still have time enough."

"But we have to begin to plan for the trip a little while beforehand, don't we?"

"Yes, we can begin right now, if you like. I thought perhaps you'd enjoy an ocean voyage. We can take a steamer direct from New York to New Orleans. It's the quickest and easiest way—the pleasantest, too, I believe. The boats are very good now and we'd have no changes to make, none of the confusion you find so tiring. Why, it wouldn't begin to be as exhausting as the trip from Sorrento to New York!"

"You mean we wouldn't travel on the Mississippi *at all?*"

It was the first time she had ever voiced disappointment at any suggestion he made. He felt sure it was the first time she had ever felt any.

"Well, we'd go from New Orleans to Cindy Lou by boat."

"But Clyde, I've been looking forward so much to going down the river all the way from St. Louis! One of our cousins, Stanard Daingerfield who lives in Louisville, has written me about a new floating palace that's named the *Richmond*. He traveled on it last year, and he said he'd never seen anything to equal it, even in the so-called 'Golden Days' of steamboating—that it really would beggar description! I admit I didn't want to stop over in the real Richmond, and perhaps you thought on that account. . . . But this would be different. It would bring back all the happy associations and none of the sad ones. I'd taken it for granted that we'd go to Louisiana by the river, because you've spent so much time on it and love it so much. And I've been meaning to ask you whether we couldn't take the *Richmond,* because that would mean so much to me and because—"

She broke off, looking at him with an expression in which bewilderment was mingled with appeal. He could not wonder at this: so far, he had forestalled her every wish before she could express it; now she had voiced a wholly reasonable desire and he did not know how to answer her, much less how to grant the favor she asked. She still had no inkling, obviously, of the way he had spent his time on the Mississippi; she would have to know someday, he fully meant to tell her himself—someday. But not yet. Not until he had proven himself worthy of her lasting love. So far, as she said herself, he had given her a glimpse of fairyland; he had taken her from scenes of tragedy and ruin, from associations with defeat and death, from a life of privation and toil, to a gorgeous and triumphant metropolis where she was lapped in luxury and laden with gifts. To be sure, he had done more than that: while treating her with the utmost tenderness, he had given her buoyant companionship and initiated her into secret delights. But he could have done all this, even if he had not changed the pattern of his former life; indeed, almost any man, who was rich and vigorous, and whose intelligence and kindliness had not been engulfed by his wealth and his virility could have done that much. And, in the long run, Lucy would instinctively feel that her husband had failed her if he offered her only prodigality and passion. She would not only want—but need—to respect and admire the man she had married, to value his opinions, to defer to

54

his judgment and to find quiet communion as well as overpowering rapture in the intimate hours which they shared.

"Besides," she went on, while Clyde was still groping for the words in which to answer her, "I've been hoping you'd show me St. Louis. You've been to Sorrento, you've been to what's left of Amalfi. You've told me it interested you to see where I grew up, to learn more about the life I led as a girl—a very happy life until I. . . . That is, until we knew there was going to be a war. It would interest me just as much to see how you grew up."

Clyde knew she had almost said, "It was a very happy life until I was persuaded to marry a man I didn't love." Ordinarily, a reminder of the compulsion which had been put upon her would have roused him to such indignation that he could not have thought of anything else until his wrath subsided. As it was, his resentment was swallowed up in consternation. While he had been trying to frame an answer to her first suggestion, his thoughts had been racing toward a compromise: he really needed to go to Pittsburgh, to see how the new ventures on which he was embarking were getting on; if they made the first part of their journey by train, and then took one of the smaller packets as far as Cairo, or even as far as Memphis, the danger of discovery would be greatly lessened; it was on the real floating palaces that he had operated. Besides, he had never had either a "capper" or a permanent partner; only at rare intervals had he joined forces with another member of the outlaw fraternity to bring off some special project. Moreover, he had been wonderfully successful in the matter of masquerading. During the course of his career, he had, at various times, impersonated a lumber-jack, a government agent and a wealthy planter, and had played the role of each so convincingly that detection had been infrequent. Even when it had occurred, he had seldom run into real trouble, for he had never deliberately invited it. He had been proud of the dexterity which was partly inherent and partly the result of long practice; so he had always preferred to keep his winnings dependent on skillful, rather than fraudulent, manipulation, and had derived far more satisfaction from a game in which he could match his wits against those of a reasonably adroit antagonist than from one in which he had a miserable "sucker" for his opponent. Not that he had ever allowed another professional to victimize him; he was not above resorting to shady practices himself, when confronted with a crooked gamester bent on winning by foul means, if he could not win by fair ones; but he could still flatter himself that he had been primarily an expert cardplayer. Surely, if he were aboard the *Richmond* only a few days, he could manage somehow; indeed, once they were aboard a more modest steamboat, Lucy could even be persuaded that it would be senseless to go to all the trouble of transferring to a larger one. . . . Yes, he would be almost sure that some such plan

55

could be carried through without disaster. . . . And here she was saying she wanted to see St. Louis because that was where he had grown up!

Abruptly, he motioned to their waiter to bring the bill and rose, with equal abruptness, before he remembered that, of course, he should have waited for Lucy to give the signal that they were to leave the table. He hardly spoke on their way back to the hotel and, once they had reached their suite, he went straight to his dressing room. Lucy was already in bed when he rejoined her. She had lowered the lights, but she had not extinguished them, and she had not composed herself for slumber, by lying relaxed on her side, with one arm under her head, but was sitting up, with two pillows behind her. Even in the semidarkness Clyde could see that her expression was troubled. She held out her arms to him.

"Darling," she said softly. "I've offended you in some way, haven't I? You must know I didn't mean to. But please forgive me, anyway. I'd rather die than hurt your feelings."

"You sweet angel, you haven't hurt my feelings," he answered quickly; and, as he spoke, he knelt down beside her. At the moment he felt that only on his knees could he accept her embrace. "But. . . . Do you remember a long while ago, even before we were engaged, I offered to tell you something about myself, and you stopped me? You said there would be time enough for that when you consented to marry me—that is, if you did consent. Then, after you did, the right moment never seemed to come. But I haven't willfully tried to deceive you, dearest, I know you'll believe that."

"Of course I believe that. I believe everything you say to me. And I don't want you to tell me anything until you feel the right moment has arrived."

"Are you sure you mean that?"

"As sure as I am that I love you with all my heart and soul."

He swallowed hard. "All right. Then I won't try to tell you much tonight. But I will tell you this much: there isn't anything in St. Louis that you'd be interested to see, or happy to see, because it's connected with me. The first home I can remember—in fact, my only childhood home—was an orphanage and a very bleak, barren one at that. I think I know who my mother was, but I don't even know that much about my father. The woman I believe was my mother stopped coming to see me when I was around ten years old. I asked questions about her and no one at the orphanage would answer them. I waited and waited for her to come back and finally I ran away. I hoped I'd find her, but I never did, and after a while I stopped looking. I could take care of myself all right by that time anyway."

"Oh, Clyde, you mustn't tell me any more tonight! I couldn't bear it! And of course we mustn't go to St. Louis—ever—ever—ever!"

56

She was weeping, weeping with grief because of his childhood misery and his childhood loneliness. Her tears moistened his face as she pressed her own against it. She was not shocked by the disclosure of his dubious background, she found nothing shameful in his doubtful paternity; her only feeling was one of infinite compassion, infinite loving-kindness. . . .

Finally, when she had grown calmer, she disengaged herself and moved away a little, slipping one hand under her pillow.

"I haven't any handkerchief," she whispered almost whimsically. "A woman never does have one, does she, when she really needs it? Would you get me one, Clyde? I keep them in the top drawer of the dresser. . . . Oh, thank you, darling."

She was smiling up at him now and the smile was an invitation. He knew that her grief had spent itself, that she was ready to show her love for him in other ways, that she did not want him to kneel beside her any more, but to take her in his arms. The rapture with which she received him, when he did so, disclosed not only the ecstatic response on which he had come to count; it also revealed a passionate determination that he should find, in his joy with his wife, compensation for every sorrow that all others had given him. The revelation was one of a new heaven and a new earth. Never had she seemed so completely his as in the time that followed.

 CHAPTER III

THE QUESTION of going to St. Louis was not raised again; but a day or two later, Clyde told Lucy that he had tentatively reserved seats for the following Monday on one of the "Silver Palace" cars which ran via the Pennsylvania Central Railroad between New York and Pittsburgh. He believed she would find the journey very different from their first hard train trip, between Richmond and Aquia and between Washington and Jersey City. The Silver Palace cars were said to be almost as comfortable as anything the most luxurious steamboats had to offer: a certain multimillionaire by the name of Stoddard was pouring out untold wealth in railroad expansion and was most insistent on this phase of its development. Moreover, she would not be confined to the cars throughout the fifteen-hour journey; schedules had been conveniently arranged so that travelers should be able to stretch their legs a little when they got out at

Harrisburg for dinner and at Altoona for supper. On the other hand, if she would prefer the experience of traveling by night, in one of the new Pullman sleeping cars, they could leave New York at seven in the evening on the Pacific Express and get to Pittsburgh around ten in the morning. The mechanism which provided for both upper and lower berths was really very ingenious, and sheets were now supplied, which was a great innovation—"Old Number Nine," the first Pullman sleeper, built ten years earlier, had been equipped with mattresses and blankets, but no bed linen and sometimes—well, he would not go into details. Lucy would not mind the change of climate, for this new car was heated with a hot-air furnace under the floor—another great innovation and an immense improvement on the small wood-burning stoves, one at either end of Number Nine. The Pullman sleeper he was suggesting also had black walnut woodwork, handsomely inlaid, French plush upholstery and a Brussels carpet, not to mention a spacious washroom. What did she think?

He could see that it was difficult for her to decide; and he teased her a little because her ultimate decision was in favor of the day trip. He was not sure, he told her, whether this was really because she wanted to see the countryside; he thought it was partly because she did not like the idea of dressing and undressing on a train. Well, of course, she replied, with one of the blushes he found so entrancing, she would not really disrobe; she would just change from her traveling costume to a dark dressing gown and loosen her corset. But, inevitably, there would be a little awkwardness, the next morning. . . . He laughed and said there was no more reason why she should not go to bed comfortably, in a nightgown, on a Pullman sleeper than at the Fifth Avenue Hotel; but he could see she did not feel that way about it and he did not urge her. After all, he could not assure her that he would have a separate dressing room on a train; they would have to share a compartment; and though they had now been married several weeks, they had never yet seen one another unclad. He realized that Lucy had been brought up to believe that no woman of refinement revealed any more of her body than she could help, even to her husband and her physician. Someday, he hoped, she would feel different about that, just as she already felt different about the marriage relationship. But he knew the time had not yet come for this. If he tried to hasten its coming, he might lose everything he had gained; he could not even talk to her about it yet, as he had talked to her about the consummation of their union. He did not want to. He wanted the next revelation of his bride to be on the same plane as those which had preceded it. . . .

So the tentative reservation for the Silver Palace car was confirmed, and the following Monday they left New York at nine in the morning. The trees were already shorn of their foliage and the level countryside, bereft of autumnal brightness, was one of almost unrelieved monotony until they had been on their way for several hours; but Lucy was fascinated by the elaborate accouterments of the car and delighted with the novel experience of eating dinner in a railroad station.

"There's a lot more style to the one in Pittsburgh," Clyde told her. "It's really about the toniest place to eat there—patronized by the local aristocrats quite as much as by the traveling public. Colonel Unger, who runs it, is a very genial gentleman, though at first glance you wouldn't think so—he's tall and erect, rather military looking, in fact. His wife's just the opposite, short and fat and dumpy and always running through the corridors around the dining room with a parrot cage clutched in her hand."

"Why on earth does she do that?" Lucy inquired.

"I haven't the first idea. Neither has anyone else that I've ever talked to. But in spite of Mrs. Unger's little oddities, that second-story dining room at the Union Depot is quite a place. I'll take you there and you'll see for yourself."

"I hope I'll see Mrs. Unger and her parrot. If I do, I'll ask her about it."

"You know you'll do no such thing."

Very probably not, Lucy finally admitted; but meanwhile they had found the Ungers and the dining room at the Union Depot an absorbing topic of conversation for some time after they had finished their dinner at Harrisburg and gone back to their Silver Palace car. The early dusk prevented them from seeing much of the mountain scenery, and the train, swaying jerkily over its tortuous roadbed, jolted them more and more. Lucy could not go to sleep with her head on Clyde's shoulder, as she had in the carriage which had taken them from Sorrento to Richmond; their elegant plush seats could be turned so that these faced each other, but there was no way in which tired travelers could sit closely side by side. Clyde was sure that Lucy would be completely exhausted when they reached their destination, well after midnight; and though she insisted that the passage over the mountains had been a new experience and that like all other new experiences she had found it thrilling, he was not reassured. His anxiety increased as they fought their way through the depot crowds in the wake of a Monongahela House runner who had met the train, and who vociferously directed them toward a waiting bus, with an occasional triumphant and inelegant aside to some rival, as the latter sought to divert his patrons by raucously voicing the claims of the Lincoln Hotel, the Union Hotel, the Mansion House or the Washington House.

"We'll be there presently now," Clyde told Lucy, as they clambered up the steps of the bus and squeezed into places on one of the narrow seats which ran lengthwise on either side. She nodded and smiled, but he realized she had not heard him, because he had whispered instead of shouting. Despite the lateness of the hour, newsboys were calling out headlines, drunken revelers were brawling in doorways, streetcar drivers were clanging their bells, and draymen were swearing at the heavy, slow-moving horses that clattered over the cobblestones. The tumult seemed all the more confusing because the smutted atmosphere made it doubly difficult to distinguish the source of one sound from another. Cindery soot pattered like raindrops against the windows of the bus; and even when a section of the crowded thoroughfare became visible through the obscured panes, the street lamps, shielded by glass bells, gave forth such a feeble flame that the darkness was dispelled for only a short distance.

Clyde did not try to speak again, but he worried increasingly. It was bitterly cold and he was afraid Lucy would be chilled through and through, besides being shaken to pieces. The cobblestone streets were terribly rough, and the jolting and jarring they had undergone on the train had been mild to what was happening to them now. He had forgotten there were so many saloons in downtown Pittsburgh, and he began to be glad that the pattering soot prevented Lucy from seeing them and the sights connected with them more clearly. He had also forgotten that there were so many livery stables; the stench of these permeated the icy closeness of the bus, making it more and more obnoxious. . . .

A loud "Whoa!" from the driver, reining in his horses, heralded the end of their painful progress. The entrance to the Monongahela House was flanked with cigar stores; a long interior passageway, lined with plush-covered sofas, led to the lobby at the rear, where horsehair supplanted the plush. Only a few loiterers remained in the chairs companionably grouped around the spittoons; these were apparently drummers, still relaxing after their day's work. Some of them had been celebrating, and the mellowness of their mood was reflected in their uninhibited comments on the new arrivals. Clyde tried to hurry through the process of registration and of disentangling baggage.

"I'm sorry there's no elevator here," he said, as he and Lucy turned toward the long stairs. "And we're on the top floor. No private bathrooms, either, though if there's a city where baths are more needed, I don't know what it is. I have got us a suite though, by going high up —that is, I've got us two rooms, and one of them will serve, after a fashion, for a parlor. But I'm afraid you'll find the Monongahela House a good deal of a comedown, after the Fifth Avenue Hotel."

"Yes, but that was fairyland," Lucy answered, her hand on the stair railing. "We didn't expect to live in fairyland all the time—at least, I didn't. And I'm glad—it wouldn't seem half so wonderful if we did."

60

She spoke with such buoyancy that Clyde could not doubt the sincerity of her words. "Do you know, lots of people in Virginia think Pittsburgh is still full of Indians?" she added when they were halfway up the second flight. "I thought so myself and I watched for them on the way up here from the depot. I saw a lot of them, too."

"You saw a lot of *Indians*!" Clyde exclaimed, stopping short in astonishment.

"Yes, darling. I tried to count them, but I had to give up, because there were so many. I can't wait to write home about them. But they were all *wooden* Indians, outside of cigar shops!"

Her laugh rang out, fresh and gay. She had not noticed the saloons, because she had been busy counting wooden Indians. And she had not minded the soot or the noise. She had told the truth: she did not need to live in fairyland all the time, she did not even want to. When they finally reached their makeshift suite, breathless from their climb, she looked at Clyde and laughed again.

"It's *all* a new experience," she said. "And it's all thrilling, just as I told you before most of all being married to you!"

Because she said all this, because she so obviously meant every word of it, she unconsciously freed him from the fear which had gradually been taking form during their passage across the mountains: in New York, his whole concern had been for her comfort and her pleasure; he felt sure that everything he had said to her revealed this, that everything they did bore out the promise of the spoken word and the loving thought behind it. Here in Pittsburgh, for the first time, he had other matters on his mind, and he had dreaded to break this to her, lest she should resent it. Now he was confident she would not. Perhaps later in the day, he told her at breakfast, the morning after their arrival, she would like to go down to the Point. The Point? Lucy repeated, questioningly. Yes, Clyde answered; the meeting place of the Monongahela and Allegheny rivers, which merged there and formed the Ohio. Pittsburghers were very proud of the Point—they called it their Golden Triangle. She must not expect to find it beautiful, in spite of the wooded hillsides beyond the trivet harbor, for even the mellow sunshine of an Indian summer day could not prevail against the spreading smudges of furnace and forge. But, such as it was, it was one of the sights of Pittsburgh and he would find time to take her there. First, however, he must go down to the foundry and from there on to the boatyards—it was necessary for him to make connections immediately with various ironmasters, boatbuilders, shippers and other industrialists. . . .

It did not occur to him that she would care to go with him and she did not suggest it. When he returned to the hotel, late in the evening, he begged her pardon for not rejoining her at dinnertime or even sending her a note—some business acquaintances had invited him to join them at Newell's. One topic of conversation had led to another and it was three o'clock before he knew it. Then he realized she would long since have gone to the dining room without him. She had not minded at all, she assured him, without making any direct answer about the dining room; in fact, she had been glad of a chance to ease her conscience by writing a long letter to her mother, whom she had shamefully neglected while in New York. Now she had described everything—the luxurious hotel, the wonderful shops, the theaters and restaurants, all the great sights. Had she told her mother about the wooden Indians, too, Clyde inquired with a grin. Yes indeed, Lucy answered, smiling back at him. Well, this letter had taken her practically all day to write, there had been so much to relate. And when she had posted it, she had sat by the window, looking out at the sunset, which had been very beautiful, and after that, at the flames leaping up from the great furnaces, which gave out a light more beautiful still. She had been entranced, watching it—another new experience. And another thrill, Clyde inquired, still grinning. Yes indeed, she had never imagined anything as gorgeous as that fiery rose color. Probably he had seen it a dozen times already, so it did not matter much that he had missed it this evening. But she hoped he was not too tired after such a long, wearing day. . . .

He was not tired at all, he assured her. But after remarking that of course it was now too late for visiting the Point, he did not suggest that they should do anything else instead; and, as soon as they had eaten their supper, he sat down at the desk she had used during the day and began to cover sheets of paper with scribbled notes and columns of figures. For a time, Lucy sat quietly beside him, doing some kind of needlework, he did not notice just what; and when he finally raised his head, after prolonged concentration on the sheets before him, he saw that he was alone and realized that he had not looked up, or even known when she left. That was a great way for a bridegroom to behave, he told himself, and hastened to rejoin her. Lucy's response to his sudden need of her seemed as spontaneous and proved as satisfying as ever; neither then nor later did he have any reason to wonder whether in her heart of hearts she had welcomed him as warmly as if he had not left her alone all day and then spent the evening figuring.

The following day was so dark that they could not believe it was already morning when they first woke. In fact, Clyde did not bother to look at his watch until after he had drowsed comfortably for nearly half an hour, he was so certain that it could not possibly be time to get up; then he had to rush off, because otherwise he would have been late for an important appointment. By noon, a steady rain had set in, and by evening, this had become a downpour. Clyde did not forget, again, to send Lucy a message; but this was only to say that he might be even later than the day before in getting back to the hotel. He assumed she would occupy herself with more letters; however, he doubted whether she would care to fill pages and pages, in writing to anyone except her mother, and he wondered, for the first time, whether she kept a diary. Most women did, he believed; and he rather hoped she followed the current custom, for, if she did, she could while away a good many hours in setting down her thoughts, as well as her "experiences." He realized that there would be no sunset for her to watch this time and that she would hardly be able to see the flames from the furnaces, either; and, intermittently, he was troubled by the thought of the tedium she was enduring. When, drenched to the skin, he finally rejoined her, he brought her a damp newspaper and pointed to an inconspicuous item, illustrated by the minuscule woodcut of a boat and appearing under the heading, RIVER PACKETS.

"For Memphis and New Orleans—" she read, following his guiding finger, "the steamer *Messenger*, Captain Jesse Dean, will leave for the above and intermediate ports on the rise.

"Ghriest & Swaney,
Flack & Collingwood, Agents.

"Is the *Messenger* the boat we're taking?" she asked.

"Yes, I hope so. If it doesn't leave too soon."

"But this notice doesn't say when it's going. It only says, 'on the rise.' I don't understand."

"You wouldn't, of course. The packets on the Ohio don't have any set schedule, like ocean liners. They go and come as the condition of the river permits. If this rain keeps up, the *Messenger* can get away fairly soon. That means I've got to keep on putting in long days at the foundries and yards, in order to finish up my business here before she pushes off. It also means that if this rain hadn't come, just when it did, we might have missed our connection with the *Richmond*. So maybe you'd better regard the downpour as a blessing in disguise, even if it does keep you cooped up."

He left her studying the notice and went into the bedroom to shed his wet clothes and take a quick rubdown. She was still reading the paper, with a rather puzzled expression, when he came back, his face glowing, his hair sleek, his linen and broadcloth immaculate.

"Come on down to supper. I need a good hearty meal and I'm sure you do, too. I'll explain to you about the rise—the raise a lot of the older captains call it—while we eat." Then, when they were pleasantly seated in the big dining room and had ordered oyster stew and roast beef, he went on, "Rains hereabouts are seasonal and they have a very important effect on river traffic. Old-timers can tell, by the amount of rainfall, just about how high the river will go. So many inches of rain mean so many feet, correspondingly, in the rise of the river."

"And they keep official records of just how many inches have fallen?"

63

"Well, not as accurately or as scientifically as you've told me your grandfather's friend Thomas Jefferson used to do it. But there's an old stone gauge at the end of Market Street, marked to show the depth of water, in feet, over the nearest sand bar. Just as soon as it indicates a rise, the waterfront starts to hum. All the commodities that have been stored in warehouses are hurried down there in drays and the loading begins. It was in full swing when I was coming back to the hotel tonight."

The oyster stew had arrived, rich and creamy, and Clyde went on talking about the busy waterfront while they ate it. When the waiter took away their soup plates and set great slabs of rare roast beef before them, he made a suggestion.

"Perhaps you'd like to try some of our special horse-radish sauce, sir? I don't know whether the lady would care for it, too—it's biting, of course. But it's getting quite a reputation for excellence."

"I'd like very much to try it. My father always liked horse-radish with his roast beef, and I used to fix it for him myself, because no one else could do it to suit him," Lucy said. "Of course I was terribly proud, but I can't pretend that I enjoyed grating the roots—I shed more tears in the process than I ever did peeling onions!" Then, as she helped herself to the relish the waiter presented and tasted it tentatively, she added, "It *is* good. Much better than mine ever was. I don't wonder you use a lot of it. But I hope your cook gets extra pay for preparing it."

"The cook gets paid plenty and I'll tell him you like the sauce. But he don't shed no tears over it." The waiter, who was conversationally inclined, welcomed Lucy's tacit invitation to explain and went rambling on. "If there's any crying done over this horse-radish, it's way out in Sharpsburg, by a young fellow named Heinz. His people have got a big kitchen garden, same as most of the folks there, and this youngster's been marketing their produce to the grocers, here in town, since quite a while back—gets up at three in the morning, so's he'll be sure to have his stuff here fresh and it can be used the same day he brings it. Well sir, this kid hit on the idea of grating the horse-radish himself and bottling it; it's all ready to use when he fetches it in, along with his fresh vegetables."

Lucy was intensely interested. She would like to see those kitchen gardens herself, she said. Perhaps she could even see this wonderful sauce in the process of preparation. If that Heinz boy could drive back and forth every day, Sharpsburg must be near enough for her to visit, easily, in the course of a carriage ride. Certainly it should be, Clyde agreed; as soon as they had finished supper, he would make inquiries about the availability of a suitable vehicle for her. If there were one, and the weather cleared, she could have a pleasant side trip; he was only

64

sorry that he could not go with her, but he would have to be in Shouse-town all day.

"Shousetown?"

"Yes, sixteen miles down the Ohio River. There's a big boatyard there where steamboat hulls are built and the framing. Afterward, they're towed to Pittsburgh for their boilers and machinery and the cabin finishing."

Inquiries at the office resulted in a favorable reply: there was no reason why a suitable carriage and a fine pair of horses with a reliable driver should not be available for Mrs. Batchelor at any time. The clerk did not think there was much to see, especially so late in the season, though he supposed some harvesting was still going on; but if the lady wanted to go to Sharpsburg, it was perfectly feasible—that is, if the rain stopped. If it did not, he would hardly advise the undertaking; the roads would be terribly muddy, the horses might flounder, the carriage might get stuck. . . .

The next morning Lucy confessed to Clyde that every time she wakened during the night she had raised her head and listened, and that she had been a little disappointed because she had continued to hear the steady beat of rain, mingled with all the other sounds. "Of course that Heinz boy must go back and forth every day, no matter what the weather is," she added, rather wistfully. "I could, too, if I knew the road the way he does, or if a city coachman and his horses—"

"But you don't and they don't," Clyde said firmly. "I'd worry about you all day."

"Why, Clyde, I'm used to country roads! I've ridden over them all my life."

"On horseback. Over familiar roads. That's different. I'm sorry for your disappointment, darling. I know you must dread another long, monotonous day. On the other hand, the harder it rains, the fewer you'll have of them. I'll go and talk with Danny MacAleer while I'm out and see what he thinks our prospects are."

"Who's Danny MacAleer?"

"Pittsburgh's unofficial weather prophet. My own guess is that there have been even harder rains above here, and that the river has risen already—enough for a light-water boat. But the *Messenger*'ll need more than that."

"How much?"

"I don't know exactly, but Danny does by this time. I'll tell you when I get home."

"Four feet and a half," he informed her that evening, adding triumphantly that Danny had confirmed his own guess about the amount of the previous rise. Even if there were no more rain—and it did seem to be clearing at last—the *Messenger* would be able to leave early on rday—the announcement was in the evening paper. Saturday would suit him to a T; he would have just time enough to wind up his own affairs. Lucy surprised him by responding that, before they left, she would like very much to see a foundry and a boatyard herself; could he manage to take her the next day, if that would be their last one in Pittsburgh? Why yes, he supposed he could, as far as time went, Clyde said hesitantly; but she would find a foundry terribly dirty. Her feet would sink down into the deep black sand which covered the stone floors; she would not be able to keep her hoops clear of it and she would ruin her white stockings; besides, she would be stumbling over crude castings with every step she took; she might very well hurt herself. She was very sure footed, Lucy replied with spirit; moreover, she was not afraid of showing her ankles in a good cause and she had plenty of stockings. And wouldn't she see anything at all that would make up for the dirt? Why yes, Clyde said again, still more hesitatingly, she might find the wooden patterns interesting; and when the pouring began, the molten metal, flowing from the great ladle into the molds, was really a gorgeous sight. Well then! Lucy persisted. But Clyde was persistent, too. It was not customary for ladies to go into foundries, he told her. The workmen went about half clad, or rather less than that; her presence would be a source of embarrassment, both to them and to her; and anyway, he was sure the grime would make more of an impression on her than anything else. He would admit that they might live to see iron make men richer than all the gold in California. However, that was far in the future. . . .

In the end she yielded, but he sensed her disappointment and blamed himself for it. Everything he had told her was true and yet, as had happened before about more important matters, he had not told her the whole truth. He could have given warning of her coming so that the men might be prepared; he could have arranged to have her arrive at the foundry just when the pouring, which always occurred at a fixed time, was about to begin; and he could have placed her advantageously, in order that she could see the "really gorgeous sight" without walking so far that she would ruin her stockings or expose her ankles. Then, as soon as the pouring was over, he could have told her there was nothing more to see and taken her away. But he was afraid that some chance remark which she might overhear, or which might even be addressed to her, would give away his precious secret, no matter how careful he was to caution everyone beforehand. So many of his secrets were disgraceful that he hugged all the more closely to his heart this one whose disclosure would be a source of pride and not a source of shame. They would be coming to Pittsburgh again, she could go to a foundry some other time. Decidedly, it was better that she should not do so now.

He tried to convince himself that this reasoning was sound; but he did not succeed very well; and the next morning he said there was hardly time to go to a foundry now anyway, as he must return to Shousetown and this was practically an all-day trip—it involved taking the Pittsburgh and Fort Wayne Railway from Allegheny City after crossing over the Federal Street Bridge, riding sixteen miles on the train, getting out at Shousetown Lane and then crossing the river again by ferry. However, if she really wanted to see a boatyard, here was her chance.

She fell in readily with his suggestion, making no further reference to the foundry, but chatting merrily about various inconsequential things. Once arrived at the boatyard, Clyde placed a chair for her in the shelter of a tool shed, spreading his fine linen handkerchief over the seat. She sat there for a long time, sniffing the pungent odor of chips and shavings, oakum and tar, and watching him while he clambered agilely into a skeletal structure of hewn yellow timbers, which looked like a mammoth rib cage. Men with adzes were skillfully flaking away bright chips of oak from this and its heavy beams rang to the stroke of metal. Eventually he returned to her, accompanied by a rather foppish-looking young man, whom he presented as Mr. Cyrus Thatcher, one of the establishment's office staff. Mr. Thatcher had sleek mouse-colored hair, which merged from his temples into sideburns and from these into a mustache, forming a single unbroken curve across his countenance, and not a lock of this curve was out of place. His coat sleeves were carefully protected by black bombazine sleevelets and he wore a stiff collar so high that when he turned his head he, perforce, turned his body as well. He bowed formally to Mrs. Batchelor and, after a few stereotyped remarks about the weather and the wonderful progress of Pittsburgh, produced a small leatherbound notebook from his pocket and jotted down entries in it, while Clyde talked to him about matters which were quite unintelligible to Lucy. For the most part, Mr. Thatcher nodded in agreement, but once or twice he embarked on a long involved argument. This went on for some minutes; then Mr. Thatcher bowed again, even more formally than the first time, and begged Mrs. Batchelor to excuse him: he was needed at the office and—if he might be pardoned the suggestion—it would perhaps be well if Mr. Batchelor accompanied him. But first, they would conduct her to the home of Mr. Porter, he added, indicating the owner's large white frame house on the hill behind the boatyard. Mr. and Mrs. Porter would be delighted to receive Mrs. Batchelor—in fact, they were expecting her. He was sure she would take pleasure in meeting them, too. . . .

When Clyde came to fetch her, sometime later, he found her seated at a table set with Royal Worcester and lavishly spread for tea, in the company of her genial hosts. Her enjoyment was so obvious that he reproached himself again for his neglect of her. To be sure, he had questioned her about a diary and, after her admission that she "did some-

67

times scribble little secrets in an old copybook," he had bought her a handsome leather-bound journal, with a minuscule golden key and a tiny heart-shaped padlock, which seemed to please her very much; she would feel much freer to write in this, she told him, than she ever had before. But he had never taken her to the tony dining room at the Union Depot, as he had promised to do, or even to Mrs. Morgan's Place, beside the Sixth Street Bridge, for ice cream; and though several of the ironmasters and shippers with whom he had spent his days had suggested that he should bring Mrs. Batchelor to their homes for supper, saying that their wives would be glad to meet her, he had declined all these invitations. Probably that had been a mistake. Pittsburgh was noted for its hearty hospitality and the huge houses of its solid citizens were well suited to dispense this. Besides, a good many important business transactions could be satisfactorily consummated when the gentlemen "repaired to the library" after the evening meal, leaving the ladies to chat in a more refined and less significant manner amidst the cluttering elegances of the draped and festooned parlor. But he had wanted to spend his evenings figuring; he had seen enough of the solid citizens during the course of the day and had preferred to be alone with Lucy, and he had been obsessed with anxiety lest she should be told something he did not want her to hear. Even now, the Porters had difficulty in persuading him to join them at the tea table. This time, however, he saw the impossibility of refusing and, to his great relief, his secret was still safe when he and Lucy bade the hospitable couple good night and went down the hill again.

It was dark now and the night shift had already begun its work by torchlight. This yard—and, in fact, most of those in the Pittsburgh area—was operating at full capacity, Clyde told Lucy on their way to the ferry, and still none of these could keep up with their orders; the men she saw at work now were getting double wages because of the hours they kept. The yard could well afford to pay them. Of course there were plenty of people who went around predicting that the great days of steamboating were over, that the war had precipitated the ruin which the railroads had already begun. He thought that even the brief glimpse she had had of the activities that evening would convince her such gloomy prophets were mistaken. To be sure, the gunboats had temporarily driven the floating palaces of ante-bellum days off the Mississippi. But bigger and better boats were being built now than ever before and business was booming again. She would see. . . .

He had to admit that she could not be expected to visualize this resurgence of past glories when they went aboard the *Messenger* early the next morning. The waterfront was actually more drab and dirty than the rest of the city and it rang with a greater confusion of sounds than the streets around the Union Depot. He was obliged to help her dodge among the drays, laden with glassware and ironware, bales of

68

paper and cases of whisky; and when they finally reached the gangplank, they were harried by a disreputable gang of water rats who lounged near by to watch the passengers embark and to make ribald remarks about them. Lucy had said, two days earlier, that she did not mind showing her ankles in a good cause and Clyde knew she had meant it then; now, as she lifted her long skirt to clear its hem of the befouled planking, he realized that she was shuddering inwardly, less because of the filth which surrounded her than because of the coarse jests and rude oglings which her passage evoked.

He had hoped that matters would improve once they were aboard the *Messenger*; but he saw, almost immediately, that this was not the sort of packet which he would have chosen for Lucy's first river trip. A three-piece "orchestra" was assailing a tune which might once have been "Robin Adair," but which retained little resemblance to it; a singularly unattractive crowd of passengers jostled them as they made their way up the grand staircase to the boiler deck; and the clerk in the little office at the left of the uncarpeted entrance regarded them nonchalantly and tossed them a key to the stateroom he said had been assigned to them, without adding that he hoped they would be comfortable and that their trip would be a pleasant one. As they walked past the potbellied stove and down the long saloon, where the tables were already set for dinner, Clyde's doubts about the merits of the *Messenger* increased; and when he opened the door of the stateroom "Maine" and saw the two narrow bunks, the built-in shelf equipped with bowl and pitcher and the three-legged stool which cramped the inadequate space beside these bunks, his disappointment deepened into acute displeasure.

"There's some terrible mistake, darling. Of course I engaged the bridal suite. It won't be luxurious, on this boat, but it ought to be a lot better than a hole like this. Just wait here for a few minutes, will you? If the porters arrive with our baggage before I come back, tell them to leave it outside in the saloon—here's some money to tip them with. A steward can look after our things later."

He hurried off, leaving Lucy seated on the three-legged stool, and made his way back to the office. The clerk, who had been merely nonchalant before, now became close to insolent, in Clyde's prejudiced opinion. Yes, he knew that Mr. Batchelor had specified the bridal suite; but it so happened that a cousin of the captain's was on her wedding journey, too. She and her husband—the son of Captain Dean's minister —were already installed in the quarters Mr. Batchelor wanted—in fact, they had come on board late the night before and were not even up yet, the clerk added with a slight leer. Of course Mr. Batchelor would be entitled to a rebate on his fare; the clerk would give the matter his attention when he was not so busy. At the moment he was fully occupied with other arrivals.

Unless he created a scene, which he had excellent reasons for not wanting to do, Clyde was powerless. With an inward vow that the clerk, the captain and the usurping couple should all have reason to regret what they had done, he returned to Lucy. Their baggage had all been neatly stowed away and she was standing by the door to the deck, looking out of the small, four-paned window. She came forward at once and handed him most of the money he had given her.

"The porters didn't expect so much," she said. "I didn't know what was fair, of course, so I asked them, and they told me. You're much too generous with everyone, Clyde—it's your one fault. They objected to putting the baggage down on the carpet of the saloon—said it would get them into trouble—so I thought I'd better let them bring it in, after all. This *is* our room, isn't it? Well, I think the arrangement of those bunks is very amusing. It would have been something like this, wouldn't it, on that night train we didn't take? Do you remember how you laughed at me because you thought I wouldn't like dressing and undressing on a sleeper? Now you'll have a chance to laugh a lot more, because I'll have to do it on this boat! But I don't care how many jokes you crack at my expense, because I think we're *both* going to have fun! And anyway, we don't have to spend all our time in our stateroom. Of course you'll want to be in the bar, with other men, part of each day, and I'll want to meet some of the ladies on board. I'm sure there must be at least a few I'd find very congenial, even if we haven't seen any who looked as if they might be. Right now, I want to see what's happening outside and I can't, very well, from here. Why don't we stay on deck until dinner's ready?"

He could not tell her that he had counted on the bridal suite not only for comfort, but for seclusion. In the spacious quarters which he had envisioned, they could have spent practically all their time; but it was unthinkable that they should do so in this miserable little stateroom. They would have to go out on deck, there was no help for it; and, for a short time, Lucy's naïve pleasure in the various sights around them diverted his thoughts from their unwelcome trend. She was much intrigued by the great gilded sphere, surmounting a high pole, which was the *Messenger*'s most extraordinary adornment; and she listened, with eager interest, to Clyde's explanation that nearly all the river packets carried some ornament characteristic of their captain's taste—usually anchors, globes or stars set in rings, but in one instance a mammoth white hat, modeled on the strange headpiece which the master himself wore. She was greatly fascinated by the various bell strokes, signaling—as Clyde also explained—that the boat was about to take her departure. Then, once they were under way, the changing pattern of the brown water, laced with creamy foam, as this was swept back from the bow, held her rapt attention. However, the *Messenger* had hardly started downstream when they were subjected to exactly the sort of an ordeal which Clyde had been dreading.

They were standing side by side, with their elbows resting on the white rail of the forward guard, when someone behind them said, in a smooth voice, "Your pardon, sir. Your pardon, madam." Lucy, slightly startled, whirled about with a little cry of astonishment. Clyde, turning more deliberately, saw a slim, fashionably dressed man standing before them, his beaver hat held at the level of his waist as he bowed.

"Colonel Ballou?" the interloper began, with a slight rising inflection.

"No, sir. Batchelor is the name," Clyde answered—with extraordinary coolness, considering that, inwardly, he was far more perturbed than Lucy.

"And mine is Fanchon, Major André Fanchon of New Orleans." The stranger waited a moment, evidently hoping that Clyde would present him to Lucy, and then bowed again. "I apologize if I have made a mistake. But I could have sworn that we were fellow passengers on the *Eclipse* in '59 or '60. I realize that is quite a while back, but still—"

"I assure you that you have made a mistake in thinking that I am —who was it? Oh, yes—a certain Colonel Ballou. As I said, the name is Batchelor, Clyde Batchelor."

"Then the resemblance to the gentleman whom I had the honor of knowing is most amazing. Possibly you have a half brother or an own cousin—"

"I regret that I am not fortunate enough to have either. And now, if you will excuse me. . . ."

He offered his arm to Lucy. She slipped her hand through it and turned compliantly away, but not before saying, "Good morning, Major Fanchon." For the first time, the indestructible quality of her courtesy was annoying to Clyde. He had certainly made it plain enough that he wished to have nothing to do with the man who had approached them, both by his failure to include his wife in the conversation and by his own curtness—and still she had spoken as pleasantly to the blackguard as if he were a long-lost friend! Clyde guided her toward their stateroom in much the same manner that he had betrayed when she innocently suggested the trip to St. Louis at their festive dinner. But before they reached it, he realized that, for the second time, he was completely unjust. Of course there had been mutual recognition between Fanchon and himself. He had indeed traveled on the *Eclipse* in '60—in the guise of a colonel from Alabama by the name of Melvin Ballou; it had been one of his most successful roles. Clyde and Fanchon, who was posing as a cotton factor, had, between them, made a very considerable killing. He even remembered the bumptious young Creole, eager to prove himself a mettlesome man of the world, who had been

71

their principal victim, and with whom they had dealt so adroitly that he blamed himself and not them when he disembarked with a heavy heart and a light purse. He must follow Fanchon at once and have it out with him.

"If you'll excuse me, my dear," Clyde said abruptly, as they reached the threshold of their stateroom. Then, realizing that he must say something more, he added, "I've a notion you're right, as usual. I ought to spend a little time in the bar, now and then. This seems a good moment. You look rather tired. I'm sure a short rest would do you good."

He kissed Lucy hurriedly and left her, inwardly cursing his inadequacy. Then he hastened off toward the doorway through which Major Fanchon had just passed, conscious of Lucy's troubled and bewildered glance. He passed rapidly through the main saloon, by the ladies who were already gathered about the stove, to the masculine bailiwick, flanked on one side by the office of the clerk, who had dealt with him in so summary a fashion, and on the other by the alcove, bridged by a counter and backed by a mirror, which served as the bar. Here a brass rail, sadly in need of polish, was raised above the floor on iron supports; and four or five passengers were using this as a footrest, while they tossed off the drams which the bartender drew from a whisky keg. Clyde saw, with relief, that the man he sought was not only among these early customers, but that he was standing near the end of the counter, where he could most easily be approached.

"I'd like a word with you, in private, at your earliest convenience," Clyde said abruptly.

The ready response to this demand was accompanied by a wave of the hand toward the counter. "No time or place like the present," the man replied cordially. "Perhaps you'd join me in a dram—the bottled whisky, of course. I've been hoping you'd see your way to—"

"I said a word *in private*," Clyde repeated. "I suggest the guard, forward. It appears to be deserted at the moment."

"Small wonder. It's the chilliest spot aboard. But as you wish. Pray lead the way. I'll follow."

Clyde stalked away from the bar, drawing his coat more closely about him by its flared lapels when he reached the open deck. Then he wheeled around and faced the interloper who had presented himself to the bridal couple as Major Fanchon.

"I've called you out here to tell you that you made a great mistake in speaking to me at all and a second one, even greater, in addressing me as Ballou, which is not my name," Clyde said coldly. "There must be no repetition of these mistakes. You will therefore oblige me, Pettigrew, by not approaching or addressing me again, whether I am alone or in company."

"Fanchon's the name, now. Major Fanchon, from New Orleans. And

72

I'm a thinkin' that if there's a mistake, I'm not the one that's making it. Hear me, now. There's a soaplock from Ohio aboard, milk fed, plump and prime for plucking. Naturally, we'd have to keep our eyes peeled for Dean, because he's the kind of captain who acts like steamboatin' and Sunday-schoolin' are one and the same. But the bartender's our cove. I tell you, it's a rich thing for true. There'd be enough for a tall poke of sparklers for the lady who—"

"I earnestly urge you not to make a third mistake, Pettigrew!"

"Fanchon, I said. And if I should not choose to accommodate my druthers to this psalm-singing play of yours?"

"That would be unfortunate. I might let the authorities at Helena know some interesting facts about the killing of a deputy marshal there in '60. I think it was '60—anyway, it was at the time of that trip on the *Eclipse* to which you referred. . . . Or I might find ways of irritating you into attacking me before witnesses, so that I could kill you—in self-defense. I think there is no need to remind you, Pettigrew, that I am a man of my word."

"*Fanchon,* dammit to hell! I suppose you realize I could rig the same description of saw on you, since I've got your notions. That makes us even Stephen."

"Not quite. I've never killed anyone—yet."

For a moment they looked steadily at each other. Then Fanchon's eyes shifted before Clyde's steely stare. He managed to shrug his shoulders, but the sneering reply he meant to make died on his lips. Instead, he spoke almost civilly.

"I see no profit for either one of us in further talk. I bid you good day, Mr. Batchelor."

"Good day to you—Major Fanchon."

Well, that had been that, and there had been no further trouble on board the *Messenger* with Fanchon or anyone else of his stripe. But Clyde had had no assurance of this, and the uncertainty kept him on edge and made him an easy prey for general dissatisfaction. He had traveled the Ohio before, and had thought it deserving of its Indian name for beautiful river; but that had been at a season when its well-wooded banks were green, not when the stark branches of the trees were leafless against a gray sky and the grass beneath them was dun colored. A cold east wind blew persistently and, from time to time, there were little flurries of snow; it was far too chilly to sit on deck, or even to walk there, for long periods. Indoors, conditions were not much better. The early dinner was bountiful, but it was unimaginative and sloppily served. The food was heavy and greasy and most of it was lukewarm when it was set before them; though Lucy made no comment, Clyde was conscious of her surprise at its mediocrity and at the multiplicity of the small oval dishes set down around her.

"This is the foundering meal you're getting—and of course served steamboat style," he whispered to her. "Dean's one of the captains that gives orders he doesn't want an inch of tablecloth showing on the first dinner aboard. The more shells, the finer the feast; the more indigestion afterward, the less interest in future meals. At least, that's his idea."

"Foundering? Shells?"

"Yes. The passengers are supposed to be so full after dinner that they can be compared to a foundering ship and these birdbaths with potatoes in one and beets in another and peas in another and corn in another are called shells."

"They must make a lot of extra dishwashing for somebody."

"He doesn't worry about that."

"Then I don't understand—"

She did not finish the sentence; but he saw her hesitate when the man on her other side passed her the butter dish and she realized there was no butter knife on it, that she was expected to cut into the pat with her own, as everyone else at the table was doing. Her bewilderment was natural, of course; one butter knife, more or less, could not possibly have mattered to the members of the cabin crew who were washing hundreds of shells. But Captain Dean's pride was centered on dishes rather than cutlery and, as a matter of fact, Clyde did not believe that anyone at the table, except Lucy and himself, had minded, or even noticed, the omission which had offended his bride's sense of suitability. In spite of the hopes Lucy had expressed, their fellow passengers seemed to be a rather sorry lot and their table companions among the sorriest of these: two New England cotton buyers, evidently brothers, whose prominent Adam's apples bulged above their celluloid collars and whose chapped hands had the look of being perpetually blue with cold; a towheaded young man—less ministerial than bucolic in aspect, in spite of his black clothes—accompanied by a pale, flatchested young woman and a sullen, pasty-faced child; a massive matron whose "waterfall" was matched by a rippling cascade of chins and who was corseted like an ironclad; and a faded, silly lady of fashion, with unnaturally bright patches of color on her wrinkled cheeks and too many rings, each of little value, on her bony, veined hands. The blackclad young man betrayed his clerical calling by asking a detailed and sonorous grace, while the stewards waited with laden arms and in obvious impatience for the "Amen!" which would permit them to unburden themselves. The child squirmed in his seat and refused to eat anything put before him; and the pale, flat-chested young woman pleaded in vain with him and looked appealingly toward her husband for help, also to no avail. The cotton buyers bolted their food with hardly a word to each other and none to anyone else; then pushed back their chairs and disappeared in the direction of the bar. On the other hand, the massive matron and the faded lady of fashion chatted

74

incessantly. Before the *Messenger* had been under way many hours, they had already sized up one of their fellow passengers to her distinct disadvantage.

"That Mme Pourrien and her three nieces!" the massive matron said gloatingly. "You'd think, to hear her brag about their 'refinement,' that butter'd be too brash to melt for them. Nieces, indeed! Baggages, every one of them. She's got them herded into their staterooms and has ordered all their vittles sent there. There's nothing green in my eye and I give you gracious leave to tell her I say so. Nieces!"

"Shameless!" agreed the gentlewoman. "But that is what one must put up with in these times, yes. Ah, I tell you fr-r-r-ankly, me, you should see them on the Esplanade in the evening, driving by in so shining carriages, with an audacity you would not believe, no. I must explain you it is for *réclame,* so that *tout le monde* can observe how new nieces, them, have make arrival at the house of Tante Frou-frou. I tell my husband, him, we must to move from the Esplanade, we have young girls in the family who should not see such things, no, never, them. But he does not wish to move to where *les Américains* live. I say that is fine biffo the war, yes, but with the *bêtes* of carpetbaggers taking over everything, even the St. Louis Hotel, them, better we should live among *les Américains* who are not Yankees, no."

She glanced in the direction of Lucy, as if to put her in that hated category. Lucy returned the look smilingly, but steadily, and turned to Clyde.

"What did you tell me your friend Mme Surget's maiden name was, dear?" she inquired. "Oh, yes, Randolph. I didn't realize before there were any Randolphs in Louisiana. So few members of the Cavalier families have married among the Creoles. And of course, next to the Lees—"

Again, she left the sentence unfinished. But, as she rose, she bowed pleasantly to the two women who were regarding her speechlessly.

"We shall look forward to seeing you again at supper," she said, taking Clyde's arm. "And at the concert afterward. There is a concert, isn't there?"

With some slight confusion, they assured her that there would be a concert and that they were also looking forward to the evening. Then there was a moment of comparative silence as they watched the unhurried departure of the bridal couple before they began their whispering again.

"Of course they're talking about us now," Lucy said unconcernedly, when Clyde and she were out of earshot. "I gave myself away by not knowing about the shells, so they realized right off I'd never been on a river boat before. And I'm afraid you and I don't act or look like people who've been married a long time. But do you care? I don't! I think half the fun of being a bride is having women like that jealous."

"Why, Lucy! I wouldn't have believed it of you! But then I wouldn't have believed you'd put 'women like that' in their places with one quite casual remark, either. I had no idea—"

"That I had a sense of humor? Or that I could be malicious about anything? Or that you'd have a good time with me? I mean, even when we weren't in fairyland, even when we weren't making love? Why, Clyde, that was terribly shortsighted of you! If we couldn't have a good time together, whatever happened, it wouldn't have been worth while getting married."

"Well, I'm ready to take oath it was worth while," he assured her, with conviction.

He had done nothing to relieve the monotony of her days in Pittsburgh, but somehow she beguiled the tedium of the afternoon and the banality of the evening for him. She was not very good at games, he knew that already, she reminded him; but sometimes, in bad weather, she had played chess with her father, who always won and who enjoyed it. Perhaps Clyde would enjoy it, too? The chess game, which he did win, but with enough effort to make it interesting, lasted until early evening, and afterward, Lucy said she would like to see the pilothouse and have some of its mysteries explained to her; when Clyde took her there, she seemed to grasp its functions without difficulty. At supper, she dealt gently but efficiently with the sullen child, whose parents still seemed cowed by him, and entered easily, both as a listener and a talker, into the conversation, which had become more general than at dinnertime. The towheaded young man identified himself as the Reverend Thaddeus Willswood, only recently ordained and on his way to Arkansas, where he had been called to ride a circuit of churches out of Marked Tree. His wife Maria had formerly taught at the district school in the village near his father's farm. The cotton buyers were less autobiographical, but divulged the hope, which came as a surprise from such a quarter, that they might be able to organize a quartette. The massive matron and the faded gentlewoman continued their comments on their fellow passengers, though less acidly than before; evidently Lucy's remarks about the Randolphs had not been without their effect. Clyde was still glowing with secret pride as he accompanied her to the inevitable concert and sat beside her during four-handed pianoforte versions of "The Battle of Prague" and "The Last Link is Broken," followed by an elocutionary proclamation, with appropriate gestures, to the effect that "It was the schooner Hesperus that sailed the wintry sea." When the concert was over, Lucy said that, in view of the early hour they had been up that morning, she thought they should consider it was now bedtime; and, after an exchange of half-serious, half-jesting remarks about their "separation," Clyde clambered into the

76

upper berth and settled down for the night more philosophically than he would have believed possible.

He was wakened from his first deep sleep by the consciousness that the boat was no longer moving. There were none of the sounds which presaged the normal approach to some regular landing, and his long acquaintance with every form of possible disaster on inland waterways made him immediately alert. He did not want to alarm Lucy needlessly and, at the same time, he felt he would be unforgivably careless if he did not investigate the cause of the boat's interrupted progress. The stateroom was provided with no light except that which came in through the transom; but his eyes were accustomed to such dimness and, after focusing his gaze carefully on his watch, he was able to make out the time. It was just after midnight. Of course it was possible that the engineer had decided to strengthen the strap iron to one of the pitmans, before proceeding farther, but this was unlikely at such an hour, unless the *Messenger* were actually in danger of "running through herself." Perhaps a valve on the "doctor" that fed water to the boilers might have jammed, or a bearing might be running hot. In fact, any one of a dozen minor mishaps might have occurred, which could be remedied on the spot, without dockyard facilities. However, he would not feel easy until he knew exactly what had happened. Moving as quietly as he could, in the hope that he would not disturb Lucy, he slid to the floor. But she was already awake.

"Is something the matter, Clyde?"

"I don't think so. But I'm going to find out. Don't worry. I'll be right back, whatever it is."

He had slipped into his trousers and shrugged a coat over his nightshirt while he was speaking. The saloon was empty and quiet when he entered it; there were no signs of excitement or sounds of confusion anywhere. He had almost reached the bar before he even saw anyone; then he encountered a solitary member of the cabin crew, sweeping up some broken bottles.

"What's happened?" he inquired curtly.

The man stared at him blankly for a moment and then gave a cackling laugh. "Ain' nuthin' happened," he croaked, " 'ceptin' that Cap'n William alluz wants we should choke a stump on Sundays, him, and Captain Jesse, being his brother, humors him. Likely you ain' never traveled with him before. Come midnight Saturday, he just pull up to de bank, wherever us is, and stay dere till de nextes' midnight. Yassuh. Has services in de saloon, too. Just like us was ashore in a sho' nuff church. Hymns and preachin' and all de rest. *Yassuh!*"

". . . And we're not even to Wheeling yet," Clyde told Lucy disgustedly, slamming the stateroom door after him. "At this rate, we'll spend the rest of our lives on the Ohio River."

77

"Hush, dear! You'll wake up everyone. . . . Does this mean we'll miss our connection with the *Richmond?*"

"It could, very well. But we did have a couple of days to spare, if I reckoned right."

"And you said I wouldn't like the wait in Cairo anyway."

"Kay-ro, darling. You're not in Egypt or even in a Select Southern Seminary for Young Ladies. You're in the Middle West, where people don't see any reason why you shouldn't pronounce 'ai' the same way in the name of a town that you pronounce it in rain and pain."

"All right, I'll try to be logical. But however you pronounce the name of this town, you said it was a horrid little hole with mud even on the walls of the houses."

"Well, yes. Cairo's pretty mucky—two big rivers overflow it every spring. The first people who tried to settle there gave it up as a bad job and so did a second set of pioneers. But it looks as if the third lot were going to hang on. I think they deserve some credit."

"Of course they do. And I don't suppose that Jamestown, or even Richmond looked like much when they weren't any older than Cairo. But since that isn't very attractive—yet—aren't we just as well off on the *Messenger* as we would be there? And if we've got two days to spare, and the captain's only stopping for one, why shouldn't we still make our connection?"

"Lucy, you're altogether too logical now."

"I'm sorry."

"And altogether too lovely."

"I'm glad."

Sunday was not as bad as he had expected, after all. Captain Dean read from the scriptures with the ease of long familiarity and the young Methodist clergyman preached a simple, but rather moving, sermon. Although plenty of the passengers had been ready with sentimental songs, it appeared that not so many knew the good old hymns; and when volunteers were called for, Lucy hesitantly said she would try to play them, if there were really no one else, and Clyde derived the same pleasure from seeing her at the piano on the *Messenger* that he had when he saw her, similarly engaged, at Sorrento. Under the influence of her persuasive touch, the saloon was presently ringing to the sound of "Onward, Christian Soldiers" and "All Hail the Power of Jesus' Name," with everyone joining in the chorus. Thus encouraged, she consented to play again later in the day, a different kind of hymn— "Abide with Me" and "Lead, Kindly Light" and everyone joined in those, too, with the happy result that, the first tensions having thus been eased, the passengers seemed on better terms all around. They began to pace the decks with each other and to call each other's attention to points of interest along the riverbank; and by Monday they had begun to coalesce into various intimate groups. Games of every sort were in progress; the New England cotton buyers had organized their male quartette; and an informal sewing circle, whose members cheerily exchanged patterns and gossip, met in the ladies' parlor every morning. Though Clyde's obvious reluctance to have Lucy leave him prevented her from joining this regularly, she did so occasionally, overriding his objections by insisting that she wanted to be friends with everyone and renewing her suggestion that he should spend more time with other men.

"I don't want to spend more time with other men. All most of them do is to lounge around on the main deck and shoot their guns at anything they feel like trying to hit, from driftwood to ducks. The exception's a man who lies in his berth all day, playing a fiddle. His roommate's nearly crazy, and some of the passengers have bribed the stewards to keep closing his door. You don't suppose I'd enjoy being with him, do you?"

"No, but—"

"I want to spend all my time with you. I'm sorry you don't feel the same way about spending all yours with me," he said, almost accusingly. Then, as she protested, half playfully, half seriously, that he was not being fair, he added, "Never mind me, darling. I seem to be getting up on the wrong side of the bed these days—not that there's more than one side I can get out, from that horrible little bunk. And then you're not in it, which makes matters all the worse. Of course I want you to be friendly, but you can be friendly for both of us, since I'm such an unsociable cuss. And you can't make me believe that most of those old cats are really congenial to you. What about that war horse at our table? Mrs. Goldthwaite, is that her name? And her Creole side-kick, Mme LeFevre? Judging from the remarks they make at meals, they never heard that charity's a virtue."

"We-e-ll, I admit those two do gossip a good deal. But most of the others—"

"Never mind about the others. What do those two gossip about?"

He caught the look of surprise on her face. He should not have shot the question at her like that. No wonder she was astonished. She must be asking herself why on earth he should be interested in the malicious chitchat of the sewing circle. But it was too late now to bite back the words.

"We-e-ll," she said again. "That young Methodist clergyman, for instance—the one who sits at our table and preached such a nice sermon. They claim he isn't an ordained minister of the gospel at all."

"Any more than Mme Pourrien's young charges are really her nieces?" Clyde answered, his reply a half question. "I rather like him, though I don't care much for the way he says grace. Somehow he sounds as if he were asking the Almighty's blessing on just our group and leaving all the others to their fate. However, they apparently don't realize their peril; they always begin eating without waiting for him to finish and what with the clattering dishes, I doubt if they even hear him."

"Clyde! You shouldn't joke about a thing like that!"

"You're right, I shouldn't. . . . Well, at that, it's quite possible he's an impostor. . . . What else?" Now that he had made the mistake of beginning, it would be better to have the thing out.

"They've talked a good deal about a young man from Dayton, Percival Fremont, I think his name is. Not in a very complimentary way, either. They describe him as being 'all scent and soaplocks,' whatever that means. It seems his father's the owner of a big stove foundry, that he's taking a lavish cargo of castings down to New Orleans and that he has 'a pocketful of rocks in his jeans.' However, Mrs. Goldthwaite seems to think he won't have the 'rocks' much longer, because he's been playing cards or dicing every day and far into the night and because—"

"Yes?"

"Because most of the time Major Fanchon's playing or dicing with him. The—the gentleman who spoke to you just after we left Pittsburgh. I haven't seen him since, except at a distance. Perhaps you wouldn't remember."

"Yes, I remember. What about him?"

"He's another person the gossips insist isn't who he's pretending to be. They say he claims to be a New Orleans sugar factor and that he's really nothing but a professional gambler with a very bad record for—well, for cheating. And—and fighting, too. They say they wouldn't be a bit surprised if Captain Dean put him off the boat."

For the first time, Clyde made no immediate answer. Lucy, whose look of surprise had gradually faded, went on of her own accord, after a moment's pause.

"I thought you were rather cool to him, Clyde, that morning. To tell the truth, I felt you were almost uncivil. But of course I realized there must be some good reason. Now I think I know what it is."

He swallowed hard. Perhaps the moment for which he had waited, the moment for full confession, had come already, sooner than he expected. He had known for a long while now that Lucy had married him for love and not for money; but neither had she married him for his past. Their marriage would survive that knowledge; he knew this, too. But he was still uncertain whether her love could do so. And that love, a kind which he had never dreamed would be his portion, was the one thing he did not dare to hazard on any chance. Not yet. Unless someone else had betrayed him, he would continue to keep his shameful secret. But it was quite possible that such betrayal had occurred already. He attempted a laugh, not very successfully.

"And in the midst of all this scandal, you haven't heard anything slanderous—about us, have you? Overheard, rather—naturally, those old harpies wouldn't say anything to your face."

"Oh, but they have! Not slanderous things, nice things! Of course they spotted us right away as a honeymoon couple; but that was my fault, showing how bewildered I was by a dinner served steamboat style. If I hadn't done that, perhaps it wouldn't have occurred to them it was strange you didn't spend most of your time playing cards and telling stories in the bar. But I roused their suspicions. As Mrs. Gold-thwaite put it, 'Any man who would stay by his wife, like he was a sick kitten and she was a hot brick, even when one of those scrawny Canterbury sisters is clawing the keys out of that poor old piano, is either a honeymooner or a saint. And I'm telling you Colonel Batchelor is a sight too good looking for a saint.' "

Lucy's mimicry of the old gossip ended in a laugh, as carefree as Clyde's had been forced. He had realized, from the beginning, that her disposition was unusually even and pleasant, but he had thought of it as grave rather than gay; since their marriage, its sunniness had seemed to increase from day to day and it had remained entirely unaffected by his recent irritability, of which, indeed, she seemed quite unconscious. Apparently, she derived pleasure from even the most commonplace sight: a snow-mantled riverbank, a sky streaked with turquoise and crimson at sunset, a flight of wild geese in V-shaped formation, a stop at some landing where tides of arriving and departing passengers met and eddied and freight was carried ashore by shuffling roustabouts. The *Messenger* had been rounding out from Cincinnati while they were talking, and she had stood watching the scene as intently as if the docks at Pittsburgh and Wheeling and Marietta had not already acquainted her with its basic pattern. The night was dark and such light as there was came from the torch baskets, which had been thrust into the riverbank by means of the long rods to which they were attached. The fire in these baskets had been kindled with pine knots to which resin was added; and now the flames leaped high above the iron holders. In their fitful glow, the shawled figures of the roustabouts were now vivid, now obscure. There was something eerie about the sight; and the mournful chant which accompanied the "coon-jining" made it all the more uncanny. Lucy watched it with fascination.

"Mrs. Goldthwaite kept calling you 'my handsome colonel' until I corrected her," she said at last, speaking more soberly than she had before. "I told her you'd been connected with the Supply Department of the Army in an important civilian capacity, but that you'd never held military rank. She was perfectly satisfied with my explanation, even though I didn't tell her which army. Perhaps I should have. But somehow. . . ."

Nothing had roused her suspicions about his past. Yet she had not

81

been able to confess that it was the Union Army with which the man she loved had been connected. In spite of all her tenderness, all her passion, all her adoration, she still found this hard to accept; she was still trying her best to forget it.

"You're—you're not ashamed of me, are you, Clyde, because I didn't tell her—everything?" Lucy asked in a troubled voice.

He had tried to assure her, more earnestly and more eloquently than he had ever spoken to her before, that shame of any sort was utterly alien to the temple of love where he had enshrined her. Later, in a calmer moment, and apropos of nothing in particular, he said that almost nobody told the whole truth about anything, and, in fact, it was probably just as well that nobody should. He reminded her, laughing almost naturally this time, that he had never told her the whole truth about himself yet, but that no doubt Mrs. Goldthwaite would ferret it out and pass it on to her before they reached Cairo. Mrs. Goldthwaite had ceased to talk about him much, Lucy reported; she was so excited because her prediction about Major Fanchon had come true that she had spoken of almost nothing else in the sewing circle.

"It seems he'd been stirring up fights among the Negroes on the lower deck and betting on the winners. Mrs. Goldthwaite called it 'a scandal to the jay birds.' Then finally, last night, he offered a demijohn of liquor as a prize to whichever one of the Negroes won in a fight where they all had their hands tied, and could only hit each other by butting."

"Lucy, I'm not surprised that you're shocked, but you don't need to be so stricken. The Negroes really enjoy those fights. However, I suppose Captain Dean came along at the wrong moment?"

"Yes, or the right one, whichever you choose to call it. Anyway, he ordered Major Fanchon off the boat then and there. He didn't even wait to get to some dock. He just pulled up beside the riverbank, the way he did Saturday night, only you didn't wake up this time."

"No, I didn't. . . . Well, Captain Dean's action doesn't surprise me, either. It's not an infrequent occurrence for the master of a boat to take action like that."

He spoke nonchalantly, but the nonchalance was assumed. Actually, he was hard put to it to conceal his overwhelming relief. With Fanchon gone, with Mrs. Goldthwaite's attention diverted, with the end of the trip to Cairo already in sight, he had little left to fear aboard the *Messenger*. He no longer clung to Lucy's side "like a sick kitten leaning up against a hot brick" or remained stubbornly in the stuffy little stateroom, pretending to work at the inadequate table, but began to move more freely among his fellow passengers. If the periods he spent in the bar were brief, if he expressed a preference for chess rather than

82

cards, that was his privilege. After all, he was admittedly a bridegroom, with a bride of whom any man might be proud. He told himself that there was probably not a single male passenger who failed to regard him with envy.

The limitations of their quarters and her own sensible attitude in regard to these had done a good deal toward lessening Lucy's self-consciousness about the lack of privacy; but Clyde realized she had not wholly overcome this, and mindful of a modesty which he respected, made a practice of taking a turn around the deck every morning and again every evening, so that she might have their tiny stateroom to herself while she dressed and undressed. At first, these promenades had been more or less solitary, for his attitude discouraged friendly advances; but as he showed himself less forbidding, some other man had usually joined him, and they had talked about matters of mutual interest as they walked. Clyde had come to enjoy these conversations and to anticipate them; therefore, he was feeling vaguely disappointed, on the eve of the *Messenger*'s arrival at Cairo, because he seemed to have the deck to himself again, when his hat was suddenly snatched from his head. He whirled around, with a hasty exclamation, to see a young girl standing close beside him, her back to the side of the boat and her hands resting lightly on her hips. It was too dark for her features to be distinguishable and her hair seemed only a part of the surrounding obscurity; but her lips were a startling scarlet in her white face and her skin seemed luminous in itself. A great deal of this was visible, for her dress was extremely low cut; and the gleaming flesh-colored satin of which it was made enhanced the effect of nudity and luminosity. She moved forward a little and, as she did so, Clyde could see that her hair was very black and her waist almost unbelievably small. Suddenly something about her evoked the stabbing memory of an episode which he had done his best to forget and which he had hopefully believed would never be revived. He turned quickly away, without a word. The girl caught at his arm.

"Don't you want your hat back, m'sieu?" she asked. "Madame might wonder where you left it."

"And your 'aunt' might wonder where you got it," he said coldly, "which would be quite all right, of course, if she sent you out here. But I rather think you're doing this on your own. If I'm not mistaken, you're being saved for New Orleans."

"What will you give me if I hand you back your hat and don't make you any trouble with Madame?"

"I think you'd better give it to me without doing any bargaining. I can make a good deal more trouble for you than you can for me. You'd better believe that, because it's true."

The girl laughed and, releasing his arm, sprang forward and started

83

to toss his hat overboard. But he was quicker than she was. It had barely skimmed the railing when he caught it. Then, with his other hand, he seized her wrist.

"No, I'm not going to hurt you," he said, as he saw her jeering expression change quickly to one of fright. "But I am going to give you a word of advice. The next time a man plainly shows you he's through with your kind, don't monkey with him. You might not get off so easy again."

He strode away, even angrier with himself than he was with the girl. She had upset him more than he would have been willing to admit, not because she had been successful in rousing the slightest shameful desire, for she had not; but because she had so successfully roused the memory of a past shameful desire. If he could have followed his inclination, he would have gone to the pilothouse—since he no longer felt secure on deck—and remained there until his mood was calmer. But Lucy would be wondering what had become of him—in fact, she was probably worried already, because his absence had been more protracted than usual. He still seldom left her for long, and he had noticed that, when he did, she was apt to look troubled on his return, though she did her best to conceal this. Once he had asked her, jokingly, if she thought he had fallen overboard; and though she said quickly, "No, of course not," she added, after a minute, "You see I can't help imagining. . . . I know it's silly, but I love you so much, the thought that anything might happen. . . . I've never been happy like this before. I can't believe, even yet, it's real—that it's going to last. . . ."

Since Lucy felt like that, he had no right to give her a moment's unnecessary concern. He could not do so now. He went back to the saloon and, when he re-entered their stateroom, found that she was not already in bed, as she usually was at such times. She had on her nightgown, but she was sitting on the edge of her berth, her nightgown open at the neck, and she was engaged in brushing her hair, which was still unbraided and fell over her shoulders and arms in long golden waves. It was the first time that Clyde had seen it like this, though he had greatly longed to do so, and the loveliness of the sight far exceeded his expectation. He leaned over and placing his hands on either side of the white part, let them slide slowly down, bringing her closer and closer to him while he did so. Then, drawing her to her feet, he enfolded her in a fond embrace.

Suddenly, he was conscious of some change in her person, a change so slight that he could not instantly identify it. Then, with a start, he realized what it was: there was a firmness to her bosom which it had lacked when they were first married. He drew away and looked down at her searchingly. The only light in the room was that which came in through the transom; but he knew, even though he could not see, that Lucy was blushing as she had never blushed before and that the rosy

84

color suffused not merely her face and neck, but that beautiful trans-figured bosom. Nevertheless, she did not draw away from him, and she did not instinctively try to cover herself more completely, as she would have done such a short time before. Instead, she returned his look, with adoration in her gaze.

"I—I waited up for you on purpose," she said. "It needn't have taken me so long to brush my hair. But I thought perhaps if you came in while I was still fixing it, you—you'd do exactly what you have done. Of course, it's too soon to be sure, even though it must have happened right away—that is, if it did happen. But I hope—I believe—Oh, if God will only be good to us! I—I prayed for this! Long after you went to sleep, that—that first night, I lay awake—praying. Not just that we'd have a child, but that you'd given me one *then,* at the same time that you'd taken away my fear of fulfillment and shown me what it meant to be a woman!"

He could not answer her, he could not voice his happiness or speak his love. But this time, it was he who lay awake, exultant, long after she was sleeping peacefully. It did not matter any more if that riffraff in the bar despised him as a quitter and a coward, a former go-getter who now let everything slip through his fingers, a hard hitter who had gone soft because a pretty woman had enslaved him. It would not even matter overwhelmingly—though he must never let Lucy know this—if she could not carry their child full term. Neither must he let her know that, deeply moved as he was by what she had told him and by the man-ner of its telling, the reasons for his joy were different from hers. He, too, had hoped that their first union might be fruitful. But this was less on her account than on his own. Indeed, if he had given thought to it, he would have shrunk from the prospect of her suffering in childbirth; but he had wanted immediate evidence of his virility, he had craved another proof of his power to wring from a reluctant fate everything life had to offer. In marriage, as in everything else, he had triumphed.

 CHAPTER IV

IT was midmorning when the *Messenger* rounded to for a landing at Cairo's levee, shouldering a place for herself among the steamboats tightly ranked along the entire length of Commercial Street. The mate had already marshaled the roustabouts, so that they would be ready to run out the gangplank after the boat had completed her turn against the current; the hoarse bellow of her whistle and the anguished squall of her orchestra had heralded her approach to shore. Now the seething babel which was apparently an essential element in all landings mounted in pitch and volume. On the levee—so low that it provided no more than a sloping approach to the flat bank—a number of young tatterdemalions were capering about in high glee, jigging and turning cartwheels; on the railroad track beyond, a small locomotive with a turnip-shaped stack was switching a string of dingy freight cars back and forth.

"Look at that waterfront!" Clyde exclaimed triumphantly. He and Lucy were again standing beside the rail of the forward guard, as they had when they left Pittsburgh, and his sweeping gesture of satisfaction included both the long line of steamboats and the chugging little train. "Now can't you see why I don't hold with the crapehangers who insist that the great days of steamboating are over? That railroad over yonder's nearabout the first one built full length in the Mississippi Valley, running the same way as the river. It comes all the way from Chicago. And did it kill the steamboats? All I ask you to do is look at that waterfront again."

A little cry from Lucy terminated this triumphant questioning. Following her glance, Clyde saw that she was looking past the drab little town, downstream to the point where a river, mightier and muddier than the Ohio, caught and reflected the November sunlight.

"Yes!" he said. "That's the Father of Waters. You can't see the place where the Mississippi and the Ohio come together, over there to the left, because of that packed file of steamboats. But you will see it, once we're on our way south from here. And if luck's with us, that'll be in a few hours now."

Luck was indeed with them, for, on disembarking, they learned from the wharfmaster that the *Richmond* would arrive sometime that afternoon. "Times have certainly changed," he conceded sociably. "Not too long back, all we could've told you was she hadn't come till yet. But now, the telegraph brings us news from up the river at St. Louis and elsewhere 'most before it happens, seems like. Yes'r. She'll be comin' 'round the p'int d'rectly the Halliday dining room closes after dinner, give or take an hour either way, and you nee'n' to tote your grips off the wharf boat, sir, lessen you've a special mind to. I'll jes' keep my eye on 'em for you, whilst you'n' your good lady pass a pleasant time of day strollin' 'roun'n' about our fair city. . . . 'f I was to make so bold, I'd segest you walk down yon to where the levee turns. That's where Fort Defiance was, and if I was to tell you. . . ."

"Thank you very much," Clyde interrupted when he saw the stream of conversation was not likely otherwise to be shut off. "We'll do as you say, and if you'll kindly let us leave the baggage, that will be a help. . . . Would you like to come, Lucy? I want to see what arrangements they have here for moving cargo from steamcars to steamboats, and the other way round, too. It'll be right on our way to the fort."

"Of course I'd like to come."

There was no hesitancy about her answer; but they had gone no distance at all when Clyde realized that, from her point of view, the "stroll" must inevitably have been a mistake. Freight-laden, horse-drawn drays churned the waterfront into a sea of sticky mud; and spindle-shanked pigs fled squealing from the heavy wheels of these "floats," hotly pursued by mangy curs. A blowzy old slattern, her underlip bulging with packed snuff, gave her deserted bird's nest of a hat a more rakish tilt as she passed them and spat voluminously in their direction. Everything that distance had softened or hidden, when viewed from the deck of the *Messenger,* was now revealed in dismal detail.

"I expect we'd better go right to the Halliday after all," Clyde suggested.

"Well. . . . Perhaps we had. At least, perhaps *I'd* better. I don't want you to miss seeing anything you want to. But this mud—"

"Remember I forewarned you. . . . It's a good thing, after all, that Captain Jesse always 'chokes a stump' on Sundays. I don't need to be told that you'd rather spend two hours than two days here."

He took her by the shortest possible route to the hotel and installed her in a suite, remembering, just in time, that she would have been loath to set foot in it if he had told her it was distinguished primarily for its occupancy by General Grant during the swift campaigns which had resulted in the capture of Fort Henry and Fort Donelson. When he was assured of her comfort, he left her, to pursue his investigations as to the shipping of cargo; and when he returned, he spoke of these with the same enthusiasm that had marked his satisfied observations earlier in the day.

"It's about what I thought," he reported. "They'll never work out a smart way to transfer goods from the cars to a steamboat, as long as they can't run the tracks beside the river, because the river's not the same height two days hand running—halfway up the houses in the spring floods, and way out by the sand bars in September droughts. So stuff has to be unloaded from the cars into drays, and then from the drays onto the boats, and that's just too much handling to pay. To my idea, folks will decide to ship all the way by either boat or rail, and if I've got to make a choice, I'll put my money on the steamboats to win—with maybe barge tows to give them capacity. . . . Well, I didn't mean to run on like this when you must be starving to death after all these hours of waiting. Let's go down to dinner."

Dinner was surprisingly good and as bountiful as it was excellent. The item of "cold jellied buffalo" at the top of the menu caused

Lucy to exclaim she had not realized they were *that* far west! And she was slightly disappointed when Clyde laughingly explained that the buffalo in question was only a kind of fish! There was catfish, too, cut in steaks and beautifully browned, a choice of three roasts, and for entrees, spitted pigeons and calves' tongues. Half a dozen kinds of pie and as many varieties of cake brought the banquet to a leisurely end; and when they left the dining room, the afternoon was already half gone. Clyde had rather expected to find, at the desk, some word about the *Richmond*'s expected arrival and he was not disappointed; a lookout, keeping watch from a northern mansard window, had already sent word that the *Richmond* had passed the island and was rounding the point: this meant that there was no time to lose. Clyde paid the bill and he and Lucy hastened back to the wharf boat to reclaim their luggage.

As the *Richmond* came floating into view, her clean-cut bow swelling gracefully back toward her great wheels, she rested with such apparent lightness on the water that the effect was almost one of some ethereal craft, gliding toward the shore of a magic lake, rather than that of a powerful river boat, slowly approaching a dingy city wharf. Clyde, who was watching Lucy as intently as she was watching the boat, heard her catch her breath in a little gasp of ecstasy. She had told him in New York that he had taken her to fairyland; but he knew that the splendor with which he had surrounded her there paled, in her eyes, before the radiance she now beheld. And here, too, was the embodiment of all he himself had tried to capture forever, in choosing, as their abode, a mansion modeled after such a vision.

He could see that the spell was still unbroken, after they had gone aboard and were passing slowly through the main cabin to their stateroom. All the wonders of which she had heard, but in which she had hardly believed, were now holding her enthralled. Here was the thick-piled, rich-colored carpet, extending the entire length of the vast channel-like saloon. Here was the rosewood furniture, elaborately carved and upholstered in satin damask. Here was the concert grand piano, also of rosewood, also elaborately carved. Here was the great series of golden chandeliers, glittering with glass prisms, bright with a thousand burners. Here were the skylights of tinted glass, emblematically depicting scenes and products of the Southland—the cotton fields, the orange groves, the avenues of magnolias in full bloom. Here were the gilded mirrors and moldings, the fretwork and marquetry, the panels depicting the city of Richmond, to which this floating palace owed her name, and the city of New Orleans, which was her home port. Lucy felt for Clyde's hand and squeezed it hard; he could see that her lips, usually so firm for all their sweetness, were trembling a little and that tears were glistening on her lashes. But she did not speak to him, and she seemed hardly aware of the other passengers

88

moving to and fro in gay little groups, of the hurrying porters laden with baggage, of the stewards already standing respectfully at attention beside the long array of white-covered tables, and of the colored orchestra which, this time, was not doing violence to a pleasant tune, but performing melodiously. Clyde was conscious before she was of a fine-looking man who gave them a quick look and then turned toward them with outstretched hands.

"Lucy! I've looked and looked for you! But I thought you'd be getting on at St. Louis, and when I didn't find you. . . ."

Without finishing his sentence, he threw his arms around her and kissed her warmly on both cheeks. Then, releasing her, he turned to Clyde and again held out his hand.

"Mr. Batchelor—or may it be Cousin Clyde from the beginning? Stanard Daingerfield of Sapphire Downs, at your service. Lucy and I are kissing kin, as you must have gathered just now. It was a disappointment, a very great one, that I had to miss your wedding—a confounded race track complication. But we'll make up for it! I said so to myself when I got Cousin Sophie's letter, telling me you were taking the *Richmond* on my recommendation, and I say it again to you now."

He wrung Clyde's hand, beaming on both of them with unmistakable good will. "Have you seen your stateroom yet?" he went on, scarcely giving them time to return his greeting. "No? Well, after you get Lucy settled there, Cousin Clyde, you'll find me waiting for you at the bar. Yes, yes, I know this is a honeymoon. Even so, a man needs to get with other men once in a while, if only to make him appreciate a lovely lady more when he rejoins her. And you *have* got a lovely lady here and no mistake. Marriage must agree with her. I never saw her look as charming as she does now; and even if I'm getting to be an old man, and am a blood relation of hers besides, I can understand that you'd be loath to leave her. But I've some friends aboard I want you to meet. You'll like them and they'll like you. Shall we say in half an hour? Oh, incidentally, of course Captain Neal will be expecting you to sit at his table. No doubt he'll be paying you his respects and telling you so himself, as soon as we're under way. Meanwhile. . . ."

He waved a cheerful farewell and disappeared in the direction of the bar. Lucy looked up at Clyde with a shining face.

"Stan's my favorite cousin," she said happily. "I thought we might find him aboard—in fact, I meant to watch for him, but I was so entranced with everything, I forgot. You're glad, too, aren't you, Clyde? You know I told you about him, I said it was he who first suggested—"

"Yes, I remember," Clyde answered. He must not speak to her curtly again, he would not. But his mind was in a tumult. He had known, immediately, how to deal with Fanchon; for years, they had played the same game and spoken the same language; now he was confronted by a situation with which he was far less qualified to cope. Stanard Daingerfield was no faker, no cheap skate, no pretender to honorable rank; this man was genuine through and through, warmhearted and likable—the sort of man whom Clyde had never had for a friend and whom, all his life, he had yearned to claim as one. But how could he accept such friendship, now that, at last, it was offered? Those other men of whom Stan Daingerfield spoke—was there not sure to be among them at least one who would recognize him, possibly one whom he had victimized? And the *Richmond*'s captain, "Stut" Neal, had been on the river for years. He had started out as a poor boy and had worked his way, by slow and painful steps, up to his present proud position as the designer, owner and master of the finest river steamer afloat. His path and Clyde's had crossed more than once before. Now that these paths had crossed again, what would he do or say, in the light of those past meetings?

Clyde was so preoccupied by these disturbing thoughts that he forgot to look at the names on the doors of the staterooms they went by; if Lucy had not paused by the one labeled VIRGINIA, he might have passed that, too. But, fortunately, something impelled him to stop before it was too late. "Yes, this is ours," he said hurriedly. "I thought perhaps it would please you to be back in the Old Dominion again, at least by inference. You know the roustabouts call this boat the 'Rebel Home,' so you ought to feel at ease everywhere on it; but, of course, I hoped you'd be especially so in our own quarters." He had succeeded in keeping the curtness out of his voice, he was thankful for that. At the same time, he was all too well aware that it was toneless. And he had expected to speak with such loving lightness, as well as such pride and joy! For, on this ship of her dreams, he could once again offer Lucy a fitting habitation. This stateroom, unlike the one on the *Messenger,* was both spacious and luxurious. It was draped with damask and Brussels lace. In the foreground were some comfortable chairs, a marble-topped center table and a mirrored wardrobe; at the rear, half concealed by a rich hanging, was a double washstand equipped with a porcelain toilet set and, beside it, a double bed, with a spotless linen sheet folded down over a silken counterpane and big square pillows peeping out on either side of an embroidered pillow sham. Here they would sleep together again, instead of being separately confined in narrow, rigid berths. Here—or so he had planned—they would eat their meals, in comfort and privacy. And here he would tell her the great news—second only in significance to the great news she had told him—which he had been hoarding for the time when he could say, "So the *Richmond*'s come up to your every expectation, has it? I'm very glad. I'll agree it's a fine boat. But wait until you see the *Lucy Batchelor.* . . ." Then, when she looked at him in rapturous amazement, he would continue, "You must have thought I was neglecting you in Pittsburgh. Yet, all the time I was out with young Thatcher, who's a lot smarter than he looks, and those shippers and ironmasters you didn't even meet, I was going over plans—I was working out designs. I was making arrangements for the financing. . . ." And she would catch her breath and throw herself into his arms, laughing and crying at the same time, because of this culminating gift—a boat which would bear her name.

Well, of course, that scene could still occur, just as he had visualized it; nothing in his triumphant utterance should betray his inner tumult. Of course Lucy would lie beside him again, with her head on his shoulder and his arm around her as she drifted off to sleep; no interloper could penetrate their private paradise and prevent that. And of course they could still have some of their meals at that little marble-topped table—it would not be considered a discourtesy if they breakfasted by themselves at least, especially if they invited Daingerfield and perhaps one or two of his friends to some of their other meals; the table would seat four comfortably and could, at a pinch, accommodate six. Meanwhile, the sooner the inevitable showdown was over, the better it would be for everyone.

"Well, I suppose I'd better be on my way," he said with an attempt at levity which did not fall quite as flat as he feared. "We were hardly aboard the *Messenger* when you insisted the bar was the place I belonged. That time, I tried to hold out, but now that your cousin Stan has the same idea, I know I might as well give in, first as last. Not that I wouldn't a lot rather stay right where I am. But I'll be back as soon as I can and, at least, I'm not leaving you in a cell like the one on the *Messenger.*"

"Don't hurry. I know you and Cousin Stan will find lots of things to say to each other. And I want to unpack. I think the pink net dress with the black polka dots, that I wear with the little black net jacket, would be just the thing for the captain's table, don't you?"

She was singing "Lorena" under her breath as she opened the lid of her small square trunk, obviously happy, both in her actual occupation and in the prospect of a gala evening. Clyde retraced his steps through the long cabin and entered the bar, which was no mere alcove, like the one on the *Messenger.* Contrary to current custom, the *Richmond* had two offices, one on either side of the entrance to the gentlemen's cabin, and, at the rear of the starboard office, was a third compartment of similar shape and size. Here an enormous oil painting, representing the Bacchanalia, as envisioned by a contemporary artist, surmounted a mahogany sideboard, decked with a sparkling array of glassware and rows upon rows of bottles. The multicolored liquors, with which these bottles were filled, caught and reflected the rays of the sun, streaming in from the cabin window; and in front of the sideboard stood Billy, the head bartender, and his two assistants, all busily engaged in filling orders. The bar was already crowded, but Daingerfield and the man with whom he was talking were outstanding among the others. Clyde, who had always taken immense satisfaction in the fact that he had never resembled the pale-faced, sable-clad gambler of tradition, was struck by the lack of any likeness between Daingerfield and the conventional Kentucky colonel, complete with goatee, frock coat and soft black hat. Lucy's kinsman was smooth shaven, and the ruddiness of his complexion was accentuated by the blondness of his hair, which drifted back from his forehead in soft abundance. His portliness enhanced his air of dignity rather than detracting from it; and his hands and feet, which were slender and shapely, looked all the smaller in comparison to his substantial build. He was dressed in a heather mixture sack, so high buttoned as almost to conceal the matching waistcoat, but setting off the bronze-colored ascot, loosely knotted below the V of the immaculate collar. He wore no rings, but the folds of the ascot were fastened with a stickpin headed by a large black pearl; and as he thrust one of his small hands into a front trouser pocket, to extract a fine linen handkerchief, the black silk ribbon of a watch fob, adorned by a golden seal set with a large precious stone, was casually revealed. The man with whom he was talking was almost bald, and his skin seemed tightly stretched across the dome of his head. His frame was spare almost to the point of emaciation—and though he looked the scholar, it was the scholar who had spent too much time indoors. Only his deep blue eyes gleamed with the clarity of great vitality.

"I agree. There's no profit to be made at Metairie, either in purses or bets," Daingerfield was saying to this companion. "There's not much spare money in circulation down yonder yet—couldn't be, less than five years after the war. But I figure I can get a good price for this colt at Saratoga after he's been conditioned by a winter's racing in New Orleans. . . . Ah, Cousin Clyde! I was wondering what was detaining you—or rather, I would have been, if I hadn't known! Carteret, let me present Mr. Clyde Batchelor of Cindy Lou Plantation, Louisiana. He's recently married my cousin Lucy Page of Sorrento—you know, Sophia's daughter. So of course that brings him right into our fold. . . . Cousin Clyde, my friend Judge Carteret Paine of Frankfort. And when I say friend, that's no figure of speech, as you'll see for yourself when you've joined us in a drink of his bourbon. He takes along a supply of it, ample for us and our friends, whenever we travel. What's more, he puts aside two casks from each year's run for me, and holds them for ten years before shipping them on to Sapphire Downs. Then, when they're emptied, I send them back to him, to be used over and over again. His father and mine followed the same practice. It's fifty years since some of the casks I have now were first coopered and charred of good white Kentucky oak. Billy— a julep for Mr. Batchelor. And I'm counting on you to convince him he's never really tasted one before!"

"Yes, sir! Right away, sir! A Special Superior for Mr. Batchelor. Yes, *sir!*" The bartender deftly took some pieces of ice from a cedarwood tub, wrapped them in a napkin and reached for a heel-worn wooden mallet. With this in hand, he paused and looked at Clyde, one eyebrow cocked inquiringly upward. "With or without a jigger of rum, Mr. Batchelor?"

"Are you out of your mind, Billy?" exclaimed Daingerfield in the same instant in which Judge Paine cried: "Lord God of Hosts!"

"Without, of course," Clyde said mildly, as soon as he could make himself heard.

"I only asked because some of the gentlemen . . . " the bartender began defensively, but Clyde interrupted.

"Some of the passengers, you mean. No gentleman would debase the judge's superior bourbon with. . . ."

"To be sure," agreed Billy. There might have been just a hint of suppressed mirth in his tone. "A Special Superior for Mr. Batchelor, coming right up." The mallet banged down upon the wrapped pieces of ice.

"Excuse me, Judge," Clyde smiled, turning from the bar and extending his hand. "I'm mighty proud to meet you, sir. Perhaps, one of these days, when you and Mr. Daingerfield visit us at Cindy Lou, I'll be able to return your hospitality—though not with anything as fine as your bourbon, I'm sure."

"Why not?" rejoined Carteret Paine. "I'd be a low sort indeed if I couldn't send a cask to Cindy Lou as a welcome-to-your-new-home gift for Stan's cousins."

"Your Special Superior, Mr. Batchelor," interrupted Billy, passing a tall tumbler crowned with aromatic green across the bar. In the one brief instant which thus brought them face to face, Clyde noted that the carefully curled mustache, which had once been merely brilliantined, was now also dyed, that the greatly thinned soaplock must now be held in place by bear's grease, that the diamond which gleamed from a scarlet cravat was larger—and more obviously flawed—than the one he himself had affected before meeting Lucy. Without a visible sign of recognition, however, he took his drink, murmured "Thank you!" and rejoined Daingerfield and Paine. Together the three walked to the gentlemen's lounge at the after end of the main cabin and took seats at an unoccupied table among those where others were playing cards, or merely chatting over their drinks.

"I was just telling the judge about a colt I've got aboard," Daingerfield went on. "I must take you down to see him—you'll find him as

93

fine a piece of horseflesh as you ever clapped eyes on. Sapphire Sky, I've named him. Lucy'll want to see him, too. She's a good judge of horses as well as a first-rate horsewoman—couldn't very well be otherwise, with her background. A great land lover, too, like most Virginians. She'll be out riding the crops with you. Of course, she'll have to learn about cane and perique—that's what you raise, isn't it? But it won't take her long. When I think of what she's done to bring back the soil at Sorrento. . . ."

He paused, taking a long, leisurely pull at his julep. Clyde was thankful for the respite. The conversation had taken a turn very different from the one he expected, but momentarily he forgot his original reasons for concern in regard to it. *Horses!* Lucy would expect to find horses, fine saddle stock, at Cindy Lou; and fatuous fool that he was, he had made no provision for this! There were draft animals on the place, and some sort of mounts for the overseers: the stock that went with the land when he bought it; but while priding himself that he had not overlooked the smallest item which could add to Lucy's pleasure, it had never occurred to him that they should have a stable of their own. He had bought horses for the Army—not many, because mostly he had bought mules; however, there had been some horses, too. And he had been to the race track in New Orleans every so often, because such visits fitted in well with his major pursuits. But traveling the river, and moving about from place to place, as he had, without any sort of roots, he had regarded horses merely as a commodity to be secured, at will or at need, from the nearest livery stable. Not that this had always been possible. Ruefully, he recalled the irritating lack of rigs available at the Grand Hotel Pierre Chanet, and then his thoughts strayed in the even less welcome direction of his first visit to Cindy Lou—there was enough to worry about in the present, without dwelling on the past. He had a great deal still to learn before he would fit into the pattern of the country gentry. And the worst of it was, that Lucy. . . .

"By the way, I happened to hear yesterday that the Duncan Kenners are giving up their stable at Ashland. Of course I've no idea what you need, Cousin Clyde—perhaps you're overstocked already. But it just occurred to me that it might be a lucky break for you."

Daingerfield took another long, leisurely pull at his julep and saluted an acquaintance who had just entered the bar. The newcomer glanced from Daingerfield to Clyde and then, instead of coming on toward their table, entered into jovial conversation with Billy, the bartender. Clyde had seen the look and felt himself growing hot under the collar. There was no question about it; he could not let matters drift along like this, while he and Daingerfield chatted casually about old bourbon and fine horses. But in spite of his resolution, the reference to Kenner halted him. Again he thought, involuntarily, about his first

visit to Cindy Lou and Dorothée's boast of visiting at that beautiful
near-by plantation called Ashland, before the owner had gone to
Europe as Jefferson Davis' minister. Later, Clyde knew, the entire
property had been confiscated; and he had also heard that, though it
had eventually been returned to its righful owners, they had not been
able to disassociate it with mournful memories and preferred to spend
most of their time elsewhere. But he had never heard of their stables.
Evidently, from what Daingerfield said, these had been fine ones. The
new-found "kinsman" was right; this was a lucky break.

"No, I'm understocked," he said. "I mean, for the stable. Have you—
could you get in touch with Kenner right away and—buy up everything?"

Daingerfield laughed, easily. "That would saddle you with rather a
large order, wouldn't it? There, I didn't mean to make a bad pun.
Of course, I can get in touch with Kenner, if you like. We're kinsmen,
too, and I served under him, abroad, for a while, after Davis decided
he had more use for me as a diplomat than as a soldier. It was a good
deal of a blow at the time, though I'm proud to remember it now.
Well, as I said, I can get in touch with him if you like. But if time is
of the essence, I think it would be better for me to wire my New
Orleans agent Moise Riviere, from Memphis, and tell him to pick
out whatever you need. Could you give me an idea of about what that
would be?"

"No. I'd be grateful for suggestions."

It was the judge who glanced appraisingly at him now. But this
time Clyde did not care and Daingerfield, apparently, saw nothing
strange about the abrupt admission.

"Then I'd say perhaps. . . . Two walking horses for you, a gaited
saddle mare or gelding for Lucy, a pair of matched hackneys for
carriage service, a Shetland pony for Bushrod—no, wait! A couple of
Shetland ponies! Cary'll be in the saddle, too, before she's much older
and you may as well be ready—meantime, both ponies could be used
in a governess cart. Would such a selection suit you?"

"It certainly would. And if you would tell your agent to send those
horses to Cindy Lou, straight off, by boat, so that they'd be there
before us, that would suit me mighty well, too."

"It's as good as done. And now, what about coming down to the
main deck with me and having a look at Sapphire Sky?"

"I'd be glad to."

"You joining us, Judge?"

"Good Lord, man, don't I see enough horseflesh on shore without
climbing all over a steamboat to look at a colt I've seen off and on ever
since he was foaled? Talk about a busman's holiday! I was just getting
ready to order another julep. Sorry you and Mr. Batchelor won't join
me in a second round. Nobody can fly with one wing."

"You see a julep once in a while ashore, too, don't you, Carteret? Well, we'll let that pass—and rejoin you later for that second round."

Daingerfield set down his empty glass and rose. Then he threaded his way, without haste, among the crowded tables, stopping every now and then to speak with still other acquaintances, to all of whom he presented Clyde as his kinsman. Instead of walking out to the guard, however, he eventually turned in the direction of the main saloon.

"Come and have a look at my stateroom, on the way," he said. "It isn't quite as grand as yours and Lucy's, but it's pretty comfortable, at that—all of them are on the *Richmond*. I want you to get it located, so you can look me up any time you're in the mood—I'm not afraid you'll wear out your welcome, with the counterattraction you've got waiting for you in the Old Dominion." Then, as he threw open the door of a stateroom which was, indeed, both spacious and pleasant, he added, "Sit down and make yourself at home. I've got some of the judge's bourbon here, too. I won't bother to make a julep or send for one. But a small shot's never amiss with a little talk."

He brought a bottle and two glasses from the washstand, poured out the liquor and sat down beside Clyde at the little table. "As a matter of fact," he said, savoring his drink, "when bourbon's as good as this, I believe I prefer it straight. What about you?"

"It's prime bourbon, all right," Clyde agreed. "In fact, I don't remember ever having tasted better, Mr. Daingerfield."

"Mr. Daingerfield? Here I've been calling you Cousin Clyde straight from the start. Isn't that all right?"

"It's more than all right. It's—it's—" He left his sentence unfinished and took another drink. "The only thing is—well, I don't know just how to say it. But I'm still not right down certain you could really want me to call you Cousin Stanard."

"Cousin *Stan*," corrected Daingerfield. "The family decided long ago Stanard was too much of a mouthful. And the family includes you now, too, of course. But I do know what's likely to be troubling you. No, hold on!" He raised his hand in a gesture of protest against interruption. "Let me be the one to say it. I'd be a sorry specimen if I put that particular monkey on your back by way of welcoming you. You were thinking, no doubt, that I might have confused you with someone I knew by—er, reputation!—years back. I want to set you straight about that. I did my level damndest to get to your wedding, but since I had to miss it, I want to make up for that as well as I can now. And I want to begin by saying how happy I am to meet, at long last, and for the first time, the man my cousin Lucy married—the man who's taking his first trip down the river, with his bride."

For a few moments, Clyde stared unseeingly at his glass. At length, with his eyes still fixed on his drink, he said slowly, "I hope there'll never be a time when you'll change your mind about being happy to

96

meet me. Because what you've just said means more to me than you'll ever realize."

"I don't expect to change it. I believe I can still tell the difference between a hawk and a hack saw. Besides, if we do have to rake up the past, my own conscience isn't too clear. None of us out here had the first notion how hard things were going with Cousin Sophie and Lucy—if we had, they'd have had all the help they needed. Of course you can say it's partly their fault for being too plagued prideful to let their own kin know how much they needed help. But it's a lot more the fault of the kin who didn't take the trouble to find out. You did."

"I don't deserve any credit for that. I went to Sorrento because I was in love with Lucy. And of course, since I was in love with her—"

" 'You can give without loving, but you can't love without giving,' eh? Yes, I know the old saying. But it didn't apply in my case. A long, long time ago, I was in love with my cousin Sophie. She never had eyes for anyone else, from the moment she met Virginius Cary. Besides, I was younger than she was; she thought of me just as a kid and a kinsman. But it was different with me. She was the most beautiful creature I ever saw, though I suppose you wouldn't guess it to see her now, after all the grief and privation she's been through. . . . Well, anyway, I never married. But still I didn't go to Virginia, after the war, to see if I could do anything for her. I got back to Sapphire Downs as fast as I could and I've never left it yet, except to further my own fortunes, selling hay at Louisville and tobacco at St. Louis!"

He set his glass down on the table with a bang. "One look at Lucy was enough to tell me all I need to know," he said. "She's got roses in her cheeks and stars in her eyes. She was a lovely looking young girl, but she was a little on the solemn side, if you know what I mean —not stiff, but very serious. She didn't have any color and she was so slim you felt she might break in two. You've changed all this. Of course you've given her fine clothes and handsome jewels, but dammit all, Forrest Page did that much! He was a rich man, too, when the war broke out, and I saw her when she was a bride before—Lord, what a difference now! She's radiant with happiness—happiness you've given her. If you'd never done anything else—or no matter what else you had done—you'd do to take along. At least that's my judgment, and I'm not often mistaken."

"Thank you," Clyde said again. "I—I do think she's happy. And of course you understand that I don't want anything to happen that would make her less happy, that it's on her account. . . ."

"Of course. If you were by yourself, you'd have a free hand, you wouldn't have to step carefully. As it is, you can't afford to risk having your apple cart upset. . . . Well, perhaps I'm mixing my metaphors, but I get your meaning and you've got mine. We're seeing this through together, you hear?"

97

Clyde was very deeply moved, so deeply that he would have been glad to leave, ending the talk on this note. But he knew that however Stan Daingerfield might feel, there were others to be reckoned with.

"You said Captain Neal had asked Lucy and me to sit at his table," he began.

"So he has. I'm sitting there, too. And I've already put a bee in Stut Neal's big hat. When I got through explaining things to him, he agreed with me that he'd never met my cousin Lucy's husband, either. He and I've been closer than molasses and corn pone a good many years now. With me at his table, he'd be slighting me—wouldn't he?—if he didn't invite my cousin and her new husband to sit there, too. It only stands to reason and it's all settled, fair and square and no king's-ex!"

When Clyde returned to the "Old Dominion," he found that Lucy had a change of clothing laid out for him and that she was already dressed for supper in the pink net with the black polka dots. The stewardess had helped her unpack, she told him—the nicest old colored woman she'd seen since she left home. She had not worried over his absence, he could see that, as she had when he left her for any length of time on the *Messenger;* and the thought crossed his mind that she had not divulged all her reasons for her former uneasiness, that she had guessed more about his acquaintance with Fanchon than she had admitted, and that she felt very differently when he went to the bar to meet her cousin than when he had sought out his erstwhile associate. But he did not dwell on the question or permit it to depress him; with Daingerfield as his ally, he would be able to meet any immediate situation and the future would take care of itself. He still intended to tell Lucy everything, someday; meanwhile, whatever she might have divined certainly had not affected her spirits and that was all that mattered. Daingerfield was right; there were roses in her cheeks and stars in her eyes; she was radiant with happiness.

As the evening advanced, there seemed to be more and more sparkle to this radiance. Their companions at the captain's table, besides Stanard Daingerfield and the judge, were an English novelist and his wife; a celebrated Italian singer, who was including Memphis and New Orleans in her concert tour; the elderly relative who acted as her duenna; and a former Senator from Mississippi, with his daughter, who, since the end of the war, had been living in France, but who were now returning to their home in Natchez. The service and the *décor* were in every way worthy of such a distinguished company. This was no "foundering" meal, nor were any "shells" in evidence. The superlative supper was served in restaurant, not in steamboat, style; the gold-lined silverware, engraved with the letter *R,* was exquisite in design; and the porcelain and crystal, similarly marked, would have done credit to any perfectly appointed establishment. Moreover, conversation was easy and delightful from the moment the elaborately pleated napkins were unfolded, to the one when the captain gave the signal to clear a space for dancing. The former Senator immediately asked Lucy if she would honor him and Clyde, with equal promptitude, bowed before the Senator's daughter. Stately quadrilles and lancers were interspersed with lively polkas and languorous waltzes; and the program came to an end with the spirited execution of the pawpaw patch. By that time, everyone in the grand saloon was in such good spirits as to be well disposed toward everyone else; and when the great diva consented to go to the piano and sing some of the arias for which she was most famous, this evidence of her graciousness and talent made a fitting climax to a period of flawless pleasure.

The captain, in bidding his guests good night, had tactfully assured them that he expected to see none of the ladies and "only the unattached gentlemen" at breakfast. So the first meal which Clyde and Lucy had together at the little marble-topped table was all he had pictured it in coziness and intimacy. Indeed it was he who finally suggested that they should take advantage of the ladies' and gentlemen's baths located, respectively, beside the nursery and the barbershop, and that after that they should finish dressing and go out on deck. A newssheet, entitled the *Richmond Headlight,* had been delivered to them with their early coffee, and Lucy was still reading aloud from it, with an eagerness which amounted to fascination, long after they had finished the copious repast of chicken with gravy and biscuits, and hot cakes with sausage, which arrived later.

"Listen to this, Clyde: 'Paris is to have, in January, a dry goods store with twelve hundred salesmen.' That's even more than at any of the New York stores, isn't it?"

"I don't know, but I should think so."

"'The Government has advice of the fact that several Spanish men-of-war are on their way to New York. Not doubting their friendly intentions for a moment, the Government has ordered a fleet of ironclads to that village to render them due honors.' Does 'that village' mean New York?"

"I suppose it must, but that certainly is a queer way of referring to it."

"Oh! . . . Here's almost a whole column devoted to murders! 'A. F. McCurdy, a merchant tailor of Cardigan, Ohio, killed his son Thursday afternoon by shooting him through the head. A family difficulty is said to be the cause of the rash act. . . . In Johnson County, Arkansas, a few days ago, a dispute arose between Mr. Johnson and three men who were packing cotton for him, concerning its weight, when they attacked him with knives, and he defended himself with one, and the result was that two of them were killed and he was cut in more than twenty places, but not fatally.' What terrible people there must be in that part of the country, Clyde!"

Clyde rose and leaned over her shoulder, scanning the column from which she was reading. Then he laughed. "Evidently, you didn't notice the first of those entries, honey," he said teasingly. "Listen to this: 'At Fluvanna Court House, Va., on Wednesday, Captain Richard Harlan was shot and killed by Washington Shares. The parties were highly respectable. The quarrel grew out of a law suit.' It sounds to me as if there must be terrible people in Virginia, too," he went on, in the same bantering tone. "Washington Shares may be considered highly respectable at Fluvanna Court House, but if he is, I'd say that was just a local idiosyncrasy. Now, now—you know I'm only joking! Evidently, you didn't read the last entry in the column, either: 'A good wife makes the poorest and most desolate home a paradise, and moulds the most negligent and indifferent husband into a tender and thoughtful companion. The influence of woman—quiet, imperceptible and all-persuasive—is irresistible when directed by woman's instinctive tact and affection.' Well, I agree with every word of that anyhow. . . . But, listen, we mustn't sit here and read that newspaper all day. You must get out and have a look at the landscape. You'll find it very different now."

"How different?"

"Well, we're farther away from the banks, of course, because the river's so much wider, and that makes it seem as if we were moving more slowly than we did coming down the Ohio—though, as a matter of fact, the *Richmond*'s going along at a pretty smart clip. And there won't be any more bustling, large city landings till we get to Memphis, and you'll find that different, too, from Louisville and Cincinnati. Meantime, there's mile after mile of bristle brush thicket, cottonwood and willow. But somehow, the scenery isn't monotonous. At least, it's never seemed that way to me. There's a restfulness about it, if you know what I mean."

"Yes, I know what you mean. I'll go up to the ladies' observatory for afternoon chocolate and watch it from there. That'll give you a chance to meet Cousin Stan and the Senator in the bar before dinner. I heard the Senator invite you, as we were saying good night."

The Senator had invited him to have a drink, the English novelist drew him into conversation about perique, but it was Stan Daingerfield who suggested a poker game and called on Billy for cards and chips. There would be six of them at the table, Stan said: Senator Fletcher, the returning Mississippian; the English novelist whose name Clyde seemed unable to remember; Clark—"Captain" Clark—whom Daingerfield had saluted in the bar on the occasion of Clyde's first meeting with Cousin Stan there, but who had coolly turned to join another group; Judge Paine, Stan himself and Clyde. For one momentary flash, Billy's imperturbability was lost in the glance of involuntary inquiry he shot at Clyde. But this met no answering gleam. Clyde's expression remained as blank as rain-washed glass.

"Wake up, Billy!" snapped "Captain" Clark. "Didn't you hear Mr. Daingerfield? We want two new decks and a case of chips."

"Certainly, sir; right away!" The bartender's moment of indecision had passed and, as Clark, having received the desired supplies, handed the racked red, white and blue chips to Paine, he said, "You pass them out, seh; since this heah's to be a frien'ly pastime, I sh'd jedge a hunnerd apiece would jes' about cut the mustard. . . . Or perhaps Mr. Batchelor would prefer to bank the game?" Clyde shook his head in denial, and watched almost absently the fashion in which Clark broke the seals on the two decks—one blue, one red—tore off the inner waxed paper wrappings, flipped out the jokers and shuffled. Yes, they were readers. He could identify them from the backs clear across the table. But Clark was shuffling them honestly. Was it possible Billy, the barkeeper, had introduced the readers for his—Clyde's—benefit, and that "Captain" Clark was not the sharp gambler Clyde took him to be? More probably, concealed somewhere upon his person, Clark already had the cold deck, which would be substituted at a given moment for the one with which the game began. Meanwhile, Clyde considered, he could make certain, thanks to the familiarly marked cards, that he did not win, and at the same time he could keep Clark from fleecing any of the others.

The play and the talk that companioned it shifted and progressed. Senator Fletcher was saying: "Nothing is further from the fact than our notion that the French, as a nation, are immoral. We have no more right to judge France by what visiting Americans see in Paris than our British cousins have to judge us by what they might see on the Bowery." Judge Paine opened a cigar case, and withdrew from it a satiny blond claro. Clark, deck in hand and ready to deal, ceremoniously produced a match, struck it, and leaned across the table to proffer the flame. In doing so, he knocked some of his chips to the floor and, after the judge's cigar had taken on an even glow, Clark shook out the match and leaned down to retrieve them. Instantly Clyde was aware that, during the fractional moment when Clark's actions were concealed as he fumbled under the table for his chips, the deck in his hand would be switched for another in which the order of cards had been prearranged—the traditional "cold deck" of the sharper.

Reading the backs of the cards as they were dealt around the table, Clyde realized that Senator Fletcher was the one who had been selected for shearing. That would have been fairly obvious, in any case, he reflected, for Clark did not really know whether Clyde Batchelor was what he now seemed to be or what, by repute, he had been. Thus

Clark would neither chance failure by trying to fleece him, nor risk reprisal by victimizing those who might be under his protection—his kinsman and his friend. That left only the novelist—Grindle, the name sounded like when the others addressed him—and Senator Fletcher. The novelist might be too unskilled to be lured by whatever inviting bait the sharper planned to use; that left the Senator in the position of chosen victim.

Clyde noted that Fletcher had been dealt a pat full house—a hand that would beat anything but four of a kind or a straight flush. Paine, Daingerfield and Grindle held merely cards, but Clyde had been dealt five miscellaneous spades, and to himself, Clark had given the four, five, six and seven of hearts. That made the line of the planned drama plain as a pikestaff. Senator Fletcher, holding an almost invincible hand from the outset, would bet heavily before the draw. So would Clyde, if he were an innocent, since his hand, likewise pat, was nearly as good as the Senator's. Moreover, if he were not an innocent, he would bet high anyway, to tempt additional Fletcher bets into the open, and would later demand a cut of the winnings. Meanwhile, Clark, pretending dismay, would mourn the ill chance which had dealt him a hand he could not afford to abandon. Reluctantly, protestingly, he would call the bets his two opponents continued to force upon one another. When the money was all in, Clyde and the Senator would stand pat; groaning, Clark would discard one of his five pasteboards; but the one he would draw in its stead would be either the trey or eight of hearts, giving him the winning straight flush.

Clyde winced as he thought of the dollars he must sacrifice, but there was solid assurance in the look he gave Cousin Stan when the latter tossed away his cards after Senator Fletcher had pushed a hundred dollars into the pot with the remark, "Any ribbon clerks or other fainthearted counterjumpers had best stay out of this one. It's marked, 'For Men Only'—one hundred dollars, and there's more where that came from."

"Up a hundred," Clyde countered stolidly.

"Too rich for my blood," sighed Judge Paine, flipping his hand to the center of the table. Grindle hesitated before following suit, and Clark looked at his hand with well-feigned woe.

"Smack where the hair's shortest," he wailed. "I got no more business in this here pot 'n a rabbit's got at a houn' dog's kennel, an' I can't afford to drop. Go easy on a poor orphan child, gentlemen. I got to call."

The betting swiftly reached a climax; the disordered pile of chips and bank notes at the table's center rose swiftly in height. Finally, the last bet was in. Clark picked up the deck and turned to Senator Fletcher.

"Cards?" he asked. "I'll play these," the Mississippian proclaimed triumphantly, and Clark conceded, "I was sure you would, seh." Turning to Clyde, he inquired, "Cards?" Instead of saying, "Mine's pat, too," Clyde picked up his hand, peered cautiously between the squeezed edges, and, with a sudden look of consternation, burst out, "Good Lord! I must have overlooked my hand!" In what seemed to be a sudden fit of temper, he slammed his cards among those already in the center of the table and snapped, "Give me five fresh ones. I've paid for the privilege of looking at another hand, even if I haven't the ghost of a chance to do anything more."

Clark did not actually gulp, but he looked as though he had. Clyde's demand meant, of course, that neither the trey nor eight of hearts, now unquestionably the top two cards, would find their way to Clark, whose hand, therefore, would remain a "bobtail," worth exactly nothing. What Clark had planned to do, no doubt, was to pass Fletcher the deck, with the request, "You deal me one off the top, please, seh. I jes' naturally don't have the heart to do it to my own self." And the Senator, having himself dealt him the top card, which would be either the trey or the eight of hearts, could therefore not be suspicious of the chance that had topped his pat full. Only now, the trey and the eight would both have to be dealt to Clyde—by Clark.

"I'm waiting—Captain," Clyde said, his equanimity seemingly restored. "Five off the top, if you please."

Thoughtfully, Clark dealt the cards, one at a time, across the table, picked up his hand for a farewell glance, and then went through with the projected play by turning his four hearts face up, discarding the fifth card, a club, and passing the deck to the Senator. "You give it to me, seh," he said. "The topmost one, and if it's right, I'll bet; if not . . . easy come, easy go, like the soldier said when he spent his month's pay, the whole seven dollars, in a single night. . . . Well, well, well, another club. I was afraid so, but a gentleman can't lay down a four-card straight flush open at both ends, seh. . . ."

"I told you this was for men only," rejoiced Fletcher, sweeping a miscellany of cards, chips and bank notes toward him. "Reckon I'll be able to lift a mortgage or so now, when I get back to old Oktibbeha." He began to sort and stack his winnings. Clyde rose.

"I expect this'll have to do me for a while," he confessed, warmed by a gleam of understanding—and admiration—in Cousin Stan's gaze. "I could have bought Mrs. Batchelor a right pretty bauble for what the Senator's got in front of him."

"Let's not break up the game. . . . You can't quit now," urged Clark anxiously.

"It's like the Senator said—Captain," Clyde responded. "I'd better stick to the boys' games. I'm not quite up to these 'for men only' deals."

"We might as well all draw the fires," chuckled Daingerfield, rising and clapping Clyde heartily on the shoulder. "Enough's a plenty. I'm going down to see how they're treating Sapphire Sky. Care to join me, any of you?"

Clyde did his best to hide the sense of satisfaction he felt over the outcome. Clark would never know, of course, whether Clyde's act had been calculated, or whether the cards had been so ineptly stacked as to justify what had followed. But, as Clyde turned to accompany Daingerfield, he noted that, though Billy had turned his back to the bar, the mirror revealed, under the dyed mustache, the bartender's lips parted in a wide and gleeful grin.

They reached Memphis late that same afternoon and again the wharf scene fascinated Lucy. She had seen cotton bales occasionally in Richmond, and had once been taken through a spinnery in Gastonia while visiting one of her schoolmates there. But never could she have imagined so vast an acreage of bales, all alike, their coarsely woven covers of brown jute bulging out between iron tie straps. As far as she could see along the levee, both upstream and down, the bales formed a brown-and-white prairie, its several sections marked by snapping flags or painted standards representing various playing cards in their several suits. In the midst of this prairie, brawny roustabouts chanted mournful improvisations as they manipulated their cotton hooks with remarkable dexterity and skill; and, under the spell of this music, enormous bales actually seemed to dance up the gangplank.

"De Great I-Am say yeah, man! He done tell me his ve'y own se'f I got a bale to tote to Misto Jack o' Di'mon's. Got to tote Misto Jack o' Di'mon's bale lessen de Great I-Am say put de bale down. Po' man, oh, po' sinner, got a bale to tote to Misto Jack o' Di'mon's an' cain' put de burden down tellst de Great I-Am say go yonnuh wid all de Jack o' Di'mon' bales. Oh, Law-awd, tell de po' man whe' at you wants Misto Jack o' Di'mon's bale put!"

"What do you suppose some psalm-singing daown-East spinner would say," chuckled Clyde, "if he knew his cotton was all being shipped to one of the Devil's picture cards?"

"I suppose he'd be very indignant," conceded Lucy. "Why on earth should they use playing cards instead of big numbers or letters?"

"Because the roustabouts can't read, but every one of them knows the cards, frontways, backways, and everywhichaways. Tell 'em to take a bale to Number Fourteen and like as not he'd fetch up in Arkansas. But tell him to take it to Mr. Jack of Diamonds, and he'll go there like a martin to his gourd."

The chants rose and fell, and though the stream of incoming bales was rarely interrupted to permit other cargo to be discharged or brought inboard, the expanse of bales still seemed unbounded. "That's one commodity the railroads or nothing else will ever take away from the rivers," Clyde observed as he and Lucy leaned forward to look down upon the swarming activity. "As long as cotton is ginned, it will be shipped by boats. River steamers to New Orleans. Ocean cargo vessels to Liverpool or Boston, or round the Horn to China and India. If you think Memphis is something, wait until you see it in New Orleans! There's a special breed of work-along-shoreman—screwmen, they're called—who load cotton in the ocean vessels. They take jack-screws and tighten those bales down into the hold of a ship till it's a caution. Why, there have even been cases when a ship's timbers were sprung and strained, so tightly were the cotton bales stowed. They get top wages, those screwmen. A silk-hat crowd of workers."

The great singer disembarked at Memphis, to everyone's regret; she had inspired affection as a woman, besides rousing admiration as an artist; and she would soon be returning to Italy, which meant that most of her fellow passengers would never see her any more—though, to be sure, with improving conditions, the grand tour would soon be a possibility again. At Natchez, Senator Fletcher and his daughter left the boat and this was likewise a matter of general regret. But after all, Natchez was not far from any given point in Louisiana; there would be visiting back and forth between plantations. For the time being, however, all that the southbound passengers saw of Natchez was a line of brick front houses, set shoulder to shoulder, like stair-steps, on a stately ascending roadway cut into the face of an abrupt bluff. This was Natchez-under-the-Hill, Clyde told Lucy; the city proper was out of sight, beyond the top of the bluff. . . . Baton Rouge was built on a bluff, too, she discovered afterward; but there, the city's principal landmarks—among them the dilapidated pseudo-Norman castle which, before the war, had been a capitol building—were clearly visible. Lucy found the sky line an arresting one, both in itself and its contrast to the flatlands on the opposite shore, which faded back from the low levee into misty cypress swamps. She stayed on deck, chatting with Cousin Stan, while Clyde went ashore to send a wire to Convent, announcing their impending arrival at Cindy Lou. A telegram, he explained, would be relayed by courier; they would find everything in readiness for them when they reached home. . . . As Clyde moved away, he heard Daingerfield say, "That means he's arranged a royal reception for you, my dear. I'm looking forward to it myself—it ought to be quite a spectacle, seen from the *Richmond.*"

"Why not come ashore with us and have a share in it? You know you'd be more than welcome."

Daingerfield laughed. "Later, my dear. And I'm looking forward to it. But on your first night in your new home? Don't be absurd, Lucy. Besides, I've got to get in touch with my agent Moise Riviere the first thing tomorrow morning."

Clyde could not hear the rest of the conversation. Later, he asked Lucy what she and Cousin Stan had talked about while he was gone.

"He said he was very fond of me—that, as he didn't have any daughter of his own, he'd like to put me in the place of one, as far as possible. I was touched, Clyde, because he said it as if he really meant it."

"I'm sure he did. I'm touched, too."

"And then, he said something else. He said, 'I like your husband. I like him very much. I was prepared to welcome him into the family, of course, for your sake, from the first. Now I'm prepared to welcome him into it for his own. You've found yourself a real man, this time, Lucy. He'll never fail you, he'll never even disappoint you. It goes without saying that you'll never fail him or disappoint him.'"

Clyde swallowed hard. "And what did you say?"

"I said I knew he was right. I said I knew the failures and disappointments of my life were all behind me now. I thanked him. And he wanted to know what for."

"And then you said—"

"Why, for accepting me as a foster daughter," she said. And looked steadily into his eyes.

It was almost midnight when the *Richmond* swung around the bend which brought the Big House at Cindy Lou suddenly into sight. There was a lamp in every window from the belvedere to the basement and little lanterns were set along the railing of the great curving staircase which led from the gallery to the garden. The terraced walk between the house and the landing was flanked with field hands, each holding aloft a flambeau; and the flames from these spread out to meet the flames rising from the torch baskets by the gangplank. When Lucy stepped from this to the shore, on Captain Neal's arm, she stood for a moment, gazing at the dazzling sight with a speechlessness more expressive than any cry of rapturous wonderment could have been. Then, still without speaking, and completely forgetful of her escort, she turned and looked at the lofty pattern made by the twinkling lights which outlined the pilothouse and the decks of the *Richmond* in tiny points of radiance. Clyde made no effort to shatter the magic moment by speech. But finally her brimming eyes met his, revealing the unity of their thoughts: land and river, boat and house, were all part of the same pattern, and their own loves and their own lives were part of it, too.

CHAPTER V

THE *Richmond* sounded its last warning bell, Captain Neal went back to his post on the roof, the paddle wheels began to turn, and the stately white boat glided slowly away, its lights duplicated by their blurred reflection in the dark water, its bow crowded by the roustabouts who had foregathered there to sing:

> *"Ah stepped across de Natchez*
> *Ah stepped across de Lee*
> *Ah stepped across de Richmond*
> *An' she flewed fum under me*
> *Ah—Annie—ah*
> *She flewed fum under me."*

Briefly, while listening to the music, Clyde and Lucy continued to watch the receding plume of spark-shot smoke which marked the boat's progress down the wide river. But the magic moment was over. Clyde turned and greeted the waiting Negroes.

"Good evening," he began cheerily. "Miss Lucy—Mrs. Batchelor—and I are happy to see all of you. But you'll get to know her a lot better in the morning. Meantime. . . ." He turned to Lucy. ". . . Will you excuse me just a moment, honey, while I explain to them about the luggage?" he asked. Then, raising his voice, he called, "Zack! Where are you, Zack?"

"Heah's me, suh," a deep musical voice replied from the darkness.

"This way, then," said Clyde. His words trailed off into indistinct murmurs as he took the servant back to the heap of trunks, satchels and bags which had been put ashore by the *Richmond*'s porters. So he was sure Lucy did not hear his anxious whisper, "Zack, tell me quickly—have any horses been shipped here the last day or so? Just nod your head—or shake it." Then, as Zack gave the hoped-for signal, accompanied by a broad grin, Clyde turned back to Lucy and, drawing her hand through the crook of his arm, said tenderly, "Come, dear. We won't stop to see the gardens or anything else now. It's late and everything will still be here tomorrow. Besides, I can't wait to claim the privilege of carrying you over the threshold."

When he set her down, it was in the drawing room, which was not dim, as he had first seen it, but superbly illumined by its crystal chandeliers, so that its arcade of pillars and its frescoed walls were brilliantly revealed. Lucy looked about her with delighted appreciation and told him she was surer than ever that he meant to have her live in fairyland. But he suddenly realized that she was very tired; there had inevitably been a letdown after the excitement of their arrival, and she was really overwhelmed by the splendors revealed through their approach to their new home and their entrance within its walls. He suggested that she should not try to see the rest of the main floor that night, but let him take her straight upstairs; the next day they would make a "tour of inspection," both inside the house and over the grounds. She agreed, almost eagerly, that this would be much the best plan. Belle drew a bath for her in the great marble tub of which Clyde was so inordinately proud; and soon she was settled among her pillows in the immense bed with the canopy lined with azure satin, after the most approved fashion for a *lit de ciel*.

Clyde was not sorry that Lucy's weariness had furnished a pretext for postponement. He felt that, with one exception, the results of his foresight, consultations and expenditures were pleasingly evident. But the space created for a library, when he moved the furnishings of the gaming room to the ground floor, had presented a major problem to him; he knew little and cared less about books. So he had installed a few handsome bookcases and decided to tell Lucy that he had purposely left these only partly filled and had attempted no other furnishings, while waiting to find out what, if anything, she desired to bring from Sorrento. Therefore, he was greatly relieved, the next morning, when, after one casual glance about the great square room at the left of the front door, Lucy said there would be plenty of time to talk about all that later, when it was not so beautiful outside. Then she went back into the hall and, turning toward the gallery, closed the door after them. The view from the gallery was certainly very pleasant: the terraces had taken shape, the fountains were playing, the trees and shrubs set in their appointed places, and many of the flower beds were in bloom; although there had not been time for the grounds to make any show of luxuriance, this was already foreshadowed. From the gardens, Lucy wanted to go on to the orchards and from there to the stables; the horses which Moise Riviere had succeeded in securing and shipping, at top speed, were already in roomy stables, from which they were led out, one by one, for her enthusiastic inspection. With the only tinge of regret that she expressed about anything, she whispered to Clyde that she supposed she should not do any riding for the present. Fortunately, she could not foresee the miscarriage which, in spite of every precaution against it, occurred early in the new year, temporarily clouding her happiness and, for a much longer time, limiting her outdoor activities.

Meanwhile, it interested and occupied her to remedy the inadequacies of the library's equipment. The handsome bookcases Clyde had already installed were filled with such promptitude that he instantly recognized the necessity of supplementing these. Mrs. Cary had maintained that Lucy was entitled to take as many of her grandfather's books as she chose from Sorrento, since she had insisted that Colonel Page's library must be kept intact for Bushrod. In Mrs. Cary's opinion, this was an evidence of fine feeling which should not go unrewarded; and she knew it would mean much to her daughter if, in her new house, the bride could have around her the well-worn volumes to which, from child-hood, she had been accustomed. Alexander Peyton had not been out-standing as a scholar; but he had considered a general acquaintance with the classics and with current literature a requisite in the well-ordered life of a country gentleman; and he had never regarded lightly his respon-sibilities as a landowner, a justice of the peace and a church warden. His library reflected his standards, his tastes and his sense of duty. With Shakespeare's plays and the King James version of the Bible as its twin cornerstones, it grew to include the complete works of Scott, Byron and the other British writers of their period. It also contained La Fontaine's *Fables* and Racine's plays in the original French, besides numerous acceptable translations of other foreign authors; and, along with these, were ranged Mayo's *Guide to Magistrates*, Gunn's *Domestic Medicine* and Frank Van Dever's *Sermons*.

Mrs. Cary had been right in believing that it would mean much to Lucy if she could have part of her grandfather's library with her in Louisiana; and, in making her selections, the bride had included not only the classical fables, plays and novels, from which he had read aloud to her on long winter evenings, and the *Medical Companion*, with the contents of which her mother had acquainted her gradually, but Byron's poems, which she was not supposed to have read, and some of the old lawbooks, which she had really never read. Like Alexander Peyton, she was cultured and conscientious rather than scholarly; but she loved the sight of the beautiful tawny old volumes bound in half calf or suede, on her well-filled shelves, whether she ever looked inside them or not. They adorned the great square room from which the gaming table had been removed, and gradually she embellished it still further with huge globes, chaste marble busts and old etchings. All of these seemed to har-monize wonderfully well, both with the books and with the rich draperies and heavy carved furniture. Clyde came to share Lucy's pride in the library and to watch for the sales which were all too often precipi-tated by fallen fortunes and—acting on Lucy's suggestions—to make wise purchases which filled the gaps in her own collection. But he never took the same degree of enjoyment in this room that he did in the rest of the house, which, as season succeeded season, more and more completely filled its builder's dream that—according to Dorothée—it should be a bower of beauty and a center of enjoyment, even of revelry, not only for its owners, but for all their friends.

To be sure, during the earlier years of their marriage, the Batchelors did not have many visitors. Cousin Stan almost always stopped off for a few days when he was on his way to and from Kentucky, bringing with him an atmosphere of great good cheer and casks of Judge Paine's bourbon. Captain Neal and the officers of the *Lucy Batchelor* and her sister steamboats, which were built soon afterward—the *Cary Page* and the *Sophia Peyton*—also came frequently to Cindy Lou; but Mrs. Surget was the only lady living in the immediate vicinity who dropped in often and who was regarded by Lucy in the light of an intimate friend. Lucy realized that her lack of verbal fluency in French —which she read with ease and wrote with grace—and the fact that she was an Episcopalian instead of a Catholic automatically created barriers between herself and her neighbors and that the trying period of Reconstruction was not conducive to conviviality; but she would have been amused, rather than offended, that Creoles might consider themselves the social superiors of a Cary. If she missed the greater degree of intimate and informal sociability to which she had been accustomed in Virginia, she never said so, and it did not occur to Clyde that she did. She seemed to feel his company all-sufficient, his devotion completely satisfying; indeed, he had the impression that guests would have appeared to her like intruders in this fairyland of his creation, that she desired to share it with no one except those nearest and dearest to her, who, when all was said and done, were only Cary and himself. Cousin Mildred Caskie had brought both children to Louisiana, in accordance with the prenuptial agreement, as soon as the bride and groom were really settled; but, when she returned to Virginia herself, after one of the long visits typical of the period, she took Bushrod with her. As things turned out, he was comparatively little at Cindy Lou after that; it had been decided by all concerned that it was best for him to go to school in Virginia, where he could have greater educational advantages, and to come to Louisiana only for his longer holidays. But part of these vacation periods were spent at Sorrento, quite logically, since this property would someday be his and thorough acquaintance with it was highly desirable. So months at a time went by in which his mother and sister and stepfather hardly saw him.

Apparently, his mother did not resent this, for his prolonged absences were another matter on which she did not comment, and nothing could have suited Clyde better than to have Bushrod in Virginia. The boy was rapidly outgrowing his less pleasing attributes. He no longer whined or sulked; in fact, his manner was unusually suave for one of his age. The sallowness of his childhood had now changed to a clear pallor, which rather enhanced the dramatic quality of his good looks. His dark eyes were keen, his mouth mobile and his expression watchful. He was slender, but exceptionally well proportioned and, despite the air of indolence which he affected, he played an excellent game of tennis, rode horseback with the careless ease of a born equestrian and danced with almost professional perfection. Without being a brilliant scholar, he did reasonably well in his studies; and without being outstandingly popular among companions of his own sex, he was liked by most of his classmates and was a great favorite with their sisters—whose parents, for some reason they did not attempt to explain, viewed him with less enthusiasm. His grandmother adored him and his mother viewed his faults indulgently; but Cary had never accorded him the respect normally shown by small sisters to their older brothers and there was still no real harmony between him and Clyde.

Cary's relationship to her stepfather was, however, entirely different. In a sense, she was even more of a companion to him than Lucy, for the little girl tagged everywhere at his heels, while her mother was occupied with the meticulous supervision of the great house; and, as soon as Cary was old enough, she rode with him whenever he went about the plantation or on jaunts up and down the river road. Lucy did not ride any more. She had stopped, immediately, when there was first a prospect of another child, hoping against hope that the doctor she had previously consulted might have been mistaken, that she could, after all, give Clyde a son of his own. Her hopes had been vain, not only then but later; nevertheless, she clung to them for a long time; her repeated disappointments were the sole cloud on her happiness and she could not bear to admit the permanency of its shadow. Eventually, her physician suggested that she would be wise to forgo riding, in any case. Her general health was good and remained so, if she was spared fatigue. But she easily became exhausted, and the handling of a spirited horse, or even a gentle one, was too much for her limited strength when this was constantly overtaxed in many other ways.

So it was Cary who went everywhere with Clyde, and to whom he talked about local happenings and the management of Cindy Lou and the lore of the countryside as they "rode the crops" along the headlands which separated the various fields and, later on, along the experimental levees erected in an effort to stay the might of the spring floods. Apparently, the beloved child, like the man who adored her, never wearied of ranging the countryside, of gazing at the shifting panorama which the landscape provided, of learning its secrets, of exploring its splendors. Together, they always found something wonderful to do, something wonderful to see, something wonderful to discuss. . . .

For months on end, of course, the sugar crop received their absorbed attention—the first tender shoots, "the fine stand of cane," the rows of tall stalks falling to the ground under the gleaming knives. Then, in mid-December, when grinding was drawing toward its close, perique came into its own, and the progress of this, from seedtime to harvest, seemed even more thrilling to Cary than anything the cane fields and the sugar mills could offer.

First the tiny sandlike granules were mixed, in equal parts, with wood ashes. This, Clyde explained to Cary, was in order that the seeds might be more widely separated in the sowing. She nodded her understanding and watched, with the same intensity that he did, while the mixture was carefully scattered over long, narrow beds and covered with palmetto leaves. Then she waited for the bright days when the leaves would be lifted to admit the warm winter sunshine and asked her stepfather anxiously, on chilly nights, whether they had not better go and make sure the covers had been replaced. Clyde always assured her that the palmetto leaves were back exactly where they belonged; but sometimes he took her to look at them, just the same. He knew she would sleep better if she saw for herself that the little plants, which had sprung from the tiny seeds, were all right.

Next, Cary waited with impatience for April to come, for then the seedlings would be taken from their long, narrow beds and planted in the fields, which were already prepared to receive them. By that time, the bright stalks of cane would already be springing up from the old rows of stubble, so that the growth of the two crops could be watched simultaneously for many weeks. But by late June, near the Feast of St. John the Baptist, the perique crop was ready to harvest, while the cane would remain in the fields until near the Feast of Toussaint, which fell on the first of November.

Cary would have liked to dismount and get out among the children who were shown how to break the suckers carefully from each stalk of perique, so that not more than twelve leaves would remain on any one; Clyde had explained to her that this was done in order to insure the size and strength of the plants, and she wanted to help, for she took immense pride in their vigorous growth. But he also told her that, while it was right and proper for some children to work in the fields, others must learn "to plant from the saddle" and that she was one of those who belonged in the latter group. When she said she did not see why, he told her that she would someday, and that, meanwhile, he hoped she would take his word for it. When he put it that way, she said of course she would. She would take his word for anything.

Perique, like cane, was cut with wide, cleaver-shaped knives. This was done when the sun was high, so that the leaves would be wilted by the time the cut stalks were taken to the drying sheds; on the other hand, after the dried leaves had been stripped from the stalks, they were cleansed and gathered into "twists" very early in the morning, while they were still pliable from the dew. So, with the coming of summer, Clyde and Cary were up even earlier than usual, first to watch the harvesting and then to follow the carts in which the leaves were hauled to the drying sheds and unloaded beneath canopies which protected them from the sun. Women were waiting to drive nails into the butts of the stalks and suspend these on wires, where they remained for about two weeks. Next, men came and took the dried stalks from the wires and beat them on logs to remove the dust which had collected on them.

After that, they stripped the leaves from the stalks and moistened them under a very fine spray before turning them back to the women, who sat at long tables and, by deft flicks of the wrist, removed the center veins—a process which Cary watched with endless fascination. Even after this work was completed, she loved to linger in the curing sheds while the twists of tobacco were placed in strong wooden boxes, with oaken blocks on top of the bundled leaves. Long poles were laid over these blocks and weighted down with heavy stones, so that the tobacco would be pressed in its own aromatic juices. Then, every so often, these stones were removed, to release the pressure on the leaves. The brawny men who lifted off the weights let Cary "help" them and, afterward, they showed her how the packed leaves, once the pressure was lifted, would suck back part of their own moisture and soak it up again. She came to understand that it was this process of alternate pressure and release which finally gave the tobacco the rich flavor which was so highly prized; and she thought it was very wonderful that anything that looked so simple should be so important.

Her interest did not end with the curing. She found endless excuses for visiting and revisiting the warehouse, to watch the packaging of the perique—after it had been properly pressed—into the five-pound bundles, tightly bound with ropes and canvas, which were called "carrots" and in which it was eventually marketed. "Please, Papa!" she would say coaxingly. Once in a while, Clyde demurred, reminding her that they had been to the warehouse only the day before, that nothing was happening there which she had not seen many times already and that it was more important for him to inspect the cane carts which were under repair, or the powerful "sugar mules" which had just been shipped in from Missouri. Then, still more engagingly, she would prattle about the "nice funny sweetness" of the scent which permeated the warehouse and which he knew she loved to sniff, or remind him that the last time they went there she had not "helped" weight down a single lever; and she would end by creeping into his lap and snuggling close to him while she whispered, "*Pretty* please!" between the kisses with which she showered him. So he would forget about the carts and the mules and remember only that Cary was the darling of his heart and that he could deny her nothing.

The wild creatures which belonged to the land, as well as the crops which grew on it, were a source of never-ending joy and wonder to the little girl. Clyde had not long been familiar with these birds and beasts himself, since he had not been raised as a countryman; but he took pains to learn about them as rapidly as he could, from Lucy, from the neighbors and from the Negroes, and then proudly passed on his new-found knowledge to Cary as fast as he acquired it himself. One day, as they were skirting the angle of underbrush, along two intersecting ditch banks, a little brown quail apparently tumbled out of the thicket onto the turf at the very feet of their horses.

"Oh, the poor little thing!" Cary exclaimed. "It's been hurt."

"No, she hasn't," Clyde chuckled. "But she's got a nestful of babies somewhere near here and is pretending to be helpless, so that we'll follow her instead of finding them. Come on, honey. Let's let her have the fun of feeling she's fooled us. Slowly, now."

Fluttering in seeming panic along the ground, the little quail managed to remain just beyond reach until she had led them far from the precious brood; then suddenly, she rose with a drumming of wings, which startled the horses, and flew away across a broad drainage canal.

"Isn't that smart though?" Cary cried delightedly. "Do all quails know how to do that, Papa?"

"Most mothers know just how to shelter their babies," Clyde told her. "One of these days you'll be keeping a youngster from trying out bright new ways to get himself killed. Then you'll realize how that mother quail felt when we came riding up to her nursery."

Even more fascinating to Cary than the wild creatures which belonged to the land were the human beings who belonged to it also, and who were not afraid that she might do them harm, like the mother quail, but who returned her friendliness. There was Moppy, the wizened Negress who always wore a shapeless calico garment and three hats, one perched on top of another. Whenever she met Clyde and Cary on the river road, Moppy snatched off two of her hats, extending one, upturned, to Clyde, and the other, also upturned, to Cary, with the single wheedling word, "Mishay!" Clyde always dropped a silver dollar into the hat nearest him and handed another dollar to Cary, so that she could give Moppy one, too. Then the wizened Negress mumbled blessings on their heads and told them she had cast her spell on them "for true." The first time this happened, Cary was very much astonished, both at the size of her stepfather's largess and at the deference he showed the weird woman. But he explained that he had met Moppy the first day he had gone down the river road, seeking his fortune, and that he had had all the good luck she had wished him; so he had been grateful to her and generous toward her ever since, and he intended to go on showing his gratitude by generosity as long as Moppy lived. After that, Cary understood and herself treasured Moppy's good wishes, feeling sure these would bring her luck, too.

Besides hobbling Moppy with her three hats, there was Milly Sue, as mountainous as Moppy was wizened, who did not beg and who always carried a small white blossom in one huge black hand. Milly Sue was remarkable in that she could walk among her many hives without getting stung and she never referred to her bees except as "my little folkses." Clyde and Cary did not meet her by chance on the river road, as they met Moppy, who never revealed her abiding place. They went to Milly Sue's cabin on purpose to inquire whether she was getting palmetto honey from her bees, because, if she were, they would ask Belle to make hush puppies for breakfast; there was nothing in the whole world better for breakfast than hush puppies with honey.

"Sho 'nuff," Milly Sue would say, raising the fragile flower in her hand toward her broad blob of a nose and sniffing at it as she chuckled a greeting. "My little folkses done be making plenty honey, them, for most three weeks now. Ah specks Ah'd better clean up on 'em beehives after you-all gone away, cose dey's fractious today by the long dry spell. Soon as ever a shower of rain fix it so dey don' have to work too, too hard, dem, dey be's feeling more better."

Then there was Aunt Vicey, who was an herb woman, and whom they saw both on the river road, where she went to gather sassafras leaves, and at her cabin, where she pounded them after drying them in the shade. She also went into the swamps, to look for bay leaves and other plants from which she brewed herb teas that were highly regarded. Clyde and Cary did not often see her when engaged in such a search, partly because they themselves spent less time in the swampland than on the river road and in the quarters, and partly because Aunt Vicey preferred to do her searching, like her brewing, in secrecy and they respected her feeling about this; they knew it was different from Milly Sue's pride in her skill with bees, which she was only too glad to proclaim, and from Moppy's begging, in which she felt no shame. On the rare occasions when Cary, who was a very healthy little girl, had one of her infrequent illnesses, Aunt Vicey always came at once to Cindy Lou with some of her brews, and Lucy did not hesitate to give these to the child. They never did her any harm and sometimes, surprisingly, they seemed to do her good. Cary herself believed quite as implicitly in Vicey's herbs as she did in Moppy's blessings.

Lucy had never tried to keep Cary away from the noisy, tumultuous life of the quarters and Clyde was glad of this. The little girl was at ease among the women who sat stuffing black moss into ticking for mattresses, or bent over their open hearths as they prepared their food and heated their sadirons, and even more at ease with their children. She loved the pickaninnies who tumbled about the dust-packed yard and was loved by them in return. The arrival of each new pinkish-brown baby was a source of rapture to her, even when she was puzzled because their mothers did not seem to be much pleased about it—like the time when Ginny Lou's fourteen-year-old daughter Ma'y Lou, who delighted in making sugar-tits for all the babies in the quarters, suddenly appeared with a bouncing little boy of her own, and Ginny Lou grumbled that Ma'y Lou never had no business finding no woods baby; but then all girls was sinners nowadays.

"Moppy must have wished Ma'y Lou luck, too," Cary told Clyde enviously. "More luck than she did me. I want a little brother the worst way. And I've looked and looked all through our woods, over and over again, and I've never found a baby. Next time I see Moppy—"

"All right, the next time you see Moppy, you can complain to her, if you want to," Clyde told her. "But we haven't time to worry about that now. Did you hear that favorite whistle of yours? We've got to hurry if we're going to get down to the landing before the *Cleon* gets in."

He knew there was no surer way than this to make Cary forget about the woods baby. The *Cleon* was the mail boat and Cary always wanted to be waiting to see it appear around the bend. She wanted to see the roustabouts lolling among the cotton bales and the hogsheads of sugar. She wanted to see the men whose occupations were more important moving about in the pilothouse and the texas; most of all she wanted to see Captain Mossop and his daughter Marianna.

Captain Mossop was the owner of the *Cleon* as well as its master, and Cary considered Marianna one of the luckiest children on earth, because she could ride on her father's boat every day, if she wished, and very frequently she did. She was always very much dressed up, much more dressed up than Cary, for Lucy believed that children's clothes should be kept simple. Apparently, Mrs. Mossop, who was never in evidence, had different ideas, for Marianna was invariably clad in a white dress with a great deal of trimming, including fluttering blue ribbons; she also wore a large, floppy hat. She was older than Cary and Cary considered her very beautiful. Marianna spent most of her time reclining in a deck chair and drinking lemonade. The lemonade was served in a tall glass and plump red cherries floated on top of it. Whenever Cary came on board the *Cleon,* Marianna summoned a steward to bring a second tall glass of lemonade, and Cary sat down beside her hostess and tried to sip and drink slowly, as Marianna did. But the lemonade was so delicious that this was very hard for her to do. She wanted to drink it down in great gulps; she was sure it was the best lemonade in the world.

Sometimes Clyde teased her a little about the *Cleon* and Captain Mossop and Marianna and said she was a greedy little girl; she proved it by liking the *Cleon* better than any of the many other boats that stopped at the Cindy Lou landing, delivering plantation supplies or picking up carrots of perique, instead of merely bringing mail. He told her he could not see why she liked it better even than the *Morning Star*, whose pilot Dick Blair had made up a special rhythm of whistle blasts as a welcome to Cary, telling her that it was their very own "rooty toot" and that no one else up or down any of the rivers was permitted to use that signal. Cary was proud because Dick had selected her for such an unusual honor, but she still thought the *Cleon's* whistle was deeper and mellower; it was never sharp, like the whistle of the *Morning Star* and those on many of the other boats. And though she liked Dick very much, it was true that she did not regard him with the envious awe which Marianna inspired in her breast. It was not until she was quite a big girl that she changed her mind about Marianna, and realized that her idol was silly and vain and condescending, and that Dick was merry and kind and capable. She confessed this to Clyde and he told her he had known all along that sometime she would feel differently, not just about Dick but about nice young men in general.

Unlike Clyde, Cary loved the land and its crops and its creatures more than she did the river. He could have taught her to love that, too, he told himself, if he had dared to talk about it more freely, or to take her on enough trips to familiarize her with its beauties and its wonders. But he was afraid that some story, harmless enough in itself, might prove to possess dangerous ramifications; and he had come so close to betrayal, on his wedding journey, that he was loath to risk further encounters and further disclosures which might rouse Cary's suspicions. Even after all these years, Lucy had never voiced any; but he knew hers must have been roused, and he was thankful to feel that Cary's trust in him had never been put to a similar test. She had been less than three years old at the time of the *Lucy Batchelor*'s maiden voyage—too young for participation in any of the attendant festivities. To be sure, she had been taken aboard, eighteen months later, when the *Cary Page*, its paddleboards painted with a huge peacock, its flags proudly flying, its approach heralded by a booming cannon, had made its first dramatic stop at the Cindy Lou landing. She had been given a sip of the champagne cup in which the captain toasted her and everyone had made much of her. But she confessed, several years later, that all she could really remember about the party was the confusion of sounds caused by the great jangling of bells as the vessel came to a halt, mingling with the cheers of the passengers and the crew, and her own tiredness after she had been led from one end of the boat to the other, amidst continual exclamations of admiration in which she did not especially share. Then, when the *Sophia Peyton* had been launched, two years later still, it was her grandmother and not herself who had been the center of attention. Most of the guests, in Cary's opinion, were very dull elderly people, who could not be expected to act as if they were having fun, though she supposed that, in their own queer way, they must be. . . .

Secretly, Clyde was pleased when he found that Cary felt like this; and afterward, there were no more gala landings and pompous launchings, for his interest shifted from floating palaces to towboats and barges, and these did not call for the same kind of *réclame*. It had always been his way to better himself as conditions changed and, once he had designed, owned and operated the three finest steamboats that had ever graced and glorified the Mississippi, and made money on them, despite the encroachments of the railroads and the gloomy prophecies of his would-be competitors, he was ready to turn his attention to another form of river transportation. So he organized an inland navigation company, calling it the C & L; invested in a new fleet of steamers which flew its house flag; and opened an impressive office in New Orleans, near the Bienville Street levee, staffing it with a port captain, a port steward, a bookkeeper and a host of clerical workers. The navigators, pilots, mates, roustabouts, barkeepers and other functionaries who manned the C & L vessels were hired from this command post. Here also, freight was accepted and billed: purchases of supplies that ran the gamut from fuel contracts along the river's length to liquor for the bar, valve parts for the steam engines, provisions for the galley, lime rods for the calcium searchlights and cup grease for the bearings of the titanic twin pitmans.

The profits of this venture, like those of all his previous ventures, were both speedy and substantial. When it came to large commodity shipments, such as grain from the Missouri River Basin, iron and coal from Pittsburgh, and cotton from the South, he could still underbid the best offers the railroads could make and continue to show an impressive percentage gain. The card of the C & L Navigation Company first appeared in the *Picayune* amidst a host of similar notices, giving the schedules of other river boats, ocean liners, sailing vessels and barks. These occupied a full page and he spread the sheet out before Lucy with a thrill of pardonable pride; as against this lordly display, only two railroads besought public patronage in a few inches of typed space, tucked away obscurely in a corner of the financial page!

Although his presence was, of course, periodically required in New Orleans, Clyde directed the affairs of the new company almost entirely from Cindy Lou. The office which adjoined the gaming room was large enough for all practical purposes and he equipped it for efficiency with a roll-top desk, a good-sized safe and a number of tavern chairs. Moreover, the ground floor, besides the premises which he had appropriated for his special needs and the laundry, wine cellar and store closets, contained four bedrooms, a bathroom and a dining room suitable for the use of business visitors. He could summon members of his staff to Cindy Lou whenever he chose, with the knowledge that they would be comfortably housed and still not infringe upon Lucy's privacy. No arrangement could possibly have suited him better. He was satisfied and stimulated beyond measure by his latest success; at the same time, he was increasingly reluctant to leave his home and his family; and the less Cary saw of barges and towboats and their personnel, the better he was pleased.

As the years went on, he was more and more sure his reticence and his hesitation had been wise. It had, perhaps, been less wise to express his doubts as to the practicability of the new levees. But one spring day he spontaneously voiced his anxiety. He had always encouraged Cary to talk freely with him; it seemed natural for him to talk freely with her in return.

"These levees may be fine things," he said, shaking his head and then looking out toward the clover-covered embankment. "But I'm afraid they'll have their drawbacks, too. Now, when the river spreads, it does so gradually and the overflows are never very deep. But the trend is toward a higher and higher levee. If there were a crevasse—and there's bound to be sooner or later—it would do a great deal of damage."

"What's a crevasse?"

"A breach in a levee—that is, a big gap where turbulent waters come boiling through and rush all over the countryside. There's never been one, in this vicinity, since we've lived here. I hope there never will be. But I wish I felt surer of it."

"What does tur-bu-lent mean, Papa?"

"Rushing and riotous. The way the waters become at the bottom of a cataract. That may happen because there's been so much melting ice, way up north, after a long, cold winter, that the river was swollen to unnatural size."

"You'd never think the river would be tur-bu-lent, would you? It looks so smooth and slide-y."

"Yes, it does, right now. But it's given trouble, ever since its banks were settled. There have been lots of wrecks on it, too—it's full of snags, it's often completely engulfed by fog. And sometimes, in the old days, bands of river pirates swarmed onto the beautiful steamboats from their skiffs and seized the strongboxes in the pursers' offices and robbed the passengers of their gold and jewelry."

"Oh, Papa, how exciting!" Cary looked away from the levee, which she could not visualize as a menace, no matter how carefully Clyde explained about crevasses, and gazed at him with rapture. "You mean to say there really were river pirates? They weren't just in stories, like fairies? Belle's talked to me about pirates, too, but I thought it was all make-believe."

"I don't know what Belle's told you about them, but they were real, all right. They were a reckless, evil lot and it was mighty hard to rid the river of them. They holed out in deep swamps and on small islands. They could hide for a long while that way. But eventually, steamboat captains began mounting small cannon on their forecastles and that precaution marked the decline of piracy. In due time, all the miscreants were scattered, if they weren't caught and killed."

"Belle says it was the pirates who killed people. She says they gutted their victims, so the poor people would sink to the bottom of the river.

She says there was a pirate named Murrell who boasted no one he robbed had ever floated up to tes-ti-fy."

"Belle shouldn't tell you things like that. Your mother wouldn't like it."

"Well, *I* like it. Belle says Murrell stirred up the slaves, too. He planned to make them rebel against their cruel masters. She says he meant to found a black empire and rule over it. She says—"

"I'll have a word with Belle about the stories she's telling you."

"Oh, Papa, please don't! *Pretty* please!"

"Cary, I—"

"Well, you just said yourself that the pirates were real. Didn't you ever hear about Mr. Murrell?"

"Yes, I've heard of him."

"All right, you tell me about him."

"He had a very sad end, which he richly deserved," Clyde said, trying to speak severely. "He was a boastful man and he tried to impress a young recruit into his band by telling all kinds of lurid tales about his past. The recruit was really a spy in disguise; he betrayed his leader and exposed the plan of an uprising. Murrell was convicted of stealing slaves and clapped into prison. He coughed away his life there and died while he was still a young man."

"Yes, but before that, didn't he have a very exciting time? Didn't he travel up and down the river in all sorts of disguises? Didn't he even have a trip to Mexico?"

"I believe so. But eventually, as I said—"

"He stole gold and jewelry, too, didn't he? Not just slaves. Belle says he had a wonderful time with his money. She said he had so much he couldn't begin to use it all, no matter how much he spent. She says he hid part of it. She says there's buried treasure right here on Cindy Lou!"

Cary was still looking at her stepfather with sparkling eyes, still speaking with a joyous excitement quite untinged by fear or horror. Clyde, cursing himself for having given color to Belle's story by introducing the subject of pirates himself, tried to shrug the matter away. It was just as he had thought. A seemingly harmless tale might have all kinds of ramifications.

"Well, of course there are always legends about what pirates have done with their loot. And the Negroes love to embroider them. But I wouldn't put much stock in this buried treasure if I were you, Cary."

"But you've heard about that, too, haven't you?"

"Yes, I've heard about it. I've even heard where it's supposed to be located—out in the rear areas of the plantation, where there's a big gravel bed, so that the land can never be productive."

"Couldn't we go there and dig?"

"We could, but we'd have nothing except exercise for our pains.

We'd have to get rid of an enormous deposit of gravel before we'd even get down to the bottom."

"Well, if you don't want to dig there, can't I go and dig by myself?"

"Certainly not. You know you and I always go everywhere together. But I tell you what: someday when I'm not too busy with the sugar crop, and you don't coax me into taking you to the perique warehouse, we'll go out to that gravel bed and I'll sit and smoke while you dig. If you dig far enough, all by yourself, to get below ground and find the buried treasure, you may keep every bit of it. How's that for a bargain?"

"Oh, Papa, it's *wonderful*. I can't wait to start!"

Within a week, she had cajoled him into taking her out to the gravel bed. But, after an hour's digging, she was ready to admit that she was pretty tired and that she would like to go home for tea. Of course, they could come again some other day. And they actually did do so, two or three times, quite close together. After that, these special outings were spaced farther and farther apart and, eventually, when Bushrod had ridiculed them on one of his rare visits, Cary ceased to suggest them. She and Clyde sometimes referred to the treasure again, in a semi-serious way. But she had become more vitally interested in matters closer at hand and she was also indirectly responsible for the emergence of her mother and stepfather from the seclusion which they had found so satisfying.

It was never suggested that she should go to school in Virginia; neither Clyde nor Lucy could have tolerated such a separation. But when she was ten years old, she began to attend the Academy of the Sacred Heart at Convent, a short distance up the river. With the same swiftness that she had won Clyde's heart, she endeared herself to her teachers and her schoolmates. Soon she was chattering in French with almost the same ease that she spoke English and was visiting at all the near-by plantations and at some of those more distant; for the "First Families," who had sent their daughters to the academy from the time of its foundation, had never lost the habit of doing so. It was natural that these visits should be returned; and though some of the more conservative Creoles hesitated to accept the hospitality of "outsiders," the girls and boys who went to Cindy Lou brought back such glowing accounts of it that all those who had not helped to make up the party were frankly jealous and complained long and bitterly to their parents, as Clyde and Lucy learned gradually, in course of time.

Everyone had such a good time at Cary's house! There was actually a tennis court; no one was expected to be satisfied with croquet or with battledore and shuttlecock. And, after a match, there was tea, not coffee. Mrs. Batchelor served tea every day, not just when she had company—on the terrace if the weather was pleasant, in the drawing room if it was not. And she did not have just squashy little *petits fours* with it, either. There was always a big loaf of homemade *pain de mie*, set out on a round board with a carved rim, and Mrs. Batchelor buttered the bread as she sliced it. There were likewise several kinds of jam to go with the bread and, in season, big bowls of sugared berries or peeled fresh figs with cream to spread on top of them, so thick that you had to spoon it out of the pitcher. There were scones and cookies and big frosted layer cakes. And while you were eating, you could watch the peacocks. They didn't just strut around the terraces, screaming. Every once in a while, they flew right up in the air, with their great tails floating out behind them. Sometimes, you could see as many as eight or ten of them, all ranged along in a row, on top of the cistern, and, at night, they roosted in the trees. It gave you sort of a queer feeling to see the white ones up there, when it was getting dark, because they did look like little ghosts—at least, what the Negroes said little ghosts looked like. Just the same, it was all nonsense to say peacocks were unlucky. Mrs. Batchelor made fans out of the feathers they dropped and also kept great clusters of feathers in vases, on the drawing room mantel, and she wouldn't have done that if they could have brought bad luck to Cindy Lou. She was a lovely lady, always pleasant to everybody, and so pretty, too. And would you believe it? She went to New York to buy all her dresses, but they came from Paris in the first place and so did Cary's. Mr. Batchelor got his clothes from London. He was fun, too. In rainy weather, when the crowd could not have tennis matches or ride horseback or do anything else outdoors, he took them to the gaming room and played casino and dominoes with them and showed them card tricks. He knew any number of card tricks and was terribly good at them. Later on, there was a huge supper, with oyster patties and chicken salad and beaten biscuit and Sally Lunn and all kinds of blanc-manges and creams, even ice cream as a matter of course, and at least three kinds of cake. There were ten house servants at Cindy Lou and they never seemed to mind how much work they did or how late they were kept up. Mrs. Batchelor and Cary both had their own personal maids and Mr. Batchelor had a valet. The guests had special maids and valets assigned to them, too, who were at their beck and call, no matter what time they went to bed. Usually this was pretty late, because they danced until all hours in that big ballroom with the colored lights and, of course, that was the greatest fun of all. Cary was a wonderful dancer. . . .

Clyde could picture the badgered parents listening with compressed lips, if they were the stern, silent type or, if they were not, permitting themselves a few scathing remarks: about the kind of people who had money nowadays and the questionable sources from which it came; about the lack of good taste exemplified by a huge house built in Steamboat Gothic style, and a fountain dominated by the cast-iron figure of a little girl, dressed in the current fashion and holding an umbrella over her head; about the absurdity of having peacocks strutting around on a series of terraces and a maze—a "puzzle garden" as the youngsters called it—for an outstanding feature of the grounds. It gave him no little satisfaction to realize that, all the time, these die-hards knew they would have to give in sooner or later and let their sons and daughters go to Cindy Lou, if they were to have any peace in life; and still more satisfaction when he found out that, while they continued to hesitate, their hands were unexpectedly forced.

In 1884, the daughters of General Lee came to New Orleans to be present at the unveiling of their father's statue and to attend the Carnival celebrations. In the course of a conversation with a distinguished escort, during a lull in the preliminary proceedings, one of them unwittingly asked an embarrassing question.

"I had been rather expecting to meet a Miss Cary Page. You know her, of course."

"I am afraid I do not. But I am sure I should. What is her father's Christian name?"

"Her father is dead. But he was Colonel Forrest Page, a very distinguished member of my father's staff. Indeed, he gave his life for the Lost Cause. That is to say, he was not killed in battle, though he was wounded four times. He died later as a result of these wounds."

"I am distressed to learn that the daughter of such a gallant officer should not have been included among those invited to meet you before the unveiling and to be present at the ceremony. I do not understand how she could possibly have been overlooked, how we could have failed to know that this young lady was now living in New Orleans. If you will give me her address, I will see that the omission is rectified immediately. Cards for all subsequent festivities will be sent to her by special messenger."

"I believe she does not live in New Orleans, but on a plantation at a short distance from here. However, the river families usually come to New Orleans for Carnival, do they not? Mrs. Page, who was a Miss Lucy Cary, the daughter of General Virginius Cary, remarried, several years after the colonel's death. If I am not mistaken, her second husband's name is Clyde Batchelor and their plantation is called Cindy Lou. But the children of the first marriage have, of course, kept their own father's illustrious name. The son Bushrod is now a student at the University of Virginia. I have met him several times—indeed, I am distantly connected with him and his sister through the Washingtons. But I have never met Colonel Page's daughter, who is quite a little younger. I should like immensely to do so."

Miss Lee's escort put his memorandum pad back in his pocket, smothering a sigh of relief. "I begin to understand the—the omission," he said, adding quickly, "the difference in name, you see. We had no reason to suppose that Miss Page would have any special interest in the unveiling. I believe it is generally taken for granted that the young lady is Mr. Batchelor's own daughter. Mr. and Mrs. Batchelor have lived—rather in seclusion. Also, from what you say, Miss Cary Page must still be—ah—quite young. It is not our custom to ask girls under sixteen to Carnival balls."

"She must be just about that now. In fact, I am certain she is at least that old, if not a little older. I know she is expected at the university for Easter Week."

"I assure you, Miss Lee, that the invitation will still go by special messenger, even though this means sending it halfway to Baton Rouge and not down the next street."

All this, of course, Clyde did not learn at the same time or from the same person; but he was gradually able to piece the various scraps of information from various sources together, and derived both amusement and satisfaction in doing so. From then on, Cary's name had never failed to be included on a Carnival invitation list, and she had been a Maid in several of the most exclusive courts. Her first appearance as such had been the year that her classmate and dearest friend Armande Vincent, whose family owned Victoria Plantation, just above Cindy Lou on the river, had reigned as Queen of Carnival. That same year, it became common knowledge that Armande's brother Savoie was deeply in love with Cary Page.

Both families, of course, had been aware of his condition for some time and neither had been altogether happy about it. Lamartine Vincent, the father of Savoie and Armande, had necessarily seen a good deal of Clyde Batchelor because of their joint interest in perique; and the Vincents, as a family, had always been civil to the Batchelors. But there had been no visiting back and forth between the two plantations until the youngsters began it; and though Lamartine and his wife had fallen under Cary's spell, as everyone else did, they had done so reluctantly; the girl did not represent the sort of alliance to which they had aspired for their only son. Clyde and Lucy, on the other hand, while admitting Savoie's attractions and finding no fault with either his intellect or his character, were appalled at the idea of having their adored daughter become a member of any family in which she was not fully appreciated. Therefore, the Vincents and the Batchelors were equally pleased because, year after year, Cary declined to lend a willing ear to the pleadings of Savoie.

She had plenty of other suitors, some of them better qualified than he to win her, in the opinion of her mother and stepfather. On Bushrod's rare visits to Louisiana, he had nearly always brought fellow students home with him, and most of these youths promptly fell in love with Cary. After her first Easter Week, the number of these swains doubled and redoubled; and each succeeding spring, when she returned from her gala trip to the university, more young Virginians seemed to find a sojourn in Louisiana imperative for one reason or another. When

Bushrod began the practice of law in Richmond, where any number of openings had awaited him, his acquaintance increased still further, in both size and stability; so did the number of his sister's suitors. Even in a state where Lee was regarded as a great general largely because Beauregard had spoken well of him, the historic names of these young men carried considerable weight and their presence at Cindy Lou greatly enhanced its prestige. Young Creoles who had hitherto hesitated to pay their addresses, either because they were cautious by nature or—more frequently—because they were restrained by their parents, now flocked around Cary; and in most cases their parents were more than willing to have them do so. Occasionally, Clyde, with the girl's best interests at heart, would ask her if she did not find Valois Dupré or Nial Stuart or Andres Santana a likable sort of fellow. Sometimes she consented to discuss the qualifications of these aspirants to the extent of saying that Valois was a city slicker and she was a country mouse; that Nial was puffed up with pride because of alleged descent from Bonnie Prince Charlie and she preferred married ancestors; and that Andres overlooked the fact that buccaneering days were past and that sensible girls liked their suitors to have mild manners however much their morals might be on the shady side. Usually, however, her only response on such occasions was to sit down on her stepfather's knee and ruffle back his hair, meanwhile looking smilingly into his eyes.

"You're not trying to get rid of me, are you, Father?" she would say. And then they would laugh together, as if she had made a very original and very amusing remark. "Why should I marry anyone when I'm so gloriously happy at home? How could I care for any other man as much as I care for you?"

"You might care for him in a different way, honey."

"Well—when I do, I'll let you know. I'll tell you before I tell anyone else—even the man in question. It'll be our secret for a while, yours and mine. Now I'll tell you another secret." At this point, she would cuddle closer to him and whisper in his ear. "You've spoiled me for every other man because you're so wonderful. I've tried to find someone who could stand comparison with you and I can't. I'm afraid the mold's broken."

How many years was it now since Cary had first said that to him? Rousing himself from his pleasant torpor, Clyde tried to think. Five? No, it must be more than that! Ten? Why yes, at the very least. Cary had been a toddler when he bought Cindy Lou and married her mother. And that was in '69. And this was '94. Twenty-five years—a quarter of a century! And what good years they had been, pleasant and profitable in almost every way! Not perfect, of course: there had been the repeated disappointments about a child of his own. There had been the lack of harmony between himself and Bushrod. There had been the aloofness of their Creole neighbors. And there had been some material causes for discouragement: a few crop failures, a few steamboat disasters, a few unprofitable investments. But the urge to gamble was still strong within him; and though the media and methods he used had changed, the thrill he derived from taking big risks on the chance of making big profits had never lessened, and he did not expect to hit the jackpot every time—all he asked was the traditional six out of ten. Besides, of what consequence were these grievances and losses compared to all the happiness he had enjoyed with Lucy and Cary, all the pride he had taken in their home, all the satisfaction he had derived from his growing importance in the community, all the success he had achieved in nearly every field of endeavor which he had entered? Nothing, he told himself, and meant it. Absolutely nothing. . . .

And now this was '94. Savoie had been in love with Cary ever since she was sixteen and here she was twenty-six. It was impossible, but it was true. Clyde lay back in his easy chair, thinking fondly about Cary and wishing she would come and chat with him now that he had taken his nap. It was very pleasant under the big tree at this time of day. The heat of noon had passed, and a little breeze had sprung up from the river. Presently he would go into the house and see what Lucy—dear, dear Lucy—was doing; but not quite yet. She was probably still resting; it seemed necessary for her to rest longer and longer all the time. She had not been quite as well as usual lately and that troubled him. But he must remember she was not a young woman any more. It was hard for him to do this, because she was so much younger than he was. He was now a man of advancing years. He had admitted as much to himself before he fell asleep. . . .

"Did I wake you, Father? Or were you just daydreaming?"

He looked up with a slight start. There was Cary, for whom he had been longing, standing close beside him; and up to that moment, he had not even been aware of her presence. He gazed at her, filled with a great sense of contentment for, though he knew he looked at her with eyes of love, still it seemed to him she was more beautiful than ever before. Her hair was fair, like her mother's, but there was more gold in it. She wore it parted in the middle, and cut to form a brief, ringleted bang above her forehead. The ringlets still reminded him of those which had framed her face and covered her head when she was a baby, for they had never lost their fine, silky texture, though now she had so much hair that, in the back, it was gathered into a great knot above the nape of her neck. Her eyes were not gray, like Lucy's, but a deep, bright blue, and when she was especially happy or excited, there was a sparkle in them, such as he had never seen in other blue eyes. She must be especially happy or excited at the moment, for they were sparkling now. Her cheeks were always rosy, but the color in them seemed to have deepened, too, and somehow there seemed to be new grace in her figure. She always carried herself well, but modern clothes did not give the feminine form the glamour in which hoops had invested it. However, Cary did not need clothes to give her glamour; she had it anyway. She was wearing white this afternoon, as she frequently did: a high-necked dress with a gored skirt and enormous puffed sleeves, in the very latest fashion. The belt to it was fastened with a fancy buckle; and though it encircled a neat waist, this was not a small one by earlier standards, and Cary did not seem to mind at all. There were several little holes in the belt which would have permitted it to be pulled in more closely, and Cary never took advantage of them. She had told her stepfather herself that her waist was twenty-two inches around. . . .

Well, she was a beautiful girl just the same, more beautiful in some ways than her mother had been at the same age. There was more sparkle to her, not just to her eyes but to everything about her; more spontaneity, more vitality. But then of course Cary had never pinched pennies or nursed a peevish invalid; she had never gone hungry or borne children after prolonged travail. She had never lost other children because her strength had been sapped away from her. What was more, she had been brought up by a man who had never tried to make her feel that it was not quite ladylike to talk with him about anything candidly and without affectation. . . .

"I've come to tell you a secret, Father," Cary said joyfully.

She sat down on his knees and smiled into his eyes. Then she put her face close to his and whispered into his ear.

"I've decided to marry Savoie Vincent," she told him.

BOOK TWO

Summer, 1894–Spring, 1897

ACCOUNT RENDERED

MOMENTARILY, Clyde was so stunned that he could not answer. For years, he had expected her to tell him that she had fallen in love; for years, he had told himself that it was high time she married and, since she had only to choose among any number of suitable applicants for her hand, that she should not indefinitely delay doing so. But her heart had remained untouched for such a long time that he had really begun to think no man would ever win her, that he himself would never lose her. Now that he suddenly learned he was mistaken, the news came as a shock.

Cary seemed to sense this, for she made no tactless attempt to hasten his response. Instead, she nestled more closely to him and waited for it, without visible impatience. Presently, he kissed her and, after another slight pause, managed to speak, though he found it was an effort, and not an altogether successful one, to keep his voice steady and make it sound natural.

"Why, that's—that's great!" he said. "I'm sure you'll be very happy. Savoie's a fine boy—I should say a fine man. You couldn't have made a better choice. Doesn't your mother feel that way about it, too?"

"I haven't told her yet. She's still resting. Besides, don't you remember, Father, I've promised you over and over again that I'd tell you first? But of course Mother knows—that is, I'm sure she's guessed. Women are better about guessing such things than men are—just as men are better about lots of other things!" She ruffled his hair. "Savoie knows, too, by this time—or he will, pretty soon. I sent Zack up to Victoria with a note right after dinner."

"And you told Savoie, in this note, that you'd made up your mind to marry him at last?"

"No, I just asked him if he wouldn't like to come to supper this evening. But he'll guess, too, even if he is a man. I've kept telling him he came to supper too often. He'll know, now that I've actually invited him, there must be a special reason for it; and there couldn't be but one reason special *enough*! Just the same, I thought he'd rather hear what it is than read it. Don't you agree with me?"

"Yes, honey, I do. After you've once told him you love him, the same words will look mighty good to Savoie in a letter. But you're right; he'd rather hear them than read them, the first time."

"I'm glad you think I didn't make a mistake—about that or about deciding to accept him, either. It means a lot to me, Father, for you to think I've done the right thing."

She kissed him again and, slipping lightly from his arms, drew another chair close to his and seated herself, taking his hand.

"As soon as Mother comes downstairs and Savoie gets here from Victoria, we'll hold a formal family council," she said. "But, meanwhile, you and I might start making plans, don't you think so?"

"If you're asking me whether I'd like to have you sit here beside me and chat with me, the answer is yes, I'd enjoy it very much. But unless I'm greatly mistaken, you've got everything pretty well planned already. What you want to do is to tell me about these plans, so that I'll be prepared to agree with you when your mother and your beau get here. Especially in case they shouldn't agree."

Cary laughed, and Clyde realized, with a pang, that Cary's laugh affected him in much the same way as her mother's voice. He loved the very sound of it.

"You're a pretty good guesser, after all," Cary said. "Well, this is what I thought: I thought we'd be married around Christmastime or maybe New Year's. Of course, we've got to have a home wedding, because Savoie's a Catholic and I'm not. But the drawing room would be a beautiful place for a wedding, don't you think so?"

"I certainly do. And I have a preference for home weddings anyhow, because that's what your mother and I had. No argument so far."

"Well, naturally the Vincents would have liked it better if Savoie and I could have been married in church, just as they'd have liked it better if I'd been a Creole," Cary went on, with characteristic candor. "But we'll make the wedding so beautiful they'll forget about their little disappointments. Of course, you'll give me away and—"

"You're sure you wouldn't rather have Bushrod do that, darling? After all, he's your own brother and I'm just—"

"Don't you dare say it! You're my *real* father, the only one I've ever known or ever wanted. There's not a girl I know whose father's meant as much to her as you've meant to me. But I know any number of girls whose brothers are more important to them than Bushrod is to me—Armande, for instance. Of course, I hope Bushrod will come to the wedding. I think Savoie will ask him to be a groomsman. But it wouldn't break my heart if he sent word, at the last moment, that he couldn't manage it. I think he's got a sweetheart of his own, at last. If she didn't want to come to Louisiana, perhaps he wouldn't want to leave her."

Privately, Clyde was of the opinion that Bushrod had already had several sweethearts, if such they could be called. Lately, rumors had reached Cindy Lou that Bushrod was courting an enormously rich New Yorker, and Clyde had been slightly uneasy about these rumors. From the little he had learned about the girl, whose name was Mabel Stoddard, and whose father George Stoddard was a railroad magnate, Clyde did not feel she was the type that would really appeal to Bushrod's somewhat flamboyant taste, or that would fit especially well into the social pattern of Richmond. But there was no sound reason for this uneasiness, and it was not difficult for him to put disturbing thoughts from his mind. He had done so in this case.

"But why shouldn't she want to come to the wedding, honey?" he asked now. "I should think she'd be tickled to death at the chance to meet Bushrod's family under such festive conditions."

"We-e-ll, let's talk about that later. As I was saying, when we got sidetracked, of course you'll give me away. And whether Bushrod appears or not, I'm almost sure Grandmother will come to Cindy Lou at last. She's always promised me she would, when I got married. Grandmother'll make a great impression on the Vincents and everyone else. Mother's so gentle, she's never tried, and anyway, she's never cared. She's been too happy with you, just as I have. But Grandmother'll let everyone realize that she was born a Peyton and that her husband was General Cary and that we're kin to the Washingtons and the Lees on both sides of the family. She'll take it as a matter of course that she'll go to visit the Conrads, too, while she's in Louisiana, and when she does, that'll make another impression."

"I didn't know you set such store by impressions, Cary."

"I don't, personally. But I know it'll mean a lot to Savoie and I think Grandmother's a wonderful old lady—I'll be glad to see her appreciated. Incidentally, I'm going to wear her wedding dress—that is, if I can get into it. I don't suppose I can, without letting it out. But there must be enough satin in the skirt to make the bodice bigger!"

Cary laughed again and again Clyde thought, with a pang, how silent Cindy Lou would seem when that laugh no longer rang through it.

"If I'm married at New Year's, I can wear a crown of white camellias," she said. "They'll be beautiful with Grandmother's rose point lace. We'll have a cluster of them on the bertha and we'll scatter them around the bottom of the veil, wherever we tack it to the train. I'll have my bouquet made of them, too. Of course, Armande will be my maid of honor and she'll carry a bouquet of pink camellias; her headdress will be made of them and the ruffles of her skirt will be caught up with them. She'll be in pale blue. And the bridesmaids will wear a deeper shade of blue and carry deeper pink camellias. Can't you see how we'll all look, Father?"

"I certainly can—more beautiful than ever and that's saying a good deal. All your friends are lovely looking girls, Cary. But none of them can hold a candle to you."

"You say that because you love me."

"I sure do love you. But that's not the reason I say it. I say it because it's true."

"Well. . . . Speaking of candles, of course we'll have candlelight everywhere. And a wonderful supper, with magnums of champagne. And dancing with fancy figures and all kinds of favors. Naturally, I'll give Armande and my bridesmaids nice presents, but these favors will be extra."

Just then one of the great peacocks strutted across the terrace and came to a stop in front of them, spreading his tail to its full size. "Look at the old dandy!" Cary exclaimed. "No wonder people talk about being 'proud as a peacock'! If he isn't showing off, I never saw anyone do it. And he's given me an idea—why not have peacock feather fans for favors? I don't see why I never thought of it before. Don't you think they'd be very striking?"

"Very. But you know, honey, some people think peacock feathers are unlucky."

"And some people think the same thing about opals! Don't you remember telling me, Father, when I was just a little girl, that nearly everyone is superstitious about something, but that it isn't always the same thing? We'll have to hope that none of the girls who come to the wedding is superstitious about peacock feathers, because I intend to have those fans. I can see them, too, as they'll look in the ballroom—perhaps used in a special minuet, with the dancers wearing rainbow-colored dresses! And, in the middle of the ball, Savoie and I will make a dash for the door and drive away in a carriage that's literally covered with ribbons and flowers."

"Yes—yes, of course you will."

"Savoie's always said he wanted to take me to Europe on our honeymoon. And I want to go. You wanted to take Mother, didn't you, Father? And she wouldn't, because I was an impediment."

"You were never an impediment, honey. You've always been the light of our lives."

"Well, of course you'd say that. But the fact remains that Mother never did get to Europe. You're such an old stay-at-home, you won't leave Cindy Lou if you can possibly help it! And of course Mother never leaves you! So, before Savoie gets to be a stay-at-home, too, and before I have any impediments of my own, I think we'd better make the grand tour. I think we'd better take our time about it, and do some visiting in France and Italy besides doing a lot of regular sightseeing. Savoie keeps telling me about all the invitations we've had, from relatives and friends of the family. One of them is from the Marquise de Chanet. She wants us to come and stay at her chateau."

"The Marquise de Chanet?"

"Yes, you know who I mean! The lady who sold you our house, when she was Mme Labouisse. You must have heard that she remarried after she went back to France! I suppose it isn't strange that she didn't keep in touch with you—after all, she never met you except that once. And she never met Mother. But she's always kept in touch with the Vincents—of course, she was their neighbor for a long time and her present husband's a distant relative of theirs, too. She's urged them again and again to come and see her. Savoie thinks we ought to. He thinks it would be fun to visit a French marquise at her chateau. I think so, too. Don't you, Father? What's the matter? You look as if you didn't like the idea."

"Nothing's the matter," Clyde answered, rather abruptly. "Except that I should think you'd want to know a little more about—about this marquise before you decided to stay at her house. After all, it's a long time since the Vincents have seen her."

"Yes, but she's sent them pictures—of herself and her husband and her son. She's beautiful, Father! Didn't you think so when you saw her?"

"As I recall it, I thought she was attractive. I don't believe I would have called her beautiful."

"Well, probably you didn't notice particularly. Because you were very much in love with Mother then, weren't you? And you weren't thinking of Mme Labouisse except in terms of someone who had a house to sell that you wanted. . . . Well, I think her pictures are beautiful anyway, and I like the looks of her husband and her son, too!"

"How old is this son? Won't Savoie regard him as a menace if he's so good looking?"

"Don't be absurd, Father! I don't know how old Pierre de Chanet is—vaguely, I'd say about my age—no, of course he's a little younger! And Savoie knows that, now I've finally made up my mind, I won't change it. Besides, I won't see this young marquis until after I'm married. So that takes care of that! . . . And I promise you we'll go and have a good look at the chateau and all its titled occupants, before we decide to stay there. But I'm equally sure that, in the end, we'll want to. And naturally, visits like that will prolong our trip, so we'll be gone quite a while. I thought that, perhaps, in the meantime, you'd build us a house."

"You wouldn't be happy to live at home, Cary, after you were married?"

He did not speak abruptly any more, but his voice still sounded a little strange. Cary was afraid that, perhaps, she had hurt his feelings.

"It isn't that, exactly. But, if we lived at Cindy Lou, the Vincents wouldn't like it, and if we lived at Victoria, you and Mother wouldn't like it. Either way, Savoie and I would be conscious of that dissatisfaction and we'd feel a little guilty about it, though it really wouldn't be our fault. And anyway. . . . Yes, I think we'd be happier in a home of our own, where we could do exactly as we pleased. Of course, if there's any reason why you don't want to build one for us—"

"And of course there isn't. Of course I want to do everything I can, Cary, that you think would contribute to your happiness. . . . You didn't want this house to be far away, did you?"

"Why no! I want it right here on our land. It would have to be, wouldn't it? That is, it would have to be on our land or the Vincents'. Savoie's never wanted to be anything but a planter and I don't want him to be. After all, he's a planter's son and I'm a planter's daughter and we've both lived on plantations all our lives. They've been very happy lives. It's natural we should want to go right along in our fathers' footsteps."

"Lamartine Vincent is a man of considerably more importance than I am, Cary. I don't know that he'd feel flattered to have you speak about us in the same breath, that way."

"Well, of course, Victoria's a larger plantation than Cindy Lou. I know it raises more sugar and more perique. But the grounds don't compare with ours, or the house. Why, they don't even have a camellia garden! And don't forget about our buried treasure!"

"Perhaps there's been a mistake about the location of the buried treasure, Cary. Perhaps it's on the Vincents' land and not on ours."

"Oh, it couldn't be! How can you say such a thing, Father? You've always believed it was ours, just as I have. You've always said that someday we'd find it, not far from where we're sitting at this moment!"

"I haven't said that in a long while, Cary. After all, we've lived at Cindy Lou nearly twenty-five years now, and we haven't found a sign of buried treasure yet."

"That was because you wouldn't dig for it with me, and I got tired of digging for it alone! But that doesn't mean you've stopped believing in it, does it, Father? Why, every time anyone's made fun of us. . . ."

It was evident that she still clung to her childlike belief, which he had been the first to encourage. Well, after all, her unquestioning faith in the buried treasure had as much foundation as her unquestioning faith in him. Since he would have gone to any lengths to prevent shaking the one, why should he shake the other?

"I know, honey. Well, we'll go on hoping and I'll go and watch you dig again, any time you say the word. Perhaps Savoie would help you now. You'll have to admit that you can't expect manual labor from a poor, feeble old gentleman like me."

"What do you mean, a poor, feeble old gentleman? You're getting lazy, that's all! You could dig every afternoon, instead of sleeping for hours and hours!"

"I suppose I could. But I'm not going to—not even if you say, 'Pretty please!' You're an awful tease, Cary, do you know that?"

"Well, you'll soon be rid of my teasing. I'll be saying, 'Pretty please!' to Savoie instead of to you."

He sighed. "I suppose you will. And I might as well confess I'll miss the teasing—like everything else about you. But I haven't got to worry over that for six months yet, from what you tell me. Meanwhile, what about this house I'm to build for you? It's to be on our land, I understand that now. I suppose you've picked out the exact location. So no doubt you've also decided precisely what type of a house you want."

"Right again. I want a house something like this one, but smaller and simpler. Savoie and I wouldn't need a ballroom, because we could always use the one here. So that would take off a whole story—and a corresponding amount of gallery and railing. I think I'd like it all white, too, instead of different colors, like this one—white and glistening. And I'd like a summerhouse in the garden—what they call a gazebo in Virginia—like the one at Sorrento. Oh, I know everything will be perfect if you do the building for me!"

She leaned forward, pressing both his hands in hers. He returned the affectionate pressure and then, shaking his head, rose with a deprecatory smile.

"It won't be perfect, but I'll do the best I can for you, honey, you know I will. And of course I'll have your mother's help while you're gone—that'll make a world of difference. I think maybe we'd better go and find her now, don't you? She'll want to have a word with you herself, before Savoie gets here."

When they entered the hall, they saw Lucy coming toward them from the dining room and Clyde's gaze rested on her with the proud admiration which had remained undiminished through the years. As in the case of many fair women, the white showed very little in her still-abundant hair; it simply altered its general effect, making her appear more truly a *blonde cendrée* than when she was younger. Her skin was as smooth as ever; none of the telltale little wrinkles which result from anxiety or overwork or suffering, more often than from age, had appeared around her eyes and mouth, for Clyde had seen to it that she was spared all that; and the tapering slenderness of her white fingers was intensified by the beautiful rings he had given her. But she was most fortunate in the natural grace of her slim, straight figure. Perhaps because Cary's remarks about her grandmother's wedding dress were still fresh in his mind, Clyde thought of the garnet-colored silk Lucy had worn when she married him and wondered whether she had kept it. He rather hoped she had, and that she would wear it again for the splendid ceremony that was to take place in the frescoed drawing room. There would need to be no letting out in the case of this dress; and, in a very special way, the bride's mother would be able to bear comparison with the bride, in presenting a picture which not only recalled but revived the charm of bygone elegance. He would certainly ask Lucy about the garnet silk, as soon as they were alone; she might tease him a little, reminding him he had said, when they were on their honeymoon, that she was not to wear made-over dresses any more. And he would reply, also jestingly, that this one would not count, because she had made it over before they were married, and she would never need to make it over again, with a waist like hers! The prospect of such a bantering exchange was very pleasing to him until a second memory, evoked by Cary and obscuring the first, flashed through his mind: lovely as Lucy's figure was and always had been, it was not the one which had met the supreme test of a standard for the feminine figure which, though now outmoded and forgotten, had once possessed the power to make him lose his head completely. His passion for Dorothée had been as brief as it was violent; he had not even given her a passing thought for years. Now, reluctant as he was to do so, he could not help dwelling on her irresistible fascination.

Lucy's approach put an end to this unwelcome train of thought. She had been on the point of joining them on the terrace for tea, she said. But it was beginning to look like rain. Perhaps they had better go into the library, rather than risk having a shower come up, just after they had got comfortably settled.

The fact that she suggested the library was significant. Her husband and her daughter both realized this, for it was still the room they used least and, as such, most suited for special occasions. She composed herself in a large armchair and listened, without interruption and almost without comment, while Cary talked excitedly, pouring out her plans. It was only when the girl paused, asking the same breathless question that she had put to her stepfather—"Can't you just see it all?"—that Lucy smiled, and that Clyde missed something in the smile, just as he had been conscious of the fact that, until then, though Lucy had been gravely attentive, she had not smiled at all.

"Yes, I can see it all, Cary," Lucy said, in her quiet way. "And of course your father and I will try to see that everything is exactly as you wish." She had always spoken to Cary of Clyde as "your father," never as "your stepfather"; and of all the ways in which she had shown her appreciation of his devotion to her daughter, this was perhaps the one which pleased and touched him most. "But I cannot help thinking—"

"Mother, you don't mean to say you're not delighted! Why, you've told me again and again how much you liked Savoie!"

"I do like Savoie—in fact, I'm extremely fond of him. And I am sure you are fond of him, too. But you have had a great many suitors and sometimes, under these circumstances, though a girl naturally feels very much flattered, she also becomes confused and fails to make a wise choice. I cannot help thinking that, if you were deeply in love with Savoie, it wouldn't have taken you ten years to find this out."

"But you kept Father waiting a long time, too!"

"Not ten years. And not because it took me a long time to find out whether I loved him. I found that out inside of ten minutes."

Never, in all her years of married life, had she said this before. Clyde's heart bounded with triumphant joy as he listened to her, and a tingling sensation, of which he had not been aware for a long time, permeated his entire being. Had he thought of himself, a few hours earlier, as a man of advancing years? Why, that was absurd! He was a man in the prime of life, and Lucy was his dearly beloved. . . .

"However, there were many other considerations, which fortunately do not exist in your case, Cary—chief among them the fact that, at the time, I was married to someone else, as you know," Lucy went on. "I believe I will not be guilty of disloyalty to—to the dead, if I admit to you now that I never loved my first husband as I loved—as I still love my second one."

Again Clyde's heart leaped in his breast. The disturbing visions which had risen to trouble his spirit when Cary talked about Bushrod and Dorothée had faded from his consciousness. Indeed, he had almost forgotten that the present conference had started for the purpose of discussing Cary's impending marriage to Savoie Vincent; he had begun to feel that the real reason for it was another revelation of Lucy's love for himself.

"I was—very young when I married Forrest Page," she was saying. "He was a kinsman of mine—what we call a 'kissing cousin' in Virginia. And he volunteered for service in the Confederate Army immediately after the fall of Fort Sumter. Well, you know all that, too. But you do not know how much pressure was brought upon me to marry him before he went away, not only by him, but by—by others. I was told that, if I did not consent to an immediate wedding, he might never know the fulfillment that comes to a man only through possessing a wife and having her bear his child."

So there had never been spontaneity in Lucy's feeling for Forrest Page, her marriage to him never a sacrament in any true sense of the word! She was admitting herself what he had always suspected: that she had been coerced into wedlock, and the child conceived on her bridal bed was no more the product of joyous union than the one begotten by a man determined to prove his authority over a wife until he lay dead beside her! Clyde's feeling of revulsion against Forrest Page had long been submerged by his love for Cary and his complete happiness with Lucy. Now, it suddenly surged through him again, filling him with fresh rage toward Bushrod's father and renewed resentment of Bushrod himself.

"I'm terribly sorry pressure was put upon you, Mother, and I'm sorrier still if my father caused you any unhappiness." Clyde was quick to notice her choice of words. Cary had referred to Forrest Page as her father; and she had not done it because she wanted, or intended, to hurt her stepfather's feelings, but because her own feelings were hurt. "I honestly don't see though that there's any connection between what you've just told me and my decision to marry Savoie. Certainly, no one's forcing me to do that."

"No, not in the way I was forced. But except for Armande, all your friends of your own age are married already." Armande's betrothed had died of yellow fever, on the very eve of their intended wedding; although five years had now passed since this tragedy and it was assumed she had received nearly as many proposals as Cary in the meanwhile, she had never even considered accepting any one of them and it was taken for granted that her heart was buried in the grave. Lucy paused for a moment, as if in respect for Armande's faithful grief, and then went on.

"These friends have begun to tease you about being always a bridesmaid and never a bride. They've contrived to make you wonder whether you really are on the verge of becoming an old maid. It's absurd for you to feel that way, but it isn't unnatural. And Savoie's gone on pleading and pleading. He's very attractive and very persuasive—in fact, I'm surprised that you haven't weakened before this. But that doesn't make me any more certain that you're really in love with him. Only that you're ready for love, like any normal girl of your age, and that you're fonder of Savoie than anyone you've seen yet or anyone you believe you're likely to see. You've become impatient for fulfillment, too."

Lucy did not flush as she made this outspoken observation, more amazing, coming from a woman of her natural reserve, than all the extraordinary remarks she had already made. But Cary was flushing, more with annoyance, Clyde rightly guessed, than with embarrassment. His own feelings had undergone so many rapid changes, in the course of the afternoon, that he had now reached a state of mental confusion, which was very rare for him. He was not certain whether he was more desirous of soothing Cary, or of reassuring Lucy, or of trying to prevent a sudden rift between the mother and daughter who had always been so close to each other and to him.

"If you really feel that Cary should wait a little longer, Lucy, before coming to a final decision—" he began hesitatingly. But, at that moment, the door of the library was flung open, unceremoniously, and Savoie Vincent burst into the room. He did not even seem to be aware that Cary's parents were present. He rushed up to her and threw his arms around her.

"Darling!" he cried rapturously. "Oh, Cary, I'm the happiest man on earth!" Then he said nothing more, because he was kissing her and she was returning his kisses and words had no further meaning for him.

Lucy did not say much more, either, after Clyde led her from the library, closing the door behind them. If she were really troubled, he suggested, trying to guide her toward the stairs, perhaps he and she had better talk all this over by themselves, in the privacy of their own room. Or perhaps, she had better lie down again; she still looked very tired. No, Lucy replied, she had nothing more to say; she feared she had said too much already. She could see that Cary's mind was made up. . . . And they must not forget that they had to be fair to Savoie, too. Cary had given him her promise now, so preparations must be made for a festive supper. Would Clyde go to the wine closet and get out a bottle of their best champagne, so that it could be properly chilled? Or maybe two bottles would be better, because someone might drop in unexpectedly. Indeed, it would be quite in order if Mr. and Mrs. Vincent should call later in the evening. And no, she was not at all tired. Surely Clyde did not think she was so decrepit that she needed to spend half her life on the chaise longue, even if she did have a son more than thirty years old!

He did not think she was decrepit at all, he told her. In fact, she still looked young enough to be Cary's sister instead of her mother; what was more, young enough to make her husband forget that he was an old man. He would give her convincing proof of his forgetfulness, right then, if she would let him. She shook her head, but she did not do so reprovingly, so he went on talking in the same vein, but even more boldly; and presently, they were laughing together at the idea that an elderly couple should be so much in love. . . .

Supper was very festive, as Lucy had said it should be. There were no inopportune visitors, but Mr. and Mrs. Vincent did call to express their pleasure at the good news which their son had hastened to share with them before he left for Cindy Lou. They were easily persuaded to remain for the evening meal; so, though only six sat down at table, it was spread with fine lace and set with Sèvres porcelain; and its splendor of adornment, together with the quality and quantity of the dishes which made up the repast, gave it the atmosphere of a banquet. Cary outlined all her plans again, and everyone agreed that they were delightful, except that Savoie thought they should have the wedding a little sooner. But Cary retorted that she did not intend to let him cheat her out of the fun of being engaged, and asked him how could Father get their house built, if they gave him only a moment's notice? For that matter, how could she get a trousseau ready? It took time to assemble a dozen dozen of everything, though of course a mere man could not be expected to know that! In this, Mrs. Vincent backed her up, and the three ladies eventually withdrew to make up lists of wedding guests and bridal linen and attend to other items, dear to the feminine heart in connection with a wedding. Meanwhile, the three men went down to the gaming room and talked about politics and crops and shipping over their cigars and their brandy. They had already drunk port at table, after the ladies had left them; but the gaming room, which Clyde had equipped and arranged to suit himself, was his favorite setting for postprandial conversations, just as the office which adjoined it was his preferred place for transacting business. He had insisted that the floors in both should be made of the old rose-colored brick, which he had found where Marchand Labouisse had set up his kilns; and in the center of the gaming room he had placed a huge round table, made of figured gum from the sawmill at Gramercy, which Brunswick of Cincinnati—the same cabinetmaker who had turned out his billiard table—had made for him from his own design. The walls were lined with Currier and Ives prints of river scenes—"Midnight Race on the Mississippi," "Bombardment of Island No. 10," "Low Water on the Mississippi," "High Water on the Mississippi," "Maiden Rock"—and over the mantel hung an oil painting of the *Lucy Batchelor*—a work of art which Clyde viewed with special favor. But his greatest source of pride was the rosewood cellarette— a converted armoire which contained an impressive array of decanters, whisky bottles, brandy flasks and square faces of Holland gin, ranged above a second set of shelves where wine bottles were cradled on their sides with the necks pointing slightly downward, and still another section filled with goblets, tumblers and stemware of every sort and description. He opened this cellarette and turned to his companions.

"Your pleasure, gentlemen?" he asked. "Or may I suggest that, in view of today's happy event, we toast the future in the finest available? I still have a few—a very few—bottles of Napoleon brandy. How could there possibly be a more suitable occasion for opening one of these?"

"There couldn't!" Mr. Vincent exclaimed. He cupped his hands about the bell of his glass, warming it before he began to savor its contents with obvious delight. "Not many a man is toasted in such liquor as this, on the occasion of his betrothal," he told his son, raising his glass. "It's a privilege to propose one to you and your beautiful bride-to-be."

"Couldn't you make it just to Cary, *mon père*, so that I could drink the toast, too?"

"Or why not make it simply to the future?" Clyde suggested. "A bright and happy future to all those we love and all those who love us?"

"By all means," Vincent agreed, a trifle testily. He was not accustomed to correction by his son or by his associates—especially those associates whom he regarded with slight condescension, as he did Clyde Batchelor. But Savoie flushed.

"Thank you, sir," he said, looking toward his future father-in-law. "I—I don't know just how to answer, but I appreciate what you did—what you said, very much."

Clyde was not sure whether the flush came from embarrassment or pleasure, or a combination of the two, but in any case, it was becoming. He had always taken secret pride in the fact that he himself had never in the least resembled the popular conception of a "typical gambler" who was very generally visualized as slim, dark and sallow faced, invariably clad in black broadcloth and frilled linen and seldom disposed to remove his tall silk hat. On the other hand, he took an equal amount of satisfaction in the fact that Savoie so perfectly looked the part of the "typical Creole." His features were finely chiseled, his eyes dark under black brows which had a slight upward turn toward the temples, his equally black hair, worn rather long, curly at the ends. Normally, he did not have much color, but his pallor was clear and healthy. He wore his faultlessly cut clothing with ease and grace, yet nothing about him remotely suggested the popinjay or the tailor's dummy. Unquestionably, this was an aristocrat, "to the manner born"; but he was more than that. There was a sort of inner light which illumined his person, bespeaking the thoroughbred in thought and deed, as well as in appearance. Lucy might be justified in her doubts about Cary's choice, but only because the girl had taken so long to make up her mind. There was nothing in Savoie himself which the most captious parent could have wished to have altered. Clyde raised his goblet.

"Well, here we go then—a bright and happy future to all those we love and all those who love us," he said ceremoniously.

The three men sat for some time, discussing the topics of the day and the part which Savoie was to play in the management of both Victoria and Cindy Lou, after his marriage. But eventually, he showed signs of impatience and, asking his father and his future father-in-law to excuse him, he went upstairs, and found Cary in the hall. She had begun to wonder what had become of him, she told him, and had missed him so much that she had almost decided to go down to the gaming room, since, evidently, he had no idea of coming to the drawing room. But it was a beautiful night; why couldn't they leave their parents to talk on and on, while they themselves strolled in the garden? A fresh breeze was blowing from the river, so there would be no mosquitoes.

Savoie commended the idea very highly, and the stroll was the first of many similar idyls. The period of their engagement was an extremely happy one for both of them, but especially for Cary. Savoie remained restive, because of its length, and occasionally this restiveness took the form of moody silence, or of pleading for less delay, or of an attempt at more ardent love-making than Cary approved. But she was always able to charm away his black moods, and to put a tactful end to his pleading and to keep his love-making within bounds; and, as for herself, she was enjoying everything about her betrothal: the raillery of her friends, the teacups they sent her for presents and the luncheon parties they gave for her; the big Tiffany solitaire which Savoie placed, with great ceremony, on the third finger of her left hand; the shopping tours for sheets and towels and table linens; the fine stitching on drawers and corset covers, ruffled petticoats and long-sleeved nightgowns, most of which were convent made, but a few of which she and Lucy made themselves; the special attention to the lace-trimmed, hand-tucked "wedding set" of finest batiste. She watched, with excitement, while the ground was broken for her house, and with still greater excitement as the house itself began to rise, spacious and symmetrical, in conformity with her wishes. And, when the wedding invitations were actually out, and gifts of every description began to pour in, she insisted on opening each package herself, on arranging every scrap of silver—down to the last bonbon spoon and pickle fork— exactly as she wanted it.

In all this time, there had been only one real cloud on her happiness, and Clyde had dispelled that for her. She had written promptly to Bushrod, telling him of her engagement, and his answer had been anything but satisfactory. Of course, he sent her all sorts of good wishes; but he told her not to count on his presence at her wedding. Things were not going particularly well for him in Richmond; he had hesitated to let their mother know, because he did not want to worry her, and he had not told Clyde, either, because he did not want his stepfather to think he was asking for help. (He had never called Clyde "Father," as Cary did; for a long time he had used "sir" as a form of address, and had always managed to make it sound mocking instead of respectful. In writing or speaking, he had referred to "my stepfather." Eventually, Clyde himself had suggested that, since Bushrod was now grown up, he might as well say "Clyde.") But, to tell the truth, he was devilish short of money; if he could scrape enough together, he thought he might move to New York, and see if he could not do better there than in Richmond, which was really a petty, provincial place. But such a move would take every cent he could beg, borrow or steal.

Cary showed this letter to Clyde, who read it through with an expressionless face and then handed it back to her, still looking completely blank. He would like to think over its contents a little, he said; meanwhile, he hoped she would not divulge these to her mother. Shortly thereafter, he announced that it would be necessary for him to take a brief business trip north; it would have to be very hurried and, therefore, he thought it would be better if he went alone this time; later on, if Cary could tear herself away from Savoie, they would all go to New York together and make the final selections for her trousseau. It was by no means unusual for Clyde to absent himself on short trips, in connection with his shipping interests, and neither Cary nor Lucy showed, or indeed felt, any suspicion of an ulterior motive on his part this time. But, the evening after his return, he took occasion to talk confidentially to Cary, when they had been over to inspect the progress of the new house and were walking home together. Except for them, the river road seemed deserted; therefore, they were safe in assuming that no one else was within earshot.

"I found I had to go to Richmond while I was north, so I dropped in on Bushrod," he said, speaking quite casually.

"Why, Father, I'm awfully glad! Did you find out exactly what was the trouble there?"

"Yes, I did, and I'll tell you about it if you'll let it be one of our secrets."

"Of course I will. . . . But do you mean a secret even from Mother?"

"Most emphatically. Do you promise?"

"Yes, I promise."

"Bushrod was badly in debt. I've paid off his debts, but I agree with him that it would be just as well if he left Richmond."

"Why, Father?"

"Because he doesn't enjoy a very good reputation there."

"He doesn't. . . . I don't understand, Father. Merely his name. . . . And he had any number of offers when he graduated from the university."

"I know. But a name isn't enough in itself any more, if it ever was. I've always thought there had to be something to back it up, in the long run. And he couldn't get as much as one offer now to save his skin. In fact, he was asked to resign from the firm of Custis and Dabney. And he'd already been asked to resign from the Westmoreland Club."

"But *why*, Father?"

"Because. . . . Why, Moppy! I didn't hear you coming up behind us! And I haven't run into you on the road for a year or more. Where've you been all this time? And how've you been?"

"Ah've been po'ly with de mis'ry, mishay. Ah don' get around like Ah'd make out to do, not no more, no."

Characteristically, she did not answer his first question; they had still never discovered where Moppy lived, and the thought crossed Clyde's mind that probably they never would now, and that there might be some sad reason for her secretiveness. Her voice quavered as she spoke. Obviously, she was very feeble; the "misery" to which she

145

referred was not merely a favorite fable, as it was with so many of the Negroes when they did not feel like working. She leaned heavily on a stick as she fumbled for the two hats which she extended, in turn, to Clyde and Cary. She must have approached them very slowly and painfully; it was not strange that they had failed to hear the soft shuffle of her feet on the dusty road.

"Well, here are three dollars today, one for each hat, instead of two, one for me and one for Miss Cary," Clyde told her, feeling in his pocket and extracting the clinking coins, "like what I gave you before I had Miss Cary here with me, remember? Why, Moppy, that was nearly thirty years ago and you looked to me like an old woman then! How old are you now, as close as you can reckon?"

"Ah'se too, too old, mishay," Moppy quavered, peering up at him from under her wide hatbrims, "but thankee and may the Big Hand bring you the bestest luck."

"Let's hope it will. And anyway, you've got a claim on me, seeing as how you brought me such wonderful luck that first time I saw you. Listen good now, Moppy. I don't want you just to take a chance of meeting me on the road any more. I want you to come to the big house at Cindy Lou every Friday. You'll be expected and you'll get a week's rations and three silver dollars. If you can't come, send someone I'll know is there in your place. But you've got to do something for me, too. You've got to bring Miss Cary as much luck as you brought me. She's going to have a house of her own pretty soon, right here on the river road, and a fine handsome husband and nice youngsters, we hope. You'll make a charm for them, won't you?"

Moppy had continued to peer up at him while he talked to her, but there was increasing blankness in her gaze, as if she had not understood very well. She mumbled, "Sho'ly, missy, sho'ly, sho'ly! The very goodest luck!" Then she turned and shuffled off again, still noiselessly and still mumbling. Cary seized Clyde's arm.

"What was it you started to tell me about Bushrod, Father, when that senile old hag came sneaking up behind us?" she asked impatiently.

"Now, now! Moppy didn't mean to sneak. She couldn't know we were talking secrets."

"Well, I asked you why Bushrod had been made to resign from his firm and his club and you only got as far as 'Because' when. . . . I believe you were really glad to be interrupted! Aren't you going to finish what you started to say?"

"You're right, I don't want to, but I'm afraid I'd better, honey. He was asked to resign because he'd been gambling."

"But lots of men gamble, Father. Most of the men we know play cards for stakes or bet at the races, or something. And quite a few of them go into debt."

"I know, Cary. But the men you're talking about don't cheat."

"You don't mean to say *Bushrod cheated at cards*!"

"Yes, that's just what I mean."

She was looking at him in horror. He tried, not altogether success-fully, to smile at her reassuringly.

"I'm sorry I had to spell it right out for you, honey. I wouldn't have, if I could have helped it."

She continued to stare at him, her expression still horror stricken. Her face showed all too plainly her conviction that her brother had committed an unforgivable sin. If he had told her that Bushrod was drinking too heavily, or that he had become entangled with a girl who was not his social equal and whom he had no intention of marrying, Cary would have understood and been lenient. She had been brought up to recognize and admit that, unfortunate as it was, gentlemen sometimes did do such things, and the ladies of the family forgave them. But no gentleman ever cheated at cards. What was more, no matter what the state of his finances, no gentleman left a "debt of honor" unpaid.

"I'm afraid it had been going on for some time," Clyde continued, speaking as gently as he could. "But it wasn't found out immediately—in fact, not until just before Bushrod wrote you. So it's been possible to clear up—and hush up—everything fairly quickly. I hope Bushrod's learned his lesson. I think perhaps he has. Of course he's terribly ashamed—terribly humiliated."

"Do you mean because of what he's done or because he was found out?"

"Well—both, I believe. But he's making a new start now. This girl we'd heard rumors about—Mabel Stoddard. That may be a very good thing for him, you know. Because her father's the rock-ribbed, right-eous type. He wouldn't stand for any nonsense in his daughter's husband. And I think Bushrod wants to marry Mabel, very much."

"But he'd have to tell her beforehand what he'd done! He'd have to tell her father, too!"

"Well—" Clyde said again. "Well, perhaps he should. And then again, perhaps he shouldn't. It wouldn't do any real good. And it might do a great deal of harm."

"You mean it might hurt his prospects?" Cary asked scornfully.

"Yes, but not only that. If he's really turned over a new leaf, there's no use dwelling on what's past. Please believe me, honey. I know more about these things than you do."

He drew her arm through his and started, in a leisurely way, down the road again.

"Don't you worry about Bushrod," he said soothingly. "I tell you I've paid his debts, I've smoothed over his departure from Richmond, I've seen to it that he'll get a good start in New York. Of course, the next move is up to him. But let's wait and see if he doesn't make the grade before we pay him any more mind. And above all, don't give him away to your mother. I won't tell her any lies. I've never done that. But I won't tell her the whole truth. I hope you won't think any the less of me when I admit I haven't always done that, either. I don't want her troubled just now and I'm sure you don't. She isn't as well as I'd like to see her. I'll just tell her Bushrod's made a change for the better, which he has. Don't you agree with me that's the thing to do?"

Reluctantly, Cary did agree, and she did not again bring up Bushrod's name, on her own initiative, or betray her feelings about him when Lucy told her, very happily, that she had received a letter saying he was engaged to be married and that he hoped they would all come to the wedding, which was to take place in the near future. That should be very convenient for them, Clyde thought, because they could attend it and do their final shopping for Cary's trousseau at the same time. Bushrod was writing to Savoie also, asking him to be one of the groomsmen, provided he could tear himself away from the plantation long enough.

Upon receipt of this letter, Savoie renewed his mutterings about the delay in his own marriage; if Mabel Stoddard could get ready for a wedding in such short order, he failed to see why Cary could not. But he accepted the invitation, and they all had a very exciting trip to New York, though, as Lucy mildly expressed it, "the Stoddards were not exactly what they had expected." They were strict Baptists, with very rigid ideas about amusements and entertainment; Mabel had never played cards or danced or been to the theater and neither had any of her intimate friends; no alcoholic beverage of any description was ever served at the Stoddards' table or accepted if it were offered them elsewhere. Mabel herself was another source of astonishment; she was heavy and plain and she had no grace of manner or sprightliness of speech to make up for her lack of other attractions. After returning from their first formal call at the Stoddards' huge, gloomy Fifth Avenue house, which was swathed in dark draperies and overhung with immense, mediocre oil paintings in heavy gilt frames, Cary spoke her mind to Clyde on the subject of the match.

"If Mother thinks I'm not in love with Savoie, I wonder what she thinks about Bushrod! I'll admit he's putting on a pretty good imitation of the tender passion—he always was a smooth one—and that Mabel's fallen for him, hook, line and sinker. But no man could possibly be in love with that girl! Girl! I'll wager she's forty if she's a day. And I'll wager she never had a beau in her life before, either!"

"No takers, Cary. On the other hand, she's an only child and her

148

father's a widower, pretty well along in years. Don't overlook that when you're talking about Mabel."

"I don't know what you mean. I don't like her father, either. I think he's a hard, grim, horrid old man."

"Yes, honey. But he's also a multimillionaire and Mabel, presumably, is his only heir."

"So you think Bushrod's marrying her just for her money?"

"Well, what do you think?"

It was hard for them to think anything else, so Lucy and Savoie, who did not know as much about Bushrod's financial situation as Clyde and Cary, were greatly puzzled, for Bushrod had never been unappreciative of pretty young girls with merry ways. Lucy was troubled, besides; without knowing the nature of Bushrod's ulterior motive, and in spite of his impeccable behavior, she was sure he must have one. But she kept her troubles to herself, not even speaking of them to Clyde; and everyone with whom she came in contact, even Mr. Stoddard, who was indeed a hard, grim old man, felt the irresistible influence of her gentleness and her charm, as he had already felt the insidious power of Bushrod's plausibility and persuasiveness. The magnate was also aware that the group from Louisiana gave a cachet to his daughter's nuptials which they would otherwise have lacked and which he did not fail to evaluate. Mabel had insisted on having a church wedding, with all possible ostentatious correlatives. She wanted everyone she knew to see the prize she had captured and Bushrod, to do him justice, looked his handsome best. He had the face and the figure—as well as the manner—to set off fine London tailoring, and Mabel's heart swelled with pride and triumph as she went down the aisle on his arm, conscious of envious glances on every side. But unfortunately, the groom's undeniable attractions did not suffice to offset the bride's lack of these. Her heavy lace veil, her stiff satin dress, her enormous round bouquet, far from giving an illusion of youth and beauty, accentuated her stocky figure and rather flat face. Her bridesmaids, of approximately her own age, were either short and stout, like herself, or tall and scrawny; and their fluffy pink dresses were wholly unsuited to their years. Only Cary, as maid of honor, was a vision of loveliness in the wedding procession; and at the stolid reception which followed the ceremony, only Cary, her mother, stepfather and fiancé, gave a slight sparkle and a certain degree of ease to the assembly. When the bride and groom had left, Mr. Stoddard, who had suddenly become a rather lost and lonely figure, urged his new connections by marriage to remain for dinner with him; and, from kindness of heart, Lucy accepted the invitation in behalf of herself and the others.

The decision was unfortunate. Savoie and Cary were both bored and restive at table and, though Mr. Stoddard did not notice this, because of his preoccupation with other matters, Lucy was quickly conscious of their attitude and troubled by it. Clyde, generally so sensitive to anything which threatened her peace of mind, was less attuned than usual to her feelings of the moment, because Mr. Stoddard had almost immediately put him on the defensive regarding the status of steamboats, and he was afraid the conversation would take a turn which might cause her anxiety. In his attempts to change its trend, he overlooked not only the uneasiness of his stepdaughter and her fiancé, but the distress of his wife.

"This steamboating of yours must be a pretty expensive hobby, these days," Mr. Stoddard had remarked, quite without preamble. The indicated comments on the marriage ceremony, the wedding reception and the display of presents had run their natural course and had even been slightly prolonged by some tactful compliments from Lucy on these general subjects. But after that there had been moments of strained silence which even her *savoir-faire* had not eased, and it was at this stage of the proceedings that their host had made his sudden pronouncement. "To tell the truth, I was surprised to learn you hadn't got out from under, while there was still time, and gone in for something more profitable. Now I suppose all you can do is to grin and bear your losses."

"Apparently your sources of information aren't very reliable," Clyde retorted quickly. "I'm happy to say that I've made a good deal of money out of steamboating. My first packet, the *Lucy Batchelor*, paid for herself in one year; my second, the *Cary Page,* earned four times her cost in two years."

"All right, all right! But that was a long time ago, wasn't it? What have they earned since? And what about the third steamboat and the fourth—I take it there was a third and a fourth."

"I'll try to answer your questions one at a time, Mr. Stoddard. Of course the *Lucy Batchelor* and the *Cary Page* haven't gone on showing the enormous profits they did at first. But they're both still on the river and they're both still carrying plenty of passengers and freight to suit my purposes. I never built or owned a fourth boat of the floating palace type. The third one, the *Sophia Peyton,* didn't do quite as well as the first two, but she did clear an average of twenty thousand for five years."

"Well, I know that's about the average life of a steamboat. I suppose at the end of that time she struck a snag or blew up. So, if she cost you better than two hundred thousand, as I presume she must have, then you lost at least a hundred thousand on her."

"Excuse me. She didn't strike a snag, she didn't blow up, and I didn't lose a hundred thousand on her. But a drunken pilot did run her up a cutoff as high water was dropping and put her aground just below Helena. That was in the spring of '79 and there she had to stay until the January rise of '80, with a part crew aboard. What it cost to overhaul her, from the oakum calking the river shrimp had eaten to the machinery parts that had to be replaced, would near have paid for a new boat. And she never was the same again. Lucy and I talked the situation over with my mother-in-law, because we didn't want to do anything that would hurt her feelings, and she was very sensible about it. She herself asked if the *Sophia Peyton* couldn't be remodeled for some other sort of service, instead of being all redecorated. And that's just what was done. She was put into use as a towboat for the C & L Navigation Company which, as you probably know, I own and operate."

"And in a minute you'll be telling me that's been a profitable venture, too. . . . Eh, what?"

Mr. Stoddard had interrupted himself to answer the butler who bent over him, whispering in his ear. "Oh, all right! . . . Seems we're having coffee in the parlor, instead of at the table," he said, turning back to Clyde. "I know that's the style, but I've never liked it, and I meant to tell the servants that now Mabel was married and I could do things my own way again, I'd go back to having it in the dining room, right with the main course, too. But I've had so many other things on my mind today. . . . Well, shall we move along? Perhaps you'll pour the coffee for me, Mrs. Batchelor?"

Lucy said she would be glad to do so and, sitting down on a low bench, busied herself with the silver service which the butler put before her. It was chilly in the vast gloomy room, and involuntarily she glanced in the direction of the fireplace, thinking perhaps she might suggest that a cheerful blaze would seem pleasant to all of them. But the hearth, like the mantel above it, was banked with a profusion of white roses, now somewhat past their first freshness; she did not like to intimate that their removal would be an improvement. Cary and Savoie retreated to a sofa in a dimly lighted corner; and Clyde, having selected a chair which seemed to offer at least a modicum of comfort, withdrew a cigar from the case Lucy had worked for him, snipped off the end with a gold-mounted cutter and struck a light on the sole of his shoe. It was not until he had looked about in vain for some sort of a receptacle in which he might place the charred remains of his match that he realized smoking was not customary in this sanctuary, though one look at his host, who had meanwhile tugged at a brocaded bellpull, would have quickly disclosed his mistake. Mr. Stoddard's expression had hitherto revealed only a satisfied sense of superiority; now it was disapproving; and the tone in which he addressed the butler, who had departed after setting down the coffee service and now reappeared, was very close to sanctimonious.

"An ash tray for Mr. Batchelor, Griffin."

"An ash tray, did you say, sir?"

"Yes. An ash tray. As you see, Mr. Batchelor wishes to smoke."

Clyde was ready to admit the possibility of a mistake, but he thought he detected a slight arch in the butler's eyebrows which had not previously been there. At all events, Griffin's tone, like Mr. Stoddard's, was almost sanctimonious as he answered.

"I'm very sorry, sir. I don't think we have an ash tray in the house."

"We must have something that would serve as a repository for ashes. Please bring it."

"Very good, sir."

The butler departed, to return with a small saucer of the same pattern as those which companioned the coffee cups. Clyde, without indicating in any way that he attached the slightest significance to the absence of ash trays, resumed the thread of conversation where it had been broken off when they left the dining room. He was determined that the subject under discussion should not be dropped until he was sure he had quieted any fears which Stoddard might have roused in Lucy.

"You spoke of steamboating a few minutes ago as if it were a hobby, Mr. Stoddard," he said pleasantly. "I therefore take it you think it's dead, as a business. I'd like to assure you that it isn't. It's only changing, as it has been for some time already. That's why I went in for towboats and barges."

"All right. If it suits you better, we'll say it's only changing. But you'll have to admit it's the railroads that are doing the changing."

Mr. Stoddard leaned back in his Gothic chair with a look of righteous triumph, at the same time putting the tips of his spread fingers and thumbs into precise contact with each other. Clyde's answer was still good humored.

"They're changing, too, if you come right down to it, aren't they?" he asked. "And, if I'm not mistaken, they'll have to change a lot more —for the better—if they're to stay in business. Wasn't it the railroads' rebates to favorites and other such capers that helped put Grover Cleveland back into the White House?"

"That's a very one-sided view, sir." The spread fingers had begun to tap against each other as if in irritation. "You talk like a Populist. Sound finance demands—"

"Perhaps we'd better not get off on the subject of politics, Mr. Stoddard," Clyde interrupted. "Especially since 'sound finance' came so close to scraping me down to the bare bones two summers ago that I still get cold chills whenever I think of it." He was suddenly conscious of Lucy's startled gaze. Hang it all, he had said the wrong thing after all! But there was no help for it. Now he had started, he would have to go on. "A good friend of mine Valois Dupré, who's an enormously successful contractor, tolled me into the cotton market for a flier that was going to put us in the class with Gould, Morgan and all the rest. He—"

"Speculation!" muttered Stoddard, making a small clicking sound of disapproval. "Speculation is like any other form of reckless gambling. It's as different from sound finance, or good investment, as one pole is from the other. Tch-tch-tch!"

"Well, it was 'sound finance' that put sand in my gearbox," Clyde chuckled. "This was back in '92, and cotton had dropped to six cents a pound, because everybody figured that if Cleveland was elected, the Democrats would shoot the tariff full of holes. But old man Dupré, who is very sharp about such things, said, 'No! Cleveland is a conservative at heart, and as soon as the country finds that out, prices are bound to start up. What's more, they'll be even surer to bounce back up if Harrison is re-elected!' "

"It would have been a fine thing if he had been. Even those wild-eyed shouters for free silver out west would admit it now," said Stoddard.

"Well, the point is that Dupré had already bought I don't know how many cotton contracts at six cents, the price was by then up to eight, and his reasoning sure seemed to be tight at the seams. So I had my broker take ten thousand bales for my account."

"At eight cents? You mean you engaged to pay out nearly half a million dollars on some man's guess at the future?" Stoddard asked incredulously.

"I wouldn't have had to pay it unless I actually took the cotton, you know," Clyde protested, "and I hadn't the first idea of doing that. Anyway, Cleveland did make it plain he wasn't going to let anybody tinker with the tariff, so the price of cotton started up immediately, and every rise meant money in my pocket—or would have meant it if it hadn't been for the sound financiers back east."

"What did they have to do with cotton, pray tell me?"

"It wasn't cotton the sound financiers were playing with, but the thing you've just been pinning all those medals on. Railroads. Most especially the Reading Railroad which went busted like a smashed tumbler."

"They had overextended themselves, buying what were supposed to be coal lands," Stoddard interjected hastily.

"Probably so. But they did start a general panic, and by the time half the railroads—not the steamboats, mind you, but the railroads— were in the hands of receivers, cotton was back down to six cents. I didn't wait for it to go any lower, and sold mine for whatever I could get."

"Why that was. . . ." The finger tips tapped against one another more urgently. "Let me see, that represented a loss of. . . ."

"Of a lot of hard cash," Clyde interrupted ruefully. "More than I cared to part with, I do assure you. But I had good luck in other ways that year. I got the highest price ever for my tobacco on an export market, and we had a high yield of cane, so I managed to pay off the banks and salt away something of real value to boot. Especially a lesson. I learned not to buck another man's game, deciding that from then on I'd stick to what I knew about. Like planting. And steamboating."

"But that is what I've been trying to say!" Mr. Stoddard exclaimed, the disapproval in his voice less marked than it had been at any stage of the conversation. "You pocketed your loss on cotton in order to escape further losses still on what was plainly an unprofitable venture. Why will you not do the same thing with steamboating, which is even more certain to be unprofitable?"

"That's where I don't agree with you," Clyde replied stubbornly. But he had decided not to argue any further. How could he make this old bigot, immured in his gloomy house, understand what the wide and sunlit river meant to a man who had traveled it from his youth? How could a Croesus, measuring everything in dollars and cents, visualize the triumph of an adventurer who had flown his own flag from the three finest packets afloat between Minneapolis and New Orleans, to say nothing of the great fleet of towboats and barges which had supplemented these? It was futile and pointless, and it had been from the beginning; he should never have allowed himself to be drawn into such a discussion. He glanced toward Lucy and she rose at once; obviously she had been waiting for a chance to give the signal for departure. She bade their host good night and thanked him for his courtesy with her usual graciousness. But there was a pinched look to her face, as if she were cold as well as tired; and when she and Clyde were seated side by side, in the hack that was taking them back to the Murray Hill Hotel, he could feel her shivering. No wonder, he said to himself savagely; that baronial hall where they had wasted so much time had been as cold as a tomb. He must get her to bed at once, and see to it that she drank a hot lemonade, well laced with spirits. But Cary, who did not seem to realize the extent of her mother's exhaustion, complained that she and Savoie had thought of course they would all go to the Hoffman House for a champagne supper, to make up for the sickly fruit punch which was all they had had to drink so far.

"Can't Savoie and I go by ourselves if Mother's too tired to go with us and you want to stay with her, Father? I see lots of girls in New York having tête-à-tête midnight suppers with their beaux."

Lucy and Clyde exchanged glances. "Why, yes, I think you might, this one time," Lucy said, after a moment's hesitation. "That is, if you really feel the evening wouldn't seem complete to you without a champagne supper."

"Well, that's the way I do feel."

There was no doubt that she meant it; champagne suppers at midnight, along with their various other extravagances had become almost a necessity to Cary. It was the prodigality of their own program which made their stay in New York exciting, and not anything connected with Bushrod's marriage, which remained a mystery to Savoie, an annoyance to Cary and a source of worry, though for different reasons, to both Lucy and Clyde. From the time of his own wedding trip, Clyde had insisted that "New York was a place where you went to spend money; otherwise, it did not have much meaning." He had always acted accordingly, reserving one of the most luxurious suites in the hotel favored by fashion at the moment, buying the best seats for current theatrical attractions, and insisting that the lavish purchases he made for his wife and stepdaughter must be supplemented by purchases even more lavish on the part of Lucy herself and—as soon as she was old enough—Cary, too. But he had never even approached his present extravagance, partly because he had never had quite so much incentive to do so, and partly because, while Lucy had always acted as a restraining influence, on account of her quiet tastes, Cary was now urging him on to more and more reckless expenditure. She did not actually cuddle up to him, showering him with kisses and whispering, "Pretty please!" as she had in her childhood. But though her methods were different, their meaning had changed very little and the results were also much the same.

None of this was distasteful to Clyde. He had thoroughly agreed with Cary that they must not give Mr. Stoddard the idea that there was any lack of money in the family; the Batchelors' entertainments, prior to the wedding, had been as profuse as the restrictions imposed by the Stoddards would permit, and their gifts to the bride and groom numerous and costly. Then, after Bushrod and Mabel had departed on their wedding trip, Cary's outfits and Cary's amusements became her stepfather's first concern. He wanted her to have a handsomer trousseau than any of her friends who had previously married, handsomer even than Mabel Stoddard's, if she had seen enough of that to judge what it was like. (Cary had and did.) He wanted her to enjoy herself, to see every worth-while play in New York, to dine and sup at every fashionable restaurant, to dance with Savoie to her heart's content.

It was Lucy's continued exhaustion, still unconfessed but now all too obvious, which finally took them back to Louisiana. The new house had come along well during their absence, better than they had expected, and Cary was delighted with it; in every way, it carried out her ideas and fulfilled her expectations. The Steamboat Gothic influence was still evident in its general style, but this had been modified and simplified. The central staircase, leading from the ground level to the main floor, did not divide into two separate flights of steps, though its width and grace gave it importance; fluted columns framed the front door, but they did not surround the entire structure, which was long and low, with wings stretching out on either side of the main part; and the ornamental railings which adorned the short gallery and screened the dormers were chaste of design. Within, there was a library on one side of the front door and a drawing room on the other, as at Cindy Lou; but both were of the same moderate proportions and of rectangular shape. The dining room stretched across the width of both and of the entrance hall, in back; and a pantry connected this with the kitchen, at the extreme rear. Each of the wings leading from the front hall contained a good-sized square bedroom, with its own boudoir and bath. Cary and Savoie were to occupy one wing; it was tacitly understood that, though now designated for guests, the other would be the future nursery. There was plenty of room for company in the dormer rooms, which were larger than they appeared from the outside; and a third bath had already been installed in the upper story, with the convenience of visitors in view. In fact, the construction was so far advanced that it would soon be possible for Cary to move in some of the furniture which she had selected in New York and which was being held until an order was given for its shipment. The prospect of this delighted her. She wanted to have everything in place before she went to Europe, so that her new home would be ready for immediate occupancy on her return, and she was sure, if she did not see to arrangements herself, that they would not suit her. She was soon very busy about these, and with all the preparations for her wedding, which was now near at hand. As she had predicted, her grandmother, who had steadfastly refused to go to New York for Bushrod's "marriage to a Yankee," had consented to come to Louisiana for hers to a "southern gentleman." The old lady had brought the rich ivory-tinted wedding dress of the thirties with her and supervised the alterations which made it possible for her granddaughter to get into it. She also did what was expected of her by renewing ties of relationship with the Conrads; and she duly impressed the Vincents, besides fitting into the pattern of life at Cindy Lou—all without effort to herself or strain on anyone else. She was Cousin Sophie to most of the surrounding gentry and—what was more significant—she was Miss Sophie to her son-in-law and to all the household staff. Her imperturbability, her dignity, the elegance which she never failed to achieve despite her lack of modishness, the measured tones in which she spoke, the stateliness of her bearing and the way she held her handsome head, all had a marked effect on everyone with whom she came in contact, and added to the general regard in which the Batchelors were held, besides contributing an important element to the family circle. It was not until Bushrod arrived with his bride that the effort and the strain began.

The effort was definitely not on Mabel's part. Though she obviously doted on her husband, whose manner toward her remained impeccable, she had come to Louisiana in a mood of condescension, if not actually one of disparagement; nothing roused her admiration, nothing was even quite satisfactory to her or convenient for her. It offended her sense of modesty to use a bowl and pitcher—not to mention other articles with which the bedroom commode was supplied—in her husband's presence or to have him do so in hers; she had supposed that, of course, a private bathroom would be available and probably a dressing room as well. She pronounced the habits of taking early morning coffee in bed and after-dinner naps as "slothful, if not downright sinful." She did not like Ivy, the quadroon maid who had been assigned to her; in her opinion, the girl was lazy, inexpert and disrespectful. Mabel was also affronted by the constant drinking and nightly dancing at Cindy Lou; she was not content with turning her wineglass upside down at table and sitting tight lipped while all the others sipped juleps and chatted merrily, or with "retiring" when dancing began, audibly expressing her belief in the old proverb that early to bed and early to rise makes a man healthy, wealthy and wise. She made pointed remarks about the evils of intemperance and the stimulation of the waltz, reminding her hosts that even such a roué as Lord Byron had not hesitated to condemn this form of "the Terpsichorean Art" as "lascivious." When she finally hinted that Ivy was probably closely related to some male member of the family or of the neighbors', Clyde could no longer restrain the mounting exasperation which, up to that point, he had managed to keep in check. He summoned Bushrod to the office adjoining the gaming room at a time when he had been able to make sure they would not be interrupted or overheard, and announced that, while he regretted Mabel's lack of contentment, they were all doing the best they could for her at Cindy Lou, and that if she could not adapt herself to plantation life it would perhaps be better to take her to a hotel in the city.

"She's making your mother unhappy and I don't need to tell you I've never allowed anyone to do that," Clyde concluded. "Not that I've known anyone who wanted to, before. She's also upsetting Cary, who's entitled to all the pleasure she can have, just now. You'll have to tell Mabel she's either got to put up or shut up."

"I don't propose to have you give orders to my wife, through me."

"All right. Then I'll give them to her direct."

"I wouldn't advise you to do that, either."

"Why not? After all, this is my house and she's abusing my hospitality."

"She doesn't care much for your brand of hospitality. When it comes to that, I don't care much for it myself."

"Then, as I suggested before, we might all be happier if you and Mabel would leave Cindy Lou."

"Do you want to create a scandal, just before Cary's wedding?"

"It won't create a scandal if you merely say Mabel's never been to Louisiana before and that she thought she'd like to see something of New Orleans. Some people may be slightly astonished at your choice of the St. Charles Hotel rather than Cindy Lou, but they'll put it down to peculiar Yankee tastes."

"I don't care to have my wife accused of peculiar Yankee tastes. I'm quite capable of creating a scandal myself, on rather different grounds."

"I don't doubt it for a minute. In fact, as I recall it, you did, not so long ago, in Richmond."

"I wasn't referring to my own conduct. I was referring to yours."

"There's nothing scandalous about my conduct. You know as well as I do that the hints Mabel's been giving are groundless as well as insulting."

"I wasn't talking about Ivy, either—or about anything you've done lately, for that matter. I was referring to your—earlier career. If Cary took my Richmond peccadilloes as seriously as you claim she did, how do you think she'd feel about your prolonged—and highly successful— prewar activities on the Mississippi steamboats?"

"If you say anything to Cary that will shatter her faith in me, I'll kill you! And you'd better believe that, because I mean it!"

Clyde had sprung up, the suppressed hatred of years suddenly unleashed. Bushrod remained quietly seated and his recoil, if any, from the threat of physical violence was so momentary as to be imperceptible. He looked up at his furious antagonist with a slight smile.

"Which would, of course, create no scandal at all," he remarked sarcastically. But he did not raise his voice, and when he went on he did so almost agreeably. "I must hand it to you, there's been remarkably little so far. I don't know what you told Mother before you married her, or what she suspected, but my guess is mighty little. I think your aristocratic Creole neighbors may have been slightly more suspicious, judging from their cautiousness in admitting any of us to their inner circle. But they haven't known for sure, either. And Cary's never had the slightest inkling. It would be unfortunate if anything should leak out, after so many years of successful silence, just before her wedding to the scion of an old, respected family."

Clyde was still facing his stepson with fury, but he was now almost as angry with himself as he was with Bushrod. Never, since the day he had left Sorrento without seeing Lucy, had he felt so defeated; his failure to act quickly and efficiently in an emergency infuriated him; and it infuriated him still more that Bushrod should remain so calm in the face of his own towering rage. It had always been a matter of pride with him that he was slow to anger and that he could control his expression and conceal his emotions whenever he chose to do so. Now, he had not only been driven to fury, but he had betrayed the fact. Reluctantly, he recognized that, quite aside from the advantage which Bushrod's youth and physical fitness gave him, he was the son of a man who had four times voluntarily returned to the battle front after being seriously wounded, and that his grandfather and all his uncles had been killed in the vanguard of a valiant army. This young scapegrace did not belong to a breed which flinched from danger, and his attitude toward an assailant whom he considered his inferior was very like that of a duelist who declines to cross swords with anyone he despises. Bushrod might be a cheat and a blackmailer, but he was no coward and nothing could alter the fact that, by birth, he was a gentleman and that, no less than his mother, he had been schooled to self-control.

"Of course, I've known for years," Bushrod went on, as Clyde continued to rage inwardly. "As a matter of fact, I think I guessed when you first began to show me and the other youngsters card tricks—you see, you're responsible for my first interest in gaming, and I should think you'd be proud that I proved to be a pretty apt pupil. I've always meant to tell you, someday, that I knew. But I've waited for a really opportune time. I'd made up my mind, when I had that little run-in with my fellow blue bloods in Richmond, that if you didn't help me out I'd mention the matter then. However, my letter to Cary brought you posthaste to Virginia, as I thought it would, so I waited for another crucial moment. I'm mighty glad now that I did."

"What'll you take to get out of here, today, and not come back until the night of the wedding?" Clyde asked, violently.

"And then, just for the wedding? I follow you. And I think I might be receptive to inducement. My father-in-law's turned out to be a terrible tightwad. He's glad enough to have Mabel and me live with him, in his great mausoleum of a house, because otherwise he'd be completely alone; but he has the strange idea that a man ought to support his wife, even when the man's a pauper and the girl's father a modern Midas. I could use a little ready cash, very easily. And it wouldn't trouble my conscience to accept it. After all, if I'm not mistaken, you promised my mother, when you married her, that Cary and I were to share and share alike. You've squandered a fortune on Cary, just to gratify her whims. And you've never done anything for me, except to send me to school, so you could get me out of the way, and settle my trifling debts in Richmond, so that there wouldn't be a scandal. Well, to get me out of the way again and to avert a much greater scandal—that ought to be worth quite a little to you. I'd say twenty thousand was a very modest figure."

"I'll give it to you the day after Cary sails for Europe, if you've behaved yourself and kept your damned mouth shut in the meanwhile."

"Oh, no, you won't! You'll give it to me now—in cash. And then you'll pay for that suite at the St. Charles you're so insistent Mabel and I should take. After all, I didn't suggest we should leave Cindy Lou. That was your idea. And of course you'll meet any little incidental expenses we might incur in New Orleans."

The insolence of this demand was enhanced by the fact that Bushrod had remained quietly in his seat and that the slight smile had never left his lips. But, by this time, Clyde had ceased to care about his stepson's manner and cold rage had taken the place of tumultuous anger.

"Very well," he said evenly. "I will pay you off—now—on condition that you and your wife leave Cindy Lou immediately and do not return until just before Cary's wedding; also, that when you take your departure afterward, it will be for good. You will get the twenty thousand, but not another cent. And that means you had better not run up any bills in New Orleans with the mistaken notion I'll pay them as little incidentals."

He had walked to the safe while he was speaking. Its heavy outer door was open and, after swinging this back as far as it would go, Clyde unlocked the inner door with a small key that hung from the end of his watch chain. One of the compartments thus revealed contained a jewel case. From another, he withdrew a japanned dispatch box and, taking from it several flat packets of bank notes, he checked the markings on the narrow brown paper tabs which bound them, tapped them against the edge of the desk to bring them into alignment, and pushed the sheaf across the table toward Bushrod.

"Ten thousand dollars," he said curtly.

"Twenty thousand was the figure," retorted Bushrod. Then, as he saw Clyde draw pen and inkwell to him, he added hastily, "No checks. Cash."

"Of course there will be no checks," Clyde replied, looking at his stepson with frank contempt. "Checks are returned by the bank when they are canceled. Do you think I'd care to risk having such a one fall into your mother's hands by some chance? At the same time, there isn't more than ten thousand in the house, and you already have that. I am about to write out an order on the C & L Navigation Company to deliver another ten thousand cash to bearer. And that will be all. No further cash, no incidental expenses, no future payments."

"Suppose I don't choose to accept the cash under those conditions?" Bushrod inquired. But he had risen at last. "Aren't you forgetting who has the whip hand?"

"No. I'm not forgetting. Because I'm not sure who has it and you can't forget something you don't know. I'm surprised you feel so certain about the matter yourself."

He was as calm as his stepson now. Neither of them spoke again, and, when Bushrod turned and left the office, Clyde continued to stand by his desk before the open safe.

With the departure of Mabel and Bushrod, the strain at Cindy Lou slackened, and its atmosphere again became one of basic harmony with pleasurable overtones of excitement. It was not until the day before the wedding that anything further happened to cause even a ripple of disturbance. Then Cary came to her stepfather, betraying a degree of agitation which bore no relation to the hectic activities which she had so greatly enjoyed.

"Father, the fans have all disappeared."

"The fans? What fans?"

"The peacock feather fans, of course. We were going to have the dress rehearsal for the rainbow minuet tonight. So I told Zack to go and get the box that had the fans in it and bring it up to the ballroom. It's been in the big storeroom, next to the wine closet. He came back and told me it wasn't there any more."

"Well, somebody must have moved it then, to make way for all those packages that your wedding presents are coming in, after the presents have been taken out of them. There shouldn't be much trouble in locating it."

"But there *is*! That's the point. I've looked everywhere myself and I've made all the servants look. And they just keep shaking their heads and saying, 'It's one of those mysteries,' the way they do if we leave Cindy Lou when the fig trees are ready for the first big pick of the year, just right for preserving, and come back, two or three days later, to find every last ripe fig gone."

Clyde, who had been working on his ledgers, laid down his pen and carefully closed the book in which he had been making entries. "I'll find your fans for you," he said, "or rather, I'll see that they're found for you, in short order. Go tell Zack I want to see him here at once."

After Cary had left to follow Clyde's directions, he opened the ledger again, and was apparently still absorbed in it when the troubled Negro came shuffling into his presence. Then he slammed the two sides of the book together and stood up.

"Miss Cary tells me that a box containing presents for her friends has disappeared," he said curtly. "If it isn't found within an hour and brought to me here, you'll be out of a job. That's all."

He sat down again, reopening the ledger. It was only a matter of minutes before Zack returned to the office, his face betraying his misery, his hands fumbling at his battered hat. "Us doesn't want all Miss Cary's nice lady friends to get conjured," he said wretchedly. "Peacock feathers am unlucky—everybody knows dat. Us ain' never liked dem birds, struttin' 'round. But long as de feathers am on de birds, or on de chimney piece, us reckoned dey couldn' do much harm. Ain' never, neither. But fans, what ladies carries in dey hands, an' touches dey cheek with—"

"Miss Cary wants those fans used at the dance after her wedding. You bring them back here this instant. You know where they are and I know that you know. Miss Cary isn't interested in your damn superstitions and neither am I."

"You done listens and Miss Cary, too, when Ah talks to you 'bout de buried treasure. An' seems like Ah done hear you believes it be bad luck to have a white horse 'board a steamboat, lessen a red dog comes a'runnin' down to de landin', barkin'.'"

It was almost uncanny, the devious ways in which the Negroes on the place possessed themselves of information which their masters would have preferred to keep from them. Zack was right in believing that Clyde himself was not unmoved by certain old superstitions still current on the river: besides subscribing vaguely to the one Zack had mentioned, he did not relish a five-handed game, and he had never willingly taken great risks at cards on a boat with a name which began with the letter M. Determined not to betray his annoyance at the butler's perceptive powers, he regarded his servant with a blank stare and answered coldly.

"That'll do. You know I don't take any back talk, Zack. Bring me that box of fans."

Zack had brought back the fans, looking more miserable than ever; but there had been no further "back talk," nor did any other incident arise to mar the pleasurable preparations for the wedding. Cousin Stan had arrived, as usual emanating good cheer and laden with casks of Judge Paine's finest; Mr. Stoddard had come down from New York in his private car, which had been switched off on the plantation spur at the Victoria sugarhouse; then he had made the *beau geste* of putting it at the disposal of the bride and groom—secretly except in as far as their parents were concerned—so that they might be spared the practical jokes to which they would have been subjected if they had taken the same train by which many of the visitors would go home. He did not suppose it would do him any harm, he said, in an expansively jocular manner which was rare for him, to travel in an ordinary drawing room himself, for once. When Mabel and Bushrod returned from New Orleans, they betrayed no resentment at this generous gesture and both appeared not only willing but eager to make themselves helpful during the last-minute rush; and the great day dawned cool and clear, with just enough crispness in the air to stimulate such activities. The camellias were at the height of their bloom, and when the bride and her attendants were dressed, it was

Lucy herself who put on the crowns and handed them the bouquets she had made for them, then fastened the loose flowers lightly into place on veil and ruffles. Finally, she sent the other girls to "let Grandmother see how lovely they looked before they went downstairs," and, left alone with Cary, put her hands on her daughter's shoulders and looked fondly into her eyes.

"Don't hold it against me any longer that I questioned whether you were really in love with Savoie," she said. "I couldn't stand it if you went away from me bearing a grudge. Someday you'll understand that I only said what I did because I wanted you to be as happy in your marriage as I've been in mine."

"I do understand, Mother. I didn't at first, but I do now," Cary told her; and for a moment they clung to each other, their eyes wet. Then they kissed and parted. And Cary did not need to ask to which of her marriages her mother had referred.

The late moon had already set when the last guests left, for dancing had lasted until all hours. The rainbow minuet had raised a storm of applause; it was pronounced the most charming and original feature at any remembered wedding. The girls who had wielded their fans in time to the music carried them lightheartedly away, as, aided by their willing escorts, they climbed into waiting gigs, cabriolets and surreys which were to carry them to the station and up and down the river road.

Lucy stood in the doorway, smiling and waving her handkerchief, until the last guest was out of sight; but Clyde, who was standing beside her, smiling and waving, too, had not failed to notice her growing pallor and other telltale signs of exhaustion. He put his arm around her and, drawing her gently toward him, kissed her cheek.

"There, that's the end at last. I'm ready for a good rest and I know you are. What about letting me carry you upstairs?"

"What nonsense! I would, if I were ill. But I'm perfectly well—just a little tired, that's all."

"That's plenty. Come on now, no more fooling."

Before she could protest again, he picked her up and, when he put her down, triumphantly, it was on their bed. Her own maid Delphie was waiting respectfully beside it. He waved the quadroon away.

"That'll be all for tonight, Delphie—this morning, rather—until Mrs. Batchelor rings for coffee. No—wait a minute. Make a tisane and put it in the *veilleuse* Mrs. Surget gave her last Christmas. A hot drink would do her good right now."

Delphie nodded her understanding and took her departure. The order did not surprise her. It not infrequently happened that the Boss Man waited on his lady himself and that he recommended a tisane as a sleeping potion for her. When the maid returned, her mistress was already settled among the pillows and, after the door had been silently closed behind the turbaned figure for the last time, Clyde poured the contents of the little painted pot, shaped like a nun, into a cup and handed it to Lucy with a look of loving solicitude.

"Try to drink all of this, if you can, darling. I know you need it."

To please him, she managed to swallow it, sip by sip, though it went against her to do so; and, though she lay down, docilely enough, when he finally took the empty cup from her, and composed herself to slumber, in her customary way, with her cheek pillowed on her arm, it was a long time before Clyde was satisfied, from her quiet breathing, that she was really asleep at last. He spoke to her softly several times, calling her by name; when she neither stirred nor answered, he was partially reassured. Then he bent over and kissed her on the forehead; she gave him no caress in return, as she always did even when she was only half awake. He could safely leave her now.

Taking off his shoes and carrying them in his hand, he tiptoed from the chamber and down the stairs, through the hall—still strewn with scattered rice and fading flowers—and into the dining room, where the magnums stood empty and the fallen remains of the towering wedding cake were crumbled over the wrinkled white cloth and the tapers were guttering in the sockets of the silver candelabra. None of the servants was up yet; no attempt had been made to straighten out this repulsive disorder. But the Negroes had all done well; there had been no complaints about the hard work, no more whispering about "conjures," either. The tired men and women were entitled to their tardy rest. Clyde had no desire to disturb them.

He put on his shoes again, went out into the kitchen and made himself some coffee. Then, carrying the pot with him, he continued on his way to the office, entered it and, having mended the dying fire, unlocked his desk. When he had taken his ledgers from this, he sat staring at them, his coffee untasted.

He was a ruined man. He had never been able to deny Cary anything she wanted and she had never questioned his ability to supply it. Well, she still had not questioned it, up to the time she left him. It had not occurred to her that the Big House was already mortgaged and that he would also have to mortgage the coming crops in order to build and furnish her house and buy her trousseau—in fact, he doubted whether she had listened when he was telling Stoddard about his flier in cotton. That was natural enough—she had been restless and resentful that evening; she and Savoie had sat, billing and cooing on a sofa, apart from the others, while he himself had been drawn into that cursed argument. He was glad that no shadow of suspicion, concerning the state of his finances, had ever crossed her mind. And now she was amply provided for. But there was still her mother to think of—Lucy, who asked for so little, but who also trusted him implicitly, and whom he had just left peacefully sleeping, unaware that trust and peace were both so gravely jeopardized.

Of course Cary's extravagance and the luxury with which he had insisted upon surrounding Lucy were not alone responsible for his plight. Although the largest single cargo of cotton—more than nine thousand bales—ever shipped on the Mississippi was carried by his *Cindy Lou,* he had invested too heavily—and too late—in the fleet which flew the C & L flag. From time to time he had considered the possibility of selling his barges and towboats and chartering others as these might be needed. Indeed, he had already reduced the number of such vessels in his fleet; by chartering additional ones for seasonal shipping peaks, he had even managed to pay actual operating costs out of current revenues. But he had never been able to make up his mind to abandon packet ownership altogether; neither had he consented to remodel either the *Lucy Batchelor* or the *Cary Page* for towboat service, as he had the *Sophia Peyton.* Quite aside from the natural sentiment he felt for them because of their sponsors—and all that this sponsorship had represented in the early days of his marriage—he was inordinately proud of the fact that they were the oldest passenger steamboats on the river. They had not only escaped all the usual disasters caused by snags, collisions, fires and explosions; they had given the lie to those scoffers who prated about the flimsiness of steamboat construction. Essentially, they were as sound, more than a quarter of a century after they were built, as when they had slid off the ways. And now. . . .

Clyde took a telegram from his coat pocket and sat staring at the envelope. It was the only one that had come addressed to him the day before, and it was merely a stroke of luck that he had happened to notice it and extract it from the sheaf of congratulatory messages for Savoie and Cary. Even so, he had not read it immediately. It was almost time for the ceremony to begin and he had thrust it, still unopened, in beside his handkerchief. It was not until he had occasion to use this, sometime later, that, inadvertently, he had pulled out the two at once. Then he had ripped open the envelope and the words inside had suddenly leaped out at him:

CARY PAGE AMONG TWENTY STEAMERS CAUGHT IN ICE GORGE AT SAINT LOUIS TODAY STOP TOTAL LOSS STOP LETTER WITH DETAILS FOLLOWS

He did not need the letter to tell him what had happened. There had been a similar catastrophe at St. Louis once before and he had been there at the time. During a bitter cold winter, ice had formed to the depth of two or three feet in that part of the Mississippi and, after a sudden rise of water, this ice had begun to move. Some of the steamboats in the port had been shoved ashore; others had been torn from their moorings and pushed toward the lower dike. As the ice drifted faster, it broke up and began to gorge; piles of it, rising to the height of twenty or thirty feet, fell on the steamboats and buried them. He had been a young man at the time of this disaster and he had tried to forget it, exactly as he had tried to forget other dreadful sights. Now he seemed to hear again the grinding and crashing of that murderous ice.

Clyde sprang up, tearing the telegram into tiny bits and flinging them into the fire. If he let himself go like this, he would soon be envisioning all the horrors he had ever seen. He tried to think collectedly, but his thoughts brought him no comfort, for they conjured up a picture of the *Lucy Batchelor* sinking, shattered, beneath the river's swirling brown surface, or burning to the water's edge. No doubt word of some such disaster was already on its way to him, and then there would be a third piece of evil news—as Zack had so shrewdly guessed, he had never rid himself of the old steamboating superstitions, and none was more credulously accepted than the saying that all bad luck went in triplets. Even if this did not hold true, it would be years before he could mend his fortunes with bumper crops and record prices for sugar and perique. His cash resources had been stretched to the very limit and Bushrod's cupidity had stripped him of nearly his last money reserve. The twenty thousand he had given his stepson for hush money represented almost the last of his ready cash; the little he still had would be more than swallowed up before the bills for the wedding had been paid.

At the moment, he could think of only one way which could save Lucy from want. Sitting there alone, with the open ledger before him and the untasted coffee beside him, Clyde knew that if he could find no other he would again take that way, hoping against hope that his devious path might still be undiscovered.

 CHAPTER VII

E ventually, from sheer exhaustion, Clyde fell asleep, still sitting in his swivel chair. When the telltale figures on the thumbed sheets before him began to blur, he stretched his hands over the desk, the better to shut out those symbols of disaster. Then, by slow degrees, his head dropped lower and lower until it rested on his arms. By that time his thoughts were no clearer than his vision. He was beset by vague but horrible nightmares and, though he struggled to free himself from these, he did not know whether they were dreams or realities. Finally he ceased to struggle and oblivion engulfed him.

With the first stirrings of returning consciousness, he shifted uneasily in his seat, aware of strangeness, but as yet unable to grasp where he was or what had brought him there. After moving his head restlessly about, he raised it from his arms and, beginning to blink, still almost unseeingly, he sensed rather than saw that sunlight was streaming into the room. Then he realized that Lucy was standing on the farther side of the desk, looking down at him with loving and compassionate eyes.

He sprang up, with an exclamation that was both bewildered and apologetic. At the same time, almost instinctively, he drew the scattered sheets together and thrust them into the ledger, closing it over them.

"I—I must have fallen asleep," he stammered.

"Yes," Lucy replied. "I hope you had a good rest. I know you needed it. I've brought you some coffee. I thought perhaps you'd rather have it here, now, than wait until you come upstairs."

Apparently, she did not feel there was anything peculiar about his presence before the disordered desk in the office at such an hour, or the fact that he was still wearing the clothes which he had worn at Cary's wedding. She began to pour coffee from a pot which she took off a tray that had been set on a small near-by table and handed him a steaming cup.

"It'll taste mighty good," he said, accepting it gratefully. "But you shouldn't have bothered, darling. You were worn out yourself."

"I'm not, any more. You made me so comfortable that I couldn't help having a good sleep. I slept for hours. But I've been up quite a while, too. When you come upstairs, you'll see that everything is in pretty good order already."

"You don't mean to say you've been overtaxing your strength, getting that mess cleaned up!"

"No, dear. I haven't overtaxed my strength at all. I've merely supervised some very willing and efficient workers. Though, as a matter of fact, I'd have welcomed a little exercise. I've been growing lazier and lazier, you've pampered me so. But I've been meaning for quite a while to ask you if you'd mind having me lead a more active life again. Now that Cary's married, I think this might be a good time to make the change."

She had seated herself in a chair between the little table and his desk and poured herself some coffee. Now she leaned over to refill his cup. He had emptied his quickly, still standing and looking at her with mingled bewilderment and concern. But, as he began his second serving, he, too, sat down and, between slower sips, continued to regard her in a troubled and questioning way.

"I'm not quite sure what you mean, Lucy," he said at last. "Of course I want you to do whatever's most pleasing to you. But you know you're not very strong and—"

"I know my strength is limited. But I've been wondering whether we need to continue, indefinitely, to keep house on such a lavish scale. I mean, I thought we'd been doing it largely for Cary's sake. We didn't do it when we first came here, before she was old enough to want so much company and so many diversions. As a matter of fact, one of the reasons I was afraid she wasn't in love with Savoie was because she seemed to get more pleasure out of all the general excitement connected with her engagement than she did in being alone with him. A girl who's really in love doesn't think of her fiancé primarily in connection with presents and parties and pretty clothes."

It was very seldom that Lucy spoke at such length. Nevertheless, after a brief pause to permit a comment from Clyde, if he wished to make one, she went on again.

"Perhaps that is somewhat beyond the point which I was trying to make. I started to say that, unless you'd find it dull, I should enjoy a period of quiet while Cary is abroad. Of course, we'd welcome any friends who chose to come here and we'd do local visiting, occasionally, ourselves. But we wouldn't give big parties, or take long trips. We could explain that I wasn't well enough. I'm not. That is, I'm not well enough to do things like that and other things I'm interested in, too."

"Such as what, darling?"

"Well, I'd like to do some gardening myself, if you wouldn't mind, instead of just telling a gardener what I wanted done. I used to do a great deal, when I was a girl; I've had a hankering, lately, to take it up again."

Clyde nodded. "Anything else?"

"Well, yes. I thought I might even do a little riding again. You know I stopped in the first place because we both felt I shouldn't take risks, as long as there was any chance. . . . And of course there isn't any more. And then later, Dr. Bringier suggested I didn't have the strength to ride and do so many other things, too. But, as I just said, if I wasn't doing so many other things . . . I could ride with you around the plantation, the way Cary used to. I wouldn't interfere with anything. But of course I always rode with my father and my brothers, at Amalfi, when I was growing up. I'd enjoy doing it with you at Cindy Lou."

"And I'd enjoy having you. Don't ever imagine, for a moment, that I'd find it dull with no one but you for company. If there's any better company than you are, I haven't discovered it." He was smiling and he realized, with astonishment, that the smile was unforced, though it was only a few hours since he had believed he would never be able to smile, naturally, again. "Of course, we'll have to find just the right horse for you," he went on. "And you must promise me that you won't overdo, that if you find you're getting tired, you'll tell me right away. I'm afraid you'll be awfully stiff at first. But that'll pass."

"Stiff and sore, too!" Lucy looked across at him and laughed. Then she lifted the lid of the coffeepot and peered inside. "We seem to have emptied this, between us," she said. "Don't you think perhaps it would be a good plan to go upstairs now? I'm sure you want a bath, and I have clean clothes all laid out for you. Now I must get Belle her supplies, or we may not have anything to eat today. I certainly don't want that to happen. Especially as I thought it would be pleasant to have a cozy noon meal in the library. I've got the gate-legged table drawn up in front of the fire there, set for two."

That day marked the beginning of an era; from then on the library became the chosen center of their daily life. The other rooms on the main floor were indeed already in perfect order when they reached this; the scattered rice, the faded flowers, the guttering candles, the wrinkled linen had all disappeared while Clyde had been agonizing over his ledgers and fighting his way through dim nightmares. There was no reason why he and Lucy should not have been formally served an elaborate midday repast in the dining room or partaken of a copious tea later on in the drawing room. But, somehow, it seemed natural to follow Lucy's suggestion, and soon the experiment had become a habit. With its establishment, the house acquired an air of added warmth and intimacy. Moreover, the quiet conversations beside the open fire—talks which seemed to follow spontaneously after the cozy meals—were conducive to the discussion of many subjects which there had seemed no logical reason to bring up before. And eventually, Lucy broached one which, startling as it seemed at first, marked another fortunate turning point in their married life.

"I still seem to have a good deal of spare time on my hands," she remarked one evening. She had begun her gardening in good earnest, with special attention to the camellias, which were now at the height of their bloom; and as there had been no trouble in "finding just the right horse" for her, she was riding regularly with Clyde around the plantation, revealing an interest in its products and an understanding of its problems of which he would not have supposed her capable. "You see what a difference it makes, not having the house crowded all the time," she went on.

"I certainly do. And I'm certainly enjoying it the way it is now."

"So am I. But I have too much leisure, especially as I don't have to rest as much as I used to."

It was quite true that Lucy seemed to be stronger than she had in years. Clyde waited, without apprehension, for her to tell him how she would like to employ her superabundant leisure.

"So I have been wondering if I couldn't be of some help to you with your accounts. My own don't take me any time at all. My father taught me something about accounting and I used to work with him on his ledgers when I was a girl. Later, after he and my brothers were killed, I kept all the accounts, at Sorrento and in Richmond both. Mother can do it if she has to, and of course she has had to, since you and I were married. But she never liked doing it, the way I did."

"Thanks for thinking of it, Lucy. But I'd rather keep the ledgers myself. That's a man's work."

He had not meant to speak brusquely, but she had taken him entirely by surprise and had come closer to causing him displeasure than she had ever done before. Had she been any other kind of a woman, he would have thought she was adroitly seeking a pretext for discovering more about matters beyond her province than he had ever seen fit to tell her; and though everything about Lucy's character precluded such a suspicion, this still did not make her suggestion a welcome one. She did not answer and, almost immediately, he regretted his words, especially the closing ones; she had told him she helped her father with the plantation ledgers and he, Clyde, had told her that accounting was not a woman's work. She might well feel he was implying she had been unwomanly to attempt it, or that her father, whom she had greatly loved, had been lacking in manliness to require it of her. Either implication would be unfair and might presumably hurt her feelings. He strove to make amends.

"I'd forgotten, if I ever knew, that women did that kind of work on Virginia plantations, Lucy," he said. "But I can see now it might have been necessary, during the war. And that very possibly a father might have thought it was good mental training for his daughter, even when it wasn't necessary. The situation's different in Louisiana and between husband and wife. But I didn't mean that what you did at Sorrento wasn't suitable."

"I know you didn't, Clyde."

She picked up the embroidery frame that she had laid aside and resumed her fine stitching. Lucy was an accomplished needlewoman, and Clyde had always admired her handiwork very much. It had never occurred to him before that she did not really care greatly for embroidery, that she did immense quantities of it only for lack of anything better with which to occupy her time. But it occurred to him now. It even occurred to him that she might actually prefer accounting to embroidery. Besides, though as he had said to Cary, he had not always told Lucy the whole truth, he had never lied to her, either; and he had come uncomfortably close to doing so in saying that the reason he did not want her to help with the ledgers was because accounting was a man's work.

"The fact is," he finally blurted out, "my ledgers are in pretty bad shape. I wouldn't be particularly proud to show them to you, if you're a good accountant. I'm not."

"I was afraid they might be rather disorganized, from the glimpse I had of them the morning after Cary's wedding," Lucy replied. "That's why I thought I might be of some help to you in straightening them out. And then of course the loss of the *Cary Page* must have meant another complication, besides being such a terrible shock. But it was just a suggestion. . . . I think it's about time we had a letter from Cary, don't you? I mean, a letter posted from abroad. If she wrote one on shipboard and posted it as soon as she landed—"

"Lucy, I didn't mean to tell you, I didn't want to, but perhaps I'd better, after all. My accounts aren't in bad shape because I'm not capable of keeping them. I've kept them all right. But they have a good many entries on the wrong side of the ledger. In fact, at this moment, there's so much red ink in evidence that the books look as if they were dripping blood."

"Well, almost everyone's do, at one time or another, don't they? But that isn't too serious, is it, when a man has plenty of resources and his credit's good?"

"No. But I haven't plenty of resources and my credit isn't much good, either—at least, it won't be, as soon as my creditors find out I can't meet my current obligations. And that'll be any day now."

For the second time, Lucy laid down her embroidery frame. Then she drew her chair closer to her husband's and took his hand.

"You said you didn't mean to tell me this and, of course, I don't want you to tell me anything you'd rather not," she said. "I've always told you that and I've always meant it. But now that you've told me this much, couldn't you tell me a little more?"

"I suppose so. As far as that goes, I can say almost everything there is to say in one sentence. I'm head over heels in debt."

"Well then, of course those debts must be paid."

Her expression, though serious, had lost none of its serenity. He began to feel that he had not made the gravity of the situation clear to her, after all.

"Didn't you understand what I was saying?" he asked sharply. "I can't pay my debts. I haven't anything left to pay them *with*. The house is already mortgaged. There's even a mortgage against this season's crops. I'm ruined. There's nowhere I can turn."

"You know you could always turn to Cousin Stan, that he'd be glad to help you."

"I seem to remember that he didn't give much help to you and your mother when you needed it badly."

"Clyde, he didn't know we needed it badly. We didn't tell him."

"Because you were too proud to let him know! Well, don't you think I have any pride?"

"Of course you have. A great deal. Perhaps too much—as we did. Please be just, Clyde. What I said is true. Cousin Stan could give you help and he'd be glad to. But I'm very thankful that, if you don't want to tell him your need, at least you've told me. Because perhaps *I* can help, perhaps you'll let *me*. Have you forgotten about my money?"

"Your money? What money?"

"The money you gave me when we were married. You said that was mine."

"Of course it was yours. But that was just pin money."

"Then you must have expected me to buy a great many pins, darling, all set with precious stones."

"Lucy, I've never known you to joke about a serious matter before. When I told you I was ruined, I was in deadly earnest."

"I know you were and I'm not joking. I'm in deadly earnest, too. I could have dressed Cary and myself and run the house, too, on what you gave me. That's what I thought, at first, you expected me to do. Then I found out you had no idea of letting me carry the household expenses. And you insisted on buying so many clothes for both Cary and me, yourself, that there wasn't anything left for me to get—that is, anything except an extra party dress for Cary, once in a while, as a special present, and a corset or some other undergarment that you didn't think of for myself. I've sent money to Mother occasionally— sometimes because I thought a gift would please her and sometimes because I knew she really needed funds. She hesitated, at first, to accept anything from me, but I finally overcame her objections. Of course, I've made presents to friends from time to time and I've given regularly to certain charities. But I've never spent more than a thousand dollars any one year—usually not quite that much."

"You've never spent. . . . Good God, Lucy, I settled fifty thousand on you! That means you've had an income of more than two thousand a year for twenty-five years! If you haven't been spending it, what in heaven's name have you been doing with it?"

"I've been saving it and investing it. Or rather, Mr. Vincent's been doing that for me. You said you didn't ever want to hear of it again. So I never talked to you about it any more, after that first time. But I thought it would be all right to talk to Mr. Vincent about it, because he would know how to handle it so much better than I would. Part of it's in government bonds and homestead shares, part of it's in railroad stock—Mr. Stoddard's railroad. And some of it's in a savings bank—I mean, two or three different savings banks. Mr. Vincent seemed to feel that would be safer."

Clyde's mouth had been gradually growing drier and drier; by now, he could hardly swallow, much less speak. He sat staring at Lucy, still unable to believe what she was saying to him.

"If we took money from the savings bank—some from each one—right away—say fifteen thousand dollars altogether—that would help satisfy some of your creditors for the moment, wouldn't it?" she inquired, as if the withdrawal of such a sum were the most natural thing in the world. "Then, as soon as you've gone over your accounts again, you could decide how to apply the rest of it so as to bring Cindy Lou and the Navigation Company and all the rest of our affairs back to where they were before those debts you've been talking about got out of hand. We'll meet this situation somehow, so there's really nothing to worry about. Don't you agree with me?"

"No, I don't. I can't let you lend me that money. If something should happen to me, it's all that stands between you and actual want at this moment. I'm not at all sure that even that big a loan would pull me through, as matters stand, and. . . ."

"But darling," she interrupted, "I'm not offering to lend it to you. I'm *giving* it to you—giving it back, rather—for just the same reasons you gave it to me, so many years ago. Because I know you need it—and because I want you to have everything you need."

He tried to answer and could not. At last he found his voice.

"Lucy—I—I—" he began. But he did not finish after all. He could not say he would not allow her to pay the debts which were due to his stubborn refusal to admit that the great days of steamboating were over, to his unbridled indulgence of Cary's every whim, to his insistence that Lucy must have luxuries she did not even want and to his own love of ostentation. He knew she did not think of the present emergency in that light. She had simply foreseen, from the beginning, that the time might come when he would need her help to save their home—his and hers—and she had prepared for this, not only with prudence and understanding, but with unwavering love. He could not insult that love. He could only take her in his arms and fold her to his heart, saying nothing and thanking God there was nothing he needed to say.

Now she would never have to know how he had been led into temptation that terrible morning after Cary's wedding, how nearly he had succumbed to it in the course of the weeks that followed and how miraculous seemed his deliverance from evil.

Of course there was no question, after that, as to whether she should help him with the ledgers. She joined him in the office every morning, having set the household machinery in motion for the day while he was taking his first ride around the plantation. They did

173

accounts together until dinnertime. Then Lucy took a short rest and, later in the afternoon, worked in her garden or accompanied Clyde on his second daily round before they went back to the office for further work on the ledgers. Grinding was over; the machinery had been cleaned and the sugarhouse was quiet and empty. But the perique seedlings were now sprouting in the long beds where the minute grains, mixed with wood ashes, had been sown during the week preceding Cary's wedding; and, in the course of a ride about the plantation, Clyde and Lucy halted their horses beside one of these beds just as the women workers were lifting the palmetto leaves that had covered them through the night.

"This warm sunlight we're having will bring those seedlings along in a hurry," Clyde observed. "Barring a late freeze, we ought to have a fine lot to set out very soon now."

"Yes," Lucy agreed. But she continued to look down at the seedlings as if she were not wholly satisfied; and presently she said, rather hesitantly, "Of course you know a lot more than I do about all these things. But I can't help feeling that these palmetto leaf coverings are terribly primitive. I know they've always been used. But it seems to me that cold frames would protect the small plants much better than they do, and cold frames could be used over and over again. That would save a lot of work, too. I realize field labor doesn't seem to cost much, but just the same, it adds up. If you'd look at the ledgers with me—"

"Stop right there, Mrs. Moneybags," Clyde interrupted. "What you say makes so much sense that I could kick myself from here to Burnside for not having thought of it of my own accord, long ago. While you're resting this afternoon, I'll draw up a schedule of the lumber, nails, window lights and so on that I think we'll need, and if it meets with your approval, we'll drive to Gramercy tomorrow and buy them all."

"But we won't need them until next winter," Lucy protested. "Why should we put out the money now?"

"Well, I'll tell you why I think we should. I've been studying about a replant bed, to have ready in case something happens to part of our seedlings: a sort of growth-insurance policy. And, instead of having palmetto leaves for protection, those seedlings will be put in the new cold frames. Check, partner?"

"And double check, darling."

A few months later, as Clyde was finishing a detailed letter to a St. Louis factor about the favorable prospects for the season's perique crop, Lucy glanced up, with a sigh of satisfaction, from the ledgers on which she had meanwhile been working. She did not speak until

Clyde had folded the bulky sheets into a heavy buff envelope and carefully sealed this. Then, when he, too, glanced up, she smiled at him in triumph.

"I thought you might like to know that for the first time we are no longer operating in the red," she announced. "I mean that for the first time more money is being taken in than we're putting out. Of course we still have the back debts to clear up; the principal, I mean. But we now have an operating profit to set aside for it."

"I'm pleased—and I'm grateful. If it hadn't been for you, the pages in that book would have kept getting redder and redder, instead of blacker and blacker. But taking in just enough to apply on the back debts isn't making a profit. We can't do that till I stop being a willful sentimentalist. So I'm stopping right now."

"I don't know what you mean, darling. Besides, I like to have you sentimental. I wouldn't want you to stop."

"I'm not going to stop being sentimental about you. But neither am I going to cling any longer to steamboating—just because I can't make up my mind to surrender the memory of the river's heyday to the reality of its decline. It's going to take every first, last and in-between jitney we can make on cane and tobacco to keep the C & L Navigation Company a going concern. We shouldn't go on doing it."

"But Clyde, we can't—we mustn't—"

"Yes, we can. Yes, we must. Hold on, honey, let me have my say out. First, we sell all the boats—every barge, every tug, every steamer that floats long enough to carry our flag. We still stay in business, but only when it pays us to do so, like during cotton shipping time; and we *charter* boats to handle that. We won't have any trouble disposing of the fleet. There's no end of smaller rivers—the Arkansas, the Ouachita, the Yazoo—that the railroads haven't reached yet, where boats are still needed. So, we sell ours and that gives us some ready capital to use for equipment here on the plantation—like jackscrews for pressing out the perique during the curing process, for instance. The beams, weighed down with rocks, that we're still using, are just as 'primitive' as the palmetto leaves we gave up. Don't you see? And, of course, that's just one example. We'll be able to modernize all our facilities."

"We'd be able to reduce the port establishment in New Orleans, too, wouldn't we?" Lucy asked thoughtfully. "I mean, those clerks and purchasing stewards and freight agents."

"Reduce? We could get rid of them all. Desk room in some office on Levee Street and one bookkeeper would be as much of a staff as we'd need. No constant repair and upkeep costs. . . . I tell you it would be the making of us as a going concern! We would cut out the unprofitable part of the operation, keep only the money-making end of it, and instead of working ourselves near to pieces for cane and tobacco profits to take up the C & L deficit, we'd have a third profit to add to the others, with a fine bonus of fresh capital right now when we need it."

"Darling, I'd never in the world have suggested it, even though I know you're as right as can be. But will you do me one favor?"

"Only one?"

"Yes—a big one, though! Will you promise me *not* to sell the *Lucy Batchelor*—on my account?"

"Promise you to. . . ." He rose, strode to her side of the table, took her hand and pulled her to her feet so that he could clasp her closely in his arms. "You think you're pulling the wool over the old man's eyes, don't you?" he asked fondly. "But you're not. You realized I'd rather lose a leg than that boat, didn't you? And you wanted to spare my feelings, knowing I'd never make the suggestion myself; so you put it that this would be a favor to you. Well, you can bet your sweet life, I will never sell the *Lucy Batchelor*—never in this world, honey! We'll bring her up here from New Orleans with a full crew of the oldest employees in our service, and we'll serve a banquet in the saloon for all our friends hereabouts, with every chandelier blazing and the orchestra playing. Then we'll tie her up across from Cindy Lou, where she'll be out of the main channel, and as often as need be, we'll over-haul her. We'll keep her in condition, so that if, at any time, we need to use her again, or want to use her again—and it's within our means—we can. Meanwhile, she'll remain afloat, with the C & L flag flying, as long as there's a you, or a me, or a Cindy Lou where our children and grandchildren, or their children and grandchildren, live."

So the fleet of barges and towboats was sold and the *Lucy Batchelor* was brought to Cindy Lou, where as Clyde and Lucy agreed, she belonged—it was all very well for a gay young girl to go jaunting up and down the river, but an old lady ought to stay at home, except for an occasional brief pleasure trip! And these the *Lucy Batchelor* con-tinued to make, going to near-by towns and throwing her lights on the pavilions where dancing was taking place on shore, or carrying groups on holiday excursions. She did not seem like an abandoned boat; rather one which was resting on her many laurels. Sometimes, after the "heat and burden of the day" were over, Clyde and Lucy rowed out to her and had their supper aboard; occasionally, they even stayed overnight there. As a matter of general practice, they went alone; but every now and then, they invited friends to accompany them—not for a big banquet, but for a quiet meal and a quiet evening. And, whether they went or not, Zack kindled anchor lights at dusk each evening and returned every morning to extinguish them and to convince himself that all was well aboard. And, just before they went to bed, Clyde and Lucy stepped out on the gallery and looked at the reassuring lights.

Meanwhile, Clyde's amazement at Lucy's sagacity in regard to his business interests and the work on the plantation continued to increase as time went on; but he was even more astonished at the reduced cost of their living expenses, now that she had taken charge of these. As far as he could see, the table she set was no less lavish than it ever had been; the daily dinners which were put before him were as carefully planned, as perfectly prepared, as beautifully served as heretofore. But almost everything they ate came from the plantation now; and though the wines they drank were sound, they were not vintage, and champagne had ceased to be among them. There were no more big parties and very few small ones; the Batchelors continued to return the hospitality of their neighbors and to extend it to other friends who had long taken a welcome at Cindy Lou for granted; but they issued almost no invitations on their own initiative, and eventually two of the younger servants, to whom Cary's continuous party-giving had been a source of pleasurable excitement, rather than one of burdensome toil, began to show signs of restiveness. When this happened, Lucy suggested that Mrs. Vincent, who had always preferred to spend more time in the city than on the plantation, might find them useful in New Orleans. The results of the suggestion were highly pleasing to all concerned; and this first break in the ranks of the household staff seemed to lead logically to a second one.

"Of course, Belle and Zack and Delphie would never be happy if they were separated from us, and we'd never be happy, either," Lucy said to Clyde one evening, as she finished making the entry of the servants' wages in the ledger. "But I think the others would be perfectly delighted to move over to Cary's new house, just before she comes home. And I think she'd be perfectly delighted to find them there. She'd have friendly, familiar faces around her from the very beginning, and she wouldn't have to waste any time or use up any energy getting strange servants accustomed to her ways. How does the idea strike you, Clyde?"

Although she had taken over practically all the household management, Lucy still never made any radical change in it without consulting his wishes. Her question was not merely a matter of form; she was genuinely eager for his approval.

"Why, it strikes me as a fairly good one," he answered. "I suppose we could get along all right here with three servants, living the way we do now, or if we couldn't, Ivy'd probably be glad to stay, too, though she's younger and less of a fixture than Belle and Zack and Delphie. I should think Cary'd be tickled to death to have the others, as you say. I don't believe they'd mind the change much, either. After all, they'd be less than a mile away. As a matter of fact, they'd probably be proud as Punch to find you thought they were capable of doing the job and besides, nothing seems to please these darkies more than to feel they're 'in' on a love affair."

"Then I'll speak to Mrs. Vincent the next time I see her and make sure she approves of the idea, too. She might have been planning to send someone from Victoria."

"She might, but you know as well as I do it's unlikely. She hasn't the knack of handling servants that you have, Lucy. I doubt if she has any to spare. She certainly was glad when you offered her Patsy and Amos."

"Yes, but she needed them in New Orleans. She might feel differently about the plantation. However, I think you're right; I don't believe she will. But it would certainly be more courteous to ask her. Then, if she agrees, I'll speak to the servants about the plan."

"You didn't think of consulting Cary, too?"

"I thought of it, naturally. But I don't know that it would be much use."

Lucy looked away, and though Clyde did not hear her sigh, he knew that the feeling which makes mothers sigh over their daughters was in her heart. Cary had proved a very poor correspondent. Not only had she failed to write the letter on shipboard, to which Lucy had so eagerly looked forward, but she had written very few since then, and they had not contained much actual news. For the most part, they had been brief and exclamatory. Everything was heavenly, everybody was wonderful, Cary was crazy about France. Eventually it developed that this "craze" had caused her and Savoie to change their plans about going to any other country, at least for the present. They lingered a long time on the Riviera, because the sunshine was so marvelous and the life so gay. According to Cary, half the crowned heads of Europe were vacationing there, not to mention various Russian grand dukes and high ranking members of the British nobility. All entertaining was on a prodigal scale, really superb; and as for the opera at Monte Carlo! Well, no one would ever think the French Opera House in New Orleans was worth a second glance after seeing that. There were any number of yachts in the harbor at Nice, and Cary and Savoie had been invited out on several of them. The Southern Yacht Club would not seem like much, either, any more. And so on and so on.

In spite of all these attractions, the bridal couple finally reached Paris for the spring season, and though no further references were made to sunshine, life was apparently even gayer than it had been on the Azure Coast. When they left the French capital, after Bastille Day, it was to begin their round of visits among friends of the Vincents' who owned chateaux. Post cards depicting these fluttered in from the Norman countryside and the Loire Valley. But it was not until Cary and Savoie reached Monteregard, the De Chanets' estate in Charente-

Maritime, that anything like a real letter came in. Cary had written then—

Dearest Father and Mother,

This is the most wonderful place of all. You approach the chateau through a beautiful forest of ivy-wreathed oaks and there's something actually magical about the effect of the sun shining through their greenery. Finally, you come to a great stone portal which leads to a paved courtyard, and you drive through that toward a tower which surmounts a wide gateway—a lot like the famous clock towers in medieval cities. That brings you to a second courtyard, larger than the first, which has dependencies facing the tower and a raised triangular garden facing the chateau proper, on the fourth side.

You go into an imposing stone hallway with a curving staircase, and on one side of that are the library, with more books in it than I've seen in any other French house, and the old kitchen, which is now the dining room, and which is all hung with shining copper. Both these rooms have beamed ceilings, gorgeously painted, and you think there couldn't possibly be anything more beautiful anywhere. But that's because you haven't yet seen the Louis XVI drawing room and the Louis XV study and the Louis XIV bathroom on the other side of the hallway. I must tell you right off, before you get the wrong impression, that the Louis XIV bathroom isn't used for bathing any more—there are plenty of modern bathrooms upstairs—and, to tell you the truth, I don't see how it would ever have been very practical for that purpose. To be sure, there is a tub in it—covered over now with a heavy, hinged oak lid—but it's in a recessed archway which is decorated with a series of rather harrowing paintings of religious character, separated from each other by golden bands. All four walls of the room are decorated in a similar way, and so is the ceiling, except that on the ceiling the paintings are circular and the gilding much more elaborate; and over the mantel, there's a wonderful portrait of some early De Chanet who looks quite delightfully worldly and wicked, as if he'd enjoy peeking at some lovely lady who imagined she was bathing in private. The room's octagonal in shape and about three times the size of our library, with long windows looking out on the inner courtyard at one side and on the other toward the great sunken garden that stretches out to the reflecting pool and the fountains beyond it. (I'll simply have to leave the description of that to some other time, or I'll never finish this letter.) We could hardly tear ourselves away from the view to go upstairs, but when we did, we found ourselves in a Louis XIII bedroom and that was just the beginning of what we saw! Really, I learned more about French history and medieval architecture and period decoration in that one afternoon than I ever did in all the years I went to school.

We had to hurry and wash up and go downstairs, because the De Chanets were awaiting us in the drawing room, with refreshments—not with a copious tea, as you would have done, but with delicious little dry cakes and a bottled drink called Pineau, of which we'd never heard before. Of course, Charente-Maritime is cognac country, and Pineau is a mixture of cognac and fresh grape juices—very good, indeed. As for the De Chanets themselves, words fail me. The old marquis—he isn't really old, but I have to call him that to distinguish him from Pierre—is the most courtly gentleman I ever met. Such manners and such a *manner!* The marquise must be as old as Mother, I suppose, but you'd never believe it. There isn't a white hair on her head or a line on her face and what a *figure!* Of course, Mother's is awfully good, for her age, but the marquise's is extraordinary. She's very vivacious, always saying amusing things, laughing herself and making everybody else laugh, too. No one could ever have a dull moment in her company. Her son is a lot like her, I mean he's also very good looking and very good company. It turns out he's only twenty-five, but you'd never guess it—these Continentals seem *adult* so much earlier than boys at home and are so much more *sophisticated*. He's a wonderful horseman and I've had great fun riding with him. You know I've always been a little disappointed that Savoie doesn't care for horses, but then of course you can't have everything in one man and aside from that, he's *perfect,* just as I knew he would be. He thinks of nothing but my pleasure and happiness, so he's delighted that I've found someone to go with me on those long rides that I adore and that are just a torment to him, and he and the old marquis—who isn't really old at all, as I said—have a great time puttering around the place while Pierre and I are off in the woods.

You never saw such woods. As I said before, there's a look of magic about them and they stretch in all directions. You can ride through them almost endlessly, without taking the same road. Or, if you'd rather, you can tether your horse to one of the ancient stone seats surrounding a little grassy plot, so well hidden that it seems as if it were meant to be secret, and walk down a narrow winding path that's bordered on one side by the river, thickly fringed with underbrush, and on the other by a series of prehistoric caves, which keep getting bigger and bigger the farther along you go. The largest one of all is called the Cathedral, because it has a lofty vaulted top and long narrow passages lead out of it in several directions. Pierre said I mustn't ever venture into one of these passages, because I might get lost or something. I asked him if anyone ever had, and he wouldn't tell me. But he did tell me the legend of the Blue Pool which the river widens to form at the foot of the caves. According to this legend, a De Chanet lady who lost her lover flung herself into this pool several hundred years ago; and ever since then, a spring has bubbled up from the place where she was drowned. Of course, that's just silly superstition, but all the same, I think the story's quite fascinating, don't you? I'm sure there's also one connected with those passages, and I mean to find out what this is, someday, too.

Anyone who wants to is allowed to come and picnic in these caves and we saw piled sticks left over from old fires, neatly gathered together and laid with fresh wood, all ready for new fires—no untidy messes of paper boxes and broken bottles, the way it would have been at home. Pierre says that, besides the peasant picnickers, who come just for the day, gypsies used to come there in large numbers, and that a few of them still do, once in a while. He said they never presumed or pilfered and that they made a lovely sight, at night, gathered around their campfires, which they watched carefully. He said it was great fun to share the suppers they cooked in open kettles and join in their dances and their singing. It sounded as if he'd enjoyed being with them very much, so I asked him if he really made friends with them, when he was a boy, and he laughed and said yes indeed, that was putting it mildly—he lost his innocence because of a gypsy girl. I wasn't quite sure what he meant by that, so I asked Savoie after I got back to the chateau and he and I were alone in the Louis XIII bedroom. Savoie was quite annoyed. He said it undoubtedly meant that Pierre had lured some poor, defenseless young gypsy who caught his fancy into one of the more remote caves and seduced her. Then we almost quarreled because, from the way Pierre told the story, I gathered it was the girl who had done the luring. Anyway, whatever happened, it was a long time ago, and probably no worse than lots of people do—certainly not worth a quarrel now. Besides, Savoie is so sweet, I don't want to quarrel with him.

Pierre says the hunting here is something I simply mustn't miss, all the picturesque medieval customs in connection with it are still kept up, so I believe we'll come back here for that—if we actually get away in the meantime! But we just seem to put off our departure from day to day, though I really ought to get back to Paris to buy some clothes, everything in my trousseau is so *old fashioned* already. Of course, I found it really wasn't up to date, by French standards, as soon as I got here and now it looks *positively provincial*. To begin with, my underclothes are all wrong.

Corsets are cut and boned to give a "straight front" effect, and the least little bulge over the stomach betrays the fact that you don't have on the right kind. Of course that's had a great effect on tight lacing, because it doesn't do any good to pull in your waist if that simply makes you stick out somewhere else. Sleeves are *much* bigger and skirts have more gores in them, daytime clothes very plain, maybe just a little black braid on blue serge, waists lighter material—lighter weight and lighter color, both—than the skirts and jackets, evening clothes very elaborate, stiff satins, lots of pearl embroidery, that sort of thing. The marquise has given me the names of several "little" dressmakers who she says will do very well for me, and she also suggests that I try one or two of the "important" ones who are beginning to take away some of Worth's clientele—Redfern and Doucet, for instance, though she hardly ever goes to anyone but Worth herself and Savoie says there's no reason why I should, either. But I do want to get enough pretty things to last a long time, since I suppose there's no telling when we'll get back to France. Savoie says he'll *try* to arrange for a trip every other year, which, as you know, is the custom in lots of Creole families. But he hasn't definitely *promised*, so I'm going to be on the safe side, and I'm afraid if I bought a dozen dozen of everything from Worth's, that would seem to him like too much of a good thing, even if he is the most generous, devoted husband that any girl was ever lucky enough to get.

Well, you can't complain that I haven't written you a long letter this time, not that you actually have complained, but somehow I've had the feeling you thought I might write oftener. I don't believe you wrote many letters though, when you were on your honeymoon, so there! And unless you'd been to France yourselves, you honestly couldn't realize how impossible it is to get a quiet moment for anything like letter writing. Not much like good old sleepy Cindy Lou, where nothing exciting happens from one year's end to another.

Loads and loads of love to you both. Your own

Cary

P.S. The marquise would like to be most cordially remembered to Father, whom she recalls most pleasantly. I think she was a little piqued when I told her he didn't seem to remember her very well, so I was sorry afterward I didn't tell a lavender lie about that. She also wants me to say she hopes to have the pleasure of meeting Mother in the not too distant future. If the old marquis finds he can leave the estate, the De Chanets *may* come to Louisiana next year, to return our visit. Wouldn't that be wonderful?

This letter had been received several weeks before the discussion about the servants and there had been no word from Cary since. Presumably, she and Savoie were still visiting the De Chanets, unless they had returned to Paris for the purpose of replenishing Cary's outmoded wardrobe; and, in any case, it was evident that they would be at the chateau for the hunting season. At this rate, they would hardly be home for Christmas, and Clyde and Lucy had both counted confidently on having them back by early autumn. Besides, the letter had been disquieting in more ways than one, and Lucy and Clyde both worried about it, without confiding to each other their worries, which were not the same. Accustomed as they were to mutual confidences, they found that, this time, they could not share their troubled thoughts.

When Lucy's idea about staffing the new house was submitted to Mrs. Vincent, the latter pronounced this excellent. It would take a load off her mind, she said, to know that Lucy had provided so effectively for the comfort of Cary and Savoie. Personally, she wanted to spend more and more time in New Orleans; she felt she owed it to Armande. It had been not only natural, but fitting, that Armande should grieve a long, long time for her lost fiancé; but after all, it was perhaps a mistake for anyone so young to bury her heart in the grave. Mrs. Vincent had begun to feel that if Armande went out more she might again meet someone who would appeal to her and who would be worthy of her. As long as Cindy Lou had been such a center of gaiety, Mrs. Vincent had felt that any effort to provide further diversion for Armande would be wasted effort. However, now that the Batchelors were living so much more quietly—and she could well understand their preference for doing so—and that Cary and Savoie would be preoccupied with each other on their return—if they ever did return—Mrs. Vincent thought that really. . . .

Lucy agreed wholeheartedly with her friend. Up to the time of Cary's wedding, she herself had viewed Armande as inconsolable; but about then she, too, had begun to think that, possibly, the days of the girl's insusceptibility to solace might be numbered. True, Armande had turned a deaf ear to numerous suitors; but that was when her grief was fresher and also—though perhaps this had nothing to do with the case—when she was younger and suitors more numerous. She was still very lovely looking, with the same soft dark hair, large brown eyes and clear pale skin that characterized her brother; but she was now nearly twenty-eight years old, and beauty of this character was apt to fade early, if marriage and motherhood did not bring it into flower. The very fact that she was less surrounded than a few years earlier might indicate that she was already beginning to lose some of her allure for the opposite sex, and perhaps she was conscious of her lessening charm; if she were, like any normal woman, she would regret this. It was conceivable that the marriage of Cary—her only remaining classmate who, up to that time, was still unwed—had left her not only singularly isolated, but singularly thoughtful. Her face did not have the mobility which made Cary's seem to sparkle and she was not given to sprightly talk like Cary, either; but her serenity and her silence suggested an intensified pensiveness, rather than the lack of reflective powers. Was it really worth while to make a cult of the dead? Was virginity, while undeniably a virtue, dependable as an attraction after a certain age? Was not normal human companionship, between a man and a woman, better than lifelong loneliness, even if it were not permeated with romance? As far as that went, why should any girl suppose that, once having achieved the married state, she could not still inspire and return passion, even if this had seemed impossible beforehand? And was any woman complete until she had borne a child?

Such were the questions which Lucy thought Armande might very well be asking herself. And since, at the moment, there seemed to be a scarcity of suitable young men among the neighboring families, New Orleans was probably the logical answer. Lucy assured Mrs. Vincent that she understood perfectly and that she would, indeed, do everything possible to provide for the comfort of the bride and groom, whose return, she felt sure, would not be much longer postponed. When her plan for installing some of the servants at the new house was explained to them, they received the news with the pleasurable excitement which Clyde had foreseen; and from then on, Lucy was more frequently there, stocking the place with supplies and adding to its ornamentation. Since Cary, while she enjoyed having flowers both for her personal adornment and for the decoration of the rooms she inhabited, freely admitted that she really was not "a gardening sort of a girl," Lucy planned and planted another garden; and she revealed so much skill and taste in the process that Clyde asked himself, more than a quarter of a century late, whether he would not have been wise to let her develop the original design at Cindy Lou. There were no exotic trees and shrubs in the new garden, no terraces, and only two small fountains, one in the center of each parterre before the house. But the whole effect was happily harmonious.

Lucy wrote to Cary, telling her of the progress that had been made, with the hope that this might rouse her daughter's interest to a degree that would make her want to see it for herself. Cary's tardy reply, obviously dashed off at top speed, gave no such indication. Of course she was pleased at the report about the grounds; but she wondered if Father had stressed the fact that she especially wanted a summerhouse, like the gazebo at Sorrento. There was no mention of it in the letter, though she had talked with him about it when the question of the new house first arose and several times after that. She wanted one more than ever now, because it would help to remind her of the beautiful pavilion at Monteregard. Not that there would be any real resemblance, naturally. But, incidentally, she had decided to name her own house Monteregard, instead of Tunica, as Father had suggested. She did not think there was really anything very romantic about an Indian name, even if it were associated with the locality; and the name Monteregard would always recall to her the happiest days of her life.

Lucy replied with reassurance as to the gazebo; she had not mentioned it before, she said, because she supposed that Cary would take it for granted her wishes in this respect would be carried out by Pierre Chauvin. He had faithfully reproduced the Sorrento gazebo; the new one was at the farther end of the garden, and its location would make it an ideal objective for short strolls, besides providing the most effective setting for it. Lucy was sure Cary would be delighted with it. As for the name, of course Cary had a right to choose any she wanted for her new home. Lucy did not refer to the fact that Clyde was a little disappointed at the abandonment of Tunica, which really "belonged," for Monteregard, which did not belong at all. . . .

Christmas brought with it a cable of holiday greetings from the wanderers, and just before New Year's Lucy and Clyde sent them a cable in return, extending all good wishes on the occasion of their first anniversary. However, since the Christmas dispatch had made no mention of home-coming, it seemed better that the one destined to arrive on New Year's should not do so, either. But when the Vincents and the Batchelors met, according to their custom, to see the New Year in together, Mr. Vincent made a pronouncement.

"I hope neither of you will feel that I am in any degree niggardly," he said, looking first at Clyde and then at Lucy. "But I've written Savoie, telling him I don't intend to supply him with any further funds for European travel—at the moment, I mean. Of course, he and Cary may want to go abroad again sometime, and if they should, I'll do my best to make it possible for them. But they've been gone a year already, and I think that's quite long enough for Savoie to be out of touch with what's happening on the plantation, quite aside from what he's spending—in fact, I think it's too long. I rather took it for granted that he'd be home for grinding, if not before, and I believe you did, though, as far as I know, nothing definite was said to that effect. And the boy's been pretty extravagant. I wouldn't be so astonished at what he's spent if he and Cary had traveled extensively on the Continent, as we thought they would do; but they haven't even been out of France, and a large part of the time they've been visiting. Of course I expected them to stay at first-class hotels, of course I expected Savoie to buy any little thing for Cary that caught her fancy, of course I wanted them to have a good time. But—well, I'll be frank with you. Savoie exhausted his first letter of credit before they'd been gone six months. He asked me to arrange for a second one and I did. Now that he's asked for a third one, I've told him to come home."

"It isn't as if Savoie were an only child," Mrs. Vincent added hastily. "Armande wants to go to New Orleans in time for the Twelfth Night Revels and to stay through Mardi Gras. I want to have her. It's a long while since we've spent the entire Carnival season in town. She and I are planning to leave Victoria day after tomorrow, and Lamartine will join us as soon as grinding's over. Of course, we'll be delighted to have Savoie and Cary come and stay with us for any or all of the balls that they'd especially enjoy. But since his father's going to be away, it does seem doubly important that Savoie should be on the plantation most of the time. And though we both hate to keep bringing it up, there *is* the matter of expense. We want to do quite a little entertaining for Armande in New Orleans, and then there'll be her clothes. And of course there may still be the question of a dowry and a trousseau and a wedding someday. We have to provide for that."

The Batchelors assured their guests that they understood perfectly and that they felt the Vincents were not only completely right, but completely reasonable in the stand they had taken; in fact, that they themselves were in entire accord with this. Now all four must get together and plan for a housewarming. . . .

Later, when they were alone, Clyde and Lucy spoke more candidly to each other. He blamed himself, Clyde said; if he had not always indulged Cary so, if he had not actually encouraged her to be extravagant, this would never have happened. They must make her understand that his own financial excesses had very nearly brought about his ruin; they must prevent her from leading her husband into similar folly. It would be hard for them to tell her all this and hard for her to listen; but it must be done. Yes, and that was not all, Lucy replied. It was kind of Mrs. Vincent to say that Cary and Savoie could come to New Orleans as often as they chose, for the Carnival balls. But there was no doubt that Savoie's place was really on the plantation, that he should stay there steadily while his father was gone; and naturally Cary should stay there with him. She should not continue to feel that her life must be a round of gaiety, in order to be pleasant. She was old enough now to settle down. It was too bad that, apparently, there was still no prospect of a baby. That would have solved so many problems. . . .

They went on talking to each other like this for hours. But still neither of them voiced the dread each of them most deeply felt.

It was early February when Savoie and Cary finally reached home. Savoie had written his father a rather aggrieved letter, saying it had not been possible to get immediate reservations, but he had finally succeeded in booking passage on the *Xenia*, from Bordeaux direct to

New Orleans. They would greatly have preferred, Savoie added, to take *La Touraine,* the newest and fastest steamer of the French Line, from Le Havre to New York, and to spend a few days there before coming on to New Orleans by train; but this would have involved additional expense, which he realized would be either resented or begrudged. He did not mean to be disrespectful to his father, but, like Clyde, he found it impossible to deny Cary anything she wanted to have or do; and, unlike Clyde, he had not yet had time to discover that such a course of action could prove extremely unwise. He went on to insist that it was quite natural Cary should wish to remain in New Orleans for Mardi Gras; and after they reached his parents' house, he dwelt with pride on the number of call-outs she received at every ball she attended without, apparently, stopping to think that Armande might well feel chagrined by the fact that her sister-in-law's popularity was so much greater and more conspicuous than her own.

For Cary was really creating a sensation. She had always been stylish as well as pretty; but now there was a *soignée* look about her that she had lacked before. She was wearing her hair in a new way, piled on top of her head—instead of coiled just above the nape of her neck— and brushed back from her forehead in a high pompadour, instead of curling around it in soft little ringlets; this ultrafashionable coiffure, still quite a novelty in New Orleans, made her stand out in any group of girls, however pretty, who were less strikingly individual. So did her smart Paris clothes, representing styles which had heretofore not reached New Orleans, except by hearsay and through the pages of fashion magazines, and which showed her fine figure and set off her dazzling color to the greatest possible advantage. She wore a different ball gown every evening, and each dress was more becoming, more elaborate and more sumptuous than the one in which she had previously appeared. She also wore very handsome jewelry, and the amount and variety of this increased as the season progressed. There was murmuring, here and there, to the effect that some of the favors Cary Vincent was receiving were more costly than it was customary or suitable for a young married woman to accept; but none of these murmurs was voiced in Savoie's hearing and, for the most part, they were quickly hushed. Savoie himself belonged to several Krewes; so did his father and so did his various cousins. What could be more natural than for a man to shower his bride with gifts and for his kinfolk to vie with each other in giving her a royal welcome home?

Cary herself revealed no unseemly degree of satisfaction over the furore she was causing; indeed, she seemed almost indifferent to it, as far as any special participation in it was concerned, eagerly as she craved constant excitement. Opinion was divided as to her attitude. Her detractors said that she now accepted admiration as such a matter of course that she had become blasé; she took it for granted that every man who met her would fall a victim to her charms. Her defenders insisted of course she was still so much in love with her husband that she was hardly aware of anyone else's attentions. Savoie's parents, who had always done their best to seem kindly disposed toward her, now vied with each other, in self-control, as far as she was concerned. They did not admit in the family circle—much less outside of it —that they were disappointed in their only son's wife, and that this disappointment was rapidly becoming tinged with displeasure, as the balls which were to have provided such advantageous opportunities for Armande proved to be instead merely a series of *mises en scène* for Cary. Clyde and Lucy, who had come to New Orleans to meet the bridal couple, and who had been persuaded to prolong their visit at the Vincents' spacious establishment on Elysian Fields, were quite as gravely concerned, though for different reasons. They could not help feeling a certain amount of pride in their daughter's success. But Lucy, especially, was troubled over Cary's restlessness, and both she and her husband were secretly hurt because the girl insisted on prolonging her stay in New Orleans, instead of hastening to the new home which they had made ready for her with such loving care. Every time this was suggested to her, however, she found some new reason for continuing her ceaseless round of gaiety.

"Why, Mother, you know you wouldn't want me to miss the Proteus parade! There's a rumor that one of the floats is going to represent peacocks and naturally. . . ."

"I've no doubt it'll be very beautiful and very original. But it's a long time, Cary, since you've seen our own peacocks."

"They've been there still longer, haven't they? I suppose it's safe to assume they won't all have flown away when I do get there."

"Of course they won't all fly away. But now that you've been to the Atlanteans and Momus—"

"*And* the Elves of Oberon *and* the first Nereus! Still, you wouldn't expect me to leave before Proteus and Comus, would you? Or the Rex parade? You know perfectly well, Mother, that unless you're in New Orleans for Mardi Gras, you might just as well not have come to Carnival at all."

"Then you'll start for home on Ash Wednesday?"

"Well, of course Savoie always wants to go to church on Ash Wednesday. And then that rich bachelor from Washington, Wallace Ashby, makes a habit of giving an enormous luncheon at La Louisiane on Ash Wednesday, and he's invited us this year, for the first time. I think it's quite subtle of him, don't you? I mean, to have a luncheon at all on Ash Wednesday. Because it's sort of a dare. Everyone's crazy to go, he's such a wonderful host, and just the same, on a solemn fast day. . . . It puts all the devout Catholics to a terrible test and some devout Episcopalians, too."

"I shouldn't have thought Mr. and Mrs. Vincent would approve of your accepting an invitation to a luncheon on Ash Wednesday, Cary."

"I don't believe they did. In fact, I'm quite sure they didn't. Armande didn't, either—but then, she didn't get an invitation! And, after all, Savoie and I have got to live our own lives, haven't we? Besides, we have to eat somewhere and there's no boat on Wednesday. The *Stella Wilds* doesn't leave until Friday."

"You could come by train."

"Yes, we could, but you know we'd much rather travel by boat, just as you and Father would."

"Then you'll come Friday?"

"Well, of course, if you insist. . . . "

Lucy turned away without saying anything, much less insisting, but Savoie and Cary took the Friday boat anyway. It was soon evident, however, that this was less on account of any impatience to reach home than because New Orleans was "dead as a doornail, now that Carnival is over," as Cary put it. Evidently, she hoped to find more of an outlet for her restless energy in the country than she had in the city. She expressed herself as being delighted with everything at the new Monteregard; but she did not take the prideful joy in getting settled there that Lucy and Clyde had hopefully expected. Instead, leaving her trunks still packed and her household still unorganized, she spent most of her time on horseback, not riding the crops, as she had formerly done, but galloping, with apparent aimlessness, up and down the river road. She did not even go to the warehouses to see the more modern appliances with which perique was now handled, or to the quarters to renew her friendship with Milly Sue and the "little folkses," Aunt Vicey and her magical brews, and all the others. She spoke impatiently to poor old Moppy, who was now so infirm that she could hardly hobble and, far from making much of the new pinky-brown pickaninnies, she merely remarked that the supply of woods babies was apparently more abundant than ever, and that Ma'y Lou would soon be hard pressed to make enough sugar-tits. When this happened, Clyde felt sure something was seriously wrong; but, instead of asking her point-blank what it was, he decided to lead up to the cause of her trouble by indirect means. Giving the impression that he was meeting her quite by chance, he joined her one evening on the road, above Burnside; and, after begging her to change her canter to a jog "out of respect for the infirmities of her poor old father's advanced age," inquired casually whether she still played catch and toss with the notion that they might have buried treasure on their land.

"Why, I don't know," she said, looking at him without much show of interest. "I haven't even thought of it lately. Of course, I'm old enough now to see that we couldn't go digging at random through a mass of gravel. But Murrell really did exist, didn't he? And probably he really did bury part of his surplus treasure, just as the darkies claim. I suppose some day we might run across an old map or a set of directions or something. . . . Why?"

"Because I think maybe we have got a treasure-trove, but that we don't need to dig for it, after all. Valois Dupré—I don't mean that old beau of yours, I mean his father—has an idea it's right on top of the ground and that we've been overlooking it, all these years."

Cary shrugged her shoulders. "Valois Dupré never really qualified as a beau of mine and you know it," she said. "I wish you wouldn't refer to him that way. And what would a city politician like his father know about land in the country? I don't see how he happened to find out about the Cindy Lou treasure in the first place."

"Easy there! I keep telling you I'm an old, old man and bruise easier than I used to. Valois Dupré, Jr. isn't in Savoie's class, I'll admit that; but he's a nice fellow just the same and a mighty promising young lawyer. As for Valois Dupré, Sr., he's no beer-bellied ward boss, even if politics do interest him enough so that he wants to play the game both for fun and for keeps. And I mentioned the Cindy Lou treasure to him myself."

"But whatever for?"

"Money and the need for the same. I'd lost some at Metairie that afternoon—no, it was the other track, the one beyond Esplanade. I remember now. Young Valois had ridden in the Gentlemen Jockey Race and won it, so his father invited several of us home to celebrate. After dinner, we played cards."

"And did you lose then, too?"

"I'm very much afraid you're right. That's just what I did."

"It seems to me you nearly always lose nowadays. But you certainly are still lucky in love."

"I am that. Anyway, having lost at the track and then again at the card table, I made some remark about what happens to a country mouse like myself when the town mice get him into their clutches. And in the same joking way, I said I might have to make a real pass at digging up my buried treasure, gravel or no gravel. Then I noticed that Valois—the older one, I mean, was pricking up his ears like a terrier. I thought it was the reference to the treasure that had interested him, so I made an excuse to linger after the other guests had gone and told him how Murrell was supposed to have used the streams and swamps at the upper end of Lake Maurepas for a hiding place—Blood River, Blind River, the Petite Amite and our own Bayou Boisblanc. I said every one of our darkies would take a conjured oath that at least one shipload of Murrell's treasure is still buried somewhere along our Bayou Boisblanc frontage. I also said there was no way of disproving this, since that part of Cindy Lou is one big gravel bed which nobody could dig up—it would cost more to go through it than any one shipload of treasure would come to. And Dupré called me a damn fool for looking under the ground when the treasure was on top of it."

"How silly of him," Cary said disdainfully. "If it had been on top, we wouldn't have missed seeing it, all these years." She was speaking in the same tone she had used when dismissing the subject of her recent Carnival triumphs. Clyde recognized the inflection with apprehension; Cary was getting tired of his talk and of their slow pace. Presently, she would be cantering off, on some pretext of haste, and he would have lost his chance to lead up to the question he wanted to ask.

"Maybe we didn't recognize the treasure when we saw it," he said hurriedly. "It seems gravel is worth a lot of money, especially if it's anywhere near New Orleans. Most of the craft that come there now are steamships, and they don't need the same sort of ballast sailing ships do—their machinery is heavy itself, and it's easy to pump water into the ballast tanks or out of them. That's why New Orleans doesn't get loads of granite blocks any more and has to look elsewhere for cobbles or use bricks to put on the streets; you can't leave city road-ways a mass of mud any more, with steppingstones at the crossings. So people are putting clamshells down, or gravel, if they can get it. Washed gravel is a much better capper—a chunk of gravel doesn't have one side all hollowed out, the way a clamshell does."

"Dupré meant the gravel itself was the treasure then?" Cary asked, indifferently.

"Yes. For here's gravel, lashings and lashings of it, right where it can be washed and loaded onto schooners and brought straight to New Orleans through the old Carondelet Canal or the New Basin. So the long and short of it was, Dupré paid your mother and me a visit while you and Savoie were in Europe and, after looking over the ground, he offered me a very tidy sum for the rear section of Cindy Lou—that Bayou Boisblanc piece, I mean; the only part of the place we've thought of as worthless, right along, because nobody can grow the first thing on gravel. I should have said worthless aside from your treasure."

"And you didn't take him up?"

"Of course not. He called me every description of simpleton he could think of, but he also said his offer stood, any time I'd care to take him up, because cities would be needing more and more gravel, and after that, the turnpikes would need it, and so forth and so forth. I expect he thought I was just holding out for a higher price and I didn't tell him different."

"There *was* another reason? You kept that Bayou Boisblanc piece, when you were offered a good price for it, just because you thought I still believed I'd have the luck to find buried treasure there?"

"Well, partly—just partly, of course. More because Cindy Lou means so much to me—to all of us—that I'd almost as soon think of selling one of the family as any of the land that's part and parcel of the family, too. . . . You do still believe in the treasure, don't you, Cary?"

"More or less. But I'm not so sure I'll be the one to find it. I'm feeling rather out of luck, these days. . . . Do you mind very much if I leave you here, Father? I seem to be almost home and I do want one good canter before I get there. Sorry you don't feel like having one with me any more."

She must have given her horse a quick cut with her riding crop, for he reared suddenly and then plunged forward at breakneck speed. Clyde made no attempt to catch up with her; he was completely baffled and he was more hurt than he would have been willing to admit. How could a girl whose mere expression of a wish had always been enough to assure its fulfillment say, even in jest, that she was out of luck? And Cary had not spoken jestingly—she had spoken bitterly. She had everything in the world to make her happy—loving parents, a devoted husband, countless friends, a beautiful home, the assurance of plenty—and she was young, lovely and in perfect health. But she was not happy and she was not pleased and touched because he had saved the land for her; she did not feel any longer about the land as he did. . . . Yes, certainly something was seriously wrong. He would not beat about the bush any more. He would ask her point-blank what the trouble was, after all. . . .

When he did so, she did not come and nestle in his lap, as she would have before she was married; neither did she bury her head on his shoulder and pour out her little troubles, confident that he could smooth them all away for her, as she would have done then. Instead, she stood in front of him, twisting a dainty, lace-trimmed handkerchief around her fingers. Somehow, the gesture seemed out of harmony with her fine carriage and beautiful clothes and the new way she was doing her hair, all of which made her seem so much more sophisticated than she used to be. It was a childish gesture. Then Clyde saw that the handkerchief was wet as well as rumpled and knew that she must have been crying, which was very unlike her. She was not crying any longer; the eyes which met his were not tearful but defiant. Yet he felt surer than ever that she must be very unhappy, so he spoke to her gently and with increasing persuasiveness.

"Tell me what the matter is, honey. You know I've always told you that you could talk to me about anything, anything in the world, and that I'd understand."

Cary rolled the handkerchief into a hard little ball and tossed it on the table between them. "All right," she said, and her voice was hard, too. "I suppose I'd have to tell you sometime. Perhaps it might just as well be now."

"I think it had much better be now. Because the sooner I know what's troubling you, the sooner I can do something about it."

"There's nothing you can do about this."

"Of course there is. But not until I know what to do."

"You can't help it, can you, if I didn't want to leave France?"

Clyde laughed indulgently. "Why of course you didn't want to leave France! You were having a glorious time and you were on your honeymoon. Every girl wants to prolong her honeymoon, if she can. And I certainly don't see why you can't. From the look of Savoie, I think he'll go on acting like a bridegroom for a long, long while! You've had your fine trip and now that you and he are in your own home, the house that's exactly what you wanted, it'll seem so good to you, presently, to be there that you'll wonder how you possibly could have stayed away so long."

"No, I won't. I'll keep wishing and wishing I could have stayed away longer. I'm not glad to be home."

"Why, Cary?"

"I've told you. Because I didn't want to leave France."

She came a step closer to him, and he saw that her face was hard now, too, indeed that it had become so hard as to obscure all its fresh and glowing beauty. "I didn't mean to tell you until I'd found out whether there was something *I* could do about it," she said. "And I haven't yet. But you've bullied me into talking. The reason I didn't want to leave France is because I'm in love with Pierre de Chanet."

If she had suddenly doubled up her small hand and struck him between the eyes he could not have been more shocked. But he managed to speak almost instantly and his words revealed that the first effect of her outburst had been to arouse concern for Lucy rather than sympathy for herself.

"Don't you dare let your mother guess this! If she did, it would kill her."

"I don't want her to guess it. I didn't want to tell you, but you made me. Just the same, I don't think it would kill her if she did find out. She fell in love with you, didn't she, while she was still married to my father?"

"Don't you dare make a comparison like that, either, Cary! You married Savoie of your own free will, when you were twenty-seven and when he'd been your patient suitor for ten years! No one urged you to do it. In fact, your mother warned you that you couldn't really be in love, that you wouldn't have kept him waiting so long if you had been. She tried to dissuade you from the marriage on that account— not that she had anything against Savoie, Lord knows! She herself was married, under pressure, when she was only sixteen. Her bride-groom left her, a week after their wedding, to join the army, and he never was at home again, except on sick leave, until his last illness. When I first saw your mother, he was a hopeless invalid. She'd never led a happy, normal married life. Nevertheless, I didn't speak a word of love to her until her husband had been dead a year and a half. I wouldn't have insulted her by making love to her while he was still alive, and she wouldn't have listened to me if I had. My God, I never even *saw* her alone! And here you are, trying to justify your out-rageous confession by pretending there's some similarity between your mother's case and your own!"

The angry words poured from him in a torrent. Cary answered with comparative calm.

"All I said was that she fell in love with you while she was still married to my father. You may remember that she told me so her-self, in your presence, when I decided to get engaged to Savoie. I didn't say the details were all alike. I think that's beyond the point. Anyway, there's no use in making long speeches on the subject."

She turned, as if to leave the room. Clyde stepped over to her and put his hand on her shoulder, not roughly, but with sufficient firmness to halt her.

"There may not be any use in making long speeches, but you and I are going to thrash this thing out right here and now. Sit down, Cary. You said, a few minutes ago, that you hadn't meant to tell me about—about this mess until you'd found out whether there was anything you could do about it. That means you must have been trying to do some-thing. I'd like to know what."

"I've been doing some reading," she replied, disregarding his order to be seated and still standing as if bent on escape at the earliest oppor-tunity. "And I've made a few inquiries. But very discreetly."

"What *kind* of reading? Inquiries from *whom*?"

"I've been reading everything I could find about divorce—"

"About *divorce!*"

"Yes. Not that I've found much. I thought there'd be something in those old lawbooks of Grandfather Peyton's, but there wasn't. So I wrote to Grandmother."

"You wrote to your *grandmother!*"

"Oh, I did it very guardedly. I just told you my inquiries had been discreet. I said I'd got interested in Grandfather's library, just as Mother always has been, but I wondered if there weren't some volumes missing, that we were supposed to have, because so many legal sub-jects weren't even mentioned in Mayo's *Guide*. Grandmother wrote back that the *Guide* was issued primarily for the convenience of jus-tices of the peace and didn't contain information about anything over which they didn't have jurisdiction."

"Even if it had, that wouldn't have done you any good. You don't need to struggle through any more lawbooks. In the first place, you're not a resident of Virginia, you're a resident of Louisiana—where the laws are different. But, even if they weren't, I can tell you right now there isn't a court anywhere that would give you a divorce from Savoie. He hasn't been unfaithful to you. He hasn't abused you. He isn't a drunkard. He hasn't committed any sort of an infamous crime. He's passionately in love with you and he has been for years. He never looks at another woman. What's more, as far as I know, there isn't a single serious flaw in his character. I've met a good many men in the course of my life, Cary, and I can tell you he's one in a thousand. But, even if you could find grounds for a divorce, and could get one somewhere, you'd be a pariah the rest of your life as a divorced woman. There's never been a divorce in your family or in any family you know."

"There you go, making another long, useless speech. I didn't say I had anything against Savoie. I'll admit all his perfections. But I think they're tiresome. If he were a little more daring and devilish, he wouldn't be so dull. I didn't suppose I could divorce him. But I thought, perhaps, in time, I might persuade him to divorce me."

Again the sensation that she had struck him was so strong that Clyde found it difficult to combat. Involuntarily, he tightened his grip on her shoulder, forcing her down into a chair. It was only when she gave a little cry that he realized how rough he had been.

"I didn't mean to hurt you, Cary," he said; but his voice was as harsh as his action had been. "Just the same, I do intend to thrash this thing out with you. I can't believe you're really trying to tell me that Savoie has grounds for divorce."

Cary did not answer.

"Has he?" persisted Clyde inexorably.

"No-o-o. Not—not exactly."

"You mean that this—this Frenchman told you he was in love with you and that you listened, but that's all?"

"Not quite."

"Then what do you mean?"

"Well, we flirted a little. He kissed me once or twice—maybe more than that. I didn't exactly slap him in the face. I guess I must have kissed back. And when we were riding in the woods. . . . Well, it isn't hard for a man to put his arm around a girl, if their horses are close together. You know that. Then, there are those famous grottoes at Monteregard. We—we dismounted once or twice to explore them. And of course we danced a lot. Dancing can be just as impersonal or just as personal as you want to make it. You must know that, too. Some gypsies came and camped in the woods and they invited us to join in their merrymaking. That was one of the times when dancing became—fairly personal."

Something very like disgust was welling up within Clyde now, mingling with his fears. It was sickening as well as unbelievable to learn that this beloved foster daughter of his, the child of a great tradition, whose rearing had been gentle, whose surroundings had been sheltered, and whose mother was the embodiment of both steadfastness and refinement, had so far cheapened herself. But though Cary was telling him all this with reluctance, she was doing it without any show of shame or repentance. Indeed, she was actually hoping that her contemptible folly might furnish her with freedom.

"If anyone else had told me this about you, Cary, I wouldn't have believed it," Clyde said. His voice was still stern, but there was real sorrow in it, too. "I'd have given him the lie. And I was right in the first place, when I said that if your mother knew this, it would kill her. You must be completely blinded by this—this infatuation of yours. If you weren't, you'd be the first to recognize your own conduct for what it is and condemn it. And you'd realize that the only kind of a man who could be jointly responsible for it was a despicable cad."

"I won't let you say that about Pierre! He isn't a cad! He's a witty, charming, cultured gentleman."

"I'll take your word for it that he looks that way to you. I don't believe he looks that way to anyone else who knows him well, except perhaps his—his mother." Clyde found that the last statement had been extremely hard to make; but he went on with less difficulty. "Was it your idea that if you could succeed in getting Savoie to divorce you, Pierre de Chanet would marry you?" he asked sarcastically.

"Why, of course! He's crazy about me! He's told me so over and over again!"

"I don't doubt it. But has he told you that if you were free, or could get free, he would want you for his wife?"

"Not in so many words. But—"

"Not in so many words! Of course he hasn't! And of course he never will. Doubtless, he'd like very much to have you in his collection of mistresses; considering how 'adult' and 'sophisticated' he is—to quote from one of your letters—he's probably had several since he 'lost his innocence.' And he's doubtless very much surprised and slightly chagrined because you didn't succumb to his charm as rapidly and as completely as most of the women he's wanted. But he'd never marry a woman who'd been divorced by her husband, naming him as corespondent. He wouldn't forgive her for making a scandal out of a secret liaison. You'd better believe me, Cary. I know what I'm talking about."

"I'm sure you think you do. And I'm sure all your advice is very well meant. But I've had about as much as I can stand of it just now. Would you mind very much letting me leave?"

She rose, facing him defiantly again. He walked quickly to the door and stood with his back against it.

"I'll let you leave if you'll give me your word of honor you won't say anything about this to your mother or Savoie or anyone else."

"That's easy. I've kept telling you that I didn't want to talk with anyone about it, and that I wouldn't have done it now if you hadn't made me."

"Very well. But I want you to promise me more than that. I want you to promise me you'll stop acting as if something were the matter. You'd already roused my suspicions. Presently, you'll rouse your mother's and your husband's. Then they'll start asking you questions, just as I did, and they'll find a way of making you answer, just as I did. After that, there really would be trouble."

"All right. I'll do my best to act like a dutiful daughter and a rapturous bride. Will that satisfy you?"

"I suppose it will have to."

He stepped aside and opened the door for her. It was the first time they had ever parted without either a farewell caress or a loving glance, and he watched her leave with a heavy heart, knowing that such glances and such caresses were now a thing of the past between them, and that a glowing and precious element of his existence was gone forever because this was so. But he was not prepared for the final bolt which Cary shot when she had reached the hallway.

"After all, I won't have to pretend very long. I had a letter from Pierre this morning, saying that he and his mother had decided not to postpone their visit to the United States until next fall. The old marquis doesn't feel that he can leave the estate, but they're coming anyway. They must be on the water already. If they are, they'll arrive in New York next week and in New Orleans the week after. Of course they're planning to come to Victoria, too. Then Pierre can tell you himself what his intentions are. He may be more convincing to you than I've been."

Cary had shown no enthusiasm for an immediate housewarming; instead she had insisted she would rather give her first big party a little later on, when she was more thoroughly settled. In the light of her outburst to her stepfather, he had no difficulty in guessing that, being interpreted, this meant she intended to have it after the arrival of the De Chanets and to make it as sumptuous as its setting would permit. The idea sharpened his sense of harassment. He was unable to dismiss the scene with Cary from his troubled thoughts for more than a few consecutive moments; and he began to feel that he should have received her horrifying disclosure very differently: instead of upbraiding her and denouncing Pierre de Chanet, he should have shown sympathy with her plight and understanding of it. Without condoning her actions or the marquis', he could have told her that he knew, all too well, how unbalancing a sudden infatuation could prove; and then he could have persuasively assured her that, fortunately, such seizures were almost invariably of brief duration, and that when their victims had recovered, they were generally the first to realize that their aberrations, however violent, had no relation to true love or even to genuine passion. If such statements proved unconvincing, as they well might have, he could have gone a step further, and confessed to her that he was only too keenly aware how nearly fatal such infatuations might be. . . .

The more he thought all this over, the more firmly convinced Clyde became that he must talk with Cary again, along different lines; but the opportunity to do this eluded him. It had been understood, when the bridal couple returned, that they would come to Cindy Lou every other day for either tea or dinner, and he had felt sure that he could get Cary away from the others, on one pretext or another. But he neither saw her nor heard from her for three days after their stormy interview. As casually as he could, he asked Lucy if she supposed anything were wrong at Monteregard; her reply was unhesitating and untroubled.

"If there were, we'd have heard of it immediately, either through Savoie or through one of the Negroes. I think perhaps we've been a little too insistent, Clyde, about seeing Cary. Of course we've missed her terribly, and it's natural for us to try to make up for lost time. On the other hand, it's equally natural for her to want to be alone with her husband. I certainly wouldn't have promised to see anyone else, as often as every other day, just after you and I were married."

"Well, perhaps you're right. And thanks for the compliment, my dear. I appreciate it."

The conversation switched to other subjects, but Clyde was still unable to put Cary out of his mind and, the following morning, while Lucy was busy with household matters, he stopped at Monteregard in the course of his ride around the plantation. Savoie was at home and greeted his father-in-law cordially, though the young husband also appeared rather troubled.

"Cary doesn't seem to be very well. She's been completely prostrated, these last few days, by a terrible headache. I thought I ought to let you and Mother Batchelor know; but Cary's kept insisting her migraine would pass, pretty soon, and that, meanwhile, she didn't want to bother her mother."

"Have you sent for Dr. Bringier?"

"No, Cary didn't want me to do that, either. She maintains that she's just nervous and tired and that she wants to be let alone." Savoie's troubled expression became more marked. "She doesn't want to see you or her mother. She doesn't even want to see me. She just lies with her eyes shut, even though she's got all the shutters closed to keep out the light. She won't eat anything, and I can't tell, when I go to her bedside, whether she's really asleep or whether she's just pretending to be, because she doesn't want to talk."

"It seems to me you ought to get hold of Dr. Bringier whether Cary's willing or not. But I'll ask her mother what she thinks, and let you know."

A fresh concern was now added to the many which Clyde already felt. At first, he was inclined to believe that Cary's indisposition was merely a form of anger, and that she was pretending a degree of malaise which she did not really feel, in order to avoid seeing him. But he quickly dismissed this theory as unconvincing. Cary was too restless to spend several days on end closeted in the dark unless she were really ill. He charged Savoie to keep him informed and hastened back to Cindy Lou.

To his surprise, Lucy took the news quite calmly. When Clyde broke it to her, she was sitting in the library reading a letter and, after putting it aside in order to give him her attention, she resumed her perusal of it, merely saying she did not believe anything serious was the matter with Cary and that Clyde should not worry too much. He waited, hoping that when she had finished her letter she would discuss Cary's symptoms more fully with him, but, when she looked up from it a second time, she plainly revealed that her thoughts were still on its contents, rather than on her daughter.

"I'll go over to see Cary this afternoon, if you'd like to have me," she said. "That is, I'll go over to Monteregard. I don't think I'd better disturb her if she's asleep, or even if she's pretending to be asleep. Probably it's not exactly a pretense. More likely, it's a feeling of drowsiness that gives a certain amount of relief from the discomfort she'd otherwise be feeling, so that naturally she doesn't want to be roused. But I'll look over the situation. Meanwhile, I'd like to talk with you about this letter I've just had from Bushrod, if you can spare the time."

"Of course I can spare the time," he replied, sitting down beside her, and trying to repress the feeling of mounting antagonism that the mere mention of his stepson's name never failed to rouse. "Is Bushrod ill, too?"

"No, apparently he's well and—strangely enough—in very good spirits."

"Why do you say 'strangely enough'? Bushrod's usually in fairly good spirits, isn't he?"

"Yes. But it's hard for me to understand how he can be now, Clyde. This letter tells me that he and Mabel have separated."

"Separated!"

"Yes. Of course that comes as—as a good deal of a shock to me."

Lucy was still holding her letter and, though Clyde purposely avoided looking at her too closely, he could tell from the slight rustling sound of the sheets that her hands were trembling. Her voice was trembling, too.

"Apparently the main reason there is no question of a divorce is because that is contrary to Mabel's principles," she went on, trying in vain to speak steadily. "Personally, I can't help believing the poor woman's still deeply in love with him. But, from what Bushrod says, she seems to think he has behaved very badly."

"Do you know in what way, darling? Or would you rather not talk about it? Don't tell me anything you don't want to."

"I want to tell you everything—that is, everything I understand. It isn't very clear to me. Perhaps you'd better read the letter yourself."

She handed him the sheets bearing the letterhead of the Hoffman House and folded her hands in her lap. Then she bent her head and sat motionless while he read.

Dear Mother:

I am dashing off these lines to you on the eve of sailing for France. It's only fair that if Cary can have a year abroad, I should have one, too, don't you think so? I rather hope to get to all the cities she went to, and perhaps others besides, though, unfortunately, my itinerary won't include visits at historic chateaux, as I'm not as well provided with letters of introduction to members of the French nobility as she was. My trip will be different from hers in another respect also, for there'll be nothing of the honeymoon character about it. On the contrary, I'm going alone.

The fact is, Mabel and I haven't been hitting it off so well, and after a number of arguments that have got us nowhere, we've agreed to disagree. Of course, I've never seen eye to eye with her father about anything, and the bigoted old tightwad has kept denouncing me, in Mabel's hearing, for every little diversion I've managed to wedge in, and every trifling sum I've managed to spend, by hook or crook, without his approval and permission. The first result of this was that she took to giving me certain lectures on the same subjects after he finally left us alone, and I got fed up with them. So finally, I told her to shut up. That sent her sobbing back to Father and presently he convinced her she ought to get rid of me. I moved over to the Hoffman House with his entire approval, which suited me all right, too, for a time; but there doesn't seem to be anything special to keep me in New York indefinitely, and I suggested that I'd like to go to Europe. At first, Mr. Stoddard felt this might be quite a strain on him, financially; but eventually I convinced him that it wouldn't cost him any more, in the long run, than to have me hanging around here. He consulted some stodgy old lawyer on the subject, in his interests and Mabel's, but I handled matters for myself; and I think it speaks pretty well for my legal training at the good old University that I got the better of him on all counts, except that the separation isn't official, as I'd have liked it to be. As a matter of fact, I can't blame the stodgy old lawyer for that. Apparently he pointed out that there were certain advantages to such an arrangement. But they didn't go down with the pillar of the church.

I'm heading first to Paris, but I don't know just how long I'll stay there, and though I think Monte Carlo will be my next way station, I'm not sure of that, either, so I suggest that when you write you address me in care of Baring Brothers until further notice.

Your last few letters haven't been very detailed, but I take it you're still living high, wide and handsome at Cindy Lou and I wish you joy of it.

Your loving son,
BUSHROD PAGE

"It's terrible," Lucy said in a low voice. "But I'm trying hard to tell myself that it might have been a great deal worse. There might have been children involved. There might have been an open break. There might even have been a divorce. I think that would have killed me."

"Please try not to feel so badly, darling. It's clear there isn't going to be an open break, much less a divorce," Clyde said, hoping that he was speaking the truth. He was still holding Bushrod's letter in his hand, but he was thinking of Cary and what he had said to her about her mother.

"Of course Mabel wasn't just the type I'd have chosen for Bushrod, but she did think the world of him and I suppose every woman feels as I do about the girl her only son marries," Lucy went on. "Very often she feels that way about the man her only daughter marries, too. I'm trying hard to tell myself we ought to be thankful that Savoie's everything we could possibly wish. But that doesn't seem to help as much as it should, either. Cary seems so restless and discontented."

"She'll settle down after a while, you'll see," Clyde said, again hoping that he was telling the truth. "I think perhaps it would have been better if she hadn't gone abroad at all," he added. That much, at least, he could say with complete conviction. "If she'd gone straight to Monteregard—which wouldn't have been Monteregard in that case, but Tunica—she wouldn't have had so much trouble getting adjusted. She's been unsettled by all these foreign ways she's seen."

"Yes, I think she has. I think you're right—it would have been better if she hadn't gone to France. I can't help feeling it would be better if Bushrod didn't go, either. And I'm very much confused. Quite aside from—from the disgrace of this separation, it seems to me most unwise for him to leave New York when he's hardly begun to build up his practice. Won't he lose all his clients? And what will he live on while he's in Europe? If Cary and Savoie spent so much money that Mr. Vincent had to intervene, I don't see how Bushrod—"

"Lucy, this won't be pleasant for you to hear and believe me, it isn't easy for me to say. But, if I'm not mistaken, Mr. Stoddard's paid Bushrod to get rid of him."

"Paid him!"

"Yes. In other words, Bushrod's become a sort of—well, a sort of remittance man. As long as he stays in Europe—or somewhere else at a comfortable distance from New York—Mr. Stoddard will make him a regular allowance. But, if he goes back there, if he tries to—to resume his marital status, the money will stop. And Bushrod would rather have money than Mabel. Of course, I'm just guessing. But I think that's the way things are."

"But he didn't have to take money! He could have come home! He could have lived with us and practiced law in Louisiana."

"Yes, he could have," Clyde answered, suppressing the impulse to say, "Thank God, he didn't!" He tried to choose his words carefully. "But he would have had to study the Napoleonic Code and that's quite a change from the English common law and after that, it would have taken him even more time to build up a practice here than it did in New York. Meanwhile, I'm afraid he wouldn't have been contented. It would have meant a confession of failure and no man likes that. The last time he was here he came in a private car, with a millionaire for a father-in-law and an heiress for a bride. It would have been a good deal of a comedown to arrive alone—and to tell the neighbors why. Besides, you and I aren't living high, wide and handsome just now. We're trying to live as economically as we can, and Bushrod likes luxury. I doubt if he'd have been satisfied with our present simple form of existence at Cindy Lou."

"I suppose it is doubtful," Lucy conceded. "And we couldn't have changed our way of living, just to please him. Because, as it is—"

"As it is, we're keeping our heads above water," Clyde said. "Barely. There's no leeway yet—you know that as well as I do, honey. But thanks to you, I don't think we'll go under. I'll never be able to tell you, Lucy, what it's meant to have you stand by me the way you have. But there's something else I can tell you: this last year at Cindy Lou has been about the happiest one of my life, in spite of all the worries. Because you and I have been closer together than we ever were before, and that's saying a good deal. I can't help being glad that there's been no third person— no matter who—to claim part of your time and attention any more."

"It's been the happiest year of my life, too. I think we *have* been closer together than ever before. But that's not just because there hasn't been anyone except you to claim part of my time and attention, Clyde; it's partly because you've let me share your adversity as well as your prosperity. You know you never have before, though you agreed to, when we got married. Don't you remember? We took each other for richer or *poorer,* for better or *worse.*"

"But you'd been so poor before we were married, darling. You'd been through so many hardships. I didn't want you to have any more poverty or any more misery."

"I know. I've always understood. And I've always loved having you feel that way. Just the same—"

"Yes?"

"Well, of course it doesn't seem to me as if we'd been poor this last year. *Really* poor, I mean. And I've been glad the money we did have came from the land, our own land, and not from—anywhere else."

He gave her a searching look without making any immediate answer. Then he blurted out, "Just what do you mean by that, Lucy?"

"Well, I was brought up on a plantation, you know. I have a special feeling for crops and timber lots and gardens and so on. Nearly all Virginians are great land lovers."

"So I've heard. But I don't think that's *all* you meant, Lucy."

"No, it isn't, quite. Perhaps I said more than I should have. I didn't intend to ask you an indirect question or to force your confidence— truly I didn't, Clyde. I spoke almost without thinking. But what I did say came straight from my heart. And I thought perhaps, now that we are so much closer together than we ever were before, now that we have started to share everything, good as well as bad, I could share my thoughts with you, too."

"You're right. You can. You should. I want you to. I've waited and waited for the right moment and now it's come." He stood in front of her, looking down at her fixedly, his arms folded across his chest. "I got my start on the sidewalks where I could shoot craps better than anyone else in my gang," he said abruptly. "I did pretty well in dives, too, as soon as I was old enough to stay inside them, without getting kicked out. And then I realized that a shanty boat could be a gold mine, too, though Lord knows none of them looked much like one."

Suddenly, the words came tumbling out of themselves, so fast that he was almost incoherent. He was telling her about his "understandings" with the captains under whom he had worked; about the bartenders who "co-operated" with him; about devices for stripping and stacking cards; about the games where thousands of dollars had been lost and won in the course of a single night; about the investment of winnings in ways that had been almost unbelievably successful; about the various disguises he had worn so effectively and changed so frequently that he had delayed or prevented detection. He did not tell her—as indeed he might have—that much of his phenomenal success was due to his extraordinary expertness in all games of chance and not to any predilection for crooked practices. He did not remind her that gambling was, in itself, regarded as no cardinal sin, or claim that, by and large, the gamesters on the river steamers could stand up well under comparison with almost any of the other "gentlemen" aboard. He glossed nothing over, he pleaded no extenuating circumstances. The story was saved from sordidness only by its essential drama and by the impetuous sincerity with which it was told. Lucy sat very quietly, her hands folded in her lap; but she did not bend her head, as if to keep him from seeing a stricken look. Her face was raised and her gaze was on her husband. However, she did not speak, even when he finally paused for breath.

"And then, along came the gunboats," he went on. "Next—well, I don't know whether you can stand this part, Lucy—about what I did during the war and immediately after it. I've told you now about what I did on the river, but I don't know whether I can tell you why it was better we shouldn't live in Virginia."

"You don't need to. I think I know. At least, I've guessed. I'd guessed part of the other, too. And part of it I've been told. When Cousin Mildred brought the children down, after we were married—well, you know how a lot of women get to talking together, when they haven't anything else to do, and of course all day long, in the ladies' cabin on a river boat. . . . Cousin Mildred wouldn't have told me what she'd heard, if she believed it. She likes you too much for that. She put it all down to idle gossip. She was very indignant about it."

"So, you've known—all these years?"

"I haven't *known*. I said I'd *guessed*."

"And you loved me in spite of what you guessed?"

"I couldn't help loving you—from the very beginning. You know that."

She rose and put her arms around his neck, her clear gaze still meeting his eyes.

"Just the same, I'm glad that money's gone. And I'm glad you've told me all this yourself. Aren't you, Clyde? It won't weigh you down any more, now that it isn't a secret. And I'm afraid it has before. All these years when you've been trying so hard to do right and succeeded so well. But since you've made a clean breast of everything—"

She left the sentence unfinished, because it did not seem to need finishing. Obviously she took it for granted that her statement was conclusive, that he had made a clean breast of everything and that his heart would be lighter from then on. Only Clyde knew that his heart would never be really light, that there was one secret he could not share with her; of course he had not told her about Dorothée.

At all events, his partial confession had diverted her thoughts from Bushrod and for this Clyde was duly thankful. But, as the day wore on, it was increasingly clear to him that she kept reverting mentally to the distressing letter she had received—and dwelling on the disgrace that it revealed—with more intensity than she thought of anything he had told her about his life on the river and with more concern than she thought of anything he had said about Cary, whose illness was a source of much anxiety to him. Late in the afternoon, he reminded her that she had promised to go to Monteregard; when she pleaded fatigue, for the first time in months, he knew that she was emotionally exhausted and, far from insisting she should go out, he urged her to rest. He made sure she was comfortably settled, and then set out for Monteregard himself.

He was met on the gallery by Savoie, whose troubled expression had given way to one of beaming pride. Yes, Dr. Bringier had been there, he said. No, there was nothing to worry about, nothing at all. Cary was awake now, and she would like to see her father. She wanted to tell him herself. . . .

Clyde went quickly down the hall and knocked on the door of the boudoir leading to the large bedroom in the left wing which Cary had chosen for her chamber. As he entered in response to her bidding, he saw that its shutters were no longer closed and he was conscious of the elegance of its furnishings and the luxury of all its appointments. At the same time, he was far more forcibly struck by its state of disorder. The toilet table was littered with gewgaws, the chaise longue was strewn with soiled clothes and, though Cary had been home for several weeks now, trunks and hatboxes, partially disgorging their contents, covered every available foot of floor space. The bed did not look as if it had been properly made in several days, and Cary herself was wearing a rumpled pink satin robe, which left her neck and arms bare, and her hair was tumbling in an uncombed mass over her shoulders. In all the years of his marriage, Clyde had never entered the room which he and Lucy shared, without finding it in perfect order. As for Lucy, her hair was always neatly parted and braided in two long plaits before she retired, and her frilled, featherstitched nightgowns, which fastened closely around her neck and wrists, were permeated with the fragrance of lavender, mingling with the fresh scent of fine cambric which had been laundered with meticulous care. Cary had been brought up to take similar standards for granted and Clyde was appalled to see how far she had departed from them. But he was even more appalled by the manner of her greeting. She sat up among her pillows and faced him with the same angry defiance she had shown, a few days earlier, in the gaming room.

"Well, I hope you're satisfied now!" she exclaimed furiously.

"I'm glad to see you're feeling better, Cary," Clyde answered noncommittally.

"Glad I'm feeling better! I'm not feeling better! I'm not going to, either—that is, not for a long while. But I'm awake, if that's what you mean. The miserable old doctor woke me up, all right."

"I'm sorry he disturbed you. I suppose he felt it was necessary."

"It wasn't necessary at all. If you hadn't insisted, Savoie wouldn't have sent for him. I could have had at least a few more days of peace. And now Savoie's acting as if he were never so pleased about anything in his life."

"Cary, you know Savoie was distressed because you weren't feeling well. That's why he sent for Dr. Bringier. He didn't do it to annoy you. If he's pleased, it's because you're really better, because the doctor's reassured him."

"He's pleased because the doctor's told him *I'm going to have a baby*! He doesn't care how much discomfort I have now, how much suffering I'll have later on. He's kept telling me, month after month, ever since we were married, that he hoped pretty soon. . . . And then acting disappointed when he found it hadn't done him any good to hope! Well, he's got his wish at last! I'll probably go on feeling the way I do now, if I don't feel even worse, for weeks and weeks, according to Dr. Bringier. I won't be able to ride, or dance, or do any of the things I really enjoy. I won't be able to give any parties or go to any. I may not even be able to stand the sight of food or walk across the floor without feeling dizzy. And then I'll begin to get heavy and presently I'll be hideously misshapen. Well, you were right! Pierre de Chanet won't want to marry me. He won't even want to see me, and I won't blame him!"

   CHAPTER VIII

CARY'S ANGRY prediction about the manifold discomforts in store for her proved well founded. Like many another girl, conspicuous for glowing health, she speedily developed almost every unfavorable symptom peculiar to pregnancy. The severity of the prostrating headaches, which, from the beginning, had seemed to her almost unendurable, increased to such a degree that she was almost frantic with pain; and her aversion to food soon took the form of morning sickness and, shortly thereafter, showed signs of developing into pernicious vomiting. If maternity had been an experience she had long and ardently desired, she would probably have borne these trials with patience and fortitude, feeling that the much-wanted child would more than compensate for all her sufferings; and, in that case, her mental attitude might have had beneficent results; but her furious resentment naturally affected her physical condition adversely. Her physician, like her husband and her parents, found it impossible to relieve or help her, and he voiced this feeling to Savoie as he was leaving after one of his frequent visits.

"I'll admit it's never easy for a young woman when things go this way, but it doesn't need to be as difficult as Cary's making it. . . . I suppose it isn't necessary to tell you she shouldn't be left alone."

"We're only too glad to take turns staying with her. But she doesn't seem to want us to."

"Well. . . . Whether she wants you to or not, I think that's what you'd better do. And by 'you' I mean some member of the family, Savoie—or possibly Mrs. Surget, if she'd come. I know your servants were with the Batchelors a long time, that they're capable and devoted and that you trust them. But I wouldn't trust them too far, just now."

"You—you haven't said this to Cary's mother, have you?"

"Not yet. But after seeing your wife today, I think I'd better." In the doctor's own opinion, there was no excuse whatsoever for Cary's outrageous attitude; but noticing Savoie's stricken look, he did his best to pretend that there were extenuating circumstances. "Of course, when a girl's as sick as she is, she doesn't think clearly," he said. "She can't. But be patient a little while, Savoie. And try not to blame her any more than you can help. Tell yourself she isn't responsible."

"I don't blame her," Savoie said dully. "I blame myself."

"Good Lord, why should you?"

"I knew she didn't want to have a baby. And I did."

"Well, she was twenty-seven years old when she married you," the doctor remarked dryly, unconsciously repeating Clyde's words. "It isn't as if she'd been sixteen. She certainly must have realized—"

"I suppose she did, in a general way. But she hoped this wouldn't happen quite so soon. In fact, not for several years yet. Even a few months would have made a difference. You see, some French friends of ours, who were very kind and cordial to us, are arriving any day now to return a visit we made them. Cary'd counted on giving them a good time—on having a good time with them herself. As a matter of fact, I had, too. But somehow the prospect of a son means so much more to me than any company could—"

"Quite natural, too. These French friends of yours—they're not the De Chanets by any chance, are they?"

"Why, yes! Do you know them?"

"I knew the noble marquise when she was Dorothée Labouisse," the doctor replied, the dryness of his tone becoming more marked. "And I understand she did very well for herself after she sold Cindy Lou to your father-in-law. Went back to France a rich woman and started cutting quite a wide swath. Eventually married into the *petite noblesse* —or was it the *grande noblesse*? Either way, she must have got a lot of satisfaction out of it. I've always understood her own family was nothing much to brag about and that she didn't have a cent to her name when she caught the fancy of poor old Labouisse. Well, she had some pretty arid years after he died. I suppose we shouldn't blame her for making hay when the sun began to shine again."

"She's a very charming woman and her second husband's a distant relative of mine," Savoie said a little stiffly. "He's a very distinguished gentleman and, incidentally, *grande noblesse* is correct."

"Yes? Sorry I forgot about the relationship. But, after all, it is distant. The name's a curious coincidence, isn't it? I mean, that there should be a Pierre de Chanet in France right now—or rather, actually on his way over here from France. History does repeat itself. Excuse the cliché. . . . Well, I think I'd better be on my way to see your mother-in-law and tell her that her daughter'll bear watching. Don't forget that I've told you the same thing."

The doctor nodded and took his departure, leaving Savoie even more uneasy than he had hitherto been. He went into Cary's room and sat down by her bed, gazing at her with pity and self-reproach. If she realized he was there, she gave no indication of it. But when Titine, Ivy's sister, who had been put in charge of the chamber work, tiptoed in an hour later and began to move about, almost noiselessly, in an attempt to restore some degree of order, Cary sat up suddenly and sharply rebuked her.

"Haven't I told you to leave things alone? I'm nervous enough anyway without having you set my teeth on edge by rustling around like that!"

"Ah doesn't want to harm you' pretty teeth, no, Miss Cary, but de las' time Miss Lucy were here, she done say Ah was a pure disgrace, me, to her teachin', leavin' you' nice things strewed aroun'. Ah 'specks she comin' back again, soon-soon, her, an' Ah doesn't want her tellin' me dat no mo', no. She liable to take me out de house an' send me to de fields."

"*I'll* send you to the fields if you don't obey my orders. This is my house and you're working for me now."

"Yassum, Miss Cary," Titine conceded doubtfully. "But Miss Lucy done tell me, her, it don't make no mind iffen you is *comme ci, comme ça*, Ah got to readen things up, me."

"And I told you to get out of here!"

Cary picked up a Book of Devotions, somewhat incongruously reposing on her bedside table and, before Savoie could take it from her, hurled it at Titine. It missed its mark, but it had the desired effect. Titine scuttled from the room, dropping an armful of clothes in her flight, and did not return, even to summon Savoie to dinner. It was Lucy who brought her back, some hours later.

"Go and get something to eat, Savoie," she said, putting her hand lightly on his shoulder for a moment. "I had my dinner and a good rest before I left Cindy Lou. Why don't you take a nap yourself? I know you must have been awake most of the night. I'll stay with Cary this evening and every evening until she's better."

Savoie rose, looking a little doubtfully at Cary; but, as she still paid no attention to him, he managed, in a rather halfhearted manner, to return his mother-in-law's encouraging smile and walked away taking care to make as little noise as possible while crossing the floor.

"Now, Titine, let me see how quickly you can put this room to rights," Lucy went on, when the door closed behind him. "Meanwhile, if you'll pass me her brush and comb, I'll get the snarls out of Miss Cary's hair. Then I'll sponge her off and, after that, you can help me to get her into a clean nightgown and change her bed."

"I don't want Titine clattering around and making a lot of noise," Cary said angrily. "I've told her so already. I'd rather you didn't interfere with my servants, Mother. And I don't want you to touch me, either. I want to be let alone."

"I shan't interfere with your servants when you're in a condition to direct them yourself. Until you are, someone else will have to do it for you and I seem to be the logical person. I'm sorry if that isn't pleasing to you, Cary. And I'm also sorry that you don't want me to take care of you. But I'm acting under the doctor's orders now. He feels we've let you have your way too long already for your own good. That's why we don't intend to do so any longer."

Titine had already handed Lucy the brush and comb. Without saying anything further, the latter leaned over the bed, turned Cary on her side, and began to separate the tangled strands of hair.

"Hereafter we can do all this when we see you're practically asleep," she said. "Then it won't disturb you so much. And we'll try to do most of it on alternate days—you'll find there's a sort of ebb and flow to your worst discomfort. I don't know why there should be, and as far as I've ever heard, doctors don't know, either. But it helps, when you're having an especially hard day, to keep thinking that the next one won't be quite so bad. . . . Oh, I'm sorry! That *was* a bad snarl! We won't let your hair get in this state again. . . . Do you know, Cary, I think you have the most beautiful hair I've ever seen? It has everything—color and natural wave and softness and yet it's long enough for you to sit on. I don't think I've ever known anyone else whose hair had all those qualities. Mine certainly hasn't. It never was as golden as yours, even when I was very young, and it never curled around my face, the way yours does."

She went on serenely, undeterred by Cary's stubborn silence and intermittent retching, until the golden hair lay in two long, smooth plaits over the rumpled nightgown. Then she handed the brush and comb back to Titine, who had already succeeded in picking up most of the scattered clothes and had begun to dust.

"Now if you'll bring me a big bowl of warm water and a washcloth and some soft towels. . . . There must be some cologne water on Miss Cary's dressing table, too, Titine—yes, that's the bottle I mean. If I pour some of it in the water, it'll smell sweet and be refreshing and it will prevent her from catching cold, too—don't forget that, in case she should want you to bathe her sometime. While you're about it, you'd better give me a fresh nightgown for her, one with sleeves—aren't there some in that farther armoire? You know where the clean sheets are, of course. We'll put those on the bed as soon as I've finished giving Miss Cary her bath." Lucy turned from the maid to her daughter. "You've forgotten, haven't you, darling, that I used to bathe you like this when you were a little girl and had fever? Of course, you didn't have it very often, because you were a very healthy child. And now you're a very healthy young woman. I know just how unpleasant this awful nausea is, but it only lasts a few weeks or at the most a few months and presently you'll forget all about it. I know, because I did, under the same circumstances. It wasn't until your father came and told me how badly you were feeling that I remembered—back to the time I first knew I was going to have a baby. But I remembered, too, how pleased and proud I was and how much that helped."

"Well, I'm not pleased and proud. I'm disgusted," Cary muttered, speaking for the first time.

"Nonsense! You're disappointed because you'd looked forward to having a good time with your French friends. And you may yet. Probably they'll stay for a few weeks in New Orleans, since the Vincents are still there, before they come on to Victoria. And by that time you may be feeling much better. I just told you that sometimes this nausea only lasts for a few weeks—almost never beyond the quickening. Now. . . . Let's not try to talk any more. You see it didn't take long, after all, to get you all fixed up. I'll just sit here beside you, and watch you, and when I can see you're almost asleep, I'll moisten your lips with a little water. You won't even know I'm doing it and presently you'll pass your tongue over them and swallow almost unconsciously. Perhaps, by tomorrow night, I can give you a little broth, the same way."

It was longer than that before Cary was able to take the broth, but she did not again try to keep her husband and her mother and her maid from her room. Clyde was the only person she steadfastly refused to see and, after two or three futile attempts at persuasion, Lucy and Savoie ceased to insist that she should do so. Clyde himself, while hurt at Cary's attitude, divined that she was still nursing the anger he had roused when she confessed to her infatuation for Pierre de Chanet, and that she was trying to even the score with her stepfather for his uncompromising stand, by the only means within her power. His own concern, as always, was primarily for Lucy.

"I'm a good deal more worried about your health than I am about Cary's," he told her bluntly. "Dr. Bringier says he's seen any number of women, as sick as she is now, who made up for lost time by eating enormous meals later on and were able to nurse big bouncing babies for months. But he thinks—and I agree with him—that it's too much of a strain on you to spend every afternoon at Cary's bedside."

"It seems to me he was the first to suggest that Cary shouldn't be left alone. Savoie takes care of her at night. He sleeps—or rather he stretches out—on the day bed at the foot of the four-poster. He never leaves the room from the time I come home until Mrs. Surget gets to the house, about nine the next morning. And *she* stays until I get there. I don't think either of them can stand any longer hours."

"It won't hurt Savoie to be short of sleep for a while. And there must be some other reliable woman, with nursing experience, who could relieve you one day and Mrs. Surget the next."

"Dr. Bringier doesn't know of any in the neighborhood. And he admits it wouldn't be wise to introduce a total stranger on the scene just now. I'm all right, Clyde, really I am. Remember this isn't the first time I've gone through a siege of nursing and been none the worse for it afterward."

"You were younger then," he muttered. It was very seldom that she referred, even indirectly, to her first marriage; but he still felt a twinge of jealousy on the rare occasions when she did do so. "You're neglecting your garden," he grumbled. "That biggest Alba Plena should be pruned, and not one of the camellias has been mulched with oak leaves and bagasse, in spite of the fact that hot weather's just around the corner. Last year, all the work was all done by this time; I ought to know. . . . You made me turn over two of my best field hands to you smack in the very middle of chopping time. Remember, though, when you showed me the flowers last December and asked me if that sight wasn't worth the time of a couple of hoe hands? It was, too. I had to give you right, honey. But none of it's being done this year, and what about next winter's buds? You've spoiled me so, I hate to think of what we'll be missing."

"Isn't it more important that I should take care of my daughter than of my camellias?"

"I suppose so. But you're neglecting me, too."

"You know you don't really feel that way about it, Clyde."

"No, of course I don't," he said quickly. "But I don't see why Mrs. Vincent or Armande shouldn't return to Victoria for at least a few days and spell you."

"Why, have you forgotten? The De Chanets arrived in New Orleans last week. Mrs. Vincent and Armande both have their hands full."

Clyde had by no means forgotten about the arrival of the De Chanets, which had been well heralded, both in letters from the Vincents and in the public prints, where much had been made of it. The Vincents were delighted with their distinguished guests, whom they found charming in every respect. It was a shame that Savoie and Cary—and of course Mr. and Mrs. Batchelor—could not have been on hand to welcome them and to be present at the entertainments given in their honor. Mrs. Vincent had decided that it would be well to begin with a reception, so that the De Chanets could make the greatest number of desirable acquaintances in the least possible time. This function had already taken place and the De Chanets had, of course, been deluged with invitations to the opera, to the races, and so on. The Vincents were now planning a series of dinners; the first one was to take place the following Tuesday, a company of eighteen; everyone who had been asked had accepted with alacrity. Portrait sketches of the marquise and her son, made in the Vincents' drawing room, had been reproduced in the social columns of the *Daily Item* and the *Bee*; and the De Chanets had also given out interviews to representatives of the press, in which they had paid the Crescent City and its leading citizens all the compliments which were taken for granted on the part of visiting celebrities, and made none of the tactless remarks which would have caused widespread resentment. All in all, it was obvious that the Vincents were fairly basking in reflected glory; and though of course they were very, very sorry that poor dear Cary should be so miserable, at such an inopportune moment, this regret was obviously not weighing them down too heavily. It was Clyde's private opinion that they might quite properly have taken time out to come to Victoria, leaving their guests behind them, now that the latter were so well introduced and so adequately provided for; and it was this feeling that he had voiced. Since Lucy apparently did not share it, he murmured something unintelligible and would have changed the subject, if she had not pursued it.

"As a matter of fact, I'd much rather they didn't come to Victoria right now. I think the quieter Cary keeps, the better."

"On general principles, I agree with you. But I don't see why it should upset her, just to see her mother-in-law."

"I don't think Cary feels very close to Mrs. Vincent, Clyde. I don't think she ever has."

"Well, she and Armande are certainly bosom friends."

"Yes, but Armande isn't in the proper frame of mind to make a good nurse right now. She's definitely restless herself."

"I suppose you mean that she's husband hunting."

"I wouldn't have put it quite that way. But—yes, that's what I do mean. Not that she'd marry anyone who asked her, just for the sake of being married. But if the right man *did* happen to come along, I don't believe she'd keep him waiting very long while she thought over his proposal."

"In other words, you think it's more likely she'd interrupt him to say yes? Well, perhaps the next time you hear from the Vincents, you'll also hear that there's been an answer to the maiden's prayer. Let's hope so, for Armande's sake."

He spoke lightly, but not sarcastically. He had always liked Armande well enough, though he had never been really attached to her, as he was to Savoie. When Lucy told him a few days later that she had heard from Mrs. Vincent again, and that the latter had written to say the hopes he had expressed for Armande were fulfilled, he took the letter from his wife without either undue interest or undue curiosity. As far as he had any feeling about it all, this was one of relief at the prospect of finding in it less news about the De Chanets than had filled the last few communications from the same source.

"So she's got a man at last! Well, I'm glad to hear it."

Lucy did not answer. He gave her a quick look and plunged into the letter.

Dearest Lucy:

I feel I must call you that, after all these years when we have addressed each other with formality, because I am now writing you with the same joy in my heart that I should experience if I were sharing glad tidings with a beloved sister. You will understand my emotion, for you, too, know what it is to rejoice in the happiness of an adored child. Yes, those are indeed my tidings. With the glad consent of my husband and myself, and with the full approval of his mother, who expresses herself as more than ready to take Armande to her heart, my darling daughter has become the betrothed of the Marquis Pierre de Chanet. . . .

"Oh, my God!" Clyde exclaimed. Then, instantly fearing that his vehemence might have betrayed that the news was more of a shock to him than seemed logical, he added hastily, "Why, they've hardly more than met! The man hasn't been in New Orleans a fortnight yet! She can't really know him, in that length of time."

"It doesn't necessarily take long for two persons to fall in love," Lucy answered, with a calmness that seemed to bear no relation to her customary serenity. "You and I both realize that. Go on reading the letter, Clyde."

It was a case of love at first sight on both sides (Mrs. Vincent continued) in fact, both Armande and Pierre insist that they knew, with the first glance they exchanged, that they had met their fate. However, with due respect to *les convenances,* Pierre waited a week before asking my husband for Armande's hand. Naturally, Lamartine could offer no reasonable objections. The alliance is, in every respect, suitable. Pierre is the scion of one of the oldest and most illustrious families in France; he is the sole heir to a substantial fortune and a magnificent estate; he is himself cultured, charming and witty. . . .

And the last time I heard him described like that, Clyde said to himself, groaning inwardly, *it was Cary talking to me. Now he's going to marry Cary's best friend. The poor girl isn't even going to have the consolation of believing that the reason he didn't want her any more was because she was sick and disfigured. He didn't even wait to see her before he succumbed to Armande. There won't be that much salve to her hurt pride.*

. . . and of course, completely *comme il faut* in every respect (the letter continued). After speaking to Lamartine, Pierre cabled his own father—all this before formally addressing Armande. But his eyes had already told her of his love, even though his lips had not, and she waited without impatience for him to declare himself.

"My God!" Clyde exclaimed again; and this time he felt no compulsion to qualify his outburst. "She actually waited ten days or so! Why, that girl's patience is nothing short of miraculous, is it, Lucy?"

"It has been," Lucy answered, in the same strangely calm way she had spoken before. "She's been patient a long while, Clyde, waiting for something like this to happen. Now that it has, you can't blame her because she acted—rather precipitately. You talked the other day, jokingly, about the answer to a maiden's prayer. Well, every girl prays for a Prince Charming, whether she admits it or not. But she doesn't dare expect that her prayer will be answered as literally as all this. Armande's not only getting a 'cultured, charming and witty' man for a husband; she's getting a title, a fortune, a storied chateau, a *forêt de legende.*"

"And, incidentally, she may be getting a damn scoundrel."

"I think we'll have to dismiss that possibility. I don't think we're in any position to discuss it. Do you?"

She met his eyes steadily. *So she guessed,* he said to himself. *She guessed from Cary's letters. I didn't, but she did. The only thing I thought of, when I read them, was that Dorothée, who was just a light of love, had feathered her nest with money she got from me, and that Lucy, whom I worship, had been bowed down with cares she shouldn't have had. Besides, Cary's letters frightened me. They made me afraid that, if Dorothée came here, she'd say something or do something that would give me away, so that Lucy would find out, after all these years. That's what those letters meant to me. And I'm not free from fear yet. I shan't be, until Dorothée's gone back to France. Perhaps I never shall be again. There may be some aftermath of her visit. . . . Well, Lucy*

214

hasn't guessed about Dorothée and me yet, thank God. But she did guess about Cary and Pierre. I knew she was worrying over those letters, but I didn't know why. Now that I do know, I can't tell her that her fears were well grounded. I can't betray Cary's confidence by telling Lucy her daughter confessed to me that she'd been false to her heritage and her upbringing, I can't say she cheapened herself by letting this Frenchman fondle her, I can't say she was actually willing to go through the scandal of a divorce if it would take her into his bed. And Lucy's right, we can't tell the Vincents Pierre's a scoundrel. If we did, they'd naturally want to know why we thought so and we'd have to tell them that, too. We'd have to say that Cary wanted to get rid of their son and go to Pierre. So we've got to let this marriage of Armande's go through. We've got to let her find out for herself about Pierre. Well, probably she'd rather do that than not get married at all, since she's so eager to do so. We can ease our consciences by trying to think that anyway. Perhaps the title and the fortune and the chateau will make up to her for the misery she'll go through, every time her husband's unfaithful to her. Partly anyhow. And whether it will or not, there's nothing we can say, nothing we can do, because of Cary....

He was aware that Lucy was speaking to him. "You haven't finished reading the letter, Clyde," she reminded him. He picked it up again.

The old marquis sent his blessing (the letter went on) and said of course he would come over for the wedding. He hadn't felt he ought to leave the estate, at this season, merely for a *visite de politesse*. But, naturally, a wedding is something quite different. So we are planning to have it in the late spring, at the cathedral. What a shame that Cary cannot be in the cortege, which we want to make as impressive as possible! Armande has always counted on having Cary act as her matron of honor, but under the circumstances....

Well, she'll be spared that humiliation anyway. She won't have to go to the wedding and chatter and laugh and pretend. She'll be glad, after all, of the refuge her darkened room gives her, she'll be glad she can't leave her white bed, she may even be glad at last that a child is coming, because that will take her thoughts away from Pierre de Chanet and what he's done to her.

... under the circumstances that is, of course, impossible. However, we are writing by this same mail both to her and to Savoie, saying we hope she will release Savoie from her bedside in order that he may come to New Orleans to salute his sister and congratulate his future brother-in-law, with whom he is, of course, already on terms of warm friendship. Indeed, as Pierre and the

215

marquise have both pointed out, the fact that Cary and Savoie spent so much time at Monteregard—I mean the *real* Monteregard—makes the De Chanets feel that their connection with our family is almost a *fait accompli* already. We are very happy that these are their sentiments and we feel sure you will join with us in urging upon Savoie the propriety of a prompt visit to New Orleans since, with all the preparations for a large wedding in the near future, we can see no immediate prospect of coming to Victoria.

Farewell for the time being, dearest Lucy. I shall write you again very soon to let you know the progress of all the exciting events here. Meanwhile, I shall await with eagerness your answer to my letter, for I know that in it I shall find an echo of the rejoicing which rings through mine.

As ever, devotedly your friend,
AURELINE VINCENT

"So they've written to Savoie and Cary by this same mail," Lucy said, taking the letter from Clyde and putting it back in its envelope. Her fingers did not tremble as they had when she heard from Bushrod. They were steady, as her eyes had been, and as her voice was now.

"Yes. When you see Cary this afternoon—" he had almost said, "you'll find out how she's taking it." He had checked himself just in time.

"When I see her this afternoon, I'll tell her that of course Savoie must go to New Orleans immediately," Lucy said. "Naturally, I can't leave Cary. But I think you should go with him."

"I'll be damned if I will!"

"It's one of those things that has to be done, Clyde. Isn't it?"

"No. I'm sorry, Lucy, but this is one of the few times—"

"Then I'll go, after all. I'll have to leave Cary with Mrs. Surget. Or trust her to one of the servants, in spite of Dr. Bringier's feeling about that. I think, as a matter of fact, that it will be quite safe to do so now. I'll make all the necessary arrangements when I go to Monteregard—the *mock* Monteregard—later in the day. Meanwhile, I'd better begin my preparations to leave for New Orleans with Savoie."

She rose and moved away from him, without haste and without any evidence of inner turmoil. He strode after her and laid his hand on her arm.

"Lucy, if—if you feel this way about it, of course I'll go, so that you can stay with Cary. But it's the hardest thing you've ever asked of me."

"Yes," she said, slowly. "It is."

And he knew she meant, not as he had, that the doing would be hard for him, but that the asking had been hard for her.

She went up to their room with him to help him with his packing. She was taking clean shirts from the armoire and handing them to him, so that he could put them in his valise, when Delphie came to the door and passed him a note. It was written in pencil on a small piece of folded paper and it contained only one sentence.

Dear Father—
Will you please come to see me?

CARY

He left Lucy to finish the packing without his help and hurried to Monteregard. Titine, who opened the door for him, said that Mr. Savoie was sleeping and that Miss Amy was with Miss Cary. He went through the hall and his old friend met him just outside the threshold.

"I really think Cary's better," she whispered happily. "She's hardly looked at the mail, since she's been sick, until today; but she's read two letters that came in this morning over and over again. Then she said she wanted a piece of paper, so she could write you a little note, asking you to come and see her. I know it's been one of her sick fancies that she hasn't wanted to see you until now. So I believe the change is a good sign, don't you?"

"I hope so. I can tell you better after I've talked to her."

He nodded and went into the room, closing the door carefully behind him. Cary was sitting up in bed. Her face was almost as white as her pillows and there were dark circles under her eyes. He would not have believed that a few weeks of illness could so completely change a being who had fairly radiated vitality, and his heart smote him at the sight of her. But, in spite of the tragic transformation, the pale girl who stretched out her slim hands toward him was the Cary whom he thought he had lost forever and who was now miraculously restored to him. As he put his arms around her, she buried her head on his shoulder, and her tears came freely, in a cleansing flood.

"Savoie hasn't guessed and we mustn't let him—ever," she whispered brokenly. "I think Mother may have, but I can't risk telling her, in case she hasn't—not when she's almost heartbroken already about Bushrod. But you *know*. You *understand*. Oh, Father, I need you so much. You won't fail me, will you?"

CHAPTER IX

As it turned out, Savoie did not get off immediately, and when he took his reluctant departure for New Orleans, he went alone after all. Lucy did not continue to insist that Clyde should accompany him, after she realized what her husband's presence meant to Cary; and, on second thought, she decided to postpone her own trip a few days more, meanwhile sending by Savoie pleasant letters and appropriate gifts. In a note to Mrs. Vincent—whom she addressed as Aureline for the first time, taking her cue from the latter's note to her—she said she would come to New Orleans to present her compliments to the marquise and offer her good wishes to Armande, in person, just as soon as Cary's health would permit and that she really believed this had already taken a turn for the better. Meanwhile, she sent the marquise and Armande the same assurances, and did not fail to add how greatly she was looking forward to meeting the former, and how delighted she was that a real Prince Charming had at last made his way to Armande through a forest which so many other suitors had found impenetrable.

The cordial and charming tenor of these notes was doubly convincing because they were accompanied by a large box of variegated camellias, beautifully packed and artistically wrapped, and by a heart-shaped diamond brooch, which not only had considerable intrinsic value, but an exceptionally romantic history: it had been presented to an ancestress of Lucy's on the occasion of the lady's betrothal to a favored courtier by King Charles I himself, at the same time that the courtier received a land grant in Virginia. In every way, the brooch was a gift which a prospective marquise could not possibly fail to feel was well worthy of her future position, and which was received with genuine enthusiasm by Armande, and viewed with great approbation by everyone around her.

"It is really too sweet of your mother-in-law to give it to me," Armande told Savoie, after opening, with an exclamation of pleasure, the small, well-worn velvet box which contained the brooch. "Especially as she has a daughter of her own and may have a granddaughter—or several of them, for that matter! I do think she's very generous."

"Well, I agree with you," Savoie concurred. "As far as that goes, I think Cary was, too—Mrs. Batchelor consulted her, of course. And Cary said she would be glad to have her mother give it to you."

"Cary is an angel," Armande said, putting on the brooch. Then she added, turning to her fiancé, who was standing attentively beside her, "Of course you found that out, while she was visiting at Monteregard.

I'm so glad she was married already—otherwise, I know I wouldn't have had a chance!"

"I grant you that your sister-in-law is very charming," Pierre answered unhesitatingly. "But *you* are the angel, *coeur de mon coeur!* The angel I always hoped I might find on earth, while never quite believing I should encounter her before I reached heaven. However, even this hope, even this half belief, sufficed to make me persevere in looking for her. And of course I shall thank *le bon Dieu* to my dying day that I did! No, believe me, *chérie,* no one could have diverted me from the search which has been fulfilled by you!"

He bent over her and, undeterred both by Savoie's presence and by the fact that their betrothal was not supposed to become official until the arrival of the old marquis, imprinted a long and loving kiss on her ready lips. Savoie turned away and left the room. He thought the caress in very poor taste and he was feeling generally out of sorts. His sister's acceptance and return of such open and premature displays of passion, his mother's gushing exuberance over the match, and his father's unconcealed satisfaction in it, were all displeasing to him; even the marquise, whom he had admired very much at the chateau, now seemed to him unduly arrogant, as if she were trying to impress Orleanians in general and the Vincents in particular with her superior importance. He found the endless discussions concerning wedding plans trivial and boring; and, in the absence of the ladies, his future brother-in-law made certain suggestions about nocturnal "sight-seeing" which were definitely shocking to him, though Savoie was no prude. He tried to tell himself that anxiety about Cary, whom he had been most loath to leave in any case, was largely responsible for his frame of mind; but two reassuring letters, one from Dr. Bringier and one from Clyde, made him all the more eager to go home. Now that Cary was improving, he longed to be with her, quite as much, though in a different way, as when she had been so ill. She was still in bed, she was still very weak, and the adverse symptoms still persisted; but the latter were lessening in severity and she was able to retain a little nourishment, if it were given to her when she was already drowsy. Her stepfather had stroked her arm one evening, merely as a gesture of affection, and the touch had proved unexpectedly soothing. Now he was doing the same thing more or less systematically, to induce the helpful drowsiness. Moreover, there were brief intervals when Cary was actually quite free from the hateful discomfort, though wide awake; and during these intervals she listened, with pleasure, while her stepfather read aloud to her, or inspected, with interest, the carefully kept ancestral baby clothes which her mother brought to show her, and discussed the garments which they must soon start making in order to supplement these. Savoie thought it would be very pleasant to sit beside Cary's bed and stroke her arm and read aloud to her himself, though hitherto he would have considered such a caress very tame and normally he was not much of a reader. He also thought he would enjoy seeing Cary, who was almost as expert a needlewoman as her mother, though she did not so often engage in such work, sewing on baby clothes. There was something very feminine and appealing about the sight of a pretty young woman so engaged. . . .

It had been agreed, before he left home, that he should remain in New Orleans until Lucy could join him at his parents' house on Elysian Fields, or he would have found some excuse for returning to his wife, in spite of the good reports which were reaching him. As it was, he fretted and fumed until word arrived of his mother-in-law's imminent appearance on the scene, and he was overjoyed at the general contents of this note. Cary continued to improve, Mrs. Batchelor said, and they were all hopeful that the time was not far distant when she could move from her bed to her chaise longue for a little while each day. After that, the next step would naturally be to get her out on the gallery, where she could have the benefit of sunshine and fresh air; and then they must begin to think about the proper nourishment and the proper exercise to build up her strength. Naturally, as her mother, Lucy felt she should be close at hand to supervise this gradual progress; and she was therefore sure that the Vincents and the De Chanets would understand why she felt she must limit her visit to three days. She still enjoyed river travel more than any other form of transportation; so, if convenient for the Vincents, she would arrive the following Monday on the *Stella Wilds* and leave Friday on the same boat.

Savoie met her at the levee and plied her with questions, all of which she was able to answer most satisfactorily, though her replies still further whetted his desire to get home. Once arrived at the Vincents', however, Lucy talked very little about Cary; instead, she listened, with every appearance of attentive interest, to the endless discussions concerning Armande's trousseau, the marriage ceremony and the wedding reception, which Savoie found so tedious. Though she made no suggestions except when asked for them, she hesitatingly advanced certain ideas which proved very helpful, and in many other little ways revealed her real desire to be of assistance. Pierre pronounced her the most charming woman *d'une certaine age*—except, of course, his future mother-in-law and his own mother—whom he had ever met. Mrs. Vincent received the implied compliment to her mature attractions with genuine pleasure, for she herself really admired Lucy; the marquise, in one of the rare intervals when she was alone with her son, voiced more tempered enthusiasm of his verdict.

"I know you feel you must be polite to these people, *mon cher*," she told him. "Just the same, you do not need to perjure yourself. I admit Mme Batchelor is all very well in her way. But she has no chic. I could swear the dresses she is wearing are at least two years old, even allowing for the time it takes French fashions to reach New York. And her hands are those of a workingwoman. I understand that she does a great deal of gardening. But if she really cared for her appearance, she would wear gloves while she was grubbing in the earth."

"Perhaps she doesn't really care for her appearance. Perhaps she thinks other things are more important."

"What could be more important to any woman—that is to say, any woman possessed of normal vanity and natural feminine instincts?"

"I don't pretend to know. But I have understood there are such women."

"And she wears almost no jewelry," the marquise continued. "Just a few mediocre ornaments that look as if they were heirlooms, valuable only for the sake of sentiment. I distinctly remember hearing Cary say, while she was visiting us, that her stepfather had loaded her mother down with jewelry. I wonder what she has done with it all?"

"Perhaps she keeps it in a safe. I understand some women do that, too."

"The proper places for jewels are at a woman's throat, and on her breast, and in her ears. And of course on her hands." As she spoke, the marquise twisted the rings on her beautiful white fingers, so that the diamonds in the settings caught the light, and then raised her hands to touch her glittering earrings, almost caressingly. "They are no good in a safe. Are they, Pierre?"

"Again I would answer that I do not pretend to know, but that I understand some women think so."

"Well. . . . All I can say is that those are very dull thoughts. I did not have the impression that Cary entertained similar ones. Indeed, I thought, when she visited us, that her jewelry was very creditable—not astonishing, but adequate."

"There I agree with you. Savoie gave her a handsome parure for a wedding present. And I understood that her mother turned over to her all the jewelry that came from the family of her father—I mean her own father, the Confederate colonel, not Mr. Batchelor. Apparently, the amount of this was, as you say, 'adequate' even if it was not 'astonishing.'"

"As a matter of fact, I was somewhat surprised that there was so much, and all in such good taste. I remember Cary told us that she had most of the old gems reset, at Cartier's after she reached Paris—she thought her mother's feelings would be hurt less, if the work were done abroad, after her own marriage, than if it were done at Tiffany's, when the two were shopping in New York together. Just the same, I imagine that Mrs. Batchelor's feelings were hurt. She is the sort who puts sentiment above taste, as you can see by those ornaments she wears herself, which I mentioned a moment ago. . . . Well, I am

221

glad Cary shows more sense. And I am hopeful that Armande will, too."

"If you are thinking of good sense in terms of a taste for jewelry, I am quite sure she will not disappoint you. Her mother has already given me to understand that Armande will expect a parure for a wedding present, at least as handsome as the one Savoie gave Cary, and preferably handsomer. Of course, she did her hinting very delicately. But her meaning was unmistakable."

"Your father will probably begrudge such an expenditure—now if she had insisted on some indicated renovations at the chateau, he would not have said a word. But I am pleased rather than otherwise. Armande's attitude does show sense—sense and spirit. I should not care at all for a dull, sentimental daughter-in-law."

"You have not found Armande dull so far, have you?"

"No, not exactly—so far. But she does not seem to have a great deal to say for herself. Now Cary is much more sprightly—or rather, she was. How tiresome that she should have got herself in such a fix, just at this time! When I planned this trip, I was rather looking forward to more of her lively chatter—as I believe you were, too."

"'Homme propose—' " began Pierre. His mother interrupted before he could finish the quotation.

"At the risk of making a bad pun, I am going to confess that I did not think the man about whom I was talking came to the United States for the purpose of proposing to Cary's best friend. I thought his original intentions were somewhat less honorable—and infinitely more exciting. And I doubt whether God had much to do with disposing of poor Cary by causing her to become *enceinte*. I think for that we must blame Savoie who, Lord knows, is very dull indeed. Fortunately, however, he is neither suspicious nor perceptive by nature. Well. . . . No doubt everything is turning out for the best. Armande has an excellent background and a suitable dowry. She is lovely to look at and she is grateful to you for having looked at her. She will make a very tractable and a very presentable wife. She will not plague you by talking about the tedium of life in the country, as I have sometimes plagued your poor father. She will adorn the chateau and her presence there will make it possible for me to spend more time in Paris. She will probably have as many children as you wish, quite uncomplainingly—it is my recollection that Creole women are very prolific. And she will not begrudge you your little diversions while she is *hors de combat*—she will take those for granted, too. I think Savoie is probably the first male of his family who has not had his little establishment on Rampart Street and, believe me, Armande knows all about such things. Her mother will leave to you the privilege of initiating your bride into many mysteries, but will not have failed to tell her daughter that a husband's peccadilloes must be overlooked—as long as he does not commit them too openly, *bien entendu*. Since it was high time you thought of marriage, it is perhaps just as well, after all, that it is Cary who is *hors de combat*. Yes, as I just said, I am sure everything is turning out for the best in our present venture."

As a matter of fact, the marquise was not feeling quite as complacent as she tried to sound, or rather, as she tried to give the impression that she was trying to sound; and her son, who understood her very thoroughly, was well aware of this. She had enjoyed the experience of creating a sensation in the society which had once turned a rather cold shoulder on her; and she foresaw, in her only son's marriage to a wealthy and doting girl, certain distinct advantages to herself as well as to him. But she missed the excitement she had anticipated. She had taken it for granted that most of her time in Louisiana would be spent at Victoria, close to the mock Monteregard and to Cindy Lou. She had visualized a resumption of her son's flirtation with Cary and of all sorts of delightful but hazardous possibilities in consequence. Savoie could not remain blind forever; sooner or later, he might challenge Pierre to a duel, and Pierre was one of the best swordsmen in Paris. Clyde and his dull, virtuous wife would not be blind indefinitely, either, and they would shudder at the very idea that the fair name of their cherished daughter might be jeopardized by a *crime passionnel*. The marquise would have taken no slight satisfaction in striking at them through Cary. She really rather liked the girl; but this liking was not sufficiently strong to outweigh her long-nourished sense of injury because Clyde had remained essentially true to his betrothed, in spite of his brief deviation from complete loyalty. She had never forgiven him for this faithfulness and she had never ceased to resent the other woman's hold over him. Now that she had seen Lucy, she was disposed to be less forgiving and more resentful than ever. It was nothing short of ridiculous that a man who could have had his choice between Dorothée Labouisse and Lucy Page should have selected the latter, and not only selected her but given her unswerving devotion for a quarter of a century. Certainly there was a score to even there.

Moreover, she could visualize the possibility that this score might be evened, not only indirectly, through Cary, but directly, through Clyde. After all, he was not immune to temptation—no one was in a better position to realize this than she was. Probably very few temptations had offered themselves in the course of the humdrum life he had so inexplicably chosen. But she was not yet ready to admit she was past the point where she could offer distraction or rekindle dormant embers. She and her elderly husband had long since ceased to stimulate each other and, with reluctant wisdom, she recognized the fact that the days when she could hope to stir any man's senses were now numbered. But they had not ended, even though they would in the near future.

She had wanted and intended to improve the present. And she had had no opportunity.

As long as Cary was immured in her dark bedroom, Clyde would remain at Cindy Lou and the Vincents would continue to say that there was no sense in going to Victoria. And presently, the marquis would arrive from France, and the wedding would take place, and Armande and Pierre would be off on a honeymoon. Her husband's presence would be a handicap to the marquise, perhaps not an insurmountable one, but still one which would present complications. Besides, he would wish to make his sojourn in the States as brief as possible; he was never content for long away from his chateau and his forest, his meadows and his marshes, and she would have no excuse for prolonging her own visit past the point of his departure. Pierre would be beyond Cary's reach, too; it was doubtful whether he and his bride would return to Louisiana at all after their wedding journey, especially as Armande had expressed such impatience and eagerness to see the real Monteregard. Even if they did return, Cary would be unsightly by that time. No duels would be fought over her; nothing would shake her husband's complacent faith in her or shatter her parents' pride. And Clyde and Lucy would go on and on, contentedly leading their Darby and Joan existence.

The consciousness of that placid, uneventful domesticity was what rankled most. If once—just once—she could have troubled its tranquillity, the marquise would not have asked for more: that would have been enough to shatter Lucy's security, to test Clyde's susceptibility and to prove her own diminishing, but still dangerous, powers. She rose from the armchair where she had been sitting while talking to her son and while brooding over her disappointment, and, walking over to the great cheval glass, which stood in a corner of the room where the light was excellent, she regarded herself long and critically. The results of this survey were not only reassuring; they were encouraging. Given the one opportunity which was all she asked, she felt sure she could still provoke passion and gratify desire.

Granted that the passion would be as ephemeral as it was intense, the desire solely one of the flesh; that was the way it had been before; and yet, after all these years, the memory of it stabbed at her vitals, the yearning for its renewal was still unappeased. She still seemed to feel Clyde's fingers digging into the small of her back, she could still evoke the delicious sensation of compliance with which she had yielded to his embrace. So powerful had been his domination, so instantaneous her response to it, that there had been no need of words to express their mutual understanding and their mutual craving.

She remembered that in the brief interlude between his kisses when he had given her a chance to speak she had managed to murmur, "But I have not shown you the whole house yet. Perhaps when you have

224

seen the second story, you will feel it is inadequate." Vivid as all the rest was, she did not remember what he had said in reply, or indeed, if he had said anything; only that they had gone up the stairs together, and that his arm had been tight around her all the time, pressing her close to him; that then they had been in her room and that presently, when his hands encircled her waist again, he had laughed exultantly at finding it even smaller without the stays than with them; and finally, that her pliancy in the garden had been mere acquiescence compared to her eventual state of complete self-abandonment. . . .

Hours later, Clyde had roused himself from his slumber of satiation and muttered that he must get back to the hotel. Then, belatedly, as he stood fully dressed before her in the first glimmer of the dim light that presaged the dawn, he had asked her whether any of the servants slept in the house, whether someone might have been aware of his presence and might now be aware of his departure. She had been able to reassure him: Belle was the only servant she had left, and Belle went back to her own man and her own dusky brood in the otherwise empty quarters by midafternoon. Indeed, she usually went as soon as the midday meal was over; she had remained to serve coffee the day before very grudgingly; her mistress did not pay her enough to exact favors from her. There were not any dogs on the place, either; no inopportune barking would betray the departing visitor. Sometimes the neighbors had remonstrated, saying that no woman should remain by herself at night in that great lonely house; there was no telling what might happen. But Dorothée had never been afraid; indeed, she had rather vaunted her valor. And now she was thankful for it. If she had been a timid woman, scared of her own shadow, she would never have had the joy of experiencing such a rich reward for her courage. . . .

Clyde's response to this rapturous declaration was far less impassioned than his previous behavior would have led his hostess to expect. He left her almost abruptly, with no warm assurance of an early return and no farewell embrace. In fact, he seemed eager to be gone. But that might well have been on account of impending dawn. Dorothée lay quietly in bed, listening as he went down the stairs and out of the front door, which he did almost noiselessly. Then she heard the click of the garden gate and that was all.

She was drifting off to sleep again when she remembered what he had said before she swooned into his arms: that, as a proof of good faith, he would give her forthwith five thousand dollars to bind their bargain for the sale of the property. He had not spoken of money or of Cindy Lou since then. What a ghastly trick of fate it would be if he had changed his mind, if he would now want to keep her on the plantation, if she could not go back to France after all! Shivering with dismay, she sprang up and opened the shutters, letting daylight flood the dim room. Then she looked wildly about her. But she did not have to search long. Propped up against the mirror of her dressing table was one of the envelopes which she kept in her near-by desk. Clyde must have taken it from there while she was still half asleep. It was sealed and it had her name scribbled on it. She tore it open feverishly, counted the thousand-dollar bills which it contained, and then recounted them, thinking that she had made a mistake—or that he had. There were not five, but six. And, after a moment, she understood. . . .

For the next three or four days, she waited and watched in vain for his return. When he finally came, he was not on foot and alone, but in a smart gig, accompanied by a certain Gilbert Ledoux, who was one of the best-known notaries in the parish. His call was as formal as if they had been meeting for the first time, and as if her sale and his purchase of Cindy Lou were the only matter of mutual interest. He was pleased to say that investigation of the title had shown it to be completely clear; he was now ready to pass papers, if Mme Labouisse were also prepared to do so. He believed that fifty thousand dollars was the sum on which they had agreed as the purchase price and he had already paid five to bind the bargain. So, according to his reckoning, he still owed her forty-five thousand, which he was ready to pay now. He spread the money out before her and the notary began to rattle documents. Her signature would be required here and here and here. . . .

It was all over so quickly that she could hardly believe it had happened. It was she who asked the only questions which caused a slight delay in the final arrangements.

"I shall need a little time to pack my personal belongings. Would a week seem too long?"

"Of course not. I do not wish to inconvenience you in any way. You must not overtax your strength."

"I appreciate your consideration. Shall we say ten days then?"

"That will be quite satisfactory. Indeed, I shall be glad of the opportunity to familiarize myself somewhat with local conditions, before coming here to live."

"Did you wish to have the house closed when I leave it? Or would you care to have my servant Belle stay on as caretaker? She is lazy and shiftless, like all the Negroes hereabouts, but she has never stolen anything, to my knowledge, and that is more than I can say for most of them. And she is familiar with the place. She might prove useful."

"I agree with you. And I wish the place to be in the best possible order. It is my intention to bring my bride here in the autumn. Perhaps I did not mention to you before that I am engaged to be married."

"No, you did not." The words came so quickly that Dorothée instantly feared her answer might have betrayed the fact that his announcement had come not only as a surprise but as a shock. She pressed her lips together, forcing herself to say no more, and looked away, lest the expression of her face might also be one of betrayal.

"It must have slipped my mind," Clyde said evenly. She did not dare glance at him, but it occurred to her—she did not know why—that if she had, she would have beheld that same blankness which had caught her attention on the occasion of his previous visit. How was it Americans described it? Oh, yes—"poker faced." She was sure his expression was poker faced as he went on.

"I have asked M. Ledoux if he could tell me of some lady in the neighborhood who might be willing to supervise the preparation of the house for Mrs. Batchelor. He suggested the widow of a physician, a Mrs. Surget, whom I am sure you know, as she lives not far from here. Since I had the pleasure of seeing you before, I have called on this lady and I am happy to say that she has consented to help me. I shall leave the matter of hiring suitable servants in her hands. But I think there is no doubt that she will wish to keep Belle who, as you say, is honest and familiar with the place. I gather that she has done cooking for you, as well as other work. In your opinion, if she had no other work to do and received some expert instruction, could she become a really first-class cook? I feel it is very important that we should have one. My fiancée tells me that if there is a good cook at the helm, the rest of the household staff can be dealt with very easily."

"I must remind you, monsieur, that I am a Frenchwoman and that to the French cooking is a fine art. When I told you that there were no longer any royal dinners at Cindy Lou, I also told you that this was because I had not the heart for them, after the death of my poor husband. But I can assure you that what little I have eaten has still represented a cuisine that was *soignée*. It will not be necessary for Mrs. Surget or anyone else to give Belle 'expert instruction.' I myself have given her that."

Her voice was trembling with rage now; she could not control it and she did not care. So that colorless relict of a country doctor, that cold pillar of righteousness, Amy Surget, had been selected as possessing the high qualifications requisite to prepare properly for a chaste bride! The offer had probably come just in time to save La Surget from starvation, for her impractical husband had never tried to collect his bills and there was little or no land connected with their house; he had chosen to ply his profession in the country because he preferred this to the city—as if that in itself were not enough to show what manner of man he had been! He had left his widow practically penniless not because, like Marchand Labouisse, he had spent money elegantly and prodigally, but because he had never cared for it or any of the goodly things it could provide. And now Amy Surget would be creeping around Cindy Lou, snooping in every corner where dirt might be lurking, probably scrubbing floors and woodwork herself because she would not trust the darkies to get them clean enough without her good example! Worse than this: she would be spreading the word around that she had found the house filthy, that it was cluttered with trash of all kinds, that much of its seediness was due to neglect and that a little prudence and a little industry would have prevented these telltale signs of deterioration!

Well, Dorothée would not give her that satisfaction at least! She would not need more than a few hours to pack her clothes—she had not many left and most of the shabby old trunks she would take with her on her departure would be practically empty. She would spend those ten days which she had at her disposal in giving the house such a cleaning as it had never had before, even though this might mean that she, and not Amy Surget, would be the one to go down on her knees and scrub! And before she left it, she would give a dinner which would prove to this *parvenu,* this *nouveau riche,* this coarse creature who had treated her like so much trash, that she was a *grande dame,* after all, one with red blood in her veins, to be sure, but a *grande dame* just the same and not a *cocotte.* He could not refuse to dine with her— not if she invited the notary and the doctor's relict and the Vincents to dine on the same night! And they could not refuse, either, though they had shown her little enough friendliness throughout the desolate years. Now that she was off to France, a rich, beautiful, independent woman, they would view her differently. And she would find a way, even with all these superfluous guests, of taking aside the one guest who mattered, of proudly returning to him that extra thousand dollars, of telling him that a woman like her might, under certain very exceptional circumstances, grant favors, but that she never sold them. . . .

These were the thoughts which had raced through her volatile mind while Clyde was civilly assuring her that he regretted his mistake in so much as questioning Belle's complete capability as a cook; it was only that he wanted to be certain. His fiancée was a Virginian, and Virginians also set great store by a cuisine which was *soignée.* Dorothée countered by extending, then and there, her invitation to a farewell dinner, the exact date of which should be determined by the convenience of Mrs. Surget and the Vincents. Both men, taken by surprise, which M. Ledoux betrayed and Clyde did not, accepted it and took their leave of her; and having thus easily secured their assent, Dorothée dispatched beautifully written little notes to Mrs. Vincent and Mrs. Surget. Their acceptances were also unhesitating, as Dorothée had foreseen. Fired by such enthusiasm for her project that she remembered to be angry only at intervals, she set to work on the house.

Belle proved unexpectedly co-operative. She not only worked herself, with a zeal which belied the reputation her mistress had given her for laziness, and which was all the more astonishing in view of her unwieldy proportions; she also found ready helpers among her cronies and progeny, who had learned by the grapevine that there were prospects of remunerative employment at Cindy Lou, and who were eager to prove that they were qualified for it. Before a week was up, the house was clean as it had never been before, the woodwork sweet smelling from soap and water, the windows shining, the brass and silver glittering. Every cupboard, every armoire, every drawer had been opened, aired and washed; even the dark store closets had lost their cobwebs and their mustiness. And still Dorothée had time to spare. As she sank back, surveying her handiwork with weary satisfaction, another idea occurred to her.

Why should she not improve the days which would still intervene before her farewell party by going to New Orleans and buying herself a completely new outfit? She had heard that, even during the war, a few beautiful French clothes had somehow been smuggled into the Crescent City, through the roundabout route of Texas via Mexico, or more directly through the blockade. She had never put these rumors to the proof because she lacked the money to do so; but there had been no reason to doubt their truth—and the war had been over four years now; so opportunities for adornment must certainly be more favorable by this time. And certainly, she did not lack money. She would not start off on her travels or give her farewell dinner wearing her old, rusty, outmoded black; it was falling to pieces anyway. And, after all, her husband had been dead eight years now. She had never intended to wear crape all her life, like these lugubrious Creoles who made such a cult of mourning, because they had nothing better to do; and even they would make allowances for her, as a Frenchwoman; she could safely experiment with soft grays, pale lavenders and pure whites. . . .

But when she reached the dressmaking establishment that had been recommended to her, it was not the soft grays and the pale lavenders and the pure whites which caught her covetous eye and held her fascinated gaze. It was a gorgeous outfit, imported on purpose for a popular actress to wear in a current play, where she was to have portrayed a wealthy woman of fashion. The actress had died, suddenly, just as the play was about to open, and the wardrobe had been left, intact, on the dressmaker's hands.

It contained "walking" dresses and "carriage" dresses and ball dresses and a dress purporting to grace a royal garden party; also calling costumes and *robes d'intérieur*—among the latter some which might logically be worn for informal dinners and some which suggested the intimacy of the boudoir—for the play was a daring one. The actress had been a slender, striking brunette, and every item in the collection had been designed to show off her figure and her complexion to the best possible advantage on the stage. There were no colors or styles suggestive of half mourning. Brilliant reds and greens predominated, and the lines and cut were as provocative as custom would permit.

Dorothée tried on all the splendid creations, not hurrying over the process, but in the same leisurely, gratified way in which she might have savored some sweet, heady wine; they fitted her and became her as if they had been made on purpose for her. Finally she stood before the *couturière* clothed in crimson satin made with an off-the-shoulder neckline, a long, tight basque, and a trained skirt whose fullness was drawn back over the hips and finished with cascades of fluted ruffles.

"How much will you take for the lot?" Dorothée inquired without further preamble.

The *couturière* gasped and, recovering, named an astronomical figure. Both women enjoyed to the full the subsequent bargaining. The *couturière* pointed out that the wardrobe consisted wholly of exclusive models from a world-famous Parisian house, that the materials and workmanship were of the finest, that the styles were those of day after tomorrow, that such a complete collection had never been seen in New Orleans before and probably never would be again. Dorothée pointed out that there were very few women in the Deep South—if, indeed, there were any, besides herself—who had any present use for such an extensive wardrobe, that if she did not take the collection it would have to be sold piecemeal and that this would take a long while to do—by the end of which time the styles would no longer be those of day after tomorrow, but of year before last. She further called attention to the conservative taste of the Creoles, the amplitude which their figures were apt to attain when they had passed their first youth and—last but not least—their straitened financial circumstances since the war. How many customers did the *couturière* suppose would come to her carrying reticules bulging with bank notes?

As she asked this question, Dorothée unclasped her handbag to extract a wispy handkerchief; then she snapped it to again, but not before the *couturière* had seen the yellowbacks which it contained. Quickly, she suggested a compromise price. Dorothée shook her head and began unhooking the crimson basque. The *couturière* gave a little cry, indicative of the ruin which was staring her in the face; then, sobbing that she had no choice but to give pleasure to such a charming customer, she capitulated. Dorothée reopened the reticule.

"Very well. You may send the collection to my apartment at the Hotel St. Louis, just as it is, today, except for this one dress, which I shall expect tomorrow. Meanwhile, I wish you to make two slight alterations in it."

"But the fit, like Madame's figure, is already perfect!"

"I appreciate the compliment. Nevertheless, I wish you to make it an inch and a half smaller around the waist and that much lower at the neckline."

"Then Madame would never be able to get into it! And she would never be able to wear it in public!"

"That is my concern, isn't it, not yours?"

Her mood was exultant as she left the dressmaker's and continued her shopping. She bought a huge Saratoga trunk and a smaller one, designed especially to hold headgear, underwear and accessories. Besides a divided tray for hats, the latter contained a special compartment for gloves, another for hosiery, another for shoes and still another for an umbrella. Dorothée bought everything she would need to fill these separate compartments; and finally, she bought new stays.

It was a thousand pities that Madame could not give her time to make these to measure, the *corsetière* told her; no ready-made stays would do her figure full credit. Dorothée agreed with her, but said that, unfortunately, she must return to the country the next day. She asked the *corsetière* to measure her waist before she took off the old stays and then she stood, clad only in her fine chemise and her silk stockings and her high-heeled shoes, and waited for the new ones to be adjusted. When they were in place, she asked to have her waist measured again.

"It is half an inch smaller now!" the *corsetière* told her with satisfaction.

"That is not enough. Draw in the lacings until it is an inch smaller still."

The *corsetière* cried out in protest, much as the *couturière* had done, though for a different reason. But she obeyed, and no cry came from Dorothée as the lacings did their cruel work, and the two sides of the stiff stays came closer and closer together until at last they met. The *corsetière* seized her measure and cried out again, this time in triumph.

"Madame is very brave and behold her reward!" The *corsetière* marked the measure and handed it to Dorothée. "So few of my customers know the truth of the saying, '*Il faut souffrir pour être belle!*' It is not more than Madame can bear, the pain of such compression?"

"Of course not," Dorothée answered proudly. It was true that she was suffering, but she would not let the *corsetière* loosen the new stays, much less remove them. It seemed to her that the pain they gave her was somehow akin to the other, still deeper and sharper, which gnawed at her vitals, and that only with the assuagement of that should come release from anything that was part of her purpose.

The conviction of this still sustained her when she welcomed her guests on the night of her farewell dinner. She was wearing the red satin dress, and she was aware that all eyes were resting on it, as she had intended they should. It mattered to her not one whit that those of Mrs. Vincent and Mrs. Surget were so soon averted. She expected—

at least she hoped—that she need never see Amy Surget again; and since she had already secured from Mrs. Vincent a letter presenting her to the De Chanet kinfolk in France, that lady's usefulness to her, for the time being, was past. Mr. Vincent was a man of the world, not easily shocked, except when it came to a question of his own woman-kind; he would have spoken sternly to his wife, if he had seen her in such a dress, and sent her back to her dressing table for more illusion, before going out with her; but he would think none the less of his hostess for her bared bosom, so white against the crimson of that basque, which tapered almost to nothing from the full breast to the tiny waistline, only to expand as suddenly again below it. Gilbert Ledoux was nothing but a local notary, a provincial; his opinion, good or bad, did not count, though, as a matter of fact, there was unconcealed admiration as well as unconcealed astonishment in his gaze. It was only Clyde who counted. And Dorothée could see that Clyde was in a fever of restlessness. He looked at her and then looked away, only to look again.

She put him opposite her at table, which was only natural, since hereafter that would be his place, as the host of Cindy Lou. But though she was duly attentive, first to Mr. Vincent, at her right, and then to Gilbert Ledoux, at her left, in tactful rotation, she caught Clyde's avid look upon her and, tossing her head ever so slightly, neglected to return it. The dinner was perfect and he complimented her on it, as the others did. But though he drank freely, he neglected his food, as he did the ladies on either side of him; Dorothée wondered whether his straying, sensual thoughts were as obvious to them as they were to her and, in deciding that they were not, also decided that she would not have cared, even if they had been.

The avid look followed her as she gave the signal for the ladies to retire to the drawing room, leaving the gentlemen to their cigars, their port and the stories customarily exchanged on such an occasion, which were reputed to be offensive in character to delicate feminine sensibili-ties. Dorothée recognized the resemblance of this gaze to the one Clyde had directed toward her on the occasion of his first visit; but it was more intense now and more purposeful. The cigars, the port and the stories consumed far less than the usual amount of time; but Dorothée's astonishment at the reappearance of her male guests was well feigned. Perhaps it would be pleasant to play a few hands of cards after they had finished their coffee, she suggested; it was too bad there was no game in which six persons could all engage at the same time—except poker, with which, of course, none of the ladies was familiar. But they could play whist at one table and bezique or cribbage at another and change partners frequently; perhaps such changes would actually add to the atmosphere of festivity, by making their friendly little gathering seem more like a large party.

Her suggestion was accepted, and so was the further one that, at the beginning, Mrs. Surget and Mr. Batchelor should play cribbage together, and that the others should make up the foursome of whist. It was very late before the logical rotation brought her and Clyde to the small table. As he held out her chair for her, he adroitly slipped a tiny piece of paper into her hand. He must have scribbled it very swiftly, sometime while places were being changed, for though she thought she had kept him under close observation and had, indeed, noticed how steadily he was winning, she had not seen him do any writing. But she already realized that his movements were sometimes almost uncannily quick.

It was ridiculously easy for her to dispose of the note in the bosom of her dress at the same time that she reached for the handkerchief which, though apparently so fragile, served so many useful purposes. But she had no immediate chance to look at her billet-doux, for she did not trust any aptitude she herself might have for legerdemain. Her guests had all gone, praising her party and wishing her a pleasant journey, before she dared look at the note. It contained only four words: *"You win, damn you!"*

She went about the main floor in a leisurely way, extinguishing all the lights except for one lamp in the hall, and that she dimmed until it shed only a faint radiance. She assured herself that the dining room and kitchen were not only orderly but empty. Belle and her cohorts had done their work well, but there was no question that now they were gone. Lastly, Dorothée tried the front door, not to make sure it was locked, but to be certain it was still on the latch. Then she went to her own room and undressed. She had bathed just before dinner, but now she sponged herself off again, with perfumed water, and lay down on her Empire bed to wait.

She did not have to wait long. She was sure that Clyde would not have left the hotel, where Gilbert Ledoux would have dropped him off on the way home, until everyone else in the building was asleep. Still, she did not see how he could have got back there, in Ledoux's gig, and then come down the river road on foot so quickly. But from the way he mounted the stairs and burst into her room, the swiftness with which he could move was again borne in upon her.

"You she-devil!" he said, and seized her.

His precipitance failed to frighten her, his assault gave her no feeling of outrage. As long as he had come back, after all, as long as her will had prevailed against his, this was all that mattered. In a way, his very violence bespoke the futility of his rebellion against her. Now that he recognized its futility, he meant to make her pay for it instead of paying for it himself and she accepted this as a tribute. It was not until at last they spoke together that she was conscious of hurt.

"This time," she murmured, clinging to him, "this time, you'll stay."

"Stay!" he echoed sharply. "What do you mean, stay?"

"I mean, of course, that we were destined for each other. I knew it from the first. It took you longer to find this out. But you must know it now, too."

"I know I'm leaving Louisiana tomorrow morning—this morning, rather. Before you have a chance to make me play the fool again. What happened before was just an explosion. I'm not blaming you for that, or myself, too much, either. But you planned and plotted for this. You laid a trap for me. I saw it and I walked into it just the same."

"If I hadn't thought you really loved me, at least that you would—"

He laughed, harshly. "You didn't think anything of the kind. You're not in love. You're in heat. And God! What a beast I've been myself!"

He was gone almost as precipitately as he had come. She had tried to keep him, throwing her arms around his neck and telling him that she was ready to give up everything for him, even her return to France, that she would not ask for marriage, for any kind of public recognition, if only they could be together in secret. To the same degree that she had flaunted her flesh to tempt him, she now groveled before him. He released himself and left her, without another word.

She had never forgiven him for treating her like a wanton. It did not occur to her that she had behaved like one.

Now, twenty-seven years later, the Marquise de Chanet stood before her cheval glass, in the home of the girl whom her son was about to marry, again "planning and plotting." Nothing that had happened since she left Cindy Lou had served to erase the memory of that passionate interlude or quench her desire for revenge. To all appearances, her life had been not only a pleasant one but a highly successful one. She had left Louisiana and reached France without any untoward incident and, upon her arrival in Paris, had installed herself at the Hotel Bristol; then she had presented her impeccable letters of introduction without delay and with gratifying results. The Marquis de Chanet, whom she met almost immediately, had, like Marchand Labouisse, fallen in love with her at first sight. Before the Franco-Prussian War had cast a blight over her second blooming, she had already remarried and was installed as the chatelaine of Monteregard, far out of harm's way. In due course of time, she had given the marquis the requisite heir to the title and the estates and he was properly grateful. Nothing else had ever been asked of her. She had been the recipient of benefits, not the bestower of them, for a long, long time. Nothing had marred the serenity of her existence or jeopardized the security of her position. And still she had not been content. There remained that ancient grudge to pay off.

And when at last she thought the time was ripe to do so, she had been thwarted. She was stuck in this dull New Orleans house, every bit as dull as Monteregard. She was forced to smirk and smile at countless ladies' luncheons, at countless pink teas, at countless stiff soirees. She had been in Louisiana for weeks and she was no nearer accomplishing the purpose for which she had come than when she landed there. Or so it seemed. . . .

And then, out of a clear sky, came a letter from Cary herself, only a few days after her mother and her husband had gone home. She was much better, not well enough yet to travel, of course, but sufficiently improved to be up on the chaise longue for a few hours each day. Since she could not come to New Orleans, she hoped very much that the Vincents and the De Chanets would come, as soon as possible, to Victoria. Savoie joined her in expressing this hope and in sending fond greetings.

 CHAPTER X

THE VINCENTS and their guests reached Victoria to find Lucy's unfailing thoughtfulness made manifest in many ways. She was not there when they arrived, but this was obviously a sign of delicacy rather than neglect; she had brought flowers from her garden, admittedly far superior to the one at Victoria, and the fresh vegetables in which Cindy Lou also excelled. A ham, cured at Sorrento and cooked by her favorite method, freshly caught fish, and one of her famous Spanish creams were all ready to grace the supper table; and in the most charming of notes, she wrote expressing her pleasure at having her neighbors home again, and said that she would call the next day to make plans.

She came late in the morning, on horseback, cool and slim in her linen habit, a gray veil floating from the small hat neatly set on her netted braids. She dismounted with the grace of an accomplished horsewoman and, patting her horse affectionately as she surrendered it to a waiting groom, looped up her long skirt and ascended smilingly to the gallery. Mrs. Vincent had settled herself there with her needlework —a garment she was making for the expected baby—directly after breakfast, and had taken it for granted that the Marquise de Chanet would keep her company there, though she had seen that, as usual, the Frenchwoman's restless hands were idle. The gentlemen were out on the plantation somewhere, Mrs. Vincent told the visitor, a little vaguely. Her husband had found a great deal that required his attention after his long absence and had needed Savoie with him. Pierre, who was seeing cane and tobacco fields for the first time, had been interested in joining his hosts; so of course Armande had been interested in joining Pierre!

She could well understand all this, Lucy rejoined; and she was sure that Aureline and the marquise would understand that Clyde was busy about the plantation, too, and that this was why she had come alone. She had, however, stopped by to see Cary on her way to Victoria, and was glad to report that her daughter continued to show improvement, and was hoping very much that her mother-in-law, the marquise and Armande would take tea with her late that afternoon. Dr. Bringier had advised her not to try to see many persons at the same time to begin with; but she hoped very much to receive the gentlemen as well, in a day or two.

Again, there were expressions of mutual understanding; but the marquise could not bring herself to put much enthusiasm into her acceptance of Cary's invitation. Tea had never seemed to her a very stimulating beverage; and the prospect of drinking it with four other women, one of them half sick and another sighing for her absent fiancé, was far from satisfactory. Neither did the only other suggestion which Lucy made hold out much promise.

"I do hope it will not be painful to you to see your old home in our possession, madame," she said solicitously. "I know I never could have gone into our Richmond house again, after it passed into alien hands! I thought that perhaps a *fête champêtre*. . . . Since the war prevented you from developing the garden, which must have been a great cross to you, I believe you might actually enjoy seeing how faithfully the original plans were carried out, as soon as it was possible to do so. Later, I could not resist the temptation of introducing a motif which would remind me of Sorrento, my mother's plantation on the James; so I added an herb garden and a sundial surrounded with roses. Later still, I became greatly interested in the cultivation of camellias, as I told you in New Orleans, and now a good deal of space is given over to them. But none of these additions has interfered with the harmony of the first design. At least, I hope and believe they have not."

"Indeed, they have improved it," Mrs. Vincent hastened to say. "Everyone who has seen it concedes that, thanks to you, the garden at Cindy Lou is the most beautiful one at any plantation hereabouts. I think your idea of a *fête champêtre* is delightful, Lucy, and very practical, too. Like our first reception in New Orleans for the De Chanets, it will serve to present a far greater number of our friends to them, at one and the same time, than would be possible at a dinner party. And of course the dinner parties will come later. You agree with me, I am sure, madame, that dear Lucy has made an excellent suggestion?"

The marquise had no choice save to agree, but again, real enthusiasm

236

was lacking in her acceptance, and she added that Mrs. Batchelor must not suppose, for a moment, that it would cause her any pain to see the interior of the house. On the contrary, she was most eager to do so. She understood that the former gaming room was now the library and that the gaming room had been moved to the ground floor. Since she herself had actually been the one to suggest, the first time Mr. Batchelor came to see her, that this change would be an improvement, she was naturally curious to see how it had worked out. And then the ballroom. . . . That, like the garden, had been in an unfinished state when she left Louisiana. As Mrs. Batchelor said, the terrible war had imposed so many hardships! But she had heard glowing tales of the magnificence the ballroom had eventually attained and of the splendid functions that had taken place there.

"Yes, Cary was very fond of dancing and of course we tried to give her every possible pleasure," Lucy said, gathering up the white chamois gloves which she had laid aside when the inevitable "small blacks" made their appearance. "But of course she cannot dance now, and I am afraid it would be a quite natural grievance to her if we gave a ball she could not attend. We are all making her our first consideration at present. I am sure you will understand that, too. Not that this will interfere with your seeing as much of the house as you would like, now that I know of your interest—indeed, our little fete need not take place wholly outside. I was simply thinking of what would give you the most pleasure. . . . Well then, I will tell Cary that she may expect you this afternoon? Around five? And I shall look forward to seeing you myself again then, too."

Her mount was brought around and she sprang into the saddle so swiftly that she hardly seemed to touch the horse block or the groom's outstretched palm. Then she was gone, with a final wave of her white-gloved hand, her gray veil floating out behind her. Mrs. Vincent, gazing after her with affectionate admiration, was amazed, on turning, to catch a look that was half sullen and half hostile on the face of her remaining guest. Mentally, she groped for the possible cause of this and, when she thought she had found it, tried tactfully to remove it.

"Lucy Batchelor is one of the sweetest women I have ever known in my life," she said, "and one of the most hospitable, too. But, as she told you, her first concern just now is for Cary and I am afraid the poor girl has really been very ill. I'm afraid, too, that the Batchelors have found it necessary to curtail their expenditures somewhat; they have been living very quietly ever since Cary was married, and have given no large, lavish parties. My husband knows more about their private affairs than I do, because he has often given them financial advice, upon request; but of course he has regarded everything he has been told as confidential. However, it is common knowledge that a great deal of Mr. Batchelor's fortune was tied up in steamboats, and the days of their prosperity, like the days of their glory, are gone, alas! forever. If he has been obliged to retrench, Lucy is the sort of wife who would help her husband in every possible way."

The marquise made a reasonably adequate rejoinder, saying she was sure she would enjoy the tea with Cary and the *fête champêtre* very much; also that she was sorry Cary was not as much better as she had somehow expected from the girl's letter, and that it was indeed unfortunate if the Batchelors had lost the greater part of their fortune. Then she changed the subject by talking about various characteristics of the Paris social season, which would soon be in full swing. Mrs. Vincent, whose parents had been among the wealthy Creoles that visited France every other year—a habit which the Vincent family had never acquired—began sighing for the delights of which her marriage had so early deprived her and which the marquise all too vividly recalled. She was glad Savoie and Cary had been able to enjoy these the previous year, she said, a little enviously, especially as, with the turn things had taken, it was doubtful whether they would be able to go abroad again very soon; and she was gladder still that Armande would be able to have these pleasures right along. But she herself was going to miss her daughter terribly. She could not bear to think of the parting which was now so close at hand.

"You will come to visit her. You will persuade your husband that he should make those biennial trips."

"I shall try. Yes, now that Armande will be in France, I believe he will permit himself to be persuaded. There never were a father and daughter more devoted to each other. In fact, our whole family is singularly united. As I said before, the parting will be hard indeed."

This was a new tack, even less to the taste of the marquise than Mrs. Vincent's previous outspoken satisfaction over Armande's engagement and impending marriage, which hitherto had included no dolorous references to separation. The titled guest found a pretext for retiring to her own room to rest briefly before dinner, and later, while the others were resting, she managed to have a few words with her son, to whom she confessed she feared the visit in the country was going to prove disappointing. He shrugged his shoulders.

"When we were in New Orleans, you kept saying you wanted to visit Victoria. *Eh bien,* now we are at Victoria and that does not suit you either."

"Of course I thought, from Cary's letter, that she was up and about at last; I did not picture her as still lounging around, nor did I suppose she had so much false modesty that she would decline to receive gentlemen *en negligé.*"

"As I understand the situation, it was not 'false modesty' which caused Cary to limit the number of her guests, but her physician's advice. I think undoubtedly she will ask the rest of us within a few days. Evidently, you and I did not interpret her letter in quite the same way. I thought she was making a real effort to sound cordial at the earliest opportunity, not that she was prepared to go in for immediate entertaining on a lavish scale. As for the 'dimmed glories' of Cindy Lou, I had suspected something of the sort, partly from chance remarks of Armande's and partly from Mrs. Batchelor's lack of jewelry, taken in connection with those remarks. She is exactly the sort of woman who would strip herself of every form of luxury, if she thought she could help her husband by so doing."

"Are you actually taking sides with these people against your own mother?"

Pierre, who had been sitting in a relaxed attitude, smoking a cigarette, extinguished the cigarette and rose. "This is the second time you have referred to 'those people' in an extremely disparaging way," he remarked coolly. "Yet they are exactly the same people whom you were so determined to visit, and you declared yourself delighted at my proposal to Armande. It seems to me it is your attitude which has changed, *ma mère,* and for no very sound reason. As for taking sides, I'm not conscious of doing that, either for or against anyone. But I'm ready to repeat what I said once before: that I think Mrs. Batchelor is one of the most charming women I ever met in my life. However, the more I see of her, the more I am persuaded that the word 'charming' is inadequate to describe her. She has charm, certainly. But she also has character. She commands my utmost admiration and respect."

To the best of Dorothée's recollection, her son had never spoken to her in this vein before, and she found it anything but pleasing. It was particularly distasteful to hear Lucy Batchelor's charm extolled by Pierre, immediately after listening to Mrs. Vincent's fulsome praise about her sweetness; and the marquise did not care a fig about the character of this paragon. She was already in a bad humor when the ladies set out, that afternoon, for the mock Monteregard in Mrs. Vincent's phaeton; and the tame visit which she had foreseen did nothing to improve her mood.

The day was warm and pleasant, and Cary received her guests on the gallery, where she lay on a glorified hammock, clad in a negligee of shell-pink chiffon and cream-colored lace, which was extremely becoming to her. Her mother poured tea for her, using an ancestral silver service which, along with the heirloom jewelry, she had turned over to Cary on the occasion of the girl's marriage; and an impeccable maid passed beaten biscuits stuffed with ham, toasted English muffins spread with butter and marmalade, and dark rich fruitcake. Cary drank her tea *à la Russe,* with lemon in it, and said she had learned to like it that way—in fact, she highly recommended it to the others; and if she ate less than they did, she did this inconspicuously. When they had finished, she said she had thought the marquise might be amused by the gazebo, which was something of an incongruity in Louisiana; she was sorry that her garden was nothing much to see as yet, but the marquise would find that the one at Cindy Lou would more than make up for any disappointment at the new Monteregard; and she was really rather proud of her house, which she realized neither Mrs. Vincent nor Armande had seen since her return from France. She was sure they would want to inspect the improvements she had made in it, now that she was settled there, and she hoped the marquise would also enjoy going through it. Her mother would conduct them, if they were perfectly sure they did not care for any more tea. . . .

The marquise was bound to admit that the interior of the house, no less than the exterior, was extremely pleasing. The furnishings throughout were extremely tasteful, many of them old English pieces, which, like the heirloom jewelry and the fine old silver, had obviously come to Louisiana via Virginia; but these had been supplemented with comfortable modern upholstery, bright rugs and soft hangings, which mitigated their austerity. All in all, greatly to her disappointment, the marquise could find nothing which did not bespeak taste, culture and tradition. She had no choice, when the ladies returned to Cary's hammock after their tour of inspection, but to echo the Vincents' enthusiastic approbation of everything they had seen, even though she did so rather halfheartedly. However, she could not resist the temptation of adding she was sorry Pierre had not been with them.

"But of course you will come again," Cary said cordially. "I shall be able to assure Dr. Bringier that your visit has not tired me in the least, that, on the contrary, it has given me the greatest pleasure. So I am sure he will let me make the next one more of an occasion, even if he is a regular old dragon. He is spacing his calls farther apart, now that I am so much better; but he will be looking in tomorrow morning, all ready to rebuke and warn, as usual! When he finds nothing to rebuke me for or warn me about, he will leave defeated. And then I shall send you a little note, asking you all to hasten over. Meanwhile, please give my regards to Pierre, and say that I am looking forward to seeing him."

She rose and walked to the top of the steps with them, looking even more lovely while she moved than while she was lying in her hammock. "I'm so glad you like the house," she said, glancing proudly around her. "However, I have just been telling Father that I thought I'd like to have a supplementary flight of steps built at the rear of the wing back of the drawing room. It would be so convenient for taking the baby straight from the nursery through the garden to the gazebo for his outings without bringing him into the front of the house, when there was company, or when there was any special reason for saving time. Since Father built the house for us, and I told him it was perfect just as it was, I didn't like to make even a slight change in the design without consulting him. But he agreed with me that it's an excellent idea. What do you all think?"

Though there were different degrees in the shade of interest that was expressed, everyone agreed that the idea was a good one. As Cary was saying good-by, Savoie rode up, shouting a welcome, and Cary persuaded them to wait until he could join them on the gallery. He hastened to do so, embraced his wife warmly and his mother and sister affectionately, and then laughingly asked the marquise if she would permit a similar salute. He apologized briefly, and without any show of real concern, for his appearance, saying that he had been in the saddle practically all day and that it was very warm in the fields already; he thought Cary was extremely tolerant to say nothing about the disastrous effect his dirty riding clothes might have on her elegant laces, and put his arm around her again as he spoke, gazing at her with loving pride. Really, he had never seen her in anything more becoming than that negligee—he would be sorry himself to have it ruined. And wasn't it wonderful that she was so well on the road to recovery? He put the question generally, apparently without expecting any special answer or caring much whether he had one or not. His complete and rapturous satisfaction with his wife was transparently evident. Contemptuously, the marquise set him down as uxorious; she doubted whether anyone could shake the faith of such a fond fool.

Savoie himself brought the promised invitation from Cary the following day. Dr. Bringier had been obliged to admit that she was getting better and better. She was going to sit up for supper with Savoie that very evening, for the first time in nearly two months. She was still not too sure of herself, the earlier part of the day, or she would suggest midday dinner on Sunday, so if they would all come Saturday night instead. . . . It would be just a very informal evening meal. But she would look forward to it. . . .

"Which is more than I shall do," the marquise told her son. "But at least I am thankful we will not be obliged to sit through one of those deadly Sunday dinners, after Mass, which have not a single redeeming feature, unless they have changed very much. And I doubt it. This whole region seems to be in the same state of desuetude as when I left it."

"Well, if you want to go back to New Orleans, you have only to say so. It is my impression that Mrs. Vincent does not care any more about the country than you do."

"No. . . . But her husband keeps harping on the need for his supervision, and there is another couple to whom separation never seems to occur! Then there is that silly *fête champêtre*—I suppose we would be considered insufferably rude, if we left before it took place. We have not heard anything more about it, but no doubt all sorts of elaborate preparations are being made to serve fruit punch and ladyfingers to large numbers of the local gentry."

"You say 'another couple.' Were you mentally comparing the Vincents to the Batchelors?"

"Yes. Have you any reason to consider the mental comparison inept?"

"I have not had the pleasure of meeting Mr. Batchelor yet. And after all, Mrs. Batchelor did leave, not only her husband, but her sick daughter, in order to bid you welcome in New Orleans. As for the *fête champêtre,* I do not believe the refreshments for that will be as insipid as you are indicating, either. But, even if they are, the gardens, by all accounts, are well worth seeing. And, as I have said before, I find Mrs. Batchelor's company delightful in itself."

Decidely, these tête-à-têtes with Pierre were getting her nowhere and neither was anything else. Savoie had explained his father-in-law's failure to call immediately by the exigencies of work on the plantation, to which Lucy had previously referred, and by the fact that Cary was still so dependent on Clyde's company that he spent every moment he could spare with her; no one seemed to cheer her as much as her father, Savoie said, quite without any note of jealousy, but rather as if he were gratified at such filial appreciation. These explanations seemed to the marquise mere pretexts. She was sure that Clyde was deliberately avoiding her, and had begun to tell herself that he did not intend to come at all, that he was actually afraid to face her, when she saw him from her window, walking across the lawn, toward the house, deep in conversation with Mr. Vincent.

She would have recognized him instantly, anywhere. He was a little heavier than when she had last seen him, but not much, and his added weight was becoming. It gave him an air of stability well suited to a substantial citizen, and he carried it off well; if such had been the current fashion, he could still have worn a gold watch chain dangling across the white expanse of a figured waistcoat. He was dressed country style now, which of course was suitable; he no longer affected urbanity, but preferred to be included among the local gentry to whom she had referred so scornfully. The sun was shining on his bare head, and she could see that his reddish-blond hair was as abundant as ever; probably there was a good deal of white in it, but, if so, it did not show at this distance, and doubtless would not show at close range, any more than his wife's did. His color was ruddy, his step brisk; all in all, he looked a good ten or fifteen years younger than his slender, stooped companion. Every now and then the two men stopped, and while Mr. Vincent fumbled with a handkerchief, Clyde Batchelor slapped his leg with his riding crop or drew patterns with it on the grass. The marquise could see that his hands, like his face, bore no telltale signs of age; evidently, if the rumors about his fallen fortunes were true, he had found some compensations for his lost wealth, since everything about him bespoke contentment and well-being. When he and his host had almost reached the house, they stopped for the third or fourth time and their colloquy became more animated; then they suddenly turned and hurried off in the opposite direction. Just then, the marquise heard a knock at her door.

"Missis done send me to tell you de phaeton waitin'," announced the servant who entered in response to an impatient order.

"The phaeton?"

"Yassum. Missis done ask me if you clean forgot you'all gwine take coffee with Miss' Surget dis ebenin'."

Yes, of course, that would have to be the day they were going, by appointment, to visit Amy Surget, whom the marquise had so ardently hoped she would never have to see again, but who had called, promptly and correctly and—also promptly and correctly—invited them to her house! If the marquise pleaded a sudden headache and said she could not go, after all, then she would have to remain in her chamber all the rest of the evening; if she went out with Mrs. Vincent, Clyde would undoubtedly have left the premises before they returned. Either way, she would miss him. She snatched up her parasol and left the room, slamming the door after her.

On her return, her son greeted her with smooth speeches. Mr. Batchelor had been to call, but had not come immediately to the drawing room, because Mr. Vincent had persuaded him to go to the warehouse first. The last of the previous year's perique crop did not appear to be curing properly, and it seemed wise to talk over the matter on the scene of the trouble, the better to get at the cause of it. Mr. Batchelor regretted that he had missed the ladies, but he would look forward to seeing them at his daughter's house on Saturday evening, and at his wife's *fête champêtre* the following Tuesday. Meanwhile, Pierre had greatly enjoyed meeting him. The deserted males had drunk juleps, made by a recipe of Mrs. Batchelor's, and these had been excellent. Also, Mr. Batchelor had proved a very interesting conversationalist—in fact, the most interesting Pierre had met since coming to the United States. His viewpoint was far more cosmopolitan than that of most Louisianians, possibly because he had traveled a great deal more than most.

The marquise flounced away from her son and went back to her room, slamming the door again. Then she decided to have the headache after all. It proved so severe that she did not recover sufficiently to leave her room until it was time to start for Cary's supper party. Meanwhile, she received a letter from her husband, which had been delayed by the necessity of forwarding. He had secured passage on the

S.S. *Nicholai II* from Bordeaux and expected to be in New Orleans within a fortnight of the day he had written. This meant he would be arriving there the latter part of the following week.

Decidedly, she did not have much time to lose.

The Batchelors had arrived at little Monteregard before the Vincents and the De Chanets, and were already in the pleasant drawing room, drinking vermouth. This time, Cary was fully dressed and was wearing one of the most attractive models she had purchased in Paris—a white grosgrain silk trimmed with coquettish little black velvet bows. Both her mother-in-law and the marquise were quick to observe that her figure had not altered in the least, that indeed her dress fitted her a little too loosely; but this, they both decided with equal swiftness, was to be expected—it was too soon for any real change in her form and she had lost weight during her illness. But she looked bewitchingly pretty, and the black velvet bow which quivered above her pompadour gave the finishing touch of chic to her costume. She and Savoie welcomed his parents and sister affectionately and their guests with appropriate cordiality; then Lucy and Clyde came forward and, quite as naturally, Lucy kissed dear Aureline on both cheeks, as the latter expected of her, pressed the lovely hand of the marquise and extended her own for Mr. Vincent and Pierre to kiss in turn. Clyde had never followed French fashions in hand kissing, and no one who knew him expected it of him any more; after all, he had never been to France, he was not a Creole and he had married a Virginian. It therefore seemed perfectly logical to everyone but the marquise that he should shake hands heartily with both men, bow, somewhat formally, to the older ladies and give Armande the brief, affectionate hug of a privileged friend. Savoie poured out more vermouth, as he broached the subject of his hunting dogs, which had not yet been brought over from Victoria; Clyde began to talk with Mr. Vincent about getting out more lumber from the swamp, for the "improvements" Cary wanted; while Lucy outlined the developing plans for the *fête champêtre*. The men then drifted into a political discussion about Senator McKinley and the sugar tariff, while the ladies, led by Mrs. Vincent, reverted to her favorite subject of the wedding. It was typically provincial, the marquise thought, again contemptuously, that the sexes should separate in this way at a social gathering. She would have supposed that Mrs. Batchelor, with her much-vaunted tact, Mrs. Vincent, with her pretentious urbanity, or Cary, with her admittedly greater sophistication, would have prevented such a division. As for Clyde, he was either deliberately avoiding her, or else he was stupidly following the custom of the countryside. . . .

The same impeccable maid who had served tea a few days earlier announced that supper was ready. In spite of Cary's deprecatory statement that it would be "just an informal evening meal," the marquise was again obliged to admit to herself that she could find no fault. The supper was bounteous and imaginative and it was perfectly served, while the delicate porcelain, the heavy silver and the well-rubbed mahogany all showed to great advantage in the soft candlelight. The table was circular, and around it conversation became more general than it had been in the drawing room; but it was still impersonal until Mrs. Vincent once more steered it to her favorite subject of the wedding. It was also she who announced that the marquis was already on his way to the United States, and that, therefore, the visit to Victoria must be curtailed. Of course they would all stay until after the *fête champêtre,* which dear Lucy had so thoughtfully arranged; but as soon as possible after that, they must be on their way to New Orleans. They hoped the others would join them shortly thereafter; so many pleasant prenuptial parties had been planned in Armande's honor by her friends.

"My love, I must remind you that Savoie and I should not both be absent from the plantation, for any length of time, at this season. . . . I tell my wife this every year," Mr. Vincent remarked, turning from her to the company at large. "I have been doing so for at least a decade —ever since Savoie was old enough to share with me the responsibility of supervising the crop. And still it makes no impression."

He spoke with proper playfulness, so that the observation would not seem like a public rebuke; still it was quite evident that he was in earnest. Clyde instantly followed up his statement with a similar one.

"Since I haven't a son to whom I can relegate authority, I'm in even a worse fix than you are, Lamartine. I'm looking forward to the day when my grandson will take over for me, but unfortunately that's a long way off. I'll get down to the wedding, of course, but it'll be a case of going to town one day and coming back the next. Lucy and Cary are planning to stay a little longer, but that's so Cary can rest up before and after the great event. We can't have this girl giving out on us again, now that we've had such a struggle to get her on her feet and have been successful at last."

He reached for his stepdaughter's hand and pressed it affectionately, his smile bespeaking the same solicitous fondness as his gesture. Really, he was as doting in his way as her husband in another, the marquise told herself impatiently. Releasing Cary's hand with a final pressure, Clyde made another unwelcome announcement.

"By the way, Mrs. Vincent, it's more than kind of you to urge us to stay with you, but you'll have your house—as well as your hands— full with this wedding. Lord knows, I'll never forget the upheaval we were in when Cary got married! And Lucy says you'll need to set aside at least two rooms, just for the wedding presents—which I can well believe, when you're marrying off such a popular daughter!" This time he reached for Armande's hand and, though the gesture revealed none of the tenderness which had been so apparent when he took Cary's, it bespoke sincere friendliness and good will. "So I've written the St. Charles for rooms. . . . Yes, Lucy said you'd protest; just the same, she agreed with me it was best I should do so."

Mrs. Vincent was, indeed, protesting and calling upon everyone else to do the same. While the clamor was at its height, the marquise sat silent, reflecting that she was the only woman at the table to whom Clyde had not spoken directly and warmly. As if he had read her thoughts, he looked straight across the table toward her, meeting her eyes squarely. *So you think I'm afraid of you,* the look seemed to say. *Well, you're wrong. I thought, before you came, that I was going to be. But I'm not, after all. I've found out that you're not a menace to my happiness any longer. There's nothing you can do to hurt me, no matter how hard you try. What's more, you're not a temptation; you're not even an attraction. You're a vindictive, venomous, vain, middle-aged woman whose evil thoughts show in her face, who dyes her hair to hide the white in it, and puts on too much rouge, and starves herself to keep slender without realizing that hunger makes her haggard. The reason I haven't talked to you is because there's nothing I want to say to you or to have you say to me. The reason I haven't looked at you is because I hate the sight of you. It's as simple as that. I told you twenty-seven years ago that I was through with you and you wouldn't believe me. But you'll have to believe me now.* Aloud, he said, "I should think you ladies would like to hear something about weddings in France. None of you've ever seen one. I'm sure the marquise could give you all kinds of fascinating details. I'd enjoy hearing about them myself. What about you, Lamartine?"

When Mrs. Vincent gave the signal for departure, the marquise was still trying to fight down her futile rage, at least to the point where it would not betray her; but she was seething within. She had only one crumb of consolation, and this was in the reflection that at the *fête champêtre* Clyde could not possibly elude her; she would ask him to show her the gardens and, as her host, he would not be able to decline. But again she was outdone. She had hardly arrived at Cindy Lou when she made the contemplated suggestion; but it was still so early that no other guests had arrived and Lucy was not preoccupied with her duties as a hostess; Clyde seemed to take it for granted she would accompany them. He had never learned the names of half the things his wife had planted, he said; Lucy would have to tell these to her visitor herself. It was too bad the camellias had now gone by; they were really the greatest glory the garden had, except the roses, which were fortunately in full bloom. No doubt she had a rose garden at Monteregard? Cary had not said much about the gardens; would the marquise herself tell them what species of plants she had found most successful?

"I suppose Cary had more to say about our so-called *forêt de légende*," the marquise observed. "That seemed to intrigue her more than the gardens—that and our famous grottoes. Before she finally left, she had explored all those quite thoroughly. Of course, Pierre was delighted to act as her guide."

"Yes, she did tell us about those. They must be remarkable. No wonder she was fascinated—and of course your son was a most ubiquitous host. No one could doubt that he would be, even after meeting him casually. . . . Ah, Lucy! You forestalled me! I was just thinking that perhaps the marquise would condescend to wear one of your tea roses. Is that Amy just driving up? I believe it is, but I cannot see who is with her. I suppose we must think of getting ready to receive."

So the stroll had come to an end because of that wretched woman, who was certainly always in the wrong place at the wrong time, and afterward there was no chance for another ramble. Clyde received with his wife, and quickly revealed that he had considerable *savoir-faire* as a host. Though he singled out no one for special attention, he gave every guest a sense of personal welcome. And, like Cary's supper party, the *fête champêtre* as a whole left nothing to be desired from the viewpoint of acceptability. The marquise found that the beauty of the garden had not been overpraised, and that her slurring remark as to the probable character of the refreshments had been quite undeserved: the punch was made with champagne, and bourbon was also provided in great abundance. There were a dozen different kinds of cake and as many sorts of sandwiches, besides chicken salad, cold ham, daube glacé, shrimp aspic, jellies and creams and, indeed, everything that could make a cold buffet complete and attractive. A Negro orchestra, stationed on the small second-story balcony at the rear of the house, played and sang picturesquely and melodiously; and as the brief twilight faded, candles were lit in the hundreds of Japanese lanterns strung among the trees. The evening was a perfect one, and the guests lingered on and on; but the marquise was all too well aware that this was due to a sense of general enjoyment, rather than as a special compliment to her; and when Mrs. Vincent, for the second time, gave an inopportune signal for departure, the marquise voiced a complaint.

"Mrs. Batchelor promised me that I should see the interior of the house. Naturally, I'm interested in doing so. After all, it was my home for nearly ten years! And I have not been inside the door!"

"Lucy is still in the receiving line—really, it is a great compliment, the way her guests are lingering! But I do not feel it would be proper for us to outstay everyone else and, in any case, she will be exhausted after the fete is over. I'm sure Clyde will insist that she should go to bed immediately. He takes the greatest care of her—it is certainly very touching! And, as you see, he makes a practice of receiving with her. . . . But perhaps Cary would take you through the house—I will ask her if she feels able to do so. Of course, I would not consider it delicate to suggest that I should do the honors."

Cary would be glad to show the marquise the house, she said unhesitatingly, when the question was put to her. She had come to the *fête champêtre* rather late, and she had neither stood in the receiving line nor done much walking about; but she had managed to give the effect of the helpful daughter of the house by shepherding small groups to pleasant places under the trees, where wicker furniture was cozily arranged, and by having refreshments brought to guests there. The friends who surrounded her when Mrs. Vincent came up were laughing heartily over some sally which they protested they could not repeat for her benefit because it was much too modern in tone. Nevertheless, they welcomed the older lady warmly to their midst, and she agreed to stay with them while Cary was gone.

"Since we're on ground level now, would you like to begin with that floor and work your way up, or would you rather do it the other way around?" Cary inquired. As she spoke, she picked up the scarlet parasol which had been unfurled to an immense size as long as the sun was out, but which was now lying beside her on the settee. She was in white again, a lingerie dress this time, its scalloped flounces and eyelet embroidery scarlet edged, a wide scarlet sash around her secretive waist. To the marquise, there was something arrogant about her appearance; she seemed almost to be flaunting her unimpaired figure and her ready resumption of the gaiety upon which her illness was said to have had so sobering an effect.

"By all means let us begin with the ground floor. I'm especially eager to see the gaming room. Perhaps your father has told you that I suggested its present location," the marquise replied, assuming something of the arrogance which she was imputing to Cary.

"Father didn't. He hardly ever talks about the dim, distant past. But Mother said you mentioned it yourself, the first day she called. Well, here it is. I hope you will think the results were worthy of your idea."

Cary opened the door and drew back, so that the marquise might precede her. Dorothée sauntered in and glanced around her. Then she shrugged her shoulders. "I see that it's changed in more ways than in location," she observed. Her tone was not actually aggrieved; at the same time, it suggested that she did not consider the changes an improvement. "The original furnishings seem to have been rather relegated to the background—not that the new center table isn't handsome in itself. But it rather crowds the room, don't you think so?"

"I never thought it did. But perhaps that's just because I've been used to seeing it here so many years. And then, I've an affection for it

248

because Father designed it himself, and because we've all had such good times playing games around it."

The marquise shrugged slightly again. "Those river prints are rather crude, aren't they?" she remarked, moving closer to the wall and inspecting them critically. "Hardly worthy of that magnificent armoire which, I am glad to see, is unaltered. And that painting of the *Lucy Batchelor*—is it the work of some local painter?"

"No. As a matter of fact, it's an Emil Bott. He made a special trip to Louisiana in order to do it. Father and I like that very much, too. But of course there are lots of people who don't admire Bott's special technique. . . . Would you care to see the wine closet and the store-rooms? I'll send for the keys if you would. Father used to pride himself on having all the best vintages, but that was mostly for the benefit of my winebibbing friends. He and Mother are both naturally abstemious, so I don't know whether they've bothered to restock since my wedding, and I do know we cleaned the place out pretty well then. However, Mother's sure to have rows and rows of preserves—figs and kumquats and everything else you could think of."

"Thank you. I should not like to put you to the trouble of sending for the keys."

"It's no trouble. But of course I realize that, compared to the *caves* at Monteregard, our wine closet wouldn't look like much, even at its best; and I can imagine that jams and jellies wouldn't be exactly in your line. Shall we go on to the library? Perhaps that will interest you more than the gaming room—after all, when you suggested the location for one, you more or less automatically suggested the location for the other, didn't you?"

The marquise agreed that they might logically visit the library next, and this time expressed herself as delighted with what she saw there: the great globes were especially noteworthy; but everything about the room had *cachet*.

"I think so, too," Cary answered. "Of course, the library's primarily Mother's creation—as you know, there was none when she came here, so this room was practically bare after the furniture for the gaming room was moved. Father and Aunt Amy did the best they could, getting the house ready for her, but they knew she'd rather take charge of this herself. It reflects her personality, doesn't it? Of course, she's got no end of *cachet*."

Cary walked over to the window and looked down into the garden. She was holding her scarlet parasol, and it was conceivable that she was using it as a means of support while she walked. But it did not have this effect.

"She and Father are really a wonderful couple, aren't they?" she inquired. "Just look at them, madame! Don't they make a picture standing there, with the big dark tree behind them and the bright

249

flowers blooming all around them and the light from the lanterns shining down from overhead? I don't wonder no one wants to go home! Everybody loves them. And perhaps it sounds like a silly thing to say, but everyone *respects* them. They've stood for so much in the community. . . . Well, I didn't mean to get sentimental, but somehow, seeing them as they stood there. . . . Shall we go on to the drawing room?"

"I understand that and the dining room have hardly been changed at all. Suppose we leave those for later inspection, if there is time. I'm really more interested in seeing what has been done upstairs."

"Just as you like. Of course, there are only four upstairs chambers—strange in such a large house, isn't it? Why, as you've seen, I have as many in my little one! Do you care which room we visit first?"

"Yes. I should especially like to see the one on the right at the rear."

"Just as you like," Cary said again. "That's always been the guest room. The other rear room's normally Bushrod's—my brother's. But he never was here much, even before he married, and he hasn't been back at all since my wedding. So that room's virtually another guest chamber. As far as that goes, mine is, too, now. But I'll go on thinking of it as mine, and I know Father and Mother will, too; I'm sure they'll always keep it just as I left it and call it 'Cary's room' and not put guests in it unless there are so many they can't be accommodated elsewhere. I'll show it to you afterward, and the view you get of the river from there, in case you've forgotten how beautiful it is. I love the river, just as Father does. . . . But this is where you wanted to go first, isn't it?"

Again Cary threw open a closed door. There were subdued lights in the room and pale flowers—evidently it had been readied for the possible convenience of some guest at the *fête champêtre* who might wish to retire briefly in order to "fancy up." But it had the telltale look of a room that is seldom used and never really lived in. The house was in shining order throughout, but elsewhere it lacked the sterile immaculacy of this one. The marquise drew back with a little cry.

"But this is entirely changed! My beautiful Empire furniture is not here! Where was it put?"

Cary shook her head. "Why, I don't know! Those convent beds have been in it ever since I can remember. I'm sure I'm not mistaken, I've heard so many persons comment on them. I don't need to tell you that most typical Louisiana beds are immense, that generally, only nuns slept in narrow ones, and that when a convent was dismantled, and other people bought those, they were regarded as a curiosity. . . . Well, of course sometimes 'youth beds' were narrow, too—my own was, for that matter. It was just as pretty as it could be. I've kept it and I'm glad I have—I'll enjoy seeing it in use again. But it's years since I've slept in it myself. I have a spool bed in my room now."

"A spool bed! You mean that cottage type Jenny Lind is supposed to have favored?"

"Yes. I happen to favor it, too. Perhaps it's an odd taste, but I do."

"And that magnificent Empire furniture—it simply disappeared?"

Cary shook her head again. "I'm sorry, I don't know. It certainly isn't here. The storerooms are cleaned religiously every year, and I've seen my 'youth bed' put in the sun, along with the other pieces that aren't in use, and then put carefully back in storage again. There isn't any Empire furniture among them. And, as you'll see for yourself, Bushrod's bedroom set is quite good Mallard and Father and Mother have a superb Seignouret."

"Then I shall inquire from your father what has become of my valuable possessions, and ask to have them returned, since he so misprized them."

All the frustration of the past weeks suddenly burst its bounds. Standing on the threshold of that room which had been the scene of her most voluptuous delights, and which was now so cold and conventual in its austerity, the marquise was beside herself with rage and beyond watching her words. Cary answered her coolly.

"Are you quite sure you want to do that? I mean, Father bought everything from you outright, didn't he—the plantation with all its equipment and the house with all its furnishings? If there were some things that he didn't care for or couldn't use, there was no reason why he shouldn't dispose of them, was there?"

"There was every reason why he should not make kindling wood of the furniture in my chamber and put the beds of nuns in its place! It is a personal insult! I shall tell him I found it so, no matter how hard you try to stop me."

"I shan't try to stop you. I shouldn't think you'd want to, that's all."

"That's all! That's all! Let me assure you, my fine young lady, that is not all! You have been bragging about your mother's 'cachet,' you have told me how greatly 'respected' your father is in this community. Well, your mother did not have enough cachet to keep her fiancé faithful, and your father would not be so much respected if I told all I know about him. This mutual show of conjugal devotion is very touching, I admit. But I could pull the props from under it in one minute. There would be no forgiving and forgetting then in your mother's case, I promise you. And as for your father, he would be glad to slink away in shame!"

She paused, breathlessly, and glared at Cary as if defying the girl to put an end to her torrent of speech or to prevent her from dashing down the stairs and denouncing her host in his own garden. The fact that Cary continued to look at her coolly and speak to her calmly increased her fury to the point of frenzy.

"I'm not sure I follow everything you're trying to tell me," the girl

251

said quietly. "It's hard for me to believe you want to proclaim that something shameful happened in this room, while you were living here, which involved my father. Because that would involve you, too, wouldn't it? I shouldn't think any woman who's passed, more or less, for a lady would want to destroy the illusion by announcing that she's not. As I've said, Father's never talked much about the dim and distant past, and anyway, he isn't the kind that would ever kiss and tell. But I suppose various kinds of women were mixed up in his early life—there are in most men's early lives, aren't there? Even so, they know the difference between the various kinds, don't they? I mean usually. Perhaps Father was mistaken about thinking you were a lady, at first. But he never, never would have made a mistake like that about Mother."

"If you think I'm going to stand here and let you insult me—"

"I'm not trying to insult you. And I've told you already, I'm not trying to stop you from doing anything you want. But I believe it's a kindness to try to make you understand that Father thinks the sun rises and sets on Mother's head. He always has; he always will. That doesn't mean he mightn't do things he was ashamed of afterward—especially if he had a lot of provocation. But he wouldn't ever slink away in shame any more than he would kiss and tell. If you really do want to go out in the garden and shout to everyone who will listen that he made kindling wood out of your bedroom furniture, why don't you do it?"

As if she were actually encouraging the marquise to take such vehement action, Cary closed the door of the guest room and moved in a leisurely way toward the stairs. There was no question, now, that she was leaning on the scarlet parasol and that she was glad of its support. But for all that, her words continued to come easily and quietly.

"There's one thing you're right about though," she said. "That's the part about forgiving and forgetting. Of course Mother wouldn't *forgive* Father for something that happened more than twenty-five years ago. You don't forgive people you love. You just love them. And you don't have to force yourself to forget something that doesn't matter anyway. Besides, if you think this announcement you want to make would come as a surprise or a shock to Mother, perhaps I ought to warn you that I believe you're wrong. Naturally, she's never mentioned the matter to me, but if I'm not terribly mistaken, she's known all about it for years. I didn't know it until a few weeks ago, when I overheard Belle talking about you to her daughter Titine, who's my maid now. They thought I was asleep and they didn't notice that my bedroom door was open, either. Probably something accidental like that happened in this house, too. I know Belle wouldn't purposely do anything she thought would make Mother unhappy. But Negroes have a sort of sixth sense about love affairs, especially illicit love affairs—what they don't know, they guess, and they're awfully good at guessing, particularly when they combine it with a little eavesdropping. And they do gossip among themselves about what they've guessed, or overheard, or seen, when no one knew they were looking. And sooner or later, someone overhears *them*. . . . Well, shall we go downstairs? Evidently, there's nothing more you want to see here."

The marquise gripped the newel post. "So your mother is sacrosanct," she sneered. "But what about you? Is it conceivable that, in your case, a man might have some difficulty in deciding what kind of a woman you were?"

"Why yes," Cary answered unhesitatingly. "Yes, it's quite conceivable. Only, in my case, he'd find out that even if I gave a wrong impression at first, I really was a lady after all. Because you see, that's what I decided I wanted to keep on being. Of course I was born one, and that's an advantage to start with. For a while I thought maybe such an advantage wasn't important. But fortunately I found out my mistake before it was too late. And who do you suppose helped me to do it when no one else could have? Father! He was quite insistent on the point. So that—" Cary concluded, her foot already on the first step, "will give you some idea of what he thinks of strumpets."

 CHAPTER XI

THE HOPE which the marquise had expressed to her son of an early return to New Orleans, after the *fête champêtre,* had been repeated, without overmuch finesse, to her hostess, in whom she found a ready listener. Yes, the sooner they were off, the better, Mrs. Vincent agreed heartily; it was all very well for Lamartine to keep harping on the necessity of overseeing the crops at this season; men never realized how much was involved in preparing for an important wedding. Besides, Savoie and Mr. Batchelor were quite capable of looking after the land, between them; now that Victoria and Cindy Lou were, to all intents and purposes, one and the same plantation, the situation was entirely different from that which had prevailed before the two families were allied by marriage; and if Lamartine did not agree with this reasonable viewpoint, he could stay by himself at Victoria, where the servants dear Lucy had trained so well were quite capable of taking care of him. For that matter, he could stay with Savoie and Cary at the new Monteregard; after all, the *lune de miel* was now long since over, the household well organized; the *jeune ménage* should not object to a visitor. . . .

With the two ladies in such complete accord, plans had been made for them to take their departure the day following the *fête champêtre*. Armande and Pierre were to accompany them; and Mr. Vincent had raised no objection to the prospect of a period of comparative solitude at Victoria—in fact, his wife had somewhat indignantly gathered that he would enjoy it. Cary had also inferred that Savoie was far from displeased at the arrangement; although he had not actually said so, she had guessed, without too much trouble, that the more he saw of the De Chanets the less he liked them, and that his devotion to his mother and sister was suffering from the strain of listening to the interminable discussion of nuptial preparations. She had never seen him in better spirits than when he took his customary affectionate leave of her before going out to ride the crops, the morning after the garden party; and his good humor was enhanced by the consciousness that Cary seemed more like herself, in every way, than she had in a long while. Her malaise had apparently disappeared completely; her color was good and so was her appetite; she rose soon after her husband, joined him in a substantial breakfast and chatted with great sprightliness about the success of the *fête champêtre* over their hominy grits, cakes, cuite and coffee. Savoie was whistling as he went down the steps of the gallery, and he turned back twice to wave a gay farewell to Cary, before he finally cantered out of sight.

When he had gone, Cary found time hanging rather heavily on her hands. It was only a matter of minutes for her to set her well-oiled household machinery in motion; after that, there was absolutely nothing of urgent nature for her to do. Though she was now feeling so well again, she was debarred from riding, and she had also been warned to undertake no further strenuous exercise of any kind for the present. Nearly all the flowers in her garden had been sent to Cindy Lou, the day before, to supplement her mother's in the scheme of decoration; it did not take her half an hour to gather and arrange those which were left. Her mother would be resting, she knew, at her father's insistence, and Clyde himself would be out with Savoie. Her mother-in-law and Armande and their guests would be in the last throes of packing; she had said good-by to them all the evening before, in order to make sure she would not be a hindrance rather than a help at the last moment. There were no other neighbors near enough to make mere morning visiting feasible and Savoie would be expecting to have her with him by dinnertime. Suppressing a slight sigh, which came from boredom rather than actual discontent, she took her sewing basket and went out to the gazebo.

Thanks to Lucy's teaching, she was an expert needlewoman; but fine sewing had never held the attraction for her that it had for the

women of her mother's generation. She stitched away rather intermittently, laying down her handiwork every few minutes to look at
the satisfactory, but unstimulating, scene before her, and trying to
refrain from daydreaming because such dreams seemed so persistently
to take her in a direction from which she was resolutely trying to
withdraw. At the same time, she could not help wishing that some
unexpected diversion would present itself, though if she had been able
to guess the form this diversion would take, she would have tried to
suppress the wish with the same perseverance that she was trying
to suppress the daydreams. While she was growing increasingly restless because of unbroken monotony, she became conscious of approaching footsteps, and looked up from her sewing to see Pierre coming
toward her down the garden walk.

She sprang up, her genuine surprise mingling with an unwelcome
sense of shock and a still more unwelcome pang of pleasure. Swiftly
and involuntarily, as she had so often done before, she compared his
air of sophistication and accomplished ease to Savoie's more ingenuous
and less urbane manner. At the same instant, she thought for the first
time, with gratification, that Pierre looked far more like his father
than like his mother. To be sure, he had her fine high coloring; but
the two men had the same graceful, though wiry, build, the same
proud carriage and the same inescapable charm. The smile with which
Pierre now greeted Cary, in response to her startled and stammered
welcome, was dazzling in its effect. She tried to tell herself that this
was merely the result of extraordinarily white teeth beneath a closely
clipped but very black mustache.

"Why, Pierre! I thought you had gone back to New Orleans!" she
exclaimed inadequately. In her sudden rise, she had dropped her workbasket, scattering its contents in every direction. Before replying, he
stooped over, retrieving the strawberry-shaped emery, the tomato-
shaped pincushion, the scissors simulating a tiny bird with a long beak,
the jewel-topped gold thimble, the various packets of small needles
and the many spools of fine thread. Having restored all these objects
to their proper places, he handed her the basket with a sweeping bow;
she did not notice until afterward that he had not replaced her handiwork.

"I had expected to go," he answered imperturbably. If he had noticed her confusion, as she was sure he must have, he gave no sign
of this; and he did not make even an indirect reference to the fact
that he had gathered up the small belongings which had been strewn
over the floor of the gazebo because of her precipitate movement.
"However, this morning my mother sent out word, through the maid
who took in her tray, that she was completely prostrated by migraine,"
he went on. "It was quite out of the question that she should travel,
it was even impossible for her to drink black coffee. This sudden in-

255

disposition was, of course, somewhat upsetting to the general program."

"Has Dr. Bringier been called in?" Cary inquired, again quite inadequately.

"No. My poor mother declined to consult a physician. I went in to see her, after her message had been delivered, and gathered that she was suffering from a *crise de nerfs* as much as from anything else. She not infrequently has those, sometimes on very slight provocation, if I may say so. This time it appears that the sight of her old home was too much for her delicate nervous system to support without injury. Personally, I do not see why it should have upset her. I have never heard her express the slightest affection for Cindy Lou, or any regret because she had sold it—indeed, I had always gathered that your father's purchase of it was more or less providential. And certainly, he and Mrs. Batchelor have maintained it beautifully. I was charmed with it, myself."

Cary, who, by this time, had begun to recover her composure, made no immediate reply, and nothing in her face revealed either sympathy or surprise. Indeed, her expression had suddenly become singularly noncommittal.

"As a matter of fact, I am charmed by everything connected with this region," Pierre continued. Cary had not asked him to sit down, but he seemed to take it for granted that she would be glad to have him do so, and had seated himself beside her; it was then that she noticed, for the first time, the piece of fine cambric which he was still holding in his hand. "So I am very glad of the pretext, which my poor mother's indisposition gives me, for lingering in the vicinity a little longer."

"But I thought Armande had made an appointment with her dressmaker for tomorrow."

"She had. She left on the morning train. Since obviously she could not go alone and since her mother, without showing herself remiss as a hostess, could not leave mine, Mr. Vincent most reluctantly accompanied his daughter."

"Surely Armande must have taken it for granted that you would accompany her, too!"

"By no means. A man who reveals himself neglectful, as a son, is a very poor prospect as a husband on whose sympathetic devotion a wife can unfailingly count. Armande required practically no argument to convince her of this. She understood my position almost before I had explained it to her: I could not leave my mother unassuaged in her sufferings; my duty to remain with her was very clear."

"I don't see why. You've said that she didn't want a doctor, and that quite often she has slight nervous upsets which, obviously, you don't take very seriously."

"Ah! I should have been more careful not to sound contradictory. But somehow, I thought that while Armande required very few explanations of my attitude, you would require none at all."

"I'm afraid I'm not as subtle as you give me credit for being. I still don't see the slightest reason why you shouldn't have gone on to New Orleans with Armande today. From what you've said, I should think your mother would probably be well enough to follow tomorrow or the day after. In the meanwhile, if she doesn't even feel like drinking black coffee, no doubt all she wants is to lie still in a dark room with a handkerchief wrung out in cologne water on her forehead."

"But I have told you quite candidly that I was charmed with this region, that I welcomed a pretext to linger longer in it."

"Yes. But of course you're even more charmed with Armande than you are with this region. What's more, you're engaged to her."

"Your second statement is correct. Your first leaves something to be desired in the way of complete accuracy. I have never thought you were subtle; indeed, I have always found your naïveté one of your most appealing attributes, Cary. But surely you're not such an ingénue that you require an explanation as to the real reason that I was glad to stay over a day at Victoria without the pleasant, but somewhat handicapping, presence of my fiancée and her father."

Pierre looked at her with a smile that was even more engaging than the one with which he had greeted her. But this time Cary did not think of it merely as dazzling; she also thought of it as dangerous. She had seen that look on his face before, when they were riding together in the enchanted forest, toward the gypsy camps and the wooded slopes leading to the grottoes which fringed the river that widened into the Blue Pool, where a girl who had lost her lover had drowned herself, long, long ago. . . .

"I don't believe I'm altogether an ingénue," she replied, with a calmness she was very far from feeling. "I don't believe you mother thinks so, either—in fact, I'm very much afraid that her *crise de nerfs* may be partly due to some remarks which I made yesterday. Since you're such a devoted son, I doubt whether your regard for me would stand up under the knowledge of just what those remarks were. In the light of them, and of your mother's illness, I don't think it's fair for me to detain you here. I think it would be far better for you to go back to Victoria and see if there isn't something you can do—what was the expression you used?—to assuage her sufferings."

As she spoke, Cary made a movement as if to rise and bring their interview to an end. Pierre leaned forward and, still holding the piece of cambric in one fine, flexible hand, laid the other over both of hers.

"Cary, I need assuagement myself. I need your assurance that you understand."

"Of course I understand," she retorted, withdrawing her hands from his reach. "A girl doesn't have to be a complete nitwit, even if she is an ingénue. And I've just told you I'm not even that."

"You're by no means a nitwit and, if you prefer, I will concede that you're not an ingénue, either," he replied, with surprising quiet. He did not try to take her hands again. However, something about the very fact that he refrained from doing so made his speech more compelling. "But I am more and more convinced that you do not understand—at least, not what I want you to."

"Very well. Then I will listen while you explain. But I would like to go on with my sewing while you do so. Will you please give my work back to me? I'm afraid I didn't thank you properly for picking up the other things. Perhaps that's why you've kept on holding the cambric—to remind me of my manners."

"Not at all. I have been holding it because it was yours, something with which you were intimately connected and—as such—precious to me." He spread the cambric over his knees, scrutinizing it for the first time. "I've been holding it all crumpled up," he remarked apologetically, smoothing it out as he spoke. "I did not realize what it was—I thought probably a chemise for yourself. Now I see that it is a baby's dress. Is that why you want it back, Cary? So that you will be reminded, while I am talking to you, that you are going to have a baby?"

"No. I'd rather keep busy, that's all. I don't need any reminder that I'm going to have a baby—or that I'm married to one of the best men in the world."

"But you are reproaching yourself because you feel that sometimes you forgot about your married state and your husband's great qualities, while you were visiting at the chateau?"

"Yes. I reproach myself very much for that. I always shall. But at least I don't intend to have any more reason for self-reproach on that score."

"I don't intend that you shall, either. But neither do I intend to leave you without convincing you, if I can, that what happened between you and me last year was important to me, that I didn't regard it like one of many pleasant amorous episodes and nothing else—nothing more."

"It isn't in the least essential that I should know how you regarded it, Pierre."

"Indeed it is. It is very essential to me, as I shall try to explain, if you will give me a chance. And I believe it is essential to you also. I believe you will be much happier in the future if you know that I never thought of you as a light of love—not even potentially. I thought of you—and still think of you—not only as one of the most desirable, but as one of the most companionable, one of the blithest, one of the

258

loveliest women I have ever met in my life—a woman whom I should
have been proud to have for my wife, if she had been free. I'm speaking in deadly earnest now, Cary. Don't you believe me?"

She turned her head away, without answering. Again he leaned
forward and took her hands and, this time, she did not withdraw
them.

"Please look at me, Cary. Please answer me. I asked you if you
didn't believe me."

"You make me believe you—almost," she whispered, still without
looking at him.

"That isn't enough. I want to make you believe me—not almost, but
wholly. Because I swear that what I'm telling you is true. If I swear
it, won't you believe me?"

"Ye-e-s, I think so."

"And won't you admit that if you do believe me, you'll be happier
than you've been in a long while? Happier than since you knew you
were going to have a baby? Happier than since you learned Armande
and I were engaged? Happier than you've been at all since you knew
there wasn't any escape for you and since you began to think that I'd
held you cheap?"

"Yes," she said again. But this time, though she still did not turn
to look at him, it was not because of hesitancy and doubt, but because
there were tears in her eyes which she did not want him to see, even if
he knew they were there.

"Then I can be very candid with you, which is what I hoped. I did
not look on you as a light of love; I would have asked you to marry
me if you had been free. But since you were not, I did think that, in
time, I might persuade you to become my mistress. I do not mean one
of many loose women with whom I had transient affairs; I mean
what used to be called, in the days of royalty, a *maîtresse en titre,* a
great lady who was completely loyal to her lover, whose station and
standing were understood and, strange as it may seem to you, respected. There are still many such women in France, even if that
special designation is gone. Indeed, there is hardly a Frenchman of any
standing who has not had, or does not have, such a woman in his life.
It is more or less taken for granted that he should. And it does not
create a scandal, as I now understand it would—and does—when such
an arrangement is made in the United States."

"And do you mean to tell me that the mistresses of these prominent
men are still respected, too?"

"Yes, in a way."

"It must be a very strange way. . . . What about their husbands?"

"Well, of course the husbands. . . ." For the first time, Pierre himself hesitated. "Perhaps we had better not try to go into the husbands'
side, in such cases," he went on a trifle hurriedly. "After all, I was only

259

trying to interpret the lovers' side—the *real* lovers, not the incorrigible libertines. So I will repeat that, when I came to Louisiana, it was with the hope that I could persuade you to become my mistress—my dearly beloved, highly regarded mistress. And I had hardly landed when I was told you were *enceinte*."

Again he smoothed the baby's dress across his knee. "It was a blow, I admit," he said, "a very great blow. Not only to my love, but to my pride. I had thought of you as waiting to welcome me, of counting the days until we could meet again."

"I was," Cary said in a low voice. "I shouldn't have been, but I was. I was even poring through old lawbooks, trying to find out whether I couldn't discover something in them that would prove Savoie had cause for divorce."

Pierre released her hands, and though he did not actually draw farther away from her, somehow he gave the effect of doing so. "Ah, divorce," he said in a changed voice. "There I must differ with you, Cary. If you had been free when I met you, as I have just told you, nothing would have made me happier than to have you for my wife. But marriage with a divorcée—especially with a woman whose husband had divorced her for cause—that would have been quite impossible for me."

"So my father said. He said that was the way you'd feel about it," Cary remarked scornfully.

"You discussed the matter with your stepfather? I'm rather sorry you did that, Cary. Inevitably, he must have formed a very low opinion of me. And from the way you spoke just now, I gather that he was fairly successful in turning you against me. I was conscious, of course, that you were avoiding me, but I thought that was because— well, because of Armande. Let me finish what I started to say. I was counting the days until we could meet again, and I was confident that when we did I could persuade you to become my mistress. I thought we would arrange to see each other, very discreetly of course, but constantly and—intimately. Then I thought you would persuade your husband to bring you back to France, in the near future, for another long visit, and that thus we could resume our liaison. I thought this delightful arrangement could go on and on. It never entered my head that you would already be with child—Savoie's child. Of course it should have. I can see now that the wonder is you weren't *enceinte* much sooner, that you did not either have a baby while you were still in France, or hasten your return so that you might have your *accouchement* at home. This present pregnancy of yours might well have been your second. It is evident that you are destined for the role of *mère de famille,* not of *grande amoureuse.* I was very blind not to realize that in the first place. And when my eyes were opened, I confess that I was very angry—unreasonably, with you; logically, with myself. And it was quite natural that when I was in such a frame of mind, I should succumb very easily and quickly to the charms of a girl like Armande."

"I see," Cary said, still scornfully.

"There is no reason why I should not say that she fell in love with me at first sight, since she and her mother have both said the same thing themselves," Pierre went on, disregarding the scorn this time. "And of course, that was not only very flattering to me, since she is such a beautiful and accomplished girl, but very soothing to my pride. I responded instinctively to her affection."

"Just the same, I don't suppose you tried to seduce her."

"Certainly not. A gentleman does not make improper advances to his fiancée, when she is a *jeune fille bien elevée*. It would be offensive to his principles. Besides, what would be the point? She will soon be his bride in any case. Why should he deliberately lessen the triumphant joys of his wedding night by anticipating them?"

"I don't know any reason why he should. But then I don't know, either, why a gentleman should deliberately set out to make another man's wife disloyal to her husband. And I don't believe, Pierre, there is anything you can say that will make me understand, or that there's anything to be gained by continuing this conversation any longer. I hope you won't try to see me again, either, no matter how long your mother's illness detains you. In fact, I shall tell the servants to say I'm not at home if you call. Now, if you'll please give me back my baby's dress. . . ."

She rose and stretched out her hand. As Pierre surrendered the piece of cambric, he pressed her fingers, but he found he could not continue to hold them unless he did so forcibly. He looked at her reproachfully and shook his head.

"It grieves me very much to part from you like this," he said reproachfully.

"It grieves me, too," she answered. But her voice was not reproachful. It was still scornful. "However, we are not saying good-by to each other for good," she added. "I shall be seeing you again at your wedding."

It was universally and enthusiastically agreed in New Orleans that the wedding of Pierre de Chanet and Armande Vincent was the outstanding social event of the spring season.

For the occasion, golden ornaments from the cathedral treasure had been brought forth and set on the high altar, where they glittered in the radiant candelight. The archbishop, always a majestic figure, seemed to have achieved added stature and dignity as he stood at the entrance of the sanctuary, clad in full pontificals, awaiting the arrival of the bridal procession, which advanced toward him to the strains of Meyerbeer's "Prophète." First, clad in their multicolored

261

medieval costumes, marched the two huge Swiss guards, who acted in their official capacity only at the most important ceremonies. Then came the twelve ushers, in formal evening dress, their *glacé* gloves and stiff shirt fronts in complete harmony with the waxen tone of their white boutonnieres. They were followed by the twelve bridesmaids, in white *mousseline de soie,* their "half veils" confined with wreaths of white roses and garlands of roses linking them together in couples. Next came two little flower girls, also wearing "half veils" and wreaths of roses, but dressed in sheer mull instead of *mousseline de soie*, as being more suited to their tender age, and scattering petals from gilded and beribboned baskets, instead of carrying garlands. They in turn were followed by the bride, on her father's arm, a coronet of diamonds encircling the rose point lace which fell in creamy cascades over her shoulders and flowed out behind her to the full length of her court train; and last of all, in accordance with time-honored custom, the groom's mother, escorted by the groom, and the bride's mother, escorted by the groom's father.

Though the stir which the De Chanets had at first created had begun to subside somewhat by the time the wedding took place, the appearance, in juxtaposition, of the old marquis and the young one gave rise to whispered remarks that both were certainly looking their polished best. The ushers had all appeared correctly attired to the last detail, until Pierre came up the aisle; now, by comparison, not one of them seemed perfectly turned out. As for the marquise, her costume left nothing to be desired in the way of chic. But the great surprise, the really startling sight in the cathedral, had been the appearance of Cary Page Vincent.

Naturally, the news that she was *enceinte*, at last, had spread, and there had been much murmuring—some of it sympathetic, some of it satisfied—because, in consequence of her condition, she would not be in the cortege and this created a vacancy for a "real Louisianian." It had also been vaguely assumed that if she did come to the wedding at all, she would be wearing some sort of a loose wrap, no matter what the weather, and that she would be seated inconspicuously. The ladies who had been busily ticking off time on their fingers had somehow overlooked the fact that she could not yet be far enough along to have a noticeably altered figure. The more general assumption had been that she would not put in an appearance at all. According to rumor, she had made a great deal of fuss about her morning sickness—as if nine out of every ten women did not have it and some of them practically every year, during the early stages of their married life! But then, everyone knew that Cary Page had always been an *enfant gâté*. . . .

She entered the cathedral on her husband's arm. The organist was already playing the chords which presaged the beginning of the special music for the cortege and everyone was on the alert for its arrival; therefore, all eyes were on the center aisle and the older and more hidebound contingent among the guests gave an audible gasp. Instead of some nondescript dark-hued sacque, Cary was wearing a dress which was almost exactly the color of her hair. This, in itself, was a drastic departure from custom. Baby blue was traditionally the favored color for blondes; they might, occasionally, switch to a very pale pink or a very delicate green, for the sake of change; but yellow was something that they never, never wore! Yet, here was Cary wearing it, one might almost say flaunting it, in the face of the public; and strangely enough, the effect, if it had not been so startling, would have been distinctly pleasing. The dress was made with enormous sleeves, and, below them, Cary's wrists and arms were encircled with glittering bracelets. The bodice was cut surplice fashion, with a V-shaped neck just low enough to set off a heavy gold necklace to great advantage; and the folds of the satin were so arranged as to display the shape of the breast in the most effective possible manner. If Cary's figure could have been said to possess a fault, heretofore, this was because it had lacked the allure of full-blown femininity; now the curves of her bosom were beautiful. Moreover, she had achieved a "straight front" unparalleled in New Orleans for its perfection, and her many-gored skirt flared out from her trim waist, catching every variation of light as she moved. Two small yellow wings, evidently the plumage of some bright bird, fastened together at their base with a bow of yellow ribbon, constituted her headdress; the feathers were poised delicately over her hair, creating the illusion not only of added height but of swift and effortless motion. They made the laden hats worn by other women look top heavy and grotesque. She was carrying a large bouquet of yellow roses, from which streamers of golden gauze fluttered; and, as she progressed, she glanced brightly from side to side, smiling and bowing to acquaintances. When she finally reached the front pew, she slipped her arm easily from Savoie's, releasing him so that he might hasten to the rear of the church and join the cortege; then she sank gracefully to her knees, after laying her bouquet on the seat beside her. Her bracelets tinkled pleasantly as she crossed herself. She knelt for some moments, and this position afforded an excellent view of her flawless profile and equally flawless figure. Finally she rose and, picking up her flowers again, turned in the direction of the aisle, just as the archbishop emerged from the sacristy and the organist began the march from "Le Prophète."

"What an entrance!" a cousin of the Vincents', who was seated slightly to the rear, whispered to his wife. "If you ask me, Savoie's wife has stolen the show."

"I didn't ask you," she answered in an annoyed undertone. "If you ask *me*, I think all that was in the worst possible taste—making herself so conspicuous at another girl's wedding! Even if it hadn't been for her condition—"

"No one would have known about her condition if a lot of old wives didn't seem to think it necessary to shout it from the housetops. As for being conspicuous, a girl with looks like that can't help it. She'd stand out in any crowd. I don't wonder she's been such a belle, ever since she let down her skirts and put up her hair."

He was not able to say any more, at the moment, because the cortege was already halfway up the aisle; his wife was nudging him and various other women were casting venomous glances in his direction. For the most part, they had not been able to hear his words distinctly; but they had experienced no difficulty in getting the drift of his remarks and they resented it, just as his wife did. *The jealous old harpies,* he said to himself, resolving to seek Cary out at the reception and feast his eyes on her when she would not be gliding past him so rapidly that he could hardly get a good look at her. But he found it more difficult than he had foreseen to carry out his resolution. A number of other gentlemen had apparently been inspired by the same idea, as they watched her progress up the aisle, and he found her already surrounded, the center of a convivial group which was sipping champagne and nibbling at *petits pâtés aux huitres* and squares of *massepain.* Cary had a champagne glass in her hand, and every other moment or so was raising it to acknowledge a toast; whenever she did so, she made some witty little remark or one that gave the effect of being witty because of the arch, amusing way in which she said it. The Vincents' cousin tried hard to catch her eyes and succeeded—all too briefly; Cary smiled at him and raised her glass and made one of her droll little speeches. The newcomer felt very much encouraged; but almost immediately there was another claimant for her attention, and presently he decided it was no use, this was the way things were going to be as long as the reception lasted. . . .

As he turned away, he was rewarded by a tidbit of gossip which he had not previously heard, and which temporarily did something to compensate for his disappointment, as far as Cary was concerned. It had leaked out that in spite of all its glittering appearances, the wedding had not been a complete success from the viewpoint of either the groom or his father. The old marquis had hoped very much that his daughter would let bygones be bygones and attend her brother's wedding with her husband and their two girls. His *daughter!* But surely Pierre was an only child! Yes, the only child of a second marriage. But it seemed the old marquis had been married before, to the Princess Asceline de Herbemont, who had died when her baby girl, whose name was also Asceline, was only a few weeks old. So, as the widower did not feel equal to rearing an infant of such tender age, the dead wife's parents had taken charge of the poor little thing and

264

she had remained with them at their chateau in northern Indre. They had regarded their son-in-law's second marriage as a *mésalliance,* and had never forgiven him for contracting it. On the other hand, his delight over the birth of Pierre had been so great that he had made no immediate effort to regain possession of his daughter; and the present marquise had said quite frankly that she did not want to be saddled with a half-grown stepdaughter, or to be snubbed by some decadent old aristocrats who imagined themselves to be better than she was. So matters had drifted along: little Asceline had never gone back to Monteregard as a child or a young girl; and, eventually, she herself had married, a certain Etienne d'Ambly, who also possessed a very fine chateau. After her marriage, she had been respectful to her father, agreeable to her half-brother and civil to her stepmother when they met by chance in the same social circles; but she had never invited them to her own fine establishment in Morbihan. Doubtless she had so often heard them disparaged that she had ended by believing it would be better if the estrangement, already of such duration, should be prolonged indefinitely. Tardily, the old marquis had tried to bring about a *rapprochement*; now that it was too late, he realized how much he wanted the companionship of his daughter and how greatly his granddaughter might have contributed to the happiness of his declining years. Moreover, Pierre was very proud of his sister's aristocratic connections and superb property. He had done everything he could to persuade her that their father needed her; and all he could do was write a letter, wasn't it, to convince her that she and her family should come to his wedding. However, all his efforts had been in vain; the princess had sent Armande a correct note and a handsome gift; but she had remained quite unmoved by the pleas that her attendance would add prestige to the marriage ceremony.

The Vincents' cousin, like the friends who related all this, relished the flavorsome gossip to the full; but it did not prevent him from hankering for a chat with Cary, and he lingered in her vicinity, hoping for better luck than he had had before. However, he seemed doomed to disappointment, for eventually Savoie came up and said that Armande was ready to cut the cake and wanted Cary to be there when this was done. She linked her arm through his and went off with him, calling something back over her shoulder which the Vincents' cousin did not quite catch, but which he gathered was very gay, like everything else she had said, and perhaps the least bit risqué, too, from the way it was received by those who did hear it. He also wanted to see the cake cut, so he wedged his way into the dining room; but it was very crowded, and he could not get anywhere near the table himself, though he could catch a glimpse of Cary, for her yellow satin dress and the wings in her hair made her outstanding among all the girls in white *mousseline de soie*, with wreaths of white roses on their heads. Some of the "half veils" were torn now, and some of the wreaths were askew, and the general effect was not as ethereal as it had been in the cathedral; even the bride, upon closer inspection, was not such a dazzling figure as he had previously thought. Of course, since he was a Vincent, he had a feeling of pride in her rose point— no other New Orleans family owned so much of it; and as he happened to be something of a lapidary, in an amateur way, he could appreciate the value of the diamond parure—it was seldom indeed that the groom's present to the bride included a tiara as well as a necklace, a brooch, earrings and bracelets. But the truth was that rose point in such immense quantities lost its light, lacy look, and that a seven-piece parure was also too much of a good thing. The radiance which Cary seemed to emanate had remained quite undimmed, however. It gave luster to all its surroundings.

And then suddenly the luster was gone, for Cary had disappeared. . . .

It was Savoie who persuaded her to slip away unobtrusively and to go back to the St. Charles, without waiting for the bride and groom to take their departure. Neither her mother nor her stepfather made any effort to hurry her, though when she complied, pleasantly, with Savoie's anxious advice, Lucy returned to the hotel with her and helped her undress. The bodice of the yellow satin, which fastened down the back with large hooks and eyes, was lined with stiff taffeta, rigidly ribbed with whalebone inside, and was kept in place, over the binding of the separate skirt, by a two-inch waistband of strong webbing, which fitted very snugly and which was also secured by hooks and eyes. As Lucy managed, with an effort, to undo the last of these fastenings, she peeled the bodice away from the corset cover which concealed the "straight front" corset and tossed it on the nearest chair.

"It won't be but a minute now, darling. Start undoing your corset cover yourself."

Obediently, Cary untied the pink bow of the baby ribbon run through the eyelet embroidery which formed the border of the corset cover and started on the buttons which went from the bow at her bosom to the waistline. Meanwhile, Lucy had unhooked the skirt of the yellow satin, and Cary had stepped out of it, so that her mother could lay it over the back of the chair where the bodice had already been tossed. After that, there were the strings to four starched petticoats to untie. But at last Cary stood clad only in chemise, corset and ruffled drawers.

"I'll cut the lacing, darling. It'll be quicker."

"No, don't. I'll take my drawers off, too, if you don't mind. Then I can unclasp the corset all right."

The drawers fastened with a string, too. This was tied in a hard knot and it took their combined efforts to loosen it. But finally the frilled drawers dropped to the floor. Never, since she was a little girl, except during her recent period of invalidism, when Lucy had been obliged to bathe her, had Cary's mother seen her daughter as nearly nude as she was now, and to both of them, the exposure of her thighs resulted in self-consciousness. To lessen this, they simultaneously endeavored to unclasp the corset. Just as they succeeded in doing so, Cary fell to the floor in a dead faint.

"Naturally, the corset was much too tight for her," Lucy told Clyde, when he came back to the hotel, several hours later. In accordance with the wishes which both Cary and Lucy had expressed, he had remained at the wedding reception until after Pierre and Armande had taken their gay departure, in a shower of rice and confetti. "That webbing belt, too. . . . If dresses could only be made in one piece! Perhaps they will be, someday."

"Yes, perhaps they will," Clyde answered abruptly. He crossed the floor and opened the door which separated his room and Lucy's from the one which Savoie and Cary were occupying. He knew that Cary would be alone, for Savoie was still at the reception, discussing with his parents the great success of the wedding and sipping one last glass of champagne, when he, Clyde, had left it. Clyde thought that, possibly, Cary might still be awake, that he might have a chance to talk with her. But she had sunk into the profound sleep of complete exhaustion, and lay with her head cradled on her arm and her golden hair bright against her pillows. He closed the door noiselessly and turned back to Lucy.

"She won't have to wear those tight, stiff clothes again until after her baby's born, will she?" he asked. Then, without waiting for an answer, he added, "But I tell you, Lucy, it was one of the proudest moments of my life, when I saw her come sailing up the aisle of the cathedral in that gold satin dress."

"I know it was," Lucy replied. And neither of them suggested that the tight corset might not have been the only reason for Cary's fainting fit.

 CHAPTER XII

THE LATTER part of Cary's pregnancy proved as painless and pleasant as the first part had proved troublesome and trying. True to her mother's prediction, none of its distressing symptoms lasted beyond the quickening, and most of them had ceased to cause her much discomfort before then. She carried her child well, with almost no real disfigurement until she was near her time; up to then she merely appeared heavier than before and the added weight was not unbecoming. Her color was good, her expression cheerful and the charm of her manner had never been so marked; if it lacked a little of its former sprightliness, it had also gained in gentleness and grace; and if her step was less light and rapid, her carriage had more dignity. Clyde, watching her with loving pride, told himself that she was growing more like her mother every day; and though Lucy, when he said the same thing to her, answered a little sorrowfully that she had never qualified for the comparison, he retorted that he was talking about mental and spiritual attributes, not physical ones.

Meanwhile, however, Savoie's adoration was permeated with anxiety. He kept meeting men whose wives' *accouchements* had been accompanied by horrors which they described in great detail, or who had actually died in childbirth; the thought that Cary might suffer such anguish and that he would be responsible for it—the fear that he might altogether lose her—haunted his days and nights. When her pains began, Dr. Bringier's assurances that everything was proceeding satisfactorily, and that a rather slow labor was often really preferable, in the case of a first child, to one that was more rapid, only served to infuriate the tormented husband.

"Why don't you *do* something for her? Once in three hours you come out here, rubbing your hands as if you were immensely pleased about something and say, 'Everything is perfectly normal and I think that in about three hours more. . . .' I sit here with my eyes glued to the clock, and when the three hours are up, you come out here and say the same thing over again! Don't talk to me about a *first* child! I tell you this is going to be an *only* child! I wouldn't have Cary go through this again for anything in the world!"

The doctor turned away with a slight smile, but refrained from making the answer which, twenty years earlier, had been his stock reply under such circumstances. He glanced toward Clyde, expecting that the older man would return his look in kind; but Clyde, though he refrained from expostulation, was obviously quite as wretched as Savoie.

He's telling himself, for the first time, he's glad his wife never had a child by him, the doctor thought sagely. Nothing will ever convince him that there's no hell she wouldn't willingly have gone through if she could have given him a son. His train of thought was interrupted by a muffled cry which, though quickly smothered, reached the room where they were sitting. Savoie bounded from his seat.

"Can't you give her chloroform? Can't you put an end to that torture by taking the baby with instruments?"

"Yes, of course I can give her chloroform, and I will, by and by—

in whiffs, when she's further along and really needs it. But I'm not going to until she does—it would simply slow things up. And of course I could use instruments. But I'm not going to risk tearing her to pieces and injuring the child unless and until I'm sure she can't get her baby into the world herself. And I think she can. I've told you half a dozen times already that she's coming along finely."

He left the room abruptly, slamming the door after him. A few minutes later, it was reopened by Lucy, who regarded the two miserable men seated there with compassionate understanding.

"Dr. Bringier tells me he doesn't seem able to convince you that everything's going just as well as possible," she said. "He thought if I told you I wasn't at all worried, it might help to reassure you. And I'm not. Of course, Cary's suffering. She has to, you know. But she's taking it all splendidly, doing just what the doctor tells her to and helping herself along. I think it would be a relief to her, though, if she could scream once in a while without being afraid you'd hear her. Why don't you go out in the gazebo for an hour or two?"

"*An hour or two!*" Savoie echoed. "An hour or two *more?*"

"I should think it would be at least that long," Lucy said calmly. "She wasn't in her second stage when I came in here and until she is—"

"What do you mean, her second stage?"

"I think perhaps I'd better let Dr. Bringier explain to you, later on, if you don't know. You may go in and see her for a minute, if you want to, but I really believe—"

"Of course I want to go in and see her. I'll probably never see her alive again."

Savoie rushed out of the room, slamming the door even harder than the doctor. Lucy put her arm around her husband's shoulder.

"Do get him outside. I don't suppose you could persuade him to play cribbage, or chess, or do anything except worry and rage, but if you could it would be the best thing in the world for him."

"I don't see how I could do anything like that myself, but I'll try, if you think I ought to."

"I do think so. Thank you, darling."

She lingered a moment or so longer, laying her cheek affectionately against his. Then she left, not hastily and noisily, as the others had done, but in her usual serene way. Clyde, making a determined effort, pulled himself together and, after a little rummaging, found a crib and some cards, a chessboard and some chessmen, and carried them out to the gazebo, where he laid them down on one of the seats while he returned for a table. Next, he went to the kitchen, where he found the entire household staff gathered together in a state of idle but gloating expectancy, the enjoyment of which was enhanced, rather than lessened, by the consciousness of Cary's prolonged travail. Somewhat curtly, he ordered drinks and sandwiches brought to the gazebo, adding that Dr. Bringier and Mrs. Batchelor might be calling for coffee at any time, and that he hoped it was not necessary to say there should be broth on the stove and custard in the cooler. Then he went back to the gazebo. When Savoie rejoined him, mopping his brow and cursing, Clyde had the table set up, the chessmen in place and the drinks already poured.

"Here you are," he said, handing his son-in-law a glass whose alcoholic content was practically undiluted. "When you've swallowed that, see if you can't beat me, for once in your life. Want to bet on it? And want to bet that Lucy'll be bringing us good news before we've finished the game?"

Savoie did not want to bet, he did not want to play either chess or cribbage, he did not even want to drink; in fact, his hand shook so that he could hardly hold the glass. But somehow, Clyde managed to prevail. When Lucy finally came to them, they did not hear her light step until she was halfway across the garden. But as they leaped to their feet, upsetting the table and spilling and scattering everything on it in their haste, she called out to them in a glad voice.

"A beautiful big boy! And Cary's as right as rain! She'll want to show her baby to you yourself or I'd have brought him with me."

Lucy had not exaggerated in her joy; the baby was undoubtedly a fine specimen and Cary a radiant mother; instead of being exhausted by the ordeal through which she had so triumphantly passed, she seemed exhilarated. To be sure, once she had proudly displayed the newborn child, lying in the curve of her arm, to her husband and father, she had fallen into a deep, profound slumber which lasted so long that Savoie, hovering entranced near her bedside, became impatient for her awakening. He felt he could not wait to tell her that he adored her and that she had made him the happiest of men. It did not matter that he had told her this countless times already; that was before she had made his happiness complete, for he worshiped her now as the mother of his son. Words would be lacking to express all this, yet he yearned to try; when she finally opened her beautiful eyes, smiling up at him, he could only stammer out his rapture.

He had supposed she would seem very fragile to him for a long time, he had feared that he would hardly dare to touch her, and that even if he did dare, he should not, because she would still be very weak and very resentful, since he had been the cause of all her suffering. He thought he must be very gentle and very patient. But as she lay in bed, with her golden hair spread out over her white pillows and the baby at her full, beautiful breast, she seemed to him more vital, as well as more desirable, than ever before; there was nothing about her to suggest frailty. It took him days to grasp the fact that childbirth had done her no harm, that, instead, it had given her physical fulfillment, and that far from resenting maternity, she was glorying in it. He felt that some miracle had come to pass when he found that she shared his sense of ecstatic thanksgiving.

"Why do you keep telling me how much you owe me?" she asked him one evening, jestingly. She had made such a rapid recovery that she had dispensed with the monthly nurse ahead of time and begun to train Titine's sister Tudie to help her with the baby; and although Dr. Bringier was extremely conservative in such matters, he had not tried to confine her to her room as long as he did most of his patients. He had, however, wrung a promise from her that she would breakfast in bed, rest every afternoon and retire immediately after supper, threatening her with the greatly dreaded "loss of milk" if she did not compromise with custom at least to this extent. She had consented, on the condition that Savoie would sit beside her and chat with her after supper "until a normal bedtime"—a condition she need hardly have imposed, since he never willingly left her side. "Don't I owe you just as much as you owe me?" she went on laughingly, stretching out her hand to him.

"I don't know what you mean, darling," he answered, pressing the extended hand fondly.

"Well, Larry's wasn't a virgin birth, you know. You had something to do with it, too."

They had agreed to let Clyde name the baby, since he had never had a son of his own, and Clyde, of course, had asked Lucy to make the choice. After some hesitation, she had suggested Lawrence. It did not sound like a Louisiana name, she knew, and she would understand perfectly if, on reflection, Cary and Savoie would rather have one that did. But it had been a name of frequent and important occurrence among the Peytons and the Carys, as it had among the Washingtons. Her favorite brother, the one who had been killed leading a cavalry charge at Manassas, had been the last Lawrence Cary, and he had never had a son of his own, either. There had been a Lawrence Peyton in the Revolution and a Lawrence Cary who was a colonial governor. In fact, the first Cary to come to Virginia—the one whose bride had been given the diamond brooch by the King of England—was named Lawrence, too. She had hoped that she herself. . . .

Everyone had instantly agreed that Lawrence Cary Vincent would be a perfect name for the new baby and he was baptized, with due pomp and ceremony, in the parish church of St. Michael's at Convent. The religious ceremony was followed by a large reception at the new Monteregard, during the course of which the baby, clad in robes of ancestral lace, was shown off to a host of admiring beholders. All the guests agreed that this christening was a most auspicious occasion on which to gather friends and relatives together for the first time in the

271

newly established home. No one regretted any longer that the proposed housewarming had never taken place. Besides, the present function served a dual purpose: it was not only a christening party, it was a *bon voyage* party. Mrs. Vincent had prevailed at last, and she and her husband were off to France to pay Pierre and Armande a long visit— and, incidentally, they might even visit the Princess d'Ambly, for Armande, with her never-failing tact, had actually succeeded in bringing about the long-desired *rapprochement* between the two branches of the family, when everyone else had failed. It was really wonderful, nothing short of miraculous. What was more, Armande was "expecting" already, which, Mrs. Vincent kept archly telling everyone who would listen to her, was just what she herself had expected! She hoped that, once she got her husband away, he would consent to remain abroad for a good long time—not only long enough to visit the D'Amblys as well as the De Chanets, but also long enough to attend a *French* christening. Of course, nothing could be nicer than the one they were celebrating now. Still, with a magnificent private chapel in a historic chateau for a setting—well, the next one in the family would be exceptionally thrilling!

Everyone agreed with her and, by the time the christening party at the new Monteregard was over, the same persons who had said that Lawrence Cary Vincent was a perfect name for the new baby were also agreeing, over their champagne, that they must find a nickname for him. With comparable unanimity, it was decided what this should be; so, by the time Cary was jesting with Savoie about his share in producing such a wonderful infant, "Larry" came readily to her lips. She said she had always despised parents who referred to their offspring as "it," and that parents who merely said "Baby this, Baby that" were almost as bad; she was very glad the whole question had been taken out of her hands.

"I never thought of it that way before," Savoie told her, in a wondering voice.

"That I ought to be grateful? Or that the baby's been called by a sensible name from the beginning?"

"That you ought to be grateful to me, of course. I don't think you should—I don't see how you can be. You had all the pain and I had all the pleasure."

"Oh, Savoie! It's beneath you, conversationally and mentally both, to use that old cliché! Besides, from what Mother's told me, you didn't enjoy the day Larry was born very much yourself."

"No, but—"

"That's what you meant when you talked about the pain, isn't it? As to the pleasure—"

She stopped, looking up at him with sparkling eyes.

"I was terribly slow about making up my mind to get married, wasn't I?" she asked. "Perhaps I was a little slow about grasping all the advantages of the married state, too. I'm sorry."

"I wasn't reproaching you, darling. I just said I knew—"

"Well, I wouldn't blame you if you did reproach me. But you won't have a chance to reproach me any more. Because I realize those advantages now. And I'm determined to make up for lost time."

He was still holding the hand she had stretched out to him. He pressed it again and raised it to his lips.

"Don't you think you might give me a real kiss? You haven't, you know, since Larry was born."

"Why yes I have! I've kissed you every day—several times a day."

"Not the way I'm talking about."

He rose and looked down at her. Never had he seen such welcome in her face and, as he bent over and kissed her, he could feel the welcome in her lips, too. He straightened up again, swiftly.

"It's—it's too soon," he said thickly.

"Is it? Do you really think so? I should have supposed you would think it wasn't half soon enough," she answered.

"I mean, if—if anything should happen. . . . It might be bad for you."

But, looking at her again and seeing the way she looked at him, he forgot he had meant to be very patient and very gentle and remembered only how much he wanted her.

Well, yes, Dr. Bringier conceded dryly, when, rather shamefacedly, Savoie sent for him again; it was sooner than he would have advised, if he had been consulted. But it was no sooner than he had anticipated. He had been expecting to be called in, about this time, ever since Savoie had raved and ranted about an only child; he had never known that to fail. He would have liked to see Cary nurse Larry through the following summer; but the baby was in such splendid condition that it would do him no harm to shift gradually to cow's milk. As for Cary, it was obvious that she was made for maternity. She was in a very different mood than before, wasn't she? Yes, that was what he would have thought. And he doubted whether she would have much trouble with morning sickness this time. As for her confinement, she would probably just kick off her slippers and have the baby. He would tell her so, since he might not even get there himself; but now perhaps he had better be getting in and looking her over. . . .

There was no question at all about the different mood. When Cary said she was very glad she was going to have another baby, she did so in such a way that the doctor could not possibly doubt that she meant it. Indeed, when she added, quite spontaneously, that she hoped she would have a very large family, he permitted himself the jest of saying it was too bad she had started in so late; she probably would

273

not be able to have more than ten or twelve, unless she had twins; whereas, if she had married at sixteen, like her mother, she might have had twenty. Cary retorted that, quite likely, there would be twins, sooner or later, possibly more than one set. Then, without even mentioning faintness or morning sickness or anything else of the kind, she went on to say that she hoped, this time, she would have a girl, so that she could name it Lucy. She had already told her mother and her stepfather about her prospects and they were pleased, too. They did not think it was too soon for her to have another. Something in her tone seemed to dare the doctor to say again that he thought so and he did not accept the dare. He was really very fond of them all and he was glad they were all so happy. It was not his policy to pry into the private affairs of his patients; but, like most family physicians, he could not help learning a good deal about these. He knew, for instance, that Clyde had suffered great financial reverses after fighting his way to a fortune and that Lucy had endured many trials with great fortitude; he knew that Cary had been a spoiled child and that, besides causing her parents considerable anxiety, she had given Savoie a run for his money, though Savoie was as fine a fellow as ever lived, even if he were not overburdened with brains. But Cary was settling down at last; she was proving to be a good daughter and a good wife and a good mother after all; there was not a family the doctor knew on the river road more deserving of happiness or with a better prospect of it. . . .

And then Savoie came galloping up to Dr. Bringier's house late one night, when the exhausted physician had finally sunk into bed after a long, hard day, and implored him to come posthaste to Monteregard. Larry, who had never been sick for a single hour, had suddenly been smitten with some strange and terrible illness. Mrs. Surget, who was visiting them, had said at first that it was only croup, and Tudie had agreed with her. They had fired a kettle of water on a small oilstove, under a blanket, so that the steam would envelop the baby in his crib, and had prophesied that this treatment would quickly bring relief. Instead, Larry's breathing had become more and more labored. Then Mrs. Surget had begun to talk about membranous croup, and had admitted steam would not loosen that. Tudie had not said anything more; she had put her apron over her head and groaned. Now the poor baby seemed to be strangling. . . .

While Savoie rattled distractedly on and on, Dr. Bringier had been flinging himself into his clothes. He did not underestimate the gravity of the situation. Unless there were apparently a question of life or death, no Creole planter would have come pounding up the river road himself to summon a doctor, instead of sending one of his servants; and even allowing for Savoie's constitutional excitability and natural anxiety, the symptoms he described were unquestionably alarming.

"Sulie's hitching up the buggy right now," the doctor said, shrugging himself into his coat and abruptly interrupting Savoie's torrent of talk. "I'll be at Monteregard almost as soon as you can get back there yourself. Meanwhile, the best thing you can do, my friend, is to go home and let Cary know I'm on my way. I tell you frankly I'm afraid, from what you say, your baby is bad off. But don't repeat that, you hear? Membranous croup? Bah! There is no such thing! Diphtheria, more likely. A killer. But don't repeat that either. After all, I've nothing to go on as yet but your incoherencies. Now hurry along. You're doing no good here."

Larry was still hooded in Mrs. Surget's improvised steam tent when the physician entered the nursery and, bending over him, curtly ordered the hissing kettle and the small oilstove removed. The baby's face was purple, his lips blue, his struggle for breath already nearly futile. Only an occasional wheezing rattle showed that he had managed to suck a bit of air into his straining lungs.

"As I thought," Dr. Bringier announced tersely. "Diphtheria. No use wasting time on medication. I've only one chance of saving him. That's by making a cut in his throat and inserting a tube. If I can do that quickly enough. . . . If not. . . ."

He did not finish the sentence. Cary buried her face against Savoie's shoulder to smother a wild surge of sobs. Beneath the damp fabric of his shirt, she could feel the trembling of his body; and suddenly she knew she could not count on him for support in this dreadful moment. Instead, she must somehow summon strength to meet it unaided.

"No time to lose," she heard the doctor saying as she raised her head. "First, let's get this table cleared—and be quick about it! Now, Mrs. Surget, you and Tudie go back to the kitchen and stay there until I send for you. Meanwhile, put some water on to boil." Then, when the old family friend and the young colored mammy had tiptoed obediently from the room, with fearful backward glances toward the crib and the baby's stricken parents, Dr. Bringier added, "They mean well, but I couldn't risk Larry's life with either of them. I've got to have intelligent co-operation. One of you'll have to give it to me."

While he was speaking, he dragged the marble-topped center table nearer the mantel and speedily transferred the two lamps which stood on the dresser to the mantel shelf. "Got to have light, too," he grumbled. "And I can't afford to take a chance of having either of you keel over, maybe, with a lighted lamp in your hand, at the sight of a little blood."

"Blood!" echoed Savoie. "Larry's blood! Oh, my God!"

"*Tais-toi!*" the doctor exclaimed sharply, as if he had been speaking to a troublesome child. "You can go to pieces later on, if you have to,

Savoie. For the moment, your son's life may depend on your self-control."

He had continued to work quickly. A sheet, hastily snatched from the crib, already covered the table. Another, folded and refolded into a narrow pad, was placed near one end of it. Shiny instruments rattled and clinked as they were laid out. When all were in readiness, the doctor detached his stiffly starched cuffs from his shirt and rolled up his sleeves as he walked toward the bathroom. Cary and Savoie could hear him moving about there, running the water and scrubbing his hands. But the sounds seemed distant and meaningless. They were drowned by the agonized stertor of Larry's gasping, which went on and on. Until then, Dr. Bringier had acted with almost unbelievable rapidity; now, the suffering baby's parents felt that he was not acting at all and Savoie impulsively started toward the bathroom himself, thereby blocking the path of the returning physician. He jerked his head, motioning Savoie out of his way and, lifting Larry from the crib, placed him on the table in such a manner as to bring the narrow pad beneath his shoulders and permit the small head to loll back.

"I'll prop back his chin myself, but one of you'll have to hold his arms against the table," Dr. Bringier announced. "I expect it'd better be you, Savoie. After all, you're a good deal stronger than Cary. Remember that the child's got to be still while I cut. Pin his shoulders down tight. If he jerked, I might not be able to help hurting him—bad, I mean."

Savoie approached the lighted table, bent forward and placed his corded hands over the baby's soft little arms. But he was still shaking, and suddenly he released his grip, swayed backward and crumpled in a heap beside the table, while deep racking sobs came from him.

"Oh, Jesus God! I can't do it!" he cried. "A knife in that baby's throat! No! No!" Dr. Bringier looked past him contemptuously and saw that Cary was already close to him, placing a steadying hand on his bowed head.

"It's all right, darling," she said soothingly. "Don't worry. I know how you feel. But I can keep him quiet. I've done it lots of times already." She took hold of the strangling baby's arms and pinioned them to the table. "Go ahead, Dr. Bringier," she said, still composedly. "Everything will be all right. Only please hurry."

She looked down at her child, marveling at the strength he showed in trying to escape her. She did not see Savoie, who had somehow got to his feet and stepped out of the way. She did not see Mrs. Surget and Tudie, who had crept back as far as the dark doorway, and stood, with their hands pressed hard against their lips, staring in horrified fascination at the lamplit scene by the mantel. But she saw the doctor's clean, gnarled fingers press Larry's chin up and back, and a dazzling gleam of light from a polished blade. Then she saw a welling line of

276

red follow the knife's gliding stroke. She saw a hand pull back the slipping edges of the wound, probe briefly at the pulsing tissues beneath, and finally drive the blade down and back. . . .

She saw no more, because she felt as if she were commencing to spin in a slow vortex, and she stopped looking down at Larry and pressed her eyelids together as though Larry's life depended now upon her sightlessness—as indeed she feared it did. Dimly, though unquestioningly, she realized that as long as the pulsing red wound and the gnarled fingers which probed it and the gleaming knife above it remained invisible, she could hold on. So she did not see a polished tube worked through the incision, or a smaller tube deftly adjusted within it. At last she heard a voice saying, "Just a minute longer. This is what is going to tell the tale." But still she did not open her eyes, lest nameless horror should engulf her and sweep her away to some remote region where she could no longer grasp small struggling arms and fight for a tiny, flickering life. . . .

Then, abruptly, Larry's tortured gasps and his pitiful writhing ceased at the same instant, and someone was speaking again, saying she did not need to hold the baby any longer, and someone had put an arm around her. . . .

She did not instantly recognize the voice as the doctor's, because it was not harsh any more, but very, very gentle; and she did not instantly realize that it was Savoie who was embracing her, because the arm which encircled her was steady and not trembling. But she dared to look at last and, through a blur of unshed tears, she saw a glint of metal at her baby's white throat, just at the place where she had so often nuzzled it to make him gurgle with laughter. She rubbed her eyes to make sure that this and everything else she saw was not a delusion. For the baby's face had lost its deadly purplish cast and was pink and warmly alive again. His little body no longer twisted and writhed in agony; instead his small breast rose and fell in the peaceful rhythm of effortless breathing, and his eyes were closed in deep natural slumber. . . .

"You can't blame him for dropping off, either," Dr. Bringier chuckled, shooting his cuffs over his knuckles and snapping the steel fasteners into his shirt sleeves. "I expect he's been through more than he'll ever be called on to undergo again. At least, I hope so. But he's still going to need a great deal of attention right around the clock. And, judging by what happened here a little while ago, I'm afraid you're the only one that can give it to him, Cary. But I know now I can count on you."

The doctor had begun to move the miscellany of bright metal from the table and stow it back into his black leather bag, item by item. In the course of this process, he selected a short, shining tube and held it up for Cary to see. He did not look toward Savoie at all.

"Here's a twin to the one your baby's breathing through now," he explained. "The upper part of his throat is still closed by the false membrane. So, naturally, he can't cough to clear his breathing passages of secretion. You'll have to do the clearing for him during the next ten days. A breathing tube like this is inside a larger one that will stay in his throat until he's well. That's so the small tube can be changed without hurting him, since it touches only the larger tube, not the baby himself. When you can tell from his breathing that the passage is getting clogged with secretion, take out the small one and put this one in. I'll show you how it's done before I leave. Then clean the old tube thoroughly and use it to make the next exchange. Larry won't mind. Matter of fact, it's so much less effort to breathe through a tube than through a nose and throat, that when it's time to take out everything, we'll first have to block the tube partially for a day and then shut it off altogether for another day. By that time he'll be using his own natural air passages again and we can remove all this hardware and let his throat heal. There won't even be much of a scar. . . . Now, if Mrs. Surget and Tudie really did put water on to boil, how's for dripping some of it through a coffeepot? I think we could all do with a drink."

For more than a week, Cary watched over Larry night and day, ministering to his every need. Not once, during this interval, did she complain of morning sickness or dizziness, though it was obvious enough she suffered from both, nor did she refer in any way to her own condition. Then, when the silver tubes had been painlessly removed, and Larry was well on the road to complete recovery, she suddenly fainted dead away, for the only time in her life, except on the day of Pierre's wedding. Savoie carried her to bed and undressed her; and when she struggled back to consciousness and instinctively tried to rise, she realized that it was her physician and not her husband who was sitting beside her, and that the fingers on her wrist were there to feel her pulse and not to caress her.

"Lie still, Cary," Dr. Bringier said abruptly; and, as she continued her vain effort to sit up, he added, more sternly, "Larry's pulled through and it's thanks to your care, even more than his fine physique. But you've got to turn him over to someone else now."

"There isn't anyone else. You've said yourself, over and over again, that Tudie was developing into a fine nurse, for a well child, but that she didn't have enough experience yet to take care of a sick one. And none of the other servants—"

"True enough. But—"

"And you've said Mrs. Surget was beginning to feel her age and show it, too, so much that you didn't—"

"That's also correct, but—"

278

"Well, then—"

"Will you kindly let me finish what I started to say, Cary Vincent? There's your mother. She's as good a nurse as I ever saw. She has a natural gift for it and she's had plenty of experience besides. Instead of just letting her spell you, for an hour or two at a time as she has been doing, you'll have to let her take Larry at night, from now on."

"You mean send him to Cindy Lou!"

"Certainly not. I'm not proposing to move him. He's out of danger and I think he'll make a rapid recovery; children go downhill fast, but they have remarkable powers of recuperation. However, though it's no longer necessary that anyone should sit up all night with him, he still requires considerable care. And you can't give it to him."

"Yes, I can."

"I'm telling you that you can't. You might faint again—at a very bad moment, not just for you, but for Larry. And you've got another child to think of now. You want this new baby—it means more to you than Larry did, before he was born. It would be a hard blow to you if you lost it. And I'm telling you that you very well may, if you go on as you have been doing. What's more, if you lost this one, you might never have another—don't forget what happened in your mother's case. And then what would become of that big family of yours, I'd like to know?"

The latter part of the doctor's speech sounded less severe than the first; there was even an obvious attempt to introduce a mildly jesting note. But this superficial lightness in no way obscured the underlying gravity. Cary sank back on her pillows.

"Who's with Larry now?"

"Both Savoie and Tudie. Mrs. Surget's in the house, too. She's still able to help another nurse, for a few hours at a stretch, in the daytime. But you're right; I can't give her any more night nursing."

"Mother isn't here?"

"No. Larry's sleeping peacefully, so she went back to Cindy Lou to have dinner with your father. I told her I'd stay with you until she got back, that I wanted to talk to you like a Dutch uncle, without any interference. And I know she thinks your father needs her, too—he's got his hands pretty full with the spring crop, what with Lamartine Vincent gallivanting around France and Savoie refusing to stir out of this house. And I believe he's expecting some business visitor, due to arrive at any moment. But I'm going straight from here to Cindy Lou myself on purpose to ask your mother to come back to Monteregard, now that you're awake and I'm through talking to you—I promised her I would. I'll also tell her she must be prepared to stay overnight—over several nights. But first, I want you to promise *me* you won't get out of that bed, except to nurse Larry, until I give you permission. You'll find you won't be able to satisfy him anyhow, when he's well

279

enough to be a little hungrier. I'm thankful we got him started on cow's milk before all this happened, because your supply will have to be materially supplemented from now on. Even if you hadn't worn yourself out, you wouldn't have had enough for him much longer. So let your mother start feeding him at night. I'm telling you the truth, Cary. It's not just a question of what's best for you; it's also a question of what's best for Larry—and for the new baby."

He had hard work wringing the promise from her. Indeed, it was not until Savoie joined them briefly, and added both his assurances of Larry's continued and peaceful slumber to those of the doctor, that she agreed to stay where she was, at least until the baby wakened and cried for her. Before that happened, her mother arrived, and proved more successful than either of the others in coping with Cary. Lucy had never enlarged, before, on the poignancy of her disappointment in her failure to give Clyde a child; but she did this now, and in a way so infinitely moving that Cary could not keep back the tears while she lay listening to her mother; and, as she was quietly weeping, her thoughts turned more and more to those children, still unborn, who would be the outward and visible sign of her fulfillment as a woman and of her triumph as a wife. Gradually, a fierce desire to safeguard the future flooded her being and helped her to forget her anxiety of the present.

"Anyway, you and Father have had each other," she said at last, knowing that she was speaking inadequately and believing that she was also speaking inconsequentially.

"Yes. We've had each other," Lucy said. And, brief as the answer was, its adequacy was complete.

"Did he mind too much, having you leave?"

"Oh, no! He agreed with Dr. Bringier that I should. But he wanted to come with me. I had hard work dissuading him. However, Valois Dupré has just arrived at Cindy Lou—he was to be in Baton Rouge tomorrow and, apparently, it's very important that he and your father should have some sort of a consultation before then. Besides, there's no reason why your father's rest should be disturbed because Larry needs care—he couldn't help anyway. An aptitude for nursing is not among his many talents." She rose. "I think I will go to the nursery now," she went on. "If Larry finds me beside him when he wakes, he will be less likely to cry for you. After all, he recognizes me now and we are pretty good friends, too. If he seems contented and comfortable, I will send Savoie in to you and keep Tudie to wait on me. Please believe me, darling, Larry will be all right."

"I do believe you, Mother. And thanks for talking to me the way you did. It helped a lot. I promise you I won't try to get up. I'll lie still and take good care of little Lucy while you're taking care of Larry."

They kissed and clung to each other for a moment; then Lucy left the room and, for a little while, Cary lay quietly, thinking less of the sick child, with whom she had been so wholly preoccupied during the last few days, than of the new life within her, of her husband's overwhelming love for her, and of the tardy quickening of her own response to him, which had already transfigured their marriage relationship, and which gave such rich promise of future harmony and future fecundity. How much more fortunate she was than her mother had been! It was true that Lucy and Clyde had been ideally happy together; but Cary realized now that this happiness had never been quite complete and, with thankful wonder, she told herself that hers was—or that it would be, as soon as she was sure, beyond any shadow of a doubt, that all was well with Larry.

When Savoie came back to their room from the nursery, an hour later, he was able to give her this assurance. Larry had not cried at all when he wakened; he had indeed recognized his grandmother—the precocious intelligence of that child!—and had been glad to see her; he had even drunk the milk she offered him, with apparent relish. Then he had dropped peacefully off to sleep again. Mrs. Batchelor had almost completed arrangements for the night. Tudie had brought in more milk, which had been put in the beautiful *veilleuse* Mrs. Surget had given Larry for a christening present; it would be kept at just the right temperature and he could have more whenever he was hungry. Now Mrs. Batchelor had packed Tudie off to bed, telling her to get a good night's rest, and was herself preparing to retire. She sent her love to Cary, and promised to let her know instantly if Larry should take a turn for the worse; but she confidently expected him to keep on feeling better.

"And I think so, too," Savoie concluded hopefully. "So there's not a thing on earth for you to worry about, darling."

"No, I don't believe there is."

She was beginning to feel sleepy herself. She had fought off the drowsiness natural to her condition all the time she had watched beside Larry. Now she could succumb to it. The sensation was delicious.

"Can I get you anything? Is there anything you want?"

"You can't get me anything and the only thing I want is to know you're here with me. It's bedtime for all of us, isn't it?"

"Very nearly. We can call it bedtime if you want to."

"I do want to. For over a week—"

For over a week their every thought had been of Larry. Now at last they could think of each other again. They went to sleep in each other's arms.

In the nursery wing, on the other side of the house, Lucy remained wakeful for some time. She had spoken the truth when she said she felt there was no further cause for anxiety; still, to make assurance doubly sure, she sat beside Larry for more than an hour, listening to his breathing and occasionally feeling his forehead. His breath came softly and regularly, his forehead was faintly moist under his clustering curls. The awful periods of strangulation were over, the burning fever had completely subsided. There was no doubt now that he would sleep peacefully for hours. Besides, his crib was drawn up close to the big bed; she would hear his slightest cry. It was needless for her to sit up any longer; in fact, it would be much better if she, too, rested as long as possible, so that she would be refreshed the next day.

She prepared for the night in her customary, calm, orderly way, hanging up her dress, folding her underwear over the back of a chair, brushing and braiding her long hair and sponging herself off, before slipping into her clean cambric nightgown. Then she knelt down to say the Lord's Prayer, adding to this her more personal petitions for those who were nearest and dearest to her; she gave thanks for Larry's recovery from mortal illness, for her daughter's growth in grace, for her husband's devotion, for everything good that had come into her life; and she did not fail to add a plea for a return to the fold by Bushrod, the black sheep. Finally she rose from her knees and, after one last look at Larry, blew out the lamp and lay down in bed. The faint glow from the *veilleuse,* formed like a Madonna, shed its soft light over the slumbering child.

She did not fall asleep instantly. She had always been sensitive to her surroundings and, aside from her feeling of responsibility, she had a feeling of strangeness. She had never occupied this room before, at night, and it was a long while since she and Clyde had been separated. In the early days of their marriage, she had not always been able to accompany him when he traveled on business, because she could not leave Cary; but ever since all his interests had been concentrated at Cindy Lou, she and he had been together almost constantly. She thought of him, alone, too, and knew that he must have the same feeling of strangeness that she did, and the same feeling of isolation.

She forced herself to lie quiet and relaxed, instead of following her impulse to toss restlessly from side to side, or to become tense under the strain of solitude. She prayed again, short, formless little prayers this time; and between them, she raised herself on her elbow and looked down at Larry, to find that he had not stirred since she last looked at him. Finally, soothed by the beneficent stillness of the night, she slept. When a slight, sudden puff of wind upset the *veilleuse,* she did not hear its soft fall. The sound was muffled by the silken scarf covering the chest where it had stood and it did not tumble to the floor. But the milk from its little pot and the oil from its lamp flowed out of it together, and on top of the oil floated the tiny lighted wick.

A second gust of wind sent the burning oil farther on its wicked way, setting fire to its surroundings.

Lucy never knew whether it was the sound of a banging shutter or a sudden scream from Larry which wakened her. The two came together, and she leaped from her bed into a room already ablaze, realizing with horror that there was not a second to lose. The first little licking flames from the lighted wick, rippling into larger and larger waves, had quickly reached the draperies. Escape through the dressing room was already cut off, for the curtain which hung at the doorway was afire. Lucy snatched the screaming child from his cradle, enveloped him in a blanket and rushed toward the door leading to the rear stairway.

By this time, the sudden windstorm had reached the proportions of a gale, and it was all she could do to battle her way across the garden. She did not dare lay Larry down on the cold ground; but once she had reached the gazebo, he would have shelter from the storm, inadequate to be sure, but enough to serve until she could summon more help. She had not paused, even to put on slippers, and, in the darkness, she could not choose her path. She kept stumbling, and once she fell; but she struggled to her feet again, unconscious of any hurt, and hurried on. Though her first dazed, waking thought had naturally been for Larry, she realized now that she must get back to the house and warn the others. Again, there was not a second to lose.

Her foot touched the step leading into the gazebo before she saw it. Wrapping the blanket more firmly around the still-screaming baby, she laid him on the floor; and, as she did so, she tried to murmur a few words of comfort. But she did not dare stay to soothe him, and his pitiful cries followed her as she turned and ran back toward the house. Darkness was no longer a handicap, for the whole nursery wing was now ablaze, and flames had already reached the rear of the building; but she could see that the great, outer stairway, leading to the main floor, was still clear. Surely she could get up it, battle her way through the hall and reach the wing where Savoie and Cary were sleeping—if they still slept. She could only pray that the wind had wakened them, too, that they had already made their way to safety. But, even as she prayed, she feared her prayers were vain; if Savoie and Cary had come out through the hall, she would already have seen them; and there was no stairway leading directly from their quarters to the ground. Unless they had leaped from a window, they could not have reached it. And such a leap, for Cary at least, would have been only one degree less dangerous than fire itself.

Lucy reached the great, outer stairway, mounted it two steps at a time, and gained the front door. Doors at Cindy Lou were never locked, but Savoie had always followed his father's custom of bolting everything at night. Desperately, Lucy threw her weight against the solid panels; then, realizing the complete futility of pitting her slender strength against such solid structure, she doubled up her fist and struck one of the glass side windows to the door with all her might. This time, her effort was successful. The blow shattered the glass, and she thrust her hand and arm through the opening and managed to reach the bolt and draw it back with her bleeding fingers. Then the knob turned easily under her hand and the door opened, releasing clouds of smoke. She stepped across the threshold and ran down the length of the hall, until the smoke stifled her and she fell.

 CHAPTER XIII

IT HAD become second nature for Cary to stretch out her arms toward Savoie as, still deliciously drowsy, she began to nestle around in the morning. He was invariably wide awake already, for he instinctively kept the "planter's hours" to which he had been accustomed since childhood; but he was careful to remain completely motionless, until the welcome signs of his wife's imminent awakening encouraged him to turn toward her. Then he drew her to him, first burying his head in her breast, and then kissing her shoulders, next her throat and lastly her lips. She was naturally a very lazy girl, she was apt to tell him; however, no amount of somnolence could have been proof against the persuasive powers of that culminating kiss. She had to wake up, so that she would get the full benefit of another like it. . . .

She was waking now, but it was not a kiss that had roused her and her arms encountered only a strange void as she stretched them out. When she became fully conscious of this, she also became conscious of pain, a pain which was dull rather than poignant; and there was a strangeness about the dullness, too, as if it were not really part of the pain. It was a little like the dullness that came from the chloroform she had been given when she was in the last stages of labor, merciful but stupefying. Yet, it did not seem quite like chloroform, either; and of course she was not in labor, it would be months yet before that happened again, and she had been assured that, this time, it would be much easier than before anyway. She was trying to decide what the dull pain could be, still without bothering to open her eyes and still groping aimlessly for Savoie, when someone took her hand and called her softly by name. Since that was not Savoie's way, nor his voice which she heard, she reluctantly opened her eyes at last and saw that her father was sitting at her bedside. And next, before she could ask him why he was there and why Savoie was not, she realized that she was at Cindy Lou instead of at Monteregard, and that she was lying alone in the little old spool bed that had been hers before she married.

"Cary," Clyde was saying again. "Cary, my darling. . . ."

It was Clyde's voice, there was no doubt of that, yet there was something strange about this, too. Everything was very strange. She did not understand at all. She had always thought with great affection of her own room at Cindy Lou and of the little old spool bed where she had slept alone; but now that she was back at Cindy Lou, in the spool bed, the strangeness troubled her. She was not happy about it because she was so puzzled. She tried to question her father, but her own voice seemed strangest of all, and the dullness of the pain did not keep it from getting worse, now that she was wider awake.

"Monteregard was—damaged by fire, during a storm at night," Clyde was telling her. At least that was what she understood him to say. She was not quite sure, because everything still seemed so strange, and she was so bewildered and suffering so much. "It seemed better for you to come—to come home for the present."

"But Savoie didn't stay at Monteregard without me, did he?"

"No. He's at Cindy Lou, too. But he had to fight the fire, you see. It's hard work, fighting fires, you know that. So he's—resting now."

"I don't see why he couldn't rest here, beside me."

She did not understand why she should begin to cry. If she had been able to follow, accurately, what Clyde told her, there was nothing he had said which should cause her grief. Of course it was unfortunate that there had been a fire at Monteregard; but fires were not infrequent occurrences, in plantation houses, and happily they did not often amount to much. She was sure her father would soon repair any damage that had been done and then she would go back to Monteregard and she and Savoie would be together again. Meanwhile, she ought to be thankful that her old home was so close that she could return to it, in any emergency, thankful that she was in the pleasant room which had been hers for so long, thankful that Savoie was resting comfortably, after having helped to put out the fire. Probably he had been afraid of disturbing her by coming to her room when she had gone to sleep. But how could she have come from Monteregard from Cindy Lou without waking up, without knowing there was a fire?

She tried to puzzle it out, but she could not and presently, in spite of the dull pain, she went to sleep again. When she waked, the pain was worse, but she was able to think more clearly. She began to remember now: she had been sound asleep, after many nights that were wakeful, because she had been watching over Larry and. . . . Suddenly, she screamed.

"Larry has died! Larry has died and you haven't told me!"

"No, darling, Larry hasn't died. He's much better—completely out of danger. But he's sound asleep, in Bushrod's room, and Tudie's there with him. She's taken wonderful care of him ever since—well, ever since we brought him here. Dr. Bringier says he couldn't be in better hands. You don't want me to wake him up, do you, when he needs sleep so much?"

"I don't believe he's all right. I shan't believe it unless I see him."

"Cary, I swear that I'm telling you the truth. Did I ever lie to you?"

"No, but I don't understand. . . ."

She must not cry again, she would not. She bit her lips to keep them steady and tried to go on remembering. Yes, she had been sleeping very, very soundly, after her nights of vigil; and then she had been roused by Savoie, who was shaking her, so that she would wake up; and the room was full of smoke, so full that it choked him while he tried to talk to her, to tell her that the house was on fire, that she must leave it at once, by a window, and he would go through the wing into the hall and make sure that her mother had left the other wing with Larry, by the steps on the farther side. He was convinced this was what would have happened, but he would go and make sure, as soon as he had seen her safely on the ground. She had tried to argue with him that she must go through the house with him, and he had told her there was no time to talk; he had picked her up and carried her to the window. . . . She tried and tried, but she could not remember anything after that. She turned again to her father, who was still sitting quietly beside her, with his head bowed, and this time she did not cry out, and she did not find it so hard to question him, either.

"Things are coming back to me, Father."

"I knew they would, if you wouldn't try to hurry yourself, darling."

"Mother carried Larry straight down the new staircase, didn't she?"

"Yes. That's just what she did. We can't be thankful enough you thought of having it built."

Briefly, Cary was conscious of immense thankfulness herself. But now that she found she could, she wanted to go on asking questions.

"Then it was no trouble at all to get Larry out of the house?"

"No. Your mother took him straight to the gazebo. He was sheltered there from the storm and safe from the fire."

"And what did Mother do next?"

"Well, naturally, after she was sure Larry was safe, she hurried back to warn you and Savoie."

"And I suppose it was while she was hurrying back that the smoke waked Savoie and that he waked me?"

"Yes, that must have been the way it was."

"He said he would go through the house to make sure Larry and Mother were all right. Probably she and Savoie met in the hall."

"Yes, Cary, they did."

"Then she's resting now, too?"

"Yes, Cary."

"But what happened to me? That still isn't clear."

"You were—hurt, falling from a window. Perhaps you were unconscious before you fell. You'd already swallowed a good deal of smoke, more than you realized. Or perhaps the fall caused your unconsciousness, and you had a slight concussion. We don't know. It doesn't matter anyway."

"But I was unconscious when I was found?"

"Yes. I picked you up myself, I brought you over here. You never stirred until you waked up a few hours ago and asked for Savoie."

"Was that *hours ago?*"

"Yes, Cary."

"Has anything happened since?"

"Well, Dr. Bringier's been here to see you again."

"Again?"

"Yes. Of course we sent for him right away. And he gave you something to deaden your pain right away. He's kept on giving you something. He'll continue to do so. He—we won't let you suffer any more than we can help."

So it was medicine that was responsible for that dull feeling, some kind of medicine which was very powerful, even if it were not as powerful as chloroform. But now that she could think more clearly, Cary could not help wondering why she should still be in so much pain. The pain was there all the time—not just when she moved a little. So evidently she had not broken any bones. She did not believe that burns could be causing the pain, either. Like everyone else, she had burnt her fingers, occasionally, and though the burns had been slight, they were unforgettable. The pain she felt now was not like the pain they gave. This was like only one other that she had ever had, not exactly like it, either. But then, the effect of the powerful medicine was not exactly like the effect of chloroform. . . .

"Father, you don't mean—"

"I hoped you wouldn't guess, darling. Try not to grieve too much. Remember you've got Larry."

"But—" It was no use. No matter how hard she bit them, she could not keep her lips from trembling now. "But this time I was *glad!*"

"Yes, Cary, I know."

"And Savoie was so glad, too. And Mother. Mother'll be terribly worried, Father. You see, she told me to be very careful, because if I had *one* miscarriage, then probably. . . . She's been so terribly disappointed herself, Father, because she didn't give you a child."

"She did give me a child. She gave you to me. You're my child, Cary. You always have been. But you're doubly my child now."

There were tears on her face and they were not her own. And suddenly she understood everything.

Everything except that she herself was dying.

She was not sure how long it was before she understood that, too, because time meant nothing to her any more. Every now and then Titine or Mrs. Surget came into her room and did things which, apparently, seemed to them necessary. They gave her broth and gruel, and sponged her off with sweet-smelling water and changed her nightgown and her bed linen. She accepted their ministrations with docility, but she never craved their company and she was always secretly relieved to have them go away. Her feeling about her grandmother and her cousin Mildred, who had come down from Virginia and were occupying the room with the convent beds, was more neutral. She did not really crave their company, either; on the other hand, she was not actually relieved when they left her. She took a certain vague pleasure in their talk of Sorrento, as it was now, and of Amalfi, as it once had been; but she had no desire to share in this conversation or to expand it. When Tudie brought Larry in to her, early every morning and again just before bedtime, she was glad to see him; but she did not resent it at all when Dr. Bringier said the baby must not stay with her too long at a time, because it would tire her. She did not feel she needed to see him long at a time to assure herself that all was well with him now. Neither did she feel that she needed to see, for long, the priest who had married her to Savoie and who had also baptized Larry, or the rector of the little Episcopal church which her mother had faithfully supported, and of which she herself had been a nominal, and rather casual, member. She recognized that they were both good men and that they were both devoted to her personally, besides having her spiritual welfare at heart. She thanked them for coming, but she did not suggest that either should come a second time. They did not add to her sense of peace or her sense of happiness. It was Clyde that she wanted with her.

She and he talked to each other freely about everything again now, just as they had before she was married; and she thought it was when he told her about her mother's funeral, and her husband's, that she began to realize he would have no one to talk to in just that way, after she died. She was troubled because she was afraid he would be very lonely then; but otherwise she was not troubled at all. It did not tire her or make her sad to talk; on the contrary, it exhilarated her, because she was glad to feel she was giving her father some comfort. She knew he had hesitated to avail himself of this comfort, because he had asked Dr. Bringier if talking would do Cary any harm. He had put the question almost in a whisper, when the two had gone out into the hall; but Cary had heard it, and the doctor's answer to it.

"You're sure it wouldn't help if she could conserve her strength?"

"She hasn't any strength left to conserve. I'll keep her as comfortable as I can, with drugs. It's your job to keep her as happy as you can, in any way that you can."

So Clyde came back into Cary's room and talked with her until the merciful drugs had done their work and she was drowsy again. He did not pretend to any false cheerfulness; instead, he paid her the tribute of sharing his sorrow with her. And when he paused, after talking to her about the past, and about her mother, she talked to him about the future, and about Larry.

"You said I was your child, Father, and I'm glad you did, because I've always felt as if I were. You said Mother gave me to you. Now Larry must be your child. I'm giving him to you."

"I'll be an old man, Cary, long before Larry's grown up. I feel like an old man now."

"But you're not old. Grandmother really is old—over eighty. I couldn't ask her to take Larry. I couldn't ask Cousin Mildred to do it, either. Cousin Mildred seems almost as old as Grandmother, though of course she isn't. Perhaps that's because she's never really lived. It's funny, isn't it, that spinsters always seem older than married women the same age?"

"I never thought of it before. But you're right, they nearly always do. And yet, their delicacy's never been outraged by a man's grossness, they've never been through the agony of childbirth."

"Perhaps that's the very reason why. Men and women need each other, don't you think so, Father? Doesn't a man's grossness, as you call it, help a woman to overcome false shame? Doesn't her delicacy help him to overcome what some people call 'baser passions'? Not that I like those words. And I don't like grossness. Savoie wasn't gross. You aren't, either."

"No woman ever really knows any man, Cary."

She sighed. "Perhaps not. But what she does learn about them helps her a lot. And certainly, every woman needs to have a child. I can't be thankful enough that before—"

She did not say, "before I had to die." She left a good many sentences unfinished now, partly because it did tire her, a little, to talk, after all; partly because she did not want to cause her father pain; partly because she knew he would understand her anyway.

"Besides," she continued, reverting to what he had said about growing old, "it'll make you feel younger, having a baby in the house. You'll take wonderful care of him."

"I'd do my very best for him, of course. But your grandmother may feel that wouldn't be good enough. She may feel he'd be better off at Sorrento than he would here. Even though she is so old, she's very wise and very experienced. She'd know to supervise his care. She could give him the right background."

"I'll tell her I don't want him to go to Sorrento. I'll tell her I want him to stay here, that I'm sure you'll take good care of him, that he'll have all the background he needs. I don't believe backgrounds mean as much as they used to. Anyway, Sorrento doesn't mean a thing to me. She doesn't mean a great deal. That is, really. Of course she's my grandmother, I respect her and all that, but it's you I love, it's Cindy Lou that's my home. She'll understand."

Clyde swallowed hard. "Well, perhaps she will, darling. But don't forget Larry has another grandfather—a *real* grandfather."

"Don't say 'real' that way, please, Father."

"I won't, Cary, again. But Lamartine Vincent's going to feel he's got a claim on the boy, and rightly—his only son's only son."

"Armande may have a son, too. We ought to be getting news from her any day now."

"Yes, that's so."

They had not spoken of Armande before, since speaking of Armande meant speaking of Pierre, too; and though nearly all the barriers of speech were down between them, that one still remained. Cary had never mentioned Pierre's name to her father since the scene in the gazebo. But now, at last, she did so.

"There's something I want to tell you, Father."

"Then you must."

"Pierre came to see me before he went away. I mean, he came alone. It was the morning after the *fête champêtre,* when his mother wasn't well enough to go back to New Orleans. He came through the garden and found me in the gazebo. He did it deliberately."

"If I'd known that, Cary—"

"Yes, and that was why I didn't want you to know—then. But it's also why I do want you to know—now. Because, you see, he told me he loved me."

"He had no right to tell you that."

"No, I suppose not. And you weren't mistaken—he wouldn't have married a divorced woman. He told me so himself. He said he came to Louisiana hoping I'd become his mistress. But he also told me that if I'd been free, when he first met me, he'd have wanted me for his wife. He never thought of me as—well, as just another woman with whom he'd have enjoyed having an affair. So I'm glad he told me. I knew I had the best husband in the world and I did all I could to be worthy of him—after I realized how close I'd come to—well, to un-utterable folly. It wasn't hard, either, except—except when I first knew he loved me, even if he didn't have a right to."

"Why, Cary?" Clyde could not help asking. But he knew without being told.

"Because I loved him. I tried hard not to, honestly I did, Father. Pierre was going to marry Armande. And you helped me over that bad time. Then, afterward—well, when a girl's husband loves her the way Savoie loved me, she can't let him down. She doesn't want to. And what she gives him in return isn't pretense. It's sincere—as far as it goes. But just the same. . . ."

"I've been afraid this was the way it was, Cary."

"But Savoie never knew. He never guessed. You know everything, Father, you guess everything. I'm so glad you do and that Savoie didn't."

It was first evening when they talked together like this and later Cary fell into a quiet sleep. Clyde continued to sit beside her, and about midnight Dr. Bringier, who had been called far up the river road on an emergency case, came in to see her before finally going home. He looked at her and shook his head.

"I don't think I'll need to give her anything after this. Of course, I'll stay downstairs. But she isn't suffering now and I don't think she will."

"No, I don't think so, either," Clyde answered.

There was still no light breaking through the darkness when she wakened again. She felt for the hand that she knew was already stretched out to receive hers.

"Father, I want to thank you for not saying anything against Pierre. Of course I know he couldn't hold a candle to Savoie. But somehow, if you love a man, you just love him anyway."

"I know that, Cary. Because your mother just loved me—anyway."

"But you never did what Pierre—"

"I never tried to win a woman away from her husband. But it so happens I never wanted to. I did other things just as bad, when I did want to. Men don't all sin in the same way."

"I don't think of you as a sinner. I'm not going to. But since you're speaking of them. . . . You've cabled Bushrod, haven't you? It's only fair he should know."

"I realized that. So I did cable him and I've been expecting a cable in reply. Of course he couldn't get here before your mother's funeral. But he's probably on his way home now."

"I hope. . . ." Her voice trailed away into silence. Clyde wondered if she were hoping the same thing he was, that Bushrod would not get to Cindy Lou until after she died, that he and she could have these last precious hours to themselves. But she had drifted into semiconsciousness again and she never told him what it was she hoped. The next time she spoke to him, it was about something entirely different.

"We never found the treasure, did we, Father?"

"No. But it didn't matter. We've had so much, without it."

"I know we have. But I wanted the other, too. Treasure, buried in the ground. Not dirty gravel on top of it. I've never told you, Father. . . . I'm so glad you didn't let Dupré have that land. And so sorry I didn't act as if I were, that day you told me about his offer."

"Don't be sorry, Cary. I understood afterward—when you told me about Pierre."

"Yes, but you were hurt just the same. That's what I'm sorry about. Because you've never hurt me. You're right, though—it doesn't matter now about the buried treasure. I'm not disappointed because I didn't find it, truly I'm not. You know I told you, that same day I was so hateful—"

"You weren't ever hateful, darling."

"Yes, I was. Anyway, I told you then I'd stopped believing that I'd find the treasure myself. And you're right, it doesn't matter now, because Larry will find it. I'm sure he will. Because of course it's there. . . . You won't forget what I said about Larry, will you, Father? That he's yours now and that no one must take him away from you."

"No, Cary, I shan't forget."

They continued to talk about Larry for some minutes. Cary's mind was completely clear. Though there was still no word from Bushrod, the expected message from the Vincents had come in, telling them that Armande had a son and that his name was Pierre Lamartine. Cary was sure this was going to make Clyde's guardianship of Larry far easier to safeguard and Clyde was inclined to agree with her. He could visualize, as she did, that the Vincents might be spending more and more time in France, that their most absorbing interest would be centered in Armande and her children.

Cary was calm and contented as they dwelt on this, and afterward she fell into another deep sleep. When she began to stir again, she held out her arms and Clyde thought she was groping for Savoie, as she had the first time she wakened after the fire. But he was mistaken.

"Pierre," she said distinctly, "Pierre!" She paused a moment and then she went on, still in a clear voice, "It's terribly dark, in this passage, isn't it? Of course I was warned that it would be, that I shouldn't go beyond the great chamber of the cave. It's a little frightening, isn't it? At least it would be, if I were alone. But since you're with me at last, dearest. . . ."

She died in Clyde's arms, just before dawn. He laid her gently back on her pillows and went out of the room, closing the door very softly after him. The feeling that she must not be disturbed persisted so strongly that he continued to move as quietly as possible while going down the stairs and out into the garden. It was very still there, too. But the morning was a beautiful one, and the first rays of the sun were already gilding the grass and the flowers; and suddenly Clyde saw, with surprise, that Lucy's favorite camellias had burst into bloom, almost overnight. The garden was transfigured by their loveliness. He stopped and stripped the snowy blossoms from the laden shrubs, and when he went back to Cary's room, his arms were full.

"This time," he murmured to himself, "this time they can't hide my dead away from me, before I've even had a chance to say good-by. This time they can't tell me I mustn't see her. I can strew flowers all around Cary, while she's still lying in her own bed—her mother's flowers. Then I can sit and look at her this once more. No one will come to disturb us for hours yet."

With the tenderest care, he placed the flowers around the quiet form, laying a cluster of buds on the still breast and putting a single perfect blossom between the hands which he folded himself. Then, long and lovingly, he looked down on his daughter. Never, in her most radiant moments, had she seemed so beautiful to him.

BOOK THREE

Spring 1897–Spring 1918

CREDIT EXTENDED

CLYDE could not understand, in the days after Cary's death, how it could ever have been his desire that Cindy Lou should be filled with merrymaking guests. He wanted to have his home to himself, except for Larry; he longed unutterably for silence and solitude.

Not that he thought for a moment that his mother-in-law and her elderly cousin were deliberately outwearing their welcome; he could understand the reluctance of Miss Sophie to confide the new tombs of her daughter and granddaughter into his sole custody, her still greater reluctance to entrust him with the care of her infant great-grandson; and he knew that her cousin Mildred shared her feelings, in so far as it was possible for a woman who had never borne or lost a child to experience the emotions of one who had known travail and its triumph and the grief which belongs with both. And certainly there was nothing about the bearing or behavior of these two black-clad old women to suggest they thought he himself should try to surmount his sorrow and, putting his grief resolutely behind him, look hopefully toward the future; on the contrary, they respected and understood his loneliness and his loss, as he did theirs. But any alien presence in the shadowy house seemed intrusive to him now. It was still peopled with his dead. He needed to commune with them in peace.

He had reached a point where the urgency of this need was so great that he had almost decided to confess it to his mother-in-law when she relieved him of the necessity by telling him, one afternoon when they were leaving the dining room, that she would like very much to have a quiet talk with him, and asking him when it would suit his convenience for her to do so. He had been sitting at the head of his table, with his mother-in-law at his right and Cousin Mildred at his left, averting his eyes, as far as possible, from Lucy's empty chair opposite him, yet unable to bring himself to order its removal; and the hushed meals had been the most trying periods of all. The erstwhile cheerful servants crept noiselessly around the table, offering food which nobody wanted; and though the three who were seated at the bereft board all tried to ease the situation by sporadic attempts at conversation, there were long pauses between forced comments and equally forced replies. This was not the sort of silence for which Clyde yearned; it was even worse than clatter and chatter would have been. Yet they found no way of overcoming it; they were all engulfed by it; they seemed to sink deeper and deeper into its abyss. The chasm between himself and the stern old gentlewoman who had opposed his marriage to her daughter had narrowed with the years; but though he had come to admire her highly and believed that she no longer resented him, they had never been on easy or affectionate terms with each other. He answered her now with the formal courtesy which had always characterized their association; however, the fact that she had spoken as if she were asking a favor of him was unexpectedly heart warming.

"Any time that would suit you would be agreeable to me, of course," he said. Then, as another empty, cheerless afternoon seemed to stretch out endlessly before him, he added, "Would you care to talk with me right away?"

"Thank you. I should like that very much."

She had not lowered her voice in making her request, and now she glanced toward Cousin Mildred, who instantly murmured that she had a slight headache and would like to retire, if Cousin Sophie and Cousin Clyde would excuse her. Then she scurried off toward the stairs.

"Perhaps we might have a little fire in the library," Miss Sophie continued. "It is still rather cool for this time of year—or aren't you finding it so? At all events, there is something cheering about a fire."

They had been using the drawing room when they met for tea and when they received visits of condolence. Clyde had found both experiences appalling. He still seemed to see the beautiful painted parlor arranged for a funeral; he still seemed to smother in the heavy scent of banked flowers. On the other hand, he had not entered the library since Lucy's death; the door had not even been opened. Hardly less than the chamber they had shared for so many years, this had been essentially their personal room. When he was alone, he had sat in his office; but he could not ask his mother-in-law to go there. She was right—the library was the proper place for their talk. It would be hard to go in; but once there, it would be less oppressive than the drawing room.

He opened the door and stood back for her to precede him. Evidently no one had remembered to close the shutters here; at all events, they were opened now and the late afternoon sunshine was pouring into the room. It was in perfect order, but its order was homelike and not artificial: Lucy's workbasket still stood on the little table beside her favorite chair, and on another table, near by, lay the book from which he had been reading aloud to her when they had last sat there together. The place was full of her presence, but it was a presence which had no relation to the closed casket and the sickening scent in the drawing room. He was conscious of overwhelming relief, almost of thankfulness, as he bent over and touched a match to the neatly laid fire. When he straightened up again, having assured himself that it would burn, he saw that his mother-in-law was already seated; and, as soon as he had drawn up a chair, she spoke, without waiting for him to do so.

"I received three letters this morning, which I should like to discuss with you," she said. "One of these was from my overseer. He says I am very much needed at Sorrento. I will not burden you with the details of the situation which requires my presence, especially as I feel completely capable of coping with it, once I am on the spot. But I think the sooner I *am* there, the better."

"Is it a situation in which I could be of any help?" Clyde inquired. He could hardly have responded otherwise. Yet the thought of leaving Cindy Lou was even more unwelcome to him than the requirement of sharing it.

"Thank you. But as I just said, I feel quite capable of coping with the situation. However, I should be much obliged if you would make the necessary travel arangements for Mildred and me. We can be ready to leave whenever you can get suitable reservations. I should prefer not to stay at a hotel, just now, if that can be avoided—in other words, if we could take a train from Convent for New Orleans that would make good connections with one going north from there—"

"I'll see about it the first thing in the morning, Miss Sophie. Not that I want you to feel hurried, you understand."

He hoped he spoke with conviction and, in one sense, he spoke with complete sincerity. He did not want her to feel hurried—that would be inhospitable and unfair. But to have Cindy Lou to himself again. . . !

"Yes, I do understand," she said quietly; and suddenly he knew that she did and that the understanding had in it no element of hurt feelings. "Of course, if everything were not going well here, I would not leave," she continued. "But I am satisfied that it is. Your servants are capable and devoted. Tudie is developing into an excellent nurse. I do not think she will need any advice or help in her care of Larry, but if she does, Mrs. Surget and Dr. Bringier are both close at hand. Besides, Larry is a remarkably vigorous baby. I doubt if you will have any anxiety on the score of his health. But I know you will watch over him with the utmost care. You have inspired me with a great deal of confidence, Clyde, through the years. I know that Lucy found complete happiness in her marriage with you and that you were a true father to her daughter. You never failed her in any way and you will never fail Larry, either, I am sure of that."

"Thank you," Clyde said in a low voice. He would have liked to say more, for he had never expected his mother-in-law to say as much. But he could not.

"So it is not with anything connected with Larry's immediate welfare that I wish to talk with you," Miss Sophie went on. "It is about his future prospects."

"His future prospects?"

"Yes. I assume that, of course, he will be one of your heirs. But I have been wondering whether, in the interests of complete justice, I should not make him one of mine, also."

"I'm afraid I don't quite follow you, Miss Sophie. You're right, of course, in assuming that he'll be my heir. But—"

She raised her hand and something about the gesture robbed her interruption of all discourtesy. "Let me explain. You knew, of course, that Lucy wished to have Bushrod inherit Sorrento and Amalfi. Cary was so young when she left Virginia and was there so little afterward that she never had any special feeling for my plantations—all her interests were in Louisiana. Besides, she was amply provided for, both by you and by her husband. So it was understood between Lucy and myself that Cary should not have any share in my property. But this understanding was never put into writing—at least to my knowledge. Was it, to yours?"

"No. Lucy never discussed the matter with me, beyond saying what you've just told me—that she wanted Bushrod to have Amalfi and Sorrento. That seemed to me eminently fair. As you say, Cary had no special interests in Virginia and she was provided for here."

"And you are very sure that Lucy left no will or even any memorandum?"

"Reasonably sure. She never spoke of that, either. And I think I'd have been bound to know it, if she had. She wouldn't have done a thing like that secretly—in fact, I don't think she could have. She talked with me freely, she respected my judgment. She certainly would have asked my advice and we'd have consulted a lawyer together. We—it was our habit to do things together."

"I know," Miss Sophie said; and again Clyde was moved by the consciousness of her understanding. "Nevertheless, in a case like this, we must take every precaution. I assume you haven't looked through her desk—or in any other place where she might have kept papers?"

"No. I haven't touched anything that belonged to her. I—I can't."

"Would you like me to do it for you? I realize how painful all this is for you, Clyde. It is painful for me, too, of course. But this is your first experience of the kind, and I have had to meet others like it, many times already. If it would help you—or relieve you—to have me—I will not say to put Lucy's personal belongings in order, for of course she always kept them in perfect order—but to have me go through them and decide what should be done with them—her clothes, as well as her papers—"

She paused, and Clyde knew she was thinking of those other personal belongings which she had been obliged to go through—her husband's, her four sons', probably her parents' as well. No, bereavement and tragedy were nothing new to this aged woman, who still bore herself with such calm dignity. He was shamed by her fortitude, but he was grateful for it.

"Thank you," he said again. "It would help me—it would relieve me very greatly." Then, with an effort, he added, "I suppose some of the clothes should be given away—those which we would have no special reason for keeping and which might be of use to someone else. And probably some of the papers should be carefully preserved and others destroyed. I will leave you to decide about all such things."

"I will try to merit your confidence. . . . And now, let us go back to this question of inheritance. My will, as it stands, leaves everything to Lucy. My first thought was that, in altering it, I should leave everything to Bushrod, in accordance with Lucy's expressed wishes. Now I am not so sure that it would be right. It is true that Cary did not need my plantations or care for them. But it is no longer a question of Cary—it is a question of her son. Is it conceivable to you that he might care for them, or need them?"

"I hadn't thought of Larry in connection with Sorrento and Amalfi. I'd only thought of him in connection with Cindy Lou. But yes, now that you speak of it, I can see it's conceivable that he might care very greatly for them, that he might even need them. I'll do the best I can for him, you know that; you've been good enough to say so. I think I have enough so that he'll never lack for any essentials. But of course I can't be sure. I nearly went under once before. I would have, if Lucy hadn't been here to help me. And now, there isn't anyone. . . . Besides, I'm not a young man any more. I'm—well, I'm pretty close to being an old one, though I don't like to admit it. If I should die—"

"I have faith that you won't die, and I have faith that you'll never go under, that you'll be able to give Larry all the necessities of life, even if you can't give him all the luxuries. At the same time, I can't lightly deprive him of the heritage which might be his in Virginia. I know that, as a Virginian, I'm prejudiced. But I still feel it to be a very special heritage."

"Yes, you're right. It is—a very special heritage." He looked across at her and, as he did so, he felt that she herself personified much which gave that heritage a special value. "Of course Cary entrusted Larry to me on her deathbed," he said. "As I said before, I've never thought of him except in connection with Cindy Lou. But if it were for his welfare—"

"That's what we must decide. We must weigh one advantage against another. Let me repeat that I would not lightly deprive Larry of his Virginia heritage. On the other hand, if Bushrod were the sole inheritor of Sorrento and Amalfi, it might simplify things for you."

"I don't think I quite follow you."

"I believe you promised Lucy, when you married her, that her children should both be your heirs, that they should share and share alike. Cary is dead, and what you would normally have given her, naturally goes to her son. But Bushrod is alive. He will certainly expect his share."

Clyde rose, thrusting his hands behind him, so that his mother-in-law should not see how convulsively he had clenched them. He could still control the expression of his face—that much, at least, he owed to his career as a gambler; but at this moment his hands might very well betray him. *Bushrod's share!* As if the wastrel had not already had more than was due a scoundrel of his stripe—the substantial sum which had settled his Richmond debts, the twenty thousand he had extracted from his stepfather just before Cary's wedding! Clyde knew that if he told Miss Sophie about this, she would feel that any promise he had made was already more than fulfilled. But how could he tell her that her only grandson, for whom her unshaken love was the only weak spot in her armor, had been expelled from the gentlemen's club where membership was part of that Virginia heritage in which she felt so much proper pride? How could he denounce Bushrod for what he was—a card cheat and a blackmailer? She had already bravely borne, in her lifetime, more than any woman should be called upon to bear without breaking. Now that life was drawing to an end and, after losing her home, her husband and her four sons in a horrible war, she had lost her only daughter and her only granddaughter in a holocaust which, though less widespread, was equally horrible. He could not give the blow which all too literally might be the death stroke, even to save Larry.

"Certainly Bushrod will expect his share, ma'am," he said gently, though a little heavily. "And certainly he shall have it. A promise is a promise."

"Of course. I was quite sure you would feel that way about it. That is why I brought up the subject; and that is what I meant when I said I thought I might suggest something which would simplify matters all around." Clyde was caught off guard by the directness of her gaze; the wise old eyes were wells of understanding and—could it be possible? —of sympathy. "Before there was any question of Larry, Lucy wanted Bushrod to inherit all the Virginia properties, in which Larry now has a right to share," Miss Sophie continued. "I am eager to follow Lucy's wishes, and you have been good enough to agree this should be done. But it would be manifestly unfair to Larry if, after being excluded from the Virginia heritage, he were still expected to surrender part of the Louisiana heritage as well. In a word, it should be made plain to Bushrod that if he takes full title to both Sorrento and Amalfi, any claim he might otherwise rightly have to a share in Cindy Lou is thereby canceled. That was what I meant when I referred to simplifying the situation for all of us."

For a moment, Clyde stared at her dumbly. The waves of relief and of thankfulness which had swept through him while she was speaking left him, literally, bereft of words. With the same calmness that had characterized everything she had said in the course of the interview, his mother-in-law returned his look. It was he who broke the silence.

"Miss Sophie," he said huskily, "I want you to know I feel it wasn't only in giving me Lucy's heart that God was very good to me. I feel he was good to me in letting me know you."

"Thank you for telling me that," she said. "I knew how you felt about Lucy and, of course, there is every reason why you should. As far as I am concerned. . . ." She turned away, but not so quickly that he failed to see there were tears in her eyes and that her face had suddenly softened. "You—you are magnanimous in your estimate of me, Clyde." She opened the volume which was lying on the table beside her, the one from which Clyde had last read to Lucy, and glanced at the passage where a bookmark indicated a stopping place. Then she laid it down again. "About this will," she said, "I will take the necessary legal steps as soon as possible. Of course, under ordinary circumstances, Bushrod should be consulted. But since he will not be available immediately—and I am coming to the reasons for that presently—and since I do not feel that, at my age, I should delay any important undertaking, I shall draw it up at once—or almost at once. But it occurs to me that I may have an ally on whom you probably have not counted, and that I had better talk with her, too."

"An ally?" Clyde inquired, sitting down again and clasping his hands lightly in front of him. He was no longer afraid to have Miss Sophie see them.

"Yes. I should not be surprised if Mabel were secretly longing for a reconciliation. We are talking with each other very candidly, Clyde; so why not admit, in confidence, that Mabel has probably not had many admirers in the course of her life? She is not—well, she is not exactly the type that commands widespread masculine attention." This time, when Clyde's glance met his mother-in-law's, he saw there was actually a slight twinkle in her eye. "Bushrod's courtship, when she had almost reached the age where any woman, however fascinating, is conscious that her powers of enchantment are waning, must have seemed to her like the suit of a Prince Charming," Miss Sophie went on, imperturbably. "And whatever his faults as a husband, I have no doubt that Bushrod showed himself very charming after marriage, too. I do not see how Mabel can help missing his—ah—companionship."

"Perhaps she does," Clyde admitted. Now that Miss Sophie had presented the idea to him in this way, he did not find it surprising.

"There is also another aspect of the case which might be helpful to us. Numbers of rich New Yorkers seem to be discovering Virginia, so to speak, just now. The quantity of estates they are buying, or attempting to buy, in the Old Dominion is really amazing. I do not quite understand why they seem to fancy themselves suddenly in the role of country gentry, but the fact remains that they do." Again, Clyde caught the humorous glint in the wise old eyes. "I think Mabel would be very much gratified at the prospect of establishing herself and her husband as landed proprietors," Miss Sophie continued. "Especially as it could be done with comparatively little expense. If I'm not mistaken, she shares her father's aversion to loose purse strings. My suggestion to her would be that if she and Bushrod can agree to let bygones be bygones, they should build a house on the ruins of Amalfi, following the original plan in as far as that is practical for present-day requirements. The house would be theirs. Then, after my death, they could move into mine if they preferred—or they could hold it in trust for their offspring, if any. I suppose it is still imaginable that they might have a child. Mabel may not be as old as she looks. But, even if she is, motherhood is probably not an impossibility."

"No, I suppose not," Clyde muttered. He had never thought of Mabel as a potential mother, and he did so now with reluctance, as the beautiful maternal images of Lucy and Cary rose before him. Moreover, if Bushrod and Mabel should have a child, that would no doubt preclude any possibility that in time the Virginia estate, or any portion of it, might come into Larry's possession. But that, he reminded himself, would matter very little, if it were made certain that no claim against Larry's undisputed ownership of Cindy Lou should ever be raised. . . . With a start, Clyde realized he had not·been listening to what his mother-in-law was telling him.

". . . my purpose to stipulate," he heard her say, as his attention focused on her words, "in this will I propose to draw, that any child of Bushrod and Mabel's, or of any marriage he might enter into in the event of her death, could inherit Amalfi and Sorrento. But if he should die without such issue, the property would naturally revert to Larry."

"I see," Clyde said. He did not add anything further. He did not feel anything further was needed. He gathered that Miss Sophie did not think so, either, from the way she went on.

"Now that those questions are settled, as far as they can be in the course of one conversation," she continued, "I think I should speak to you about the other letters which reached me this morning. I said, a few minutes ago, that I would tell you why I realized that Bushrod would not immediately be available for consultation. One of those letters was from him. It seems that he has had typhoid fever—a light case, fortunately. There is no cause for alarm. But he was slightly delirious at the time you cabled him about his mother's death, and his physician—a Dr. Norchais, who seems to be a man of good sense— felt it would be better to withhold the news from him until he was stronger. So it was delayed in reaching him. I do not know why he did not ask the doctor to cable a reply for him, when he did get it, but doubtless there was some good reason. This letter from him was written before you sent the second cable, announcing Cary's death. You probably will hear from him yourself within the next day or so."

"Probably," Clyde muttered. While he had been somewhat puzzled by the delay in hearing from Bushrod, he had been too preoccupied with other matters to give it much thought; and when he did think of it he had regarded it as a reprieve. He was, therefore, inclined to regard the attack of typhoid fever as a blessing in disguise, and regretted only that the case had not been a more serious one. However, he could not say any of this to Bushrod's grandmother, whose vision, clear as it was in most respects, was naturally obscured by love when she looked at him.

"It may be some time before he will be strong enough to undertake an ocean voyage," Miss Sophie went on. "And, if you approve, I shall write him, suggesting that, before coming to Cindy Lou, he stop off to see me at Sorrento. I would then lay before him immediately the arrangement on which you and I are agreed. I believe I could do so in such a way that he would grasp its advantages and the whole question would be settled without further delay."

"That might be a good idea," Clyde answered, still in more or less of a mutter; he would have liked to say that he had never found Bushrod slow to grasp anything that was to his advantage.

"The third letter," Miss Sophie continued, as if she had now dismissed the subject of Bushrod for the time being, "was from Pierre de Chanet, who wrote to express the sympathy of the entire family. But it was more than a letter of condolence. It also contained some rather bad news."

Clyde lifted his head quickly. He had not been able to feel that the news from Bushrod was bad, as far as he was concerned, and he could not believe that any news coming from Pierre de Chanet could cause him much distress, either. But he was eager to know what form it had taken.

"Of course everyone at Chateau Monteregard was deeply affected upon hearing of our terrible losses," Miss Sophie went on. "But poor Mr. Vincent was more crushed than any of the others, especially by the death of his only son. After all, this is natural. Mrs. Vincent is closer to Armande than she was to Savoie, and Armande has her husband and her baby to divert her thoughts from her bereavement. But Mr. Vincent could think of nothing else, and his mental condition has had a sad effect on his physical condition, as so often happens. He has had a stroke. Evidently, he has rallied, to a certain extent; but he speaks with difficulty and two of his limbs are affected. Mrs. Vincent is devoting all her time and strength to him. Of course there can be no question of moving him for a long time."

"I am very sorry," Clyde managed to say. But the words were perfunctory. He *was* sorry that Lamartine Vincent, who had long been a good friend of his, should have come to such a pass through grief; and fleetingly he resolved, for the first time, to put an end to his own brooding before it could get the better of him in one way or another. But he could not feel sorry that the Vincents would not be hastening home, that he would not have to share Larry with them. His thoughts raced ahead and, in his mind's eye, he saw Mrs. Vincent, who had never cared about Victoria, relinquishing her rights in it to Larry—for a consideration, of course, but still doing it. He could see her persuading Armande to do the same. Armande was, to all intents and purposes, a Frenchwoman now. She was dressed by Worth and Redfern, she inhabited a magnificent chateau, she moved in the most sophisticated Continental society, she was addressed as Madame la Marquise. She could not have all these privileges and perquisites in Louisiana and they meant much to her. Yes, someday Victoria, as well as Cindy Lou, would be Larry's. He could well afford to do without the Virginia heritage, great as this was. He would have one greater still in Louisiana. And his grandfather, Clyde Batchelor, would safeguard it for him. . . .

"I am sure you are," Clyde heard Miss Sophie saying. He did not realize, at first, with what she was agreeing. He had been looking so far into the future that, for the first time since Lucy's death, he had been unmindful of the present. And, before he could fully collect himself, his mother-in-law had risen, saying she did not think there was anything more they needed to discuss and that she would bid him good afternoon.

A week later she and Cousin Mildred left for Virginia. In the meantime, Miss Sophie had "gone through things," as she had promised. No document of any importance had been discovered among Lucy's papers. She had saved all the letters she had ever received from her mother, from Clyde, from Cary and from Bushrod. They were separated into neat little bundles. Miss Sophie told Clyde that she was leaving his letters and Cary's in Lucy's desk, but that, with his permission, she would take the others with her. Most of Lucy's clothing Miss Sophie quietly gave away. In recent years, Lucy had bought very few new dresses, and only the ones Clyde had given her in the earlier days of their marriage had qualities that made them worth saving; these her mother packed away with loving care, labeling each trunk as she did so. There was not much jewelry, either. Miss Sophie knew that Lucy had given most of the heirlooms and all the Page ornaments to Cary on the occasion of the girl's marriage, and if she wondered what had become of the other jewels, she did not say so. Clyde thought she probably guessed.

Neither one said anything about a future meeting when they parted at the depot. They both knew there would be few—if any—such meetings. But not because of ill will. After long years of antagonism and resentment, they had arrived at mutual respect and mutual understanding. These feelings were made manifest in their farewells to each other.

On his way home from the depot, Clyde stopped at the cemetery with flowers, as was now his daily habit. Usually, he and his mother-in-law had gone there together, since the distance was too great for her to walk, and he did not like to be the one to suggest that she should be driven there by a servant. But the previous evening she had said she would like to make her last visit to her granddaughter's tomb alone, and asked if Zack could not take her to the cemetery and wait for her at the gate; the Vincents' lot was not far from there; she could easily walk that short way, with no help from anyone, even Mildred. Clyde had complied all the more readily with her request because he, too, would have preferred to make such visits alone and was thankful that henceforth he would always be free to do so.

It had been a source of great grief to him that he could not insist that Cary, like her mother, should be entombed at Cindy Lou. But he knew long-established custom ordained that a wife should lie by her husband in death, as in life; a departure from this tradition would be viewed with great disapproval throughout the countryside, under any circumstances. In the present case, when the wedded pair had perished so close together and as the result of the same holocaust, such criticism would be all the more severe and widespread—no doubt properly. So Clyde had suppressed his longing, not voicing it to anyone, and he knew he had been right in following this course. But at first his grief had been all the greater because of his inner rebellion and because Cary seemed so much farther away from him than Lucy. Now, at last, he found assuagement both in the realization that Lucy's quiet resting place was hers alone—and therefore more wholly his own sanctuary—and in the thought that Cary was sharing a noble monument, since this was her due.

He approached the Vincents' stately tomb with more calmness than he had hitherto been able to command. Usually the tall iron gates of the driveway leading into the cemetery were locked, except to permit the passage of a funeral procession; pedestrians habitually entered by one of two smaller gates, on either side of the entrance, which were difficult to operate because of the unwieldiness caused by a heavy weight, suspended on an equally heavy chain, that hung from them and closed them automatically. A mourner, burdened with flowers, inevitably found their manipulation doubly difficult. Clyde was thankful to discover that, for once, the driveway was open and walked slowly down it, shifting his great sheaf of white azaleas and purple irises from one arm to the other as he went along, and pausing, occasionally, to take some note of his familiar surroundings which, hitherto, he had hardly noticed.

As Miss Sophie had said, the Vincents' lot was not far from the gates; but a wide variety of tombs rose from the intervening terrain. Some of these were mounds, no larger than the interment of a single coffin would require, which had been rigidly cemented and starkly white-washed; others, built of mellow brick in the form of either single or multiple ovens, were crumbling with age and neglect and lank grasses sprouted from them. There were, naturally, crosses of every size and kind, some of elaborately wrought iron, some of carefully chiseled marble, some of rudely hewn wood. The cemetery was very deep, extending back almost to the cypress swamps; and it was dominated, at the rear, by the tallest and most imposing of these crosses; even from a distance, Clyde was conscious of its majestic presence. Other crosses surmounted stone books or marked the corners of the ornate railings which enclosed the larger lots. Unlike the cemeteries of Barataria and the region near Grand Isle, with both of which Clyde was acquainted, this was not rich in shadow boxes; but he saw one, containing an appealing figure of the Virgin, robed in white and cloaked in blue. Flowers grew in abundance and, for the most part, apparently untended; they seemed to slope off in every direction. If he had cared to pluck irises and azaleas at random, he could have done so and, earlier in the season, there must have been quantities of paper-white narcissuses; soon there would be even greater quantities of roses. The more modern and important tombs, which were adorned with angels and other symbolic figures, were also decorated with well-filled flower vases; Clyde was by no means exceptional in his daily ritual, though, for the time being, he was alone.

The Vincents' lot was one of the many enclosed with an iron railing; but the gate to this was left open for his convenience. The monument was a towering one: a sarcophagus surmounted by a stone urn and severely plain, except for this and the fluted pillars at each corner, in turn surmounted a burial vault, so large as to suggest a chapel, with a complete façade of pillars and elaborate carvings simulating torches. A second urn, similar in design to the other, but open at the top, rose between the stone steps leading to the bronze doors. The flowers with which it was filled had been placed there only the day before; still they were not fresh enough to satisfy Clyde. He removed them, emptied the urn of its water and refilled it. Then, with loving care, he arranged the purple and white flowers he had brought with him. He was not skilled in such arts; it was Lucy who had always arranged their flowers. But what he lacked in proficiency, he made up for in patience and devotion. When he finally turned to leave, the urn had blossomed forth in beauty.

He was in no special hurry to reach home again and, since he no

308

longer had an armful of flowers, he could wander unencumbered down the driveway. Earlier, it was the character and setting of the tombs which had arrested him; now, he found himself studying their inscriptions. Most of the names on these were French, some of them preceded by the "de" which was the indication of nobility; and, in several instances, where a birthplace was recorded, this was in France. Most of the places—Pontarlier, Bouches-du-Rhône, St. Maximin—he had never heard of before; but one—La Rochelle—struck a responsive chord. The Chateau of Monteregard, if he were not greatly mistaken, was near that port. Cary and Savoie might well have visited it when they were staying with the De Chanets. Or possibly, Cary had gone there alone with Pierre. She must have been alone with him in the dark cave of which she had spoken, almost with her dying breath. It was more than probable that she had also visited the surrounding countryside and its towns with him. Pierre would easily have found some pretext for limiting such expeditions to himself and the object of his desire. . . .

The supposition disturbed Clyde's new-found sense of calm and he decided it was high time he left this somber place before he started some other fantastic train of thought. But as he turned away from the inscription which had proved so unreasonably upsetting, his eye fell on a plain stone slab and, involuntarily, he stopped.

> "*Ici repose en paix,*" he read
> "C. Aimée Boucry
> *épouse* d'Armand de Bourgeois
> *née le 3 Février* 1806
> *décédé le 4 Novembre* 1839
> *Bonne mère Tendre Épouse*
> *et sincère amie*
> *Elle emporte au tombeau*
> *les regrets de ceux qui l'ont connu.*"

The lettering of this simple epitaph was quaint and obscure. At several points Clyde, whose French was still somewhat sketchy, had been obliged to stop and puzzle over a word which was almost illegible, as well as more or less unintelligible to him. But it was not, after all, this inscription which had constrained him to stop. It was the words above it, which were clear, clean cut and newly chiseled:

CLOSED FOREVER

He did not have the vaguest idea of who Aimée Boucry de Bourgeois could have been, or how a woman who was a good mother, a tender wife and a sincere friend happened to be buried alone; neither did he know why, more than fifty years after her death—and not until that time—her tomb had been "Closed Forever." Then and there he resolved that he would never try to find the answer to any of these questions. Simultaneously, he made another firm resolution: Savoie's parents, of course, would still logically expect burial in their family vault; but, as far as Cary was concerned, it had closed forever, not only on her beautiful body, but on all the secrets she had not shared with him.

As he approached the garden, he saw that Tudie had taken Larry out in his perambulator. The baby was bareheaded and the sun, shining on his hair, which was glossy and black like his father's, gave it an added sheen. He was wearing a little blue knitted jacket which Lucy had made for him and which was exactly the color of his eyes—Cary's eyes. He was vigorously banging a silver rattle against the strap which confined his plump little person and, as usual, he hailed his grandfather with delight. But Clyde noticed a sign of progress which had gone unobserved before.

"I didn't realize he could sit up straight, all alone," he said admiringly. "Why, he hardly touches those fluffy pillows behind him at all!"

"Yassuh! Nossuh!" Tudie agreed with pride. "Won' be no time atall afore he starts to crawl. I never see no such smart baby, me, or either one feel his strength so young."

"Could he sit up in a high chair, do you think?"

"Jes' as good as he kin in a carriage."

"Very well. Get Miss Cary's high chair out of the storeroom and put it in the dining room. I'll have Larry with me, at mealtimes, from now on."

He gave his grandson a hearty hug and turned away, in the direction of the little enclosure where Lucy lay. Then he halted and turned again. He could visit that sanctuary later, after the day's work was done. Meanwhile, many matters, too long neglected, demanded his attention. Larry had been left to him in trust, and it would need all the effort of which he was capable to fulfill that obligation. He could truly serve the dead only through his service to the living.

He walked back toward the house and entered it by the door leading to his office. Then he rolled back the top of his desk and opened his safe. The entries in the ledger were complete, through the day when he and Lucy had last worked on them together—the day of her death. As he assembled his neglected papers and carried on the figures from there, the results were so reassuring that he wondered, more logically than ever before, why he had allowed Valois Dupré to talk him into selling the narrow strip of land, at the rear of the plantation, where the gravel bed was located. He had not confessed to Cary, on her deathbed, that he had done this, because he had been greatly moved by her admission that she was sorry for what she had said to him about it, the day when they had met on the river road and he had told her of Dupré's offer. But he had promptly taken her at her word, the first time, feeling, as he thought the matter over, that he should do anything and everything he could to lighten the load of indebtedness which Lucy was helping him to shoulder—and to lift. Necessarily, he had told Lucy about the sale, because after she began to help him with the ledgers she was obliged to enter all credits and debits in their books; but she had taken the news with her usual calmness, saying—just as Clyde had said to Cary on the occasion of their last talk—that their lives had been so full of numerous treasure in any case that they did not need to dig for more. Besides, Lucy had added—considering the question from another and more practical angle—why should they give even a passing thought to parting with a few barren arpents when the sale of these helped them to safeguard hundreds that were giving a rich yield of sugar and tobacco?

Her wise and dispassionate attitude had been a source of such immense relief to Clyde that, to a certain degree, he had eventually succeeded in sharing it. But he had never ceased to chafe over the loss of anything connected with Cary, or to regret his failure to keep intact the property he had originally acquired. Now, as he looked at his orderly books, it occurred to him for the first time that possibly he might someday be in a position to buy back the tract of land where he had sat in the sun, watching his little daughter as she dug and dug until finally, warm and weary, she had flung down her small spade and come to nestle in his arms. . . . He could not buy that land yet, of course, but perhaps someday. . . . Evidently Dupré was really not much interested in the property after all. In any event, he had not even yet started the process of washing the gravel, much less loading it and transporting it. If Clyde's mind had not been so occupied with other things, he would have asked Dupré when he intended to do so. But then, they had not seen much of each other lately. The next time they met, Clyde would question his friend about the matter. . . .

Meanwhile, the longer he worked on the records and accounts which had lain untouched since Lucy's death, the more causes for reassurance he found. Over two thousand carrots of strong, dark tobacco were ready for shipment and they would bring a good price, now that two families—the Guglielmos and the Roussels—were vying with each other for dominance as perique factors, whereas the Roussels had formerly controlled the entire market. The cane fields had also yielded abundantly. Fair weather had permitted the harvest to proceed almost without interruption; not one heavy frost had closed down to threaten the tall growth, even with the coming of December. Sugar was selling at three and a half cents for plantation raws; altogether, he should realize forty thousand dollars after paying the Vincent tollage for processing. From that, of course, land taxes, labor, fertilizer and other costs of cultivation would have to be deducted; but the net profits would still far exceed his expectations.

For several hours, Clyde worked steadily and intensively on his ledgers. But when Zack came to tell him that dinner was served, he smiled as he looked up.

"I believe I have a young gentleman dining with me today, Zack," he said.

"So you does, suh, for a fac'!" Zack answered, returning the smile.

Larry was already at the table when Clyde reached it and after that, he did not dread going into the dining room any more. The silent, somber meals were a thing of the past.

 CHAPTER XV

THE NEWS which Clyde received from abroad, both directly and indirectly, continued to seem extremely important to him.

Miss Sophie wrote him almost immediately. While she was on the train, she had given a good deal of thought to their long conversation in the library, she told him. As a result of this reflection, she had decided to go straight through to New York, for she felt it was of even more consequence that she should see Mr. Stoddard and Mabel immediately than that she should give her first attention to straightening out the situation at Sorrento. She had found Mr. Stoddard more than co-operative; indeed, he had been so insistent that she and Cousin Mildred should be his guests, during their stay in the city, that it would have been really discourteous to decline. As a result of this hospitality, she had been able to have a series of discussions with him, instead of the single conference she had sought; and each time they talked with one another they were in closer agreement than on the previous occasion. Mr. Stoddard had even gone so far as to say that he thought her offer generous, and that the acceptance of it would be extremely advantageous to his daughter. With Mabel herself, Miss Sophie had not had a chance to talk, for the simple reason that Mabel had taken the first ship for France, after hearing about Bushrod's attack of typhoid fever. Bushrod had written her an appealing letter, as soon as his extreme weakness would permit him to take pen in hand—in fact, over the protests of his physician and his nurses, who insisted he should not so overtax his limited strength. He had told Mabel how much he needed her, now that he was ill and alone in a foreign country; moreover, her presence would help him to assuage his sorrow in the great loss he had suffered through the death of his mother and sister. It was really a beautiful letter, and Mabel had been very much moved. . . .

Miss Sophie did not say that Mr. Stoddard had been very much moved; and Clyde reflected, not without a certain grim satisfaction, that the harsh old man had probably not been hoodwinked for a moment, but had understood that Bushrod's allowance, as a remittance man, had proved inadequate for his extravagant way of life, and that the only way he could see to increase his income, during his convalescence—which he would not be averse to prolonging, if this could be done in some pleasurable manner—was through a reconciliation with his wife. Clyde took, if possible, an even greater satisfaction in the thought that Stoddard, shrewd as he was, had been no match for Miss Sophie. Her son-in-law could visualize exactly how she had handled that series of conferences, and how each had resulted in "closer agreement" than its predecessor. . . .

Eventually, Mabel wrote to Clyde herself, in terms more affectionate than ever before, and in a way which indicated triumphant contentment. She and Bushrod were really having a *second honeymoon,* she said. They had been fortunate in finding a *beautiful* villa, fully staffed and finely furnished, at Menton, and they were going to remain there until Bushrod had *entirely* recovered his strength. After that, they would travel for a time in a *leisurely* way; there were so many places she had never seen and that Bushrod was *eager* to show her, among them the great German spas. Of course, she had been to Europe *several* times; but her father's idea had always been just to go to the *big cities* and he had been handicapped because he had never learned *foreign* languages. She did not need to tell Mr. Batchelor that Bushrod spoke French *like a native* and that he had a good command of German and Italian as well. He was giving her lessons. Naturally, she had studied French at school, but that was not like having Bushrod for a teacher. And other languages were *so neglected* in the United States. It really was very backward, in cultural directions. . . .

Clyde smiled over this letter, too. Although geography was not one of his strong points, he did not need to be told that Menton was conveniently near Monte Carlo, and he thought it quite likely that Bushrod would not regain his strength sufficiently to travel much until he had exhausted the possibilities of the Casino, or Mabel's newly awakened patience, or both. Then, after a "cultural" interval devoted to museums and cathedrals, he would doubtless "overtax" his strength again and require the refreshment of a spa where the gambling rooms were conveniently adjacent to the mineral springs. At all events, Clyde doubted very greatly whether Bushrod and Mabel would return to the United States before autumn; and then they would very logically go straight to Sorrento, so that the plans for the new house at Amalfi might be made on the spot. This meant that they would hardly be coming to Cindy Lou much before Christmas. Nothing could have suited him better.

Meanwhile, he also heard several times from the Vincents. The first of these letters came from Armande, who told him that her father was very low; indeed, the attendant physician had come out of the sickroom looking extremely grave, and had said that it would be well to summon a priest, and that until other instructions were issued, the patient was to be given nothing except champagne. Though Clyde had never come in close contact with the sacrament of extreme unction, he was acquainted with its grave significance; the reference to champagne, however, puzzled him, until Mrs. Surget, to whom he showed the letter, clarified it for him.

"I haven't heard of its usage, in such a connection, for a long while; but I do remember, vaguely, having heard that it was customary in certain parts of France for a physician to make such a recommendation, instead of saying outright that the end was near. The family was supposed to understand, and still, feelings were spared, scenes averted and all amenities observed. You must admit, Clyde, that the French make a fine art out of *savoir-faire!*"

"All right, I'll admit it," he said. But he spoke rather grudgingly, and Mrs. Surget had no trouble in gathering that the admission carried with it no admiration, and that probably his lack of enthusiasm had other causes than the one under discussion. "Well, evidently poor Lamartine is in a bad way," he went on, looking at the letter again. "But I don't believe he's dead, after all. This was written over two weeks ago, and I haven't had a cable since. I think I would have, if the worst had happened."

Clyde's surmise proved correct. About ten days later, he received a second letter, this time from Mrs. Vincent, which told him that though extreme unction and champagne had both been administered, as directed, her dear husband had rallied after all, and was even beginning to regain some of his powers of speech, though his physical helplessness was as great as ever. "In fact," she continued, "I am writing you now in accordance with Lamartine's expressed wish. It is evident that our sojourn in France must be greatly prolonged, and that when— or if—he is able to return to Victoria, he will not be able to take an active part in its supervision. Under these circumstances, it would mean a great deal to him—and, I may add, to Armande and me, also—if you would undertake the management of the plantation, on a business basis. Of course, you have had a hand in its management for a long time already. Both dear Lamartine and poor Savoie relied on your advice and your help, and I know that since we suffered our great loss you have taken an even more active part in its direction. Grateful as we are for your good offices, we cannot permit you to continue them, as a favor, indefinitely. (Of course, in a sense, everything you would do would be considered a favor, but I think you will grasp my meaning.) We should, therefore, be most appreciative if, without false pride, you would set forth the terms on which you feel such an arrangement would be not only fair, but profitable, from your point of view."

So it had come—the chance for which he had so greatly hoped. He had not lifted a finger, he had not voiced a wish—and still it had come. For some time already, he had been taking Larry through the gardens and orchard and to the stables and dairy, carrying the baby over his shoulder when he himself made his daily rounds. More recently, he had set Larry in front of him on the saddle when he went to the drying sheds and the sugarhouse. Now, for the first time, he went farther afield with his precious charge—past the charred remains of the mock Monteregard, from which he still averted his eyes, and on to the big house and wide arpents of Victoria. The baby sat as straight on horseback as he did in his perambulator and his high chair, and he showed no fear when Spice, Clyde's favorite mount, changed his gait from a walk to a rack. Instead, Larry gave the gurgle of delight for which his grandfather had learned to listen. Clyde, who was holding him firmly enclosed in the hollow of one arm, raised the other and waved his hand back and forth in an encompassing gesture, as he reined in his horse.

"That's going to be yours someday, Larry," he said. "*All* of it! And when it is, it'll be worth more than it is today—a lot more. I'll see to that."

Larry gurgled again and pounded on the pommel. Clyde understood this to mean that the baby wanted to be off again, if anything at a smarter clip than before. The ride was resumed at a lively pace and, before it ended, embraced both plantations. Then late that night, after Larry had been put to bed, Clyde spent several hours in figuring. Before he went to bed himself, he wrote to Mrs. Vincent, telling her that he was honored by her request and that he would be glad to assume the management of Victoria on a business basis. He suggested a salary of five thousand a year. He had reckoned that with careful management he could gradually pay off the mortgage at Cindy Lou and still have enough left for Larry and himself to live on, from the proceeds of his own crops; he could even put aside a little for Larry's education. Everything that came from Victoria could be salted away for its eventual purchase. If that were done, in ten years' time he would have fifty thousand dollars, plus interest, and with fifty thousand. . . . Even if he could not live to see Larry grow up, he could live for ten years. He must. . . .

In the same mail that brought an answer from Mrs. Vincent, accepting his terms and thanking him for his co-operation, Clyde received another letter from Mabel: she felt that the summer climate of the Riviera was perhaps a little too enervating for Bushrod, now that he was so much better. They were leaving Menton for Paris the following week; from there they were going to Munich, Dresden and Berlin to see the galleries. After that, to Baden-Baden. . . .

Clyde grinned and chucked Larry under the chin.

As time went on, he had more and more reason to congratulate himself on his prophetic vision. Bushrod and Mabel landed at New York in late October and, almost immediately, proceeded to Sorrento, accompanied by an eminent architect who was enormously pleased at the prospect of constructing a mansion with all modern improvements, but modeled after the original one at Amalfi. According to him, there was no reason why work could not begin as soon as the plans were approved and, with any luck at all, the foundations could be laid before the ground froze; after those were in, building could continue straight through the winter. He was slightly puzzled because his clients did not wish to remain at Sorrento while the building progressed, as he himself thought it far and away the most impressive estate he had ever seen; and he was still more puzzled when Mr. Page refused point blank to winter in Richmond, in spite of the practicality of such a plan and Mrs. Page's avowed approval of it. However, he agreed, under pressure, that Washington was not too far off to permit frequent conferences and, since Mr. Page seemed to feel that was the ideal place to spend the winter, he would offer no objections. But a remote plantation in Louisiana—a place where there was no telephone and no mail delivery—was something else again. He would not guarantee that a move might not be made, contrary to their wishes, if they stayed there for any length of time, because he would not be able to get in touch with them readily. Of course, the alternative would be to hold up work until their return; but he understood they wished this to progress as rapidly as possible. Of course, a brief visit—one which involved an absence of ten days or, at the outside, a fortnight—would not make much difference. But he very earnestly advised. . . .

It was, accordingly, for only a brief visit that Mabel and Bushrod came to Cindy Lou late that autumn; and in spite of the fact that Miss Sophie and Clyde had both felt so sure, the previous spring, that she would never come there again, she came with them and so did Cousin Mildred. Mr. Stoddard once more offered his private car and, at the last moment, decided that he, too, would like to join the group. So Cindy Lou was filled with guests again and, this time, Clyde did not find their presence hard to accept. Even Bushrod, who revealed only his personable best, did not prove a thorn in the flesh; Clyde could afford to let bygones be bygones, as far as his stepson was concerned, now that his grandson's future was so amply safeguarded.

Miss Sophie's new will had been made, along the lines she and Clyde had discussed, and approved by all concerned. Clyde had also made a will, in which Cindy Lou was bequeathed outright to Larry. Bushrod, Mabel and Mr. Stoddard all seemed as well satisfied with Clyde's arrangement for the future as they were with Miss Sophie's. Even the provision that Amalfi and Sorrento should eventually revert to Larry, if Bushrod died without issue from a marriage sanctioned by the Church, seemed to create no hard feelings. Simpering, Mabel confided to Miss Sophie that she already had "expectations." She had not seen a specialist yet, but she was almost sure. . . . Miss Sophie passed on the news to Clyde with the slight twinkle for which he was learning to watch. He smiled and shrugged by way of reply. It did not greatly matter, after all, whether Larry eventually came into possession of the Virginia plantations; he would have enough, and to spare, with Cindy Lou and Victoria. Besides, his grandfather was so delightfully preoccupied with the present stage of his development that it was all the easier to assume that the future would take care of itself. Larry was saying a few words now, adding to their number almost daily, and his physical development was more than keeping pace with his mental progress. He was walking, too, not staggering and stumbling about and then falling down suddenly and bursting into tears, but strutting sturdily from place to place with complete self-confidence and including everyone within his range of vision with a wide, disarming grin. His table manners were equally pleasing. He grasped his silver mug firmly in both chubby hands and, after quaffing from it, set it down with a sigh of satisfied repletion; he even waved away all proffers of help in the use of his short-handled spoon. Miss Sophie declared that she had never seen so young a child show so much independence about feeding himself—and his food certainly agreed with him. His red cheeks glowed and his blue eyes sparkled beneath his unruly shock of black hair; his build was sturdy, his stature surprising. He was really gorgeous looking, as well as remarkably intelligent. . . .

Exultantly, Clyde listened to her plaudits, feeling every word to be well merited. Cousin Mildred almost groveled with admiration; and Mr. Stoddard, who had begun by saying gruffly that, while he did not actually dislike small children, he had never been able to understand the doting fondness they inspired, was soon observed to be making friendly, if covert, overtures to Larry; within a few days, he, too, was shamelessly voicing his admiration of the "fine little boy." Since Larry had inherited not only several silver mugs, but also two silver porringers, a silver plate and a complete silver *couvert,* there was nothing along these lines which Mr. Stoddard could consistently offer in the way of a gift, and it was not in his nature to think of a rocking horse or a nest of blocks. But one day, with an air of great secrecy, he went to

317

Baton Rouge and came back brandishing a passbook; he had opened a savings account, in Larry's name, with a hundred dollars.

"Of course, I wouldn't have done it if there were any danger that I'd be robbing my own grandchild," he said importantly; at which announcement, made to the family as a whole, Mabel blushed deeply and exclaiming, *"Papa!"* hastened from the room. "Well, perhaps I shouldn't have mentioned such prospects, just yet anyway," Mr. Stoddard added, looking after his daughter apologetically. "But what I mean is, there'll be plenty for the next generation, no matter how many little youngsters are coming along. And the more the merrier, I say."

No one disputed this statement or any other that he made. In fact, the visit proved so unexpectedly harmonious in every way that Clyde, to his own surprise, suggested that it should be prolonged to include Christmas. He had ordered a tree from New Orleans—it was unthinkable that Larry should not have one, even if the year of mourning had not yet run its course. He was already old enough to delight in the star which would crown it, in the glittering tinsel and the multicolored balls with which it would be trimmed and the candles with which it would be lighted. Why, Clyde could remember that Cary, at approximately the same age! . . . He was sure that Cary, and Lucy, too, for that matter, would want Larry to have his tree, that year and every year. Clyde also intended to have the house garlanded with scarlet-berried, silver-leafed youpon, just as Lucy had always done. Then of course the Negroes would expect, as usual, to make a big bonfire of roseau canes and driftwood on the lower *batture,* hard by the river. In fact, he thought the bonfire had already been laid. And after the tree had been lighted and the gifts distributed, the well-dried reeds would be kindled and their every joint would burst with a report like a firecracker, so that for a few moments the blaze would rattle like a volley of musketry. Larry would be delighted with that, too—nonsense, of course it would not frighten him! That child had never shown the slightest sign of fright about anything! And nonsense, of course he could stay up long enough to see the bonfire! It would not hurt him, for once, to go to bed an hour or so later than usual. Besides, they could have the tree by four o'clock; at this time of year, it was already first evening by then and by six o'clock it was good dark. . . .

Miss Sophie and Cousin Mildred did not require much urging to remain for the celebrations thus outlined. But Mr. Stoddard, with genuine regret, declared that he must be getting back to the office; and Mabel and Bushrod received a telegram from the architect, saying that one of the guest chambers would have to be sacrificed at Amalfi, if both his clients required dressing rooms and still insisted that he keep to the size and shape of the original house; he would not take the sole responsibility for the decision. So three of the guests at Cindy

Lou took their departure, under circumstances which still showed no strain; and Clyde admitted to himself that he was actually enjoying the presence of the other two and that he would be sorry when they left. Several times Miss Sophie suggested that she and Cousin Mildred should be getting back to Virginia; but each time Clyde persuaded her to remain until the weather was a little milder. So it was not until one afternoon in February, when he reluctantly brought her a paper whose screaming headlines proclaimed the sinking of the *Maine* in Havana Harbor, that she told him she really must go home, and that he knew that he could not and should not try to dissuade her from her decision.

"This is going to mean war, Clyde. If it does—or rather, when it does—Virginians will hasten to offer their services to the government. In that way, at least, this conflict may be a blessing in disguise—it will open new wounds, but it will heal old ones which are worse. You will find the great survivors of the Confederate Army vying with each other to assure President McKinley of their support. And you will find the sons of the men who perished in the Lost Cause doing the same. Bushrod will certainly be among the first to take such action. I must not be away from the plantations while he is gone."

"You're probably right about Bushrod. And right about going back to Sorrento, too, I'm afraid. I hate to have you leave, Miss Sophie, I certainly do. But I can see how you feel."

Her first letter to Clyde after her return to Sorrento revealed the accuracy of her surmises. Bushrod had succeeded in joining the Volunteer Calvalry, under the command of General Joseph Wheeler, who had been a friend of both his father's and his grandfather's. Before long, Mabel had joined him in Tampa, where she obviously enjoyed herself immensely, sitting in a rocking chair on the veranda of the Tampa Bay Hotel, drinking enormous quantities of iced tea and chatting amicably with the wives, mothers and sisters of other volunteers. When the cavalry embarked for Cuba she waved a tearful farewell to the *Allegheny* and returned to Amalfi, where she sang "Good-by, Dolly Gray" on every possible occasion and dwelt upon the war news with ever-increasing satisfaction. Bushrod had been among the few chosen by "Fighting Joe" to accompany him when he pushed through the surf on the beach and landed at Daiquiri; then Bushrod had gone with Wheeler on the first exploratory trip to the interior. When it became evident that the position assigned by General Shafter to the Volunteer Cavalry was such that it would probably be the last to see action, Bushrod was one of the officers to voice his dissatisfaction and to take part in a maneuver later described as "unique in military annals": the one in which Wheeler took a thousand men, outflanked General Dawson and other divisions of his own army and provoked a fight with the Spanish troops. The indiscretion of this deed was matched by its daring and surpassed by its success; every man who had taken part in it was acclaimed a hero.

As the summer advanced, the acclamation in Mabel's case became more and more emotional. The news reached Virginia that, in a moment of understandable excitement, Wheeler had forgotten in which war he was fighting and had shouted, "We've got the Yankees on the run!" When she heard this, Mabel stopped singing "Dolly Gray" and began to sing "Dixie." Apparently her own memory was not wholly reliable, for she had been born in New Jersey, but she had begun to resent any reminder of this; she now said "cyar" for car and "gyarden" for garden and joined the Episcopal church. Bushrod was promoted from lieutenant to captain and she became convinced that not only Wheeler but every high-ranking officer from Shafter down was seeking her husband's advice. Bushrod was cited for conspicuous gallantry under enemy fire and she began to visualize the ceremony at which the President would present him with the Congressional Medal, while she stood at his side. Bushrod was slightly wounded in the shoulder and she took to her bed and lay for days in a darkened room, considering whether it might not be well to order elaborate mourning, so that she would be properly prepared if she received an official notice of his death. His prompt recovery actually had in it certain elements of disappointment for her.

Meanwhile, her patriotic pride and consuming anxiety were not confined to her husband; she bewailed the suffering of all the "heroes" who shared his lot. One day she brought a copy of a certain prominent weekly to Sorrento and asked Miss Sophie if she had read the poem entitled, "The Yankee Dude'll Do." Miss Sophie confessed that she had not.

"It's terribly touching," Mabel informed her. "I thought perhaps you might have missed it, so I brought the magazine with me." Miss Sophie took the proffered periodical and began to read.

"When Cholly swung his golfstick on the links,
Or knocked the tennis ball across the net,
With his bangs done up in cunning little kinks,
When he wore the tallest collar he could get,
Oh, it was the fashion then
To impale him on the pen—
To regard him as a being made of putty through and through
But his racquet's laid away,
He is roughing it today;
And heroically proving that the Yankee dude'll do.

When Clarence cruised about upon the yacht,
Or drove out with his footman in the park,

320

His mama, it was generally thought,
Ought to have him in her keeping after dark!
Oh, we ridiculed him then,
We impaled him on the pen,
We thought he was effeminate, and we dubbed him 'Sissy' too—
But he nobly marched away,
He is eating pork today,
And heroically proving that the Yankee dude'll do."

"It's very amusing, isn't it?" Miss Sophie said, looking up with a smile.

"Amusing! You don't mean to say you think that's a *humorous* poem?"

"My dear Mabel, how can I help thinking so? 'He is eating pork today' . . . he is, too. What do you suppose my husband and my sons and my son-in-law—and all the rest of the South, combatants and noncombatants for that matter, ate during the War Between the States?"

"I don't know. Chicken, I suppose. That's what they—I mean we—eat mostly nowadays anyhow."

Miss Sophie handed the magazine back to Mabel without further comment. Mabel read the poem aloud to the end.

"How they hurled themselves against the angry foe,
In the jungle—in the trenches—on the hill!
When the word to charge was given every dude was on the go—
He was there to die, to capture, or to kill!
Oh, he struck his level when
Men were called upon again
To preserve the ancient glory of the old red, white and blue!
He has thrown his spats away,
He is wearing spurs today,
And the world will please take notice that the Yankee dude'll do."

" 'He is wearing spurs today!' " Mabel repeated triumphantly. " 'The world will please take notice that the Yankee dude'll do!' Well, the world *is* taking notice!" She left the room abruptly, taking the magazine with her, and afterward she wrote to Bushrod that he must not be surprised, when he reached home, to find that his grandmother had failed very greatly while he was gone. The war was already over when the letter reached him, and in his brief reply he said that in this case he would hasten home as soon as possible, in order to relieve Miss Sophie of all responsibility connected with the plantations. But Mabel could not wait for him to get there. Like hundreds of other hysterical women, she rushed to Camp Mohawk to welcome her returning hero, thereby greatly adding to the difficulties with which General Wheeler was trying to cope. Conditions at camp were unquestionably bad; there was a scarcity of water, inadequate sanitation, general sickness and discomfort. Mabel's enthusiasm gave way to vituperation; there was nothing she could say that was denunciatory enough to express her opinion of the President, the Secretary of War and all others in authority. With the least possible delay, she "rescued" her hero from the United States Army. Never, she declared, would she again consent to his departure from Amalfi. At last he had returned to his ancestral home, which she had made beautiful and kept inviolate for him. For the rest of their lives they would enjoy it in peace, meanwhile upholding the traditions of the past by taking their rightful places and playing their appointed roles among the country gentry.

Unfortunately, Bushrod did not see eye to eye with Mabel about all this. He found her fervor irritating rather than stimulating; and the hubbub which attended his homecoming had hardly subsided before country life began to pall on him; he was relieved when an invitation arrived to accompany Wheeler on a tour of inspection through the South, which included a series of "jubilees"; he was even more delighted when the opportunity arose to proceed with the general to Manila. Mabel was alone when she watched the new century come in, for Miss Sophie had not lived to do this and Bushrod did not return from the Philippines until nearly a month later. Then, after remaining in Virginia only long enough to make sure that everything connected with the estate was in order, Bushrod was off again, on another series of "jubilees" which eventually took him to New Orleans.

It was natural that from there he should go to Cindy Lou. Clyde freely acknowledged this, both to himself and to others; but as one week succeeded another, and his stepson still seemed content to remain where he was, the old man began to wonder why Bushrod should find country life in Louisiana so much to his liking when, admittedly, he had found country life in Virginia boring. But Clyde did not dwell overmuch on this mystery, largely because at the moment he was preoccupied by the liquidation of the C & L Navigation Company.

When the final formalities in connection with this had been consummated, he returned from New Orleans in a state of almost overwhelming fatigue and depression. The fatigue was understandable enough; his general health was good and his strength sufficed for the activities which came within the sphere of his regular routine; but under any additional exertion, he tired very quickly. Admittedly, he had reached an age where this was inevitable and perhaps the depression was inevitable, too. Of course, the C & L Navigation Company had long since ceased to be anything more than a skeletal organization. He and Lucy had acted quickly upon their decision to sell all their barges and towboats and to confine their projects on the river to chartering steamers at cotton-shipping time. Seasonal revivals of this sort had defrayed the cost of a so-called office in the rear room of a St. Peter Street building, where an elderly, stoop-shouldered book-keeper also acted as manager, accountant and janitor. Even when the railroads threatened to gobble up the little freight business there was left, a shipping contract with some planters at Hard Times Landing had produced enough revenue to provide both Lucy and Clyde with some special treat on the occasion of their wedding anniversary—the only one—at the only time—to which she would consent after they had agreed on their policy of retrenchment. After Lucy's death, Clyde had put a similar sum aside for Larry's education, on the same day, every year; but the profits of the C & L had now almost reached the vanishing point; and though the plantation was doing sufficiently well so that there was nothing to prevent him from carrying on the custom, he could no longer pretend that the money came from the moribund steamship company. In a sense, he felt that its house flag was a memorial to Lucy, even though it flew for only a brief period each autumn; and he had a further sentimental attachment to the property since it was the only one which he and Lucy had owned jointly, under Louisiana law. But increasingly he found himself able to look hopefully toward the future rather than sorrowfully to the past. There was peace again after war and the world was beginning not only a new year but a new century. What better time could there be to close forever the door of that rear room, holding fast to the belief that somehow and some-where another would open?

Over and over again, on the way back to Cindy Lou, Clyde told himself that there was only one answer to this question. There could have been no better time. He had done the wise thing, the right thing, the thing Lucy herself would have been the first to advise. Even the stoop-shouldered bookkeeper could not be a logical object of sympathy; he had a small pension as the veteran of a former war, and a widowed daughter was eager to have him make his home with her. Clyde who, as usual, had erred on the side of generosity when he severed his con-nections with his forlorn employee, had no reasons for self-reproach because the man was losing his means of livelihood. But the mood of depression continued. After Clyde reached home and responded, with as great a show of heartiness as he could summon, to Larry's boisterous welcome, he stepped out on the gallery, as was still his nightly custom, and gazed for some moments at the anchor lights twinkling from the *Lucy Batchelor*. It seemed to him that they looked a little lower than usual. That might be merely imagination; he would speak to Zack about them in the morning; but still he could not believe that anything was really amiss. At all events, he did not want to believe it. With a sigh, he turned back into the room.

In accordance with his instructions, Larry's evening meal had not been delayed until the uncertain hour of Clyde's return and Tudie was now putting the little boy to bed. Bushrod, as was his habit, had gone to one of the neighboring plantations, where a Negro orchestra, alternating with a large music box, would provide tunes for dancing and where he would be the lion of the evening. But he had left the door of his room open and evidently he had left a window open also, for cold air was pouring out into the hall. Picking up a lamp, Clyde entered the empty chamber, prompted only by the idea that he would find the source of the draft and put an end to it.

Once inside, however, he paused and looked around him. The room was in a state of complete disarray and, after closing the rear window and setting down the lamp, Clyde began, almost automatically, to pick up the stray garments which were strewn about. He was orderly by nature, and years of association with Lucy, who had been the personification of daintiness, had increased his instinctive aversion to slovenly habits. Moreover, he realized that in Lucy's lifetime no room in their house could possibly have looked like this in the evening; however negligent its occupant, some servant would have put it in proper condition during the course of the morning and returned to it, later in the day, to rectify anything that might since have gone awry. He would have a word with Delphie, who was still supposed to give meticulous care to the upper story; but there was no use in trying to do so tonight, as by this time she would have returned to the quarters. In any case, he was too tired, at the moment, to deal with a servant who had grown slatternly in her ways, now that she had no mistress to supervise her. It would be less bother to straighten things out himself.

In order to see better, he pulled down the lamp which was suspended on metal chains from the center of the ceiling and lighted it. As he swung it back into place, his attention was caught by a rectangular packet, wrapped in brown paper, tied with white cord and tagged with a blue express label, which lay on the littered center table. Frowning with impatience at himself, he turned aside; then, conscious of some strange compulsion, he looked back again; there was something vaguely familiar about the appearance of the parcel, though he did not instantly realize what this was. Still acting almost involuntarily, he picked it up and scrutinized the label.

"Ever-True Novelty Company, St. Louis," he read with growing dismay and mounting rage. Then, his fingers shaking, he untied the knotted cord and laid back the wrapping. The brown paper unfolded to disclose two dozen decks of cards—the same kind which, over and over again during the old days, he had seen slipped, by sleight of hand, into a friendly game which was taking place in the gentlemen's cabin of a floating palace.

CHAPTER XVI

His first impulse was to throw the cards into the fire, leaving the empty, telltale wrappings to confront his stepson when Bushrod returned from his night of revelry. Indeed, Clyde had already picked up the decks and stridden toward the hearth, when sober second thought brought the realization that this was no way to deal with such a serious situation. What the best way might be could not instantly be determined; but at least it was not through the destruction of material which might prove valuable evidence in an emergency. He carefully rewrapped the cards, restored the package to its original position and, making no further effort to create order out of the prevailing chaos, left the chamber and went slowly down the two flights of stairs which took him to the gaming room. Then he poured himself a stiff drink and sat, sipping it slowly, until he heard the sound of wheels outside, followed by footsteps along the gravel path. A moment later, Bushrod opened the door and walked in.

Undeniably, he made an impressive showing. His unimpaired figure set off his uniform to immense advantage; pallor gave a Byronic touch to his fine features; and the dark circles under his eyes, far from suggesting dissipation, only added to this air of romanticism; in every way he embodied the popular conception of a patriot who had suffered in a noble cause, and who was still suffering from the results of its hardships and its dangers, but who was making a valiant effort to conceal his pain under a cloak of buoyancy. And this was the dissembler who was accepting hero worship from a generous and cordial people at the same time that he was preparing to abuse their hospitality, so prodigally offered, with practices as adroit as they were dishonorable!

"Anything wrong?" Bushrod inquired, casually acknowledging his stepfather's greeting and turning toward the open cellarette.

"Not that I know of. Why should there be?"

"No special reason. Except that it's rather late. I don't usually find you up at this hour. When I saw the light here, I thought something might be amiss with you. That's why I came on to the gaming room, instead of going straight upstairs."

"I appreciate your concern for my welfare. I seem to remember another occasion when something rather different brought you to this room. You can't blame me if I still associate your presence here with a very unpleasant interview. Not that there's any real connection, of course. Though, as a matter of fact, I've got some money for you this time, too."

"Money?"

"Yes. I meant to give it to you in the morning, but if I do it now instead, we'll be square that much sooner. I don't know whether I mentioned that I intended going to New Orleans today. But that's where I've been. The C & L Navigation Company was liquidated this afternoon—at least, what remained of it. The Cooley folks bought out the name and good will, leaving me what I'd banked from last year's shipping and paying a tidy enough sum for the contracts already signed—enough to cover the coming crop."

Bushrod, who had been fingering the glass he held and looking down at the drink he had poured himself, as if he enjoyed its mellow light, glanced up with a sudden show of interest.

"And part of that tidy sum would be mine?" he inquired. "Is that what you waited up to tell me? I haven't wanted to hurry you, of course, but I've been wondering when. . . . Don't keep me in suspense. What does my share come to?"

"Six hundred and eighty-four dollars and some odd coppers."

"Oh!" Bushrod looked down again and began to drum on the table, first with a slow, rhythmic movement and then with jerky irregularity. Clyde glanced at him contemptuously and, for the first time, some of his contempt crept into his voice.

"When you say 'Oh!' like that, it's evident you really mean, 'Is that all?' Yes, that's all—and whatever it is, it's just that much more than what, under the law, you can rightfully claim. Is that plain?"

"No, it isn't. If you think I mean to sit idly by and let you pass me a sugar-tit, you're mightily mistaken."

"Very well. I'll try to explain. The steamboat company was formed after your mother and I were married, and so became community property, jointly owned, half and half, by her and myself. It was the only piece of community property we owned. I bought the plantation before our marriage. Hence that was mine alone, because it was separate and paraphernal, under the law."

"I know. Under the Napoleonic Code which so amply assures protection for married women!"

The sneer in Bushrod's tone was now as unmistakable as the contempt had been in his stepfather's. But Clyde answered quietly.

"That is correct. It is also correct that the fifty thousand dollars I gave your mother at the time of our marriage was hers. I could not touch it or compel her to give me any part of it."

"Fifty thousand dollars!"

"Actually, more than that, by quite a good deal. Your mother had invested most of it very shrewdly, thanks to advice given her by Lamartine Vincent and others. She had done this without consulting me; indeed, without my knowledge. I did not learn about the existence of that sum until you bled me of what was just about my last penny in ready cash . . . the last time we were together in this room."

"Then what's all this palaver about six hundred dollars when I have coming to me a share—at least a quarter share—of more than fifty thousand?"

"You have coming to you exactly nothing, as a matter of law."

"We'll see about that!"

"Indeed we shall. But it will be worth your while to hear me out, so that you understand what your position is. I had mortgaged everything I owned at the time of Cary's wedding to build her a house and provide the sort of marriage she had counted on. Those loans were necessary because of an unlucky flier in the cotton market and the drain of our steamboat operations on the plantation earnings. So when you blackmailed me out of twenty thousand dollars I was ruined. That was the one thing I might have used to make a fresh start. And you robbed me of it."

"It wasn't a fraction of what you should have given me, and you know it. Cary and I were to share alike as far as you were concerned, and. . . ."

"We'll discuss that some other time, if we must. Let me get on with this explanation of what utter and complete ruin I faced the day Cary and Savoie left on their honeymoon. I don't know to what shifts I might have been put—but for your mother. She had guessed something of how things stood with me, and offered to help. I told her the situation was beyond help, because I had exhausted my credit, was head over heels in debt, had mortgaged even the coming crops—and it was then that she gave me not only the money I had settled on her years before, but all the gains her wise investments and the income from these had added to the original sum."

"And you mean that was all swallowed up in your mismanagement?"

"From then on she and I managed together. Thanks to her, we paid the interest on my debts and made other pressing and immediate payments on principal. We bought some bitterly needed equipment—and before the year's end we were taking in more than we were paying out. Had she lived, not only this plantation, which she helped to redeem, but the money, which it would have repaid, would have been community property. But she—she did not live."

"How does that affect the money that was due her?"

"It means that at the time of her death she and I were technically insolvent. It means our liabilities—our debts—were greater than our assets. It means that the community, such as it was, consisted of nothing but unpaid and unpayable debts."

"But they have been paid."

"Last year's operation finally cleared away the last of the loans we made to meet our mortgages. For the first time, Cindy Lou was free and clear once more. But none of that, under the law, affects your mother's share of the community."

"We'll see about that, if there's any law in the land."

"That we will. As a matter of fact, I had your mother's succession opened before Judge Chretien. He appointed an appraiser, whose report on the insolvency of your mother's estate has been filed. But because you were abroad, I asked that the proceedings be held up. So that if you want to contest them, you can do so, at any time. Meanwhile, the solvency of the plantation made it possible for me to liquidate the navigation company at last, and while no court could compel me to give you a share of that, I was and am ready to do so."

"While you pocket the rest?"

"For Larry. As his tutor. Under the agreement made with your grandmother at the time of—of the funeral—he will be my heir to all of Cindy Lou."

"Tutor?"

"Guardian then, if that term suits you better. But the legal guardian of a minor is called a tutor in Louisiana. I hardly thought a barrister would need to be told that."

"And since when, if it isn't asking too much, have you been made my nephew's legal guardian?"

"I haven't been. That is, not officially. But I have spoken to Judge Chretien of the district court and written to Mrs. Vincent about the matter. Since the appointment won't be contested. . . ."

"What makes you so certain of that?"

"Mrs. Vincent has answered my letter, assuring me that her husband is satisfied. As you know, he's completely crippled. But, fortunately, his mind has remained clear."

"Is he the only one who might object?"

"I feel sure he is, since your grandmother had already assured me that she didn't. Don't you think I'm right?"

For a moment, their eyes met. Then Bushrod shrugged his shoulders, as if the matter were of no further interest to him.

"About my share in the proceeds from today's transaction," he said. "I suppose there's some sort of an accounting I could see, merely as a matter of form, naturally. But so as to verify the calculations."

"Certainly. In fact, Valois Dupré prepared a notarized attest at my request. I felt reasonably sure you'd make such a demand and you're entitled to an accounting."

"Of course I am. And while we're on the point, I might add that I'd like a similar statement from you, acknowledging my ownership in a part of this plantation."

"You don't own any part of this plantation. You never will. You agreed, in writing, that if Amalfi and Sorrento were left to you outright, you would forgo any claim you might have to a share in Cindy Lou."

"As you said a few minutes ago, 'that is correct.' Otherwise, you've made a mistake, and a mighty big one. I own the entire back part of this plantation—that strip of land along Bayou Boisblanc, where Cary was always setting out to find treasure—and never did!" From somewhere out in the garden came an unearthly shriek. Bushrod leaped up. "For God's sake, why don't you get rid of those damned peacocks!" he cried. "That noise would drive a preacher to drink!"

Clyde reached into a bowl which stood beside his empty toddy glass, took out two pecans, pressed them side by side into his hand and knotted his fingers over them until the shells burst noisily. Then, opening his fist, he looked at the fragments for a moment before picking out a few meats and putting them into his mouth.

"Well now, you amaze me," he said slowly. "Not by asking me why I don't get rid of the peacocks. I know you don't like them, but Larry does. So I think I'll hang onto them. What you say about the land does come as a surprise though. I know for a fact that old Dupré didn't sell you the property and no one else had a right to. Or the title, either. I take it you're not lying—this time. So somebody must have sucked you in. Instead of selling you a gold brick, or a diamond mine in Brazil, or a key to the river, someone sold you a worthless deed to Cindy Lou. Well! . . ."

"The state of Louisiana sold it to me! I bought it for the taxes. And if you think you can make a joke out of that, you're welcome to!"

"I won't try to make a joke out of it. But I'd like to hear a little more about it."

Clyde reached for more pecans, cracked them as he had the others and sat thoughtfully chewing the meats. Bushrod's sneering tone gradually rose to something very near a shout.

"I'd be very glad to explain. Dupré found a better gravel bed than yours on the Tangipahoa River—close to New Orleans, too, with a sand bar hard by. It's easy to follow how he figured things out. Here was this parcel on Bayou Boisblanc that wasn't worth a jitney to anybody, *except* as a gravel bed, and he didn't want to waste any more money on it. Naturally, he wasn't going to offer to sell it back to you and no one else wanted it. So he decided to let the state take it over for taxes. My father-in-law—not to mention my dear wife—keep me pretty short; but I manage, one way and another, to have some ready cash most of the time. So I had enough to buy in the Bayou Boisblanc property for the first verse and chorus of a short song. So it's mine. Do you understand? *Part of Cindy Lou is mine!* And I dare you to put up a fourth interest in the rest of the plantation against that part in a poker game and see who picks up the marbles!"

"And supposing I won't? After all, you just said that what you claim you own is worthless, except as a gravel bed. And it seems nobody wants a gravel bed there."

"I did say so and it's true—generally speaking. But it happens to have two other values as far as you're concerned. One is you want it so badly you can taste it. That was where you and Cary used to spend a lot of time, and anything connected with Cary, in your mind. . . . She had a few faults, too, but we won't go into those."

"No. We won't go into those."

Clyde's voice was still as even as before. Nevertheless, something in it caused his stepson to decide, rather hurriedly, that the last statement was conclusive.

"Well, there may be treasure there, too, for all I know," he said. "I mean the kind you and Cary were hunting for. But you'll admit it's pretty doubtful. However, there's no doubt at all that tract of land could be a gold mine for me—not a gold *brick* or a *diamond* mine in Brazil, but a *gold mine* right here in Louisiana. I could start a gambling house on it—a saloon, a dance hall, maybe some cribs upstairs. A neighbor to Cindy Lou, on what used to be Cindy Lou land. What would you say to that?"

Bushrod had expected that this suggestion would bring forth another cold statement made with menacing finality or even, this time, a violent outburst. Instead, Clyde merely shook his head and, for a few moments, seemed absorbed in thought.

"I don't know," he answered eventually. "I suppose if I were a 'hero,' I'd say such a venture would be unbecoming an officer and a gentleman. As I'm just an old river gambler, I look at it differently. I can't see why you bother to risk a 'gold mine,' like what you've described, against a share in the plantation. The gambling den, booze parlor and whore house would be a lot more profitable. The odds aren't good enough."

"Name your own odds, then."

"Very well. I'll play you draw poker for your claim to the Boisblanc gravel land *and* a written statement from you acknowledging the insolvency of your mother's community estate at the time of her death, against an assignment to share all of Cindy Lou's profits with you henceforth."

"An assignment to how much of a share?"

"A third of whatever's turned over to Larry, or to me as his tutor, each year. Even you are bound to realize I wouldn't cheat him."

"But what's the idea of acknowledging mother's insolvency?"

"At the time your mother's succession was appraised as insolvent, Judge Chretien wanted to have you present so that you could, if you wished, assume your share of the insolvent estate's debts. I asked that the whole matter be held up until you returned. If you will sign an acknowledgment of that insolvency, and recognition of the fact that there was no community, Judge Chretien can enter a judgment recording the fact that there is no other claimant to the estate, such as it was at the time of your mother's death. . . . That agreement against a third of all profits Cindy Lou will ever earn. What do you say?"

Bushrod made no attempt to conceal the sudden surge of elation that swept him to his feet. "Why, I say, done with you!" he cried. "What'll it be? Winner-take-all on the first hand?"

"Winner-take-all on one hand's no test of anything but luck. We'll play for chips till one of us picks a hand by his own choosing to tap out the other player for everything."

"That's all right with me. First hand, last hand, four-in-hand, any old hand. Trot 'em all out—foot, horse and heavy artillery and let the firing commence!"

"That can't all be done in a minute, as you ought to know after your recent glorious military career. Besides, there are documents to prepare and it's rather late, as you said yourself when you came in. I've been to New Orleans today and you've been—well, I don't know exactly where, but anyhow this is 'After the Ball is Over.' I wouldn't say either one of us was in the best shape to play—even for peanuts. And this isn't going to be that kind of a game. What about tomorrow night?"

"I'm taken for tomorrow. The Naquins and their cousins are making up a party to see the ball game at Donaldsonville and spend the night there."

"Day after tomorrow then. Any time you like, except tonight."

"Very well. Day after tomorrow. Though I warn you I'll be on the lookout for any rigs you may try to run in the meantime."

"Run any rigs? As if I'd need to. But you'd be well advised not to run any on me. I knew all the tricks long before you started your brief career at the Westmoreland Club. Well, that's neither here nor there. I'll be looking for you around eight Wednesday night."

Clyde twitched the reins so that they flickered along Spice's back, but the motion was quite without conscious direction. His relaxed posture in the cabriolet was as easy as the mare's gait, and she jogged along the familiar road, early Wednesday afternoon, just fast enough to outdistance the dust cloud raised by her hoofs from the powdery surface of the highway. Along one side of it ran the low, endless molehill of the levee. On the other lay the fields, separated here and there by arching, moss-hung live oaks, by the ornamental shrubbery of a plantation garden or by clustered cabins weathered to the same silvery gray as the cypress palings of the fences surrounding them. At one such cabin, Clyde drew Spice to an abrupt halt and banged the butt of his whip against the side of the cabriolet in a sharp tattoo.

"Ma'y Lou!" he called. "Ma'y Lou! Rustle your bones!" There was no immediate response, and he was on the point of raising a fresh halloo when an enormous Negress turned the corner of the cabin, billowing into sight. Her splayed feet were bare and a single shapeless garment of faded calico clung to the more voluminous bulges of her body. But a bright print cloth was tied about her head in an elaborately knotted tignon, and large loops of yellow metal dangled from the lobes of her ears.

"Bless Jesus, Mr. Clyde, you'se too welcome, suh," she beamed, "even iffen mah house is that upset I could faint. I could so. Do leave me unhook dis gate. . . ."

"No need, Ma'y Lou. I'm only passing by. But I'll be back directly, and when I come I want you to have a sugar-tit for me."

The big Negress cupped one fat elbow with her palm, whipping the other hand over her mouth as she cackled shrilly.

"No sugar-tit couldn' be for you, suh, no," she giggled, sputtering. "You just a'funnin' with old Ma'y Lou, dat you is."

"Don't act like you never had good knowledge," he said with an answering grin. "I want a sugar-tit and what I need it for doesn't concern you the first particle."

"Does you mean just a plain, everyday sugar-tit lak us gives our babies, Mr. Clyde?"

"Exactly. And I'll be back for it in less than no time, so stir your stumps."

"Yessuh, I sho'ly will. As soon as ever you gets back, suh, I has a sugar-tit tied for you."

Clyde nodded a good-by, twitched the reins and clicked a command to Spice. Then, as the mare resumed her peaceful jogging, he continued along the river road to the Grand Hotel Pierre Chanet. This hostelry had prospered greatly as river traffic fell off, for canvassers and drummers—Knights of the Grip, as they liked to call themselves—now went about the countryside in their own buggies, because steamboats were so few and far between and so unreliable of schedule. The Pierre Chanet housed a good poker game in one of the back rooms, and the traveling salesmen found it pleasant to while away the Saturday-to-Monday tedium there. This meant excellent business for the bar, as well, and here Clyde, having secured Spice to the worn cypress arc of the hotel's hitch rack, purchased a deck of cards.

"Just one, thanks, Celestin. Steamboats, either pink or blue. It makes no difference which."

He found Ma'y Lou waiting for him at the weathered fence, a clean, neatly tied bit of white cloth that looked like a miniature rag doll held proudly in her great black hand. Tucking it into the pocket of his gray moleskin vest, he gave her a silver dollar, nodding acknowledgment of her shrill thanks and a broad jest to the effect that the older the stallion, the prouder he be's to claim ary wood's colt as his own get. Then, chuckling as he thought of Ma'y Lou's parting comment, he sat back in the cabriolet, relaxed, while Spice drew it homeward through the deepening dusk.

CHAPTER XVII

Now that Miss Sophie was no longer there to continue Lucy's pleasant practice, Clyde had discontinued the ceremonious serving of afternoon tea. Instead, he had a hearty supper, early enough for Larry to be at the table with him; and while Delphie had grown slack in her ways, Belle, aged and slow as she was, had not lost the skill that went with having "a free hand and no conscience" when it came to cooking. She had never yet sent in a meal that was not a credit to her and tonight it was actually something of a feast. Dumaine, the overseer, had sent a couple of fine green trout to the Big House and these had been baked in a *sauce piquante;* fluffy white rice and Whippoorwill peas accompanied these. So did a mixture of late-gathered winter greens, which had been simmered with a hunk of fatback in an iron pot, after leaves of sweet basil, finely minced with bird's-eye peppers, and a couple of garlic pods, stuck with cloves, had been added for seasoning. Crackling bread made with buttermilk and home-ground meal went with this *pièce de résistance* and crisp waffles with pecan cuite followed it. When he had finished, Clyde pushed back his chair from the table with a gusty sigh.

"A man my age hasn't any business eating that much rich food," he said. "Remember that, Larry, when you get to be as old as I am. From the way you scoop everything up now, it looks as if you might need a word of warning."

Larry's hearty laugh showed that he understood his grandfather was "funning" even though he did not know what all the words meant; and after the two had hugged each other hard, he ran noisily off to Tudie. Clyde looked after him dotingly and turned to Zack. "Bring my coffee down to the gaming room," he said, "and light a fire in both the heating stove and the fireplace. It was hot enough through the day, but it's turned off chilly. . . . I don't expect Mr. Bushrod for an hour or so yet, but when he comes in, tell him I'm waiting for him."

"Ah done light the fires already, suh. Ah figured as how you might be wantin' 'em."

The gaming room's warmth was benign; the crackle of wood in the grate mingled cheerfully with the purr from the draft of the heating stove. The large central lamp of the girandole had been lighted and its height so adjusted that only the top of the card table came within its cone of radiance; the rest of the room remained intimately wrapped in semidarkness. With an increasing sense of well-being, Clyde let himself down into an armchair facing the fireplace. On the serving stand at his elbow, Zack placed a tray bearing a small silver coffeepot, a bowl of cracked loaf sugar, a decanter of brandy and one eggshell cup, which Clyde promptly filled with the fragrant black brew. Then, into the bowl of a coffee spoon, he dropped a small chunk of sugar, which he saturated with brandy. Zack touched the end of a *roseau* sliver to the coals and quickly applied the tiny flame to the sugar. A blue light clothed its crest for an instant, before sliding down to envelop the sides and dance lightly over the bowl of the spoon. Clyde held the small flambeau steady until the sugar lump collapsed with a sirupy bubbling, then quenched it all in the coffee, stirring the aromatic mixture and sipping it with lively relish.

"Only one, tonight," he said to Zack. "But wait in the kitchen, even after Mr. Bushrod gets here. I might be wanting you later on."

His sensation of well-being continued to increase. It would not matter how soon Bushrod came; on the contrary, the stage had been set for hours now and he was eager for the play to begin. He had realized, from the beginning, that whatever methods his stepson had in mind, the latter must have taken the precaution of working these out before he issued his challenge. Otherwise, he would not have talked so brashly. Yet a close scrutiny of the cards and chips, kept on an inlaid rack in the gaming room, had revealed nothing out of the ordinary. The cards were the same Steamboat and Congress decks Clyde always kept there and most of them were new, their revenue stamps still intact. So much for that.

An equally detailed examination of Bushrod's room had likewise brought nothing of a suspicious nature to light. The package from the Ever-True Novelty Company, which Clyde had accidentally found on his return from New Orleans, was gone; but that was to be expected. Bushrod had, no doubt, taken its contents with him when he went to Donaldsonville for a "ball" game and to spend the night and the following day with the Naquins and their cousins at an adjacent plantation. This interval would certainly be largely given over to poker. But it was here at Cindy Lou that Bushrod was preparing for the supreme gamble of his career. . . .

The answer to the puzzle was so simple that Clyde was astonished he had not found it at once; but it was not until he had passed a sleepless night, restless and irritated at his failure to solve the mystery, that he suddenly did so: the package of his discovery could not have been the first which had come to the house. There must have been at least one other—perhaps several others—and from one of these had come the decks which Bushrod intended to use now. He was far too shrewd to suppose that his stepfather would accept any he might bring into the gaming room at the last moment. The marked cards must be there already, and so placed that Clyde himself would unwittingly introduce them into the game. But he had examined the contents of the inlaid rack and everything had appeared to be in order. Hold the deal a moment. . . . Appeared to be. . . . Appeared to be. . . . Why that must be it!

Clyde had dressed hurriedly, returned to the gaming room and, from the inlaid rack, had again taken an unopened deck and peered with frowning intensity at the intact revenue stamp which sealed it. Finally he had sawed through this with his thumbnail, pulled out the contents and carefully lifted the flaps of their waxy wrapping with the blade of a penknife. No more than a glance was needed to reveal that the apparently normal latticework pattern on the backs of the cards was marked with the familiar Ever-True design, so that anyone who knew the key could read the value of each card as clearly from the back as from the front. But the unbroken government seal? . . . Of course! Bushrod would have in his possession forged—or even stolen—revenue stamps, to be applied over what was left of the torn seals after marked decks had been substituted for the original contents of the genuine Steamboat or Congress boxes. An old, old dodge. But it had come within a hairsbreadth of taking him in.

Well, forewarned was forearmed. A skilled player, knowing that marked cards which he could also read were being used against him, enjoyed a tremendous advantage over a cheat who was not aware of his intended victim's knowledge. Clyde wondered what sort of a deal Bushrod planned to use in the crucial hand. The marked cards had been rearranged; the cold deck was already stacked. And Bushrod would deal that hand. He must have arranged the packs for himself to handle with a false shuffle, being prepared to reverse Clyde's cut when he packed the cards. Clyde took two poker hands off the top of the substituted deck, turning the cards of one up. Sure enough, there it was. The hand that would be dealt him showed a pat full house—three queens and a pair of fours. Bushrod's hand held two kings, two tens and the five of diamonds. Obviously, he had assumed Clyde would stand pat. Bushrod would discard one on the draw— the five of diamonds, naturally—and would receive . . . Clyde flipped over the next card—a third king. Thus Bushrod's three kings and two tens would top Clyde's three queens and a pair of fours. Old as the hills, but suckers were still taken in by it.

Clyde riffled through the deck to draw out the fourth queen from far beneath the carefully stacked hands that topped it. Taking this card to his office, he slipped a fine-pointed new steel nib into his penholder and diluted a few drops of red ink with water from the cedar drinking keg. Turning the pink lattice of the card's back uppermost, he set to work with knife point and pen. Progress was slow; it was achieved by no more than a touch of blade or pen point at a time. But when he had finished, the markings on the back of this queen of clubs showed it to be a four; and though his eyes were tired, they twinkled as he returned to the gaming room and substituted this queen for one of the two fours that were to have been dealt him.

Otherwise, he left the deck arranged exactly as he had found it, rewrapping it in the original glassine cover which he closed fast with a drop of mucilage from the bottle on his desk. He had no way of replacing or repairing the broken revenue stamp, after he had slipped the rewrapped cards back into their flat box. But this was no great matter since it was virtually certain Bushrod would call for a new deck and ask him to take it from the rack; otherwise there would have been no reason to substitute "cold" marked decks for all the genuine ones in the rack. Moreover, Clyde could always make an adequate pretense of breaking an already broken seal. Certain of his ground, Bushrod would not be watching closely at that stage, in any case. . . . Replacing the deck in its rack, Clyde went through a rear passage to the kitchen garden where a bell swung from the top of a slender pole. He gave its cord a sharp pull and, as the bell pealed, a stableboy came running quickly toward him.

"Hitch Sugar or Spice to the cabriolet," he directed. "It doesn't matter which, but be quick about it."

What a pity it was, he reflected, as he waited for the cabriolet, that this rare jest could not be shared. So Bushrod did not mean to have anyone fob off a sugar-tit on him, eh? The joke was really too good for a man to keep to himself. Clyde went into the garden and plucked a wine-colored, belated bloom for the buttonhole of his jimswinger; then, returning to the house for his Stetson, he cocked this at a rakish angle. It certainly made a man feel young again to whet his wits.

He took the reins from the small darky, gave the cabriolet's spidery wheels an approving glance and set off in the direction of Ma'y Lou's cabin and the Grand Hotel Pierre Chanet.

This had been several hours ago and now he was seated in the big armchair, gazing quietly at the embers and sipping his coffee with that increasing sense of contentment. He was still sitting there when Bushrod came in.

"People, people, it's cold on the river!" he exclaimed, spreading his hands to the welcome warmth of the grate fire. "In that open launch of Naquin's, the wind cut through me straight to the marrow."

"I expected you rather earlier."

"God almighty! You ought to know how these Creoles are. They've got kinfolk back of every tree and tucked away in every fence corner. Before we could think of leaving Donaldsonville, we had to pay courtesy calls on Cousin Constantine and Cousin Clovis and Parrain This and Marraine That, because any relative who was overlooked would be mortally hurt. But here I am, better late than never, I reckon, and ready to receive the warm and affectionate welcome of a stepsire who loves me as though I were Bronze John's own twin."

"Coffee?"

"No, thank you just as much. But a hooker of blue ruin would be gratefully received as a sovereign preventer of *la grippe.*"

Clyde waved his hand toward the rosewood cellarette. "You'll find whatever you need there, I think," he said. "And if you're not feeling up to snuff, I wouldn't object to postponing the game until—"

"Hell no!" Bushrod tossed off a small glass of bourbon, neat, and smacked his lips. "You said you expected me earlier. I won't hold you up any longer. Bring on the cards and counters."

Clyde rose, placed the rack on the table, raised the cover and began to count out chips.

"I should think a couple of hundred dollars would be aplenty," he suggested, with just enough of a rising inflection to leave the decision to Bushrod. "I mean for the warm-up. One of us will probably make it winner-take-all before it's used up."

Clyde produced a worn pigskin portmanteau from the inner pocket of his coat and extracted a folded sheet of paper from it. "Here's the statement, all in good shape," he said. " 'Whatever money is paid to Lawrence Vincent's account from Cindy Lou Plantation, through sale, rent or crops, whether paid to him direct or to his tutor during his minority, a sum equal to one third of every such payment is to be remitted within seven days to Bushrod Page or to his lawful agent.' " Clyde tossed the sheet across the lighted table to Bushrod, who scanned the document briefly and shrugged.

"I expect it'll hold water," he observed. He scraped a chair across the floor to the table and sat down. "All right. Shall we start the sociable?"

"When I have your written agreement," Clyde answered, still standing. "This will be table stakes. Until the paper is with the chips in front of you, we don't turn the first card."

"What the hell's eating you? How could I chiprack you on a proposition like that?"

"I'll never know, because you won't have a chance to show me. Stop playing the gentleman, will you? I'm all the audience there is this time. Bring what you need in the way of paper, pen and ink from the office, and then write me a signed statement of your promise to leave and another stating your disclaimer to any part of this property. Put those statements with your chips, and afterward we'll play. Not before. And we won't play with any cards of yours. I've taken the time and trouble to go to the Chanet and buy a new deck. You needn't bother asking if I don't trust you. The answer is I sure as hell don't. I wouldn't trust you as far as I could carry the river in my vest pocket."

Bushrod rose, without answering, and, going into the office, brought

337

back a pad of ruled foolscap paper, a pen and a small bottle of purplish ink. Then he sat down and wrote scratchily, signed the two documents with a flourish and read them aloud. Clyde nodded and Bushrod ripped the paper from its pad, passed the sheets quickly back and forth over the lamp chimney several times to dry the ink, then laid them beside his varicolored chips.

"Satisfied?" he asked.

"Well, not exactly. But we can start playing any time. Here's the deck. Shuffle it yourself. Then we'll cut. High deals."

Without a word, Bushrod opened the new deck, stripped the glassine wrapping from the cards, pushed it and the two jokers to one side and shuffled dexterously, riffling the cards with practiced skill. At length, he spread them in an arc across the baize centerpiece.

Clyde turned a jack to Bushrod's six of hearts. As he shuffled the cards anew, his expression was as blank as a newly whitewashed wall; but behind that imperturbable mask he was wondering by what means Bushrod would substitute one of the marked decks for this unmarked one. He was not left long in doubt. On the first deal, Bushrod tossed two ten-dollar chips into the pot, along with two cards.

"I'll take a couple off the top, if you feel like seeing how the luck's running tonight," he said. Then, as an earsplitting screech again slashed through the quiet night, he exclaimed, "God damn those peacocks! Every last one of them would be in the market for a new neck if I had my say-so."

"But you haven't. As for this hand, I wouldn't care for any part of it," Clyde observed placidly. "I wouldn't choose to draw against you this time."

"You mean all I win is my own double sawbuck?" Bushrod asked testily. "And with three natural aces to draw to?" He made as if to display the cards, but, as though goaded beyond endurance, he tore them across and threw the pieces on the floor. Then he did the same with the two he had discarded, snatching them back from the table's center. "That calls for a new deck. And, by the way, I'm not afraid to play with your cards, even if you are scared of mine. Pick any deck you please out of your own box, for all of me."

Not so well done, reflected Clyde behind the blank front of his poker face. To be sure, tearing up an ill-favored hand and demanding a new deck was a traditional gesture. But a cleverer sharp would then have offered to bring in cards of his own. When Clyde demurred, as he was reasonably certain to do, Bushrod could have waved aside the objection with a casual, "Hell, if you're all that worried, I'm agreeable to playing with your cards. Anything for a quiet life." But he was too impatient for his grand coup to let the suggestion come from his opponent.

Clyde lifted the cover of the container and, apparently without looking, withdrew from it one of the decks. Running his thumbnail swiftly along the upper edge of this, as if he were slitting the revenue stamp, he took out the cards and shoved them, still in their glassine wrapper, across the table to Bushrod, who removed the wrapper and the two jokers and tossed them into the grate.

Bushrod riffled the cards, crisply, apparently shuffling them with his swiftly moving fingers, before offering the deck for a cut, in a way that suggested he half expected the tender would be waived. But Clyde reached across and divided the pack. He appeared wholly intent on stacking his chips in more meticulous alignment; nevertheless, he caught every detail of Bushrod's reversal of the cut: the tip of the left little finger inserted between the two portions of the deck, the swift left-hand flip under cover of the right hand, which was brought forward as though merely to take the first card in making the deal. He picked up the hand Bushrod dealt him, squeezed the edges cautiously to inspect it, closed it into a book and laid this face down upon the table before him. There lay the four queens and the single four he had arranged in this deck earlier in the day.

"I'll tap you on this first hand," he said quietly. "Do you want me to do it now or after the draw?"

Bushrod examined his cards, shifted in his chair and otherwise made a show of indecision and doubt. "That means your hand's pat," he said musingly. "What a hell of a note! A pat hand on the first deal, with me over a barrel, because I can't lay down my hand, however sorry it might be. And I don't mind saying it's a sorry two pair—the hardest hand in the deck to improve. So it makes no difference when you tap me."

"What makes you so all-fired sure my hand's pat?" Clyde challenged.

Beyond the cone of illumination, the room still lay in shadow. Then a sudden jet of yellow flame hissed from a dying ember and subsided into a dusky glow. Clyde again picked up his cards and studied them, as though seeking reassurance. Apparently still preoccupied with his thoughts, he arranged his cards face down before him, one beside the other, so that each back was plainly visible.

"I might have four and a kicker, you know," he argued pensively, "or I might have nothing but a rinctum tiddy—a cooler—a strong case of measles, having overlooked my hand, maybe. You'd never believe a body'd be gambler enough to shoot the moon on a chance. That'd tempt me to run a windy on you just for the hell of it. But whether the hand's pat flush, or four of a kind or just a wild dream makes no difference. So put up your poke right now if you aim to draw cards."

Bushrod had darted a surreptitious glance at the face-down row in front of Clyde. There could have been no error. Nevertheless, he felt the cold clutch of doubt. If by some wild mischance anything had gone wrong. . . . But no, the marks showed that his stepfather had a full

339

house: three queens and a pair of fours. Yet he swallowed several times before tossing his statements on the green centerpiece in front of Clyde.

"Domino!" he said, not very steadily. "Now—how many cards?" He picked up the deck and held it toward Clyde, waiting with his right hand poised as if to deal on demand.

"I'm pat. You were right. I'll play what I've got."

"I reckoned as much," Bushrod answered rather smugly. "Neither do I think you're running a windy. That's why I'm going to draw one card to my two pair. If what you've got is a straight, a flush or a small full house, I can improve enough to take the pot. If you've got four of a kind, or a straight flush though, I can't. Here's what I'm drawing to— kings and tens." He faced up his hand and flipped the fifth card, the five of diamonds, to one side and lifted the top card slowly from its resting place on the deck until he could read it. Then he turned it over and brought it down on the table with a resounding bang of knuckles against the wood. "And a king it is!" he said exultantly. "Twenty sweet miles of railroad track and three kings to walk them!" He cast a triumphant glance at the backs of the cards still aligned in a row before Clyde. "Well, speak up. Which of us sleeps on the levee tonight? Show me that pat hand of yours!"

Clyde faced up his cards one at a time: the queen of hearts, the queen of diamonds, the queen of spades, the four of hearts. . . . He waited, looking up to watch Bushrod's face as the last card was turned: the one whose marked back proclaimed it a four, but whose face revealed the stylized mirror images of the queen of clubs, four-petaled blossom in hand.

"Why, Bushrod!" he said mildly. "What in time's the matter with you? You're the color of a toad-frog's belly."

"B-b-but. . . ." Bushrod caught himself just in time; he had been on the point of reaching across the table for the queen. "I mean. . . ."

"I know exactly what you mean." For the first time since the game began, Clyde smiled. He turned the queen and skimmed it across the table so that it came to rest, back up, in front of Bushrod. "You mean the mark on the hindside showed it to be a four-spot? Those Ever-True people must be getting downright careless."

"You—you've had that card right from the start!"

"I expect I must have. While you were visiting the Naquins, I did a little prospecting—and bless me, if I didn't trip right over a cold deck, all stacked for the whiskery old caper that went out of style about the time McClellan was beaten for president. So I took the notion of playing fox to your possum. Well, you know as much about the rest as I do." He pushed the cards aside and, taking the document of assignment, tore it into small pieces. "I've had a very pleasant evening," he continued. "It's been worth a little trouble to show you that you'd better not step out of your class—when it comes to gambling or anything else. While we're at it, let's get one fact mighty clear: whether you believe it or not—and on that point I don't give the first God damn—I've never cheated you out of anything that belonged to you and I wouldn't have done so this time. I made a promise to myself, as well as one to your mother—well, never mind about that—you wouldn't understand anyway. But you didn't have anything for a stake tonight. Your renunciation of a share in the property is no more than you had already agreed to when your grandmother made you sole heir to both Amalfi and Sorrento. And your claim to the Boisblanc acreage is only lettuce and wind. You've got no more title to it than a field mouse."

 CHAPTER XVIII

STILLNESS SUDDENLY closed in upon the room, and in the semidarkness beyond the sharply edged cone of radiance, this silence became something almost palpable. At his stepfather's final words, Bushrod had glanced swiftly down toward the folded sheet of foolscap that had just been returned to him, conscious that his eyes might betray his thoughts. Now he tapped it lightly against the polished edge of the table.

"What you said doesn't make sense, but you evidently believe it does," he remarked evenly. "I mean about my claim to the Boisblanc acreage being nothing more than lettuce and wind."

"Quite so," Clyde agreed.

"And you gave this back to me"—Bushrod lifted the folded sheet and let it drop again—"of your own accord. I didn't so much as ask you for it."

"No, you didn't."

"Which means that even if you beat me at my own game—and you did, I'm bound to admit—you wouldn't take this quitclaim on any such terms," Bushrod went on, almost as though musing aloud. "So you gave it back to me. Is that right?"

"That's about what it amounts to."

"In other words, whatever title I may have to the Boisblanc tract, good, bad, indifferent, worthless or whatever, that title is still mine. Do you agree to that?"

"Yes indeed. You couldn't be more welcome to whatever claim you think you have, not if I handed it to you on a silver platter with *sauce piquante.* Because what you call your 'title' is still nothing but lettuce and wind and I tell you so plainly."

"And I tell *you* plainly it's as good as gold. After all, I know something about land titles—you seem to have forgotten that I'm a lawyer. And titles don't come any sounder than tax titles. I bought that Boisblanc acreage from the state of Louisiana."

"You had every reason to think so. I'll go that far with you. But fortunately or unfortunately—whichever way you choose to look at it—the title the state of Louisiana gave you wasn't worth the match you'd use to set fire to the paper it's written on—at least, if you took a notion to burn it up."

"That's impossible. The state is a sovereign and. . . ."

"If you've a mind to listen, I can explain to you. If not, that suits me, too."

"I'll lose nothing by listening, I expect. Besides, I'm interested to know just what sort of yarn you've cooked up in an effort to prove that a title direct from the state itself isn't worth the price of a matchstick."

Bushrod's chair made a scraping sound on the furbished brick flooring as he pushed away from the table and crossed one leg over the other. He still held the folded paper in his hand and he now began tapping it against his knee.

"It's really quite simple," Clyde began. "Just one sorry little mistake, made by a clerk, set everything topsy-turvy. You know how it is with a file of dominoes: maybe you knock down only one, but that knocks down the next one and so on until they're all flat. This is something like that."

"Dominoes hasn't ever been my game. And so far, I haven't heard a word to prove that a tax title isn't as sound as a nut."

Bushrod was smiling now, and his smile was condescending rather than mocking. He continued to tap his knee with his folded paper, but there was still nothing in the gesture that suggested impatience.

"I'll have to go back quite a ways in order to explain, so I'm glad that you don't seem to be in a hurry," Clyde remarked equably. "The mix-up began right after your sister got back from Europe, early in '96. I'd been hard hit, in a money way, at the time of her marriage— well, you ought to know something about that. I still wasn't out of the woods a year later, though your mother'd helped me every way she could, and by scrimping and saving we'd got to the place where we could see daylight ahead. In fact, we knew that if we could just get hold of a little more ready cash, to make some improvements. . . ."

"Weren't we supposed to be talking about tax titles? I mean about my purchase of the Boisblanc part of Cindy Lou at a tax sale two years ago?"

"Is that when you think you bought it?"

342

"Think hell! I *did* buy it!"

"All right. We'll come to that presently. About that Boisblanc tract now. Old Valois Dupré had been pestering me for a long while to sell it to him. I never would listen, because I had the idea Cary set great store by that particular tract. But when she came back from Europe she acted and talked as though she weren't even interested in it. So, as your mother and I needed the ready cash to make those improvements, I sent word to Valois Dupré that I was ready to sell him the gravel land."

"Well, I know about that already. I know he bought it from you and I know he let the taxes lapse."

"So he did," Clyde interrupted quietly. "But still they didn't lapse. That's what I'm trying to explain."

"He did . . . they didn't . . . what sort of talk is that? What's it all leading up to?"

The tapping had become a little more insistent and one slender leg was now swinging back and forth over the other. The smile was gone. Bushrod's face, as well as his gestures, reflected increasing annoyance.

"You'll see, if ever you'll hear me out," Clyde answered, still imperturbably. "Dupré bought the land from me in April of '96, and it was agreed that he'd assume that year's taxes—due in '97. Everything was shipshape and the transfer of title to Dupré was recorded at the courthouse. The cash we got out of the sale put Cindy Lou over the hump. We knew then—your mother and I—that, barring the worst kind of luck, we could pull through. And that summer we didn't have to squeeze the pennies quite so hard before we'd let one go."

"I still say all this is beyond the point. The point is that you did sell that Boisblanc tract to a man named Dupré, who let the taxes lapse."

"I'm coming to that now. During the late spring of '96, we were all more or less upset by Cary's illness and the preparation for Armande's wedding and the De Chanets' visit. Then in the midst of this general confusion, Dupré came to tell me about the other gravel bed he had found—the one a lot closer to New Orleans than our Boisblanc piece. He offered to sell my land back to me, then and there. And I had to tell him I was too hard up to buy it."

"Why, you just said you'd reached the point where you didn't need to pinch pennies any longer!"

"I said we'd got to the point where we didn't have to pinch them *quite so hard*—to the point where we thought we could pull through. But we still had to keep on pulling. So I refused Dupré's offer, even though he went as far as to say he'd sell the land back to me for a dollar and lend me the dollar to buy it with! He kept insisting that the extra profit he'd make out of the new gravel bed would more than make up for the cost of mine and that he really *wanted* me to have that."

343

"And still you refused?"

"I expect you wouldn't understand. But yes, that's just what I did. I had all I could do to keep the rest of Cindy Lou going and lay by enough for taxes on that. Valois understood how I felt, even if you don't. But he said that since I didn't want the property the state could have it, for all he cared. He was going to abandon it. It wasn't a bit of use to him, and he didn't propose to worry with bookkeeping on it. He hadn't paid the first year's taxes yet and he wasn't going to pay them—those or any others."

"So we're coming to it at last. He *didn't* pay the taxes, did he?"

"Indeed he didn't. And if one lone clerk in the office of Fernand Lemieux, the old assessor, hadn't made a mistake, your title to that Boisblanc property might have been worth gambling for in dead earnest. But see if you can follow me now: I told you the sale of that Boisblanc land to Valois Dupré was recorded at the courthouse and that the purchaser assumed the '96 taxes."

"Yes and that he didn't pay them. That he never paid them or any other taxes on the property."

"That is correct. But the tax bills were sent to him. The clerk in Lemieux's office saw that a proper entry was made on the books, so that the sheriff sent the notices to Valois Dupré at New Orleans— I assume you know that the sheriff collects taxes in Louisiana—the assessor merely computes them."

"And if those notices were duly sent, what was the mistake?"

"The clerk made the mistake. He neglected to make a second entry to the effect that my tax bill should be cut by the amount of Dupré's. So, in April of '97, when they sent Dupré his bill, they also sent me mine at the old figure—the figure based on my ownership of *the entire Cindy Lou Plantation, Boisblanc and all.*"

"And you paid it? You didn't high-tail it up to the courthouse at Convent and raise holy hell until somebody corrected the mistake? What sort of a Simple Simon do you take me for? You ought to know I wouldn't swallow a yarn like that!"

Bushrod's voice rang with the contemptuous anger which he was no longer making the slightest effort to control or conceal. He leaped to his feet and leaned across the table, gripping its polished edge and looking down at his stepfather with an expression of sneering hatred. Clyde neither moved nor answered and, just at that moment, Zack entered the gaming room with an armful of firewood. The Negro plied an iron bar among the embers and laid fresh bolts of wood against the smoldering backlog. Then he glanced at Clyde, as if in silent inquiry. But the latter shook his head without speaking and Zack withdrew. It was not until the sound of his footsteps had died away in the distance that Clyde answered his stepson's outburst.

"I said I would explain to you. Also, that I didn't give a damn

344

whether or not you believed me. Yes, I paid the full amount. That was right after your mother, your sister and Savoie Vincent had died horrible deaths. It wasn't until after your grandmother left Cindy Lou that I so much as looked at my books. Up to then, I was just going through some motions. When I got back to realities and went over my accounts, I saw right away that there must have been some mistake. But as long as the money had been paid, I decided to let matters stand as they were for the time being. I still wasn't in any mood or in any shape to take on extra problems."

"Though only the summer before, you wouldn't put out so much as one lousy dollar to buy back the land!"

Clyde looked up quickly. "I didn't propose to be the object of Valois Dupré's charity, then or at any time," he rapped out. "I'm neither a panhandler nor a blackmailer. When I set out to buy something . . . oh, what the hell! I've already said there are things you wouldn't understand. But maybe you can understand when I say that we did a lot better in '96 than we had ciphered we might. I mean your mother and I. Before the harvest, we couldn't say more than that we saw daylight ahead. But we had a bumper yield of cane that year and got top prices for our sugar, even allowing the Vincents their toll for grinding and granulating. Our tobacco crop did better still. Everything was coming our way at last. By the spring of '97 we not only saw daylight ahead, we were out of the woods. It really looked as if life would be wonderful again . . . until the fire. . . ."

Suddenly, his voice broke. But almost immediately it was under control again.

"That's got nothing to do with you," he continued harshly, glowering at Bushrod. "But it does concern you that as long as I was paying taxes on all of Cindy Lou, those on the Boisblanc tract were never in arrears."

"That's only your view of it."

"No, it's been generally admitted. When old Fernand Lemieux finally found out about the mistake in his records, he almost had a spasm. He said he would do anything I wanted him to, in order to get everything straightened out. He fired the clerk who was responsible for it. He offered to have the sheriff send Valois Dupré a receipt for all past-due taxes. All in all, he took on so bad that I told him to wait until he got quieted down before we tried to get things fixed up. And the next day he dropped dead of a heart attack."

"So the matter was not straightened out. That's exactly what I've been saying. The land was advertised for sale by the state and I bought it."

"As I told you before, you had reason to think so. But I wouldn't advise you to count on it. You see, the next time I was in New Orleans I called on Valois and explained to him what had happened. I also said I was ready to buy back the Boisblanc tract for what he had paid me in the first place. And he said no, he had made me a price on it, which was one dollar, no more and no less, and he would stick by that price. If I cared to take it for that it would be a deal. He had got mighty rich by that time, dealing in building materials, and his schooners were bringing in shell and sand and gravel from over the lake to his yards on the New Basin Canal. I knew he meant what he said, just as I had, so I finally bought back the Boisblanc tract."

"For a dollar?"

"That's right."

"And would it be too much to ask what became of your high and mighty notions of not taking handouts, or whatever you called them?"

"By the time I bought back the land I had the money to pay for it, and that made all the difference. This was in the early spring of '98, another good crop year; it was no longer a case of having to take the land for a dollar because that was all I had. If you can't see what a difference that'd make, there's no use talking about that end of it."

"Suit yourself. But what you've said still doesn't alter the fact that a year later the high sheriff advertised the land to be sold for delinquent taxes and that I bought it—and own it."

"That's the last domino that fell. Lemieux, the old assessor, was dead. His clerk, the one who made the mistake, was fired. Young Sigur Hymel, who was elected to succeed Lemieux, and his staff didn't know anything about all this. All they knew about was what stood in the office records. And, according to those records, a certain number of properties—the Boisblanc tract among them—were in arrears. So Hymel handed the sheriff a complete list of what should be advertised in the *Regisseur du St. Jacques* to be sold for taxes. Naturally, if any of those properties had been in my name I'd have seen the notice, or someone would have told me about it. But it wasn't. The name of Valois Dupré didn't mean the first thing to any of the folks around here and I didn't look at the list myself, for the simple reason that all my taxes were paid. I wasn't hunting around to grab more land off the people who couldn't keep up their taxes. Apparently, you were."

"You're quite welcome to think anything you like about my motives. That won't alter the fact that I did buy the land."

"My prior purchase of it and the record, showing that no taxes on it were ever delinquent, alters the fact, though."

"Where is the record of that sale? The first one was recorded at the courthouse. What about the second one—if there was a second one?"

"Before Valois got around to recording it, or having his attorney do it for him, the war broke out. Young Dupré was on Colonel Billy Dufour's staff in a regiment of immunes and they were among the first to be sent to Cuba. The boy's father wasn't thinking about getting an unimportant scrap of paper recorded—unimportant to him anyway.

And the attorney who would ordinarily have handled such matters for him was his son—the son who was in Cuba. So the matter was neglected. Then, by the time the war was over both he and I had forgotten about recording the transfer, although young Valois had drawn up a regular act of sale, when the deal was consummated, with all the whereases and the business about one dollar and other good and valuable considerations, so the mistaken entry on the assessor's books never did get corrected. What's more, as long as the tax notices were now going to you, it probably never would have been corrected, till either old Valois or I died. But it doesn't really signify."

"Well, something'd better signify, or I'll. . . ."

Without haste, Clyde rose. "Or you'll what?" he inquired casually. Then he stood, waiting for a reply, with the thumb and forefinger of each hand hooked into the pockets of his gray moleskin vest. "Go ahead, Bushrod. Finish what you were saying. You'll do what?"

"A man has his rights," Bushrod insisted sullenly. "And don't stand there like an old fool. You never saw the day you could scare me, not even when I was a child. And now. . . ."

"Now you're a bold hero and I'm just a decrepit old man?" Clyde chuckled in such genuine amusement that Bushrod looked up in equally genuine surprise. "Certainly I'm no bull of the woods. I never was. But Zack, who is old, too, and his son Nappy, who isn't, and who can take some of the bend out of a horseshoe with his bare hands, are still up. They wouldn't like it if anybody got to worrying their white folks too much. Sounds like storybook stuff, doesn't it? But it's real. So is what I told you about your deed to any part of Cindy Lou not being worth the match you'd strike to set fire to the paper it's written on. As for me, decrepit or not, I propose to keep my health and strength till Larry's old enough to fend for himself . . . no!"— he interrupted himself as Bushrod seemed about to speak—"you abide where you are and let me do the talking for now.

"You renounced all claim, right or interest to Cindy Lou when I told your grandmother Larry wanted and needed no part of the Virginia properties. But you tried to buy your way in through the back door and then cheat your way into more yet. If your title to the Boisblanc tract had been valid, you'd have lost it to me at poker tonight, by trying to run in some nursery tricks that wouldn't have fooled a bunch of schoolteachers playing 'Authors.' In other words, you forfeited any right to any share or part of Cindy Lou I don't know how many times over."

"Your sermons don't interest me any more than your real estate dealings," Bushrod said, rising. "If you must talk, talk to the walls. I'm going to bed. As to who has title to the Boisblanc land, I'll look into the records before I tell you what I'll do in the matter."

"You'll find it would pay you better to listen to me," Clyde went on.

Bushrod, who had already started toward the door, half turned and waited. But his bearing showed plainly that he was merely pausing, momentarily, between one step and the next.

"As I said before, you've forfeited any right or claim to consideration," Clyde continued evenly, "but I've always been willing to pay for what I want. And what I want is that Larry should be left alone by the likes of you. So I'll do this: as long as you stay away from Cindy Lou, I'll pay you an allowance that will keep you from any need to panhandle or engage in any of the other ways you've used in making ends meet. It won't be enough to fit you out with a private apartment at the Gibson House or the Waldorf . . . but perhaps you can sweet-talk or blackguard Mabel into giving you a remittance to stay away from Amalfi, except when she wants you to make an appearance there. With two remittances, you'll be secure against everything but your own folly . . . and before you go, by way of lagniappe, here's something that's about your speed. Matter of fact, you suggested it."

Withdrawing right thumb and forefinger from the pocket of his vest, he tossed a clean, white sugar-tit onto the brightly lit table. Outside in the night-cloaked garden, one of the peacocks again burst into a raucous screech. Furiously, Bushrod flung the sugar-tit into the fire and stormed from the room.

Much later, Clyde was aroused once more from the light slumber of old age by the peacocks' clamorous discord. He realized that some sort of commotion was afoot on the grounds; but his energy had been deeply drained by the events of the day and he did not rise to investigate. Not until he came downstairs the following morning, after noting that Bushrod's room, deserted, had been left in chaotic disorder, did he learn from Zack that all the peacocks had been found dead in the garden, where someone had wrung their jewel-sheathed necks during the night.

It was only after he had superintended their burial, and the rage which surged through him mingled with the consciousness that another link with the happy past was gone, that he remembered to speak to Zack about the anchor lights. He had had many other things on his mind and, subconsciously, he might have used this as an excuse for the delay: he had not been willing to believe that anything was amiss aboard the *Lucy Batchelor,* which was a still more important link with the past, and Zack had not noticed the change in her. But when they went out to her together, they both realized that there must be a slow leak somewhere, that she was gradually settling. Before expert help could locate the cause of the trouble, she had sunk without a trace.

CHAPTER XIX

I‌T DID not surprise Clyde to find Larry playing with his blocks; this was one of the little boy's favorite pastimes. Neither did it surprise the old man to find that Larry had brought the blocks to the office, instead of playing with them in the nursery or in the library, as he had done heretofore. Clyde had always encouraged Larry to stay with him and there was no reason why the child should have thought he would not be fully as welcome to bring his playthings with him as to come himself. To be sure, the box in which the blocks were kept was rather heavy; it was about a foot square and it was made of wood, ornamented with etched Oriental figures framed in bands of dark green. Originally, it had contained tea. Clyde could remember when Lucy bought their tea in large wooden boxes like that, shipped direct from China. They had used a great deal of tea in those days—a long, long time ago. . . .

That was not the point, of course. The point was that Larry, though he was large and strong for his age, could not possibly have carried that big box from the nursery—or even from the library—down the steep stairs to the office. He must have asked Tudie or Nappy to do this for him, and he must have had some special reason for it. Without impatience, but with considerable interest, Clyde waited to find out what this was.

The blocks had belonged to Cary and, as she also had been a very sturdy child, they had suffered considerable hard usage before they came to Larry. In the beginning they had been bright blue and bright red, in equal quantities, and the letters on them had all been bright black. Now the blue and red surfaces were streaked and faded and the bold lettering was faint at best, even where it had not been almost obliterated. The sharp corners of the blocks had either been unevenly chipped off or rubbed to roundness, and many of them were faded or cracked. But Larry had always played with them quite contentedly, ever since he had been old enough to play with blocks at all, and it had never occurred to Clyde before that perhaps he ought to get new ones—stone blocks, for instance, with which Larry could build houses and churches, instead of just making piles and rows. However, it occurred to him now.

"I reckon that maybe we ought to be thinking about getting you some new blocks, one of these days," he remarked. "Eh, Larry?"

Without answering aloud, Larry shook his head. He was very busy putting some of the blocks in two short rows near his grandfather's desk. He turned them this way and that and arranged them with

349

great care. When he finally looked up, Clyde saw that his cheeks were flushed and his eyes shining.

"These are *alphabet* blocks!" he said. "You didn't tell me so, but Aunt Amy did." His tone was not reproving. His adored grandfather could do no wrong in his eyes, and consequently could commit no sins of either commission or omission. Nevertheless, Clyde instantly accused himself of negligence and started to say he was sorry Aunt Amy had got ahead of him, that he should have realized Larry was old enough now to know about alphabets and not to think of blocks merely as playthings. But Larry went on so fast that Clyde had no chance to get very far. "She was surprised because you hadn't taught me my letters," Larry was saying excitedly. "So *she* taught them to me! I can say them all! A—B—C—D—E—F. . . ." Without a mistake he chanted through the alphabet to the end. "She taught me something else, too," he concluded in triumph. "So that I could surprise *you*. Look at those blocks I fixed!"

Clyde glanced down. His eyesight was not keen any more and besides, his vision seemed to be somewhat blurred at the moment. But as he focused his gaze on the blocks in front of him, he saw that they had been so arranged that the letters in one row would spell LARRY and that those in the other row would spell DADDY. Larry had always called him Daddy and not Grandfather or any abbreviation of this. And now he knew how to spell that and his name. . . .

"Well!" Clyde said, clearing his throat. "Well, you certainly have surprised me, Larry! You've given me a very fine surprise. . . . Do you know how to spell anything else?"

"Yes, lots of things. I'll show you."

Swiftly he demolished the two rows of blocks which were standing and began to arrange others. "M-A-N. B-O-Y. D-O-G. C-A-T. H-E-N. P-I-G. C-O-W." Clyde read in swift succession. Then Larry began to fumble a little. He was trying for HOUSE and HORSE and he became slightly confused. Clyde rose from his chair and knelt down on the floor beside him.

"Maybe I could help—" he suggested a little hesitantly.

"Oh, Daddy, will you? Aunt Amy said she thought you would. She said she'd ask you to get me a primer, too."

"Of course I'll help. Of course I'll get you a primer, too. It's just that I didn't realize. . . ."

This time he succeeded in saying what he had started to say before. Then, until suppertime, he and Larry sat on the floor together, arranging and rearranging blocks. And after supper, while he was reading aloud to Larry from Grimm's *Fairy Tales,* he stopped every now and then and asked the little boy to point out words that he knew. It was great fun for them both. The trouble was that Larry became so excited over it all he could not go to sleep. He did not sleep in the nursery any more, with Tudie watching over him. He slept in the youth bed which had been his mother's and which was now drawn up closely beside his grandfather's four-poster. Only this time, he kept sitting up in bed to make one important announcement after another.

"Larry, it's getting late. You won't feel like riding Tophile tomorrow morning, if you don't quiet down now."

"Yes I will, too. I always feel like riding Tophile. You know that, Daddy. But I've thought of another word. I could show you if I had my blocks here."

"Well, but you left your blocks down in the office. You can show me tomorrow."

"But I can *tell* you now, can't I, Daddy? It's a nice word. It has four letters in it."

"All right, tell me now. But after you've told me, I want you to turn right over and—"

"B–O–A–T."

Clyde did not answer. It did not matter, in the darkness, that his vision was blurred. But something seemed to have happened to his voice, too.

"Don't you think that's a nice word, Daddy? Aren't you pleased?"

"Yes," Clyde said at last. "Yes, I think it's a very nice word. Yes, I'm very much pleased."

Larry finally went to sleep, but Clyde still lay awake beside him, thinking hard. He had not paid much attention when Larry teased Zack, who was handy with a jackknife, to whittle little boats. He had thought the boy's request accidental—it might have been for animals or wagons or something else, just as logically. Afterward, to be sure, he had noticed that Larry's favorite pastime, next to riding his pony, seemed to consist in steering the little boats about in an old sugar kettle, now used only to hold rain water. But he had not regarded that as significant, either. Perhaps he should have. And of course he should have realized that a child, who could ride and swim as well as Larry could already, was old enough for book learning, too; and yet he had not given it a thought. He was grateful to Amy, of course; but he was chagrined that she should have had to point the way; he was also slightly jealous because it was she who had taught Larry his letters. Probably he himself would not make much of a teacher; but he could at least have done that much and perhaps a little more. He would look, the first thing in the morning, to see if there were not an old primer in the library. Cary must have had a primer. Yes, he remembered now, Lucy had taught her to read out of one called by the astonishing name of *Warner's Holiday Album;* and then there had been *McGuffey's First Reader*—and *Second Reader*—and *Third Reader*. They were certainly around somewhere. But perhaps now there was something newer, something more modern. He must make inquiries. And not only of Amy. She meant well, she had done her best, better than he had done himself. But certainly someone else could do better still. . . .

Larry would need other things besides a primer. A slate. Slate pencils. A blackboard. Chalk. If he could learn to spell he could learn to cipher. Well now, he had said nothing about numbers. Perhaps Amy had not stolen a march on Clyde when it came to numbers. He did not believe she had, either. Most women did not seem to realize that numbers were just as important as letters. And Larry would be quick at figuring, too. Clyde felt sure of it. He and Larry would have a good time together, over sums. Even the multiplication table . . . there must be some way of teaching a child the multiplication table so that it would not mean bewilderment and misery. He would find out. . . .

People talked about the three R's—Readin'—'Ritin'—'Rithmetic. And 'Ritin', not 'Rithmetic, came next after Readin'. Maybe. But he was not going to let any old method stand in the way of his teaching Larry to cipher—straight off, too. Besides, if he remembered correctly, Lucy had taught Cary to print before teaching her to write. Well, he could do that also—he could do both. He would get some of those ruled copybooks that had a page of letters in the front—capital letters and small letters, too, formed with an almost incredible degree of perfection and enclosed in a decorative scrollwork. Then he would practice secretly at copying these before he tried to teach Larry to do so. His penmanship had never been bad—in fact, it had once been a source of considerable pride to him. Lucy had complimented him on it more than once. But he would try to improve it. . . .

Perhaps Larry should be taught to read and write French at the same time he was taught to read and write English. That was the way Savoie had been taught, Clyde knew; if Savoie had lived he would have wanted his son taught in the same way. And Cary had not been much older than Larry when she had begun to study French. Lucy had not taught her that, because Lucy had insisted that the Madames of the Sacred Heart at Convent would do it so much better. But the nuns themselves complimented Lucy on her knowledge of French. Though she did not speak it as fluently as Cary quickly learned to do, she read it with ease and wrote it with grace. Even Mrs. Vincent admitted that. . . .

Perhaps he should write to Mrs. Vincent for suggestions. She was entitled to express an opinion about the education of her only son's only child and to expect that this opinion would be respected. Clyde resolved that he would write to her the next day—well, perhaps not the next day, because he and Larry had planned to ride out on the levee and watch Nappy catch a mess of shad sardines in the yellow flood that writhed seaward below the plantation at high water. But certainly very soon. However, it might be necessary to start on some sort of a program before he heard from Mrs. Vincent, for he had no assurance that she would reply promptly. With each succeeding season her letters had been farther and farther apart. Poor Lamartine still lingered on, a helpless cripple; and two years after the birth of the heir Pierre Lamartine, whom they called Pierrot, Armande had had another child, a little girl this time, who had been named Janine. Mrs. Vincent's outlook seemed to be bound by solicitude for her invalid husband, her pride in her daughter and her doting fondness for her two French grandchildren. She hardly ever mentioned her son-in-law and occasionally Clyde wondered whether there were any special reason for this; but he avoided giving the matter much thought. Sometimes Mrs. Vincent did refer with a certain arrogance to the reconciliation between the two branches of the De Chanet family, which Armande had effected, and spoke of the visits which Pierre's half sister the Princesse D'Ambly and her daughters—Josephine, now the Baronne de Courville, and Isabelle, who had recently married Gilles de Lorne—periodically made at Monteregard. The old marquis had died and Pierre was now at the head of the family; his son Pierrot was still the only male descendant—a fact on which Mrs. Vincent commented, with little apparent regard for the disappointment this must have caused, but rather with great personal satisfaction. However, it appeared that Josephine had a darling little daughter—Louise—who was a little younger than Pierrot and a little older than Janine, and that the three children had wonderful times together. Obviously, Mrs. Vincent was interested in Louise only because she was such a perfect playmate for the others; and though it pleased her to speak of her important connections with such families as the D'Amblys, the De Courvilles and the De Lornes, Clyde was sure that her enjoyment was based on a sensation of vicarious prestige rather than on any feeling of genuine affection. Nevertheless, the effect of such a milieu had been to alienate her from the one in which she had formerly lived and which she had never regarded as quite worthy of her. Larry, the little American grandson whom she had not seen since he was a baby; Cary, his mother, who had not—in her estimation—been the social equal of her son Savoie; and his grandparents, Lucy and Clyde Batchelor, who by no stretch of the imagination could ever have "belonged" to the Creole aristocracy, were all part of that milieu. She was only dimly aware of Larry now and she had no desire that the vague image should become more real to her. Clyde would write to her, that was the proper thing to do; however, he thought he could tell beforehand what she would say in her tardy reply: she was sorry to have left his nice letter so long unanswered, but poor Lamartine required more and more attention; and the children had had the mumps—light cases, fortunately, but one could never be too careful of adverse symptoms which might develop suddenly. Since their recovery the chateau had been full of company. Dorothée, as usual, had been in Paris, so it had been necessary that she herself help Armande oversee the household and entertain all these people who were coming and going. (Here would follow a formidable list of names culled from the *Almanach de Gotha*.) She was happy to say that Josephine's husband Jehan had been able to accompany her on her latest visit, though Gilles had been prevented from bringing Isabelle because of pressing duties on his own estate, which was one of the finest in France. Louise was not nearly as pretty as Janine, but she was a very cheerful child, and Janine, who was rather grave, needed exactly that sort of companionship. Oh, yes—about Larry! Well, of course Savoie had always had a tutor. Probably that would be the best solution for Larry, too—at least, if Clyde could find a suitable young man of exemplary habits who was also an accomplished classical scholar. But Mrs. Vincent had an idea that tutors, like servants, were not what they used to be. . . .

Lying thoughtfully awake in the darkness, Clyde dismissed the idea of a tutor then and there. When the time came, he would write to Mrs. Vincent and tell her that her surmise had been correct, that, unfortunately, he had not been able to find a suitable young man of exemplary habits, who was also an accomplished classical scholar; it would not hurt his conscience to omit mention of the fact that he had not searched for any such paragon. However, the next evening, after he and Larry had returned from their swim in the old barrow pit on the *batture*, and Larry had tumbled contentedly into bed—not excited and wakeful this time, but drowsy from fresh air and exercise—Clyde rode up the river road to confer quietly with Mrs. Surget.

She had been hoping he would come, she told him; she had not liked to hurry him, to seem in any way to interfere, but it was really high time. . . . Well, what specifically would she recommend? . . . Would he consider Jefferson College? she wanted to know. Generally boys were not received there until the age of ten or twelve, but occasionally exceptions were made for special cases. It was out of the question, Clyde answered, with more heat than he intended. He could not take Larry back and forth from Convent every day, or spare one of the hands to do so. That would mean four trips; besides, it was a long ride, too long for a little boy. As far as that went, Mrs. Surget replied quietly, Larry would not go back and forth every day; he would have to be a boarding pupil from the start. . . . All right, he might have known in advance what his answer would be to that, Clyde responded, still more heatedly; he had not the slightest idea of permitting Larry to be separated from him. He would teach the child himself, as well as he could. Of course French would have to wait. . . .

Mrs. Surget forbore to say she had known that was what he wanted to do, all along, that his call had been simply a gesture of courtesy.

Nevertheless, she smiled to herself when he had gone. Now that he had been driven to it, Clyde would probably make a very good teacher. However, she had done the driving—quietly, secretly even, but nonetheless skillfully. That was the way women often had to work. Results proved that it was not a bad way.

The lessons were a success from the beginning. Clyde emptied a ground floor chamber of its furniture and fitted it up as a schoolroom. It was one of the bedrooms which had formerly been in frequent use by his business associates, and had always been kept in readiness for their reception. Now that he no longer had such visitors or, indeed, visitors of any kind, except at very rare intervals, it had outlasted its original purpose and it should have another. The lessons provided this. Larry was delighted with his primer, his slate, his copybook, his well-filled pencil box, his varicolored chalk; he was even more pleased with the little desk, placed beside his grandfather's large one. Its opening was on the top, and there was room inside for all his new treasures, except the blackboard; moreover, there was a row of little drawers down one side, in which future treasures could be stored. This desk had been bought on purpose for him; it had not belonged to someone else first, like all the rest of the furniture in the house. It was his very own.

They did not have lessons at regular hours, but fitted them, more or less haphazardly, into the periods which the management of the plantations left free. Larry nearly always accompanied his grandfather in riding the crops and Clyde marveled at the boy's natural aptitude for the saddle. Apparently, it never occurred to him to remain on the headlands and trot sedately over bridges; if something along one of the drainage banks caught his eye, he kneed Tophile, his small plantation pony, out into the field and sent him briskly over the ditches in beautifully timed jumps. He had outgrown the fat little Shetland on which he had learned to ride, and Clyde had purchased Tophile for him in Tennessee. From the beginning, there had been an extraordinary degree of understanding and attraction between horse and rider. Almost instinctively, Tophile seemed to divine what Larry required of him; and he fulfilled these requirements with the same zest that Larry himself showed in revealing them. No day was long enough to provide all the hours which the boy wanted to spend in riding, and it did not occur to him that lessons should interfere with a pursuit which was already habitual, nor did Clyde see any reason why he should make an issue of the matter.

But though the lessons were so irregular, there were just as many of them—if not more—than there would have been if Larry had been going to school. Saturday was not automatically a holiday merely because it was a Saturday; in fact, if there were rain, Clyde and Larry sometimes spent the entire day in the schoolroom and more than made up for their absence on a Friday, which might have been such a pretty day that they had taken a picnic basket and gone in a buggy with Nappy to the ditches back of the Boisblanc area for a big mess of scarlet swamp crayfish—"mud bugs," Nappy called them. On such occasions, Larry was fascinated by the great square nets, and watched with gleeful interest as Nappy tied a piece of raw meat in the center of each and then set them all upright in the shallow water, stirring the mud beneath until it spread upward in great dark clouds. The bait was allowed to rest until these mud clouds settled. Then Nappy took a long myrtle pole and snatched out the nets, one by one. A dozen or more startled crayfish were often still gorging themselves on the bait which had lured them to their undoing, and Nappy tilted them from the net into a bucket, which Larry proudly held out toward him, and from the bucket the mud bugs were transferred to an oat sack, which was well filled by midafternoon.

There were all sorts of excursions like this; and sometimes Clyde and Larry went to the old gravel bed, where the buried treasure still lay undisturbed—if, as the Negroes continued to insist, it were really there —and Clyde watched Larry dig for it, just as he had watched Cary dig, more than a quarter of a century earlier. Larry did not tire as easily as Cary had or become so restless; he did not throw down his shovel and come to fling himself in Clyde's arms, demanding distraction. In fact, very often Clyde had to insist that Larry must stop digging, because it was getting dark and it was high time they went home. Larry always put down his shovel with reluctance; if he could only get just a little farther down, he insisted, he might find the treasure; nothing ever shook his belief in its existence.

Despite all such interruptions, however, the "book learning" progressed faster than Clyde had expected. In summer when it was very hot outdoors at midday, the schoolroom was always cool and that was a fine time for lessons; and in winter, when first evening came so early and it was cold in the fields and on the river road, it was warm and cozy in the schoolroom. So the lamps and the fires were lighted and Clyde and Larry stayed at their desks until Larry began to rub his eyes, or said, "Gee, Daddy, I'm hungry." Then they went upstairs together to their waiting supper and, very often, Clyde went to bed immediately afterward, just as Larry did. But because they both went to bed so early, they were both ready to get up early, too; and since it was still dark and cold outdoors, it seemed natural to go back to the schoolroom and stay there, with the lamps and the fires burning, until the kindly sun had brought light and warmth to the day.

So, all in all, Larry galloped through the primer at top speed and plunged almost as fast from the *First* to the *Second Reader*; and meanwhile he had learned to print every word he could read and to write a good many of them. He could also count and add and take away; and Clyde realized that in little or no time the experiments in making the multiplication table pleasant could begin. Every now and then, Mrs. Surget was invited to visit the schoolroom and remain through lessons, and she always complimented Clyde on his prowess as a teacher and Larry on his progress as a pupil and went away smiling to herself.

Eventually, they had another visitor in the schoolroom. This was Father Le Grand, the pastor of St. Michael's Church in Convent. Larry recognized him because the priest had come and spoken to them, several times, when they went to the cemetery to put flowers on the tomb where Larry's father and mother were buried. He did not understand about that very well yet. He had seen dead animals, and knew they had to be put in the ground after they had died; but he had never seen a dead person, and his grandfather had not explained to him yet what happened to persons who died, or why they were buried differently from animals; and, for some reason, he had felt shy about asking, though he asked Daddy almost everything else that came into his head. He associated the priest with the cemetery, and the thought crossed his mind that perhaps Father Le Grand was the person to ask about death, though he was not an old friend, like Aunt Amy, and Larry did not think he had been invited to the schoolroom, the way she so frequently was. However, his grandfather received Father Le Grand respectfully and invited him to be seated.

"We're almost through for the day, Father," he said. "If you don't mind, Larry and I'll finish this lesson before we go upstairs. Then I hope you'll accept some refreshment."

"Thank you," Father Le Grand answered pleasantly. "I'd enjoy that very much—hearing the end of the lesson and taking a little refreshment afterward, too."

"Go on reading, Larry," his grandfather directed.

Larry was delighted to finish the story. He had been a little afraid, when the visitor arrived, that his grandfather would say, well, that would be all, until tomorrow. It was a very interesting story about a horse named Black Beauty. He read it aloud carefully, but with eager interest, and when he had finished he looked from his grandfather to the visitor, not because he wanted them to praise the way he had read it, but because he hoped to discover that they had shared his enjoyment. He was not disappointed.

"That was a very fine story," Father Le Grand said enthusiastically. "I never happened to hear it before, either. You've given me a real treat, Larry. I'll have to see if I can't find a story you haven't heard before and read it to you someday—or send you a book that it's in, so that you and your grandfather can read it together. Do you know the story about David and Goliath?"

357

"No, sir," Larry answered.

"Or the story about Daniel and the lion's den?"

"No, sir," Larry said again.

"Well, I have a book with both those stories in it. I'll bring it to you the next time I come this far down the river road."

"Thank you very much, sir," Larry said promptly. He was quite sure he had spoken politely, yet evidently something was wrong, for his grandfather started to say something and then stopped, because the priest shook his head. However, apparently nothing was *very* wrong since both men were smiling. Larry put away all his treasures and closed the lid of his desk and slid out of his chair. Then he waited expectantly. The word "refreshment" was not one he had heard often, but he knew in a general way what it meant and he had reason to hope that cookies might be involved.

"I mentioned going upstairs, *Father,*" his grandfather was saying. He stressed the last word and then Larry understood: you did not call a priest "Sir," you called him "Father." He was very grateful because he had been permitted to learn that in such a pleasant way, instead of being reproved for making a mistake, which would have embarrassed him very much. But then, his grandfather hardly ever reproved him; that was one of the many wonderful things about Daddy. "However," Clyde Batchelor went on, "perhaps instead you'd just come into the gaming room. That's where Larry and I usually have refreshments, at least between meals. We have so few visitors nowadays that I'm afraid the drawing room's closed. But of course if you'd prefer—"

"Thank you, Mr. Batchelor. I'd consider it a compliment if you'd let me come to the gaming room."

Larry's grandfather opened the door and the priest stepped into the passageway that connected the schoolroom with the gaming room. He had never seen the ground floor of Cindy Lou before, he said; he had heard about the series of arches which gave it such distinction, besides acting as supports for the superstructure; but he had not realized that this series was so extensive or so impressive. He was using big words, but Larry knew what most of them meant; he knew that this visitor appreciated Cindy Lou, and that made him very happy. Zack, or one of the other servants, must have guessed that he and his grandfather would be going to the gaming room, even if they did have a visitor, for a glass of milk and a plate of cookies were already standing on the center table, besides the silver coffee service and a silver basket heaped with fruitcake. But his grandfather paid no mind to the coffee; he opened the door of the cellarette and asked the priest what he would like.

"If you still have some of Carteret Paine's bourbon—" Father Le Grand suggested.

"I have, indeed. And you couldn't make a better choice."

The bourbon made a rich gurgling sound as it was poured out. The two men lifted their glasses and sat down in easy chairs on either side of the fireplace. Larry stood beside the gaming table, eating his cookies and drinking his milk. He understood that it would be all right for him to do so now, though nothing had been said to that effect. In fact, nothing had been said to him on any subject. His grandfather and the visitor were talking to each other and for the moment they were not including him in the conversation.

"You said you'd never been on the ground floor of Cindy Lou before, Father. It's a long time since you've been anywhere in the house."

"Yes. Not since—"

"Not since Cary died. You were kind enough to come and see her during her last illness, even though she wasn't a member of your church."

"I wanted to come. I was fond of Cary and I thought of her as at least partly belonging to us. After all, I married her to Savoie Vincent, I baptized their son." He glanced toward Larry, smiling again, and Larry found he wanted to smile back. "But later . . . I didn't like to intrude."

"It wouldn't have been an intrusion. It would have been a very kindly act, like the other. But of course I should have realized that I ought to invite you. I'm afraid I've been very negligent about a great many things."

"Not negligent. Forgetful, perhaps. But I understood."

There was a short silence. The priest lifted his glass and took a slow sip. Larry reached for another cookie.

"Nevertheless, I decided that the time had come to jog your memory a little."

"Yes?"

"Yes. You see, having baptized Larry, I know how old he is. And as his godparents apparently haven't done it, I thought perhaps you wouldn't take it amiss if I suggested that he ought to be coming to church now and learning his catechism pretty soon. . . ."

There was another silence, a longer one this time. Neither man took a drink in the course of it, so Larry did not think he ought to reach for a cookie again, either. At last his grandfather spoke.

"You're right, of course, Father. His godparents—well, I'm not sure, but I think they both live in New Orleans. They were school friends of Cary and Savoie, I remember that much. But they haven't kept in touch with us since . . . I'm afraid they've been even more forgetful than I have."

"I can give you their names, of course. They signed the registry at the time of the baptism."

"Yes . . . well, I suppose I ought to write to them to remind them.

359

But I'll bring Larry to St. Michael's myself next Sunday, Father. Next Sunday and every Sunday from now on, unless there's some good reason why I can't."

"I was sure you would, Mr. Batchelor, when I reminded you."

"About the catechism, though. I'm afraid there are some other things Larry ought to learn first. I'm afraid he'd be very much puzzled."

"You won't let him be puzzled. We'll see that he learns the other things first, if he doesn't know them already. But perhaps he does. . . . Come here, Larry."

Larry went around the table and stood between the priest and his grandfather. The priest put his arm around Larry's shoulders and spoke to him very kindly.

"You have a Christmas tree every year, don't you, Larry?"

"Yes, si—yes, Father."

"And you hang up your stocking and get lots of presents?"

"Yes, Father."

"You know there's some special reason why you have all those nice things at Christmas, don't you?"

"Yes, Tudie told me. Tudie took care of me until I was big enough to take care of myself. She told me lots of things."

"Such as—"

"She told me Christmas was a sort of birthday party."

"I see. Well, Tudie was right. Did she tell you whose birthday it was?"

"Yes. She said a boy named Jesus was born on Christmas. A long time ago. She said his own people were very poor and he was born in a stable, with lots of animals around—cows and sheep and donkeys. But his mother was very pleased with the baby and lots of other people, besides her, were pleased. Some shepherds. They were poor, too. And some kings. They weren't poor, they were very rich. They brought the baby nice presents. And there were some other people— that is, sort of people, called angels. And there was a star."

"I see that Tudie has done her very best to teach you about Christmas. I'll give you a story about it, too, in the same book with the story about David. . . . Now, tell me something else, Larry. Did Tudie teach you to say your prayers?"

"Yes, Father."

Larry thought he heard his grandfather say something very quickly, as if he were surprised, the way he had been about the alphabet. But when Larry turned at the sound, his grandfather was not saying anything at all, and his face had a strange blank look, without any smile on it.

"What did she teach you to say?" Father Le Grand went on.

"Well, first she taught me to say,

> 'Now I lay me down to sleep,
> I pray the Lord my soul to keep. . . .'

"And did you understand what that meant?"

"No. But I said it every night because Tudie asked me to. Tudie's always been awfully good to me so I was glad to do something to please her. Then, last year, before I moved into Daddy's room to sleep, she taught me two more prayers. One begins, 'Our Father,' and the other begins, 'Hail, Mary.' Do you want me to say them to you?"

"No, not just now, Larry. But you do say them, don't you—every night before you go to sleep and every morning when you wake up?"

"Yes, Father."

Again Larry thought he heard a strange sound, but again, when he turned, his grandfather was silent and motionless.

"Do you kneel down when you say them?"

"No. I used to, when I slept in the nursery, because Tudie knelt down with me. But when I moved into Daddy's room he didn't say anything about kneeling down. So I just say them in bed."

"Well, it's all right to say them in bed. The place doesn't matter so much. The thing that matters most is just to pray. Sometimes it's easier to do it kneeling down, that's all. Sometimes if we wait until we get in bed, we're so sleepy that we don't pray very well."

"I thought of that. But still—"

Larry looked inquiringly from the priest to his grandfather. Suddenly he felt very tired, not a nice kind of tired, as if he had been outdoors all day, but a different kind of tired, as if he were going to cry. He hadn't cried in a long while, not since he could remember, and he hoped very much he wasn't going to now. He thought perhaps if they could talk about something besides prayers, he wouldn't. Or maybe they wouldn't have to talk about anything else—anything, at least, that he didn't understand very well. Maybe Father Le Grand would go away now and leave him and Daddy alone. . . .

Evidently, Father Le Grand realized himself that this would be a good idea, for he rose, still with his arm around Larry's shoulders, and said he'd enjoyed his visit very much and, now that he had found his way back to Cindy Lou, he was promising himself the pleasure of coming there fairly often. Meanwhile, he looked forward to seeing Mr. Batchelor and Larry at St. Michael's—and he wouldn't forget about the storybook.

After he had gone, Daddy did not say anything for such a long while that Larry thought perhaps he had gone to sleep. He tried to keep very still so that if Daddy was tired, too, he would not be disturbed. But at last he stirred in his chair, and Larry went over to it quickly and climbed up in his grandfather's lap. He knew he was

361

welcome to do so, though when Daddy was funning he said that Larry was such a big boy now it was hard to hold him.

"I'm afraid there are a great many things I should have taught you that I haven't," his grandfather said in a sad voice. "I realize more and more all the time—"

"Why Daddy, you've taught me lots of things! Everything I know, except the alphabet and the prayers."

"Yes, but I ought to have taught you those, too. I shouldn't have waited until after an old lady and an ignorant colored girl—"

"I think Aunt Amy and Tudie were pleased to be able to teach me *something* when you'd taught me everything else, don't you?"

"I suppose they were. But I'm not pleased."

"I don't see why not. I should think you'd be very pleased. We're having all those nice lessons together just because I learned the alphabet. And now that you know about the prayers we could say those together, too, couldn't we? Every night before we go to bed. Out loud. Kneeling down. Then we'd be sure we wouldn't be too sleepy."

Lucy had always knelt to pray and she had taught Cary to do the same. But even she had not suggested that Clyde should kneel with her or her child. She had never discussed prayer with him at all. She had known that he was without religious faith, and she had not wanted to do or say anything that would seem to put the slightest unwelcome pressure upon him—about that or anything else. But Larry did not know that his grandfather was without religious faith; Larry was unconscious of any unwelcome pressure. He only knew that he and his grandfather did things together.

That night, for the first time since he had run away from the orphanage, when he was only a little older than Larry, Clyde Batchelor knelt beside his bed and repeated the Lord's Prayer. Larry repeated it with him. Afterward, still speaking in unison, though Clyde missed a word now and then, they said the Hail, Mary.

 CHAPTER XX

WHEN LARRY was twelve years old he made his First Holy Communion at St. Michael's. The next autumn he entered Jefferson College as a boarder.

Their first parting was a terrible wrench for both him and Clyde. But though it had taken him time to do it, his grandfather learned to face the fact that Larry needed better and other teachers and also companions of his own age. He had been very shy, at first, in the catechism class, but gradually he had made a few friends. Those friendships should now be ripe for development.

The school year was a long one, beginning in September and ending in June, with no vacation at Easter and only a short one at Christmas. On the first Sunday of every month Larry was allowed to go home, and on the other Sundays and on Thursdays Clyde was allowed to see him at the college. These brief visits were tantalizing rather than satisfying. They both counted the days from September to Christmas and from Christmas to June; then they made the most of every moment they could spend together. It did not occur to either of them, for a long while, that Larry might wish to visit some of his schoolmates, or invite them to Cindy Lou. They were so happy in each other's company, after their long parting, that neither was conscious of any need for other society. In time, however, after Larry had declined several invitations quite automatically, he mentioned one of them casually to his grandfather. Clyde answered quickly.

"If you'd like to go home with Blaise Bergeron, Larry, I hope you will. I hope you don't feel you have to come to Cindy Lou."

"I don't feel I have to come to Cindy Lou. I want to come to Cindy Lou."

"Well, of course I'm glad, in a way. But you haven't seen many other places yet. Perhaps you ought to."

"I don't believe any of them are as nice as Cindy Lou."

"You can't tell until you go and see them."

Larry made no reply. Taken by and large, he had always been an exceedingly tractable boy; still, deep within him, there was a stubborn streak.

"If you don't want to go home with Blaise, why not ask him to come home with you?" Clyde persisted.

"Because I don't want Blaise or anyone else around, except you, when I come home. I see all I want to of Blaise and the other boys at school."

If he had not been good at games, this insistent periodic withdrawal from his schoolmates might well have resulted in lack of harmony with them. But he was a born athlete, and his mode of life at Cindy Lou had tended to develop his natural talents. He made both the basketball team and the baseball team in the first tryouts, and his fancy dives were a source of secret envy and constant emulation at the swimming pool. He was always close to the head of his class, when he did not actually lead it, and this might have been another menace to widespread popularity; so might his flat refusal to join the debating society, though this refusal was not due to any lack of interest in controversial matters. When topics were subject to argument, he preferred to think them over by himself, or to discuss them quietly with his grandfather. Indeed, he could appear to be completely lost in a book, unaware of the tumult raging around him, and would look up with an expression as blank as Clyde's could be at will when angry questions were hurled at him by his classmates. At home, after a talk with his grandfather, he would sometimes sit silent for hours, mulling over everything that had been said, or saddle his horse and ride off alone toward the solitary swampland, or take his pirogue and paddle away through the drainage canals and the sluggish bayous.

In like measure, he declined, courteously but with unmistakable finality, to join either of the sodalities at the college. He had a great reverence for religion, but his shyness still persisted when it came to his devotions. He was not self-conscious when the college attended chapel in a body; but it was hard for him to approach the Communion rail unless so many others were doing it at the same time that he would not be noticed in the crowd. The prayers which meant the most to him were those which he and Clyde said by themselves in the chamber which they still shared when he was at home.

It was not until Larry was halfway through his third year at Jefferson College that his grandfather Vincent finally died, and his grandmother and his aunt Armande returned to Victoria, bringing the body with them for burial in the family vault at Convent. Probably they would not even have done this if the unhappy man had not extracted from them a promise that he should not lie in foreign soil. It was Clyde's impression that Lamartine had never become as fully expatriated as his wife and daughter, that his years of helplessness had been all the more bitter for him because they had been passed amidst the alien corn, and that his unimpaired mind had been active until the end; and this impression was quickly confirmed by the demeanor of his widow and daughter. Clyde met them at the station when they arrived, accompanied by a French maid and wearing the longest and heaviest veils that he had ever seen, even in a community addicted to crape. He escorted them to Victoria and assisted in the arrangements for the interment which, in accordance with their wishes, was the most elaborate that had ever taken place in Convent. But nothing which could be called a real conversation took place on these occasions; and for a few days after the obsequies the two ladies remained secluded, allegedly in a state of complete prostration. Clyde called, first alone and then with Larry, who had been given special permission to leave college for the purpose, only to be turned away by Titine with the announcement that they had not once left their darkened chambers and that they were "takin' on somethin' terrible." However, within a week, Bassie, Titine's new husband, delivered a note at Cindy

Lou, so deeply bordered in black that there was hardly room for the superscription. Inside, the brief message, written in French, was couched with great formality: if M. Batchelor would make allowances for the outbursts of grief which they might not be able to control, and which they were sure he would understand in view of their recent great bereavement and the conflicting emotions awakened by the sight of their old home, Mme Vincent and Mme la Marquise de Chanet would be glad to receive him at five the following afternoon.

Clyde's mouth twitched slightly as he read this communication, and when he had dressed in the black suit which he almost never wore nowadays, but which had been taken out of moth balls for the funeral rites, he winked at himself once in the mirror before starting downstairs. Sugar and Spice had been appropriately covered with tasseled black netting before they were harnessed in the cabriolet; and Nappy, proudly wearing a long-disused black livery, was in the driver's seat, holding a whip which had been adorned with a large black ribbon bow of watered silk. In fact, everything had been prepared in the most approved fashion for a *visite de condoléance*. When Clyde was ushered into the drawing room at Victoria, he found, as he had expected, that the shutters were closed and the furniture shrouded with coverings. It seemed rather a pity, when he had taken pains for years to see that the house should be kept properly aired, that it should now be stifling. However, he recognized the pattern.

Mrs. Vincent and Armande came into the room together. Their elegant crape dresses were cut after a fashion which had not yet reached the river road, with underskirts so narrow at the bottom as to make walking awkward and difficult, and overskirts so voluminously folded as to give the false effect of enormous hips. They both wore onyx jewelry and carried black-bordered handkerchiefs. Clyde, who had not seated himself while awaiting their arrival, went forward with becoming gravity and Mrs. Vincent extended her hand at a level which indicated she expected him to kiss it, not shake it; Armande followed suit. Clyde had never overcome his aversion to hand kissing as a social gesture, but he decided that on such an occasion as this he would do well to respond in the manner expected. However, when Mrs. Vincent began to speak to him in French, he shook his head and answered courteously but firmly.

"I'm very sorry, madame. Of course you've forgotten, but I never knew how to speak French and I can't follow more than a few words of it. I'll have to ask you to talk to me in English."

"It's so many years—" Mrs. Vincent said, with a deep sigh. She glanced around the shrouded room, touched her eyes with her black-bordered handkerchief and seated herself on a small sofa, signifying that she wished Armande to sit beside her and that Clyde should take an armchair near by.

"Yes, it is a great many years. I am very sorry it has been so long. And of course sorrier still for the reason. I shall always think of Lamartine as one of my best friends."

"One of the best friends, one of the best husbands, one of the best fathers—"

Mrs. Vincent glanced for confirmation toward her daughter who, as yet, had not spoken at all. Clyde gathered that Armande's natural taciturnity had increased with time. At all events, she disregarded the implied suggestion that she should join in the conversation, and Clyde concluded that he had better pursue it without her assistance.

"You know I want to do whatever I can to help you," he said. "I hope you've found everything in good order here and that the servants are making you comfortable. As I've written you, some of the older ones have died since you went away, and I have not thought it was necessary to replace them, because Titine married and there was so little work to be done. I don't need to tell you that until your arrival she and Bassie have been merely caretakers. But if you require more service, I can send either Delphie or Ivy over from Cindy Lou. Belle has died, too, and of course, in my opinion, there will never be another cook like her. But she taught Ivy all she could, and Lucy found Delphie fairly satisfactory as a maid. She does not do quite so well without feminine supervision, but you could supply that—which I can't."

"I really do not have the heart to attempt it. I find that these younger Negroes make very poor substitutes for their fathers and mothers, and the Grim Reaper has taken those faithful souls, just as he has taken their masters." Mrs. Vincent paused, with such a deep catch in her breath that the sigh seemed likely to become a sob. But she recovered herself and went on, "Titine and Bassie leave much to be desired, of course. But as you know, we have our own excellent French maid Leonie with us, and since our stay will be so short—"

"Will it? I had hoped, now that you are here—"

Mrs. Vincent raised a slim white hand in protest. "You must remember that Armande has children. It did not seem best to interrupt their studies, or to subject them, while they are still so young, to the ordeal of such a melancholy journey. Of course their grandparents give them the greatest care, and the *princesse* and the *baronne* both assured us that they would make frequent visits to Monteregard during our absence. Even so, a mother's heart—"

"I understand. But since Pierrot and Janine are so well cared for, surely you don't need to worry about them. And you haven't seen anything of Larry yet. I think you'll be very pleased with him, very— very proud of him. He's a fine boy."

"Oh, yes, Larry." Mrs. Vincent glanced at Armande again and again Armande disregarded the signal. "I must see him, of course, before I

366

leave. I know you brought him here, the other day, but it was really too soon. Perhaps some day next week—"

"It would have to be a Thursday or a Sunday, and then as a special concession, because of the circumstances. The college is pretty strict about giving leave of absence, and of course Larry's had some already, for the funeral and the first call. But if you'll tell me which day would be agreeable, I'll ask the president. I'll tell him you feel you can't stay until the holidays. That is, if you're sure."

"Oh, perfectly sure!" For the first time Mrs. Vincent spoke with animation. "So shall we say next Sunday? I'm sure the president of the college will not make any difficulties, when you tell him how important it is that I should return promptly to France. And certainly I should see Larry before I go—once, anyway. Meanwhile, speaking of Larry—"

She paused again, but this time, though she did draw a deep breath, it was also a quick one. She neither sighed nor sobbed, but went on quite briskly.

"Since my time is so limited, I think we should not waste it. I think I should talk to you at once about my husband's will. It was his wish that Larry should inherit as much as would have normally gone to poor Savoie, if Savoie had survived him. That is, a fourth of all his property. I am sure you will agree this is a very generous apportionment."

"Yes, madame, I surely do."

"As to the other three fourths—" for the third time, Mrs. Vincent glanced at Armande, who stirred slightly, but who still made no other response. "Armande and I are agreed that we would like to keep the house in New Orleans," Mrs. Vincent went on. "I do not foresee any likelihood of wishing to return there. But of course there is always a possibility, and it does not involve much expense for caretakers and taxes and occasional repairs. I should be grateful if you would continue to look after such details for us in the future, as you have in the past. And it has occurred to us that you might be willing, as Larry's guardian, to waive his rights in a share of that property, if he were given, by way of exchange, a larger share in Victoria. If I am not mistaken, this would be comparable to the arrangement that was made in regard to his inheritance of Cindy Lou."

"I'd be very glad indeed to do both, madame—glad to continue my supervision of the New Orleans property and glad to exchange Larry's rights in it for a larger share in Victoria," Clyde answered, without making any comment on the latter part of her speech or even feeling any curiosity as to how she had learned of the arrangement between himself and Miss Sophie.

"I am delighted to hear it. And since that point has been settled so easily and so quickly, we can go straight on to the only other which seems to me to require adjustment. I do not care to retain possession of Victoria and neither does Armande. Would you like to buy our rights in it for Larry?"

So it had come at last, the opportunity for which he had worked and waited so long. There was no room for doubt in Clyde's mind: Mrs. Vincent had guessed how greatly he coveted this plantation for Larry and she drove a hard bargain; in order to close with her, he was forced to offer far more than the plantation was worth in dollars and cents. She laid aside all pretense of grief as she haggled and revealed herself simply as an avaricious old woman, intent on wringing all she could from him. But it was worth the sum on which they finally agreed, in other ways than money; and he had the dollars and cents ready and waiting for her demand. When she went back to France with her silent daughter, two weeks later, Larry was the undisputed owner of Victoria.

Meanwhile, accompanied by Clyde, he had paid his grandmother the one stiff Sunday visit which she stipulated. The shutters had been opened by this time and the furniture uncovered; but she and her daughter entered the drawing room in much the same manner that they had before, and made no effort to put the boy at his ease. Clyde had warned him in advance that Mrs. Vincent and Armande would expect him to kiss their hands, and was proud of the lack of embarrassment with which Larry performed the unaccustomed rite. Clyde had also told him that his grandmother had become very French and very formal, and that his aunt, who had never been talkative, was now noticeably silent; perhaps it would be well for him to begin by addressing Mrs. Vincent as madame, and wait to see whether she herself would suggest *grand'mère*. Though she did indeed make the suggestion, she did this belatedly, as if it were an afterthought. She designated a small bench, opposite her sofa, as Larry's seat, and asked him a succession of questions, without drawing either her daughter or her second visitor into the conversation at all.

"So you are my other grandson, Larry. I think you are taller than my French grandson Pierrot. Of course, you are about six months older. But you seem to me very large for your age. Have you been told that before?"

"Yes, madame."

"And you look more like your mother than your father, even if you do have his straight black hair instead of her golden curls. I suppose you've been told that, too."

"Yes, madame."

"It is very sad that you should have lost both your father and mother when you were a baby, that you can't even remember them."

"Yes, but then I've always had Daddy."

He turned to glance at Clyde, his eyes lighting with unabashed

368

affection. In fact, nothing about the call seemed to be causing him any embarrassment. He sat erect but easily on the stiff little bench, his feet crossed, his hands clasped in his lap and, except for that one glance at Clyde, he kept looking straight at his grandmother. He did not fidget and he did not stare around the room. Clyde, who was aware of the inherent shyness which Larry had never wholly overcome, had dreaded this interview for the boy. Now his relief was mingled with pride. If he were not mistaken, Larry was sizing up Mrs. Vincent quite as shrewdly and swiftly as she was appraising him, and it was evident that he was not overawed by her and that he saw no reason why he should be.

"Daddy?" Mrs. Vincent inquired, as if she were puzzled by the designation or thought it unbecoming. "Oh—you mean your grandfather! I didn't grasp, immediately, to whom you were referring. But I suppose, under all the circumstances. . . ." She shrugged her shoulders slightly, and it was then she bethought herself that Larry should not be addressing her as madame. "Of course you and your grandfather must decide between you what you are to call him," she said, condescendingly. "But I am going to ask you not to call me madame. That is most inappropriate. After all, I am your grandmother."

"What would you like to have me call you? *Grand'mère?*"

"Yes, that would be entirely proper. Do you know some French?"

"Yes, *Grand'mère.*"

"Enough to carry on a conversation with me?"

"I think so."

"Well, let us see. *Vous étudiez quoi, à present?*"

From there on, Clyde was able to follow only in a general way. He realized that Mrs. Vincent was asking Larry about his studies and his schoolmates and what he did in the way of recreation, and that Larry was answering adequately, though not expansively. Then he saw the boy's face flush with sudden color and, for the first time, heard a hesitant answer. Something had obviously gone amiss after all; he would try to find out, later, what it was. Fortunately, just then Titine came in with coffee and little cakes, and Mrs. Vincent suggested that Larry might like to pass them. As he handed Armande her cup, he smiled and spoke on his own intiative.

"I'm sorry Pierrot and Janine didn't come with you, Aunt Armande. I'd like very much to meet them."

Evidently Armande found something persuasive in his manner, for she broke her long silence. There was not much warmth in her voice, but she spoke agreeably.

"Thank you, Larry. It didn't seem best to bring them to Louisiana. But perhaps you'll come to see us some day, at Monteregard."

"Well, I don't know whether that would be best, either. Daddy doesn't care much about traveling any more. We don't even go to New Orleans, except once in a great while."

"You could go to Monteregard without me, you know, Larry," Clyde said quickly. "I'm too old to travel myself now. But I'd like to have you accept your aunt's invitation. I'd be glad to have you see something of your cousins. And you'd enjoy the trip."

"Not unless you went, too."

He was still completely courteous, but his words were conclusive. Clyde recognized the stubborn streak which, like the streak of shyness, was still there. He knew it would do no good to insist but, taking the initiative in his turn, he said he would be pleased if the ladies would come to dinner or supper at Cindy Lou, some day before their departure. Larry, unfortunately, could not be there. But perhaps they would like to see the old house again.

Before Mrs. Vincent could voice formal regrets, Armande, surprisingly, said she would be very glad to go, and that possibly evening would be the better time, since they were very busy during the day, sorting and packing the personal belongings which were not included in the sale of property. Clyde answered that he quite understood and how about Wednesday at six-thirty? He was suddenly relieved that Armande had chosen evening; by candlelight the shabbiness of Cindy Lou would not be so apparent as in the more revealing light of day. It was a long, long time since any renovating had been done inside the house. Not since Lucy had died. Many of the rugs were worn, much of the upholstery dingy. And the house had not been painted outside, either. It had begun to have a weather-beaten look, very different from the resplendency which had characterized it when Armande was a girl. Well, now that Victoria was bought and paid for, he could begin to make the superficial improvements which would restore Cindy Lou to its erstwhile elegance, both inside and out. Until now, he had limited himself to essentials in the way of repairs and replacement. The roofs had been kept tight, the timbers sound. There had been better and more machinery on the place all the time, better and more wagons, better and more livestock. The outbuildings were in first-class condition, the Negro cabins exceptionally comfortable, the land well drained. But nothing had been done in the way of embellishment.

These thoughts darted through his mind as the call came to an end. When Larry approached Armande to bid her good-by, she leaned over and kissed his cheek. After that, Mrs. Vincent could do no less; but she said nothing about hoping to see him again. She thanked Clyde for bringing her grandson to visit her and said she was gratified to find him in such obvious good health and to learn that he was making so much progress in his studies; but she confessed that she was slightly disappointed to find that he had left the locality so little and that he seemed to have formed so few close friendships. Evidently Larry's quick blush had been occasioned by some reference to such lacks. On the ride back to Convent Clyde asked Larry, as casually as he could, whether the boy felt like telling what all that jabbering in French had been about.

"I don't mind. She asked a lot of questions—whether I liked Latin, whether I had any talents—"

"Had any talents?"

"Yes. Whether I had a good voice, or whether I could play any musical instrument or paint pictures. I told her I could sing in the choir, at a pinch, and that I could strum on the piano a little, but that I didn't care about either one and that I couldn't draw anything to save my life. I told her I got along all right in Latin, because having French, too, helps, but that I'd be glad when I was through with it. So then she asked me what I did like."

"And you said—"

"I said I liked to read and to ride. And she said those were both apt to be rather solitary occupations—those were the words she used. She seemed to think I ought to be in a crowd all the time. I told her I hated crowds. And then she said she wasn't talking about crowds, she was talking about society."

"What kind of society?"

"Why—parties and stuff like that. She seemed to think I ought to be going to dances—where there were girls."

So that was what the sudden blush had meant! Like most children raised in the country, Larry had learned a good deal about sex, as he had learned something about death, from observation of the animals on the plantation. But he had never asked many questions about it or revealed any special curiosity. As far as Clyde had been able to discover, his attitude was still that of a child rather than that of an adolescent; and in view of the confidence which existed between them, Clyde thought it unlikely that the boy could be specifically inquisitive or emotionally disturbed without revealing the fact to his grandfather. The man was annoyed, almost angry, because Mrs. Vincent had raised such an issue inopportunely, even if she had done this unconsciously. He tried not to show his irritation, but to continue speaking casually.

"I suppose some of your schoolmates have parties given for them at home. I suppose boys and girls both go to such parties."

"Yes, I suppose so."

"You could have a party at Cindy Lou, you know, any time you wanted."

"I don't want a party at Cindy Lou at all. I see all I want to of the other boys at school, Daddy. I've told you that before. And I don't want to see any girls. If I had wanted to, I'd have told you that."

Clyde realized that it would be futile to press the matter and the rest of the ride took place in silence as well as in darkness. But he was deep in thought. Looking back, he remembered that he had been very little older than Larry when he had first spoken to a girl in the street and afterward gone to her wretched room with her. He was thankful that it was going to be different now. Larry would be older and more selective when he had his first experience with sex. Clyde did not even try to visualize what form this would take; but he felt sure that it would not be premature and that it would not be sordid.

He wished he might be equally sure that there would be no Dorothée Labouisse in Larry's life.

The little supper party went off as well as could be expected. Clyde invited Mrs. Surget to join the other ladies and asked her to superintend Delphie beforehand, in getting out long disused linen, china and silver and in opening, airing and cleaning the closed drawing room. There were still a few dusty bottles of sound old wine in the cellar, and Clyde himself made a careful selection from these. Ivy's supper was creditable, even though it was not especially imaginative, and the wines and service gave it a certain distinction. After supper, before conversation had a chance to lag, Mrs. Vincent suggested that since there were four in the company they might play bridge whist—personally, she did not feel that a quiet game of cards, among friends, was incompatible with mourning. Neither Clyde nor Mrs. Surget had ever played bridge whist, though they had heard of it, and Mrs. Vincent did not attempt to conceal the satisfaction she felt through telling them it had been played in France for years already; in fact, that many persons now referred to it as auction bridge, omitting the outmoded word "whist" altogether; but one could hardly suppose that in provincial Louisiana! . . . A card table was set up in the drawing room and two packs of cards brought in. Mrs. Vincent expressed surprise because these were the large, old-fashioned type, outmoded, too; and she presumed they would have to use homemade score cards. Then, with still greater condescension, she began to explain the principles of the game. She thought it would be hardly fair to cut for partners; this might result in putting Armande and herself together. It would be better if each of them took one of the beginners. . . . Well, she said, three hours later, when the homemade score cards showed that Armande and Clyde were considerably ahead of the other two, she had always realized that her daughter was a good player—evidently an even better one than anyone in the De Chanet family had imagined. Bridge was part of the daily schedule at Monteregard, but unless she were needed to make up a fourth, Armande frequently excused herself. It was ridiculous, when she could play so well.

As Clyde gathered up the cards, he happened to glance at Armande and was startled by the expression on her face. She had been caught off guard and there was something in it very like desperation. Up to then, he had been merely annoyed by her persistent silence; now, for the first time, he wondered what might lie behind it. She had been a pleasant, friendly girl, even if she had lacked animation; but her only evidence of kindliness, in the entire course of her recent stay at Victoria, had been in her farewell to Larry. And she had not only failed in graciousness; she had not once joined in her mother's complacent comments about Monteregard, she had never spoken of her husband's relatives or of her husband himself. Of her husband. . . . Clyde met her eyes again and suddenly thought he had found the answer to the riddle: she was a wretchedly unhappy woman and her husband was the cause of her unhappiness. Her reserve was not, like Larry's, caused by contentment and self-sufficiency; she had withdrawn into herself because she did not intend to be hurt any more than she had been already. Her silence was her protective armor. . . .

Clyde slid the old-fashioned cards back into their cases and followed his guests from the drawing room. Mrs. Vincent and Mrs. Surget were walking ahead, absorbed in an animated discussion of the relative merits between whist and auction bridge. Clyde fell back a step and spoke in a low voice.

"I'd like to give you something that belonged to Cary," he said. "She was very fond of you, Armande. I know she would have wanted you to have a little keepsake to remind you of her. Of course, most of her personal possessions were—destroyed. But there were a few trinkets that she never took away from here—they didn't have much value, and she thought they were too childish looking to wear after she was married. But some of them are rather pretty—a small locket set with turquoises and pearls, for instance. If it would mean anything to you—"

"It would mean a great deal. And it means even more that you've offered it to me."

"Well, could I bring it to you tomorrow? What time would be convenient?"

"If you don't mind, I'd rather come here and get it. While *maman* is resting."

He nodded and stepped forward again. He was just in time. Mrs. Vincent was already extending her hand for his kiss.

"Such a delightful evening, my dear Clyde. Really, no one can take the place of old friends, after all. It makes me feel very sad to think that the time is drawing near to part from them again."

If he had thought she was speaking sincerely, he would have been much concerned, for the final papers had not yet been passed, assuring Larry's possession of Victoria. But he knew such expressions were only part of her pose. The more he saw of her, the more he despised her for her shallowness, her artificiality, her pretentiousness. He knew she had always possessed these qualities to a certain degree, just as she had always had a false sense of values; but they seemed to have been intensified through her residence abroad. Lately he had discovered that she had also become avaricious; and now he began to wonder how great a share she might have had in her daughter's unhappiness. If Armande's marriage had been a failure, then surely her mother should have been the first to shield and support her, even, if necessary, to remove her from the scene of her misery. Instead of that, she had so obviously reveled in the prestige of prerogatives and rank that she would have sacrificed almost anything else to retain them. The more he thought of it, the surer Clyde became that she had sacrificed her daughter.

Armande had not mentioned the time of her mother's siesta, but Clyde took it for granted that this was probably in the afternoon, directly after dinner. He told Delphie to dust the drawing room again and to have the coffee service ready; and immediately after his own dinner, he changed from the clothes he had worn during his rounds of the plantations that morning and this time, when he looked in his mirror, he did so with a certain degree of satisfaction. His figure was still spare and his alpaca coat was as carefully tailored, fitting his wide shoulders and lean flanks as flawlessly as the burgundy broadcloth of yesteryear. His color was still fresh and his hair abundant as ever, though it was now silvery white instead of ruddy gold. The heavy brows over the deep-set eyes were white, too, and so was the sweeping mustache. Clyde raised his hand to this and brushed it, first left, then right, into the merest suggestion of a cavalier's twirl at the points. His fingers were bony and his seal ring was loose between the knuckle and the enlarged joint, but his carefully tended hand still suggested the dominance that had always given it virility.

Instead of going to his office to work on his accounts, as was still his habit every afternoon, Clyde awaited his guest in the drawing room. The trinkets which Cary had left behind at the time of her marriage were all together in a small carved wooden box, and he had decided to let Armande take her choice among them, instead of simply giving her the locket. There might well be something else she would prefer and, in any case, the offer of a gift had been merely a pretext to give her a chance to talk with him, if she wished to do so. He thought she understood this and that she did wish to do so, or she would not have suggested coming to Cindy Lou, instead of receiving him at Victoria. But the afternoon wore on and she did not appear. Clyde sat fingering the little wooden box, toying with its quaint golden clasp and lifting its lid; then taking out the ornaments it contained, one at a time, spreading them on the table beside him and putting them back again in a new arrangement. It was true that none of them had much value; but as he turned them over and over, he could see how they had looked on Cary when she wore them in the radiance of her youth. Besides the locket, there were also earrings, bracelets, a brooch and a ring, all set with turquoises and pearls; he remembered that these stones had been favorites of hers, at a certain stage of her development, and that every time he came home from a trip he had added another matching ornament to those she already had. He was almost sorry he had told Armande he would give her one of them; whichever she took, the set would no longer be complete without it. And he had kept it so all these years. He would never see it in use again himself, but perhaps someday a daughter of Larry's would wear it. Or if Larry should happen to fall in love, very young, with a very young girl, he could offer it to her. Sometimes boys like Larry, who were girl shy longer than most boys, did fall in love very young, and when they were finally smitten, it was suddenly and hard and their first love might be their last.

Well, it was too late now to change his mind. He had offered Armande the locket and, if she wanted it, he would have to give it to her. But he wondered what had become of her. He restored the trinkets to their proper places, closed the clasp and, setting the box aside, took out his watch. It was after five o'clock. Something must have detained Armande or prevented her from leaving the house. Possibly she had even changed her mind about wanting to come. At any rate, it was too late for her to do so now. He would go to the office and work on the ledgers until suppertime. In fact, as he was so late in starting the accounts for the day, he would go on with them, straight through the evening. Telling Delphie that she might put away the coffee service, but that he would like sandwiches later on, in the office, he descended to the ground floor.

There was thunder in the air and darkness had closed in early, though it was pierced by occasional flashes of lightning. Presently, rain began to fall. Clyde made sure that the windows and doors were tight, brought his books within the radius of the lamplight and settled down to his accounts. The results of his ciphering were gratifying. Even after paying the unreasonable sum that Mrs. Vincent had extorted from him as the purchase price of Victoria, and allowing for the loss of his salary as its manager, he and Larry would still be in comfortable circumstances. He had never mortgaged his crops again, since Lucy's death, and the mortgage on the house had long since been paid off. Any further hesitancy about improving the appearance of the place would represent parsimony. He would get hold of a painter the next day, and it was also high time that the plumbing was expanded and modernized. He would consult Amy Surget about restocking the linen closet, replacing threadbare upholstery and turning out the storerooms. The grounds, too, needed attention. There was no reason why he should not have a good gardener. Lucy's camellias required expert care and he had not the strength to look after them properly any more; none of the colored hands on the place was capable of doing so. The gardens as well as the house must be revitalized.

He became so absorbed in his figures and his plans that he failed to notice the increasing fury of the storm. The rain had been falling in torrents for some time; now it was streaming against the windows and gushing from the overflowing gutters. The wind was rising, too; not with the death-dealing suddenness which had cost Lucy and Savoie their lives, but with steadily increasing momentum. The windowpanes and blinds were rattling harder and harder, and above the noise they made came the racket of a door blown open with violence. It was not until the wind swept into the room through this opening that Clyde realized it was his door which had been forcibly unclosed and sprang up to shut it. Then, instinctively, he recoiled. On the threshold a veiled figure, robed in dripping black, was standing with arms outstretched.

 CHAPTER XXI

THE RECOIL was only momentary. Armande had not thrown back the veil, which she had stretched out her hands to raise, before he recognized the identity of his sable-clad visitor. He hastened toward her, his own hands extended.

"My dear child! Whatever are you doing, out in this storm? I gave you up hours ago! You must be soaked to the skin. Come, let me take you to Delphie. She'll find something dry for you to put on and make you a hot drink."

"Please don't bother. I've got to get back as soon as I can and—"

"*Get back!* You won't stir out of the house, not while this storm lasts. In fact, I think you'd best let Delphie get you straight to bed. As soon as the rain lets up, I'll send a message to your mother."

"Please, Mr. Batchelor! As soon as the rain lets up, I must go myself. I don't want my mother to know I've come out at all. That's why I couldn't get here sooner—she didn't take a siesta today and she wouldn't let me out of her sight. It was almost as if she'd guessed. But she went to bed early, because of the storm. She's terribly afraid of storms and, for some reason, she imagines she's safer in bed. She's got Leonie in the room with her and I've bribed Leonie not to tell. It isn't the first time. But I'd rather none of your servants found out.

You know how these Negroes gossip among themselves. Please!"

She took off her dripping veil and, leaning over the hearthstone, wrung the water from it. Then she unfastened her cloak and shook it hard. Clyde was relieved to see that it was fairly heavy and that therefore it must have given her a certain amount of protection. But her long hair, which had come unbound, hung in wet, black waves around her shoulders and he knew that her shoes must be soaked. She would certainly be chilled through and through; she might even contract a serious illness unless he could persuade her to accept help. But the same look of desperation which he had caught on her face the day before had come into it again and he hesitated to insist.

"Won't you at least take off your shoes and dry them in front of the fire?" he asked gently. "I can have one going, you know, in no time at all." He took the napkin from the tray which Nappy had brought in some time earlier, but which was still untouched, and handed her the large square of linen. "Here, take this and get some of that rain off your hair. And you won't refuse to take a drink and eat a sandwich with me, will you? I haven't had my own supper yet."

Without waiting for her to answer, he busied himself with the wood and soon had a cheerful blaze burning. Then, going to the cellarette, he filled two glasses. Armande took off her wet shoes and, lifting her narrow skirt a little, sat down near the fire with the drink in her hand. But she shook her head when Clyde offered her a sandwich.

"No, really. I don't want to eat anything. I just want to talk to you."

"I thought perhaps you did. But you could have waited until tomorrow, just as well. As I told you, I never dreamed you'd come out in this storm."

"Tomorrow *maman*'ll keep me beside her all the time, just as she did today. The number of things she's packing to take away—well, I suppose it's all right. I suppose you don't care about china and silver and linen and things like that, as long as you get the house and the land for Larry."

"Not much. Not enough to make an issue out of them. But after all, some of those things are Larry's by rights, and others I'm paying for. When your mother spoke of keeping personal possessions, I thought she meant little ornaments and family photographs that had a special significance for her. I didn't think she meant valuables and furnishings."

"No, I didn't believe you did. Just the same, unless you're willing to have the sale delayed—and possibly fall through—I—I wouldn't make any objections, if I were you. That's one of the things I wanted to tell you."

"Thank you, Armande. Well, I'll think over what you've said. I don't like the idea of being cheated by anybody—if you'll excuse me

377

for referring to your mother as a cheat. I've never let anyone get away with chiseling yet. But perhaps this time . . . yes, I'll think it over. That wasn't all you wanted to say to me though, was it?"

"No. I wanted to tell you things I've never had a chance to tell anybody and that I might never have a chance to tell anybody again. Things that have been—well, choking me for a long time."

"I'm very glad you felt you could confide in me, Armande."

"I'll have to go back a long way—to the time I got engaged to Pierre. I knew he was in love with Cary and still I accepted him."

The look she turned on Clyde now was not only desperate, it was imploring. He answered her even more gently than he had spoken before.

"Do you want to tell me why you did that, Armande?"

"Yes. Yes. That's just what I want to tell you—first. I was afraid I was going to be an old maid. I hadn't had a proposal in a long while. I wasn't grieving for my first love—the boy who died of yellow fever— any more; I hadn't for years. That was just a legend of *maman*'s, to explain why I didn't accept suitors—suitors who didn't exist."

So Lucy had been right! As vividly as if it were yesterday, Clyde recalled her summary of the situation—a summary which was almost word for word the same as the one Armande was giving him now.

"Every other girl I knew had been married," Armande went on. "Even Cary, who took so long to make up her mind—because she had so many suitors she got confused. And then she chose wrong. I don't mean there was anything the matter with Savoie, except that he lacked force, just as I do. Perhaps it's a family failing, a failing in lots of families like ours. But he wasn't the man for her. If he had been, it wouldn't have taken him so long to get her and he wouldn't have lost her so soon. Pierre was the man for her. She knew it the minute she saw him and so did he."

"She didn't meet Pierre until after she was married to Savoie, Armande. And she—she pulled herself together. She wasn't unhappy and she made Savoie a good wife. He never guessed. I don't see how you did. I don't see how you guessed I knew, either."

"The last was *just* guessing. You and Cary were so close to each other, I didn't see how she could keep anything from you. But I knew how Cary felt because I knew how Pierre felt—almost right away. It was one of those things that you can't help knowing, that's so powerful it demands recognition. I knew he'd come here, hoping to get her. I knew he took me, out of pique, when he couldn't. I knew it, and still I accepted him. And not just because I didn't want to be an old maid, either. I really loved him. I loved him with all my heart and soul. I really thought that perhaps, after a while, he'd love me."

378

"I'm very sorry, Armande, that it didn't turn out like that. Sorrier than I can tell you."

"But I didn't deserve to have it turn out like that. Because there was still another reason why I accepted him. I accepted him to take him away from Cary. I thought it was quite a triumph to do that. I—I gloated over it. You see, she'd had so many suitors, and I was so close to being an old maid, that I thought, in the end, to get the man she wanted and who wanted her—"

Clyde leaned over and took Armande's hand. "Love's a strange thing, my dear," he said. "It does strange things to all of us sometimes. If you really cared for Pierre, you shouldn't blame yourself too much."

"I really cared for Pierre, but I was a false friend. I knew that Cary was suffering and I wasn't sorry. I was glad. And she was magnificent. Will you ever forget her, at my wedding? I never shall. . . . No, I didn't deserve to be happy. But somehow I don't believe I deserved to be as unhappy as I have been."

"Why don't you leave your husband, Armande? Why don't you come home?"

"I—I can't. I can't leave my children. And I couldn't take them away. I couldn't bring them with me, even for a short visit. You don't know what pressure can be like, from a French family. And I'm a Frenchwoman now. I lost my nationality when I married Pierre. I lost my real home. And then my mother. . . . I think my father would have helped me, if he could. But he couldn't even help himself. My mother was too strong for him, too. She's the only strong one among us. She seems fragile, but she's got an iron will."

"Do you want me to try to get you your freedom, Armande? Because, if you do—"

She shook her head and, as she did so, her long locks of black hair fell over her face, concealing it for a minute. Then she lifted her hand and brushed it back.

"No," she said. "What would be the use? You couldn't do it, even if you did try. I just wanted to talk to you. Now that I've done that, I feel better."

"I'm very glad, my dear. But I still wish there were something—"

"There isn't. And I mustn't give you the idea that Pierre—maltreats me. He doesn't. He's very polite to me—most of the time. Painfully polite. But when Cary died—well, it was an awful shock to him, of course, especially—especially happening the way it did. He—he lost control of himself, he told me she was the only woman he'd ever loved. Afterward, he apologized. He never told me so again. But I can tell that he wants to, every time he's annoyed with me. Every time I don't come up to his stiff French standards of what he thinks his wife and the mother of his son ought to be. Every time he imagines I'm disrespectful to his mother."

There was a long silence. At last Clyde asked, huskily, "Are you disrespectful to his mother, Armande?"

"I don't mean to be. At least I don't mean to show it. And she isn't at the chateau much any more, she's in Paris most of the time. So it isn't hard—not nearly as hard as it used to be . . . but I don't respect her. You met her when you bought this house, and later, when she came to Victoria to visit. Did *you* respect her?"

There was another long silence. For the first time in more than forty years, Clyde thought, fleetingly, that the moment had come when he could permit himself the comfort of full confession, in a way and in a quarter which he never could have foreseen. But almost instantly he knew that it had not come after all, and that it never would. Even on the chance that he might help Armande, he had no right to give her more than the briefest of answers.

"No," he said at last. "But you mustn't ever tell anyone I said so. Least of all Pierre."

"I won't. And I won't ask you but one more question. It would help though, if you'd answer that. Do you know what it's like to live with a secret and to feel that it's your fault you have to?"

It was not until after the storm had abated and Armande had gone out into the night again that Clyde remembered he had not given her the pearl and turquoise locket after all. It still lay, nestled among the other ornaments that matched it, in the little carved box which he had left upstairs. . . .

He did not see Armande alone again and, when he took her and her mother to the station, she was once more the silent, elegant French lady of fashion who treated him almost like a stranger. It was hard to believe that she was the same woman who had come to him, in secret, through a storm, and who had sat disheveled and distraught by his hearthstone, as she poured out her heart to him. And it was not until Larry came home for his summer vacation that he and Clyde went through the house at Victoria together and rode over the land. There had been no previous opportunity to do so since Mrs. Vincent's departure, because Larry had used up all the leave of absence which he was able to get; and though they had often surveyed the plantation in the past, they had never before been able to do so with the consciousness and the pride of ownership. Both eagerly awaited the occasion.

They rode past the mule barn and the quarters into the sea of standing cane that stretched away before them to the dark line of trees where the swamps took over. Clyde was handsomely turned out in freshly laundered linen riding breeches and polished, handmade boots; and despite his years he sat his bay gelding easily. From beneath the wide brim of his finely plaited Panama, he shot a swift glance at the slim, tall youngster on the sorrel stallion beside him. What a world of difference there was between this boy and the gamin who had clawed and battled his way from the barrel house dives of St. Louis to the proud position of a landed proprietor! Larry would never need to fight for a place in the world, never need to assume a virtue he did not have; he was really to the manner born. And now Clyde Batchelor was taking his beloved Lucy's grandson out to show him the domain which that erstwhile guttersnipe, that erstwhile river gambler, that erstwhile profiteer, had won for him.

The two trotted along in companionable silence between walls of green and purple cane until they came to the heavy gates which led to the fenced lane which divided the land of Victoria from the land of Cindy Lou. Larry slipped swiftly from the saddle to open the gates for his grandfather, leading his mount across the gaps.

"No need to close them, Larry," Clyde said. "Matter of fact, I could have had that fence taken down the minute the act of sale had passed. No sense, with all the wagons and teams going back and forth, making the hands stop to open and close those gaps every time. I just kind of felt I wanted you to be with me when we finally opened them for keeps."

"Thanks, Dad. For waiting, I mean. That's swell of you. It makes me feel like—well, I reckon you know what I'm trying to say."

"Yes—and there are things I want to say. Things I want you to look at, too, closer than you ever have before, because now they belong to you. Suppose we go up on the old Indian mound, where we can get a good view and rest awhile."

The Indian mound to which he referred had long been a favorite objective of theirs. There was none on Cindy Lou and there was no other on Victoria; but it was one of several similar elevations in the vicinity, which had presumably been built by aborigines, so that they might have the security of high ground when the river flooded the lower land in the spring. Arrowheads and skeletons had sometimes been unearthed from their depths; and the Negroes insisted that strange lights, which looked like balls of fire, played over them at night, as a warning for white folks to keep away. Larry had a few of the arrowheads, which he treasured greatly, but he had never been scared by the stories; in fact, the mound, shaded as it was by pines and moss-hung magnolias, had always seemed to him a pleasant spot for a breathing space on a warm day, quite aside from the fact that it afforded the best possible view of the surrounding countryside. Now he fell in readily with his grandfather's suggestion. They slipped forward in their saddles and the horses obediently broke into a brisk trot that covered the distance between the lane and the green elevation in a matter of minutes. Alighting and tethering their mounts to a hackberry sapling, they climbed the steep slope. As they reached the crest Clyde dropped an arm casually about the boy's shoulders.

"As you know, over there's the main part of the fields," he said, pointing. "But don't pass up that woodland on the far side. One of these days, when cypress gets scarce, there's a real fortune waiting for you there. Frank Williams, over in Patterson, is close to being the richest man in Louisiana, and he came there as a sawmill hand not too many years back. Cypress did it. And his cypress isn't going to last forever. As the rest of it is logged out in other places, here's where they'll have to come for more. And don't you be in any hurry to sell. Wait till. . . ."

"I'll wait till you sell it, sir," Larry said in his newly acquired baritone. He had never before called Clyde anything but "Daddy" or "Dad." Yet Clyde found the "sir" strangely warming.

"I'm not going to be here too much longer," he told the boy placidly. "No, never mind about that"—as Larry seemed about to interrupt— "I'm in no hurry to go, and I propose to hang on as long as the good Lord'll give me leave to stay, getting a bit crankier and peskier with the years, maybe. On the other hand, I'm well past the threescore-ten the Bible talks about. I'll be seventy-eight years old pretty soon. So we've got to face facts. That's why I'm talking to you about all this, because one of these days, no matter if it's soon or it's late, the whole thing is going to be your responsibility. I'd kind of hoped to have it for mine, and to head up a great big—well, call it empire—she's all of that, now; better than eight thousand acres, and there's places in Europe where you'd need a passport to come into or leave a chunk of land that big. But it's too late for me to make it, now. All I could do was get it together, and you're bound to know who I got it together for. So I'm showing it to you. Your empire. The fields and the cypress over there. The sugar mill close by the levee, because one of these days there'll be barges bringing you cane to grind. The big house you've got to keep in prime condition, because one of these days you'll have a daughter or a son to turn it over to for a wedding present. Naturally, I'm hoping you'll keep Cindy Lou for yours. No gates between them any more. It's one place—one empire—and it's yours. . . ."

He paused, too moved to say anything more. Indeed, it seemed to him, at first, that there was nothing more which required saying. Then, as Larry remained silent, too, he added, "Is there anything else, Larry, you'd especially like to have? I mean anything I haven't told you about, while we've been talking these matters over. Because if there is, I wish you'd ask me for it. There's probably no reason why I shouldn't give it to you now, and it would please me a lot to do it."

"All right, Daddy. I'll tell you. I'd sure enough like a dog. You know I've never had one."

A dog! Yes, it was true, there had never been a dog at Cindy Lou. Oh, of course the overseer and the manager of the sugarhouse had their hunting dogs and the Negroes had their feists! But there had never been a dog, a purebred, in the Big House. Now that Larry mentioned it, Clyde could not understand why Cary had never asked for one, why he and Lucy had never been conscious of such a lack, why he had not offered one to Larry long ago. A dog would not only mean a great deal to the boy; it would also mean a great deal to him, in those long periods which inevitably lay ahead, when Larry would be gone and he himself would be alone at Cindy Lou.

"Why, of course, Larry. Of course you ought to have a dog. Of course you should have had one long ago. We'll start looking around for one tomorrow. Have you thought what kind of a dog you'd like?"

No, Larry had not gone as far as that. They discussed, at some length, what kind of a dog they should get, without reaching any decision, and concluded there was no hurry about that, anyway. Tomorrow would be plenty of time. However, Clyde asked another question.

"When I said I wanted to know if there were any special thing you'd like to have, Larry, I wasn't thinking of something like a dog. I don't mean that a dog isn't important—that it can't be, anyway. But I was thinking of something that might mean a really big investment, something that might affect your future. Is there anything of that kind?"

"Well, yes. I don't know whether it's the sort of thing you meant, but sometimes I've wondered—"

"Yes, Larry?"

"About the boats. Yours, I mean. They were all gone, you know, before I can remember. There've been nothing but pirogues around—at least that had any connection with Cindy Lou. But I've been watching the river. There are more and more towboats on it all the time. Have you noticed, too? If we could have some of our own, you and I. . . ."

CHAPTER XXII

"I DON'T know that we could begin on the river, Larry. It would mean huge investments and uncertain returns, because it's paralleled by the railroads—damn them!—along most of its major branches and tributaries. By highways, too. And those are getting better and better all the time, thanks to gravel."

"Where could we begin then?"

"On the bayous. They run through swamp country where year-round roadways can't be maintained and where wheeled traffic—other than rail, of course—is feasible only during the dry seasons."

"I see. Well, whereabouts would we start on the bayous?"

"I'll tell you what I've considered and let you say what you think of it. I've heard that a small stern-wheeler, the *Palourde,* has sunk in Lake Verret. Of course the wreck's for sale cheap. I thought I might make a deal with the Teche Lumber and Planting Company whereby I'd purchase the wreck, raise it, repair it and operate it if they'd give me a contract to haul sugar cane for them from Bayou Aux Chenes and other small waterways of the countryside to Franklin. Our boat would be just doing the towing, you understand. If the Teche Lumber and Planting Company'd agree to furnish the barges and pay seventeen cents a ton, and we could move around seven hundred tons a day, between early October and early January, I think we could gross nearly—well, let's see."

Clyde swung around in his swivel chair and, facing his desk, began to figure. Larry, who had been sitting close beside him, rose and leaned over his shoulder, watching with absorbed interest.

"A hundred dollars a month for the captain—and I think I know just the man for the job. Clovis Bourgeois, his name is. I ran into him first at Morgan City, which used to be quite a shipbuilding center for bayou boats—he was the man who generally took new boats out on their trial runs. But there haven't been any new steamers built in nobody knows when—and Clovis has been living in Madisonville, where there's a shipyard turning out small tugs and shrimp boats and such as that. He'd sell his eyeteeth for a chance to take hold of the spokes of a wheel again, and he'd know where to pick up a pilot—he and the pilot could stand twelve-hour watches, and so could the rest of the crew. The pilot would get seventy-five dollars, two oilers sixty each, two firemen forty-five each, a cook the same, eight deck hands thirty each, a cabin boy fifteen." Clyde added up the figures rapidly. "That seems to total $685.00. It would cost about $250.00 to feed that many men and the fuel—wood—could run to another ninety. Well, allow a little leeway and, say, a grand total of about $1,050.00 for expenses per month. At that, we ought to net about twenty a day."

"That's pretty good, isn't it?"

"It's damn good. Even if I had to borrow against the contract, in order to salvage the *Palourde* and put her into condition, we ought to be able to pay for her within a year, because at the close of the sugar season we should be able to get another contract."

"For what?"

"For hauling rafted cypress logs from Bayou Boeuf and other forest waterways to the sawmill at Patterson, hard by where Bayou Teche empties into the Atchafalaya."

"You said 'even if you had to borrow the money.' Do you have to borrow it?"

Clyde began to figure again. "Not if we cut some corners here. I'd meant to do a little fancying up, at Cindy Lou, now that Victoria's paid for. But if we put that off—"

"Why on earth did you want to fancy up Cindy Lou?"

"Well, it's getting pretty shabby. Nothing's been done to it for a long while—seventeen years, to be exact. I had a run of bad luck about the time—about two years before your grandmother died. We had to figure pretty close for quite a spell—and I couldn't have pulled through if it hadn't been for her. She was wonderful—about that and everything else. There never—" Clyde checked himself. He had been on the point of saying, "There was never anyone like her before and there never will be again." If he had, Larry might very logically have asked, or at least wondered, if his mother hadn't been equally wonderful. "After your grandmother died, of course I didn't care, for a long time, how things looked," Clyde went on. "And it didn't seem to matter, anyway, with just you and me here. It's different when there's a woman—a lady—in the house than when an old man and a small boy are living by themselves."

"Yes, I suppose it must be."

"Then after I began to realize it was a shame, in a way, to let the show place of the river road get so run-down at the heel, I'd also begun to wonder whether I couldn't get hold of Victoria for you. And it seemed more important to save ahead, in the hope of doing that, than to spend money in—well, in fancying up."

"I think you were right, too."

"And now, if you and I are going into partnership—"

"I'd rather have the boat, Dad, than the trimmings. I'd rather have it than anything else in the world."

His voice broke with earnestness. His black-and-white setter Nuffy, who had been lying quietly on the rug near by, with his head between his forepaws, looked up with an expression of anxiety in his great liquid eyes, and wagged his tail intermittently, in a manner that suggested troubled inquiry rather than unquestioning joy. Nuffy, who had been named Sure Enough, because of the way Larry had asked for him, but who had quickly been nicknamed, had been a member of the household for only a few weeks, but he was already attuned to his master's moods. He knew, from the tone of Larry's voice, that portentous matters were under discussion, and he was not altogether sure that they were progressing satisfactorily. Clyde leaned over and patted the dog on the head. It was understood, of course, that Nuffy belonged to Larry; Nuffy knew this and so did everyone else. But there was also a strong bond of friendship between him and Clyde. The night after the dog's arrival at Cindy Lou, he had raised his head and howled dismally several times. This had then been attributed to his natural feeling of strangeness and loneliness in his unfamiliar surroundings; but when the habit of intermittent howling persisted, in spite of his appearance of general contentment, some other cause was sought and eventually found: Nuffy's mournful cries always coincided with the passage of trains over the "Valley" or the L. R. & N. tracks at the rear of the plantation. Why these distant sounds so distressed him, when others left him unmoved, no one had been able to discover. However, Clyde insisted that Nuffy was only giving vent to feelings about railroads which a man like himself, while endorsing, must perforce conceal, whereas a dog could properly give tongue to them. In other words, Nuffy was his mouthpiece as well as his kindred spirit.

"It's all right, Nuffy," he said now, pulling the dog's ears gently and giving him a final pat. Then he straightened up. "If you really feel that way about the boat, Larry—"

"I really do, Dad. I don't know that I'd like Cindy Lou fancied up. I like it the way it's always been, even if it is sort of shabby. It won't suffer in any way, will it, if you buy the boat?"

"No, it won't suffer. At least, I suppose I ought to have some painting done, not so much for looks as for preservation. But I'll keep it at a minimum. And I won't try to do anything in the way of interior decorating or landscape gardening. I still don't feel things like that matter very much without—just for you and me. And since you like it the way it is. . . . But we'll buy the *Palourde* and put it into action. I'll get in touch with Fred Banks at the Teche Lumber and Planting Company right away. If he and I come to terms, we ought to be ready to start operations this fall."

So it came about that more than ten years after he thought he had left the river for good, Clyde Batchelor was back on it again. The first contracts for hauling sugar cane from various waterways to Franklin, and rafted cypress logs from Bayou Boeuf to Patterson were followed by other contracts still more profitable: for towing gravel barges from

Profit Island in the Mississippi, just above Baton Rouge, to Morgan City on the Atchafalaya; for hauling granulated sugar from Glenwild landing near Charenton, and rough rice from the Teche country to New Orleans; for hauling general merchandise on the return trips. All this was done with the reclaimed stern-wheeler. Then came the proud moment when Clyde told Larry that the time had come for them to expand, to charter barges themselves, and bring loads of cotton down from the Ouachita River country, after having taken groceries, dry goods and other such commodities as far north as Camden, Arkansas, on the upstream leg of the journey.

By this time, Larry was nearing the end of his high school course and all for coming back to Cindy Lou to stay. His marks had continued to be good, but this was due to a combination of pride and intelligence, rather than to any special love of studying; and though he was well liked both by his teachers and his schoolmates and had made some real friendships among them, he still preferred his grandfather's company to any other. He could not see the slightest sense, he said, frequently and vehemently, in putting up with the restrictions at Jefferson four years more. It was ridiculous to expect that he would be satisfied any longer with those stiff, short Sunday and Thursday visits—as if he ever had been really satisfied with them!—with getting home only once a month in term time, and with only two vacations a year, one of them so short that it hardly counted! He was even more vehement when Clyde suggested that it might be a good thing for him to have a complete change from Louisiana and go to one of the big eastern colleges. The last thing he wanted was a complete change from Louisiana—he had never said he was not satisfied with *that*! What he was after, as he thought he had made clear, was not more separation from his grandfather, but less. If Dad was sincere in saying that he wanted Larry to relieve him, increasingly, of the plantations' management, if they were really partners in the new C. & L. Navigation Company, then the place for him was Cindy Lou.

It was with the greatest difficulty that Clyde persuaded him to accept Tulane as a compromise. If Larry went to college there, Clyde pointed out, he would have more freedom of action than at Jefferson; though New Orleans was so much farther away than Convent, he could actually get home from there oftener and stay longer at a time—in fact, he could come as often and stay as long as his scholastic standing would permit. It was true that Clyde was more than ready to relinquish the reins of management on the plantations; but when he did so, he wanted to be sure that Larry was properly prepared, in every way, to take hold of them. He would be far more capable of handling such a task at twenty-one than at seventeen—not merely because he would be more mature and could assume authority more convincingly; but because during the interval he could learn many things, both at college and elsewhere, which would help him to be a good manager. What, for instance, Larry wanted to know. Well, there was sugar chemistry, for one thing; not that Larry would be a sugar chemist, of course; he would hire those. But it would give him a great advantage to have all the fundamentals of this and other phases of sugar processing at his finger tips; he would not be like those planters who were obliged to accept the reports and conclusions of their subordinates. By the same token, he should study business administration, enough law to cover the question of contracts, warehousing, import and export shipments, and enough about accounting practice so that he would not be dependent on such rule of thumb bookkeeping as Clyde himself had been obliged to use. Then there was something else, and it was very important: Larry should not confine his studies at the university to those subjects which would be immediately and directly of use to him in his work and his business. Clyde had never realized how much he himself had missed, through lack of acquaintance with the classics, until Larry's grandmother had brought Alexander Peyton's library to Cindy Lou from Virginia. It was true that Larry had always had the run of this, and had profited by its availability and by his natural taste for reading, as well as by the courses he had taken at Jefferson; it was also true that an awareness of great literature and an acquaintance with languages did not help a man to buy supplies for a steamboat or to purchase the best sugar mules. But such breadth of knowledge not only increased the respect in which he was held as a member of a cultured community; it enriched the counsels he could thus contribute to discussions of men and affairs and it deepened the enjoyment he took from life as he lived it. With the guidance he could get at the university, Larry would be able to widen immeasurably the horizons he had only glimpsed through his great-great-grandfather's library and through his high school course.

As far as the partnership was concerned, of course it was a real one; but Clyde was beginning to foresee further contracts, even more profitable than those they had had in the past, but very different in character; he did not feel too sure that he himself had the knowledge to deal with these changing and expanding markets, so Larry must acquire it. What changing and expanding markets, Larry inquired. For oil, Clyde told him. Maybe that was not so important now, but it was going to be. Petroleum would certainly replace wood and possibly someday even coal as fuel for boilers, just as in a few short years it had already driven whale oil out of the market as fuel for lamps. His next towboat would have oil burners under her boilers—and think of the time that would be saved by not having to transfer cordwood bolts from wood flats to his own decks, and the labor that would be saved in stoking the furnaces! Ever since that man Heywood had made his strike near Jennings a dozen years before, more and more oil had been discovered in Louisiana—all west of the Mississippi so far, to be sure, and there were those who said that would always be the boundary line of discovery. But Clyde did not believe it. He thought that one of these days it might be found almost anywhere or everywhere in Louisiana, when men developed a surer way of looking for it in the flat country. An enormous refinery was already in process of construction, unit by unit, in Baton Rouge. And there was one commodity—oil, that is—where the railroads, damn them, could never compete with the river. A tow of three barges, say, could carry as much oil as seven trains of sixty tank cars each—and think of the time to be saved in loading those barges! Only three couplings to make. One man could do the whole thing in twelve hours. On those seven trains more than four hundred couplings would have to be made and unmade, and you couldn't load more than a dozen cars at a time on any single spur anyway, so it would take a week just to fill the tank cars and another week to empty them when they got to their destination. Yes, indeed! Oil! That was the thing to bring back the river to its glory. One of these days he and Larry would take a trip to that Evangeline field—in fact, if there were no more of this talk about leaving school for good, they would take it that very summer, as soon as Larry had finished high school. Clyde had met young Heywood in Morgan City one time, and they had developed a mutual interest in the idea of transporting petroleum in barges. Of course, it was impossible to take oil from Jennings to Baton Rouge by water now; but one of these days it might not be, one of these days there might be canals. That was what Heywood had predicted; and people were already talking about an intracoastal canal that would run from Brownsville in Texas all the way to the Mississippi River at New Orleans. . . .

Admittedly, the prospect of the trip had more effect on Larry's decision than the good advice about courses in sugar chemistry and the comments on the advantages of familiarity with the classics. Clyde recognized this, but he did not greatly care, as long as he had secured the desired results. The trip took place and, all in all, was a great success. Moreover, as Clyde wisely timed it toward the end of the summer, its aftereffects were such as to start Larry off to college without too much protest. Another one of its many good results had been to overcome much of his adolescent diffidence and reserve. At Tulane he continued to do well in his studies and to make his mark in athletics; but he also mingled more willingly with his classmates than he ever had at Jefferson; he even joined a fraternity and began going to dances. Though he established no David and Jonathan friendships and singled out no one girl or succession of girls for special attention, Clyde felt the boy was making progress in the normal—and therefore in the right— direction.

This progress was facilitated and expedited by the unawaited appearance of Armande de Chanet on the scene. Mrs. Vincent had recently died and Armande arrived in New Orleans alone—except for her maid Leonie—opened the long-closed house on Elysian Fields and settled down, apparently for an indefinite stay. She offered no explanation to the acquaintances whose curiosity was aroused by this procedure, beyond stating briefly that there were certain matters, in connection with the settlement of the estate, to which she thought she could attend more satisfactorily in person than through correspondence. When pressed, she added that her son Pierrot was in college, her daughter Janine at the Sacré Coeur and that neither of them needed her at the moment; therefore it seemed a good one for returning to her old home, which she had always hoped she might occupy again sometime. Having said this much, she politely but adroitly withheld further information, and it was soon obvious that she had no intention of giving any. She did not seclude herself, but made visitors welcome, in a somewhat impersonal way, and returned, with becoming promptitude, the calls that were made upon her, using a very handsome turnout for the purpose, and dressing, almost invariably, in black velvet with touches of ermine which, as everyone knew, was not really mourning at all. She also went to Mass at the cathedral and to meetings of the Athenée Louisianais and accepted the invitations to informal soirees, extended with some hesitancy because of her recent bereavement, but with hopefulness that in course of time she might become more communicative. Though these hopes remained unfulfilled, she gave distinction to any gathering she attended because of her elegant attire, imposing presence and polished, though guarded, conversation. Moreover, she seemed quite conscious of the fact that if she accepted invitations she would be expected to return them, and inaugurated a series of quiet dinners and small bridge parties which were recherché in every sense of the word. By this time she had reorganized the dormant household staff and expanded it, taken the family silver and other valuables out of storage, and given such fine feminine touches to the double drawing rooms as to make them seem more generally inviting; and long before she became recognized, to any extent, as an experienced and charming hostess, she had taken pains to let Larry know that he would be most welcome at her house whenever he felt like coming there, and that she also hoped he would feel free to bring his friends.

Her first note, asking him to come and see her, reached him before he was even aware of her presence in the city, and he responded to it with a promptness and politeness not characteristically collegiate. He had been genuinely attracted to her during the course of their one meeting, at Victoria, and had felt vaguely sorry for her, without knowing quite why. Later he had spoken to his grandfather about this and

Clyde, without saying enough to betray Armande's confidence, had told the boy he was right, that his aunt's life was not a very happy one and that, unfortunately, there seemed to be nothing they could do to help her—which was all the more to be regretted because much of her unhappiness was not her fault. Since then, Larry had thought of her fairly often, considering the number of other things which were on his mind, and had hoped that his grandfather was mistaken, that someday they might be helpful to her after all. It was with this in his thoughts that he went so promptly to see her; and he was both relieved and surprised to find that she did not seem nearly as sad as she had before, and that evidently, far from needing or expecting help from him, she was eager to do everything she could in the way of contributing to the pleasures of his life at college.

"She said maybe I'd like a standing invitation for Sunday night supper," he told his grandfather when he went home over the week end. "Not just for myself, either—for as many people as I'd like to bring to her house. I told her I still didn't care much for crowds and, from the way she smiled, I could see she remembered that awful call at Victoria, just as well as I did. But all she said was that I'd probably be getting over such a feeling, almost any time now, and that meanwhile I could come alone, or with one or two other fellows, just as I liked. I told her I nearly always came to Cindy Lou for Sunday, and she said all right, any other night then. She made me feel she'd really like to have me and I began to feel as if I'd really like to go."

"I'm very glad. And look here, Larry, you know you don't have to come to Cindy Lou every Sunday. You know—"

"I know we've hashed that all over before and that we're not going to again. Aunt Armande and I settled on Wednesdays. I'm going to supper this coming Wednesday and Blaise Bergeron and another fellow I like, named Gus Gallion, are going, too. I didn't say I'd go every Wednesday, but it's understood I can if I want to. Aunt Armande's looked up my godparents, and she says they've told her they're going to get in touch with me; if they don't, pretty soon, of their own accord, she'll invite them to supper, too, some Wednesday when I'm there. She's even offered to fix up some rooms that I could call mine, or to let me do it—a bedroom and maybe another room, too, where my friends and I could play cards or roughhouse or do anything else we wanted. She says she's just rattling around, alone in that great house. It *is* a great house, you know—as big as this one."

"Yes, I know. Your grandmother and I used to visit there, quite often." Clyde might have added that he was rattling around alone in a great house, too, but he did not. He sat still, stroking Nuffy's head, and listening to Larry as the boy rambled on with an unusual degree of expansiveness.

"Aunt Armande said that she remembered when you and my grandmother used to visit there. She said she hoped you'd come and visit there again."

"Well, I don't know, Larry. It's a good deal of an effort for me to go anywhere these days—you know that. And now my partner's off at college, of course I'm pretty busy with that navigation company of ours, let alone the two plantations."

"Aunt Armande realizes you are. I told her about the new navigation company and she was very much interested. But I think she really does hope you'll come to visit her, Dad. I hope so, too."

"All right then, I will, one of these days, after grinding's over."

"She especially told me to give you her love, Dad. And she asked me to tell you something else. She said she brought back a lot of stuff with her from France—stuff she says really belongs at Victoria. I didn't understand what she meant, but she said you would."

"Yes, I think I do. I'll tell you about it sometime, Larry. Well . . . that's very thoughtful of your aunt, very thoughtful and very fair. I've been thinking, even before you told me about all this stuff, as you call it, that we ought to put Victoria at your aunt's disposal. Maybe she'd like to come there for week ends—or longer, if she's going to stay on."

Clyde was not among those who had plied Armande with importunate questions. He had waited for her to take her time about getting in touch with him, and he was really moved by the way she had chosen to do so. Now he would have been glad to know something about the underlying causes for her sojourn in New Orleans and about her future plans.

"I guess she must be intending to stay quite a while," Larry went on. "She said she was going to take a *loge grillée* at the opera house through the season, and I don't suppose she'd be doing that if she didn't mean at least to spend the winter. She said I'd be welcome to bring friends to the *loge,* too, any time, if I'd just let her know beforehand, so that she wouldn't have it filled already. She said maybe you'd like to go to the opera again—she thought it was a long time since you had."

"She's right. It is a long time since I have. But when your mother was a young lady. . . . I'll never forget how she looked the night of her debut. She wore a white tulle dress, looped up with lilies of the valley, and she looked like a fairy princess. I wanted your grandmother to wear white, too—white satin and pearls. But she said one white dress would detract from the other and she was right, as usual. She wore old rose moiré and cameos set with diamonds and she—well, she looked like a *queen*! They sat side by side in the front of the *loge* with your mother's bouquets heaped all around them—we always had a *loge ouverte,* because that was what your mother preferred, but of course we'd have had one for such a special occasion anyway. Your father came to the *loge* between every act and so did his various rivals—Valois Dupré, I mean the younger one, and Nial Stuart and Andres Santana, and I don't know how many others—not that they ever got very far, against your father's persistence, but they all tried to get in a word edgewise." Clyde paused and Larry remained silent, realizing that his grandfather was never happier than when reliving those golden days—realizing, too, that the old man did this more and more frequently all the time. "Well, of course I can see that a *loge grillée* would be more suitable for your aunt than a *loge ouverte*," Clyde said at last, in a tone that suggested he was reluctant to return to the present, but that he realized it must be done. "After all, she's more or less in mourning, and she can keep the grille closed, if she wants to. Naturally, I'd feel very honored to act as her escort. But I must see about some dress clothes if I'm going to start going out on the town again, mustn't I? And by the way, what about *your* clothes? The next thing you know, your aunt will be talking to you about white ties and tails. As if I didn't know. . . ."

Subsequent events proved that he did, indeed, know; and it was a proud moment for him when he and Larry, equally elegant and equally immaculate in their beautifully tailored new evening clothes, stood back for Armande, superbly gowned in royal purple, to sweep into the *loge grillée* before them, on "French Society" night, when the Creole population of the city turned out in full force to crowd the great opera house, which was properly decorated with flags and bunting. The fourth member of Armande's party—a well-connected young girl, pretty enough to pass, but not sufficiently striking to detract from the effect produced by Armande—did not really count. Neither did the opera itself, which was a very fine performance of *Thais*, with Mlle Savarenne singing the title role; and neither did the fact that at the end of the second act Mme Dalcia, who took the part of Albine, stepped before the drawn curtains, robed as La France, and sang the "Marseillaise" with magnificent effect. What counted to Clyde was that he and Larry were going out together now, as two men, and that they were fitted, in every way, to do so, not only when they rode the crops or went to see an oil field; but also when they were the chosen companions of a beautiful woman at a spectacle where all the world would be made aware of her choice.

His satisfaction over the turn things were taking was so great that he was persuaded to prolong his stay in New Orleans for several days, to act as host at one of Armande's soigné little dinners and to make a fourth at bridge whenever she was inclined to have the card table set up. She made him feel that he was flattering her by his presence, which naturally had the effect of increasing the sense of flattery inspired by her hospitality; but it was not until the last evening of his

393

visit, when her other guests had left after prolonged expressions of appreciation for a delightful evening, that she abandoned the role of accomplished hostess for that of a confiding friend.

With the exception of Leonie, who always awaited her mistress in Armande's bedroom, to help her prepare for the night, the servants had gone to bed, after leaving the double drawing rooms in perfect order, mending the fires and setting out drinks and sandwiches. Armande did not object to the smell of smoke herself, and apparently felt no apprehension lest this should cling to the draperies and upholstery, for she encouraged Clyde in the enjoyment of his cigars. He sat smoking contentedly while she excused herself to change from the black velvet dress, which she had worn for dinner, to a *robe d'intérieur,* in which she could be more at ease. When she returned, her appearance was quite as elegant as before, but it was definitely less formal; and she made a charming picture in her negligee of snowy chiffon fastened at the throat, the waist and the wrists with grosgrain ribbon bows. Its full bishop sleeves fell softly over her arms and its pleated skirt spread out like a fan when she seated herself. She had taken down her hair, and her long sleek braids were also fastened with white ribbon. Clyde realized, poignantly, that he had not seen a woman's hair, plaited for the night, since Lucy died, and that it was one of the loveliest and most intimate sights which could be vouchsafed a man. Of course Armande's raven locks could not compare, in beauty, with Lucy's golden tresses—or Cary's, either, for that matter. But then Cary had never wanted to bother with braids. Before the girl's marriage, Lucy had insisted upon them as part of a proper ritual, like prayers; and in Cary's last dreadful illness, she had lain unprotesting while Miss Sophie or Amy Surget brushed and combed the long strands and arranged them neatly. However, Clyde knew that Savoie had encouraged her to leave her golden curls unbound, and that her husband had loved to see her lying with them spread out all around her, on her white pillow, as Clyde did himself. Sometimes when she was riding, too, they escaped from their knot and their net; Clyde wondered if this had ever happened, in the woods at Monteregard, and what Pierre de Chanet had said, or done, if it had. . . .

Clyde went on puffing at his cigar, glancing every now and then with continued appreciation at Armande's filmy dress and sleek hair. He no longer found her silences oppressive, as he had when she came to Victoria with her mother. He found them companionable—not to the same degree, of course, that he so found Larry's, but to a very pleasing extent. This time, however, Armande spoke fairly soon after she had effectively disposed herself and her white draperies in the chair facing his.

"This isn't much like the last time we sat together, by ourselves, on either side of a hearthstone, is it, Uncle Clyde?" she asked with a smile.

He had still been thinking about Cary's beautiful unbound curls, and all the potentialities connected with them, when Armande broke the silence. As so often happened nowadays, it required an effort to bring himself back to the present; and this would have taken him still longer had it not been for the words "Uncle Clyde" at the end of her question. The designation was new and very, very pleasing to him. It helped to rouse him from his reveries.

"No, my dear, it isn't," he agreed. "The weather's unusually mild and pleasant, for this time of year, and there was a wild storm that night, as I remember."

"Is that the only thing you remember about it, Uncle Clyde?"

"No. I remember being very much afraid that you'd catch a bad cold. Did you? I never heard. You were dripping wet—you never should have been out on such a night."

"But I wanted so much to see you that the storm didn't matter. And no—I didn't catch cold. I very seldom have a cold. However, I was desperately unhappy, I wanted to confide in you. Do you remember that, too?"

"Yes, I remember that, too."

"Well, I'm not desperately unhappy now, but I'd like to confide in you again. Do you mind very much? I've tried to wait for just the right time."

"My dear, of course I don't mind. Of course I'd be honored by your confidence. Naturally, I felt rather curious. But I haven't wanted to question you."

"You're about the only person who hasn't. That's one reason why I feel like telling you of my own accord. Not the only reason, of course. Another reason is that I'm very fond of you."

"I'm honored by that, too. And it's a sentiment I fully reciprocate."

"We could go on paying each other compliments for a long while, couldn't we? And the best part of it is that'd they all be sincere. . . . But what I really wanted to tell you is that I've left Pierre at last."

"I'm very glad. You know I asked you why you didn't, two and a half years ago."

"And I told you I couldn't then—at least I didn't see how I could. But *maman's* death made everything much simpler for me. I don't need to pretend, to you, that this loss was a blow to me, and I don't want to pretend, to anyone else—that's why I don't discuss it. I heard someone say, a long while ago, that old age is the great test. The majority of persons are at least reasonably pleasant and reasonably upright when they're young. Then, at middle age, latent faults and failings begin to show, if there are any; and by the time a person's elderly, those faults and failings are either overcome—or intensified. An old man or an old woman who's really fine is about the finest creature there is, just as one that's handsome or beautiful at eighty is about five times as remarkable as one who's handsome or beautiful at eighteen. *Maman* couldn't meet the great test. She grew more and more shallow and snobbish every year, more and more hard and grasping, too. Her association with the French aristocracy didn't help, either. She tried to copy a sophistication and pretend to a tradition that were natural to the people she met, but that she wasn't equal to assuming. And she got the idea that more money would help—which of course it doesn't, in that particular milieu, unless you've got the other qualities to go with it. So she was disappointed and embittered and she took out her disappointment and her bitterness on me. I'm afraid she took them out on poor Papa, too, and he was even more helpless than I've been. . . . Well, we won't speak of her again—I felt justified in doing it this once, so you'd see the whole picture. But now, let her rest in peace. At least she got her final wish—a magnificent Parisian funeral and burial at Père-Lachaise, with a marble monument that's the marvel of all beholders. I'm thankful she didn't want to be brought back to Convent. I should think you'd be thankful, too. I shouldn't think you'd like to get the feeling that whenever live Vincents reappeared on the scene, they were accompanying a corpse."

In spite of himself, the corners of Clyde's mouth twitched. He did not attempt any reply.

"So with *maman* magnificently interred, everything began to seem simpler," Armande went on. "The children are both in boarding school now, and French vacations are very short. Pierre and I reached an amicable agreement about those: after this year, Pierrot and Janine will come to the United States for a little while every summer, or I'll go back to France, just as seems best, until Janine's grown up. Meanwhile, I'll look around for a suitable apartment or small house in Paris and when Janine's old enough to go out in society, she can divide her time between my *pied-à-terre* and Monteregard. There haven't been any dramatics at all between Pierre and myself—in fact, it's only fair to say that he's made no difficulties for me. Of course he never was a fortune hunter—he has more money than I have and I've got plenty. We'll appear together whenever it's necessary, and we'll be very careful to see that nothing is done that could jeopardize a suitable marriage for either or both of the children. Of course Pierre wouldn't have been so reasonable if he'd cared about having me stay with him."

For the first time, her tone was bitter—while she was talking about her mother it had been merely hard. But very soon she went on more lightly.

"I think the person who really did the most to make it all seem easy, though, was Pierre's niece Josephine de Courville. She and her husband Jehan agreed to disagree long ago. She made me see how simply it could all be done. Of course the De Courvilles have only one child—Louise—and that made things less complicated than if there'd been two, especially as they've always left Louise at Monteregard a great deal, and she prefers being there to staying with her grandmother, the Princesse d'Ambly. That's natural, for she hasn't any cousins, except Pierrot and Janine, and no brothers and sisters. She's in boarding school, too, now—at the Sacré Coeur, in the same class with Janine. They're really inseparable."

"Well, that does seem a logical arrangement all around."

"Yes, doesn't it?"

"Logical, but not especially loving."

Armande rose, adjusting her beautiful white draperies. "Uncle Clyde, do you know what you are? You're an old sentimentalist. You like to pretend you're tough and you're just as softhearted as you can be. Of course I have to admit it's no wonder—you did have a happy marriage, I mean *really*. But it's the only one of the kind I've ever seen. You know perfectly well that Cary's—no, I won't say it. However, let me tell you something else: you're one of those few who *has* stood that old-age test I was talking about a while back. You're the most magnificent old gentleman I ever saw. If I weren't afraid of running up against something in canon law I don't know about, I'd set my cap for you. Can you marry uncles if they're just make-believe uncles? I don't know! There . . . you know I was only joking. But I do love you a lot. Larry, too. Good night, Uncle Clyde."

More and more Armande became a recognized member of their small family group, from both Clyde's viewpoint and Larry's. She agreed, without making any stilted speeches to the effect that of course it was not really her home any more, to spend frequent week ends at Victoria; and gradually the mansion there, like the one on Elysian Fields, showed the excellent effects of her inhabitance. She went often to Cindy Lou as well, and continued to make Larry and his friends welcome at her town house. When the spring semester ended at Tulane, she told him he must bring them to Victoria instead, and he was glad to do so; for the first time, he also had frequent guests, quite voluntarily, at Cindy Lou. Throughout July the old plantations teemed with young visitors as they had not done in twenty years. Theoretically, Clyde was delighted; but after his long years of seclusion, he found the constant tumult unexpectedly wearing; he longed for solitude and for Larry's unshared company. The servants also showed signs of strain. As Clyde had told Mrs. Vincent, the efforts of Titine and Bassie, for a long while, had been confined to the comparatively easy task of caretaking; and though Armande brought

Patsy, Amos and Leonie from New Orleans, there were occasional mutterings about extra washing, late hours and unexpected arrivals. At Cindy Lou, no attempt was made to increase the household staff, but neither Clyde nor Larry heard as many complaints as Armande. Tudie good-naturedly accepted pointers from Leonie about waiting on young ladies, and helped Nappy serve in the dining room, the drawing room and the gaming room; Delphie got through a good deal of chamber work and dusting because none of it was done very thoroughly; and Ivy patiently cooked on and on. However, the results were a far cry from the days when every guest had a body servant, and afternoon tea was a ceremonious occasion in the terraced garden. Fortunately, none of the youngsters who now came to the plantations expected much personal attention or gave so much as a passing thought to afternoon tea. On the other hand, boys and girls were constantly dashing back and forth between the two places, more often in Model T Fords than on horseback nowadays; there were swimming parties in the old barrow pit, excursions up and down the river, shrimp and beer suppers on the *batture*, fish fries in the largest grove, tennis on the lawn; and every night, and many afternoons as well, there was dancing in the ballroom to a victrola and on special occasions to the music of a Negro band. The multicolored lights were as brilliant and kaleidoscopic as ever; but they played over dances very different from the polkas and schottisches of former times, and the only waltz in favor was called the "hesitation," and was generally danced to a tune entitled "Mighty Lak a Rose." More favored were the one-step and the fox trot and such intricate, exotic dances as the tango and the maxixe, which only the more experienced and skillful did really well. Armande was a beautiful dancer and a willing exponent of the new steps. Larry and his rapidly increasing "gang" learned more from her than they ever had from each other, and there was not a boy among them who was not pleased and proud to have her for a partner. But she did not lack partners of her own age, either. Any number of personable men in their late forties and early fifties seemed to be perpetually about; and though they played more bridge than the collegians—who were by no means at a loss when it came to cards, either—they also wedged in considerable dancing. Clyde could not imagine where they all came from, how they happened to have so much leisure and why they still seemed so comparatively young. If Armande had lacked attention as a girl, she certainly had plenty of it now—so much, indeed, that Clyde began to wonder whether her many admirers were under the impression that she was a widow. It was his first encounter with an unattached, middle-aged, married belle and he found it vaguely disquieting. Nobody else seemed to be worrying much about chaperones, for the mothers of the girls who visited assumed that Armande was fulfilling this role; but he pressed Mrs. Surget into more and more constant attendance and made a point of being present in the ball-room himself.

"You ought to be dancing, too, Uncle Clyde," Armande told him one night, as she sank down breathlessly beside him after a lively turn. "You know Rodney Ashe, of course?" she added, almost as an after-thought, as she indicated her partner. "Rodney, do get me some punch. I'm simply parched." And when the dapper, urbane gentleman had gone to do her bidding, she added, "Everyone's doing it now."

"It really looks that way," Clyde answered a little dryly. "Still, at eighty—"

"Why, you don't seem eighty! You could pass for sixty any day. And lots of sixty-year-old men are having the best time they've ever had."

"Maybe, though I doubt it. Be that as it may, if they are, remember they're *really* sixty, not passing for it."

"Not always," Armande answered, nonchalantly. "And not that it matters. Truly, Uncle Clyde, I'd love to dance with you."

"It's very hard to resist such a tempting invitation. But I think I'd better."

"You used to dance, didn't you?"

"Yes. I danced the Virginia reel with my bride, at our wedding. And while we were coming down the river, on our honeymoon, we used to join in a square dance called the 'pawpaw patch.'"

"I think that sounds fascinating! Won't you teach it to us? I'll clap for attention and then everyone—"

Hastily, he put up a warning hand and, at the same moment, double deliverance came: Rodney Ashe returned with the punch and the Negro band struck up "I'm on My Way to Dublin Bay." Armande, apparently forgetting that she was simply parched, was on her feet just in time to avoid being swung from her seat by her next partner. Clyde noticed that she was not affecting even half mourning any more. She had on a pale green satin dress with a full white lace over-skirt and transparent lace sleeves that did not reach halfway to her elbows. It was not cut unduly low, but somehow it seemed to be very revealing; and suddenly Clyde realized that this was because Armande did not have on very much underneath it. He looked around the ball-room, with new clarity of vision, and suspected that the same thing must be true of practically all the girls in the room. Apparently, they did not wear corsets—at least not the kind with which he had been acquainted—any more; there was no sign of rigidity about their cloth-ing; and though this, in itself, was perhaps an improvement, their figures, slim and supple as these were, had lost some of their feminin-ity, for with the larger waists had come smaller breasts and thighs. Possibly it was this very lack of beautiful bosoms and curving hips that made these modern maidens less seductive in his eyes than those of his own time; and doubtless it was just as well that they should be, dancing the way they did, so close to their partners that it would have been hard to get a sheet of paper between them. And as for the costumes in which they went bathing! . . . Yet Larry, as far as his grandfather could tell, was either quite unconscious of this daring lack of discretion—not to say modesty—or quite unmoved by it. Clyde wondered. . . .

Armande's birthday was late in July and, when she spoke of celebrating it at Victoria, Clyde asked her if she would not let him have the pleasure of giving a party at Cindy Lou instead. She seemed to hesitate.

"That's sweet of you, Uncle Clyde, and I do appreciate it. But it won't hurt your feelings, will it, if I say you seem the least bit old fashioned when it comes to parties? I want this one to be really gay and—"

"We'll have it as gay as you like, Armande. You haven't hurt my feelings. I'll admit I like the old ways better. This seems to me an era of restlessness rather than an age of elegance, and I enjoyed the elegance and the—well, the refinements that went with it. You—you remember my wife?"

"Of course I remember her. She was the loveliest lady I ever knew."

"Yes. Well, of course there never could be anyone like her again. But somehow I didn't suppose—"

"That the change would be so much for the worse? Perhaps we aren't as different, inside, as you think. Perhaps the change is just in our figures and in our habits." Armande laughed and Clyde smiled, indulgently if not altogether approvingly. "And perhaps there'll be another change, later on, for the better," Armande continued. "Anyhow—"

"Anyhow, I hope you'll let me give you that birthday party. We'll have a band up from New Orleans, gin as well as champagne, plenty of places for sitting out. Whatever you say."

"All right, Uncle Clyde, if you really want to. Because you *are* sweet, you know."

If he could have passed for sixty, in her opinion, she could easily have passed for thirty, in his. And obviously he was not the only man who felt that way about it. He was sure that several, Rodney Ashe among them, were seriously smitten, and that a number of others were dangerously close to it. Clyde had made inquiries about Ashe; it seemed that he was very well thought of, besides being very well off; he was a banker, of Carolinian extraction, who had made quite a place for himself in Louisiana. Clyde felt sure that Ashe must have made inquiries, too, that he must be aware Armande was not a widow. But his conduct was certainly that of a declared suitor and there was nothing in Armande's attitude to give the impression that she was trying to discourage him. He was a constant and obviously a welcome visitor at Victoria. . . .

The birthday celebration was gay enough to fulfill Armande's fondest hopes. It was primarily her party and though Larry, of course, was present, Clyde had suggested that on this occasion his aunt's friends, rather than his, should be their guests; and Larry had said sure, that was all right by him, he could have his gang any other time. Clyde was a little sorry, at the last moment, that he had never done that "fancying up" at Cindy Lou, which he had had in mind when Larry and he decided to have the barge line instead. But after all, as he had reflected before, the worn places on the upholstery and the faded streaks in the draperies did not show up much at night; and he doubted whether the assembled company was much interested in upholstery and draperies anyway. There was dancing all night, to the jazz music of a New Orleans band, and there was a great punch bowl whose well-spiked contents were frequently renewed. Armande wore a turquoise chiffon dress, beaded in gold, with a wide gold belt, a matching band of gold around her black hair and long pendant earrings. She was still as fresh and as gay, when she came to say good-by to Clyde at four in the morning, as she had been when she arrived at eight the evening before; and as she went down the grand staircase he could hear her laughing and jesting with Rodney Ashe. . . .

The next time he saw her she came into his office with a blanched face and asked him if he had read the paper that day.

"No, not yet," he answered. "I'll have to confess I've been feeling a little tired since that party of yours, so I've been taking things easy. I've spent most of the day rereading some of the letters Cary wrote her mother and me while she was on her honeymoon. I want Larry to read them, too. I want him to go to the same places that she did, because I believe that's what Cary would have wanted. Even—even to Monteregard. Since you say there isn't any strain between you and Pierre, perhaps you'll renew the invitation you gave the boy the last time you were here. Sit down, Armande, and have a julep with me. It's a warm day."

"You read about the murder of that archduke in Servia, didn't you? Before, I mean? You knew about that?"

"Yes, but that was just another of those Balkan outbreaks. There was one two years ago. Those people actually seem to enjoy killing each other."

"Uncle Clyde, you don't seem to realize what I'm trying to tell you. France is at war—at war with Germany. I've got to go back— I've got to get home as fast as I can."

Neither of them noticed that this time she had spoken of France as "home." Clyde struggled to his feet—it was harder and harder for him all the time to rise from his chair—and tried to speak comfortingly and reassuringly. But words of fright and horror came tumbling from Armande's lips and she did not even listen to him.

"Pierre's in the reserves, he'll be called out immediately. After all, he is my husband, after all, I do love him. I always have, even though I've tried to pretend that I didn't. I wouldn't have left him if I hadn't known he didn't care whether I stayed with him or not, that he never had, really. Pierrot's only seventeen, he won't have to go to war right away, but they'll be after him presently and meanwhile I don't know where he is, whether he'll be safe. Janine, either. If there were a siege of Paris, like the one in the last war with Germany, if there are battles like Sedan. . . . Uncle Clyde, you will help me to get home right away, won't you?"

Larry and Clyde both went to New York with her, because the ships that went from there were faster than the ones that went from New Orleans. She had no difficulty in getting immediate passage—most people were hurrying west, not east, across the Atlantic in those days. Larry and Clyde saw her comfortably settled in an excellent *cabine de luxe* on a Cunarder, the *Lusitania,* that stopped at Havre, and told her they were sure there was no reason why she should worry: everyone said the war would be over in three months; Pierre and Pierrot and Janine and all the rest of the family would certainly be quite safe in the meantime.

Like most of their fellow Americans, Clyde and Larry proved very poor prophets. Gilles de Lorne was killed in the first Battle of the Marne and his wife Isabelle, in Paris, when a shell struck the Church of St. Gervais, where she had gone to pray for the repose of his soul. Jehan de Courville was sent on a military mission to Washington, and on his return journey to France his ship was torpedoed. His widow Josephine, far from being inconsolable, promptly married a cabinet officer, with whom she had for some time been on admittedly intimate terms. Pierre de Chanet was slightly wounded and his son Pierrot severely wounded at Ypres; though the boy made the better physical recovery of the two, he suffered so acutely from shell shock that he was confined, for months, to a base hospital in Brittany before he could return to the front. Armande visited him as often as she was permitted to do so and, meanwhile, carried the full responsibility for the maintenance of Monteregard, the welfare of the women and children on the estate and in the neighboring village, and the supervision of her daughter Janine and her niece Louise—for the cabinet officer had made it quite clear that he did not care to be encumbered with a stepdaughter. Pierre's mother had remained in her Paris apartment; apparently she was not suffering any hardships or deprivations, but neither was she mitigating those of anyone else. The two girls were helping Armande as best they could. Of course their education had been interrupted and they were having no diversions. The young men whom they would have normally been seeing by this time were all at the front, if they had not already been killed. And something less than three years after Armande's return to France, Larry came into his grandfather's office, late one April afternoon, and told Clyde he had just heard the United States had entered the war and that he was about to start off to enlist.

   CHAPTER XXIII

He had come home the day before for his Easter vacation and, as this was Good Friday, he had gone to church in Convent. After the services were over, he had stopped in at the Valley station to see if the new bearing for a water pump, which had been delayed in transit, had finally arrived, and the telegrapher had given him the news as it was ticked off the wire.

"De kaiser, dat species of h'animal, him, he goin' find out, yes, he made a bad mis-take when he ain' satisfy, no, he already fight de Fr-r-r-ranch an' de h'English, he got to fight us, too, him, yes," the operator had sputtered in conclusion.

"And of course that means I'm going right back down to New Orleans to enlist," Larry added, in repeating this to his grandfather. "Some of the fellows have already gone in, you know, with the Canadians, and even one of the professors has been driving an ambulance."

Clyde nodded in apparent agreement. The proverbial Easter cold snap had come, and he was settled in his armchair before the fire, a cheering glass in his hand and a pile of old letters beside him.

"Of course you're going to enlist, Larry," he said. "You wouldn't be much of a man if you didn't do your duty. But it doesn't make sense to rush off blindly. I . . . I know what I'm talking about. Let's find out first of all where you're needed most."

"Now look, Dad, if you're going to tell me how important it is to raise crops and how I'm more needed at home, it won't go. I'm not a jelly bean, hanging around drugstore corners. I'm a man, and the Army needs men."

"That's right. But look at it this way. War is a disaster, like a levee break or a steamboat wreck. If the levee breaks and everybody who wants to help rushes off to do the same thing, nobody's going to accomplish anything. If a steamboat hits a snag and everybody rushes to the rail or to the lifeboats, the result is panic. Somebody has to direct the efforts to make them effective. You know that. All I want you to do is wait until we hear what our leaders in Washington want."

"But we know they are going to want men."

"But we don't know where. For instance, you spoke of the Army. But maybe men are needed more in the Navy right now. Our first job is going to be to get an army across the seas and to supply them after they get there. We're going to have to feed half the world, too. And all the sugar that is being raised everywhere—here, Cuba, the Philippines—everywhere, isn't going to be enough. It's too late for this year's crop, but by next year we ought to turn a lot of the tobacco fields into cane—it's going to be a lot easier to do without perique than without sugar. That's the sort of thing I mean. All I'm asking you to do is wait, before you join up. Wait to see what Washington wants. A few weeks won't matter. And by that time you'll have your degree."

"What's a degree but an insignificant old piece of parchment?"

"It isn't insignificant. It's a visible and tangible proof of what you've been and done before you could get that piece of parchment. I never got one—because I'd never been or done any of those things. Do you remember my telling you once that I'd hoped I'd rule—well, a sort of empire someday? And that I couldn't, because I didn't have what it takes to do that? But I got it ready for you to rule and you will have what it takes by the time you're a little older, if you keep on the way you're going."

Larry, who had been standing by the hearth, kicking at a log which had fallen forward, turned just as his grandfather attempted to rise. The effort was obviously even greater than it had been at Christmastime. Then he had made only one false start, supporting himself meanwhile on the arms of his chair. Now he made two. But Larry knew he did not want any help, that it hurt his pride to acknowledge his increasing stiffness and lameness. He finally struggled to his feet and put his hand on the boy's shoulder.

"I don't often bargain with you, Larry, but I want to this time," he said. "If Washington hasn't spoken by the time you graduate, and you still feel the way you do now, I'll say go ahead and enlist. I really think, though, that this is a case when you should follow the leader—not in any game, either."

Washington spoke, unmistakably, the following month, with the passage of the Selective Draft. However, Larry did not bring up the question of enlistment again until he was safely in possession of the "insignificant piece of parchment." But on their first evening at Cindy Lou, after the commencement exercises, Larry handed the rolled degree to his grandfather, saluted solemnly and then stood before him, grinning.

"All right, all right," Clyde said, grinning also and laying the degree carefully on the desk beside him. Then he opened a drawer of his desk and took a cigar box from it. "Go tell Nappy to bring us some coffee, will you, Larry?" he asked. "We might as well be comfortable while we talk."

"But there isn't anything to talk about this time. You said—"

"I know what I said, and I always aim to keep my promises. If you want to enlist now, I'm not going to try and stop you, like I did before. I can see how you'd feel a lot better if you did, instead of waiting until you're called, in the fall, after you're twenty-one. But I do want to have one more talk with you. So, as I said, if you'll just go and tell Nappy to bring that coffee—"

Rather abruptly, Larry left the office. It was easy to see that he was closer to being angry with his grandfather than ever before in his life. But Clyde watched his departure imperturbably. When he returned to the office the old man's cigar was burning evenly, and he was leaning back in the swivel chair whose arms, long since denuded of varnish, had been worn smooth through constant use during many years.

"I want to ask you what you think about enlarging the kitchen garden," he said, puffing comfortably. "Food is going to be mighty important, with sugar and flour rationed already, and we could raise a lot of cabbages on a small piece of our cleared black land."

"Food may be important, but I still can't see what cabbages have got to do with winning the war," Larry said, almost sulkily.

"Cabbages are only a starter. I'm saying that, because what isn't eaten can be brined into sauerkraut and provide food all through the winter. Up north they can have root cellars for potatoes and beets and such. We can't. Our winters aren't cold enough. . . . Well, here's the coffee."

For a few moments they sipped the fragrant beverage in silence. Then Larry looked up.

"I suppose that after the cabbages are harvested, the same rows could be planted to sweet potato slips, Dad," he said hesitantly. "And there's certainly no better eating for man or beast than yams. I don't need to tell you that the vines make prime hay for the mules and the milch cows, and we could turn a couple of shoats into the field to glean the roots that aren't big enough to stack away."

"That's sound thinking." Clyde put down his cup and took up the cigar he had momentarily laid aside. "Larry, ever stop to think that I'm eighty-three years old—be eighty-four this coming winter if I make it?"

"Shucks, Dad, that's only on the calendar! You're the youngest man on the place for real. Everybody knows that. Old Dumaine was saying only yesterday you'd walked his legs down to a nub and weren't even drawing a long breath, when he was looking for a hole to fall into."

"Granted that I've still got the use of myself, eighty-three is old bones and we all know it. Ordinarily, when a young man goes off to war the question is whether he'll live to come back. But when you go off. . . . Well, after all, we don't know how long this man's war is going to last, do we? We made a pretty big mistake about that once before when we were seeing your aunt off on the *Lusitania.* So the question this time is whether I'll be here until you come back. I once made up my mind I'd be bound to live till you were old enough to fend for yourself. I've done that, now. But whether I live or don't live until you come back from the war, I can't carry the whole load of the two plantations any more."

"I should say not, Dad. And nobody expects it of you. Not that you aren't still worth more than any three of the rest of us. You certainly are. But there's plenty of help on the place for you now."

"Plenty of help to do the things I say I want done, yes," agreed Clyde. "But not to do the saying—and the thinking. That's what you've been doing. Maybe you don't realize it, but you practically ran the plantations all through your last summer's vacation. A body doesn't have to draw a whole blueprint for you. Just a suggestion here and there, and you don't actually need even that. Like when I talked about the cabbages: you were right there with the sweet potato project that made the whole deal worth its salt. And there's nobody else here could do that."

"Septime would have been a whip, if he'd only stayed."

"Maybe yes, maybe no," Clyde answered with continued imperturbability. He did not fail to catch the note of envy in Larry's tone. Septime Prudhomme, the swarthy, strapping young Cajun who had formerly been the overseer at Cindy Lou, had hastened to become a marine at the first opportunity, and he, Larry Vincent, was still on Cindy Lou Plantation. Dumaine, the paunchy, middle-aged incumbent of the same position at Victoria, did not hesitate to say that he doubted whether this action had been prompted wholly by patriotism; there was a girl Septime had been going with, who was threatening to make trouble for him, and he was tired of her. But after all, Dumaine had been obliged to take over many of Septime's duties, so under the circumstances, allowances were made for his caustic remarks. Clyde answered Larry from still another viewpoint.

"Of course, Septime was a college man," Clyde went on, "studied agronomy or whatever at L. S. U., and he was a good first mate. I don't know how he'd have made out as pilot or captain, and I don't need to tell you we need someone who knows the river as well as the plantations."

This was still another phase of the situation, and one which they had failed to discuss in their previous conversation on the subject of enlistment, but which Larry was bound to recognize as extremely important. An organization known as the Commercial Solvents Corporation had been formed, not long after the outbreak of the war in Europe, which utilized molasses, as well as grain, for the basic fermentation in the manufacture of acetone. Both Louisiana molasses and West Indian molasses were pressed into service and were now being used for the manufacture of munitions by some factories near the upper reaches of the Mississippi River in Illinois. The West Indian molasses was brought by ocean vessels to New Orleans and there pumped into barges—the barges belonging to the new C. & L. Navigation Company among these—to be taken upstream to these munition plants, along with the Louisiana molasses. Far from hurting the river, the war was helping to bring it back to its day of glory as a trade artery; and what was even more important, in the light of the present discussion, was the fact that the barges were making a mighty contribution to the war effort.

"However, Captain Bourgeois can help on all that," Clyde went on, as he saw that Larry was pondering the last remark. "Matter of fact, he can run that part of the show now. And Dumaine's son Georges can learn enough to give me the rest of the assistance I'll need, even if he is only seventeen, provided you'll stick around this summer and train him. They won't call you until you're twenty-one and that'll be in October. We'll be grinding by then or soon thereafter, and Old Man Dumaine, with Tregre to superintend the sugarhouse, can take over. I won't say you won't be missed . . . but you could be spared. So it's up to you. I won't say one more word to stop you if, after what I've just explained, you decide to go ahead and volunteer anyhow."

Larry cleared his throat. "You're right—and it wouldn't be the first time or the last, Dad," he conceded. "Of course I do want to go charging off to New Orleans and tell the recruiting officer, 'Hey, give me a gun and a bayonet, so I can kill us a few Huns.' But we'll let the kaiser and Hindenburg draw a breath of relief by sending them word that Larry Vincent isn't going to join up until October."

It was long before daybreak, on a chill November morning, that Larry reported at the Convent Courthouse for induction, having duly registered two months earlier and subsequently been passed as "sound as a nut and twice as strong" by Dr. Doussan, who acted as medical examiner for the draft board.

About twenty other registrants from St. James Parish reported at the same time to Sheriff Dornier, the chairman of the local draft board, and Larry knew several of them—in fact two, besides Blaise

Bergeron, had been his schoolmates at Jefferson. One of these was Tracy Dixon, a tall, blond and rather vague young man, whose father was an official in the offices of the Colonial Sugar Refinery at Gramercy; the other was Henri Laburre, an automobile repairman in a garage at Lutcher. Tracy had stayed at Jefferson for the college course, and had received his bachelor's degree the previous June, having completed a number of courses in both moral and natural philosophy. Henri, short, stocky and already wearing a heavy mustache to make himself look older, had been obliged to drop out of his class when his father, a sawmill foreman, had been killed in a mill accident. Henri had been working ever since to help keep a large family intact. His mother was doing needlework and an older brother was clerking in a store. Always passionately fond of mechanical things and a wizard at bringing cars back to operational status, Henri hoped to own a big garage of his own, one of these days, and was already fishing around for a sales agency. Larry knew that he was not too happy about being drafted; on the other hand, he knew it never would have occurred to Henri to ask for a deferment or to declare himself a conscientious objector. . . .

Larry was also acquainted with Tony Mangiarino, a sleek-haired, good-looking chap who was very much the ladies' man and who had been captain of the Lutcher High School football team. His father was a very successful truck farmer, who sent his cabbages, cauliflower, spring onions and other vegetables in season to the French Market in New Orleans, and who was now branching out into what was fast becoming a very important agricultural development in the Florida parishes—strawberries. Tony was one of nine brothers and sisters; but in spite of the demands inevitably made by such a clan on its principal provider, the boy appeared for draft induction wearing an expensively tailored suit, and was driven up to the courthouse by his father in a shiny, seven-passenger touring car. With Tony was Fletcher Trumbull, the English teacher at the Lutcher High School—a small, spindle-shanked man in his later twenties, who wore pince-nez glasses hooked to a loop of gold wire by a fine gold chain. He was the only one of the group who appeared to be frightened—not bewildered, but really terrified; as he raised his right hand to take the oath, it trembled, and his voice broke at several points in repeating the words: "I, Fletcher Trumbull, do solemnly swear that I will bear true faith and allegiance to the United States of America; that I will serve them honestly and faithfully against all their enemies whomsoever; and that I will obey the orders of the President of the United States and the orders of the officers appointed over me, according to the Rules and Articles of War." When his arm dropped to his side again, the signet ring which he wore—and which was too loose—slipped from his finger and fell, clattering, to the floor; as he stooped to pick it up, he trembled all over.

The next man to approach Sheriff Dornier did not act as if he were frightened, exactly, but it was obvious that he was bewildered, and it presently transpired that this was because he did not understand or speak English, and that therefore the sheriff would be obliged to repeat the oath of allegiance in French for his benefit. He was short of stature, with brown eyes, red hair and a freckled nose. Larry, who had never seen him before, set him down as a farm boy from one of the brûlées back of Vacherie, where his forebears had probably burned off a section of the woodland to clear it for planting. He had a singularly pleasant face, and Larry took an instant liking to him; somehow he got across the notion that in spite of his ignorance he was willing and intelligent, and that he would be glad to do whatever was expected of him whether or not he understood, at first, what it was all about. After him came another non-English-speaking chap from the back country—a sullen-eyed, unkempt, jeans-clad swamp man. There was also a gap-toothed, whiskery specimen, who might have been a shrimp fisherman during the season, and who seemed to be very dim mentally. He was powerfully built and walked as if his shoes bothered him, which Larry thought they probably did. The last of the individuals before the sheriff was so undistinguished looking that he would have been passed over in almost any crowd, except for the cannon ball shape of his head and his large protruding ears. Larry could not seem to identify him with any special trade or locality. . . .

When the oath had been administered to all the men reporting for induction, Sheriff Dornier led them in a straggling walk, which did not even remotely resemble a march, from the courthouse to the little railroad station. It was almost time for the arrival of the Gulf Coast train, which had left Houston the night before and which used the Valley tracks into New Orleans.

"Just remember, all of you," the sheriff said as they walked along, "you're in the Army now, as much as you'll ever be. We're starting you off on your way to Beauregard by yourselves. But if you strike out on your own in New Orleans, you won't be just strays—you'll be deserters. Now, as soon as we get to the station, I'll call the roll once more and give each of you his own ticket."

When the tickets had been duly distributed, the men drifted apart. Rather forlornly, those whose kinfolk had not been able to accompany them to the station, like the sullen-eyed swamp man and the red-headed farm boy, clotted into a special group of their own. Tony was soon the center of a family circle which ranged from a worshiping small brother and a beautiful dark-eyed sister to his father, who was obviously torn between pride over this fine man-child of his and pain over the impending separation. Henri's mother was trying desperately hard not to cry, but she clutched a damp handkerchief in her needle-pricked fingers, and every now and then she blew her nose and dabbed at her eyes. The lump in Larry's throat grew bigger every time he glanced at her. He slipped his arm through his grandfather's, drawing the old man as far as possible away from the others.

"There's a lot I'd like to say, Dad, but somehow it won't come out," he began, in a low voice.

"Forget it," Clyde answered abruptly. He was standing very erect, with his head held high and his shoulders thrown back. "If we had to put everything we want to tell each other into words, we'd be wasting a lot of good time."

"I know. But somehow I'd like to say it. I mean about my not having any father or mother, and yet having so much more than any of the boys I know that did have fathers and mothers. I mean you've been more to me, you mean more to me, I mean. . . ."

"Look here, Larry," Clyde interrupted, "you're a man, going off to war, and I'm a tough old he-coon that's too mean to die when his time comes. So let's act like it—if we can."

"You a tough old he-coon!" Larry scoffed. "You're an old fraud, that's what you are. But you're something else, too—you're everything my grandmother and my mother thought you were and we both know what that was. Now you've got to promise me you'll take care of yourself, you hear? None of this getting up to ride the crops in the chill of the early morning and staying until all hours in that office. You've got plenty of men to do the leg work now. Isn't that why I stayed home all summer? To see that you would have? You take it easy."

"Say, which one of us is going out to get shot at? You're the one that's running into danger. And don't you go taking any reckless chances. I'll do my best to hang on until you get back, but all I want in this living world is to hand the whole shebang over to you to run and to worry with, while I sit on my scrawny old hind-end and look at the river and our barges on it. So don't you be too long winning this war. And if you need anything, you let me know. By the way, here's some money I forgot to give you before we left the house."

He pressed some bills into Larry's hand and the boy took them mechanically. Then, as he glanced down at the sizable sheaf, he said hurriedly, "Thanks, Dad. Thanks a lot. But you shouldn't have. My new boss pays off regularly and feeds me, doctors me, clothes me, teaches me—does all the things you did for me. I'll just keep this to buy you a nice present in Berlin."

"That'll be fine, if you can spare the time from the beer gardens. Meanwhile. . . ."

A headlight winked at them out of the morning fog, far down the tracks, and a mournful, yet curiously impatient, whistle was borne faintly across the distance. The Mangiarino tribe began to swarm around Tony, almost overwhelming him. Henri's mother flung her arms around his neck, sobbing unrestrainedly now, and he hugged her in return, while some of the other men, who had been accompanied by girls, clasped them in long-drawn-out embraces. Larry swallowed hard, but managed to grin at his grandfather as he held out his hand, gripping the other's bony fingers in his own and striving not to let the sudden realization of their shrunken flesh show in his expression.

"No matter what happens, Dad, I'll always love you better than anyone else in the world," he said chokingly. Then he turned and swung aboard the steps of the day coach. One at a time, the others were hustled aboard. Some of them were encumbered with musical instruments—guitars and banjos, even, in one case, an accordion; some were carrying paper parcels containing clothing which they did not realize they would have to send back as soon as they were outfitted. A few had old satchels and only Tony a handsome new suitcase. The coat of a very young-looking boy had a strange bulge to it and muffled sounds came from within it. When they had all gone up the steps, a flagman waved his lantern and the train chuffed into motion. A gray smudge was beginning to show along the eastern horizon, but the area beyond the lighted platform was still dark and into this darkness Clyde strode steadily. It did not matter now that his shoulders were no longer thrown back and his head was no longer held high. He was thankful to think that Nuffy would be waiting for him at Cindy Lou.

 CHAPTER XXIV

"Morning—especially this early in the morning—is one hell of a time to be getting to a place like New Orleans!" It was Tony Mangiarino speaking. "The way I hear it, they'll grab us off right at the damn station and hustle us right to the damn barracks."

"You shoulda been like we were, Blackie," gibed one of the group that had been put aboard the train at Baton Rouge. "We gave the gals a good time last night. I mean a *good* time. I don' know have I got enough man left in me to pass no army test."

"Aw, hell, you don't get no tests till they send you to Beauregard or Houston or wherever they ship us. By that time we got enough

411

food and stuff so your manhood don't have to worry you none—if you really had the manhood to start with."

"Don't you worry none about my manhood, or we can take it from there any place or any time or just as far as you want."

"Aw, save that for the Krauts, and for Christ's sake, shut up. I want to sleep."

In the rear of the coach a group began to sing:

> *"You're in the Army now,*
> *You're not behind the plow,*
> *You'll never get rich, you son of a bitch,*
> *You're in the Army now."*

Larry wondered what it would be like. The L. S. U. boys would know, of course. They had a cadet corps there. It had been fun to kid the L. S. U. "dogs" about their hayfoot, strawfoot chores and their uniforms, but most of them would be made officers straight off. Like Septime Prudhomme, the erstwhile overseer at Cindy Lou, who had enlisted in the Marines to get away from a girl and was a second lieutenant already. How did anyone who had no military training at all go about becoming an officer? Left to himself, Larry would have applied for the first officer training school at Fort Logan H. Root in Arkansas, as some of the other Tulane boys had done. But he had promised his grandfather to wait until he was drafted, and now it was too late; now he would have to peel potatoes and clean latrines—well, there were worse things. At least he'd be doing a job in the Army.

". . . and so she gives me the eye. Well, she was wearing those plaid stockings and I said. . . ."

Larry had been shoved into the same red plush seat as the man with the protruding ears and the head shaped like a cannon ball, whom he had not previously been able to identify. This fellow draftee now volunteered enlightenment: his name was Jules Robinaux and he was a refinery worker from Baton Rouge, whose family home was on the river road near Paulina, where his people had always raised perique. But the bigger wages offered by the refinery had lured him away and he hated the idea of exchanging these for thirty bucks a month. He had been saving up to get married. . . . The whiskery specimen, who was in the seat behind and who had leaned forward and listened with interest to this information, now volunteered some of his own: he had been dragged back from Manila Village in Barataria Bay, where he had stayed hoping to escape the draft; but the authorities had found out where he was and had sent a deputy to bring him back to St. James. According to his story, he had accompanied this official without protest, his attitude having apparently been that you couldn't blame a guy for trying, and that being a member of Santo Bajo's seine crew was a helluva lot better than being in the Army. Besides, you could get rousing drunk at Myrtle Grove, when you had the money. However, as long as they had sent to get him, okay, let them tell him what to do next. . . .

The group in the rear of the coach was singing again:

> "It's a long way to Tipperary,
> It's a long way to go.
> It's a long way to Tipperary,
> And the sweetest girl I know.
> Good-by Piccadilly, farewell Leicester Square,
> It's a long, long way to Tipperary,
> But my heart's right there."

The train jolted over the interlock at Kenner, went past a vegetable packing shed and so on to its stop at Carrollton. The bright sun was throwing long shadows to the west as the cars rumbled through a slum section of littered tenements and stopped with a jerk in a grimed, red brick station where a sergeant with an outjutting chin and a rakishly tilted hat was waiting at the steps of the coach and snapping, "All you snot-nosed draftees over there by that post." Behind Larry there was a murmur of resentment.

"Who does that mother-lover think he is? Take that uniform off him and I'd goddam well show him whose nose needs wiping and I don't mean maybe, either." But the murmur was discreetly low and the draftees obediently headed toward the designated post, while the other passengers—the ones Larry suddenly realized were merely civilians—filed down the platform with their baggage. When they were gone, the sergeant held up his hand for attention.

"Now get me, guys," he said sharply. "Some of you may have been big shots in your home town. You may have been used to telling other people what to do. But you're in the Army now, and the first thing you learn is to do what *you're* told. There's trucks waiting outside. We're going in them to the barracks."

"Hey, when do we eat?" asked a taunting voice from an unidentifiable source in the crowd.

"I'll answer that this once. You eat as soon as you get to the barracks."

"Eat hell, when do we drink?" called another voice, but less loudly, as though the owner were anxious not to be identified by the eyes of authority. General laughter followed. They had emerged on Rampart Street, and across the way were many saloons and package houses, quite a few of the latter frankly announcing that they would send liquor into dry Mississippi, or other dry territory, for a reasonable fee.

"Say, is this the Rampart Street I been hearing so much about?" inquired the refinery worker. "Those don't look like no whore houses to me."

"Hell, no. This is Rampart Street all right, but it's South Rampart. The district is all on the far side of Canal Street." Tony Mangiarino, the cosmopolite, was explaining. "Anyway, what the hell do you care? Who'd want to go there this time of morning?"

"Any time's a good time if you got your nature," chuckled one of the waiting group.

"All right, all right, button them lips," the sergeant shouted. "Listen to me now. When I tap you, climb into them trucks and don't drag it. You're in the Army now."

"You mean we got to stand up in them things?" inquired the young-looking boy with the bulging coat, as the first of three olive-drab trucks wheeled up the cobbled esplanade in front of the station.

"Yes, you'll stand up in them things," replied the sergeant in a mincing falsetto. "You'll stand on your head if I tell you to, and you'll. . . . Say, what the hell you got under your coat?"

"N-n-nothing, sir. I got nothing—" stammered the luckless youngster.

"Nothing my behind!" The sergeant yanked the lapels back. "Well —I'll—be—a monkey's—uncle!" he exclaimed, grinning, as a nondescript, bright-eyed mongrel puppy was brought to view, cowering trustfully back toward its master's armpit. "What the hell you scared of, anyway?" The sergeant wooled the puppy's ears. "Get in that truck, now, before I boot you into it," he added good-naturedly.

The truck ride was uncomfortable as they rumbled along St. Claude Street toward the river front, and into the shelled driveway of Jackson Barracks. There they passed the armed sentries at the entrance and drew up before a long wooden building in whose shadowy interior breakfast was spread on long tables flanked by benches.

"Go ahead. Climb out of those trucks and eat," came the next order, "but stay put until you're through."

Breakfast was plentiful and surprisingly well cooked. There were platters of ham and of fried eggs, bowls of grits, mugs of coffee, all the butter and bread anyone wanted to eat. "Say, this isn't bad," commented one of the rooks. "I can go for this chow any time, me."

"Better not hit the Java too hard though," advised the man who had said it did not matter to him what time they reached New Orleans. "They tell me it's got saltpeter in it. They put it in to take away some of your nature, else maybe you'd go over the hill after you were in camp awhile."

"Aw, that sounds like a lot of crap to me. Don't you ever think about nothin' except your nature?"

"It ain't too bad to think about and I'm only tellin' you what they say. Me, it'd take more than a little saltpeter to take my mind off what I got my. . . .

"All right, everybody out and line up, now," barked a voice from the doorway. "Come on, you rooks."

This order was preparatory to a march which took the men to a distant area where they were told to walk around picking up all cigarette butts, all matches, fragments of fallen leaves or anything else in the way of trash. After having been kept thus occupied until dinnertime, they were herded to the mess hall once more for a meal of roast lamb, green peas, mashed potatoes and coffee, brought to them by mess attendants as they sat at the tables, commenting on the general situation.

"I thought you had to hustle your own chow . . . this isn't bad at all, I'm beginning to like this man's army if they got people to wait on you. . . ." "Well, I d'know, a man couldn't work on that much food, you got to have more in you than that to do a day's chopping in the woods. . . ." "D'you reckon we could be let go to town tonight? I been hearing about those cabbyrays, all my life I been hearing about the. . . ." "No dice, boy. Tonight they ship us off to Beauregard. . . ." "Aw, how the hell would you know? . . ." "Okay, boy, okay, you wait and see."

Surprisingly enough, the prophet proved right. After an early supper the recruits were once more put aboard a train—a troop train, this time; and while they waited in the station, elderly, buxom ladies, in Red Cross garb, passed apples, cigarettes and chocolate bars in through the car windows. Larry found himself beside the youngster who still had his nondescript puppy with him, and who did not want to reach out the windows, so he passed his share of gifts to the boy. He wondered, as he did so, whether any women who were young and slender and pretty ever came to troop trains in Red Cross uniforms. He could visualize the possibility that some might look rather fetching in such a garb. . . .

An impromptu quartette, with a couple of banjos and a guitar as accompaniment, had been organized and was bearing down heavily on the harmony of "There Are Smiles That Make Us Happy" and "There's a Long, Long Trail A-winding." This quartette was soon augmented into something like a glee club, with almost everyone joining in the chorus. Larry did not take part; he was thinking about his grandfather, as the train moved on through the night, and when it lurched thunderously over the Blind River Bridge, he realized that they were passing behind Cindy Lou, and that Nuffy would be howling.

The train stopped at Baton Rouge in a sparsely settled section of the city, then headed toward the ferry on which it was carried across the

Mississippi, to the accompaniment of switchmen's dancing lanterns and the hoarse blaring of steamboat whistles. The songs in the car had stopped. At the forward end, a dice game was in progress; at the rear, a huddled group of men told an endless succession of droll tales, which they punctuated by loud guffaws. Larry joined in neither the game nor the stories; and somewhere beyond Morganza he dozed off, not to wake again until almost daybreak, when he was roused by the jolting of the cars as they were switched back and forth in the Alexandria yards for the transfer to the seven-mile spur ending at Camp Beauregard. The sun was just rising when the train stopped for good and bellowed commands to "Tumble out there! Get the lead out, you're in the Army now!" summoned the men from the coaches. Outside, they were lined up in four rows, one behind the other, where they stood shuffling their feet and feeling self-conscious, even among themselves. A truckload of men, wearing blue denim fatigue suits and equipped with shovels, rumbled by and began to jeer, "Lookit the *ears* on 'em! Lookit the *ears* on 'em!" Meanwhile a sergeant—a tall, wide-shouldered, flat-stomached man with a seamed face—was snarling at the newcomers. His hatbrim looked as stiff as if it had been cut from metal, the sleeves and yoke of his serge shirt were sharply creased and his canvas leggings scrubbed to near whiteness. His voice was a harsh, hoarse rasp.

". . . and while I've seen some lousy rooks in my time, you buck-wheats are the sorriest bunch of misfits anybody was ever expected to make soldiers outa. . . . SHADDAP THAT TALKIN' in the ranks; those guys hollering at you are on a garbage detail because they didn't shaddap when they were told. What the hell do you want to pay attention to bastards like that for?—old hands that have been soldierin', man and boy, for two whole weeks. Now you rooks pay attention to me, or I'll have somebody on the end of a shovel cleaning out a latrine. No use tryin' to learn you anything yet, so just face the same way I'm facing, that'll mean left from the way you are now, if you know your left hand from your right, that is, and follow me."

In a shuffling, awkward column of fours, the men straggled off toward a raw, wooden building, where batteries of clerks sat behind long plank tables. At these, the recruits were enrolled, given papers to carry and passed along to a door at the far end of the building, where they were divided into smaller groups, which were herded off toward different company streets in what Larry soon learned to call "the casuals." Eight were assigned to each of the pyramidal tents that lined these streets and were told to deposit their belongings on the steel cots there; then, within a matter of minutes, they were summoned out again, lined up and marched off to one of the supply buildings, where mess kits and canteens were issued to them and instructions given in the use of these. Next, holding a pannikin in one hand and a cup in the other, with knife, fork and spoon clasped against its handle, they filed down the long mess line for breakfast, which was eaten at top speed. As soon as it was over, the men were shown first the huge receptacle into which any food remnants on their pannikins should be scraped, and then the three GI cans of hot water in which they were to wash and rinse their mess kits and herded back to their respective tents, only to be summoned forth almost immediately again and marched to a bare, tunnellike building. Here they stripped for a searching physical examination, much more brisk and businesslike than the one which old Dr. Doussan had previously given Larry. "Breathe in —all right, let 'er out—pull up your left foot behind you, now the right one. All right—over there!" came the barked commands. Visual and auditory tests followed and after that the quick look at the teeth, the prodding fingers at the groin and the order, "Now cough—all right, bend forward."

Some sort of segregation was obviously in process as the line flowed steadily by—one group for dental treatment, one group with blue tickets, for venereal segregation, one group back toward the starting point. Occasionally a medical officer would growl, "You'd think they wouldn't send us a man with a heart valve like that of an old flivver," or, "If the kaiser could see this line-up, he'd laugh himself to death and the war'd be over." Between the file of recruits and the exit gate toward which they worked their steady way, a group of medical corpsmen stood waiting, apparently in gleeful anticipation, to pounce upon their hapless victims. One of them seized Larry's left arm and scratched two parallel vertical lines on it with a needle before rubbing a glass rod dipped in smallpox vaccine over these; another corpsman seized his right arm, pinched up the skin just below the shoulder, sent a hypodermic needle deftly into the tissue and pressed home the plunger of his syringe.

"Get out there and put your clothes on, Slim," a bored-looking corporal directed. "And make it good, because you won't be putting civvies on any more for a long while."

As Larry complied, he heard the thud of a falling body and turned to see a strapping, muscular figure crumpled on the floor and the corporal shaking his head. "Looks like it's always the huskies that faint at the sight of a needle," one of the corpsmen muttered. "Some soldier, believe you me!"

"Isn't anyone going to pick him up?" Larry asked the bored-looking corporal.

"Hell, no! He's all right. And don't hold up the line. Get going, you! You're in the Army now!"

Larry went back to the bench where he had left his clothes and tried to hurry, not very successfully, as he put them on, for his sense of strangeness was developing into a state of general bewilderment. When

417

his detail was reassembled, Larry noted that there were several absentees—the youngster who had played the accordion and the sullen-eyed, loose-lipped man from the marsh country, who spoke no English, were not among the others as they were marched to the Quartermaster's Building, where they filed along the counter and were issued various articles of clothing: cotton socks, long drawers, long-sleeved undershirts, breeches, khaki shirts, a blouse, a hat, a blue corded hatband, a webbing belt, denims, a blue barracks bag and three pairs of shoes, one of them hobnailed. As soon as they were back in their tents the men were told to change, and there Larry saw the accordion player and the sullen-eyed swamp man for the last time. They had been given tickets back to their homes. "Lungs," explained the swarthy little musician to no one in particular. "Ain't that a hell of a note? And I never had no idea. Me—a lunger!" It was not through calloused lack of feeling, but because they could think of nothing to say, that none of his tentmates replied. The swamp man said nothing and no one asked for an explanation.

The men were all in uniform, after a fashion, when the hard-bitten sergeant's whistle called them once more into the dusty company "street" before their own particular row of pyramidal tents. "All right, men," he barked. "Here's where you're going to be for two weeks, in the casual section, until after you've had your third typhoid shot. Now listen to me: there's an outfit over in the next street that thinks they're something, and they've sent word they got some good boxers. Any of you men know anything about fighting, you come and give me your names after mess.

"Another thing: we ought to have some kind of a company fund, so we can get a few extras for chow, maybe a baseball mitt or a football, stuff that you don't get in this man's army. You'll be doing it when you get into your permanent outfits after you leave here, and you might as well start now if you want to. Say every man puts up about ten cents a day—and you can pick anybody you want to for treasurer. The supply sergeant would be a good guy, because usually he'd know where to get hold of some grapefruit maybe, and things like that— you'd be surprised at how much you can buy when a lot of men put up a thin, slick dime apiece. But anyway. . . ."

The sergeant's harangue was interrupted by a tinny crash, as a man, one Larry had not noticed before, fell unconscious to the ground, his mess kit clattering into the dust.

"All right, all right," rasped the sergeant. "Two-three of you guys that are in the same tent with him carry him back and lay him on his bunk. That's only the typhoid shot; it gets some and it don't get others. He'll be as good as new in an hour or two—and the rest of you wipe them goddam smiles off your pans. You liable to be the next ones to get it, or if you don't get it this time, maybe you will after your second

418

shot, or your third. . . . Now about your bunks, the way they're supposed to be made up . . . and each tent picks one man to get up and light the fire in that Sibley stove in the mornings . . . you can take turns. . . . Fatigue details will be posted. . . ."

At various times in the lecture, other tinny crashes interrupted the talk. But finally the sergeant said, "Now, for Christ's sake, see if you can stand up straight, and see if you can face left, for once, and we'll march off to chow like we were gonna be soldiers someday. . . . Tai-ai-ain-SHUN! Lay-yufft FACE!"

Neither of the first two shots bothered Larry, though he felt a sudden queasiness after the third one and took to his bunk for an hour or so. He was wretchedly homesick, but physically he had never been better in his life; and he adapted himself readily to camp routine, feeling neither resentful nor distressed that all hands were required to "police the company street" or that he was frequently assigned to the latrine-cleaning detail. He was, however, appalled by the hit-or-miss fit of his uniform and made several visits to a camp tailor before he was reasonably content with the appearance of his blouse; and he occasionally experienced a pang of envy when other men received sheaves of mail and boxes of goodies or other presents. Clyde and Father Le Grand were the only two persons who wrote him regularly, and Mrs. Surget the only one who sent him presents. For the first time, he was dimly conscious of his lack in not having a sweetheart; and this sensation was not assuaged when he heard his tentmates joking about home-knitted articles: socks that did not fit, sweaters with no sleeves and—God help us!—pulse warmers. He knew that such gifts, like the fudge that was hard and grainy and the cookies which were broken to pieces by the time they arrived, had been made by someone who cared in a way that no one cared for him; the fact that this was his own fault—for he had continued to maintain an unusually objective and diffident attitude toward the opposite sex, despite numerous golden opportunities to do otherwise—did not help, either. He wished, now that there was nothing he could do about it, that he had not neglected all those golden opportunities.

This vague and intermittent discontent, however, in no way interfered either with the efficiency or the eagerness with which he did everything required of him—and often a good deal more; and his general attitude won grudging praise from the sergeant in charge of his group, when Larry suggested that he might be useful in one of the mule lines of the artillery, because of his long experience with these animals on Cindy Lou and Victoria.

"Now get me, Slim," the sergeant advised him earnestly. "If you really got a yen to be a mule nurse, tell the guys in your new outfit you was a church choir tenor, or a he-milliner or a baker. Then they'll assign you to the farriers. Tell 'em you been working mules all your

419

livelong life and they'll make a typist or a dental assistant outa you."

"But why?"

"I dunno. That's just the Army for you. Take me. I was in since long before the Mexican border business—I made expert rifleman, I been shootin' a gun since I was knee high to a wart hog, so I'm stuck here to teach rooks how to clean a latrine. . . . Say, do you realize that four batches of buckwheats I helped to break in are in France already, or at least England, and I'm still at Beauregard?" His voice rose an octave. " 'Grampaw, tell us about what you did in the great war.' That's what I'll be asked one of these days. And what'll I say? Why, I'll tell 'em how I fit the battle of the Bentley Hotel—I wish I had all the brass hats in Washington here with no holds barred, I'd have every one of them shoved down into it as far as the Adam's apple. . . . In this man's army there ain't but one God-damned safe rule. Keep your mouth shut and your bowels open, and don't never volunteer for nothing."

The day after this conversation Larry was transferred to Company M of the 156th Infantry. Then came four months of rugged training. Gradually, he acquired more equipment: his overseas pack and entrenching tools and the webbing with which to put them about him; his rifle and bayonet; long woolen spiral puttees to supplant the canvas leggings; and finally, an overseas cap in place of the campaign hat, which was saved for special occasions. Each day started with "monkey drill"—calisthenics, in which the rifle was later used, too. Then came close order drill, first by squads, next by platoons, finally by companies. He had become a corporal by the time they reached the stage of battalion practice marches. Meanwhile, there had been rifle training and endless drills in constructing all sorts of complicated entrenchment systems, with braided willow-withe fascines to hold the parapet and the parados in place, and *boyaux* for machine gun emplacements. Larry's instructors in these maneuvers were a French lieutenant, who demonstrated the use of the machine gun which had been developed from the French cavalry carbine, and a British sergeant major, who was bayonet instructor and who also trained the recruits in the use of gas masks. Larry enjoyed most of the maneuvers; however, for some reason, bayonet drill irked him. He could not have told clearly why the endless repetition of parry, lunge, thrust and jab became a form of inquisition. But it did; and it was not in the least relieved by the British sergeant major's exhortation, before sending them against the six-foot cylinder of tightly bound sticks suspended from a cross-frame that represented "the bloody 'Un," to "call 'im a son av a 'ore, call 'im a bleedin' barstid, call 'im wotever the flyming 'ell will make you believe that bundle o' faggots ryped your sister an' stick that gun-knife in 'is guts like you wanted to scoop 'em out o' 'is bleedin' belly."

He would certainly be thankful when he knew he would never have to hear all that again, Larry reflected—by no means for the first time—one afternoon when Company M was marching back from bayonet drill, with the loose, easy stride of toughened muscles and heightened co-ordination. Larry had never felt so well in his life; such a thumping big—he searched for the right word—such a hunk of man. He ate like a horse, slept like a log, rejoiced in the life that surged through all the tissues of his hard young body. If this was a fair sample, and war was hell, Larry decided he would have to lead a much more sinful life to assure himself of a pleasant future!

The column swung around a sharp detour to the left, still in route step, so as to skirt the outer edges of the grenade area, where trainees were learning that a Mills bomb could not be thrown the way a base-ball was tossed from player to player. There could be no wrist snap, or the thrower would soon have no further use of a lame arm. A long, circular sweep of the fully extended arm, like that Scottie in the kilts had shown them—that was the trick. Once you got onto it, it came easy. But a few of the men never did quite master the knack; they could not unlearn the ball-tossing technique with which they had grown up in special scorn against the stiff-arm motion "like a girl throws a ball."

The boys were using live bombs this afternoon, Larry noted. They were bursting beyond an earthen parapet which shielded the surroundings from flying fragments. Then suddenly there was a frenzied, high-pitched scream, and an explosion from within the trench where the practice squads were stationed. Instinctively, the men of M Company started to break ranks and run to the spot.

"Company, halt!" shouted the lieutenant. "Hold your ranks, there. I'll shoot the man that moves. Sergeant, take a detail of four men and find out what's happened, and whether we can be of assistance."

The sergeant called for "Slim, Whitey, Ted and Sam—on the double." As Larry sprinted across the ground, ground that thousands upon thousands of heavily shod, marching feet had denuded of its grass, he saw a motorcycle roaring away from the spot where the bomb had burst. By the time they reached the scene, a siren's wail heralded the approach of an ambulance. But there were few fragments that could be picked up, and none of these were recognizable as parts of an individual.

"It was Captain Foss," explained a frightened-looking corporal. "He was trying to explain the throw to one of the boys, and told him to go ahead and pitch his pineapple. The guy reached back stiff armed, and knocked his hand against the back of the trench and dropped the bomb. The pin pulled out when it fell. Cap came charging along the trench and knocked the guy a dozen feet away, and then fell on the bomb and rolled himself into a ball over it, like he was trying to hug it right into his belly, and that—that was it. They won't find much of him, but nobody in his outfit got more'n a scratch. That man had guts, believe you me. What a guy. . . ."

The corporal's eyes suddenly widened, tears welled out from them; his face became a weeping grimace as he turned away.

"Come on, you guys," said the sergeant. "Let's get back. There's nothing we can do around here." He clapped the weeping corporal heavily upon the shoulder as he turned away. "Happens to the best of 'em, buddy," he murmured. "Looks like the better they are, the more apt they're to be tagged."

Larry rejoined his company with dragging footsteps. The catastrophe, which had reduced the finest officer at camp to bloody, quivering fragments, had made the boy recognize, with hideous suddenness, that war *was* hell, after all, that soldiering was fraught with peril and that he himself was now a soldier. His present training, sometimes monotonous, sometimes stimulating, was merely a preparation for facing danger, mutilation, agony and sudden death. The realization was terrifically sobering.

Because he was young and healthy, because he worked hard and slept soundly, Larry was able, eventually, to overcome the depression which engulfed him after the tragic death of Captain Foss and to carry on as usual. But he could not help asking himself why, if such catastrophes were inevitable, they must "happen to the best of them" as the sergeant had said. Everyone at the camp had admired and respected Captain Foss; many of the rookies had referred to him affectionately as "a regular prince," and even Nyagolski, the Socialist, who came from the sawmill country near Urania, who used to spit when he talked about the ruling classes, never bitched about Foss. Larry felt a deep compassion for the clumsy trainee who had dropped the bomb. The poor kid must be ready to cut himself a piece of throat—his own. Larry thought that even Father Callahan, who never seemed to feel any load was too hard to handle, might find it a pretty hard job to bring that boy back to normal everyday thinking.

Next to Captain Foss, Father Callahan was the man whom Larry had admired most at camp from the beginning. A wonder, that priest, Larry mused. A real soldier of the Cross. Had his football letter from Notre Dame, built like a wrestler, realized the boys couldn't seem to talk right without cussing some, now and then, could organize a boxing tournament like nobody else could, and yet—Larry had heard it from some of the convalescents—tender as a woman with the boys in the post hospital during that frightful Spanish flu siege. And Larry knew something else, too. He had the story from Private Nathan Friedberg himself. Friedberg, an engraver, was a Halstead Street product who had bummed his way down to New Orleans, where he had found work at his trade. He was an artist at cutting likenesses of the St. Louis Cathedral into the bowl of a silver teaspoon, for example, but he was given to boasting about his prowess. Consequently, when an accurate representation of a latrine was found graven in the bowl of some tablespoons at the general's own mess, it didn't take the MP's long to find the culprit; nor was it long after that before he was tossed into the guardhouse to ponder upon the vice of defacing government property. But it was Father Callahan who realized that the sentence carried over into the high holy days of the Jewish calendar; and it was his threat to consign some very brassy hats to purgatory, despite the fact that the words were accompanied by a warming Irish grin, that secured for Friedberg a furlough from the clink and thus enabled him to attend Yom Kippur services in the temple at Alexandria.

Larry couldn't think of any other officer, or any other Catholic, for that matter, who would have known about such things, and who would then have acted on the knowledge. Except maybe Frank Waddill, a master sergeant whose name had already gone up for promotion to lieutenant. Frank and Larry had met at Tulane during the course of a warm winter evening when they walked along Walnut Street to the river and sat in a tavern garden, drinking a few goblets of beer, while the mellow peal of ships' bells and the hoot of steam whistles proclaimed the shuttling of ferryboats between New Orleans and Westwego. Frank was specializing in sonar research and was always looking for a listener to whom he could talk about this subject. "An echo bounces back the way a tennis ball does when you toss it against a wall; it bounces back from anything solid. You make a sharp, clicking sound, and if you've got the timing equipment and the detectors that are delicate enough to catch the rebound, you can tell from the elapsed interval how far away the thing is that the sound bounced back from. Like in ships, for instance. Heaving the lead to take soundings at sea used to be a slow job, and not much more accurate than if you'd sent your mother's seamstress down a rope to do it with her tape measure. But you can take an echo sounding in less than a second."

"Yeah?" Larry had inquired, without much enthusiasm.

"Yeah," Frank replied, warming to his theme. "Now it's my idea that if you'd hitch your detector to a pencil of some kind, you could make a continuous record of what the bottom of a river looked like, and think what that would mean in controlling Old Man Mississip' in flood time, all the way from Vicksburg to Port Eads. The way I figure. . . ."

Gradually, Frank had roused Larry's interest and they had become fast friends; it had been more or less of a habit for them to go to the tavern garden to drink beer and talk about sonar research. Then, for a time they had lost touch with each other, without losing any of their mutually friendly feeling. Larry was delighted when he ran into Frank again at Beauregard, though he felt that of course his friend should have been sent to the Navy. Seeing Frank on the dusty parade ground, Larry could imagine just what sort of comments his first hard-bitten

423

sergeant would have made back there in the casuals: "Like I say, that's the Army for you. He shoulda told them he was a guy who never done a thing in this world outside of make gates ajar funeral pieces with flowers. Then they'd a sent him to sea, and everything. . . . SHADDAP THAT TALKING back there!" Larry hoped that even after Frank was made an officer, with cordovan puttees and a gold-braid hat cord, they would find ways of having long talkfests some evenings; and Frank eagerly accepted Larry's invitation to visit Cindy Lou after the war and see what might be done about modernizing the sugarhouse operation at Victoria. . . .

In his tentmates, also, Larry found satisfying companionship. Among these was the farm boy from the brûlée, who was proving quite as adaptable, willing and intelligent as Larry had expected and whose progress was all the more amazing in view of his original handicaps. The youngster who had smuggled his puppy onto the train from Convent to New Orleans was another tentmate; and the puppy, which had now reached the gangling stage of its growth, far from being kept under cover, had achieved the proud position of company mascot. His presence was a constant reminder of Nuffy, and made Larry doubly homesick for his own dog; but he shared the general pride of the tent in having contributed "an extra" to camp life. His former fellow student Tracy Dixon was a tentmate, too; but Tracy continued to be vague and self-absorbed. His greatest ambition was to continue his studies along the same lofty lines he had pursued at Jefferson, and he seemed to regard the war as an ill-timed interruption of the cultural pursuits which would eventually lead to the possession of a master's and then a doctor's degree. This attitude kept him aloof from the rather earthy atmosphere created by most of the others.

Toward the end of Larry's training period—he was company supply sergeant by that time—he and other noncoms could leave camp late in the afternoon, almost any day they pleased, as long as they were back in their barracks and had reported in before taps. The first time that Larry availed himself of this privilege, he was accosted by a woman who hailed him as "Soldier Boy" and announced that she would like to adopt him. She was a female of indeterminate years, with a middle-age spread, and there could be no doubt of either her complete respectability or her excellent intentions. She quickly became voluble on the subject of her home-cooked chicken dinners, the nice, wholesome girls to whom she would be glad to introduce him and her close connection with the Y. M. C. A. Larry escaped from her grasp as soon as he could, murmuring something about being late for an appointment; and after a second experience of much the same sort, he guiltily gave his would-be benefactress a fictitious name and address and announced to his companions that he was through with Alexandria. It required a good deal of ribbing, on the part of his special cronies, to get him back there a third time. After all, he wasn't such a bad-looking number, they told him—he'd got to expect some pickups; and as long as he didn't go for the other kind, why not see if the nice, wholesome girls wouldn't fill the bill? Larry shrugged off these importunities with a good-natured retort that, even if it did seem to be taking him quite a while to find a girl he wanted, he still preferred to do his own choosing; and eventually his friends prevailed upon him to accompany them again, after he had extracted from them a mock solemn promise that he should never be left unguarded in the future.

Sometimes they left early enough to eat supper at "the Greek's," a small restaurant just across from City Hall, two blocks after crossing the Red River Bridge into Alexandria proper. At other times, they merely wandered about the streets in groups, or attended a dance at the Elks' Club. Most of the sergeants in Larry's company were older than he, and married; their wives roomed in "Aleck," and these married noncoms would leave their fellows as soon as they reached the city. The others did not visit any of the tawdry brothels in a group, nor did any of them say to the others, "Well, I'm going down the line tonight." If someone failed to go to Alexandria with them, but met them at the corner of Second and Murray streets in time to join in taking a jitney back to the camp, it was tacitly assumed he had been with a woman. But hardly anyone ever boasted of such excursions, not even by such indirections as a smirking, "Well, it comes high, but it's worth it." There was, however, one curious story which was bandied about more or less freely: a certain schoolteacher, who seemed at first glance to be the personification of primness, had proved amazingly responsive to the advances of one of the earliest trainees, though he had not expected to be taken seriously in making them. When he left Beauregard for Dix, his inamorata had amazed him still further by presenting him with a Testament for a farewell present. The first astonished philanderer had been followed by an equally astonished successor, who had received the same spontaneous welcome and the same farewell present. After that, word had got around, and there had been less and less astonishment. The Testaments were always respectfully preserved. . . .

By the time regulations permitted the outings in Aleck, the men no longer looked much like the nondescripts who had scrambled aboard the trucks at the New Orleans station. How long ago was that, Larry asked himself. Four months? Five? Yes, sir, going on five. There was a rumor in every company street that the 156th was about to move out for Camp Dix, and was going from there overseas. And certainly most of the men he knew were receiving furloughs to visit their families. He had been told that his own would begin the next week and could think of nothing but how grand it would seem to be at Cindy Lou with his grandfather again.

The next night he and his first sergeant Pete Spofford and regimental sergeant major Jack O'Bierne of the 114th Engineers went to the

Bentley Hotel in Alexandria for dinner. The dining room was famous both for its service and its cuisine, and Jack O'Bierne was a great buddy of the Irish head waiter's, whom he had known in New Orleans. Whenever a special celebration was about to be staged, any table Jack wanted was reserved for him, and apparently this was all on the house, for no one was ever told how the banquets were paid for.

So the three sergeants went to the ornate main dining room and feasted on roast turkey and oysters and raspberry parfaits and coffee, and afterward, well fed, well content, they strolled about City Hall Square until it was time to find a jitney for the drive back to Beauregard. "This'll be about the last spread for us," Larry observed, as they jolted along. "The last one on the house or somebody else in Aleck, at least. My leave is next week and after that—"

"I got bad news for you, Slim," interrupted Spofford. "I didn't want to spoil your good time by telling you before, but now we're headed back to camp you might as well hear the worst."

Fear clutched at Larry's heart. His grandfather . . . but no, they would have told him that before; and yet. . . .

"You don't get any furlough, Slim," Spofford went on.

"No furlough?"

"Uh-uh. You ain't going to Dix with the outfit. How you did it, I don't know; in fact, I'll never know how a lunkhead like you could put it over on the brass hats. I got orders for you to go to Camp Merritt in New Jersey, as a cadet for officer training. But it's only a staging area, so you won't be there long, Slim. They'll shoot you across to la Belle France to finish your course—and if you're ever going to find a girl that'll suit you, you ought to do it there."

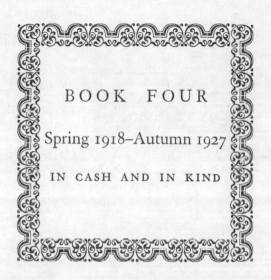

BOOK FOUR

Spring 1918–Autumn 1927

IN CASH AND IN KIND

CHAPTER XXV

On board ship
Friday, April 26, 1918

Dear Dad:

I am writing this as we are in the subzone somewhere off the coast of Spain. We expect to make port tonight or tomorrow morning. So far, there has been nothing sighted except a few battleships and a couple of empty lifeboats. I don't think we are allowed to say what ship we are on, but it is a large passenger boat and quite comfortable. We were fortunate enough to go second class, so had cabins. The ocean is wonderful and I have enjoyed every minute of the sailing, in fact I would like another week of it. I haven't been sick at all, although many of the men have. The weather has been warm and there have been very few rough seas. I would have liked to see a good storm for I love the motion of the boat. We sailed on the 16th around the middle of the night. There are about [here a small rectangular hole is cut in the letter, presumably by the censor] troops on board besides a couple of hundred doctors and Red Cross nurses. I have met quite a number of them and have seen quite a good deal of one nurse, an English girl who trained at the Massachusetts General Hospital and whose father is an English consul—or something. She is bound for Italy, so I probably won't see her again, although one never knows. We have had nothing to do except a few lifeboat drills and some calisthenics and have had the rest of the time to ourselves. All the crew of the ship are French, so we are getting quite a lot of practice in conversation. I find that my French is good enough so that I can get along fine. The O.T.C. from Oglethorpe—who are all southerners—are a good crowd, so if we are kept together I think we will have lots of fun. Anyway, I know I will always be glad I had the chance to come. We have got very little news on board, so have no idea what has been doing on the different battle fronts, but will probably hear as soon as we land. I never heard from you at Camp Merritt and wondered why. We have not been allowed abovedecks during daylight since yesterday morning and get pretty restless sitting around waiting for night to come and have some air and exercise. Everybody is rather keyed up just now and will be until we get out of this zone. They have dozens of men constantly watching and gun crews at the guns day and night. I left a postal in New York which the Gov. will mail just as soon as they get word that we have landed, so you will have that two or three weeks before this.

Since I started this letter we have got close enough to land so that the water is green instead of blue, and we are getting some of the fog which they say is natural when near shore. Just a few minutes ago the whistle blew and as three blasts are a signal to get ready to abandon the ship, it startled a lot of the passengers and they sure moved some for a minute, although none of the soldiers that I saw jumped. I have spent quite a lot, so the money you've sent me will come in mighty handy, as I don't expect we will get paid for two or three months. I will write again very soon and tell you all I can and, in the meantime, please don't worry for everything is going to be fine.

Your loving grandson,

LARRY

Cadet Lawrence Cary Vincent
Officers' Artillery Training School
American Expeditionary Forces (write in full)
France

April 28, 1918

Dear Dad:

We arrived at the debarkation camp [rectangular blackout, presumably cut by the censor] 11:30. We got into dock at 7:00 P.M. after a trip of about four hours on the boat up a river, the name of which I cannot give you. We came through some of the most beautiful country I ever saw and they tell us here that where we are going is just as fine. That river trip was really most awfully impressive and I shall never forget it. Everybody all along came to the bank and cheered us continually. We passed a U.S. construction job on the way up and the boys there sure gave us a hand and blew every whistle in the place. This country here is beautifully clean and green and with every bit of it like a well-kept park. We were told just after landing that we were chased the last night for three hours by two subs and finally dodged them in the fog. After landing, we marched for about five miles to camp and, having had very little exercise for two weeks and a full pack and overcoat, it was a rather hard trip. The people here are intensely patriotic and everybody is willing to talk to you. It is awfully funny to see some of the efforts at conversation. I can't take time to describe all the little incidents now, but when I get home I think I can amuse you for hours. We don't know how long we will stay here before going on to the school, but probably not for very long. We talked with some fellows just back from the front, also a French sgt., and from what they say, I think the Germans will soon have a most hearty respect for the Yanks, as everybody now calls us. (It sure sounded funny to me at first and the other southern boys I've talked to felt the same way, but we're getting used to it.) The Huns seem to be bearcats for fighting and don't bother to use their rifles, preferring a bayonet which has been well sharpened; so maybe that British sergeant major at Beauregard was right when he egged *us* on, though he irked me a good deal at the time. Everybody also says that the war is not far from its end, but I hope to get a whack at it before it's over. Our quarters here are very good, but of course not like Beauregard. We are in a forty-eight-hour quarantine, but as soon as it is lifted I am going to have a fine time looking this country over. I took my first bath and changed my clothes for the first time in two weeks this morning. I don't think I would ever go dirty from choice. We have had lots of fun watching the people this afternoon. They have little two-wheeled carts and the whole family gets into one and is drawn by a little donkey not as big as a newborn colt. I saw a family stop to talk to some soldiers and the donkey sat down on his haunches for a rest while the conversation went on. I will write again soon.

Lots of love,
LARRY

Saturday, May 18, 1918

Dear Dad:

We finally arrived at school last Wednesday afternoon after a day and a half on the train. The ride was rather tiresome for we were pretty well crowded and had to sit up all night, but I enjoyed seeing the country in spite of it all. From the train I saw about fifteen airplanes all flying in a bunch and it surely was a pretty sight. We started work the next morning and were glad to do it for we had done nothing for a month and that gets monotonous. This life is going to be some change for we get much better treatment and accommodations than we have had before—and they use us as though we were men, not kids. The barracks are enormous, being built around a court and made of stone. We have rooms holding from four to eight with tables, chairs, bureaus, washstands and sheets and pillows. Also maids to care for the rooms. The food is fine—with all kinds of vegetables and soups and real dishes to eat it from, also waitresses. The work is on the same lines as at Beauregard, but much more thorough and with better instructors. I have just returned from riding and we have a French instructor in that. They surely know how to ride. The country around here is very beautiful—with a wonderful climate, I think, for it has been very warm and fair since we arrived. We are situated right in a city of about forty thousand. From my window we can see a good deal of it and only a short way from us on a hill is a large castle. We expect to get three months' instruction here and then probably go right to the front. I have heard no war news for weeks, so know very little of what is going on. I haven't got any mail at all yet, although some of the men have. We haven't been paid, either, and I would have been stone broke without the extra money you gave me. You spend more than it seems as though you could for things, like underwear, that haven't been issued us cost a mint over here. I haven't seen anybody that I know, but expect to any time, for some of the fellows here have met men that they knew. Write me if they are shipping men from Beauregard yet. I wish Dumaine could see the way they work the ground over here and the crops they grow. There are no weeds and every inch is cultivated. The cattle aren't as good as what we breed, but you see lots of good horses. Please write as often as you can. I will be tickled to death to hear from you.

Love from
LARRY

Cadet L. C. Vincent
A. P. O. 718 S. A. S.
American Expeditionary Forces
France

Sunday, May 26, 1918

Dear Dad:

I wonder if you have been getting my letters. I have not heard a word from you. The daily mail was just brought around and both of the men in my room got some, but I did not. Out of luck. We have had our rooms changed and I am in a room now with two Vermont boys. We are on a regular schedule and work from 7:00 A.M. until about 5:30 P.M. We have supper at 6:30 and can do as we wish until 9:30. We don't get our Saturday afternoons off here as we did in the States, only have the evening with taps an hour later and Sundays, so I haven't been able to plan any overnight trips—if I could have, I might have got to Monteregard, but that's out of the question, at present, anyway. However, some of us quite often go to a village about eight miles from here where there is a wonderful restaurant, run by two sisters who simply can't do enough for us. There's a fine view from the terrace and we sit there and look out on the river and eat and eat and eat.

We get a holiday Memorial Day and I think I will spend it in the country. Yesterday while I was out studying field service, I saw farmers cutting their first crop of alfalfa and it smelled pretty good to me. The equitation here is great stuff, for we have good horses and excellent instructors. We do our riding in a big hall and get all kinds of suppling exercises which cause a lot of falls. One of the men that went off yesterday fell under his horse and got kicked in the head, taking a lot of skin and hair off. So far, I have managed to stay on. We hope to get paid sometime, though the Lord knows when that will be. Write as often as you can and make the letters long.

Your loving grandson,
LARRY

Dear Dad:

I got a letter yesterday from you that was written the 10th of May. It was the first one and sure was welcome, even if what you said about the high water going down at last, so that they could start loading gravel at Profit Island, made me more than a little homesick. Incidentally, that idea about the steel barges instead of wooden ones sounds mighty good, but it would be my guess nobody would be able to get steel for that until after the war is over; they are even building those Hog Island ships mostly of wood, I understand. Over here, our training goes ahead. We went out to the range this week for the first time and fired and observed fire of the French .75. They are a great little gun and better than our own three inch everybody says. That part of the work and the horses appeal to me much more than the mathematics, in which I am pretty weak. I believe we will go straight to the front from here. It looks to me as though the Allies were waiting for us to get a lot of men over with a preponderance of artillery before starting a big push and then settling the thing for good. There are a lot of wild rumors floating around today about commissions. Yesterday they collected all our recommendations and something is certainly happening which has got a lot of the men all haired up. Personally, I would much rather wait until I finish here and make good as a sergeant, then be commissioned, than to be busted after not finishing successfully.

Yesterday we went out into the country to make sketches and saw a lot of caves in the side of a big cliff. We were told these used to be occupied and I guess they were, for they had windows and doors big enough for horses and teams to pass through. We went up on top of an old mill to draw and though, as you know, I am not a Whistler by any means, I enjoyed it, for the mill was quite a sight, too. It was made of rocks and divided into rooms, halls and stairways and was evidently hundreds of years old, for the stone steps were worn down as much as six inches where people had walked.

Thursday, the 30th—the northern Memorial Day—we had a holiday and all the American soldiers marched out to the cemetery with the French and decorated the soldiers' graves. There must have been about a thousand soldiers that marched out there and it surely was impressive. About one hundred and fifty had American flags and another one hundred and fifty carried bouquets. After we reached the cemetery and were lined up around the section the soldiers' graves were in, a French general and our commanding officer—a lieut. col.—made short speeches. Then the band played while first the men with the flags filed in and each stood by a grave and then together stuck their flags in each one. After they filed out, those of us with flowers did the same. There was only one American grave, I think, and the French decorated that and it was piled high with flowers. The French people in town were awfully pleased with the whole thing. Yesterday I returned from a class just in time to see three Frenchmen given medals. That was quite a ceremony, too. One, an officer, received the medal of the Legion of Honor, the highest the French give. A civilian got two—the Medaille Militaire and Croix de Guerre. Then a private on crutches got a Croix de Guerre. They had a line of French and American soldiers who stood at "present arms" during the whole thing. A lot of officers lined up and a general did the honors.

Yesterday noon, just as we were coming out of the mess building, a Yankee aviator flew over and evidently seeing the crowd under him decided to show us a few tricks. He cut very short corners, side-slipped, looped the loop, went way up and shut off his engine and took a long dive in which he just skipped the top of the school and skimmed along the parade grounds in front of it, then went up and away. It surely was pretty and we near broke our necks watching him. When he slipped off sideways and was dropping straight down on edge, there were several of us directly under him. We kind of edged back to give him plenty of room—providing he didn't change his mind and keep on coming. He changed it though, which was a great relief to us. I guess I have told you all the exciting news. The work goes well and outside of a hard cold and couple of raw spots caused by riding, I am very well.

Lots of love,

LARRY

P.S. Just as I am finishing this, there are about a dozen of the most wonderfully toned church bells ringing all at once. Please tell Father Le Grand for me that there's a beautiful church very near the barracks—not to mention several others, one quite famous for its tapestries—that I've enjoyed seeing and that I go to Mass regularly.

June 24, 1918

Dear Dad:

I received several letters from you this week. One of the letters you sent me while I was at Camp Merritt just came, but I have never got the package you spoke of. If there are any of Aunt Amy's cookies in it, that will be just too bad, even if it finally does get here. Of course things must have been moving right along at Cindy Lou since you wrote. By this time, you are probably cutting the perique. Anyway, the kids must have suckered the plants, and I hope you can get some of the high school boys to help bring the stalks to the drying sheds, during their vacation, for I know you are shorthanded. But the crop won't be nearly as big as usual this year now that you've put all that additional ground into cane. How long it seems since we first talked about doing that! I didn't write yesterday for I went out into the country during the day and spent the evening studying for an examination. Last Monday we went through a gas attack and saw weapons of that nature demonstrated. This morning we had lots of fun riding. Our instructor took us out to an old steeplechase course where we took jumps about five feet high and did so well he told us that next time we could take some higher yet. Up to now, we have had to ride without stirrups at all gaits, but only over low jumps. Sometimes your horse goes down or feels particularly good and starts bucking, but there are very few falls. I haven't been off yet, but am knocking on wood as I write this. We just had a talk by a major on the Headquarters Staff, telling us about some of the work they are doing over here and I think the old U.S.A. is going to show them something before they get through, at that.

Your loving grandson,
LARRY

Cadet L. C. Vincent
U. S. A. P. O. 718

←————Form we have to follow.

American E. F.
France

July 5, 1918

Dear Dad:

Just received a letter you wrote the 23rd of May, and of course you won't get this one until almost the 20th of July at the earliest, so it will be two months to make a round trip by mail between me and good old Cindy Lou, where the river shrimp must really be running by this time. Is Nappy setting out his sacks with corn meal for them? Don't forget to eat some for me. Well, yesterday was the Fourth, and of course we had a holiday and quite a celebration. At ten in the morning they had a review with about two thousand men in it. Then we were all addressed by a French general and after that there was a presentation of an American flag. In the afternoon there were all kinds of races. Sprints, jumps and that stuff and then races between mounted batteries who had to harness, gallop across the field and go into action. They had a mule race that was awfully good. A lot of men, each with a mule, had to lead it across the field, around a tree and then ride it back. It was a funny sight. There was some trick riding, like one man riding three horses, standing on the two outside ones; also riding bucking horses and lassoing a running horse with a man on him. In the evening the fellows gave a show which was awfully good. Altogether it was quite a day.

There really is no news I can tell you, only the little incidents that happen in the day's work.

Love from
LARRY

P.S. Today, at dinner, they told us the water was not good. (Of course, we have been drinking it ever since the middle of May!) I am afraid I shall have to cultivate a taste for wine.

July 21, 1918

Dear Dad:

I am now a lieutenant! We were commissioned Friday and I blossomed out today in all my regalia. We finish our course in one more week, so by the time you receive this I will be somewhere else in France, or perhaps in Italy. I don't know. The war news is very encouraging now and I rather anticipate getting in on a big push. Recently we conducted fire with an aero-observer who flew over the target and sent back reports by wireless. After we finished, he looped a few loops and landed. Last week about two hundred and fifty second lieutenants came in from the States and they were all men from the third camp. They were commissioned the 1st of June and we were, too, but our commissions were held up for some reason or other. At that, these men haven't had the experience we have and we figure we are a lot better off, after all. We have got them all scared to death by telling them what they have coming to them—study, hard work, etc. I am going out to supper tonight with a French family by the name of Detain and expect a wonderful feed. I have eaten there before and the mother and daughter are both marvelous cooks.

I have two problems to work out for tomorrow, so will stop now and get at them. Just as soon as I get located after leaving school, I will write again. Don't worry for I am well and happy and confident that I will see you again before very long.

Your loving grandson,

LARRY

Lawrence C. Vincent, 2nd Lieut. F. A. N. A.
U. S. A. P. O. 718
American E. F.
France

August 7, 1918

Dear Dad:

I landed here in Camp Meucon last Monday morning and have been too busy to write before. Meucon is about five miles from Vannes, which is near the coast, so you can look it up. I am once more in school and am kind of disgusted. I hope to goodness we finish this everlasting study sometime and get to doing a little fighting. The country here is very rolling and not as fertile as where we have been. It is in Brittany and the country people's dress is rather novel. The women wear all sorts of fancy white bonnets, some enormous, some tiny, and the men wear big round hats with ribbons hanging down their backs. The brigade we are attached to has not arrived here yet, but some of the officers have preceded it and are at school with us. We traveled down here in first-class carriages and eat at an officers' mess which costs us six francs a day, but it is real American food and the first I've had since we arrived in France. We had pie for dinner and it was good, but I would gladly give all the pie in the world for one dish of Ivy's gumbo. We will be here several weeks for it takes that long to train the men and officers, but then we go to the front. They sure split us up at school for the men were sent to join different outfits anywhere from the Swiss border to the North Sea. I hit my first real case of bugs here. We had a few at school, but they soon got rid of them for us, but here I am afraid we will be constant companions. The little devils bite me, but don't poison me much and really they bother me most by waking me up at night; but some of the fellows are badly poisoned by them and suffer quite a lot. They are just common bedbugs, but most awfully active and hungry. I may have to cash another check for, as yet, I haven't been able to get all my pay and it is imperative that I have more equipment before going to the front. An officer has to buy everything he has, even his own tent and dishes, so you see it costs some money. How is everything going at home? Fine, I hope, and I bet the war news is pleasing to you as well as us. I must close now, but will try and write again soon.

Lots of love,
LARRY

Lt. L. C. Vincent
U. S. A. P. O. 779
American E. F.
France

August 26, 1918

Dear Dad:

I have not written for some time, but have been so busy that when I got through work it seemed as though I could do nothing but go to bed. Things seem to be going well with me—meaning that I am giving satisfaction—and I expect to stay with this outfit probably through the war, though one never can tell. I will tell you my schedule today to give you an idea of what I have to do, although the schedule varies and some days I do a lot of firing and mapping. Reveille was at 4:45. After breakfast, which followed immediately, we got the cannoneers and drivers out, groomed and harnessed forty-eight horses and got the guns out to the range at 7:00. The drivers came back and I had charge of them and the stables for the day. I had to give infantry drill to about seventy-five men part of the morning, take them on a hike with our gas masks on for two hours and see that one hundred and sixty-four horses were fed, watered and cared for. After dinner, I gave the drivers mounted drill, then watered and sent them after the guns. After that, had the rest of the men work at the stables on the other horses. Wound up with retreat at 5:45. Now since supper, I have had a half-hour gas drill, attended a lecture on the organization and use of artillery and now have a stack of letters about a foot high to wade through and censor. All of this on top of a trick at guard in which I had to ride forty-four kilometers and take my few hours of sleep on the floor. Don't think from this letter that I'm feeling abused, because that's not true. I am contented and perfectly healthy.

Your loving grandson,
LARRY

Lt. L. C. Vincent
Battery E. 113 F. A.
155 Brigade
American E. F., France

September 13, 1918

Dear Dad:

I am taking a few minutes off tonight to write a little. We have been very busy the last few days getting ready to go. It is quite a job getting everything packed, lashed and ready to load so that the minute we detrain we can start on the road, for there is the possibility of having to detrain under shelling. I am very limited as to space, because I can't take more than can ultimately be distributed over a horse. I know where we are going, but can only tell you that they have just started a big drive there, so we ought to hit it right in the midst of things. We leave here Sunday, the 15th, at 8:00 A.M. and travel about three days by rail. This brigade is part of the 80th Division, so perhaps you may follow our movements in the papers.

This letter is rather disjointed as I have been interrupted while writing it and have had to do it hastily, as I must also take time to write one in French to the Detains, thanking them for inviting me to spend my first leave with them. I should like very much to do that, so my visit to Monteregard may be still further delayed. Good night, Dad.

Lots of love,
LARRY

September 22, 1918

Dear Dad:

I haven't time or facilities for writing much, as all I have for a table is a small notebook and I am all curled up in a pup tent. We are camped in some woods just back of the lines and we move into position tonight. I cannot tell you where we are, but it is very famous for the battles that have been fought there during this war. From all indications, there is going to be another big one very shortly. I have seen several air battles and of course we can hear the firing here. I was out this morning doing some reconnaissance work and the Germans started shelling a hill just a short way off. They were very big shells and it kind of makes you want to duck when they come whistling over and burst close by. We are getting lots of rain and the mud is a foot deep, so we are nearly always wet and daubed with mud. We do all our moving at night, which is some job when it is pitch dark and no lights can show. I just got orders to see to the packing, so must stop now. Don't know when I can write again or when I will ever get any mail, but hope before long.

Your loving grandson,
LARRY

Another change:
Lt. L. C. Vincent
Battery E. 313 F. A.
American E. F.   O. K.
France   L. C. Vincent, 2nd Lt., F. A.

September 30, 1918
8:00 A.M.

Dear Dad:

I have got a few minutes this morning while waiting for my horse to go out for all day on a battalion problem. I didn't write Sunday because I went to town Saturday night for my last crack at civilization. You would have laughed if you could have seen how I ended up. I had hoped to spend the night in one of those marvelous French beds, but found the town was filled up and not a room left. As there was no way to get out here to camp—it was so late when I finished hunting—I crawled off in the grass beside the road, curled up in my trench coat and spent the night. I slept until seven, then went to a hotel and washed and had breakfast. Coming out on the train, I ran into three more officers who did the same thing.

It sounds a good deal like the front as I am writing this, for there is a regiment in position about a thousand yards from here and they have been blazing away for over an hour. The brigade finishes its training here in about a week and then we move up to the big doings.

From now on, don't put any P.O. number on letters for we will be moving continually and won't have the same number. I must stop now for it is time to go.

Much love,
LARRY

Lieut. L. C. Vincent
Bty. E. 313 F. A.
155 Brigade
American E. F., France

October 14, 1918

Dear Dad:

My last two letters have been necessarily brief, so tonight I am going to try and make this as interesting and descriptive as possible. There is a little lull tonight which accounts for it. To begin, I am sitting in a little hole in the ground just big enough to lie down in and about two feet deep. Protection from splinters. I haven't had a bath since September 14th and have not had my clothes off since about the 20th of September. I have been four days without even washing my hands or combing my hair. The last two days have been rather warm in respect to scrapping—and I have several times been as close as is healthy to some of Fritzie's shells. The nearest was yesterday, about ten feet, and a big one, too. You sure would have laughed to see me lying sprawled perfectly flat in the mud while it was bursting. If you have time after hearing it coming to flop you are fairly safe. To tell you somewhat of how we do this job: we move into position about three thousand yards from Fritz at night and get set. Then for the next couple of days help the doughboys hold the line while our heavies, which are less mobile and slower to move, come up to two or three thousand yards behind us. Then, when all is set, everybody opens up at once and we shove the Germans back three to five miles. Sometimes it takes a couple of days to do it, but so far they have gone. In the meantime, as the Germans begin to locate us, our position develops more business. We receive 'em as well as send 'em. Thus far, our battery has been lucky and the casualties have been light. Some of the others in the regiment have not been so fortunate. I am knocking on wood as I write this, also I pause occasionally to scratch. I sure have them—and one of the greatest joys of my life is going to be a hot bath and a bottle of larkspur.

I saw a funny one the other day which gave me a good laugh. A plane came over and dropped out a small balloon—about like a Fourth of July one—which landed in a field. About twenty doughboys, who happened to be near, started as fast as they could to see what it was. When they got about twenty feet from it, some cautious bird happened to think that it might be a Fritz plane and some trick he was up to. So they all stood around for a few minutes, first looking at the plane which was by then a long way off, and then talking the thing over. Finally they all took off their helmets, put on their gas masks and one bold lad walked up and carefully looked the thing over. There was a carton of cigarettes hitched to it. There is another side which is not so pleasant, but I will tell you a little of that. This morning I was walking across a field, chasing up some ammunition we needed, when a shell broke near by and I turned partially around to see if it would be better to change my direction. I stepped on something soft and looked down to find the head and shoulders of a redheaded American under my feet. The rest of him was near by and he had evidently been there two or three days. I had the poor boy buried. Enough of that.

I think one of the things that interests me most is to see what you can do with a horse before he drops dead from work and where one can go with them hitched to wagons and guns. I'll certainly know how to show our people what to do with mules when I get back to Cindy Lou. I have put the battery into position in the thickest of woods in rough country when it was so black you couldn't see your hand in front of you and so slippery with mud you could hardly stand up. The planes and balloons are mighty interesting, too, and nothing is more thrilling than a scrap between two planes. The figures they cut in maneuvering for position are marvelous and the final dive of the one that gets beaten makes your hair prickle all over you. I have seen quite a few of our balloons brought down in flames by the German planes— seen the observer in the balloon jump in his parachute and float down, and then seen our antiaircraft guns get the plane before it was safely away. I would give quite a good deal right now for a good soft bed with sheets and things, for this ground is kind of hard, damp and cold, but I sure can sleep on it at that when I get a chance which is not awfully often. I am anticipating a good night's sleep tonight for we attacked this morning and drove them back six kilometers and then got orders not to move up tonight for some reason or other, so hope it will be quiet. The peace news is very encouraging and we all hope they will declare an armistice before long. I am hoping to be able to dodge 'em a little while longer, for it would be hell to get bumped off so near to the end of it all.

The beautiful countryside we are going through has not a soul in it but soldiers, and the little towns which must have been so pretty are in perfectly flat ruins. I think I had better sleep now for I don't know when I will get another chance like this again. I hope this reaches you safely for it is the longest I have written for a long time. I am very well—aside from a little dysentery and a cold which go with all the rest of this. Don't worry, for I think the fighting will stop soon and then it can't be very long before I see you again. The days and nights are pretty full, for this kind of warfare is not like trench warfare—for when one is not fighting one is moving.

Lots of love,

LARRY

P.S. It's funny, since I have been up here I haven't got a letter from you. Don't worry—I am *not* going to bring home a French girl, although they are *wonders*.

Lt. L. C. Vincent
Bat'y. E. 313 F. A.
A. E. F., France

Tours
November 3, 1918

Dear Dad:

I am sitting in a café in Tours writing this and hope that the crowd around will furnish enough inspiration to make it interesting. I came down here last Thursday to go to the Observers' School after having answered a call for volunteers at the front. This flying is great stuff and although I don't think it furnishes more thrills than the artillery, one is sure more comfortable. An observer's job is to locate all things of military importance, to be a good machine gunner for the fights—and must know how to handle a plane, too, in case the pilot gets hit. I have run into about twenty-five Saumur men I knew before who are here on the same work. It makes it seem kind of like home for some of them come from Beauregard. I am sitting here writing with a lieutenant of Engineers named Frank Waddill, who was one of my buddies there and whom I also knew at Tulane, where he was hipped on the subject of sonar research. He's going to modernize our sugarhouse when the war's over. Meanwhile, he and I have been spending some nights rather wildly—but after six weeks at the front we thought it was due us. I also did Paris on the way here and it certainly is all it's cracked up to be. I had a little hard luck on the way down for every bit of my baggage, except toilet articles which I carried, has been lost. It is going to cost me three hundred and sixty dollars to get re-equipped and some more to buy my flying clothes. The govt. furnishes them now, but they are not warm enough for winter use. The Army sure uses an airman well for we have practically no discipline, the best of grub and quarters and short working hours. This is a great camp here—with lots of activity. There are usually forty or fifty planes in the air at once and the fellows have great fun after finishing their missions by chasing farmers out of the fields and scaring people on the roads. I rather doubt now if I ever see the front again, for it looks as if the war would finish *"toute de suite"* and I am sorry in one way for I would have liked to see it as a flier. The war news looks awfully good, and if it ends soon I expect to be home shortly thereafter for, although I lost all chance of promotion by leaving the artillery, I am now detached. So I ought to be one of the first to leave. Am shy of paper, so will quit.

Your loving grandson,
LARRY

Lt. L. C. Vincent
2nd A. I. C.
A. P. O. 717
A. E. F., France

November 12, 1918

Dear Dad:

I want to write you now while everything is fresh in my mind. We got the news of the cessation of hostilities yesterday and all of France has gone wild. It is the greatest celebration I ever hope to see and a most wonderful change in a nation. I was in town Sunday and everything was quiet and the people very serious and sober as all French have been. Last night all lights were lighted, you could hardly get through the streets and everybody wild with joy and, for the most part, French and Americans both quite drunk. The Americans express their joy with wild whoops and yells, while the French scamper about singing and kissing and hugging everybody. I got my share. The city was decorated, everybody in their best clothes, and fountains playing that haven't worked for months. As for my part of the celebration, I got gloriously drunk and had for a companion one of the prettiest and most stylish girls you ever saw—a vaudeville actress who is showing here now. She got drunk, too, also insisted on paying her way. The last I saw of her, I recollect having told her I would take her to America with me and she commenced crying, with both arms around me and kissing me between each sniffle—all right on the sidewalk with a million people about. I was too exhilarated to be embarrassed, but nobody paid any attention anyway. I have a hazy recollection of her saying she would blow me to my Thanksgiving dinner. It seems very wonderful to think this grinding war is over.

I am getting along well here and am making lots of friends amongst the wildest bunch of men in the world. I haven't had any mail for ages, but hope it will begin to come through before long. Write often, please.

Lots of love,
LARRY

November 17, 1918

Dear Dad:

Now that the war is finished, I guess I can tell you more of what I have done and where I have been. I landed in Bordeaux—went from there to Ussel—from there to Saumur—thence to Vannes and from there to Verdun, where we went into the lines. We were on the west bank of the Meuse between the river and the Argonne Forest. It was one of the toughest sectors on the whole front. I have seen two hundred effective men reduced to fifty in less than thirty minutes and there

443

was lots of that kind of stuff. We started with one hundred and ten horses and four weeks later had only twenty-four and our battery was no exception. I can't tell you all the things I saw for it would take reams of paper, but will when I get home. I have just finished my gunnery course which consists of range work with machine guns and then aerial fire. Now I am starting the observation course which consists of taking photos, making maps, adjusting fire for artillery and liaison with infantry. The flying is fine and I enjoy it a lot, except that now it is getting pretty cold. The course here only lasts thirty-three more days and perhaps some of us will be sent home then. The celebrating has ended now and everybody has settled down again to work. It was great while it lasted though.

Loads of love,
LARRY

December 16, 1918

Dear Dad:

Once more I have moved and this time to the most desolate place in France. I am at Le Courneau, south of Bordeaux and very near Arcachon. They closed up the school at Tours and dumped us all down here, though we wanted to go to our own outfits. This country is perfectly flat and covered with scrub pine. I have no idea when I will get home, but hope to by spring at least. Haven't had a letter in ages.

Your loving grandson,
LARRY

L. C. V.
A. P. O. 778
A. E. F., France

A. P. O. 778   January 1, 1919

Dear Dad:

New Year's Day and it is most beautiful—warm and sunny, so I am celebrating by writing. I haven't written for some time for I have been on a seven-day leave, which I managed to stretch to twelve days. I meant to get to Monteregard, but after spending two days in Saumur, I went back to Tours and never got away from there. I had a wonderful time—saw some good shows, had lots of good stuff to eat and plenty of sleep. I am enclosing a picture of the lady who was kind enough to make all this possible. She is the daughter of a French officer who was the governor of one of the French provinces in Algeria and the widow of another French officer, killed near the Marne. She has a baby a year old, is well educated, plays the piano, has a good voice and has an independent income of her own and lives in a big house just outside of Tours, well staffed with servants. Incidentally, she is much prettier than the picture indicates and one of the few French-

444

women I have seen who doesn't use make-up—she doesn't need to. We took a walk every day, went to shows in town and dined at the best hotel several times. We also went to Midnight Mass at the cathedral, the most beautiful service I ever saw. (Tell Father Le Grand that.)

No, she is not in love with me, although she did kiss me good-by at the station in front of everybody, and I found that very easy to take, for I do like her a lot. While I'm not exactly in love with her, either, I can imagine that I very well might be.

They are closing up this camp now and getting the men all sorted into districts, so they are going back to the States very soon, but as for me, I don't know. I will probably draw some job on a dock or something for a year or so, but never mind, I'll get home eventually.

Your loving grandson,
LARRY

A. P. O. 703, A. E. F.
January 27, 1919

Dear Dad:

I landed here (Gondrécourt) last Saturday after taking six days to get here. I visited the lovely widow in Tours again and stopped off in Paris on the way, also lost all my baggage for the second time. The French system baffles me—I saw everything put on the train at Tours and when we arrived at Paris it was minus—it had been dumped off somewhere in between. It is rather inconvenient for I have no clothes except what I had on and they are my best ones and I don't care about knocking around camp in them. This is a reclassification camp—all officers who have lost their outfits go through here and are assigned new jobs according to their qualifications. Most of the work they are giving out now is special work like military police, railroad transportation, baggage department, labor battalions, prison camps, etc. This is all a great experience anyway and I ought to be able to do anything when I get home, which I hope will be by fall at least. Gondrécourt is just south of Bar-le-Duc and is an enormous camp. It was one of our forward camps during the war. Jeanne d'Arc's birthplace is only about ten miles from here and I hope to see it before leaving. I have hopes of being stationed somewhere soon and staying there long enough to get some mail.

Heaps of love,
LARRY

A. P. O. 703   February 11, 1919
Dear Dad:

I got a letter of yours today dated August 11th. Outside of two or three letters all my mail has been like that. I got no Christmas boxes at all, but I wasn't surprised, for Aunt Amy was the only person I

445

knew who went in for that sort of thing. It will seem queer not to have her around when I get back and I will miss her a lot. Of course she really was a very old lady though and you're right, we ought to be able to take losses like that in our stride, even if they do hurt. But it seems real silly to be answering what you wrote me 'way last August. By this time you're not only all through grinding, and then some; you've put the seeds for the new perique crop in the cold frames by now. Lordy, Lordy, what I wouldn't give to be there with you and to go with Captain Bourgeois to get that new hundred-foot steamboat at Zanesville. You didn't tell me what you'd named her or much else about her and I certainly would like to know more.

I am still in the same camp, but have hopes of getting out soon, for I have been living an awful existence for the last two months. Absolutely no work—nothing to do but eat and sleep. You can't even get drunk in this town to break up the monotony. Speaking of drink, you ought to hear the soldiers, officers and all, express their opinions of the folks back home who have passed the prohibition law. There is going to be an awful holler when they all get home. This place is horrible— mud a foot deep and rain all the time, so you get practically no exercise and simply sit around and cuss. No passes are given here except to the permanent personnel. I have run into some of the fellows I came over with who have been sent down here for reassignment. Most of them didn't get to the front at all, but got stuck in some camp, so maybe I was lucky after all, and I may get sent to Germany eventually. Anxious as I am to get home, I'd be glad to go if I thought I could be of any real use there. I don't feel that I am here.

Love,

LARRY

April 30, 1919

Dear Dad:

Well at last I can write you in a somewhat more definite way and that means it will also be in a more cheerful vein. No doubt that will be a relief to you, for I know I've done an awful lot of griping lately and you must be sick of it. By some miracle I have succeeded in getting a ten-day leave and I suppose this means that afterward I'll be attached to a regular unit again. I may be able to tell you something more definite the next time I write.

Meanwhile, I can tell you right now that I'm going to take advantage of my leave by going to Monteregard. You're quite right, I ought to have done it before. But as you probably gathered, I had a pretty good time at Saumur and Tours from the beginning, so I couldn't resist the temptation offered in the persons of very attractive young ladies to get back to both places when I had the chance. Of course I realize by now that these attractions were just passing fancies, but they

446

sure were pleasant at the time. Haven't you told me yourself that if I ever got started in the right—or even the wrong—direction, I might like girls better than I expected? Well, you knew what you were talking about, as usual.

I've been looking up train schedules and I go from here to Paris, which is fairly simple, then after several main line changes to a place called Saintes, where I change again to a local which takes me to the small village of St. Porchaire, very close to Monteregard. I am sure to find some kind of an inn there, where the food and the beds will both be good, because that seems to be true everywhere in France. I'm not going to write beforehand to Aunt Armande, because mails are still so uncertain that I'd probably get there before the letter did and anyway, I think it would be more fun to surprise her. If she's really glad to see me, and I guess she will be, I can easily move over to the chateau from the inn. I only hope I won't lose my baggage again, for I'd hate to get there looking like a tramp. I suppose there may be some attractive girls in that vicinity, too, I mean besides Janine, who, of course, doesn't count.

Well, that will be all for now, as I'd better start packing and be on my way to Dublin Bay. (How long it seems since we used to dance to that tune and how good it would be to dance to it again!)

Lots of love,
Larry

 CHAPTER XXVI

Larry was hungry and the lunch was very good: sardines, cold sliced sausage and fresh young radishes for hors d'oeuvres; then crisply fried sole, veal steak delicately browned, a green salad, cheese made from goats' milk; to top all this off, wild strawberries with thick cream. When he complimented the *patronne* on the butter, she answered with satisfaction that it was all very well for Normans to claim the best butter in the world was made at Issigny, but everyone who was really informed knew that it could not compare with Charentes butter. The difference was caused by the fact that in Normandy the cows were left out from morning until night, whereas, in the Charentes, they were carefully brought into shelter during the heat of noonday. And the cheese, another specialty of the region—did not M. le Lieutenant think it superior to Pont l'Eveque and Livarot? It was evident that she felt

447

great pride in local products and Larry was glad that he could praise these wholeheartedly.

A carafe of red wine stood on the table and he had poured it out with a liberal hand; it was good sound wine that had a glow to it, and it suited him. But when he praised this, too, the *patronne* looked apologetic. It was nothing but a commonplace *vin de table,* not suitable to go with sole and veal; above all, not suitable for such a connoisseur as M. le Lieutenant was revealing himself to be. If she had realized in time, she would have brought him something better from behind the faggots—a vintage Montrachet, for instance, of which she happily still had a few bottles. She would make up for the omission at dinnertime. Meanwhile, M. le Lieutenant would of course have cognac with his coffee and that must be on the house. Oh, but she would insist! This was cognac country—and 1914 had been an especially good year. He could not decline to accept the country's hospitality on his first visit there!

By the time Larry rose from the table, he was so full of good food and good drink that the morning's urge for activity had materially slackened. He would have been quite content to sprawl out beside one of the little tin tables in front of the inn and bask almost drowsily in the sunshine. Not that he would be averse to passing the time of day with anyone who happened to come along; but he had no special craving for immediate companionship. It actually took a certain amount of will power to strike out for Monteregard, as he had originally planned, almost immediately after lunch; and he sauntered along, smoking a cigarette, instead of going at his usual smart clip. However, he had declined the *patronne's* friendly suggestion of a cariole and a driver who would act as a guide. The walk would do him good and he was sure he could find his way. If he had understood her correctly, he was to turn down the road which ran at right angles to the inn and proceed about a kilometer. The first fields he saw would already be part of the Monteregard property; the forest lay just beyond them.

It did not take him five minutes to get past the twin rows of gray houses which fringed the village street and which were redeemed from drabness only by their blooming flower gardens; and once he had reached the meadows which men were busily tilling and the pastures where cattle and sheep were grazing, his drowsiness was dispelled by the freshness of the breeze which still retained the salty tang of the sea. The sunny landscape changed quickly in character: the open country was soon interspersed with wood lots and he saw less livestock and no workmen. Then, suddenly, the fields were completely engulfed by trees. With a quickening of senses, Larry saw them closing in upon him.

For this was a forest unlike any he had ever seen before. Dense as it was, it had none of the gloom which enfolded the swamps and groves of Cindy Lou. The sunlight filtered in through the verdant branches of ivy-wreathed trees and lay in bright patches on the moss and ferns beneath them. All about him was the radiance of gilded greenery. But it was strangely still. Though the sun had penetrated to its innermost depths, the breeze had failed to pass beyond its network of boughs and not a leaf was stirring. If birds nested within it, their song was silenced; if foxes burrowed there, they were withdrawn; if hares sometimes scampered through it, they had leaped away. Larry paused, and when the sound of his footsteps ceased, there was no sound at all.

All at once he remembered a letter, written on paper crackling and yellow with age, which his grandfather had shown him, and a sentence from it seemed to stand out as vividly as if it had been written in letters of flame and not in faded ink:

"You approach the chateau through a beautiful forest of ivy-wreathed oaks and there's something actually magical about the effect of the sun shining through their greenery."

The mother he had never known had been right. There was a look of magic about this place, a feeling of it, too. As this feeling grew stronger and stronger, Larry remembered, not quite so clearly, something else the letter had contained: something about roads branching through the forest in every direction and about a little grassy plot, with ancient stone seats in it, which could be reached by one of those roads, though it was so well hidden that this must have been done on purpose, in order that the plot could be a secret trysting place. And suddenly he knew he would never be content until he had explored the roads of the forest, until he found this place of which his mother had written and which had been so carefully concealed from curious eyes. He was no longer in a hurry to reach the chateau or to meet his aunt and his cousins. He wanted first to find the hidden enclosure.

At the moment, only one road stretched out before him. It was straight and wide and level and was obviously designed to lead directly to the chateau. However, he had not gone much farther when he saw another, branching off to the right. He took it without hesitation, but almost at once decided that, though narrower than the first, it was also too straight and open to promise romantic possibilities. He had not pursued it very far before discovering that his surmise had been correct. An enormous kitchen garden, surrounded by outbuildings, came into view; and though Larry was still at some distance from it, a couple of workers in it raised their heads and stared at him in a way which showed they felt he was an intruder. He turned again and, after regaining the highway and walking a little farther on, saw another road branching from it, this time to the left. Its condition showed that it was less traveled than those he had seen before and it led more deeply into the woods; but when he came to a circular open space, he found it neatly clipped, ornamented with flower beds and dominated by a white marble column, for which he could see neither rhyme nor reason. Nothing about it bespoke secrecy or antiquity; evidently, for some inexplicable reason, it was a place in which the De Chanets felt a certain pride and on which they lavishd a certain amount of attention. But it had no special attraction for him.

Larry would have been glad, then and there, of a stone seat, moss grown or otherwise. He had evidently walked farther than he realized or else the afternoon was actually warmer than he had supposed, for he was hot and tired. But he was still determined to go on with his search; and after a moment he saw that the road by which he had entered the cleared circle, though it was the only one leading directly toward the highway, was not the only one branching out beyond the clipped lawn and the flower beds. There were others, radiating like spokes from a wheel. They were all very narrow and they all apparently led deeply into the forest; there seemed to be no special differences among them. If he guessed wrong more than once, as to which would take him where he wanted to go, the afternoon might very well be almost gone before he could rectify his mistake. He finally made his choice in favor of one which had a slight slope to it and which soon dwindled to the size of a path. It was thickly bordered by underbrush and the branches of the trees met and interlaced overhead. Presently Larry found that he would have to skirt large stones in order to continue on his way; then, that the branches above him were bending lower and lower. As he stooped to avoid being brushed by them, he was aware, for the first time, of a sound which was not made by his footsteps—a very slight murmuring sound, such as might be caused by the gentle flow of a small stream. Then he heard another—and it was the sound of a human voice, quickly mingled with a second one. Both were fresh and vibrant, suggesting youth, and one had a musical quality that went straight to his heart. He plunged forward, no longer mindful of impediments. The trees parted suddenly and he saw in front of him the secret place he had sought.

On an ancient stone seat before him sat two young girls, who were holding a book between them and whose heads were bent over it. One was dressed in white with black ribbons and the other was dressed in white with green ribbons. One had very sleek black hair, parted in the middle, and the other had unruly golden-brown curls which were not parted at all. That was all he had time to observe before they sprang up and he saw that one was pale and the other rosy. They stared at him in amazement, but not, he was relieved to see, in fright. Then one of them spoke so quickly that he had not been able to think of anything to say which would explain or excuse his intrusion.

"Monsieur has lost his way," she suggested. "If he will retrace his steps to the column which marks the circle from which he must have come, he will have no trouble in getting from there to the main road."

It was the pale girl with the black hair and the black ribbons who had addressed him. Now the other one spoke, too.

"Perhaps he didn't lose his way," she suggested. "Perhaps he wanted to come here all the time."

She smiled, and her smile had the same effect upon him as her voice. And he no longer had any trouble in framing an answer.

"You are right, mademoiselle," he said. "This was the very place I set out to find. Only I didn't expect to be so fortunate as to discover that it was peopled with wood nymphs."

"Well, you must have had some good reason for wanting to find it."

It was the brown-haired girl who had spoken again. She was still smiling, and the more she smiled, the lovelier she looked. The other girl seemed much graver and, though she did not speak discourteously, there was a marked coolness in her manner.

"Possibly you had in mind a visit to the grottoes. But those are best reached by another route and, in any case, the public has not been admitted to them, since the war. I am sorry to say that there can be no exceptions made to this rule. I must repeat, monsieur, that you will find it easy to reach the highway if—"

"I don't care about visiting the grottoes just now. This really was the place I wanted to find. And I don't particularly want to go back to the highway, either. As a matter of fact—"

"Monsieur—"

"Why don't you let him finish, *chérie?*" asked the brown-haired girl.

"Thank you, mademoiselle. As a matter of fact, I hope you won't feel I'm an out-and-out intruder, though I realize I should have gone to the chateau first and introduced myself properly. But please let me do that now. My name's Larry Vincent and I think one of you must be my cousin, Janine de Chanet."

He looked hopefully from one to the other. The black-haired girl, though her expression was still slightly severe, appeared to relax a little; while she regarded him silently, as if willing to believe him, but somewhat doubtful as to whether she should, the brown-haired girl laughed outright.

"If you're Larry Vincent, Janine *is* your cousin," she said. "So she ought to be the first to welcome you to Monteregard. But I can't wait any longer for her to make up her mind, so I'll do it. My name, in case you're interested, is Louise de Courville, and the relationship's very complicated—in fact, it doesn't exist at all, as far as you're concerned. But I'm very glad to see you, just the same."

Even though Janine had not been the first to welcome him, her greeting was now wholly courteous; obviously she was the *jeune fille comme il faut* of fond French tradition. She was sorry she had not realized Larry was her American cousin; but, as he himself had said, if he had only come first to the chateau and presented himself to her father. . . . She could understand his wish to see their beautiful woods, but after all, there would have been plenty of time for that afterward. And naturally, she had been slightly surprised that a stranger. . . .

"You mean there'll still be plenty of time," Louise interrupted. "So why not all go up to the house together, right now?"

As if it were futile to discuss the matter further, she turned in the direction of the path. It was so narrow, until they came to the circular open space, that they could not walk two abreast. But when they reached that point, she suggested that Janine should continue to lead the way and fell easily into step beside Larry.

"You probably wondered about that column," she said, answering his unspoken question. "There are four of them on the property—one at each of the cardinal points of the compass. They're not very old. Uncle Pierre had them set up and surrounded with flower beds. I've never quite understood why. They don't seem to me especially important."

"They provided an agreeable occupation for him," Janine remarked, turning. "I don't think you should speak so slightingly, Louise, about Papa's activities."

"I didn't mean to speak slightingly. I've always been puzzled, that's all . . . didn't the column puzzle you, Larry?" she added.

"To tell the truth, it did. But I'm still more puzzled about this question of relationship. Evidently, my uncle Pierre is also your uncle Pierre. But you said—"

"I said it was very complicated, and it is. Also, that the relationship didn't exist at all, as far as you and I are concerned. Would you like to have me explain?"

"Very much."

"Well, you knew that my uncle Pierre's father—let's call him the old Marquis de Chanet, for the sake of convenience—was married twice, didn't you?"

"It seems to me I did. I'm not sure. My grandfather's tried to explain, but—"

"I'll probably have to draw you a plan, in the end, to straighten you out. But I'll do the best I can now. His first wife was the Princesse de Herbemont. She died when her only child, Asceline, was only a few weeks old and the marquis didn't feel competent to take care of a baby. So little Asceline was raised by the De Herbemonts. When she grew up, she married Etienne d'Ambly and had two daughters herself—Josephine and Isabelle. Josephine married Jehan de Courville and Isabelle married Gilles de Lorne. I'm Josephine's daughter. So the old Marquis de Chanet was my great-grandfather. Is that all clear so far?"

"More or less. I don't know whether I can take in so many strange names, all at once, and connect them to the right people and get all the various relations straight. But I'll try."

"And I'll help you. I told you I'd draw you a plan if you wanted me to. But if you'll listen carefully—"

"I'm listening all right."

"Well, a long time after the death of the Princesse de Herbemont, the old marquis married again—a lady we always think of as an American, though actually she was French by birth, too. Her name was Dorothée Labouisse and she also had a baby—Pierre. So he's my uncle Pierre—my great-uncle rather, because he and my grandmother are half brother and sister, though she's old enough to be his mother."

"I see."

"I'm not sure whether you really do, or whether you're just being polite about it. But anyway, Pierre de Chanet grew up, and went to the United States with his mother, the former Dorothée Labouisse, and met a certain beautiful Miss Vincent, who really was an American, and fell in love with her and married her."

"And that lovely young lady was my aunt Armande—my father's sister!"

"You're right. You see, it really isn't so complicated after all. The present Marquis de Chanet is my uncle Pierre and your uncle Pierre, just as you said. But just as *I* said, you and I are not related at all!"

Louise laughed, as if there were something amusing in their lack of relationship. Larry laughed, too. For no special reason, he was inclined to agree with her.

"I've been looking forward a lot to meeting my cousin Janine," he said. "I didn't know that at the same time I was going to meet a cousin of hers who wasn't a cousin of mine, but who'd add a lot to the pleasure of making her acquaintance. If I had known, I'd have looked forward to it a lot more."

Louise laughed again and her laugh, like her voice and her smile, seemed to go straight to Larry's heart. However, it quickly occurred to him that he ought not to have spoken about anticipating the pleasure of meeting Janine without saying that he was anticipating an equal amount of pleasure in regard to meeting her brother.

"I mean, of course, I'd been looking forward a lot to meeting both my cousins—in fact, the whole family, and to seeing Aunt Armande again. I hope everyone's at home?"

Janine turned again, and this time the look she gave him was not merely reproachful, as it had been, more or less, from the beginning; it was surprisingly stern, for the expression of so young and beautiful a girl, and it was also very sad. Larry realized that somehow he had erred, even more gravely than through his intrusion; and, though he had not been much concerned over his first offense, this time he was suddenly appalled.

453

"Evidently you did not know that you were coming to a house of mourning," Janine said chillingly. "If you had inquired—"

"Probably he hasn't been any place where he could inquire, Janine," Louise interposed swiftly. "We don't know yet where he has come from, or when. He hasn't had time to tell us. We haven't even asked him. It isn't any stranger that he shouldn't know about us than that we shouldn't know about him." She laid her hand lightly on his arm, and Larry realized that she had sensed his distress. "We ought to have told you right away," she went on gently. "But there didn't seem to be just the right moment to do it and of course it's very hard for Janine to talk about it. I don't talk about it, either, if I can help myself. I try to talk about—well, cheerful things, as much as I can. I hope you will, too. But Monteregard *is* a house of mourning, a house of—of great desolation. You see, just the day before the Armistice, when everyone was so happy because it seemed certain that the end of the war was in sight—"

Janine had not turned again or spoken again. But quietly, collectedly, Louise told Larry how Pierrot had met his death: a German battery of heavy artillery, far behind the lines, had one shell left and decided to fire it in the general direction of the west before dismantling or crippling their gun. The shell landed in a ruined field, beside what was left of an old stone farmhouse, and a jagged splinter of metal, ricocheting off the stones, had struck Pierrot in the temple. . . . "It was more than his mother could bear, after four long years of anxiety," Louise went on. "Pierrot had been badly wounded twice before, once at Ypres and once at the Meuse. Aunt Armande—well, you can understand that she'd been through a terrible strain all through the war."

"And what happened?" Larry managed to ask. But his mouth was very dry, because he thought he knew already.

"Of course, it may have been an accident. She may just have slipped. Or she may not have noticed where she was going. Because she really was distraught. Not that it wouldn't have been very, very sad in any case. . . . You've heard of the Blue Pool at Monteregard, haven't you?"

Again it seemed to Larry as if he were holding in his hand that letter, yellow with age, which his grandfather had shown him; again it seemed as though he were reading those words which were so vivid, though they were written in such faded ink. "Pierre . . . told me the legend of the Blue Pool which the river widens to form at the foot of the caves. According to this legend, a De Chanet lady who lost her lover flung herself into this pool several hundred years ago and ever since then, a spring has bubbled up from the place where she was drowned. Of course, it's just a silly superstition, but just the same—"

"Yes," he answered, speaking with still greater difficulty, "I've heard of the Blue Pool."

"The day after we had the news of Pierrot's death, Aunt Armande

454

stayed in her room for a long while, with the door locked. Afterward, we discovered that she'd been writing most of the time, and though she'd torn up practically all the notes into tiny pieces and thrown them into the fireplace, one was still lying on her desk. It read, 'I haven't lost my lover, for I never had him. But I have lost my only son and that is worse.' I told you she was distraught—the note goes to prove it. She didn't lose her lover, as you know. She married him."

"It seems to me I've heard she was engaged when she was very young to a man who died of yellow fever. Perhaps she was referring to him."

"Perhaps," Louise said doubtfully. He knew she did not think this was the case, and it did not surprise him, because he did not really think so himself.

"Besides, it can't be worse to lose a son than a lover," Louise said thoughtfully. "At least, I don't think so. I think if I loved a man, I'd feel the worst thing that could happen to me would be to lose him. Not that I'd commit suicide if I did."

"I think you would feel that way." Larry did not know why he spoke with such conviction, but it was very deep. "I'm sure you wouldn't commit suicide, either."

"Well, we mustn't talk about me. I must go on telling you about Aunt Armande. She finally left the chateau without saying a word to anybody. But Justine, our portress, saw her pass through the Gate of the Lions and leave the avenue for the woods. No one ever saw her again after that, but there were footprints on the path that goes by the caves—the path that's been closed ever since. And by the edge of the Blue Pool was a scarf."

This time Larry did not even try to answer. They had left the forest now and gone through a marble portal, adorned with sculptured lions, to an inner avenue where wide lawns dotted with scattered statues stretched out beyond the trees. There was a thatched cottage just inside the portal and, as they passed it, an aged man came hobbling to the door and stared out at them, mumbling something that seemed to have no meaning. Almost instantly, a sturdy woman whose thin hair was strained back from her ruddy face and who was dressed in dingy black, appeared beside him and spoke to him soothingly before saying, *"Bon soir, m'sieu-dames,"* to the passers-by. Janine acknowledged the greeting with an inclination of the head and a murmured "Good evening," but keeping at some distance ahead of the others, she walked straight on toward the huge entrance gate surmounted by a great tower. Louise paused, her hand still resting on Larry's arm.

"Good evening, Justine," she said pleasantly. "It *has* been a lovely afternoon, hasn't it? I do hope your father's rheumatism will be much better, now that he will be able to get out in the sun again." The woman smiled and, though this smile revealed the sorry condition of her mouth, which contained only a few blackened and broken teeth, it also changed her look from one of anxiety to one of great good will. It was not hard for Larry to guess that the old man was in his dotage, and that his daughter was grateful to Louise for disregarding this and referring only to his rheumatism. "As you see, we have a visitor, Justine," Louise went on. "This is M. le Marquis' American nephew, M. le Lieutenant Vincent. You will, of course, let him in and out of the grounds without question, at any time."

"But of course, mademoiselle. It goes without saying. M. le Lieutenant must be very welcome at Monteregard."

She nodded, smiling more broadly and toothlessly than ever, and Larry felt unaccountably warmed by her friendliness. He had been so shocked, and so stirred, by what Louise had been telling him, that he was grateful for any sign of cheer. Evidently Louise was aware of this, for she looked up at him and smiled, too, and her smile was very lovely.

"We must not speak any more of these sad things," she said, "and you must not think about them too much, either. You had to know them, because otherwise you would not have understood. But please do not think that Uncle Pierre will feel you have intruded. I believe he will be very glad to see you—very grateful for your company. He is so terribly alone. I do not think he and his mother were ever very close to each other, and now she stays in Paris all the time. She has always preferred that to Monteregard and she never comes here any more. She says it gives her a creepy feeling, that it is like a tomb. I hope you will not feel that way about it; and even if you do, I believe you can help to make it seem more like a home again. I do the best I can, but of course that isn't much."

"I should think you would make almost any place seem like a home," Larry said thickly. "But if I can help—"

"Of course you can help. I'm counting on you."

Louise quickened her pace, evidently hoping to overtake her cousin. But Janine had already disappeared when the others entered the great courtyard. A high wall, jutting out from the watchtower, met the chateau on one side and enclosed the raised garden which bordered it on the other. A row of red-tiled dependencies faced the entrance; these, in turn, adjoined the chateau, which flanked the entire left side expansively between its two majestic turrets. The courtyard was vacant, and there was something overpowering to Larry about its severity and its immensity; even the greenery of its triangular garden seemed dominated by the flights of stone steps which led from one terrace to another and the great stone jars which adorned them. There was no sunshine in the place, as there had been in the forest; there the warm light had filtered through the ivy-wreathed trees and here, where he felt the stones should have been bathed in it, there was none. Everything about the place was fortresslike and forbidding and there was an emptiness to its grandeur. Had it not been for Louise, Larry would have been tempted to turn away without going farther. As if she guessed what was passing in his mind, she slid the fingers which had been resting so lightly on his arm into his hand and pressed it.

"I think Janine's already told Uncle Pierre you're here," she said. "I think she hurried ahead, on purpose. Please don't be disturbed because she didn't seem very glad to see you. Pierrot's death was a terrible shock to her, too—they were much closer to each other than most brothers and sisters. She's had any number of suitors and they haven't meant a thing to her. She never wanted a sweetheart—just Pierrot. He felt the same way about her. And now she's talking about going into a convent. If that happened, it would be still another blow for Uncle Pierre. She's all he's got left, of his own. Of course he's fond of me, but it isn't the same, it couldn't be."

Just as she finished speaking the front door opened and, as it swung slowly back on its heavy hinges, Larry saw that a tall, slender man, dressed in black, was standing in the embrasure. His hair was iron gray and there were deep lines around his mouth, but he was strikingly handsome and carried himself with great distinction. Louise pressed Larry's hand again and then detached her fingers and hurried forward.

"Uncle Pierre," she began. But the man in the doorway shook his head slightly as a signal of interruption and came toward them, looking Larry straight in the face in a way she had never seen him look at anyone else before.

"Come in, Larry," he said, holding out both hands. "You are very, very welcome at Monteregard. I should have known you anywhere for Cary Vincent's son. No one else in the world could have had eyes like hers."

 CHAPTER XXVII

As CLARITY of thought gradually overcame delicious drowsiness the following morning, Larry was aware that sunshine was streaming into his room. Since this was the case, he speedily assured himself, his first impression of the chateau as cold and gloomy must have been erroneous. He lay still, reveling in the warm light—and in the astonishing and glorious realization that he was head over heels in love.

What a fool—what a fatuous fool—he had been, not to come to Monteregard on his first leave, and at every possible opportunity thereafter, instead of wasting precious time at Saumur and Tours! Why, if he had only followed his grandfather's advice, he and Louise might have been engaged by now, they might actually be preparing for their wedding! And he could be making this visit in the role of an accepted suitor—or even a prospective bridegroom! In his blissful state, he did not stop to consider that there might have been obstacles to a whirlwind courtship. After all, nothing could have been kindlier or more moving than the welcome he had received from the marquis. As for Louise, her instant acceptance of his presence, her unquestioning cordiality, her disarming confidences and the candor with which she returned his gaze of admiration, already quickening to ardor—all these combined to convince him that he had found favor in her sight, almost as swiftly and surely as he had looked on her with eyes of love.

Janine was nowhere to be seen when her father, linking his arm into their guest's, had drawn him into the entrance hall the evening before, and she did not reappear until just before dinner. Meanwhile, after inviting Louise to join them, Pierre had taken Larry straight through the drawing room to his private study, rung for refreshments and told the servant who promptly brought pinaud and cookies that M. le Lieutenant's luggage was to be fetched immediately from the inn and placed in the *chambre charentaise.*

"I think that is the one you will like best, Larry," he said, turning back to the boy. "It faces east, so you will get the morning sun there; and it overlooks the reflecting pool and the surrounding gardens, which to my mind form a pleasanter view than the courtyard where you entered. I shall give orders, immediately, that we must have the fountains put into play again, in honor of your visit, and tomorrow night we will have them illuminated. But I believe there is a moon, and they are very pretty, by moonlight, without any artificial illumination. Am I right, Louise, about the moon?"

"Yes, Uncle Pierre. It is almost full."

"In that case, perhaps after dinner you and Larry would enjoy strolling in the garden for a little while. . . . And now, my dear boy, I want to hear where you have just come from and how long we may hope to have you with us at Monteregard. Later, if you feel inclined, I hope you will tell me what you have been doing ever since you arrived in France. Not that I expect you to go into details. But I should like very much to know about your experiences, in a general way."

The first two questions did not take long to answer. Then Pierre and Louise interrupted, almost simultaneously, with the protest that ten days were far too few for a leave, and Larry found this objection unexpectedly heart warming.

"Perhaps you'd let me come again sometime," he said a little hesitantly. "That is, if—"

Again he was interrupted. Of course he was to come to Monteregard as often as he could and stay as long as he wanted. There was no immediate prospect, was there, that he might be sent home?

"I don't think so. But that's just guesswork. The rule for dealing with soldiers seems to be a lot like that for dealing with reporters: 'Catch 'em young, treat 'em rough, tell 'em nothing.' "

They laughed, as if he had said something witty and original and, encouraged by their friendliness, he began to talk about Saumur, the riding school and the kindly people, the sparkling wines and the beautiful countryside. He did not want to talk about the weeks at the front and he thought they guessed this, for they did not press him to do so; and he checked himself, when he was on the point of talking about Armistice Day at Tours, remembering that for them it had been a time of such personal tragedy that this must still overshadow all feeling of patriotic rejoicing. When he paused, Pierre asked him a few questions about the observers' course and the camp near Bar-le-Duc; then he rose, saying that he would show Larry the way to his room, that the luggage must be there by now and that perhaps a bath before dinner would feel good. Linking his arm through the boy's again, he went with him up the great marble staircase with the balustrade of wrought iron, down a long corridor hung with family portraits and beautiful old engravings, and threw open the door of a large chamber hung with soft chintzes. Finally he led Larry over to the casement windows, which he flung open.

"Look!" he said. "Don't you agree with me that this is a charming view?"

Larry's gaze followed the sweep of his host's arm. Beyond a great parterre, studded with flower beds and small conical trees, lay a silvery expanse of water, in which the wide colonnade, the great façade, the sloping roof and the twin towers of the chateau were reflected with such clarity that the effect was one of superb duplication. Flagstone walks, bordered with verdure, enclosed this magical mirror and met at its farther end near the base of a tiered fountain, surmounted by a marble maiden, where the water fell in shimmering sheets from one brimming basin to another. Except for the sound that this made, the place was still with a stillness akin to the silence of the enchanted forest. . . .

"Do I think it's *charming?*" Larry asked, after a long pause. "I—I think it's the most beautiful place I ever saw in my life!"

"That is what your mother thought, too," Pierre de Chanet answered in a strange voice. And he closed the casement and turned back into the room.

It was only a moment before, speaking quite naturally again, he called Larry's attention to the *dressoir* which stood in one corner, and which was adorned with quaint pottery plates, set in carved racks above a wide shelf, and deep drawers with ornamental handles. It was an old custom, in Charente-Maritime, to have such *dressoirs,* which resembled buffets, in bedchambers; but Larry must not think for a moment that they were intended to supplant the large sideboards which he would find in dining rooms! Incidentally, dinner would be in an hour or so and the two girls would meet them in the drawing room beforehand for an *apéritif.* Perhaps, given the ingredients, Larry would prefer to mix a cocktail himself. Or would he rather leave all such responsibilities to his host?

Much rather, he replied. And when Pierre had left him, after telling him again how very welcome he was at Monteregard, he went back to the window and reopened it. In the soft twilight, which merged into darkness so much more slowly in France than in Louisiana, the surface of the water seemed even more silvery than it had before, the greensward a deeper emerald, the flowing fountain more limpid. As Larry stood watching, the first gleams from the rising moon widened into radiance behind the marble maiden; and he saw that between the fountain and the pool there was a stone seat, not hidden away, like those in the forest, but openly placed, as if inviting rest after a stroll along the flagstone walk. Was this really where he and Louise would be coming, after dinner, he asked himself unbelievingly. It must be, from what his uncle had said to her in the study—"Perhaps after dinner, you and Larry would enjoy strolling in the garden for a little while." Yet it was hard to realize that before the end of the day, when he had found Louise in the secret bower, he would walk with her beside these moonlit waters.

The music of chimes, followed by the striking of a clock, sounded above the flow of the fountain and served as a summons to leave the window a second time and make haste with his preparations for dinner. A bathroom, less suggestive of ancient and honorable custom than the *dressoir,* adjoined the *chambre charentaise*; and, having hastily showered and dressed, Larry raced through the long corridor and down the stairs. The drawing room door stood open and, as Larry entered, Pierre looked up with a smile from the drink he was mixing and told his guest to help himself from the tray of canapés that stood near by. The marquis had changed from his black clothes to a striking uniform and there was a row of ribbons across his breast—obviously he had received almost every kind of decoration which a grateful government could bestow. The two girls were seated side by side on a sofa, and it was Janine who was wearing black now. Larry could not help feeling that she was trying to emphasize the family mourning with all the greater insistence because her father had made an effort to lighten it; but the dress was beautifully cut, and the sheer chiffon of which it was fashioned softened the effect of her plainly parted hair and the slight stiffness of her carriage. Louise was in chiffon, too, a pale gray shot with silver, and with this she was wearing a long chain of moonstones. Looking at her, Larry felt as if she were telling him something, too—telling him that she had chosen this dress and these jewels because they were suited for a walk in the garden and that she wanted him to know she was eagerly awaiting the moment when they could wander beside the water.

Dinner was announced while they were all still sipping their drinks and Janine put down her glass at once. It was still amost full, Larry noticed, and she had hardly spoken at all. Pierre, on the other hand, had taken the lead in pleasant and easy small talk; now he motioned the servant away and assured Larry there was no hurry, nothing would spoil if they had refills. Despite his preoccupation with Louise, Larry had not failed to be conscious of their uncle's extraordinary charm, and to sense, beneath his grace of manner, a deep underlying sadness which bore no resemblance whatsoever to his daughter's parade of grief. He spoke to her very gently, as if he were sorry for her and were trying to spare her feelings in every possible way; but somehow it did not seem to Larry as if she were as close to him as Louise, to whom he kept turning with obvious affection and without restraint of any kind. Perhaps that was part of the tragedy of Pierre de Chanet's life—that his niece was really dearer to him than his daughter and that he would have been happier if he could have claimed the nearer relationship. But it could be only one part, of course—the terrible dual loss he had sustained in the death of his only son and of his wife would account for a great deal more. Not everything, though. Larry did not know why he felt so sure of this, but he did. Perhaps Pierre had hoped for several sons, which would have been quite natural; perhaps he had not only been deeply disappointed because there was only one, but unable to rise above the realization that, had there been three or four, it was improbable that he would have lost them all. Larry did not hazard any further guesses. But, inconsequentially, he remembered that Pierre had spoken twice of Cary Vincent—and that each time, brief as the comment had been, it had been deeply moving.

As if he divined that Larry was thinking about him and wished to divert these thoughts, Pierre remarked that perhaps they had better go in to dinner at the end of the current drink—after all, this was an occasion that called for champagne and they must not dull their taste for that. So they left the drawing room and passed through the hall into the great library, which Larry had not seen before, and from there to the original kitchen which, for the last few generations, had served as a dining room. An enormous hooded fireplace covered all one side of it; and, close to this, a small refectory table had been drawn up, leaving the center of the room spaciously open. A fire, kindled from small, neat pieces of wood, was burning on the hearth; and the great copper utensils, with which the remaining three sides of the room were hung, caught and reflected the light from this and from the sconces interspersed among the burnished basins and skillets and saucepans. An arrangement of spring flowers, in a large copper bowl, formed the centerpiece of the table and two smaller bowls, correspondingly filled, stood near either end. The service plates, similar to those Larry had seen on the *dressoir,* were more noticeable for quaintness of design than delicacy of texture; but the silverware was massive and crested and the crystal finely etched. Two decanters, which matched the goblets in pattern, were filled with wine, ruby colored in one case, topaz colored in the other; and as Pierre asked Larry his preference, he remarked that both were the product of the Monteregard vineyard and that he hoped his nephew would feel like sampling both—if not that evening, then all in good time.

"I am sure you had sole for lunch, and veal," he remarked. "So we have tried to vary the menu a little tonight, and let you begin with our own favorite *pot-au-feu,* in whose concoction we think our aged Alphonsine excels, and then go straight on to our duckling, of which we are also rather proud. Therefore, the red wine is quite in order, from the beginning through the salad. Later there will be a soufflé, for which we may have to wait a few minutes—Alphonsine can take no chances on the length of time we may talk; but I believe you will feel it worth waiting for. The champagne will come on with that and afterward, of course, the cognac—that is inevitable in these parts. Incidentally, it might interest you to go to the city from which this most noble of liquors takes its name. It is not far from here—just far enough, in fact, to provide a day's pleasant outing. Yes, decidedly, we must arrange such an excursion. I have several friends among the manufacturers and I really believe you would enjoy visiting both their homes and their factories which, for the most part adjoin each other, in a row facing the river. Some of them date back to the time of Francis I and many have lovely gardens. Ah—here is the *pot-au-feu!* Now tell me frankly what you think of it, Larry, and if it is not to your taste, we will find you something else."

Indeed it was to his taste, Larry answered, feeling the reply inadequate. He felt the same way about his praise of the glowing wine, the crusty bread, the succulent duck, the frothy soufflé—in fact, everything he mentioned. He felt even more strongly about the things he did not mention—the fragrant flowers, the warm fire, the soft candlelight, the gleaming copper; most strongly of all about the growing attraction which Pierre de Chanet had for him, and the tenderness, fast becoming a tumult, which Louise had awakened. Of course nothing could ever be quite perfect, he told himself; and this time it was Janine's attitude which disturbed his sense of well-being and brought a little bitterness to his brimming cup of happiness. She had crossed herself and murmured something, presumably a grace, as she sat down, and the action might have been a touching one if it had been differently performed; as it was, Larry could not help feeling that it was a deliberate rebuke to her father's conviviality, just as her exaggerated mourning had been a rebuke to his full-dress uniform. Once seated, she had kept crumbling her bread into little pieces, occasionally putting a morsel into her mouth. She tasted her soup, but she ate almost nothing else; and when her father asked her, solicitously, if she were not feeling well, she reminded him that it was a long while since she had had any appetite. She did not decline to drink a toast when the champagne was served, but Larry felt she might almost better have done so, for she raised her glass unsmilingly and barely touched it with her lips. Then, soon after coffee and cognac were brought into the library, she asked her father if he would excuse her, this time with the reminder that ever since the beginning of Lent, she had spent every evening at prayer in the chapel.

"I had thought that perhaps, since this is Larry's first night here—" Pierre began, in the same gentle, almost careful way that he had spoken to her right along. But Janine interrupted him.

"I shall, of course, include Larry in my prayers. However, with your permission, *mon père*—"

He rose, kissed her forehead and stood watching her as she accepted, without returning, an embrace from Louise, and bowed to Larry. When she left the room, instead of sitting down again immediately, Pierre glanced from his niece to his nephew, and then let his gaze rest affectionately, first on one and then on the other.

"You must both make allowances for Janine," he said. "The young —especially the female young—do not know how to make a companion of grief. They treat it like an enemy and so, of course, it becomes one. Fortunately, you do not know any of this from experience, as yet; but take my word for it. Janine is really suffering and I am afraid this makes her seem a little self-centered. Well, we will not talk about that any more—in fact, I do not think that you two should remain here any longer, chatting with a dull old man who prefers a comfortable fireside to a moonlit garden. Get yourself a wrap of some sort, *chérie,* and then take this *mauvais sujet* out of my way, so that I can read some naughty novel in peace."

"But you will tell us the name of the naughty novel, so that we can read it ourselves at some time, won't you, Uncle Pierre?" Louise inquired archly from the threshold.

"Perhaps. If you will promise not to read it aloud to each other. That I could not countenance. You must admit that I have already shown myself very broad minded, in suggesting an evening stroll."

Louise laughed and ran off to get her wrap. Larry stood very still for a moment, studying the deep-cut motto above the stone mantel. It read:

FIDE—FIDELITATE—FORTITUDINE

He was conscious of Pierre's eyes upon him as he did so and then of the older man's arm around him again.

"We have our standards, too, you see," he said, "though I'm afraid we don't always live up to them."

"Does anyone?"

"Perhaps not. But some of us come closer than others. And all of us come closer than if we were without any—even the worst of us."

"Uncle Pierre," Larry burst out, "you don't know what it's meant to me—having you welcome me the way you did, making me feel like one of the family. I've been away from Louisiana a long time and—well, I guess I must have been getting more homesick than I realized. Anyhow—" He stopped, swallowing hard. "And now, letting Louise go out with me," he managed to add, "I—I know it's very unusual, in France, for the guardian of a girl like her to—to—"

"It's not unusual, in France or anywhere else, for a man of average intelligence to see straight enough to size up a given situation," Pierre answered. "Probably I don't need to tell you that this will be the first time Louise has ever been out alone with a man. But we have an old saying, 'Bon grain fait bon pain'—good grain makes good bread. Well, I didn't need to translate—you speak French almost as well as I do. I knew your—I knew both your parents. I knew your grandmother and your grandfather, too. No, I don't need the reminder I know you'd rather not give me that Clyde Batchelor really isn't your grandfather. You're the child of his spirit, and sometimes such a one counts for even more than a child of the flesh." He paused, and again Larry thought of the impression he had received earlier in the evening that it was Louise and not Janine whom Pierre loved best in the world. "I know that you and Louise will be very happy together in the garden, this evening," he said. "And I know, too, that she will be as safe there with you as she would be here, with me. Later—some other day, I mean, of course—you will probably visit the grottoes together. But even then—" He dropped his hand and turned. "Ah—there you are, my dear. A very wise choice, that little gray fur cape. It is still chilly, after the sun goes down. I shall sit here, reading my naughty novel, till you come in, and then perhaps we may all have a nightcap together. But do not stay out too long. The aged need more sleep than the young."

That was the way it had been and now Larry lay thinking about all this as he watched the sunlight come streaming through the casements, flooding the room with its warmth and its brilliance. He was quite content to stay where he was—for the time being. Of course before long he would want to get up and go downstairs and find Louise. But first he wanted to relive every moment they had spent together from the time of their meeting in the forest to the time when they had bade each other good-by in their uncle's study.

They had not meant to stay in the garden so late. But somehow the stroll from the colonnade to the fountain had taken longer than they expected. Then they had sat down to rest a few minutes, not because they were tired, but because it seemed the natural thing to do. Once they were seated, there seemed to be many, many things that it was natural they should want to say to each other; and by and by, it seemed natural that their hands should meet, and that they should sit with their fingers intertwined, not talking any more, but in an even more blessed communion of silence. Finally Larry, looking into Louise's eyes, knew that he wanted to kiss her—more than he had ever wanted to do anything else in his life; knew, too, that she wanted to have him do so. But because she was what she was and what he wanted her to be, and not merely because Pierre had trusted her to him, he also knew that he must not do that until he had told Pierre, before he told Louise, what she meant to him and had asked for permission to marry her.

So they had come back to the study, not thwarted through the consciousness of that unshared kiss, but happy in the promise of it, and in the mutual understanding, which neither had put into words, of the reasons why it was still a promise and not an actuality. Pierre had laid aside his naughty novel, and looked from one to the other, and Larry had felt certain that their uncle not only knew how it was with them, but that he had known, from the outset, just how it was going to be. He did not reproach them for staying out so long; but he said he had found, when it got close to midnight, that he was growing thirsty, so he had had his drink without waiting for them, and now perhaps they had all better be saying good night. He would go to Larry's room with him again, to make sure everything had been prepared for his comfort; and when Larry protested, Pierre had said nonsense, he was going up anyway, for it was high time old men like himself were in bed. So they had all mounted the marble staircase together and, when they reached the top of it, Louise had thrown her arms around Pierre and hugged him hard, instead of standing solemnly before him, waiting for him to kiss her forehead, as Janine had done. Then, before she turned and ran down the long corridor, in the opposite direction from the one Pierre and Larry were taking, she had given Larry her hand and looked into his eyes again, and the promise of the kiss shone in her gaze, even more brightly than it had before.

After that, Pierre had paused at his own doorway and told Larry to come back and knock on it, if he found that everything was not all right in his room. Then Larry knew that his uncle was not going on with him, after all, because, in that case, they would have started to talk about Louise, and they had already said as much as they should to each other, for one evening, especially the first evening they had ever spent together. But Larry knew it would be all right to talk to Pierre about Louise the next day, in fact, that Pierre was expecting him to do so; he went on to bed and quickly to sleep, in spite of his joyous excitement. Now he had slept for hours and hours and it was morning again and the sun was streaming into his room and he was head over heels in love and it was a wonderful world.

 CHAPTER XXVIII

LARRY was still rapturously daydreaming when there was a knock on his door and Léonard, the houseman who had served dinner the night before, came into the room, flourishing a tray.

"M. le Marquis felt sure M. le Lieutenant would wish to have coffee and crescents in his room," he observed, setting down the tray even more jauntily than he had carried it. "Especially as such service is not too customary in the Army," he added with a broad grin.

"You're right, it certainly isn't. . . . I take it you've had some military experience yourself."

"As what able-bodied Frenchman has not, *mon Lieutenant!* Ah, well! The bad years are over now and good ones ahead—or at any rate, so we may hope!" Léonard moved the coffeepot slightly to one side, bringing a vase into better view. "Alphonsine prepared the breakfast, of course, but Mademoiselle picked the flowers and placed them on the tray," he remarked objectively. The grin had disappeared and his manner was now entirely impassive. "I thought possibly it might be of interest to M. le Lieutenant to know this. And I was almost forgetting: M. le Marquis told me to say that he hopes M. le Lieutenant will enjoy his breakfast at his leisure. But later in the morning, M. le Marquis would be very pleased to see M. le Lieutenant in the study."

"Thank you, Léonard. Tell him I'll be there inside of an hour."

So he guessed immediately, Larry said to himself, as Léonard, grinning again, saluted smartly and marched away. *Well, I'm glad he has. There's no time to lose—two days out of ten gone already, and I've got to allow another to get back to camp. Why, that gives me only a week here!* It was all very well to talk about breakfasting at leisure, but his feeling of lazy contentment was gone now. He swallowed the coffee and bit into the crescents almost unmindful of their excellence, then shaved, showered and dressed at top speed. It was well under an hour when he presented himself at the door of the study and Pierre, who obviously had not expected him quite so soon, was deep in conversation with a thickset, black-bearded man whom he introduced to Larry as Robert Sabadelle, his head forester.

"No, don't go," he said, as Larry, somewhat confused because of his involuntary intrusion, murmured an apology and turned to leave. "Robert and I had finished with almost everything that required discussion, in any case. Incidentally, it might interest you to go out with him sometime and see him in action. The beauty of our woods is not wholly accidental—we must give him credit for part of it." Then, when the forester, beaming with pride at this praise, had bowed his way out of the room, turning his soft hat round and round in his ruddy hands as he did so, Pierre went on, "We have eight families living in cottages on this place, besides a few unattached bachelors who are quartered in the tower. We try to keep the unattached spinsters quartered in the chateau proper, but sometimes the younger ones stray—well, that is neither here nor there. What I started to say was, that what with foresters and gamekeepers, gardeners and vineyardists, shepherds and stablemen, all needing to see me, or imagining that they do, I'm on call most of the time. Fortunately, Louise is very adept at running the house, considering her youth, so at least I do not have the cook and the butler and the rest of the domestic staff charging in and out of here early and late, and I have given instructions that you and I are not to be disturbed. . . . I trust you slept well?"

"Very well, thank you."

"Which goes to show you are young, healthy and essentially an Anglo-Saxon, in spite of your Creole heritage. Otherwise you would have been much too excited to sleep, judging from appearances when you came in last night—or did I misjudge them?"

"No, of course you didn't. You knew I'd fallen in love with Louise at first sight. But I wasn't so much excited as—uplifted. And I hope that doesn't sound like a silly thing to say, because it happens to be true."

"No, it doesn't sound like a silly thing to say and I know it's true. Sit down, Larry. You and I've got to talk this over, you know."

"Yes, I know," Larry answered, obeying instructions. "I was going to ask you if we couldn't, but you got ahead of me, by sending for me before I had a chance. I'm sorry. I did sleep like a top last night, but this morning, while I was waking up, I did a lot of lazy and very pleasant daydreaming. I didn't realize it was so late until Léonard came with the coffee and your summons."

"It wasn't a summons. It was an invitation—an invitation for you to ask Louise's hand in marriage, if that is what you want to do."

"You know it's what I want more than anything else in the world."

467

"Well, the idea isn't displeasing to me, either. If it had been, I wouldn't have sent you and Louise out into the moonlight together." Pierre paused and smiled so engagingly that Larry who, up to that moment, had spoken with the utmost seriousness, could not help smiling back, his heart warming more and more toward his host. "However, I think I should warn you that I am not the only person to please," Pierre continued.

"But I honestly believe that Louise—"

"There isn't the slightest doubt of it. In fact, she has told me so already—she succeeded in getting to me before Robert." Pierre smiled again, and this time Larry's heart seemed to turn over in his breast. "However, Louise is not of age and I am not her legal guardian—only a sort of foster father to her. I think you know—at any rate you should —that her mother—my niece Josephine—remarried shortly after the death of her first husband, Jehan de Courville. Louise's stepfather, Paul Carrere, has never shown much interest in her so far. But he is sure to reveal some, when the question of her marriage arises. In fact, I'm under the impression that he has been making some plans for her himself, and he is a very powerful person—which means that he would like to have still more power. It never fails. The right alliance for his stepdaughter might give it to him."

"But you wouldn't sacrifice Louise to the ambition of some revolting old man!" Larry exclaimed, his happiness suddenly engulfed in horror.

"Not willingly. Not without a struggle. But I am warning you that there may be a struggle. And probably, in all fairness, I should add that Paul Carrere is not a horrible old man. He is very personable and very gifted and he is about my age, like Josephine. Those two marriages of my father certainly made our family relationship very confusing. . . . Speaking of my father's marriages, my own mother is still living. In a sense, she is the matriarch of the family. The wishes of a woman in that position carry great weight in France."

"But surely there couldn't be any reasons why she should raise objections! I should think it was a lot more likely that she'd be very pleased, too. After all, Cindy Lou was her home once. If Louise married me the marquise might feel that it was coming back into her family, in a way. At least—"

"At least, it looks like that to you. But unfortunately, my mother and yours were not especially congenial. Not that I am blaming either, you understand. It was just one of those things."

"Why, Dad showed me the letters my mother wrote when she was visiting here and she said she admired the marquise very much!"

"Yes, I believe she did—then. Or perhaps she was in a mood to admire almost everyone and everything. She was on her honeymoon, you know." Pierre picked up a paper cutter and began to balance it on his fingers. The gesture did not seem like an indication of restlessness;

on the contrary, like everything else about him, it betokened the ability to give the impression of ease under almost any circumstances, the refusal to permit grimness or even grief to engulf urbanity. He was now wearing gray tweeds, with only a black tie and a black arm band as concessions to mourning custom, and his face was less drawn than it had been the night before; even the lines around his mouth looked less deep. "However, later on, when my mother and I went to Louisiana, the spring before you were born, she and Cary apparently rubbed each other the wrong way, on one or two occasions," he went on casually. "I wasn't present, so I don't know exactly what happened. My mother never told me and naturally I didn't ask."

"My mother didn't tell you, either?"

"No. Remember I never saw her after that spring, Larry."

"But surely you don't think merely because my mother and yours weren't congenial, as you put it, the marquise would object to my marrying Louise!"

"I don't know. I hope not—though I believe the sort of alliance Paul Carrere has in mind would have more appeal for her. In any case, we shall very soon find out."

Pierre laid down the paper cutter and straightened the big, leather-bound blotter on the desk. "It is not very often that a well-brought-up French girl attempts to circumvent her father," he said. "But Janine has done exactly that. She visited me this morning, even earlier than Louise, and informed me that she had written her grandmother who, as usual, is in Paris, and Josephine, who is also there, urging them to come here at once. She sent these letters off by the first post, before she told me about them. It seems she was very much shocked because you and Louise stayed in the garden so late."

"*Very much shocked!* Why, there wasn't a word we said or a thing we did that—"

"I know, Larry. And I think, down deep in her heart, Janine knows it, too. But she is in a very strange—a very sad state. My poor wife was also subject to such periods of depression. If she had not been. . . ."

Pierre left the sentence unfinished and Larry did not attempt to complete it for him or to answer him. If Armande had not been the victim of acute melancholia, of course she would not have committed suicide, Larry realized that. Probably she would never have left her husband, either, if it had not been for a distorted outlook on their relations to each other and on life in general. Yet it was hard for the boy, who remembered her only as kindly and beautiful and pleasure loving, to visualize her in the same light that he saw Janine. However, Pierre apparently saw them both clearly and turned the same unflinching gaze upon himself.

"I am afraid these periods of depression have been largely my fault. I have not been very successful, Larry, either as a husband or as a

469

father. That is, I certainly did not make my wife happy, and I have not made my daughter any happier, though it was different with my son. He and I spoke the same language. We were very close to each other." Pierre glanced down at his desk again, and Larry saw that his eyes were fixed on the photograph of a fair boy, who looked too young to be a soldier, though he was in unform, and whose expression, like that of Louise's, was singularly candid and cheerful. "When I say the same language, I am not thinking about French and English," Pierre continued. "Of course we are all bilingual, and even if we had not been, that would not have made much difference. I doubt whether there would ever be any difficulties between you and Louise, even if you had begun your acquaintance without the benefit of a common tongue. I had something else in mind."

"I know you did," Larry answered. Momentarily, his sympathy for Pierre had engulfed his dismay at the unexpected prospect of obstacles to his suit.

"Well, Louise and I speak the same language, too," Pierre said, turning away from the picture. His first words had been obviously spoken with an effort; but as he went on, his voice sounded quite natural again. "And I'm sure that everything will come out all right in the end. Meanwhile, I must give you two reminders, which will probably seem to you contradictory: first, you and Louise are not engaged, nor can you be, until there has been a family council on the subject; second, my mother, my niece and my niece's husband, the cabinet minister, will probably all be arriving here within two or three days, and after their arrival your style will be very much cramped—to borrow a good American expression. There is nothing, as far as I am aware, to cramp it in the meantime—except your own sense of the fitness of things. I have told Janine that I am greatly displeased by her lack of cordiality to a guest and a kinsman; I think you will find her less antagonistic from now on, especially as she has done, or tried to do, all the harm she can for the present. I shall not use up your time with any more long talks, and Louise tells me that she has unlimited leisure on her hands. I think, if you look for her, you may find her in the library, and as she is not an especially avid reader, she will probably be very glad to take a short walk before lunch. And, by the way, you might give her this— from me, of course."

He picked up a small box, covered in threadbare velvet, which lay beside Pierrot's picture, and handed it to Larry. "If I am not mistaken, the heart-shaped brooch inside this box belonged to a very distinguished ancestress of yours," he said. "At all events, the tale told of it is that it was given to such a lady by the King of England when she went with her young husband, as a bride, to claim a royal grant in Virginia. It was handed down, from one generation to another, until it came to your grandmother. Then, with great generosity, she gave it to my fiancée, instead of keeping it for her own daughter. Now I should like to give it to Louise rather than Janine, and I think my poor wife would have felt the same way, or of course I should not do so. Who knows? Perhaps it will prove to be a luck piece, and that someday your bride will wear it at Cindy Lou, which is where it belongs."

 CHAPTER XXIX

PIERRE WAS right: his mother, his niece and his niece's husband all arrived at Monteregard within three days.

The marquise was the first to put in an appearance, as the cabinet minister was detained in Paris by an important meeting, and she was not willing to await his departure, which, as a matter of fact, his wife did most reluctantly. As soon as the marquise was settled in the apartments at Monteregard which were always kept in readiness for her, though she so seldom occupied them, she sent for her son and subjected him to a tirade which became increasingly vehement when he listened to it with the air of detached indifference which had always infuriated her. After she could think of nothing more which could possibly be said to Pierre, she demanded that Larry be brought into her presence and, after inspecting him through a lorgnette, as if he were some kind of a repulsive curiosity, she began to bombard him with questions, most of them entirely superfluous.

"So you're Cary Vincent's son?"

"Yes, madame."

"And you've lived at my beautiful old home all your life?"

"Well, not quite. I wasn't born there. I was about six months old when my parents died. Since then I've lived with my grandfather, except of course, this last year and a half, when I've been in the Army."

"You don't mean to tell me that your grandfather is still living?"

"Yes, I'm thankful to say he is."

"He must be a terribly decrepit old man by now."

"He's over eighty, but he's not in the least decrepit. He still rides around the plantations every day—at any rate, he was still doing so when I went to camp in the fall of '17 and he's never written about having stopped."

"He probably doesn't want to tell you. Or perhaps he can't. Senility sometimes sets in very suddenly."

471

"I'm sure that if anything like that had happened, Father Le Grand would have written to tell me about it."

"Father Le Grand? Who pray, is Father Le Grand?"

"He's the priest at Convent who married my father and mother and baptized and confirmed me. He and my grandfather are great friends."

"I thought your grandfather was an atheist. I can't imagine a priest being friendly with him."

"Well, he is."

Larry's tone was even and his manner civil, but both gave the same impression of detachment and indifference which had so infuriated the marquise on the part of Pierre. As a matter of fact, the principal effect she had produced on Larry had been one of deep disgust. He had expected to be somewhat overpowered by her; instead, he saw nothing awe inspiring about her—a wizened old woman, with too much rouge on her withered cheeks and too many rings on her clawlike hands, whose fussy dress gapped open to disclose a shriveled neck and whose curly black wig had slipped a little to one side, revealing wisps of mousy hair underneath. She was a great one to talk about decrepitude and senility—why, she must be getting on toward eighty herself, and she certainly did not carry her years with either vigor or dignity! When Pierre had spoken about the "matriarch of the family" Larry had visualized someone quite different—a stern, forbidding sort of woman, but a person to be respected as well as feared. If he and Pierre and Louise among them could not get the better of this vapid old hag, they did not deserve to. But of course they would. . . .

"So you came here hoping to marry my granddaughter?" the marquise inquired sarcastically, rousing Larry from his brief reverie.

"No. I came here to see my aunt and meet my cousins and my uncle. I hadn't heard about Aunt Armande and Pierrot. Of course if I had, I wouldn't have barged in so unceremoniously. But I'd have tried to come, sometime before I left France, to see Janine and Uncle Pierre. I didn't know about Louise beforehand—that is, I must have heard about her in a vague way. But as she and Uncle Pierre both admit, the various relationships in the De Chanet family are awfully confusing to an outsider. I never paid much attention when I heard them discussed."

"Well, you hope to marry her now, I understand."

"Louise de Courville? Yes, I do. But she's not your granddaughter, is she? I think I have got relationships straightened out enough now to know that."

"To all intents and purposes, she is my granddaughter—quite as much as you are Clyde Batchelor's grandson."

"Oh! Well no, I didn't realize that."

"Which is quite natural, because she isn't," Pierre remarked equably.

"I'm not talking to you at present, Pierre. You and I have finished our conversation. In fact, I do not see that any useful purpose will be served by having you remain in the room any longer."

"As far as that goes, I don't see that any useful purpose will be served by having Larry remain any longer. You already knew the answers to all the questions you've asked him and you know the answers to those you still intend to ask him."

"No, I do not. No one has told me what Larry has to offer Louise—if anything. So far I'm forced to conclude that he's been presumptuous, as well as precipitate."

"I'm not sure I understand just what you mean, madame—that is, about being presumptuous. I'll admit I was precipitate. But my leave is for only ten days."

"And you imagined you could leave Monteregard, at the end of ten days, as the accepted suitor of Louise de Courville?"

"Why, yes, I did. In fact, I've been encouraged to think I might."

"*Encouraged!* By whom?"

"By Louise."

"And by me," Pierre interposed quietly. "I'll admit I haven't given much thought to practical matters. They haven't greatly concerned me. But since they concern you, *ma mère,* I wouldn't say Larry's prospects were so bad."

"I suppose you mean he'll be his grandfather's heir. Well, I haven't forgotten about the paltry sum he paid me for Cindy Lou. No doubt it's worth more than that now, just as it was then. But it isn't worth enough to make Larry Vincent a desirable *parti.*"

"Perhaps you've forgotten about Victoria, madame. That's mine already. My grandfather gave it to me on my twenty-first birthday. And he and I own a steamboat line together."

"A steamboat line! *A steamboat line!* I thought Clyde Batchelor sold that, after it nearly bankrupted him."

"He sold one, but now we've got another. And it's doing very well indeed. Of course I couldn't surround Louise with the magnificence she lives in here. But after all, this doesn't belong to her, does it?"

"The places you're talking about won't, either. I know that much about Louisiana law. They'd be your separate and paraphernal property, because you owned them before your marriage."

"I don't own Cindy Lou yet. I hope I shan't for a long time after my marriage. Because when I do, it'll mean my grandfather's dead. But then it will be community property."

"Bah! The next time you hear from Clyde Batchelor, it'll probably be indirectly, through his executor."

"I don't agree with you, madame. But if you really think there is any such danger, why not consent to an immediate wedding? As I just pointed out, any property I acquired after my marriage would belong to Louise as much as to me. So if we were married before the end of my leave, she would be completely safeguarded from the financial point of view and you could be quite easy in your mind."

Pierre laughed outright. "*Touché, ma mère!*" he said lightly. "I think Larry has you there. What do you say? Shall we set the wheels in motion at once? Of course there are certain formalities. But what is the use of having a chapel under your own roof, if these cannot be expedited, on occasion?"

"I think you must have lost your mind, Pierre. And between you and Larry, I am completely worn out. I feel the need of a long rest and shall not come down to dinner."

"You certainly won that last round," Pierre observed to Larry, as they went down the corridor together. "And I imagine you are not feeling very sorry that you were at least partly responsible for my mother's exhaustion. But do not be too hard on her. When she was young, an extremely small waist was considered a sign of great beauty— a wasp waist, it was frequently called. To achieve it, a lady went through all kinds of tortures from tight lacing, which compressed her inner organs. In the process, her disposition sometimes suffered also and became waspish in its turn. I am afraid that is what happened in this case."

"I can't for the life of me see why a small waist should be considered beautiful."

"Of course you can't. But that is because the girl you are in love with wears dresses as straight as a chemise from shoulder to hem, and thus sets your standards of the female form divine. What is more, the hemline is sufficiently high to permit a very satisfactory view of her shapely legs, which I assure you would not have been the case in the days of tight lacing—you would have been lucky if you had caught sight of anything above the ankle, before your marriage. What is more, if you tried to take your fiancée in your arms, you would have encircled stiff stays, you would instantly have been repulsed and you would have been able to get very little feeling of a warm, vital body underneath. I am told that now, even in quite conservative circles, young girls of unimpeachable character permit their accepted suitors to embrace them —with discretion, of course."

Larry did not answer. To his chagrin, he realized that he was blushing, for he could feel his face and neck growing hot. But at least it was not the heat of anger. He had been furiously angry before the session with the marquise was over, but he had managed to conceal this—or at any rate believed that he had. If he had been obliged to choose between the two, he would much rather have betrayed slightly guilty embarrassment than rage.

"However, as I reminded you before, you and Louise are not engaged yet," Pierre went on serenely. "What is more, if my mother accepts your challenge, you never will be, for you will be married before there is any time for an engagement. Well, I suppose we must await the arrival of Paul and Josephine before we go any further into this matter of marriage. But that gives you another twenty-four hours' reprieve from dismissal, at all events."

M. and Mme Carrere arrived the following afternoon and, from lunch time on, Larry waited in his room, expecting a summons as prompt as the one he had received from the marquise. But hour after hour passed, while he strode impatiently up and down or stared almost unseeingly out of the casements, and still no one sent for him. He tried to read and could not; but at last he managed to focus his gaze, if not his attention, on a beautiful white swan which was gliding over the reflecting pool, followed by her cygnets. He had not noticed them before, but that was no sign they had not been there; after his first breathless glimpse of the gardens, he had been far too preoccupied with Louise to be conscious of other attractions.

At last, when he had waited so long that he had begun to imagine all sorts of unlikely calamities, Léonard brought him a note on a crested tray. He tore it open and read it avidly.

Dear Larry:

You will be wondering if we have all stabbed each other in the heat of argument. It is not quite as serious as that, though from your point of view, I can well understand that the elimination of everyone but Louise—with the possible exception of myself—from the scene might appear an unmitigated blessing. Unlike *maman,* Paul and Josephine wished to talk first with Louise. They did not invite me to be present at this interview, but after they had dismissed her—I think in well-concealed despair—they sent for me and I was able to form a pretty fair idea of what had just taken place. My guess that Paul already had some sort of alliance in mind for Louise was correct—a very wealthy and well-born young diplomat Raoul de Bonneville, just now attached to the Foreign Office on the Quai D'Orsay, but scheduled for a post at Rome in the near future. I am sure they imagined that Louise would find such brilliant prospects irresistible, and that they were as much surprised as chagrined by her complete lack of appreciation, and her stubborn reiteration that if she could not marry you she would not marry anyone. Their attitude toward me was one of cold courtesy and even chillier criticism; they blamed me for inviting you here in the first place and for aiding and abetting your suit afterward. I hope you will not feel I failed you when I tell you my reply: that I did not invite you here, and that your suit needed no aiding and abetting from me, since you and Louise fell in love with each other so fast that everything was as good as settled between you by the time you emerged from the woods and reached the chateau. Of course I added that, though I did not expect you, your visit was the most welcome one we had had in a long while, as far as I was concerned, and that I wholeheartedly supported your proposal of marriage. So now you and Louise and I are all in the bad graces of the Carreres together, as we are in my mother's. But you need not fear that you are in for another scene, such as you had with her. Paul and Josephine will be exceedingly polite to you, because it is part of their code to be civil, even when they have murder in their hearts, and I do not think they have quite reached that stage, even yet. You will find us all assembled in the drawing room for drinks before dinner, as usual, and if you will take my advice, you will act as if you were a kinsman, taking his reception for granted, rather than an uneasy swain. Have patience, I still believe *tout s'arrangera,* though not tonight.

Yours, with affection,
PIERRE DE CHANET

So everything would arrange itself, would it, though not tonight? A likely chance! Never had the complacent French phrase, which Larry had always hated, seemed so irritating and so misleading. And how in heaven's name was he to have patience—with five days of his leave already gone and only five more ahead of him, the last of which must be spent in getting back to camp? Pierre knew better than to give such assurances and advice! Yet, as Larry reread the letter, he was increasingly and ungrudgingly aware of the kindliness with which it was permeated. "Yours, with affection, Pierre de Chanet." Yes, there was no doubt about it, his uncle was his friend, and his best chance of success lay in following the lead that had been given him. Since nothing had been said about presenting himself sooner, Larry gathered that he was not expected to put in an appearance until just before dinner and that, above all, an attempt to see Louise alone would be very unwise at this juncture. Glancing at his wrist watch for at least the fiftieth time, he saw that he still had another hour of involuntary seclusion and, sitting down beside the window, he scribbled one of his half-punctuated, unparagraphed letters to his grandfather. It was longer than usual, partly because he had not written at all since he had left camp and was suddenly and guiltily aware of this; partly because he really wanted to tell Clyde everything about his visit at Monteregard, including his newborn love for Louise; and partly because he felt the driving need of occupation. He was still writing, at last absorbed in what he was doing, when Léonard knocked at his door again and said that M. le

Marquis had sent word to say that drinks would be a little earlier than usual, because, with more of the family present, more time would be required to enjoy them before dinner.

Grateful for the warning, Larry pushed aside the sheets on which he had been scribbling, washed his hands and went downstairs, reaching the drawing room just as Pierre entered it from the study, but not before the marquise, who had evidently recovered from her exhaustion, was already ensconced in a thronelike chair. Far from giving her a regal aspect, this made her appear more artificial, more shriveled and more venomous than ever. She barely acknowledged Larry's cool, "Good evening, madame"; but when M. and Mme Carrere came in, accompanied by Louise, they shook hands with every appearance of cordiality and at once entered into animated conversation with him. Even though this was only surface courtesy, it was infinitely better than the unveiled animosity of the marquise; and if Larry had not realized that, at heart, the new arrivals were quite as hostile as she was, he would not have been too unfavorably impressed by them. Mme Carrere was beautifully turned out, and her fine figure showed off her perfect clothes to great advantage; and though her complexion and her hair had unquestionably both received expert touching up, her coloring still retained much of the same quality that made Louise's so lovely. M. Carrere's dinner jacket was a little too tight for him, and he did not wear it with the careless grace which Pierre managed to effect, whatever he put on; but, on the whole, the cabinet officer, though not as tall as his wife and considerably broader, carried himself well; and his geniality, if assumed, was an excellent imitation of the real thing. Janine, who was the last of the family to arrive, was accompanied by a plump priest, whose appearance was actually jolly. The marquise, after acknowledging his presence with scarcely more ceremony than she had Larry's, beckoned to her son and spoke to him in a stage whisper.

"I thought this was to be a family party, Pierre. You did not tell me that you had invited outsiders."

"Oh, but M. le Curé is hardly an outsider, *ma mère*! I thought it would be pleasanter to have an even number at dinner . . . also, that possibly our good priest might tell us whether he could waive some of the usual formalities, in the event that Larry and Louise should decide to get married at once."

"In the event that *Larry and Louise* should decide! Really, Pierre, you are becoming more and more insufferable every minute! This boy must have you bewitched, just as his—"

Larry had caught most of her speech. But the end of it was suddenly muffled, almost as if a silencing hand had been placed across her hideous painted mouth; and though of course nothing of the sort had happened, Larry saw that Pierre had bent over her and, while his face was hidden, something about the quick gesture seemed to bespeak threatening anger. At all events, her sharp words became an incoherent mumbling and presently trailed away into silence. Before anything else could be said, Léonard opportunely announced dinner.

The small refectory table, cozily drawn up before the hearth, had been supplanted by a large round one, set in the center of the room, the peasant pottery by fine porcelain, adorned with the family crest. The tablecloth and napkins were also crested, and the latter were so large that as Larry unfolded his he thought at first a mistake must have been made somewhere along the line, and that this was also a *nappe,* not a *serviette.* The marquise was duly seated at the head of the table, with her son opposite her, the cabinet officer at her right and the priest at her left. Larry, securely wedged in between Josephine and Janine, thought she seemed in a somewhat chastened mood; and this gradually mellowed into something approaching urbanity, possibly because her dinner companions were extremely gallant in their bearing toward her. Janine, as usual, spoke very little and never on her own initiative; Josephine, on the contrary, chatted along in a merry, effortless way, and again Larry was conscious of an underlying resemblance between her and Louise. Twenty-five years before, she must have looked and acted much as her daughter did now; what, besides age, he wondered, had brought about such a change in her? Then suddenly he thought he knew: she had not married for love, but for "practical reasons," and these had not been cogent enough, after all, to keep her and Jehan de Courville together; they had drifted apart, just like Armande and Pierre. He remembered another letter, one of those that his aunt had written after her hasty return to France, in which she spoke of Josephine's second marriage—"to a cabinet officer with whom she had long been on very good terms." Well then, she had probably been Paul Carrere's mistress before she became his wife, and that sort of furtive relationship must inevitably have had a corroding effect on a type of beauty—and of character—in which candor and single-heartedness were predominating factors. Her small talk, her chic, her faultless manner all lost their attraction for him; he understood why Louise preferred to spend most of her time at Monteregard. . . .

Alphonsine had prepared a perfect dinner and Léonard, wearing livery instead of a white coat and aided by a second houseman whom Larry had not seen before, served it with silent skill. There were no awkward pauses and Larry was obliged to admit to himself that he had no sensation of strain. This dinner, he supposed, was a fair example of what *savoir-faire,* combined with good breeding, could do to save a situation—though as far as the marquise was concerned, nothing could ever persuade him that she had been to the manner born; he was convinced it was in spite of her, rather than because of her, that everything proceeded so smoothly. He was beginning to feel an aversion for her which amounted almost to antipathy. It was no wonder, he told himself, that she and his mother "had not been congenial." How could there have been congeniality between Cary Vincent and the erstwhile Dorothée Labouisse, whom he had never once heard extolled in the locality where she had long lived? He decided that when he reached home again he would ask a few questions about her. Why, his grandfather should be able to answer them! After all, Clyde Batchelor had bought Cindy Lou from her. He must have seen something of her, and heard more, in the course of this transaction. . . .

Despite the absence of strain, Larry was relieved when the marquise gave the signal to leave the dining room and Pierre, rising with her, said that, with her permission, the gentlemen would take their coffee in the library and join the ladies later in the drawing room. Since he could not be alone with Louise, and since he knew that even an attempt to talk with her lovingly in the midst of such a gathering would have been a dismal failure, Larry welcomed the prospect of being in a group of men, rather than in mixed company. After all, he had been raised by a man; he had gone to a boys' boarding school and, even before he entered the Army, he had felt more at ease with men than with women. Perhaps he would get on better with Paul Carrere and M. le Curé than he did with the marquise and with Josephine. It was certain that he understood Pierre much better than he did Janine. Louise was the one glorious exception to his lack of understanding, when it came to women—his first real love, as he felt sure she would be his last. . . .

He was soon reassured by the general tenor of conversation, which ranged from political to military subjects, with no reference, for a long while, which could possibly be construed as personal. Pierre encouraged the cabinet officer to talk about crises, real and potential, in the government, and Carrere seemed quite willing to do so. Eventually, shifting adroitly from one topic to another, Pierre began to question the priest, whose name had belatedly been disclosed as Robineaux, about conditions in the parish, to which—so Pierre said— he feared he had not paid as much attention as he should of late. Then, remarking that of course all this was to be regarded as confidential, he asked whether, in the opinion of M. le Curé, Janine really did have a vocation, or whether he thought she was merely going through a phase, like so many girls and even some boys. The priest answered guardedly; certainly Mlle Janine was very devout, but he did not need to tell M. le Marquis that this was not enough for a vocation. To be a successful nun, a certain type of disposition was also desirable, if not actually requisite. A cheerful girl, whose own character was above reproach, but who viewed the shortcomings of others with charity, even with tolerance, was really more fitted for the religious life than one who was more morose and critical. The great Teresa herself—a pattern of austerity if there ever was one—had prayed to be delivered from gloomy saints. And, if M. le Marquis would forgive him for saying this, Père Robineaux felt that Mlle Janine was so inclined to see the dark side of things that perhaps. . . .

"I could not possibly be more in accord with your views," Pierre said heartily. "In fact, I'm inclined to believe that Janine would derive far more benefit from a love affair than from a postulancy. Do you think I could possibly be right, M. le Curé?"

"Yes indeed, quite possibly."

"She would have to be taken by storm, of course," Pierre went on, apparently warming to his subject. "But once all her false defenses were down, she might surrender very quickly. You have known of such cases, haven't you, M. le Curé?"

"Yes indeed," the priest replied again. "In fact, the surrender is—ah—apt to be almost too rapid, if I may say so. Especially in unsettled times, like the present ones."

"Exactly. I think we must be prepared for such a contingency. Now if Janine should decide, very suddenly, that she wished to be married—"

The cabinet minister made a small clicking sound, to which Pierre paid no attention. Instead, tapping the arm of his chair by way of emphasis, he leaned eagerly toward the priest.

"Let us assume, for the sake of argument, that I, as her father and legal guardian, would have no objections to this marriage and would give my wholehearted consent to it, even though my daughter were under age," he said. "And let us also assume that I would have approached M. le Maire, and found that he was disposed to be most co-operative in regard to hastening the civil ceremony. Would you, as the priest of this parish, be equally co-operative? Supposing the young man in question could not, for instance, immediately produce a baptismal certificate, would the cabled assurance, signed by the priest who performed the baptism, to the effect that he was in possession of such a document, satisfy you? Would you be willing to do away with banns? I understand that a special dispensation is sometimes given to foreign nationals who are soldiers or war workers, and who cannot be absent, for any length of time, from their posts. Of course I may be mistaken, but—"

Father Robineaux glanced hastily in the direction of Larry. He thought he was beginning to understand the drift of the marquis' comments and questions, which at first had been somewhat puzzling to him. The cabinet minister made another little clicking sound, but his fellow guests, like his host, disregarded it. Larry and M. le Curé were now smiling at each other and, though the reasons for their smiles were different, mutual good will lay back of both.

"The church should of course co-operate with the state in every

480

reasonable way," Father Robineaux said emphatically. "And in the case of our brave allies, who have done so much to rescue beautiful France from the detestable invader, the clergy, like the laity, must never lose an opportunity to show its gratitude. Of course it is also the purpose and policy of the church to—ah—safeguard young love with the proper sacraments. You may depend upon me, M. le Marquis, to serve you and yours in every way I can."

 CHAPTER XXX

"Paul is very much annoyed with you, Pierre, and I am, too. You had no business leading M. le Curé on the way you did, giving him the impression all the time that you were talking about Janine."

"It's not my fault if M. le Curé leaps to conclusions. All I did was to present a hypothetical case. Possibly the next time Larry comes here to visit he will bring a friend with him; in that event, Janine might become as much attracted to such a friend as Louise has been to Larry. It is always well to be prepared for contingencies; as Janine's father, I naturally have her interests at heart."

"You were not thinking or talking about Janine and you know it. You were thinking and talking about Louise. You have put Paul and me in a very awkward position, Pierre."

"I am sorry. I did not realize you were so easily upset. I credited you with more *savoir-faire*."

Pierre de Chanet had risen politely when his niece came into his study the morning after her arrival at Monteregard, but he had immediately resumed his seat and remained entrenched behind his desk, while regarding Josephine with a calmness not untinged with slight mockery. He now picked up his paper cutter and began to play with it, a gesture which added to her fury. Still standing upright, she confronted him.

"And I credited you with more sense," she said angrily. "If I hadn't, I wouldn't have allowed Louise to come so completely under your influence."

"Excuse me. I thought the reason you were willing Louise should spend so much time at Monteregard was not because of my good sense, but because of yours. You realized, while poor Jehan was still alive, that a *ménage à trois* is not the best sort of a home for a young girl. And after he was so opportunely killed, you realized that Paul's preferences

481

should be your first concern—also that a grown daughter constitutes something of a giveaway, as far as her mother's age is concerned. I have always admired your good sense very much, Josephine—in fact, I have often told you so. This is the first time you have ever mentioned mine. I did not suppose you thought I had any."

"I did, but I don't any more. Or any manners, either. How dare you say such things to me?"

Josephine's voice was becoming shriller and shriller. The more angry she became, the more composure Pierre displayed.

"Have I said anything that was not true?" he inquired calmly.

"It is no part of *savoir-faire* to talk the way you have been doing, whether one is telling the truth or not. You had better not mention that quality again. And since you realize that Paul's preferences are my first concern, you had better tell me how you think I'm going to meet them, in regard to this De Bonneville marriage, now that you have made it so difficult for me to do so."

"I'm not going to tell you how I think you should meet them. I'm going to tell you, most emphatically, that I think for once you should disregard them, if you are not sufficiently adroit to change them tactfully." Pierre put down the paper cutter and his manner suddenly became stern. "Listen to me, Josephine," he said, almost harshly. "You will never get Louise to marry De Bonneville now. In fact, I doubt if you could have persuaded her to do so, even before she met Larry. I think she has somehow acquired the fixed idea that love is one of the requisites—perhaps even the main requisite—for a successful marriage—possibly since she has seen one or two that were not very successful because they lacked it. Besides, I do not think that De Bonneville's type would ever have appealed to her—he is altogether too smooth a specimen to be quite real and Louise likes sincerity. Be all that as it may, she is now so deeply in love with Larry Vincent that you could not get her to so much as look at another man. If you and Paul will not let her marry him until she is of age, she will do so the day she is twenty-one."

"He may not be able to get leave the day she is twenty-one."

"Very well. Let us say for the sake of argument that he will not. I will amend my statement and say that Louise will marry him as soon after her twenty-first birthday as he is able to come for her. But I assure you I shall be very much surprised if there is any great delay. I think that at the first opportunity after his return to camp he will tell his commanding officer that he wants to get married, naming the earliest date at which his fiancée can arrange for the ceremony. And I think he will contrive to join Louise on or before that day. He is also very much in love and I think he has enough persuasive power to present his case so eloquently that no reasonable military superior of his will put obstacles in his way."

"Then the only hope you leave me is that he will encounter one who is unreasonable. Meanwhile, Paul and I will return to Paris tomorrow, taking Louise with us. I wish we were not dependent on the unspeakable train service. If we had come by car, it would have taken us longer to get here, but we could also have left as soon as we had sized up this deplorable situation."

Josephine flounced out of the study, slamming the door behind her. Pierre lighted a cigarette and, while he smoked it, pondered the situation which Josephine claimed to have "sized up." He did not consider that she had done so, and what was even more unfortunate, from his point of view, he did not feel at all sure that he could cope with it himself. However, after a few minutes' thought, he rang for Léonard and sent him to Larry with a message. When Larry appeared, in prompt response to this summons, Pierre chose his words with extreme care, while endeavoring to avoid any semblance of undue concern.

"I'm beginning to feel as though this study were the *mise-en-scène* for amateur theatricals," he said. "You know, the kind where the different characters keep coming in and going out by the same door, in such a constant stream that you do not see how they can possibly avoid bumping into each other. At the same time, the opposing forces are not supposed to have the least idea what their antagonists are up to. Well, perhaps it is not quite as bad as that but, as you know, there was a series of conferences here yesterday and now Josephine has just left and you have appeared."

"You sent for me, didn't you?"

"Yes, I sent for you, and I tried to make sure that Josephine, for whom I did not send, would be out of the way before you came through the drawing room. I was speaking figuratively rather than literally. You didn't bump into her, did you?"

"No. But I suppose I should ask to see her, shouldn't I? That is, she and her husband are expecting me to do that, aren't they?"

"They are fearing that you will and they will be indignant if you do not. In the former case, they could not very well refuse to give you a hearing, which they wish to avoid, and in the latter, they would feel you had been remiss in not asking for one. I really think your best course would be to write a very formal note, requesting permission to pay your addresses to Louise, and then to wander off in the forest somewhere and not return until just before dinnertime. Alphonsine will give you some sandwiches to put in your pocket and a canteen to sling over your shoulder, or you can take a small knapsack, if you prefer."

"But then I wouldn't see Louise all day! And I have so little time left!"

Pierre picked up his paper cutter again. "I don't think it would be wise for you and Louise to disappear simultaneously," he said. "But if you will do as I have indicated, I will try to create the opportunity for her to join you after lunch. Don't ask me now just how I shall manage. My alleged mind is already overtaxed by all this maneuvering. However, no doubt I shall think up something. Meanwhile, by way of further suggestion to you, I may add that the grottoes, especially the largest one, which we call the cathedral, have many times proved extremely satisfactory for rendezvous."

Larry remembered Janine had said, when he finally found his way to the little grassy bower, that the caves were "best reached by another route," and he thought it was quite possible that there was one which had been cut through since his mother's time. However, he also re-membered Cary's description of tethering her horse to a stone seat and walking down a narrow winding path, bordered on one side by the river, "thickly fringed with underbrush," and on the other by, "a series of prehistoric caves, which keep getting bigger and bigger the farther you go." Moreover, he remembered the sound he himself had heard as he approached the bower—the slight murmuring such as might be made by a stream or, in other words, by the river of which his mother had written. Since this was so, the grottoes could not be far from the secret enclosure. In any case, he was glad of a pretext to revisit the spot where he had first met Louise.

He went toward it without haste, but without bewilderment. He had a reasonably good sense of direction, and he experienced no difficulty in retracing his steps. But though the forest had lost some of its mys-tery for him, it had lost none of its magic. Since his arrival at Monte-regard, one beautiful day had succeeded another, and the sunlight which filtered in through the branches of the ivy-wreathed trees had the same golden quality as when he had first seen it, the mosses and ferns beneath the same gilded verdure. When he reached the bower, he sat down and basked briefly in the midday warmth; then he plunged down the path which he had not previously taken.

It was even more overgrown than any he had found already and, at times, he could not hear the murmuring of water because of crackling twigs, unless he stopped and listened. Then its sound came to him, all the more alluring because it was so faint. Gradually he became aware that a rocky wall formed the background of the greenery at his left and glimpsed, at intervals, the rippling stream beyond the underbrush at his right. He was, perforce, going more slowly now, because the path was almost impassable, and he began to wonder whether, after all, he had made a mistake in trying to reach the grottoes by this route. Then suddenly he saw a cleavage in the rock and a clearing in the under-brush. On one side of him was a low opening, overhung with dead branches, which looked all the darker because the stone which enclosed it had a glaring quality. On the other side of him was a limpid pond, surrounded by sedges and shaded by bright foliage.

So he had not been mistaken after all! Unquestionably, he had arrived at the first in the series of famous caves. The one he now saw was not large enough to enter, nor did it offer any temptation to do so. But in no time at all, he would have reached his destination—the one which had a lofty vaulted top and long passages leading out of it in several directions. Meanwhile, under his very eyes, in deadly serenity, lay the Blue Pool.

For a few moments he stood gazing at it, fascinated in spite of himself. At first he could not see a single ripple on its smooth surface. But as he watched it a tiny bubble appeared near its center and then another and another. Afterward, as surprisingly as they had come, they disappeared. However, Larry had seen enough to realize that under the seeming serenity was a whirlpool, and that once a hapless victim had been sucked under by it, rescue would be impossible. The story of the luckless lady who had lost her lover, centuries before, and who had cast herself into this pool because of the loss, might well be sheer fantasy; but the insidious force of the legend, combined with the insidious force of the water, had been strong enough to lure Armande to her death. Involuntarily, almost unconsciously, Larry crossed himself and, turning away from the Blue Pool, hurried farther down the path.

He did not stop to count the caves as he went by, but it was his impression that he passed five or six, each larger than the preceding one, before he came to the grotto which he instantly realized must be the cathedral. He believed he could easily have stood upright in two or three of the others; but he had felt no inclination to put them to the test, partly because the spell of the Blue Pool was still too strong upon him, and partly because it was only the cathedral that he was really eager to explore. It did not disappoint him. As soon as he entered it, he raised his arms as far as possible above his head and found that he could not reach the top even by doing this; and though he could not immediately adjust himself to the change from shimmering sunshine to comparative gloom, he realized that a good deal of light must actually be penetrating to the grotto because one of its immense sides was entirely open, and soon he was able to discern the vaulted formation above him and the tunnels which branched off at the rear. To his surprise, he saw that a fire, built of small neat pieces of wood similar to those used in the dining room, was carefully laid in one corner. It must have been prepared years before, since no one had been allowed to picnic in the caves since the beginning of the war. But when Larry lighted a match and poked it under the sticks, these kindled almost instantly and suddenly the cave was transfigured by radiance.

It was not a rosy light; on the contrary, the dome above him seemed whiter than ever, the encircling walls more deeply green; but both were now dazzling in their brilliance and this brilliance was not confined to the cathedral. It suffused the openings of the passages leading out of it, at the rear, giving them an almost mystical quality of allurement. Larry found himself gazing toward them in fascination. Then, telling himself that it had been senseless enough to succumb to the spell of the Blue Pool, without doing anything so preposterous a second time, he resolutely looked away. . . .

Some flat stones had been arranged to form crude benches on either side of the fire and Larry sat down on one of these, smoked a cigarette and ate the excellent lunch which Alphonsine had prepared for him. Then, unexpectedly overcome by drowsiness, he lay down on the ground, using his knapsack for a pillow, and was almost instantly asleep.

He woke with a confused sense of strangeness and could not identify his whereabouts. At first he had a vague impression that he was again on the roadside near Vannes, where he had curled up and slept, because every hotel in town was full. Then he realized that the surface of the ground on which he was lying was much harder than the grass had been, that there was not open country but enclosing walls around him and that he was in a place where he had never been before. Next he began to remember what had happened that morning: he had waited and waited for Pierre to send for him, just as he had the previous day; and when he finally went to the study, he had been told to write a formal note to M. and Mme Carrere and then to go off for the day. He had been reminded that the cathedral had "many times proved extremely satisfactory for rendezvous" and had gathered that he should wait for Louise to join him there. . . .

Well, he had waited and waited and still she had not come. In spite of the fact that his eyes were now accustomed to the dim light, he felt certain that it was darker in the grotto than when he had first entered it. He glanced at his wrist watch, whose radium dial gleamed in the gloom, and saw that the hands pointed to quarter of five. With a one o'clock lunch, lasting an hour, Louise would have had all kinds of time to reach the cathedral, even if she had not been able to make a quick getaway; and after all, Pierre had not made any promises. He had only said that no doubt he could think up something. Perhaps he had failed to do so—or perhaps the failure had lain, not in his lack of resourcefulness, but in the execution of his plan. Larry had great confidence in Pierre's capability, when it came to meeting and overcoming difficulties, but he was under no delusions as to the amount of opposition which must be overcome. He would not even have put it past Mme Carrere, in her present frame of mind, to lock Louise in her room and keep her there until she could be swept off to Paris. . . .

That was absurd, he told himself next. Eventually Louise would come, thanks to Pierre's maneuvering, and she would have some logical, probably some rather commonplace, explanation for the delay. After all, there were still nearly two hours of daylight, out of doors. It had been senseless enough, the day of his arrival, to appraise the courtyard of the chateau as grim and cold, merely because he had first seen it at a time in the evening when the sun could not possibly strike it, except in midsummer. It was even more senseless to imagine that nightfall was near, merely because he was in a cave. Nevertheless, all this waiting was beginning to get on his nerves. He should have put a pack of cards in his pocket, or some writing paper, or both. He could have sat outside, near the entrance to the cave, and played solitaire or gone on with his letter, and that would have passed the time until Louise came. . . .

Failing such diversion, he cast about in his mind for some other. Fleetingly, he considered a swim in the near-by stream and as quickly dismissed the idea. He would no sooner get out of his clothes than Louise would come; that was the way such things always worked out. Suddenly he remembered that, according to his mother's letters, the tunnels leading from the caves also had some kind of a story connected with them, no less than the Blue Pool, though what the former was she had never learned. Perhaps, by investigation, he himself could find out. The idea had hardly taken form when the passages beyond him again seemed to assume a beckoning quality.

The fire he had kindled was out. He rebuilt it from stray sticks, scribbled a note on the paper in which Alphonsine had wrapped his bottle of wine and, propping up his knapsack against one of the stone seats, slipped the note under a strap. If Louise arrived while he was engaged in exploration, she would know that he had found their trysting place and that he would soon be returning to it. But he thought it most unlikely that she would get there before he came back. After all, he probably could not go far. It was merely that his curiosity had been so impellingly aroused that he had no choice but to satisfy it.

There were three apertures at the rear of the cave, superficially all much alike. Larry entered the center one, which had a little more height than the others, and where he had no trouble in standing upright. But he had gone forward only a few yards when he was confronted by solid wall: the tunnel had come to an end so abruptly that when he turned to leave it he instantly saw the light from his little fire penetrating the gloom. The second aperture did not end so suddenly; but the stone formation overhead sloped downward in such a way that he found he could make no further progress, even on his hands and knees. Again he turned, worked his way back to the fire and went outside to look and listen for Louise. There was still no one in sight, no sound except for the rippling water and the slight crackling of the fire. He strode back into the cave and entered the third tunnel.

487

He was again able to walk upright, though he had less leeway than in his first experiment, and as he went forward he was soon obliged to stoop a little. Complete darkness enveloped him, but as he stretched out his arms he found that they no longer reached the sides of the tunnel. He stopped, lighted a match and saw that the passage had widened into a small low chamber, and that from this, in turn, two more tunnels branched out.

Since luck had come to him on the left before, after futile attempts in the center and on the right, he decided to take to the left again. He progressed without difficulty and with increasing excitement; though he had a slight sense of eeriness, he had absolutely no feeling of fear. When another lighted match revealed a second low chamber, fairly gaping with openings, it did not occur to him to pause, as it had when he reached the clear circle dominated by the columns. There his good judgment had told him that if he chose the wrong path, among those which radiated from the circle like the spokes of a wheel, the afternoon might well be gone before he could rectify his mistake. Now he did not stop to reason; he thought only of going farther and farther into the cavernous depths. He hastened toward another tunnel, tingling all over with the thrill of adventure.

He was stopped, as he had been on his first attempt at exploration, by the abrupt ending of the tunnel. This did not discourage him. After all, it was only one of half a dozen which led from the second chamber; the next time he would have better luck. He felt his way back, lighted another match and surveyed his surroundings preparatory to making another choice. Only then did he realize that though he could indeed choose among several openings to continue his explorations, he had no idea by which one he had entered the chamber. They all looked exactly alike. He could go forward, as fast as he chose; it might take him hours to get back to his starting place.

He stood very still, trying to orient himself by remembering whether the tunnel by which he had entered the chamber had been opposite the one whereby he had left it and, if not, on which side of it. He could not do so. The sense of direction on which he had always prided himself had failed him, and in his haste he had acted with great foolhardiness. Now, all too tardily, he would have to pay the penalty for this, perhaps by hours of delay. Meanwhile, Louise would be waiting for him. Soon she would be worrying about him. Not, of course, that there was any reason to worry. . . .

He took off his jacket and laid it down by the opening of the tunnel from which he had just emerged. At least he would not make the mistake of going into that one again. If his next reconnoiter proved futile, he would lay something else beside the opening to the next tunnel he tried. On the other hand, if it led him back to the first chamber he could easily return for the jacket, because by this time he would have familiarized himself with his route. Resolutely telling himself that of course everything was all right, he entered another passage.

For some minutes he went cautiously along, again stretching out his arms to gauge the width of the tunnel. He still had plenty of matches left. Nevertheless, it was probably better to conserve them. He found, by feeling, that the walls still allowed him ample space; but for the first time his hands encountered moisture and the ground was slimy underfoot. Reluctant reason told him that he could not be headed toward the first chamber, for if these conditions had existed in the passage by which he had entered, he would have noticed them before. He swung around, determined to get out of the damp hole with the least possible delay. As he turned, he slipped; then his feet shot out from under him and he went down. When he regained his foothold he felt, instinctively, for his matches. They were no longer in his pocket.

It did not take him long to find them, but when he did so it was in a small crevice where water had formed. Frantically, he tried to light them, one after the other, in the desperate hope that at least a few might have escaped damage. Every one had been ruined.

He groped his way back to the second chamber and slumped down, engulfed in merciless and menacing darkness. By feeling for his coat, he knew which of the passages he had already explored because it lay between them. But there were still three or four other passages which he had not tried, besides the one by which he had entered. There was no telling how long it would take before he found deliverance—if he found it at all. And he might very well pay for his recklessness with his life. Probably that was what had happened in this labyrinth before: some other rash fool had rushed in there, just as he had, and that was the last that had ever been seen of the hapless man. The reason Cary Vincent had never been told the whole story of the cave was because, after the story of the Blue Pool had been revealed, no one had wanted to heap tragedy upon tragedy in her hearing.

Of course he was not going to lie there like a log, conjuring up horrors. He would pull himself together and make a fresh start. Perhaps he would hit the right passage with the very first try. It would take a long while to find out whether he had or not, because he would be able to tell only by feeling when he reached the first chamber—if he did. Why, there was no if about it. Sooner or later, he was sure to find it. But it might be later rather than sooner. So there was no time to be lost. His search must begin right away. No, not right away, either. There was something else he must do first. Drawing himself to his knees, he began to pray. . . .

Prayer had been a habit for him, ever since he had learned the "Our Father" and the "Hail, Mary" from Tudie in his early childhood;

from the time of his association with Father Le Grand, it had been something more than that. But he had regarded religion with reverence and with the feeling that it was part of the natural order of things, rather than with unquestioning faith or devout fervor. Even at the front, he had never prayed for safety. Indeed, he had regarded with a certain amount of contempt the men who prayed for their lives when they never prayed for anything else; what sort of a God was it they thought they believed in, he had asked himself more than once, if they approached His throne only to ask for favors and never in thanksgiving or praise or worship? Now, for the first time, he prayed with all his heart and soul that he might see the blessed light of day again—not because he was afraid to die, but because he could not bear the thought of dying until he had proved himself a man of mettle and not merely a foolhardy boy, not until he and Louise had shared the full experience of life and love. . . .

He was still on his knees when he heard her calling to him.

The sound was faint and distant. But there was not even a momentary doubt in his mind that it was her voice he heard and that she had come to deliver him. As loudly as he could, he called back, "Louise! Louise!" The name took on new meaning and new music as he shouted. Her answering call came back to him instantly and it was louder now. He thought she might have reached the first chamber and since only two passages led from that, it would be only a matter of minutes before she could reach him, if she took the same one that he had taken. He called, "The left! The left!" But he did not know whether the words had carried, because all that came to him in return was something he could not distinguish. He tried again, in French, *"À gauche! À gauche!"* But the results were no better. Once more he heard the indefinite murmur and then there was silence. He realized that Louise must have taken the wrong passage.

A long period of blankness followed, but it did not trouble him. In one way or another, Louise would discover her mistake, return to the first chamber and try the other tunnel. He was so sure of this that he felt no anxiety, and was impatient only because the joy of reunion must be so long deferred. He waited with infinite eagerness but comparative calm, and when he heard Louise calling him again, he knew she had returned to the first chamber and that this time she would come unerringly toward him. Presently he heard her movements, as well as her voice, and then the striking of a match. There was a quick flash of light. The next instant they were in each other's arms.

CHAPTER XXXI

IT HAD become increasingly difficult for Clyde to write letters. This was partly because the physical effort of doing so was now very great; it was hard for him to sit upright at a desk. But it was even harder for him to make the mental effort of focusing his thoughts on a central subject and getting them on paper. More and more he was inclined to lounge in a comfortable armchair with Nuffy beside him— on cool days, close to his office fire; on warm days, under one of the great oaks that shaded the garden. Stretching himself out at ease, he would reread old letters which required no answers and, putting them back in their envelopes, close his eyes and relive the pleasant past which they evoked. Soon he would begin to grow drowsy and he seldom knew, nor did he greatly care, where his waking dreams ended and those which came with sleep began.

He was not lonely any more. The anguish he had suffered through the loss of Lucy and Cary, the poignancy of his parting with Larry, were sorrows of the past; one untroubled day succeeded another, with little or no variation. He was not annoyed when Dumaine or Tregre came to consult him about something on the plantations; they presented no serious problems for his consideration and they never stayed long. Since they said little or nothing to worry him and since their visits were brief, he enjoyed their company; but he almost never sent for them any more. Every Saturday, before Father Le Grand began to hear confessions, he came to see Clyde, and the old man looked forward to these visits. Less regularly and frequently, Dr. Doussan and Valois Dupré dropped in. Clyde enjoyed these visits, also. But Father Le Grand's were the only ones he would have missed if they had ceased.

He had stopped riding. But once a week Nappy drove him in the old cabriolet to the cemetery, so that he could put flowers on Cary's tomb. When he was not too tired, he stopped at Victoria, on his way back to Cindy Lou, and took a look around the Big House, to make sure everything was as it should be there. It always seemed to him as if it were. Other days, he made the rounds of the garden at Cindy Lou on foot, leaning more and more heavily on his cane. When he reached the enclosure where Lucy lay, he sat down to rest. It was a peaceful place, so peaceful that he often went to sleep there. When this happened, no one disturbed him unless rain set in or a sudden chill came to the air; then Nappy tiptoed up to him and waked him gently and helped him back to the house.

Once or twice it crossed his mind that perhaps he should let Larry know he had stopped riding, that the only parts of the plantations, except the houses and grounds, which he saw nowadays, were those he could reach in the cabriolet. It was easier to get in and out of this than in and out of the Ford—and besides, it seemed more like old times to take a horse-drawn vehicle than an automobile. The roads which transected the plantations were good, as such roads went, and he could get a fair idea of how things were going without leaving his seat. But of course it was not like riding the crops. Yes, perhaps he ought to let Larry know. . . .

But he never did. The boy was already fretting at the long, senseless delay which kept him idle in one army camp after another. If he were suddenly sent home he would see for himself how things were, soon enough, and he would have everything that needed attention remedied in no time. On the other hand, if he were detained indefinitely overseas there was no point in worrying him about conditions which he could not correct. Besides, it really *was a* great effort to write letters, in any detail or at any length.

Because he was essentially honest, Clyde admitted to himself that this was one of the reasons why he did not write Larry that he had stopped riding. But it was a minor reason; he honestly did not want to worry the boy, either about an old man's failing faculties, which were real enough, or about deterioration of the property and its equipment, which might be merely imaginary. There was only one aspect of the situation at Cindy Lou of which he deliberately avoided mention: he had received a disturbing letter from the chairman of the Levee Board that he had never answered and, since then, some army engineers had been doing surveying in the neighborhood. If the levee really were moved back, and the grounds at Cindy Lou were materially altered by such a move, it would be a shock to Larry to come home and see them changed, unless he were prepared for such a difference in them. But perhaps the levee never would be moved back, at least in such a way as to affect Cindy Lou. Clyde had not heard further from the chairman of the Levee Board and the engineers had not reappeared. Again, he decided against writing anything beyond the brief notes which he could scribble with a pencil while lounging in his armchair. . . .

And then he received a letter from Larry which roused him from his torpor and sent him to his desk with a clear head and a steady hand.

It was a very long letter, written in two main sections, and after these came a brief, hurried postscript. The first section told his grandfather about his arrival at Monteregard, his repulse by Janine, his welcome from Pierre and his immediate love for Louise de Courville. He had obviously been interrupted while writing it, and the next section had been written several days later. Meanwhile, the Marquise de Chanet and M. and Mme Carrere had all arrived at Monteregard and had all vehemently opposed his suit, which Pierre had continued to support. Acting on Pierre's advice, Larry had written a formal note to the Carreres, asking for Louise's hand; then, still acting on Pierre's advice, he had gone to see the famous caves and to wait for Louise in the largest one. There he had played the fool by trying to explore the dark tunnels which led from this; he might not have found his way back for days, he might even have lost his life, if Louise had not come to his rescue. When they returned, very late at night, to the chateau, they were both in disgrace with everyone but Pierre, and even Pierre could not and did not defend Larry's folly. The Carreres had taken Louise off to Paris early the next morning without even giving Larry a chance to see her again; and though Pierre had tried to smooth things over, the marquise had succeeded in making life at Monteregard so insufferable for Larry that he had decided to start back to camp at once. The postscript had been written after his arrival there. He had found his orders waiting for him: he was to proceed at once to Coblenz, where he would be attached to the cavalry unit of Head-quarters Staff. There was no telling when he would have leave again, when he would see Louise, when he would get home. . . .

Clyde read the letter through rapidly once and twice more slowly. Then he sat for nearly an hour thinking it over, before reading it a fourth time. He did not grow drowsy or weary as he did so; on the contrary, his thoughts came to him with increasing clarity, and he felt a renewal of strength such as he had not known for months. He rose from his easy chair under the shade of a great tree and walked into his office with a firm step. Sitting down at his old desk, he drew several sheets of paper from one of its pigeonholes and began to write.

Cindy Lou
May 25, 1919

My dear Larry:

Your letter begun on May 7th and finished May 11th has just reached me and I am hastening to reply.

First, let me say that I am glad your tedious period of inactivity is over and that you have ahead of you the prospect of interesting work in an interesting place. Under the circumstances, you certainly do not want to come home until the various complications of which you write me have straightened out, and certainly you do not want to stay at Gondrécourt any longer, either. It seems to me that Coblenz may very well be the happy medium between the two.

Next, let me say I am gladder still that you have found your true love—for, from what you tell me, I do not doubt for a minute that Louise *is* your true love and that you will have many years of the same complete happiness with her that I had with your grandmother. Do not allow yourself to doubt this, either. A girl with the courage she has revealed, first in refusing to permit herself to be browbeaten and second, in going heroically to your rescue, at the risk of her own life, will not permit minor obstacles to keep her from the man of her choice. And that you *are* the man of her choice is certainly self-evident. If you cannot go to her, she will come to you. Remember that she did so in the cave; if she could do it there, she can do it anywhere.

I am not surprised by the unfriendly treatment you have received in certain quarters; there are things which I have never thought best to tell you—and which I do not intend to tell you now—that would explain this treatment; but you may take my word for it that they exist and have long existed. Nevertheless, I am not especially alarmed by the situation, though I deplore it. Even if she had opposition on all sides, instead of on all sides but one, I am sure Louise would overcome it, as I have just said; and she has a very powerful ally in her uncle. I am greatly impressed by what you have written me about him; to tell you the truth, I did not suppose that he was so much of a man. Now I see that I may have done him an injustice. I hope I may have a chance to tell him so in person someday, but at all events, I shall write to him at once, to say how much I appreciate the confidence he has shown in you. Of course I shall also write immediately to Louise, telling her how very welcome her presence will be at Cindy Lou.

I shall ask Father Le Grand to arrange for a copy of your baptismal certificate and also, since he has easy access to all such records, of your birth certificate, your parents' marriage, etc., etc. Perhaps you do not need all these documents, but it will be better for you to have them in your possession, in case you do. On the other hand, if you require more, let me know and I will see that you have them promptly. I think it also may be helpful to you to have a letter from me, formally stating that your marriage has my full approval and that you are my heir. (Which reminds me: my will and all my other papers of importance are in order. Since I am writing you anyway, it is just as well to mention this, though of course you do not really need the information at present.)

I gather from your letter that you are very low in your mind, not only because of your discouragement about Louise, but because you have played the fool, as you put it. I agree that you did a senseless thing in trying to explore the tunnel; and I know you must feel all the more strongly about this because Louise was endangered, as well as yourself. But a man is not a fool because he does one senseless thing—or even a great many. I had so much to live down, when I first met your grandmother, that I did not see how I could ever justify myself in her eyes. What is worse, I played the fool, as you put it, even after I met her—and in a far worse way than you have ever done or ever will do. Yet somehow, because of her, I found the way to rise above my sins rather than to live them down. I happen to know that Pierre de Chanet has also, in many ways, been a sinful man, and that he was saved from even greater sin only because the woman he loved was stronger than he was. Yet, from what you tell me, I know that he, too, has risen above his sins. You have no sins to live down or rise above. You can go to Louise with a clean slate and a clear conscience. Think of that, instead of dwelling on a single act of folly, and be thankful for it. It is a reason for greater thanksgiving than you now realize, though you may do so someday.

With this letter goes my abiding love. Men do not often speak of that in connection with each other. You tried to, the day you left for camp, and I silenced you. I have been sorry since that I did. But I know what was in your heart to say. Now I am saying what is in mine. You have been the light of my life, as your mother was before you and—in a different way—your grandmother before that. Without the light you have given me, my old age would have been passed in the shadows. You made it radiant. God bless you, Larry, and make you as happy as you have always made me, and as I know you will make Louise.

Devotedly, your grandfather,
CLYDE BATCHELOR

Clyde read the letter through and hesitated. It did not sound like the way he usually talked, or wrote, either. Perhaps, for this reason, it would seem to Larry that the words lacked sincerity. Then Clyde realized that it was *because* he was so utterly sincere, because he felt so deeply and was so determined Larry should know this, that it had been possible for him to express himself with more than usual eloquence, almost as though someone more powerful than he were helping him to do so, or speaking through him. He folded the letter carefully, placed it in an envelope, sealed and stamped this. Then he laid it to one side and reached for another sheet of paper, still conscious of no weariness of either mind or body.

My dear Louise:

My grandson Larry Vincent has written me of his meeting with you and of his love for you and yours for him. I am hastening to tell you how happy this news has made me, in many ways and for many reasons.

Larry writes me that even before he saw you, the music of your voice came to him through the silences of a forest. Many, many years ago, as I was walking along a street in a city ravaged by war,

I heard a voice beyond a garden wall and my whole life was transfigured because of this. I know it will be the same with Larry. I could mention many other instances of experiences which he and I seem to have shared, and which, therefore, I can appraise at their full significance; but I know this one will suffice to show you what I mean.

I believe that Larry will have both the will and the power to make you happy. When you leave the place that has so far been your home, and come to his, your surroundings will seem strange to you at first. But soon they will become familiar and then dear because you will be living here as his wife, and his heritage and his hearth will be yours, too.

I also want you to know how warmly I welcome the thought of your presence at Cindy Lou. For more than twenty years now it has been without a mistress, and a house is only half a home that has no woman in it. You will make this house wholly a home again. I thank you beforehand because you will do this, and because of the joy and fulfillment that you will bring to the life of my grandson, who is dearer to me than any other human being.

Yours, with gratitude and affection,
CLYDE BATCHELOR

Again he read his letter through, this time without hesitation, folded it and sealed it in its envelope. He was now beginning to be aware of physical fatigue. But his thoughts still came quickly and clearly and there was one more letter that he wanted to write. He drew another sheet of paper toward him.

My dear Pierre:

The receipt of this letter will be a surprise to you, but my reasons for writing it are so strong that I trust it will not seem intrusive.

Larry has written me of your great kindness to him and of your sympathetic understanding of the problems that have arisen in connection with his courtship of Louise de Courville. No doubt you were drawn to him partly because of his own personality; at the same time I realize there were other powerful reasons why you were disposed in his favor. I will not go into these; I have no desire to do so and I am sure you would not wish it, either. But I feel impelled to tell you that when death was very near, Cary called for you by name, and that these were her last words:

"It's terribly dark in this passage, isn't it? Of course, I was warned that it would be, that I shouldn't go beyond the great chamber of the cave. It's a little frightening, isn't it? At least it would be, if I were alone. But since you're with me at last, dearest. . ."

Her passing was peaceful and even happy because she believed you were with her. I should be everlastingly grateful to you for this—and I am.

Besides writing me about your kindness, Larry has written me about his foolhardiness. I know that if it had not been for Louise, he might have lost his life in the dark passages leading from the grotto, beyond which his mother never actually went, but where, in her last moments, she believed herself to be. I was a gambler once and, like most gamblers, I held to certain superstitions. I thought I had outlived them all and I have, as far as the old ones are concerned. But to me there seems something fateful about these occurrences in the cave, something linking not only mother and son, but you and yours with me and mine, almost as if the hand of God were uniting us. It is in the hope and with the belief you will share my feeling that I have written this letter.

Faithfully yours,
Clyde Batchelor

He was very tired now. When the third letter was ready for the mail, he rang for Nappy and told him to start for the post office at once. But when Nappy asked whether he should get the cabriolet ready, Clyde said no, Nappy could take the Ford. That would be quicker, and he was not going to the post office himself. He was going out to the garden.

When Nappy came to report that the letters were in the mail, he did not find his master under the great shady tree, so he went on to the enclosure which was Lucy's resting place. As he expected, Clyde was seated beside her grave, sleeping quietly. It was still warm and sunny, so Nappy made no effort to waken him. It was a long time before the faithful servant realized that this was the deepest and most tranquil sleep of all.

 CHAPTER XXXII

THE TRANSPORT *St. Mihiel,* sailing from Antwerp to New York with returning troops, was not as comfortable as the liner on which Larry had gone to France. At least, that was the way it seemed to him. But he realized that the impression might well be erroneous because, on the eastbound voyage, he had not expected to be comfortable and had not cared very much whether he was or not, and this time he was concerned about Louise.

Not that she had said or done anything to cause him anxiety; quite the contrary. She could have had a berth in quite a good cabin, on one of the upper decks, if she had not insisted she would prefer to share one with him, which meant she would be put practically in the hold. That was where they were now, in a stuffy little hole in the wall. The sea was very rough and Louise had been sick. Larry was terribly distressed by her sickness, but Louise did not seem to be distressed at all, except because of Larry: she said she did not see how a man could keep on being in love with a girl who kept getting sick. As far as she was concerned, she had been expecting to be sick, ever since she had known she was going to have a baby. Most girls were. However, she had not expected to be sick in his face, so to speak. . . .

It was all very well for Louise to joke in this way, but Larry knew that she was sick because of the stuffiness and the roughness and not because of the expected baby. She had known for nearly two months that she was going to have a baby, and she had not been sick a minute in Coblenz or in Antwerp or on the train between the two, though that had been very crowded. She kept urging Larry to go up on deck and get some air, and he continued to sit stubbornly on the little folding canvas stool, which was the only kind of a seat available, and for which there was barely room between the berths and the opposite wall. Fortunately, she slept a good deal between the sudden attacks of seasickness which woke her up, and while she was sleeping he sat looking at her with eyes of love and marveling—as he had many times before—that anyone as wonderful as Louise should have loved him from the beginning and should have continued to love him as much as he loved her. . . .

Though he had left Gondrécourt with a heavy heart, the change of scene and the satisfaction of being on active duty again had done much to raise his spirits; merely the sight of the Stars and Stripes, flying from the mast above the Ehrenbreitstein—the great fortress which dominated the merging waters of the Rhine and the Moselle and the city which crowned their union—never failed to give him a feeling of triumph. But the news of his grandfather's death, which reached him when he had been in Coblenz less than three weeks, was a shattering blow. The cable from Valois Dupré, announcing this, of course arrived long before Clyde's last letter; and Larry had hardly recovered from the first impact of grief when his grandfather's moving message poignantly revived it.

He was writing daily letters to Louise, addressing them to Monteregard, and not infrequently he wrote to Pierre, also. From the beginning, he had found release in the composition of these letters and, from the time of his grandfather's death, it brought him even more assuagement to know that the unrestrained outpourings of his grief would be received with sympathy and understanding. When he learned that Clyde had written to his beloved and to his uncle, as well as to himself, and that these letters had meant a great deal to them, his sense of shared sorrow and, consequently, of solace became infinitely greater. Louise sent him a copy of Clyde's letter to her, which Larry read and reread almost as often as he did his own. Pierre did not quote at all from the letter he had received, but the one he wrote to Larry was the direct result of it, though Larry never knew this.

My dear boy:

Perhaps you will let me call you this, since I now have no son of my own, and since I believe I could not care for you more greatly if you really were my son.

I have been trying to think of something I could say that would help you through these next hard weeks, and I have not been able to do so, as far as any expression of condolence is concerned. I have never yet heard one myself that gave any real comfort and I am incapable of devising one. But perhaps I can say something on another subject that will serve to cheer you, at least a little.

It is this: I am more and more convinced that you and Louise were meant for each other, and that you should marry as soon as possible. If Paul and Josephine do not come to their senses—and it would not be true kindness to tell you I think they will, for I do not—I will see that Louise has a modest dot, a proper trousseau and a suitable wedding—in fact, I should be very pleased to have the marriage ceremony take place in my private chapel. Louise will be twenty-one in August, and I think we should allow her mother and stepfather that much time to change their tune, if only to save their faces—such face saving might be important to you later on. If by then they have not relented, I shall take action and I advise you to ask for leave, since I can be ready for you by the time you can reach here. On this you may count *with complete assurance*.

Devotedly, your uncle,

Pierre de Chanet

Conscientiously, Larry had acted on this advice. But the months dragged by and still the Carreres showed no signs of relenting. In August, Larry applied for leave the first week in September.

The colonel of cavalry under whose immediate command he had been since coming to Coblenz had just been transferred to another post, and Larry had not seen the new C.O. until he presented himself at this functionary's office—or rather, until he had waited in the office for more than half an hour. During the course of this unwelcome delay, he noticed that the office had undergone a considerable change since he last reported there. It had previously been conspicuously bare; now, besides the necessary maps and other military props, it was adorned with various framed photographs, citations and diplomas, and there were flowers on the desk. Larry had just decided, out of sheer boredom, that he would inspect these ornamental additions, somewhat unusual in a milieu where great stress was laid on "military atmosphere," when a door opposite the one by which he had entered was thrown open and the colonel came in.

He was wearing a polo shirt with his riding breeches, and after casually returning Larry's salute he flung himself down in his desk chair and proceeded to riffle through some papers lying in front of him. Then he signed two or three letters and read a document of some sort, before giving more than a passing glance in his visitor's direction. During this interval Larry, whose patience had already been considerably taxed, regarded his superior officer with increasing distaste. The man was undeniably handsome, but he lacked the distinction which made Pierre's good looks so outstanding; curiously enough, the general effect he produced was not only unmilitary but unmasculine. His hands were too smooth and too white, his chin too rounded, his shoulders too sloping. He could not be overweight, or he would not have been a polo player; but there was a certain softness about him generally associated with superfluity of flesh. When he finally looked at his visitor long enough for Larry to study his face, the boy saw that there were dark circles under his eyes and that the eyes themselves lacked directness.

"I understand that you have come to apply for leave," the colonel said at last.

"Yes, sir."

"But apparently you had leave no longer ago than May."

"Yes, sir. Of course I should not have asked for it so soon again, if certain circumstances had not made it seem imperative for me to do so."

"I see. And these circumstances are. . .?"

"I'm engaged to be married, and September is the most convenient time for the wedding, as far as my fiancée is concerned."

"I see," the colonel said again. "I take it then that your fiancée is an American girl, engaged in some sort of postwar work which puts limitations on her freedom?"

"No, sir. She is a French girl."

"Oh—a French girl! Then I should think it would be possible for her to arrange to be married at almost any time."

"Yes, sir, it would. Any time after August."

"And why not before August?"

500

"She won't be of age until then, and after that she'd need a certain amount of time to get ready for her wedding."

"But she can get married at any time, without waiting to become of age, provided that she is in possession of a birth certificate, that she can prove she has lived for at least a month in the *arrondissement* where the ceremony is to take place and that she has her parents' consent."

"Yes, sir, I know. But unfortunately she doesn't have her parents' consent."

"Why not?"

"Her father is dead. Her mother and her stepfather don't regard me as an especially good match."

"Why not?" the colonel asked a second time, in a tone less casual and considerably cooler than he had said, "I see," the second time.

"I think they had different plans for her. I don't know of any other reason. Her uncle approves."

"What is the name of this girl to whom you say you are engaged?"

"Louise de Courville. And I am—"

"Yes?"

"I don't mean to be disrespectful, sir, but I am engaged to her. I'm not just saying that I am."

"Yet you tacitly admit that her mother and her stepfather do not recognize any such engagement when you say they will not consent to her marriage with you. What is their name?"

"Carrere."

"And the friendly uncle's name?"

"Pierre de Chanet."

"Well, well! So Pierre de Chanet has entered the picture again."

"I don't think I quite follow you, sir."

"It isn't necessary that you should. What about his mother? Is she still living?"

"Yes, sir."

"And does she approve the match?"

"No, sir."

"And still you expect me to okay a leave in order that you may marry a girl whose entire family, with the exception of one uncle, is opposed to the match?"

"I hope very much that you will, sir."

"Well, I shan't. I think I should be doing the Marquise de Chanet and M. and Mme Carrere a great disservice by giving my consent—not to mention the girl herself. I have no doubt that the marriage which has been arranged for her is much more suitable. . . . That will be all, Lieutenant Vincent."

Larry bit his lip to keep from retorting, swallowed hard, saluted and turned to leave the office. He had almost reached the door when the colonel called him back.

"Lieutenant Vincent."

Larry swung around, a flicker of hope suddenly quivering through his despair.

"Yes, sir?" he said eagerly.

"Do you play polo?"

"No, sir," Larry answered, feeling very doubtful whether he was successfully concealing his angry disappointment.

"You've never played it?"

"No, sir."

"The general is very fond of polo. Perhaps you knew that?"

"I'd heard so, sir."

"But it's never occurred to you that it might be helpful if you played it?"

"No, sir."

"Well, it shouldn't be too hard for you to learn. I understand you're a good rider."

"Thank you, sir."

This time he knew he had spoken sarcastically. After all, there was no such animal as a graduate of the Cavalry School at Saumur who was a poor rider, and of course the colonel was fully informed, not only as to when his visitor had last had leave, but as to everything else connected with his military record.

"We could use another good player on our team," the colonel remarked nonchalantly. If he had noticed the note of sarcasm—and Larry did not see how he could have helped doing so—he apparently had not taken umbrage at it, or at least he did not intend to betray any such feeling. "Think it over, Larry." The colonel permitted himself a slight smile in answer to Larry's startled look. "I really do not see any reason why I should not call you by your Christian name when we are alone," he said. "In fact, you may call me Uncle Bushrod, if you like, under the same circumstances."

"It never entered my head that the new C.O. was my uncle," Larry wrote Pierre. "Colonel Page! . . . Why, there must be hundreds of Pages in the Army, dozens of them colonels, and he doesn't use his first name any more—it seems he's always hated it! He signs himself B. Harrison Page and all his cronies call him Harry—Colonel Harry Page, that was all I'd heard. And he'd only been here a week. Of all the cursed luck! I could have gone just as well to Kent, who was here before him, and who was a grand guy. But I waited, just as you thought I should. Not that I'm trying to shift the blame to you, of course you understand. It was just one of those things. . . . And why Page should take sides with the marquise and the Carreres, instead of with you and

502

Louise and me, is just one of those mysteries, as our people say at Cindy Lou."

Yes, it was just one of those things, Pierre agreed in his reply, without making any answering comment on mysteries. And he was very sorry that *Colonel B. Harrison Page* should be so unreasonable, not to say so lacking in understanding. However, Pierre did not see why Larry's failure to secure leave should delay the wedding. Of course it was disappointing, in some respects, that this could not take place in the chapel at Monteregard. But rather than wait on the vagaries of *Colonel B. Harrison Page,* Pierre would bring Louise to Coblenz. He thought it very unlikely that, if he took this course, *Colonel B. Harrison Page* would go so far as to create further difficulties.

In this assumption, Pierre had been entirely correct; and before his arrival with Louise, Larry had revealed an aptitude for polo which was very gratifying, not only to the general, but to a number of other high-ranking players, and had also become something of a favorite among junior officers who were not polo players. So Colonel B. Harrison Page contented himself, for the time being, with having dealt one body blow and did not attempt another. In fact, he eventually recalled Larry to his office, now even more elaborately adorned than before, and said he thought that possibly leave could be arranged after all. But by that time all necessary formalities had been met for a marriage ceremony at the Liebfrauen Kirche and for a wedding reception in the palace garden. Larry wrote hastily to Pierre and Louise, telling them that if they would prefer a last-minute change of plans, he could meet it; both replied that they would rather let the existing program stand. Louise did not go into any explanations as to why she felt this way, but Pierre gave his reasons in some detail: word had been widely circulated that Lieutenant Vincent could not leave his post at this time; it would cause confusion and needless curiosity if the information were reversed. Word had also been circulated that M. Carrere, both because of official commitments in Paris and because of the inevitably bitter feelings which still persisted between France and Germany, did not feel it best to go to Coblenz at this time. That would account quite logically for his absence and his wife's from the wedding, if it took place there. On the other hand, if it took place at Monteregard, in the face of his continuing hostility, this would make itself felt in the atmosphere, even if he attended the ceremony. At the last moment, he might very well decide to do so, rather than to give occasion for local gossip by his absence. But Pierre was not at all sure that this would have been an advantage.

"There would have been awkwardness either way," he told Larry, the first time they were able to talk quietly together after his arrival in Coblenz with Louise. "And then, there is my mother . . . of course a lady of that age could not be expected to travel any great distance, even if there were no question of national feeling involved, so you could be sure that she would not come here. But she has remained at Monteregard ever since you were there—the longest time within my recollection—and she does not seem to have the slightest idea of leaving. I think she would have contrived to make you very uncomfortable."

"She certainly did before," Larry said bluntly.

"Yes, I know. So I think it is just as well that she should not have another opportunity to do so. It affords me much more satisfaction to realize that you are having an opportunity to make *Colonel B. Harrison Page* uncomfortable—as you are undoubtedly doing."

"It affords me some, too. Not that I care much, one way or another. The only thing I care about right now is getting married. The place and the attendant circumstances don't seem to matter very much."

"It is quite understandable that you should feel like that. And believe me, my dear boy, things are better this way. . . . Now there is something else which we should have discussed before, but the right moment never seems to have arrived, up to now. That is the question of Louise's dot."

"It's not a question that interests me in the least. I can take care of Louise. If you're uneasy on that score, I can settle something on her immediately, so it won't be community property."

"I'm not in the least uneasy. . . . You are speaking rather abruptly this evening, do you realize that, *mon cher*? It is unlike you—but then, I suppose we must allow for a certain amount of edginess on the part of a prospective bridegroom. The reason I speak of her dot is not because I lack confidence in your ability to take care of Louise, as you must know—I should hardly be doing everything possible to facilitate your marriage, if I were. I speak of her dot because it is no more considered suitable for a French girl to marry without one than without a chemise . . . well, that is perhaps a slight exaggeration, but here is what I am coming to: I had thought, at one time, that I would be in a position to say she would have a rather handsome dowry—in prospect, if not actually in hand. That was when I felt quite sure that Janine intended to enter a convent. Now I am not so sure."

"No?"

"No." The corners of Pierre's mouth twitched. "Your future mother-in-law was very much annoyed with my presentation of a hypothetical case to M. le Curé—a presentation which you heard," he remarked. "But there is solid basis of fact in the old saying that many a true word is spoken in jest. The Carreres insisted on having me invite De Bonneville to Monteregard. They were obsessed with the idea that if he and Louise were thrown together in romantic surroundings she would make a comparison that was unfavorable to you, and change her mind as to whom she wished to marry. The plot was a complete boomerang. Louise, who had never been ill before in her life, as far as I know, developed some sort of a sudden fever—that is, I did not take her temperature myself, but it was so reported to me. In any event, she hardly stirred out of her room during the entire course of De Bonneville's visit. Meanwhile, since time was hanging heavy on his hands, he naturally sought diversion—and found it with Janine, who apparently forgot all about a vocation from the moment she laid eyes on him. In justice, I must say that he is not unattractive, in his way, though it is a way that would never have done for Louise. Love at first sight seems to be very much the vogue. I think he and Janine are as good as engaged already."

For the first time in the course of the conversation, Larry laughed.

"Yes, it *is* rather amusing, isn't it?" Pierre went on, his smile widening. "Except in this respect, as far as you are concerned: if Janine had entered a convent, I should have made Louise my heir. So eventually, she would have inherited Monteregard and, as its future possessor, I should have felt it proper that she should have had a very considerable dot, from me. Now as things have turned out, I shall need that money for Janine's dot, for her wedding and the contingent expenses. So, at the moment, all I can spare for Louise, in the way of hard cash, is a small sum which, if well invested, should make her independent of you as far as pocket money is concerned—I have a very strong feeling that every wife should have that much independence from her husband. In addition, I should like to give her the house on Elysian Fields, in New Orleans. I am sure Janine will never want or need that and I certainly do not. I don't know what sort of condition it's in, or whether its location is still suitable for residential purposes. If it is in good shape, and if it would meet your needs and tastes, you might find it convenient to use as a town house. Otherwise, you might sell it, and add the sum you receive for it to the one I am giving outright."

"I think you're very generous, Uncle Pierre, to give Louise so much. I want you to know I appreciate it. But even if you hadn't given her a cent, I'd have felt you'd done a great deal for her—for both of us—already. And I meant what I said before—that nothing else seems to matter very much, if I can only marry her."

That was how it had seemed to him then and, throughout the three years which followed, that was how it had continued to seem. It did not matter to Larry that he and Louise were billeted, along with two other young couples, in a small, unattractive house on the Mainzerstrasse, instead of in one of the costly, commodious ones on the Rheinenlagen where his uncle lived in comparative luxury. It did not matter to Larry that his work was increasingly monotonous and increasingly meaningless. It did not matter that he was kept on and on in Coblenz, when everyone else with whom he talked on the subject succeeded in getting sent home. It did not matter that Colonel B. Harrison Page continued to needle him in small ways and thwart him in large ones. With Louise he found complete harmony and complete happiness. Why then *should* anything else have mattered all this time? But now that the sea was so rough and she was so sick, he was troubled. He began to think more seriously than he ever had before—though of course such thoughts had sometimes crossed his mind—about what their life in Coblenz must have meant to her. Not her life in relation to him—that, he felt sure, had been as rapturous, and as rewarding, as his in relation to her; but her life in relation to its general aspects. Hitherto she had always been lapped in luxury; she had had none in Coblenz. She had been the daughter of a nobleman, the stepdaughter of a cabinet officer and the niece of a man who treated her like his own child and whose name was illustrious, whose home was magnificent and whose personality was outstanding. In Coblenz, she was simply the wife of an obscure second lieutenant. No, that was not all, either. She was a Frenchwoman by birth, an unwelcome guest in the house of a hereditary enemy, and she had lost her father and a cousin who was like a brother to her in a war with this same enemy—a war whose gaping wounds were still unhealed. Over and over again she must have been obliged to stifle her sense of strangeness, of isolation, of hostility. But she had done this so successfully, indeed so completely, that she had never betrayed any such feeling and that Larry had never been conscious until this moment of its existence, at least enough so that it troubled him.

As he dwelt on all this, with increasing concern, Louise stirred slightly and opened her eyes. Then she smiled and held out her arms to him.

"I'm feeling ever and ever so much better," she said, in answer to the question which accompanied his kiss. "No, I don't feel like having anything to eat. I feel like talking, and I certainly haven't felt much like doing that these last few days."

"You certainly haven't. But I think perhaps you ought to try to eat something before you try to talk."

"All right, if you want me to. But I'd rather talk."

"All right, if you'd rather."

They laughed together. Larry forgot that he had been troubled.

"I want to talk about getting home," Louise said.

"That's a nice thing to talk about. I'd like to talk about it, too."

"We've got four more days at sea?"

"With luck, it might be only three."

"And you think we'll have to stay about six weeks in and around New York?"

"I'm afraid there's not much chance it would be any less, even with luck. It might be more."

"But not more than two months?"

"No, I shouldn't think so."

"And then you won't be Lieutenant Lawrence Cary Vincent of the United States Army any more? You'll be Larry Vincent of Cindy Lou?"

"Yes, thank God!"

"Free to start for Louisiana?"

"Yes to that, too—and thank God for that, too."

"It'll take two more days to get to New Orleans?"

"Yes—at least the train trip will spoil two days."

"And then we'll look at the house on Elysian Fields and decide what we want to do with it?"

"What you want to do with it. It's yours."

"It's ours. . . . Well, that shouldn't take us long, should it?"

"Not if it's in very good condition or very bad condition. But if it's somewhere in between—"

"Well, let's say four days. . . . And then we'll take the train to Convent—is that right?"

"Yes."

"Just an hour or two?"

"Yes."

"And Nappy will meet us at the station?"

"Yes."

"And we'll drive to Cindy Lou—"

"Yes, we'll drive to Cindy Lou."

"And it'll be wonderful, like everything else?"

"Yes. But that'll be the most wonderful of all."

They laughed again, secure in the certainty.

 CHAPTER XXXIII

NAPPY DROVE jerkily at best, slamming on the brakes whenever he wanted or needed to go more slowly. They were riding along close to the river, and when he turned abruptly to the left, with a sudden slackening of speed, Larry thought at first that this was simply preparatory to swerving around another curve in the levee, where the road was obscured. Then he realized that they were turning into a driveway and that a great square house was looming up ahead of them. But he did not grasp that this was Cindy Lou until Nappy came to a full stop. The terraces, stretching spaciously out toward the road, were gone;

and the unkempt lawn, which now divided this from the house, had so shrunken in size that the levee seemed almost upon it. The stately avenue, bordered by majestic trees, was gone, too; the driveway into which Nappy had turned was so short that it had not taken more than a moment to traverse it. And the house beside it did not merely *look* gray, because of the deepening dusk. It *was* gray, the gray of weather-beaten clapboards and pillars that had gone long unpainted; even the green shutters, which had once been so vivid against the brightness of white surfaces, had peeled to dinginess. Larry had meant to have the car stopped in front of the house, to walk toward it through the tiered garden and then to lift Louise triumphantly over the threshold, just as Clyde had lifted his Lucy. But the place was so changed that he had not known when they reached it, and now they were at one side of the great outer staircase, at the point where it looked least impressive, even at its best. And apparently much of its grandeur was gone any-way; its newel posts, its balusters, its handrails, were drab and dingy like everything else. . . .

He became aware that Louise was looking at him in a trustful but questioning way and that Nappy had already climbed out of the front seat and was opening the rear door of the car. Larry would have to say something quickly.

"We're home, darling," he told her with an attempt at a smile. Fortunately the dim light would prevent her from seeing just how unsuccessful the attempt was. "This is Cindy Lou. I—I didn't recognize it myself, at first. You see, while I was gone, the levee was moved back, and that did away with the terraces and the *allée*. Of course I'd heard about this, in a general way, from Valois Dupré but I didn't realize what a difference all that would make. If I had, I'd have warned you. About the house, too—"

"I'm sure the house will be lovely, inside. It's sad for you, to find everything so changed. But remember I never saw Cindy Lou before, so I can't make comparisons. And I'm happy that we've reached here at last."

She leaned forward and kissed him. How like her that was, he thought, with a great surge of loving thankfulness, to show no self-consciousness, even though they were not alone, about giving him this spontaneous caress, which she knew would comfort him, and to behave as if the fact they had finally reached their destination was all which really mattered. But as he gave her his hand to help her alight and went up the stairway with her, it was she who went on chatting cheer-fully, for he found he could not say anything to show his appreciation of her attitude. This was not because of the shock which the sight of the house had given him; he was beginning to recover from that. Now it was because he dreaded, unutterably, to reach the doorway and see it empty of his grandfather's welcoming presence. Always, before this,

Clyde had stood at the top of the grand staircase waiting for him, and they had gone inside the house together. Even with Louise beside him, Larry found the entrance almost unbearably hard to face. He forgot, completely, that he had meant to lift his bride over the threshold; he turned his head away, trying not to look beyond the open door.

"Us sho' is proud to have you back, Mistuh Larry, you and Miss Louise. Us has waited de longes' for dis happy day."

It was Tudie speaking, Tudie the ever loyal, the ever kind, the ever capable. As if she understood that no one should stand at the entrance itself, since the old master was not there to do it, she had been waiting in the hall; but she came forward quickly and close behind her was Ivy. Both of them looked at Louise with eyes that were admiring and at the same time appraising; the thought passed through Larry's mind that they had wondered how far along she was and that now they thought they knew. Somehow the faint amusement which came with this realization helped him to shake off some of his depression.

"I am glad to see you, too, Tudie—Ivy, too, of course. But where's Delphie?"

Tudie and Ivy exchanged embarrassed glances. "Us sho' sorry, but Delphie, she gone," Tudie said hesitantly. "But us gwine make out all right, me and Ivy. Us got everythin' lined up."

"What do you mean, gone?"

"She done leave Cindy Lou and go to work for some po' white trash nigh to Gonzales. Us never knowed she was all that triflin'. But don' you fret none, Mistuh Larry, me and Ivy got everythin' all lined—"

"All right, Tudie, all right. . . ." It was the first time, as far as Larry could remember, that any of their people had ever voluntarily left Cindy Lou. It had never occurred to him that one would do so. He had supposed there would be plenty of service for Louise—that, while this might lack distinction, it would always be forthcoming willingly, even eagerly. Now there would be only Tudie and Ivy in that great ark of a house and before very long Tudie would be needed for the baby. Well, of course Nappy could help, except that he was probably needed all the time outside; since there had been defection in Delphie's case, this was probably not an isolated one. But there was nothing Larry could do about this situation at the moment. Louise must be made comfortable at once; she must have some supper and get to bed.

"Do you want to look around a little, darling? Or would you like to go straight upstairs?"

"I think I'd like to go straight upstairs, if that's all right. If I could just wash and get out of these traveling clothes I've worn so long, I'd feel better. That is, of course I feel all right anyway, but—"

"But of course you want to wash and change. Come, I'll show you the way."

It was not until they had almost reached another threshold that he stopped again, once more appalled. He had given no instructions as to which room he and Louise should occupy. As far as he knew, the youth bed had never been removed from his grandfather's chamber; he had continued to sleep there, whenever he was at home, until he went to Camp Beauregard. The youth bed had been altered by replacing the original rails with longer ones, and he had never minded having it narrow. It would have no logical part in the new pattern of his life; but he would hate to see it standing empty and he would hate still more to see the room without it. Besides, he could not sleep with Louise in his grandfather's bed. He would constantly keep thinking. . . Where would they sleep then? In the room that had been his mother's, across the hall? The spool bed she had loved was certainly not large enough for two persons. In the room of the uncle he had never known until they met at Coblenz? The furniture there was adequate, even very handsome. But he had always disliked it, for some reason hitherto inexplicable, but now linked to his resentment toward Bushrod Page. As to the guest room, the one with the two convent beds, of course that was unthinkable. Except during the crossing on that unspeakable transport, he and Louise had always gone to sleep in each other's arms.

It was Tudie who saved the situation. "Us figured you would want to take you bride to you mama's room, Mistuh Larry," she said. "Miss Cary done have that fixed the way young ladies likes dey rooms, and now us got another young lady at Cindy Lou, us got to aim to please her." Tudie was already advancing toward the only open door on the second story and, as Larry looked beyond her when she paused respectfully on the threshold, he instantly saw that she had made a wise choice. The spool bed really *was* big enough; the fact that it did not have the great canopy and the carved framework of the Seignouret or the Mallard made it look smaller, that was all; its low headboard and complete lack of footboard did not affect its comfortable width; and an immaculate, embroidered linen sheet had already been turned down over the quilted coverlet in a way that seemed to invite restful slumber. Moreover, everything else about the room was attractive; the chintzes were not bright any more, but age had given added softness to their color and delicacy to their design; the chaise longue, the easy chairs, the drawn draperies, all added to the general air of coziness. A fire was burning brightly on the hearth and flowers had been lavishly used for decoration. Larry saw that Tudie was right; there was an air of femininity about this room which the others had always lacked; and while he was rapidly coming to the realization of this, Louise spoke in her warm, friendly way.

"You *have* pleased me, Tudie," she said. "It's exactly the kind of a room a young lady likes—this young lady, anyway! And everything's so complete—the bed turned down, the fire lighted, the flowers all around."

"Yassum, Miss Louise," Tudie replied, beaming with relief and gratitude. "Us figured maybe you'd like to go straight to bed and have your supper on a tray. Mistuh Larry, he could eat his on a table right beside you. Ivy, she got a good gumbo made, same as Mistuh Larry used to like it, and she done her best with the rest of the supper, too, without she knowed your pleasure. She thought in the morning you an' her'd overlook the storerooms and such. But you must be tuckered for true tonight."

"I am a little tired. . . . Would you like to have supper here, *mon coeur*?"

"I think it's a grand idea." Larry would not have confessed, even to himself, that the reason he thought it a grand idea was not only because this room of his mother's had been made so inviting for the reception of his bride, but also because if they stayed here he could put off the evil moment of going into the rooms which he associated more closely with Clyde. "You've done fine, Tudie. There's just one thing lacking. I haven't seen Nuffy yet. I thought he'd be bounding out to meet me— at least, if he hasn't forgotten me, after all this time."

"Dogs, dey don' forget no more dan folkses, Mistuh Larry. But us got Nuffy tied up, 'cause us didn't know did Miss Louise—"

"But of course I want to see Nuffy! Of course I want him with us! Please go and untie him right away, Tudie!"

"I'll go myself. I don't want him jumping all over you, in his first excitement. Where is he, Tudie?"

He was in the kitchen, Tudie said, and he'd been restless all the evening, just like he knew something was going to happen. Ivy would go downstairs with Mr. Larry and she herself would stay and help Miss Louise unpack. Maybe draw a nice hot bath, too. Or would they be having supper straight off?

Again Louise consulted Larry before giving a definite answer, again he said he thought Tudie had a grand idea, this time in suggesting the bath, and again he knew in his secret heart that his reply was not wholly disinterested. Of course a bath would be refreshing to Louise, of course her supper would taste better to her after she had taken one and had been comfortably settled in bed; but he was also thankful for the chance of going to get his dog by himself. If Nuffy did remember him and greet him with barks and jumps of joy, then he would take the dog outside with him while he went to look at his grandfather's grave. He was not sure whether there was a moon or not, but the night was clear, the stars would be out, anyway. He would be able to see all right. And he did not want even Louise with him on his first visit to the little enclosure. But he would be glad to have Nuffy. Nuffy was still a link between himself and his grandfather. . . .

When he came back to his mother's room, with Nuffy trotting quietly at his side, Tudie had left everything in perfect order; Louise was already sitting up in bed, looking as fresh as a rose in her dainty crepe de Chine nightgown. Larry leaned over to kiss her, and then put both arms around her and hugged her hard; but for the third time within less than an hour, he was prompted by conflicting emotions. Louise not only looked as fresh as a rose, she smelled as sweet as one. Her bronze-colored hair was still damp around the temples and fell in a fragrant cloud about her neck; and the lace-trimmed nightgown, which was cut in a deep V and sleeveless besides, was at best a mere wisp of a garment, veiling, but not concealing, her beautiful body. From the first, their desire for the full experience of love had been mutual. Moreover, Louise had been instinctively aware that her husband's physical delight in her was akin to some other deep, almost tragic need and therefore had been all the more prodigal in her response to his passion. Unbelievably, however, Larry had taken her in his arms now only because he craved comfort. He had been to his grandfather's grave and had stood for a long while under the stars, looking at it. Then, when he had finally left the enclosure and had come back upstairs, Nuffy had bounded along ahead of him and had gone, not to the open door of Cary's room, but to the closed door of the room that had been Clyde's, and had turned to look at Larry with the piteous bewilderment of the faithful dog which grieves and cannot understand why his grief is not assuaged by the master who has never failed him before.

"Nuffy did remember me," Larry said at last, releasing Louise. "He did jump all over me, too, so it was just as well Tudie kept him tied up, until he got over his first excitement. He'll be all right now, though. Come here, Nuffy, and meet your new mistress." Nuffy, who had been sniffing around the room, obediently approached the bed and Louise turned on her side to pat him and scratch his ears. Again his look was questioning and again his trustful brown eyes sought Larry's. But this time he seemed satisfied and, after a moment, he began to wag his tail, hesitantly at first, and gradually with more conviction of well-being.

"You won't object to having him here, will you, Louise?" Larry inquired. "He—he's always slept in my room, when I've been at home, ever since he was a puppy."

"Of course I won't object. Didn't you hear me telling Tudie I expected to have him with us? Is it all right for me to give him orders, or should all those come from you?"

"It's all right for you to give them to him. I don't know that he'll mind you, straight off. But he'll learn. What do you want him to do?"

"I thought I might tell him to go and lie down on the hearth, while we had our supper. It's getting very late, isn't it, darling? I suppose we ought to think of the servants."

She was right, of course; and though Nuffy did hesitate again, for a moment, and did again look questioningly at Larry, he obeyed the second time Louise spoke to him and lay quietly on the hearth while the two ate their supper. The gumbo was very good and so were the quail in brown butter and the stuffed mirlitons—all old favorites of Larry's. Louise was lavish in her praise of them, both to him and to Tudie, who proudly did the serving. She had decorated both the tray and the little table she placed beside the bed with a few early camellias; and when Louise once more voiced her admiration of these, Tudie spoke more happily than ever.

"Miss Lucy, she used to have camellias of every prescription. Us ain' got so many now as us used to have. But Ah specks you'll be takin' care of Miss Lucy's garden now, won' you, Miss Louise?"

"I'll try. I don't know much about camellias, but I can learn."

The reference to the camellias did not hurt Larry as much as most of the reviving memories. Clyde had endeavored to see that Lucy's garden continued to have good care, from someone on the place, after her death; but the foundation of the new C. & L. Navigation Company had prevented him from spending the money to hire an expert to look out for them, as he had planned at one time. They had never been a subject of frequent discussion between him and his grandson, and their culture had not been among the activities which he and Larry had shared, for he had not known much about camellias himself. Larry was grateful to Louise for her expression of willingness to revive the garden and he reverted, of his own accord, to Tudie's suggestion about the storerooms.

"We'll look around the grounds together the first thing in the morning, if it's a pretty day—well, perhaps not the first thing. I suppose I ought to see Dumaine and Tregre as soon as I can. But sometime before evening. Meanwhile, perhaps you and Ivy would go through the storerooms without me. I don't know much about those, anyway."

"Of course. Is there anything else I could do to be helpful?"

He was silent for a moment, thinking painfully again. "I suppose you'd better go straight through the house and see what condition it's in," he said at last. "Dad—my grandfather—and I never used the drawing room much, except the summer Aunt Armande was at Victoria, just before war broke out. That was the only time we had much company. We used the ballroom, too, that summer, but I don't suppose you and I—"

"No, of course we won't be giving any balls right away. But I will see that the drawing room's ready to receive visitors. I suppose people will call, won't they? I mean, because I'm a bride."

"Yes, I suppose so. And you should always offer them black coffee and little cakes, when they do, the way pinaud and cookies are offered, when callers come to Monteregard."

513

"Thank you for telling me, darling. I'll try to do everything just as you'd like to have it done."

"I know you will. I suppose you ought to go through the linen and silver and china, too, in case we want to have people in for meals, later on. I've no idea what condition those things are in. Or the books. This climate's hard on books. And we never used the library much, either, Dad and I, after I was old enough to read to myself. Before that, we sat there every evening and he read aloud to me before I went to bed. I don't think he enjoyed it especially but my grandmother always used to read aloud to my mother, so he thought it was the right thing to do. As soon as I could read myself, I took my books down to his office and to the gaming room. Those open out of each other, on the ground floor, and he spent most of his time in them, after he got older. So I stayed there, too."

"Of course you did. As soon as I've been through the storerooms, I'll go into the library and look over the books. If I think any of them need attention, I'll tell you, and we'll decide together what to do about them. But I'll leave the gaming room and the office to you, at least until you ask me to help with them. Is that right?"

"Yes, that's exactly right. You always do the thing that's exactly right, Louise, you always think of it."

While they were talking, Tudie had unobtrusively removed the tray and cleared the little table. Then she had asked whether she should bring their coffee at any special time the next morning, or whether they would ring for it. When she had been told they would ring for it, she wished them good night and left them. As her footsteps died away in the distance, Larry rose and began to undress. He had progressed no further than taking off his necktie and unbuttoning his shirt when he realized he had said nothing to Louise about the other bedrooms.

"You'll probably want to look over this floor, too. The room across the hall was my grandfather's, and as soon as I got out of the nursery I always slept there, too, in a small bed beside his big one. We—we might leave that as it is for a while. One of the chambers at the rear has always been a guest room—it has twin beds in it, the kind that are called convent beds in Louisiana, because they were first used in nunneries. The only other narrow beds in general use were the sort I slept in—youth beds—and the accouchement beds that were put crosswise at the foot of four-posters. They look like what you call day beds in France. But in the old days here families were generally large and of course babies were all born at home, so these accouchement beds were kept handy."

"I see. A lady in bed with her husband was reminded all the time what was ahead of her. I don't think that was exactly tactful, do you?"

"No, I'm afraid it wasn't."

He spoke very soberly and then realized that Louise might think he resented her light banter, whereas he was only remembering the stories he had heard about the horrors of plantation confinements, even in the most luxurious houses, and the number of times they ended fatally for mother or child or both, at the period when accouchement beds were in general use. Louise slid out of bed and came and stood beside him in her pretty filmy nightgown.

"Darling, you know I was only joking. If you'd like to put an accouchement bed in our room, it wouldn't trouble me at all. First, because I want you to make love to me, no matter what the consequences may be. I'm sure I'd die of a broken heart if you stopped now. And second, because I want lots of children, anyway. Don't you?"

"I—I guess I do. I haven't thought much about it. So far, I've only been thinking how much I wanted you."

They smiled at each other, the brief moment of constraint gone. Louise came closer to him and put her arm around him without waiting for him to put his arm around her.

"Are there any more rooms you want to tell me about before we settle down for the night?" she inquired.

"There are a whole flock of them on the ground floor, besides the wine closet and the storerooms you've already agreed to look over. The others were originally planned for the convenience of business visitors. In the early days, the planters and the shipowners kept their social life and their business life strictly separate—there's even a dining room down there. One of the chambers was eventually converted into a schoolroom for me there weren't any more business visitors by that time." He paused. "My grandfather taught me himself until I was twelve years old," he said at last. "I guess you might pass the schoolroom up, too, for the present, if you don't mind. But there's another chamber on this floor, opposite the one with the convent beds, that you'll probably want to look over. It's the one that was my nursery for a while—until I was old enough to move in with my grandfather. I believe it was mostly used as a second guest room in the old days. But the servants always call it Mr. Bushrod's room."

"You don't mean your commanding officer at Coblenz, do you, Colonel B. Harrison Page?"

"Yes. You know he was my mother's elder brother—my grandmother's son by her first marriage. I believe it was understood, when she married my grandfather, that her children should share and share alike; so of course Uncle Bushrod was regarded as a member of the family at Cindy Lou, though as a matter of fact, he never was here much, I believe, because mostly he lived with my great-grandmother in Virginia on her plantation, which he eventually inherited. But whenever he was here, that was the room he used. My grandfather always leaned over backward in his efforts to be fair—he made Uncle Bushrod a regular allowance, even after it was agreed that the value of his ownership of Sorrento and Amalfi more than offset the value of my ownership of Cindy Lou. That was before my grandfather got Victoria for me, however, so perhaps he figured Uncle Bushrod had something more coming to him. Anyway, you know Dad's will stipulated that Uncle Bushrod should get two hundred dollars a month for life, in spite of the fact that he's married to a millionairess. I told you about it, because I thought I ought to explain why you and I might be short of cash sometimes."

"Yes, I remember."

"Just the same, I have the impression he and my grandfather never got on very well together—of course, as you must have gathered, I didn't get on very well with him myself. And anyone who couldn't get on with my grandfather—" Larry paused again. "Anyway, I was so small the last time my uncle Bushrod came to Cindy Lou that I don't remember it," he went on. "And I don't remember hearing my grandfather speak of him, except in the most casual way. The servants used to talk about him a little more, but not much. I suppose it's conceivable that he might want to come here again, sometime. Perhaps I ought to ask him, anyway. As far as I know, he's the only relative, except Janine, that I've got left. I might like him better if I received him as an uncle, instead of being under orders to him as an officer."

"You don't mind too much, do you? About not having relatives, I mean?"

"No, of course I don't mind. How could I, when I have you, how could I miss anyone?"

The words were hardly out of his mouth when he was conscious of the lie he had told her. Only as long as he stayed in this one room, only as long as Louise prodigally gave him her love, could he forget the rest of Cindy Lou and close his consciousness to the great loss which had come with his great gain. But once he was out of this sanctuary, once he had left his beloved, it would be different. He would miss his grandfather with every turn he took, with every breath he drew. Nothing, no one in the world, could wholly compensate for that loss.

Belatedly, he realized that he had not returned her caress and, as he did so, his dormant desire wakened to urgency. He had been cheated out of lifting her over the threshold, but he would make up for that now. Without a word, he swept her from her feet and started across the room with her. She laughed and snuggled her head under his chin, kissing his throat. But almost immediately, she recognized the intensity of his mood and her own changed. He still needed her more than he wanted her and perhaps he always would. Since this was so, he required, more than anything else, the assurance of her compassionate understanding and her everlasting loyalty. A lighthearted response to his love making was not enough, and it was not enough, either, that he should be able to take the unity of their yearning for granted; there must be something akin to dedication in her self-surrender. Her laughter trailed softly away into silence and she raised her head. Her lips were waiting for his to seal them as he put her down on their bed.

 CHAPTER XXXIV

Louise was still sleeping peacefully when Larry waked the next morning. Army routine had tended to confirm the habit of early rising which the schedule at Jefferson and the normal requirements of plantation life had already formed; he still found it difficult to adjust himself to the later matutinal hours natural to his wife. After lying quietly beside her for a few moments, he became so uncontrollably restless that he was afraid he would disturb her; so he slipped out of bed, scribbled a note which he pinned on his pillow and carried his clothes to the bathroom. Once dressed, he took his shoes in his hand and tiptoed through the hall and down the stairs, while Nuffy padded softly along beside him. Ivy, who entered the kitchen at almost the same moment he did, looked at him in unconcealed surprise.

"You-all didn' ring, did you, Mistuh Larry? Us didn't speck you'd be up so early. An' Tudie said—"

"No, we didn't ring, and that *was* the agreement. Miss Louise is still asleep—you'll be hearing from her later on. But I was awake and I wanted to get out and see how the grinding's coming along. As soon as you can get some coffee made, you may bring it to me—in the dining room."

"Yassuh, Mistuh Larry. Won' be but a few minutes. Will you have your grits now, too, or will you be comin' back for those?"

"I'll have those, too, as soon as they're ready—maybe with the second cup of coffee. And tell Nappy to saddle Black Jack for me, will you, when you get things started? Once I'm out, there's no saying just when I can conveniently get back—I don't want to make a special trip, just for grits. On the other hand, what about some eggs and bacon, while you're at the stove anyway?"

Ivy nodded, smilingly, and set to work; before the coffee was dripped, Tudie was there to serve it. The grits, the bacon and the eggs followed in swift succession; so did some tiny light biscuit and some fig preserves. Larry had not realized that he was so hungry; good as

517

the supper had been the night before, he had not had much heart for it. Now his healthy young appetite was asserting itself again. He pushed back his plate with a sigh of satisfaction.

"Tell Ivy that's the best breakfast I've had since I left here. And, Tudie—I'm depending on you and Ivy both to see that Miss Louise has everything she wants and needs. She was pretty tired last night. If she still seems tired when you go to her, try to make her stay in bed. The storerooms and all that can wait."

"Yassuh, Mistuh Larry, Ah sho' will."

Black Jack was ready for him when he went out and he leaped into the saddle with rising spirits. He must do something about fixing up the house, of course, as soon as possible. But meanwhile the crops were his first consideration; and he was thankful they gave him a pretext for getting away from the desolate, battered bulk which bore so little resemblance to the resplendent mansion of his grandfather's pride, but which recalled so inescapably his grandfather's presence. The first sight of the fields stimulated him still further. The stand was fine. It would look beautiful from an airplane, Larry thought to himself, remembering his flights over Touraine—as if there were block after block of deep-piled green velvet. Dumaine was a planter's planter, for true. But Christ in the mountains! He was still trying to make a crop by the same methods as Etienne de Boré. Impatiently, Larry put Black Jack across a ditch. The big gelding made the jump easily enough; but as he landed on the far bank, a flock of doves rose suddenly and he bolted, rocketing off down the bank. At first Larry gave the horse his head, sensing that he was letting off excess spirits rather than yielding to the mad panic of a runaway. But presently Larry sawed on the bridle and brought his mount to a panting halt just as they approached a newly cut stubble field.

"Satisfied now, you old jug-headed son of a bitch?" he asked aloud. "Got it out of your system? If not, I'll give you a real workout, any time you say, the way we used to do at Saumur. . . ."

He looked across the stubble where, along the farther edge, men and women, swinging their cleaver-shaped knives, were cutting cane. Others followed in their wake to strip the leaves from the heavy, polished joints of the long stalks. Still others piled the stalks so that the creaking, two-wheel carts could pick up the loads and take them through the dusty lanes to the daily stockpile around the base of the sugarhouse carrier. All this was obsolete, Larry told himself with growing impatience. In the mill proper, Tregre would have everything going smoothly from carrier to centrifugals. But out here in the field were mule carts instead of trucks, mule-drawn plows instead of tractors. Hell, didn't anybody here realize yet that a tractor didn't eat except when it was working, while mules had to be fed twice a day, the year round, whether they did a lick of work or not? Didn't anybody care that the land you used for mule feed couldn't produce a cash crop, whereas a tractor got its feed out of a tank? No wonder they'd had that knockout the year before when crops that cost four dollars to put in couldn't be sold for as much as three! The rice people had been hit worse, of course, but even so. . . . And those splintering old wooden bridges across the drainage canals and ditches! One team was kept busy just going around day after day replacing worn-out planks and stringers. Suppose cypress *was* cheap and labor didn't cost much? A good concrete culvert lasted practically forever, once it was put in. There was not only plenty of work for him to do, there were plenty of changes he ought to make. He wheeled Black Jack around and cantered toward the cane cutters, whistling a rather jerky version of "Where Do We Go From Here, Boys, Where Do We Go From Here"; and as he did so, he saw Dumaine, mounted on his walking mare, but relaxed "slaunchwise" in the saddle, while he watched the progress of the work. He saluted Larry with a wave of his worn riding crop.

"It's good to see you out here again," he observed, pushing back his wide-brimmed hat and running a bright red bandanna over his brow. "After all, like your grandfather used to say, there's no better fertilizer for any field than the eye of the owner."

"I'd like to spend a lot of my time out here, and that's the truth," Larry answered. "But don't forget I've got a mill, some perique sheds, the tobacco fields and a towboat or so that all need looking after, too. And up to now, I've had a commanding officer to make the decisions. Learning how to do that'll take me a little time. However"—he pointed back to the headland along which he had just ridden—"one of the first jobs we've got ahead of us is putting in culverts, either concrete or iron, in place of those bridges, while we're cleaning out the ditch banks this winter. And as to our seed cane, from what he wrote me I gather Septime seems to think. . . ."

"Oh, him!" shrugged Dumaine. "He's got a headful of book ideas, ever since he came back from the Army. You can't plant sugar out of those books, and what he says about our native seed cane being from a strain that's too old, and importing something that never did grow here before. . . ."

"I know, I know," Larry interrupted. "Maybe you're right and he's wrong. But suppose you stop planting until we can all get together at the house some night—you and Tregre and Septime and all the rest— and decide among us what's best. That is, I'll do the deciding, because it's my responsibility. But I want to give everyone a chance to say what he thinks, first."

"Well, then, there's one thing I want to say right now," Dumaine declared with spirit. "What we really need most, to bring these fields back to where they ought to be, is mules. You know how it is yourself,

Mr. Vincent. For sugar you need the youngest and strongest mules you can get. We didn't use to keep them after they got to be nine years old. Then we'd sell them to cotton planters, because they'd still be plenty young enough and strong enough to make cotton. But when the war came, the Army grabbed off all the mules there was, so nobody could get any. Then, after Mr. Batchelor died, we didn't like to bother you by writing you about it. But after all, we're using one hundred and eighty mules on the place, which is damn good for thirty-five hundred acres of cane—and at least a third of them are over age."

"So you mean we need at least sixty new mules, for a starter?"

"That's it."

"At a hundred and fifty each for low, that comes to—let's see, yes, sir, that's nine thousand dollars and we wouldn't get more than twenty-five hundred dollars for the old ones at best."

"But you've *got* to have mules for cane, just like you've got to have land."

"Like hell you have! Listen: new mules to be bought every year and at least one man to each pair of mules and the Lord alone knows how much acreage held out from sugar for corn to feed the mules. Why, you could do it all with fifteen or twenty tractors, run by fifteen or twenty men, with maybe two more men for a maintenance crew and with no acreage held back for feed. Don't you see we've got to run the place that way or go under? It won't be easy to find the money for the tractors, I can tell you. But at least when I've done it, I won't have poured it down a drain, as I would if I stuck to the old outworn ways."

"As far as the money goes," Dumaine retorted, "the cost of the mules wouldn't be much more than a starter. Just wait until you hear what Hermann Tregre's got waiting for you. And he's holding things down to what's needed most, such as shelling the mill. That hasn't been done since before the war and—"

"The whole mill? All nine cylinders?"

"Sure."

"But God almighty, that will come to at least ten thousand dollars!"

"Well, you're lucky a way's been worked out to slip those ridged shells, like sleeves, over the big grinding cylinder. Just think what it would have cost you if—"

"I know. But that isn't going to make it any easier to pull nine thousand or so out of a hat for your mules and then ten thousand more for Hermann to reshell the mill. Besides, I haven't heard yet what Septime wants in the way of improvements. And maybe you don't read the market reports. In case you don't know it, there was a bad break last year in commodity prices. All the clear cash profit we make out of this year's harvests we'll be able to put in our eyes and forget. The only thing that might keep us going, with luck, would be the perique, the way Septime's got it set up. I mean *lots* of luck!"

It was a good thing he had eaten a big breakfast, Larry reflected, rather grimly, as he turned home again at last; otherwise, he would have been almost starved, for, as it was, he was terribly hungry. He hoped dinner would be ready and, for the first time, he wondered how Louise had been getting along with her inspection of the storerooms— that is, if she had actually felt equal to beginning her rounds. As he approached the house, he saw that she was on the gallery, and she waved and called out to him in warm welcome. Instantly his irritation and sense of frustration about the plantation evaporated, for her presence meant that she was not exhausted, that she was ready and waiting for him, just as usual; since this was so, what did all Dumaine's griping—all Tregre's stubbornness—amount to, anyway? Nothing at all—nothing, at least, that he could not easily cope with. But he had hardly reached this happy conclusion when he saw that Louise was not alone; a stocky, elderly man had come up behind her and the next minute he recognized Clovis Bourgeois. He tossed his reins to Nappy, who, for a wonder, was waiting for him, and rushed up the steps.

"Why, Captain! What good wind brings you here?" he exclaimed, wringing his visitor's hand. "This is the man I've told you so much about," he added, turning to Louise and giving her a hearty kiss. "If it weren't for him, the C. & L. Navigation Company never could have kept going all this time. Sit down, Captain, and tell me about everything while we have a good drink before dinner."

"It'd have to be a mighty long one, if I'm to tell you all about everything before we eat," Bourgeois answered, grinning. "So I hope some of my news can wait until afterward. But I will tell you, straight off, what brought me here on the double, the minute I knew I'd find you at home. We've had a steel towboat offered us by the Nashville Bridge Company, up in Tennessee, powered with a Diesel motor, and complete. Listen, when I say complete, I mean *complete*. Put a couple of cans of beans and a ham in the galley, and you can step aboard her right this very now, and start for Council Bluffs or Wheeling or any damn place on any damn river you'd care to name. And you can pick her up for a measly twenty-five thousand dollars. She was built for some wartime outfit that busted up as soon as the war was over, and Captain Joe Chotin—I guess you'll agree he knows his ear from a hole in the ground when it comes to towboating—had the mate to her built for himself, and got a contract right away with the Standard Oil to tow their barges from Baton Rouge to Louisville."

"I like the way you say a 'measly' twenty-five thousand, skipper," Larry interrupted wryly. "Only it was just this morning I had them pick off all the dollar bills from the bushes, rake 'em in a pile and burn them. They were cluttering up the place something awful. So it will be anyway a week or ten days before a fresh crop of money grows back. . . . Meanwhile, I'm going to see about those drinks. I'm assuming Louise has already seen to the dinner."

His assumption was correct, she told him smilingly. In fact, she had some drinks ready, too—she had felt sure he would want one as soon as he got in, and Captain Bourgeois must be thirsty, too. Tudie had remembered how they used to like their liquor—so, well, here was Tudie now, with a tray. Both men pronounced the contents of the proffered glasses excellent and asked for dividends before they went inside for the dinner which obviously gave them an equal amount of satisfaction. But Bourgeois persisted in sticking to the subject of the new towboat, and it was soon evident to Larry that it would take plainer speech than table talk to divert his visitor. There was no help for it; he would have to take Bourgeois down to the office, which he so greatly dreaded to enter, and thrash matters out with him there.

"Where the hell do you think I'm going to snatch twenty-five thousand bucks without turning bootlegger?" he inquired, rather testily, when they were seated by the old roll-top desk. "I hear those boys are roping it in now that Washington is really trying to make the prohibition law stick."

"Mortgage the *Palourde* and the *Larry,* mortgage everything you've got, but raise that money, son," Bourgeois said earnestly. "You'll never get another chance like this. Listen to me, now: do you think the Standard is the only outfit that's going to be shipping barges of oil up and down this river? If you do, you're crazy. They're putting up a tank terminal at Good Hope; there's already a refinery at Destrehan and another at Norco, which I hear this big Dutch outfit, Royal Shell or something, is likely to take over and—"

"And what?"

"And one of these days there'll be oil fields right along this river. Mark my words, Larry."

"One of these days!" Larry burst out. "What'll I be doing with that Diesel towboat while I'm waiting for one of these days?"

"Charter her, if you can't get a towing contract," Bourgeois replied unhesitatingly. "Betcha Joe Chotin would charter her, just like that. And if she's yours, you could name her the *Clyde Batchelor.* I've got a sneaking hunch he'd like that."

Larry rose abruptly and turning, looked out of the low window nearest him toward the truncated terraces. The *Clyde Batchelor!* The return of that beloved name to the river! He could see the island, with its willow scrub and tall cottonwood, where once the *Lucy Batchelor* had been anchored and where she had sunk, at long last, to rest in the shallows. The island had been gradually formed as her upper works caught driftwood and trash in successive rises; new crests had been built up and the muddy water, checked by the obstruction, had deposited more and more silt there. The island was far out of the channel, and the members of the River Commission had let it remain there. They had, indeed, listened with favor to the suggestion Larry had made, while he was still overseas, that on their charts it should be designated as Batchelor's Island. And if there could be a boat by that name, too! . . . But twenty-five thousand dollars! With all the modernization for which the two plantations clamored, with all the restoration needed at Cindy Lou, with the prospect of an increasing family and the expense which this would entail, he did not see how he could rightfully spare such a sum, even if he could beg or borrow it. Still, the temptation to try was too strong for him.

"I don't know how I can do it, skipper," he said at last. "But I'll go through my account books right away—of course I haven't had a chance to look at them yet—and then I'll go over Dumaine's and Tregre's and Septime's with them, to see exactly how we stand and what corners we can cut. After that, I'll let you know."

"But meanwhile that offer might go to someone else, who'd snap it up like we ought to and—"

"We could wire and get an option, couldn't we? If I stopped wishing—and talking—and settled down to those books, it wouldn't take me long to find out what I could do. Get along to Convent and send that wire and then come back and stay with us for a couple of days, anyway. Keep Louise company while I'm figuring. I need help to prevent her from trying to do everything that requires attention here, all at once. You see, we're expecting—"

"Say, that's great news. No man's really lived until he's paddled his son across the behind for being a wild young buck—like he was himself once."

"So I've heard . . . well, be that as it may, I know Louise would enjoy visiting with you. I've told her a lot about you already. And maybe, if I get right to work, we can take the train to New Orleans tomorrow or the day after that and go into a huddle with Valois Dupré. He's better than I am when it comes to this high finance business. One way or another, we'll make strap and buckle meet."

The answer to the wire came promptly: the Nashville Bridge Company would be glad to let Mr. Vincent have a week's option on the new towboat. Without waiting for the telegram's arrival, Larry had settled down to his figuring, and by the following afternoon he was ready to talk with Dumaine, Tregre and Septime. In view of their first rather captious attitude and insistent demands, he had dreaded the interview; but he found them more co-operative than he expected. Sure, the old mules and the old machinery would go for a while longer, if they had to; crops had been raised without anything better before and could be again. Larry was reminded of men he had known in the Army, who griped when nothing much was the matter, but took it in their stride when a real emergency arose. . . .

He knew that next, in all fairness, he should talk with Louise. While he had been busy with his figures, she had been equally busy with the house. Before his first agitation over Bourgeois' visit had subsided, she had come to him with a little book, bound in red morocco and fastened with a tiny heart-shaped padlock. The hinges of its clasp had rusted with age and the padlock was, consequently, quite useless; but Louise was holding the book firmly between her fingers, taking great pains to keep it closed.

"Look what I've found!" she said excitedly. Larry, whose thoughts were centered on the new towboat, glanced at the little book without enthusiasm. However, since it was evident that Louise was thrilled by its discovery, he made an effort to show some interest.

"What is it?" he asked. "An old diary?"

"I think so. I haven't looked inside it, because I didn't know whether I ought to or not. You can see that it has a lock. I believe that in the days when ladies kept diaries, they used to write all their innermost thoughts in them. And I'm almost sure this was hidden—purposely. It was in a secret drawer—I'd have never known there was one, in the desk where I found it, if there hadn't been one almost exactly like it in a desk at Monteregard."

Larry took the little book from her and turned it over. On closer inspection he thought Louise was right; it undoubtedly was a diary, but it was obviously a very old one and he opened it without hesitation. On the flyleaf was written, in faded ink:

Lucy Batchelor
With love from her devoted husband
Clyde Batchelor

Pittsburgh, Pa.
November, 1867

The handwriting was his grandfather's, which Larry still found impossible to regard without a pang. He closed the little book.

"It does seem to be a diary," he said. "But I don't see any reason why you shouldn't read it, if you want to. It's probably just a record of rapture. My grandfather must have given it to my grandmother while they were on their honeymoon. I know she was blissfully happy, but I understand that in those days ladies were shy about saying, out loud, that this was the case, if their happiness had anything to do with their love life. Perhaps that's why they confided in diaries and hid those away. I'm sure glad times have changed. I'd much rather have you tell me—and show me—that you enjoy being married to me than to have you write about it in a book."

He handed it back to her with a smile. Her answering smile was warmly responsive. But she still fingered the diary a little hesitantly.

"You don't want to read it yourself?" she asked.

"Well, not right now, honey. You see, I'm pretty busy with all these figures. Maybe some other time. But you go right ahead."

He had not thought about the diary again for several days. Then he asked Louise whether she had found time to glance through it. He did not see how she could have, for apparently she was spending every moment when they were not together in making a thorough investigation of household supplies and a careful record of household needs. Still, she had obviously been greatly intrigued by the diary; she might have stolen a few moments, here and there. . . .

"I decided against reading it, after all," she answered surprisingly. "I know you said it would be all right and you and I usually agree. But this time I didn't agree with you. I felt sure that diary had secrets in it. As a matter of fact, I—I was so sure of it that I burned it."

"You burned it!"

"Yes. You don't mind, do you, Larry? You said you weren't interested in it, so I thought—"

"No, I don't mind," he replied, quite sincerely. Her action astonished him; it seemed both precipitate and extreme, and Louise was not given to extremes, nor had he ever known her to be precipitate, except when she fell in love with him. But he was not offended by what she had done and indeed he did not attach much importance to it. He had too many other matters on his mind and he also felt sure that by this time she must have all kinds of lists of things that she wanted and needed ready to submit to him. He had not suggested, before, that she should come to the office, but now he did so; and as she seated herself composedly beside him, he realized that this was very much as it must have been when his grandfather and his grandmother conferred together about ways and means. History certainly did have a way of repeating itself.

"I wanted to talk to you about this boat Bourgeois' so sure I ought to buy," he began. "You're my partner now and I think you should be consulted. It's this way—"

"Of course I am your partner—all good French wives are their husbands' partners," she answered. "And I think I understand already how it is, *mon coeur*. You want to buy that boat and you do not quite see where the money is coming from to do it. Well, of course I don't, either. But French girls are brought up to manage, as well as to prepare for partnership, you know, even when there's plenty of money in the family. And there wasn't much in mine. That is, of course, Uncle

Pierre has a great deal, and he's always been very generous. But my father wasn't wealthy, and after he and my mother separated, she and I lived on what she had. Then when she remarried, naturally she felt she had to contribute toward keeping up my stepfather's position, and this meant there was still less for me. I explained that to you in the beginning, and I think Uncle Pierre did, too, because otherwise I would have had much more of a dowry, and we wanted to be sure you wouldn't be disappointed."

"Good Lord, I never thought about a dowry when I fell in love with you and you know it! In the first place, there wasn't time, because it all happened so fast. And in the second place, I'd have felt just the way I do now, just the way most American men feel, I think—that they'd rather support their wives than have it the other way around."

"It isn't a question of support, it's a question of mutual contribution in France," Louise said calmly. "I wasn't thinking of making any special contribution; I wouldn't, even if I could, unless there were an emergency, because I know you wouldn't like it. But I shouldn't think you'd mind having me show you how well I could manage, without spending much of your money, until you have more. Even if I didn't have a big dowry, of course I did have more linen and things like that than we could use up in a lifetime—that part of my dot was started as soon as I was born. I can replenish a great many household needs at Cindy Lou, without spending a cent—and I'll admit a good deal of replenishing seems to be needed! Don't forget we've got all the furnishings and equipment of the Elysian Fields' house to fall back on."

"That's so. I'd forgotten about those."

This was quite true. So many questions—all urgently requiring immediate answers—had arisen since their arrival at Cindy Lou that the problem connected with the New Orleans property had inevitably been crowded out of his consciousness. The caretakers, grown old in the service of the family, had been faithful to their trust; the contents of the house, many of them beautiful, some of them valuable, were in as good condition as could be expected, after a long period of disuse in a hot, humid climate. But the house itself had deteriorated badly and the neighborhood in which it was located had deteriorated still more. In order to make it habitable, a new roof, new plumbing and much other replacement would be necessary, besides extensive repairs; and even if all this were done, its surroundings, some of them almost slumlike in character, would have made it unsuitable as a residence of the kind Larry and Louise would require for themselves and their children. Neither of them had any sentiment about the house, and after their first disappointing inspection of it they had agreed that it should be either rented or sold as soon as possible. But they were in a hurry to reach Cindy Lou, and they had left New Orleans without coming to any definite decision about it, nor had they brought up the subject since. Now Larry realized that Louise was right: whether the house was sold or rented, it should be emptied, as soon as possible, of everything that could be of use to them.

"I think we'd better decide, right now, to sell it," Louise went on. "Then we can take the money we get for it and apply that toward the purchase price of the *Clyde Batchelor.*"

"I'm not sure that's fair. Remember Uncle Pierre said if we did decide to dispose of the house, the money we got for it ought to be added to your little capital and properly invested."

"But the *Clyde Batchelor is* a proper investment! If it weren't, you wouldn't be making it."

"Well, of course I've great hopes for it. Still, I'm not sure that Uncle Pierre—"

"I am. But we can consult him if you like. After all, the money won't be available for investment right away. But I think we ought to take whatever steps are necessary to make it available as soon as possible." As if that question were now settled, Louise went on to discuss others. "So we don't need to worry about household equipment at Cindy Lou, and I shouldn't think we'd need to worry about food, either. We can raise most of what we need, can't we? I should think we could. Even if we can't, another thing French girls know how to do is to set a good table without spending too much on it—we could do that before the war and we got better and better at it all the time. Naturally, Uncle Pierre would be sending us wine from his vineyards, if it weren't for this queer American law which says you mustn't drink it—*that* I don't understand very well. But I think I can learn how to make wine. And if Tudie and Ivy won't resent having me tell them a few things—"

"Never mind whether they resent it or not. Go ahead and tell them."

"No. Not right off and not that way, darling. They've been telling me how Miss Lucy used to do things—I've encouraged them to. And I'm learning a great deal. She must have been a wonderful housekeeper, and she was older and more experienced, even when she first came here, than I am, wasn't she? But after I've learned, gradually, all that I can from the way she did things, then I think maybe I could experiment doing things—well, perhaps more in the modern manner, inside the house, just as you want to experiment in the fields and the factory."

"Louise, I didn't suppose I could possibly be any gladder than I was already that I'd married a French girl. But if you go on talking like this, I think I shall be, at that. And I think maybe I can manage to get that boat. But I don't want to do it under any false pretenses. We won't be able to go anywhere, we won't be able to do anything—"

"But why should we want to go anywhere when we've just come home? And why should we want to do anything that we won't be doing at Cindy Lou? I should think we'd have all we could possibly do, right here, this winter. And after the baby's born, we won't want to leave him, and it wouldn't be good for him to take him here, there and everywhere—now would it?"

So Larry told Captain Bourgeois to send another wire to the Nashville Bridge Company, and they went off to New Orleans together for a conference with Valois Dupré about high finance. And though, as Louise had said, there was certainly plenty for both of them to do on the plantations, Larry was obliged to leave fairly frequently after that, since it did not prove as easy a matter to put the *Clyde Batchelor* into actual operation as Captain Bourgeois had rather glibly intimated, in his excitement over the purchase. In spite of all the "management" of which Larry and Louise were jointly capable, it was impossible for them to make an immediate cash payment on the new boat, and this was necessarily bought on the installment plan. Then, after the act of sale had finally been passed, the arrangements for chartering the *Clyde Batchelor* to the Vicksburg & Bayou Sara Towing Company required prolonged adjustment. It had been decided to operate her like a tramp steamer: hauling grain barges from Minneapolis and St. Paul for the big public grain elevator in New Orleans; bringing barges of cotton from Arkansas; automobiles from Ohio and loads of coal and steel from Pittsburgh. There was also the substantial hope that occasionally they might get a tow upstream, too—when there was more oil or gasoline or both—to take north than the Chotin Navigation Company could handle in a single tow. But it took infinite time and patience, not to mention a good deal of tact, to make this hope a reality.

At last Larry started back from New Orleans on a beautiful spring day, fairly bursting with the good news that the final contracts had actually been signed, and that the decks of the *Clyde Batchelor* were really cleared for action. He had been summoned, unexpectedly, to close these last deals, and had driven down the river road in the old Ford, which he had decided would have to go another year, after all, when the question of "management" for the *Clyde Batchelor* had arisen; then he had come pelting back again, the minute his business was finished, feeling more confident of impending prosperity than he had for a long while and correspondingly happier. He had just heard that the little island which owed its existence to the first boat his grandfather had built and owned had officially been given the name of Batchelor by the River Commission; the towboat *Clyde Batchelor* was indisputably his own and ready to begin operations, flying the C. & L. house flag; and within a few weeks now, there would be an even more important namesake for the man whom he had loved and believed he always would love beyond all others. Neither he nor Louise had ever doubted that the expected baby would be a boy—they always referred to it as "him"; and the next time he went to New Orleans he would be taking Louise to the hospital, where the best available room had been engaged—for in this instance there was to be no economizing. The services of a specialist in obstetrics had been secured, too; and when this physician had last examined Louise, he had said that her condition could not possibly be more satisfactory; he did not expect complications of any sort, and she should be able to go home when the baby was two weeks old, if she took a professional nurse with her. Next, Larry reflected, there would be a gala christening which would be the first big party he and Louise had given, just as his own baptism had been the first to which his parents had invited their friends in their new house. It really was a pity that Cindy Lou had never been "fancied up" to this day—such a celebration should have a more elegant setting than they could give it. But what really counted was that they had the boat and that presently they would have the baby. And they had each other. In that last respect, history was not repeating itself, but improving upon itself. Larry did not doubt that his grandfather's marriage had been an extremely happy one. But he did not see how it could possibly have been as happy as his own. Lucy Page had been a widow when Clyde married her, and that was not like having your bride come to you as Louise had come to him. And the other marriage had been childless, while the baby who was expected so soon would unquestionably be only the first of several. . . .

The nearer Larry came to home, the higher his spirits soared, as he thought of all this. Then, as he turned into the driveway, he saw the battered Dodge, belonging to Dr. Peter Mitchell—who long before had succeeded old Dr. Bringier as the family physician— parked near the grand staircase. Suddenly, cold fear swept through him. Neither Nappy nor anyone else was in sight and the place seemed curiously hushed. He tore up the steps, two at a time, and threw open the front door. The hall, like the yard, was empty, and there was no answer to his call. But when he was halfway up the second staircase, he heard the hushed murmur of voices and then a sharp, thin wail, which pierced him like a knife. The doors of all the rooms except his mother's, which he and Louise still shared, stood open; but no sounds were coming from them. They were vacant, too. It was behind that one closed door something was happening—that something had happened. The sickening smell of ether came from it; the murmuring grew louder and more confused and the wail penetrated it more sharply. Larry stopped abruptly on the threshold, tempted to rush in but somehow withheld; and, as he hesitated, the door opened and Dr. Mitchell, wearing a blood-spattered white garment, came out.

"Why, hello there, Larry!" he said. "This is a great time for you to be showing up."

There was no note of tragedy in his voice; it was almost bantering in tone. Larry seized his arm.

"What's happened?" he asked hoarsely.

"Why, just what we've been expecting—only we didn't expect it quite so soon." As he spoke, the doctor peeled off his rubber gloves, unbuttoned his blood-stained gown and tossed both nonchalantly on a near-by sofa. "We weren't very thoroughly prepared, but everything went off okay at that. Of course, I wouldn't be out here if it hadn't. You can go in pretty soon. Don't stay but a minute though. It's been rather a long pull. However, your wife's taken it like a Trojan—never saw anything to beat it—and she's fine now. So's the baby—a bouncer." He opened the door a crack. "Mr. Vincent's back. Let him know when he can come in, will you?" he said to someone Larry could not see. Then he closed the door again. "Well, I want to go and get cleaned up. So long."

He disappeared in the direction of the bathroom. Larry waited what seemed an eternity. He thought he could distinguish Louise's voice now, above the wailing sound, but he was not sure, for he had never heard it when it was so faint. Tudie came out with a big bundle of linen, holding it as if she were trying to hide the stains from him. But she was smiling broadly.

"We done cotched us de sweetes' baby you ever did see, Mistuh Larry," she said proudly. "It were a while befo' Miss Louise could turn dat child loose, but she done grand just de same. De nurse, she'll be out in a minute now and let you in."

Again the wait seemed endless. Finally the door opened once more, and a woman who was a complete stranger came out of it, but remained standing in such a way as to block Larry's passage. Her countenance was stern, her primly parted hair was surmounted by a stiff cap and her starched dress rattled with the least movement. She looked at Larry accusingly, as if she believed his past conduct to have been something close to criminal and also as if she had little hope of his future reformation. Then she spoke severely.

"After this, I cannot permit anything to interfere with Mrs. Vincent's rest," she said. "But she has been asking for you, and Dr. Mitchell has overriden my advice and humored her by consenting to allow you to see her now. I hope I do not need to warn you that you should not say or do anything which will upset her."

"Why in hell should you think I want to upset her?" Larry asked angrily. "But I do want—"

The strange woman raised a thin hand. "And you should not raise your voice, either. Noise of any sort is a very disturbing factor, at this stage. I shall return, in five minutes, with some nourishment for Mrs. Vincent. Meanwhile—"

"Meanwhile I'd appreciate it if you'd give me a chance to go to my wife, especially as she's asked for me."

He had not raised his voice this time, but something in it evidently warned the nurse that if she did not move of her own accord, he might thrust her bodily away. She stepped rapidly to one side and Larry strode past her.

The room was still permeated with the mingled scents of ether and blood; but as Larry crossed it, he became less and less conscious of these, more and more aware of the fragrance of clean linen and new wool, and of another fresh smell, which was unfamiliar to him, and which he did not instantly recognize as the unique sweetness that emanates from a newly born, newly bathed baby. The baby was not lying, as he had imagined it would be, in the curve of Louise's arm, but in an old wooden cradle that had been drawn up beside the bed; and, in a way, he was glad. At the moment he felt that he did not want even their child to come between Louise and himself. As he bent over her, he was horrified by her pallor; but though her eyes seemed preternaturally large in that white face, they were full of love as she looked up at him, and there was nothing about her smile which suggested suffering.

"I'm afraid you'll be terribly disappointed," she said. "I know how much you wanted a boy, so you could name him Clyde. But I love little Lucy already and I'm sure you will, too. Besides, next year, we'll give her a baby brother, won't we?"

   CHAPTER XXXV

It was over two years, instead of only one, after all, before there was another baby and then it was a second girl.

It was true that Larry had been disappointed the first time. However, his disappointment had been swallowed up in his concern about Louise, and, as she had predicted, he quickly fell a victim to the charms of little Lucy, much as Clyde had fallen under the spell of Cary. But the second time, everything happened on schedule, in such a quiet orderly way that he had no cause for concern; and the second baby girl was not nearly as winsome as the first. There had been no name ready for her, because Larry had been so sure that this time the name would be Clyde; but after some hesitation and discussion, it was decided to call her Amy. After all, Mrs. Surget had left no child of her own, and Larry felt a certain debt of gratitude to her for her kindness to him during his childhood; it seemed as if he would be repaying this in some slight measure by giving her a namesake. Beyond this, he had very little feeling in the matter, anyway, for this time his disappointment was very deep. And it was not assuaged by Louise's hopeful prediction that the *next* one would be a boy.

"Perhaps we won't ever have another. After all, we didn't have Lucy right away or Amy very soon after that. And it certainly wasn't because of any preventive measures."

"No, and I'm glad that it wasn't. But I'm also glad we had those first years to ourselves. I wouldn't have wanted even a child to come between us then." She was putting into words what he had felt himself, at one time, but which he had never expressed. "And I'm glad Lucy and Amy weren't so near together that I haven't been able to enjoy them both and give undivided attention to them both. If they'd been only a year apart, I'd have had two babies at the same time— without even having had the excitement of twins! Please don't worry so, *mon coeur*. You'll have your boy yet, you'll see."

"I don't believe it. If we do have another, it'll be a third girl. We'll have a *drei Mädchen Haus,* as they say in Coblenz."

Perhaps if he had not been worried about many other things, Larry would not have worried so much about his failure to beget a son. But everything on the plantations seemed to be going wrong. The yield had been short and its sucrose content low; maybe Septime was right when he said cane got tired, and that after a certain number of years you had to try a new kind of seed to give it a fresh start. Then of course agricultural prices had really never recovered from the setback of '21. Besides, it had been absolutely necessary to replace more machinery than Tregre had indicated in his first surveys; and no one realized more keenly than Larry that his failure to modernize the entire equipment of the plantations was the principal source of trouble. Back of this failure, to be sure, lay his decision to squeeze from the turnip every drop of blood it held and thus buy the *Clyde Batchelor.* The money so spent could have been used to replace mules and carts with tractors and trucks; it could also have been used to modernize the mill, and so take advantage of the new deal everybody was talking about—making wallboard out of bagasse. The Godchaux at Raceland were already baling bagasse; but Larry couldn't swing anything like that at Cindy Lou or Victoria, because he did not have the money to shift his production line into new and more profitable channels.

He could not be thankful enough that he did not have a nagging wife, one who insisted on making a show, on "keeping up with the Joneses," as people were beginning to say. From the outset, Louise had been a blessing straight from heaven. But now Louise was ill, and of course that was the worst trouble of all. It was all very well for the New Orleans specialist, who had been consulted this time, to tell him he needn't worry. How could he help worrying, for God's sake, when the dear girl was running a temperature, when she was steadily losing weight, when her erstwhile buoyant footsteps dragged listlessly and when her lovely laugh sounded less and less often? Where in hell she could have picked up that damned undulant fever was a mystery. The doctor had shrugged his shoulders when Larry told him every cow on the place had been tested. There was always a chance. . . . However, there was no cause for concern. Recovery was slow, but it was sure —practically sure, anyway. The doctor would admit, though, that it was a tedious business, for the fever was apt to recur over and over again, even after convalescence seemed assured, and a certain amount of pain did go with it. No one could expect women, especially young women, to be resigned to such discomforts. No, Larry said savagely to himself. And no one should expect a man who was trying to pinch a penny here and a jitney there to stop worrying when, in addition to his natural anxiety about his wife, he was wondering how to pay her doctors' bills. Louise was home again now, thank the Lord—the great gloomy house had seemed like a tomb without her; but the doctor had insisted upon having her at Touro until the nature of the disease was determined beyond any shadow of doubt. And that being the case, Larry himself had insisted on a private room and special nurses. You might economize on anything and everything else, but you didn't economize on your wife when she was sick. He hadn't changed his mind about that, either. However, this didn't alter the fact that payment had been required, in advance, for the private room, and every week for the nurses. And when the doctor's first bill—also very promptly rendered—had come in, Larry told himself grimly that it must be cheaper to run a steamboat line than a doctor's office.

Increasingly, he begrudged the monthly remittance which, under the terms of Clyde Batchelor's will, went regularly to Bushrod Page. Larry did not believe his grandfather could have realized how little his uncle needed it. Mabel, who had inherited millions from her father, the railroad magnate, had died, leaving her immense fortune to Bushrod; and Bushrod had promptly married again—a young and beautiful woman, who had no money herself, but who had considerable social standing and who had promptly presented her husband with an heir. So now Bushrod had everything: a substantial fortune, a charming wife, a proud position, and an assured inheritance. Somehow Larry, without knowing quite why he felt that way, did not believe his uncle deserved any of this, much less all of it; and he was consumed with rage when Bushrod, whom he had never seen since he left Coblenz and with whom his correspondence had been as brief and impersonal as was consistent with courtesy, wrote him a smooth letter, saying that henceforth the monthly remittance would be set aside as a nest egg for the heir to Sorrento and Amalfi. Larry did not resent the belated arrival on the scene of the little boy whose birth deprived him of his own potential Virginia heritage; he himself was a Louisianian, through and through, as his Virginia forebears had believed he would be. But he felt there was no justice in a destiny which permitted his uncle to flourish like the green bay tree while he, Larry, struggled harder and harder to make both ends meet. Above all, it seemed to him like the irony of fate that he should be the one to squeeze out money to provide a "nest egg" for the heir to Sorrento and Amalfi, when he himself was heirless.

But, as his grandfather had often reminded him, a promise was a promise; and the two hundred dollars did go every month to Virginia, no matter what that meant in the way of deprivation at Cindy Lou and, after all, griping about your troubles was about the only relief you got from them, whether it was in the Army or back home, Larry reflected morosely, as he sat over his accounts one fine summer day, when he would much rather have been out riding the crops. He had quickly abandoned the use of his grandfather's office on the grounds that, while he did not want anything changed there, he couldn't function efficiently with its antiquated equipment; he needed files, not pigeonholes, and a large, flat surface to his desk, not a roll top. This was the truth, as far as it went, but it was by no means the whole truth. He still missed his grandfather so poignantly in the surroundings with which Clyde had been most closely associated that he could not shake off the sense of loss; and he still instinctively looked for the old man, indeed sometimes still started to speak to him, before the swift realization came that it was tragically futile to do so. Larry thought Louise was aware of all this, although she had never voiced such awareness. The chamber which Larry and his grandfather had shared remained closed and unchanged, though they could have utilized that space now; and when Larry spoke to Louise about the inadequacies of the old office, she said of course he needed more modern equipment, and why not install it in one of those ground-floor chambers which were still unused? The schoolroom had better remain as it was, for who knew? They might be wanting that for Lucy and Amy and—she added unfalteringly—little Clyde someday, if not for lessons, then for games. To be sure, they were having business visitors again now, but not to the extent the builder of Cindy Lou had visualized, and probably they never would. Not that there would not be more business visitors than ever before. But the speed and ease of modern transportation had rendered long visits, for business purposes, superfluous. It was a simple matter now to leave New Orleans or Baton Rouge in the morning and return the same evening, having meanwhile settled any number of important transactions; there was hardly ever an occasion for an overnight stay, so another chamber could easily be spared for a new office. As to the cost of what Larry wanted and needed to equip it, he should not think of that; it represented an investment, not an expenditure. . . .

So Larry bought his big flat-topped desk and his files, secondhand,

and they were duly installed, as Louise had suggested, in one of the rooms formerly set aside for business visitors, which still left several more available for that purpose; and Louise supplemented the new equipment in various ways. She had discovered a firm in Chicago which ground up old rugs and carpeting and made new floor coverings out of the material; so she had sent several of the most worn and ragged specimens at Cindy Lou to this resourceful and competent establishment, and the result had been one large and very presentable rug. She had also made chintz curtains out of some longer ones which she had found in a chest at Victoria, and which would bear shortening enough to do away with the worst parts; and the attics of both houses had yielded several pictures, in which Larry had seen no decorative possibilities whatsoever until Louise actually had them up on the wall, when he ungrudgingly admired them. So, taken by and large, the new office was a very cheerful, pleasant room—and a good thing, too, Larry said to himself, looking up from the discouraging figures to a shady corner of the garden, where Louise had taken the two little girls; if it had not been, he could hardly have withstood the temptation of strolling out to join her. The children were romping around her, but she was not romping with them, as she would have, before she had been so ill. She was sitting in a big chair, watching them, and since she did not know anyone was watching *her,* the expression on her pale face was unguarded. Larry's heart smote him as he looked at her. He turned back to his books and, as he did so, Tudie knocked at the door of his office.

"Yes?" he answered impatiently, without raising his eyes from the figures.

"Dey's a gen'mun say he like to see you, suh," Tudie informed him.

"Tell him to go find Mr. Prudhomme or Mr. Tregre," Larry said abruptly.

"But he want to see you," Tudie persisted. "He say to tell you his name Mr. Waddle and the last time he see you it were in Two—or."

"Waddill! Frank Waddill!" Larry leaped up and, brushing past Tudie, rushed to the doorway. The next moment he and Frank Waddill were pummeling each other heartily and calling each other by such endearing terms as you old bastard, you, and you no-count lousy buckwheat.

"Come in, come in," Larry finally insisted. "Come in and park your carcass. What'll it be? Coffee? I can let you have some home-brew, too, that doesn't taste too God-awful if you don't look at the half-inch sediment of yeast in the bottom of the bottle. And I know there's still some prime old bourbon—prewar, so help me!—back in Dad's cellar-ette. Give it a name, man."

They were soon seated in the office, with both coffee cups and tall glasses between them, talking about that café at Tours and the little

535

black-eyed girls at the next table; about poor old Tracy Dixon, who had got his in the Argonne, instead of a master's degree at Princeton; and about the way some of those armchair soldiers were trying to grab off the American Legion. Then there was a brief pause, while Frank took a long pull at his glass and Larry glanced down at the sheet of paper on which he had been scribbling when his friend arrived.

"Hell, this reminds me," he exclaimed. "I expect you're about ready to make that survey of our sugarhouse over at Victoria. Boy, there's nothing I'd rather have or need more, too, I can tell you. But there isn't a god's blessed chance." He dropped his hand down on his discouraging notations. "I've just been telling myself the bad news. I mean bad. Now get me. I'm not going to sing the blues to you, but things have just been breaking tough. I overextended myself in buying a towboat—but I'm not sorry—and I've been trying to piece out on the plantation the best way I could to make up for it. So anything that means putting up the frogskins is not for me; not now, at least. I was just sitting here, when I was told somebody wanted to see me. I was trying to figure things out. It's less than two weeks to my wife's birthday and if anybody ever owed anybody else a real present, I owe her one. But there's no way to make it; leastways not without opening a still back in the swamps and peddling out a choice lot of white lightning to the cash trade."

He paused and Frank held up a monitory hand.

"If you'd just give me a chance, stupid, I'd ha' told you I wasn't here to inspect your sugar machinery," he said. "You got bad news, you keep saying. Well listen, shavetail, maybe I got good news for you. Ever remember me telling you about that sonar stuff, that echo-bouncing business? Good Lord, man! That was while we were still in college, before ever we made the world safe for Democracy."

"Yeah, sure I remember. What was the name of that beer garden down by the ferry?"

"I forget. But it doesn't matter. This is what does: coming back from France, I ran into a navy officer name of Karcher. Listen, mah frien'. Karch started in on sonics about nine miles higher up than the farthest I got. That boy had it. And he had something else, too. He had a man name of De Gollyer. He was working on a plan to apply his sonar stuff to oil exploration."

"Oil exploration? Out in the water, you mean?"

"No. On land. Let me ask you. How much do you know about oil?"

"It's greasy, it stinks and it makes Osage Indians rich. Outside of that, precious little."

"Well, I won't try to give you a series of lectures on the subject this evening. I might later on, if you're interested then. But here's what

536

might interest you right now: Karcher and De Gollyer have found a way for getting 'soundings' on land, similar to those the Navy used at sea during the war. They map out subterranean landscapes."

"Well, what of it?"

"Quite a good deal. In this way numbers of 'domes' have been discovered, in spite of the fact that the surface failed to indicate that there were mountains of rock layers where oil and gas could be trapped, thousands of feet beneath the top soil."

"And you helped develop this plan?"

"No such luck! But as I *had* done sonar research in college, I got in with one of the major oil companies, the Old Hickory Petroleum Corporation, and now I'm at the head of what they call their Exploration Department."

"That's fine. I'm sure glad for you. Maybe for me, too. When I'm even broker than I am now, I'll know who to hit for a fast loan."

"I can do a lot better than that for you. I'm going through this part of the country leasing exploration rights."

"Come again?"

"Let me get at it my own way. Probably you know that practically everybody in the oil business has been saying the deposits on the Gulf Coast were all west of the Mississippi River. I don't believe this. So eventually I sold my company on the idea of letting me run a shooting crew through the land between Lake Maurepas and the river. Never mind why I picked this particular area. It would take me a week to explain how we draw these underground maps from drilling logs, and fill in the blank spaces by guesswork. If our shooting crews—seismographic explorers, if you want to use the broad A—find nothing, we're not out much. If they do, we're first aboard the gravy train, with all the desirable spots under lease."

"You mean you want permission to make those bounce-back records on Cindy Lou and Victoria, and maybe find oil there? Hell, yes. Help yourself to the roasting ears."

Waddill threw back his head and laughed.

"Lord, but you're an easy touch!" he cried. "Lucky for you I won't take advantage of a partner who fought the battle of Murray Street with me in Aleck. How many acres have you got here?"

"Call it eight thousand and you won't be far wrong. Three thousand at Cindy Lou and the balance at Victoria, give or take a few hundred either way. It would need a survey to show whether the land outside our levees—the *batture,* you know—had been building up or eroding away."

"Good. Then here's my proposition. I'll pay you fifteen cents an acre for the right to make seismographic explorations on your land. That will be at least twelve hundred dollars cash on the barrelhead, here and now, this afternoon, if you sign the agreement. I've got copies of our standard exploration lease forms in my brief case out in the car. You get that much, win, lose or draw. . . . What's the matter?"

"Nothing's the matter. I was just thinking."

"All right, go ahead and think. Mind if I have another drink while you do it? This stuff isn't bad at all."

Without waiting for an answer, Frank refilled his glass. Larry, who had been staring at his friend, looked down at the sheet he had shoved aside and, picking up a pencil, scribbled on it again. Then he sat staring at the result.

Twelve hundred dollars! Twelve Hundred Dollars! TWELVE HUNDRED DOLLARS! Why that would be enough for . . . for a gala trip to New Orleans during the last few days of Carnival and the right dresses to wear to Momus and Mystick and Proteus and Comus— perhaps an evening wrap as well. Or, if Louise would rather go to New York and see some shows, but have fewer dresses, that could be managed. Larry wouldn't feel any compunctions about using Frank's money for something like that, because it would be so much velvet and you didn't put velvet into necessities. You might even put it into jewelry, if Louise would rather have jewelry than a trip. He'd never given her any jewelry, not once since they were married. But now— well now, of course he still couldn't get her a bracelet with baguette-cut diamonds, or anything on that order, but maybe he could get her a sapphire clip or something like that. Or if she'd rather blow in every-thing on a party—the sort of party they used to have at Cindy Lou— they could give one of those, with an orchestra and champagne and everything. At least, he thought they could. He had never paid for that sort of a party himself. Perhaps it cost more than he thought. Besides, he remembered with a pang, maybe Louise wasn't well enough to give a party—or to go on a trip. Anyway, she had never seemed to be dependent on excitement of that sort for pleasure. Probably she would rather redecorate one of the threadbare rooms—or could she do more than one for twelve hundred dollars? Even one room would be worth it. Then, with a less passing pang, he realized that the twelve hundred dollars might have to be used, after all, for more hospital bills . . . and that even twelve hundred dollars might not be enough. . . . He looked up.

"And if there should be oil?" he asked quietly.

"If our shots show that there's a dome or some other structure here, we'll make a regular mineral lease with you that'll come to real money. Offhand, I'd say that if the structure looked favorable, we might pay you a dollar and a half an acre for the right to sink one or more oil wells on your place in a year. If we hit, you're in the big time, because an eighth of all the oil would belong to you, and that's no chicken feed.

If we don't, you'll be better off to the tune of twelve hundred dollars, anyway. So what can you lose? Let me get that lease form."

There would be only one way, Larry knew, by which he could make Louise accept a present of any value. That would be to put it beside her plate and let her find it there, when they went in to supper on the night of her birthday. She would pick up the little box and thank him rapturously, even before she undid the ribbon with which it was tied or folded back the tissue paper in which it was wrapped. As he had so regretfully meditated, he had given her very few presents; but she had always shown immediate and wholehearted appreciation of every little thing. What mattered was that he had wanted to make her a present; the form it took was unimportant—at least to her. Larry did not feel that way about it. He was immeasurably thankful that he could make her a real gift at last.

He held back her chair for her and leaned over to kiss her. They had decided that this should be a party, with all the best silver and china and linen and all the things they liked best to eat, and that they would dress up for it; but it would be a party just for themselves. After Louise was seated and he had kissed her, Larry lingered beside her, instead of going to his own chair at the other end of the table. Louise caught sight of the little box and picked it up.

"Darling, how sweet of you! I can't wait to see . . . but whatever this is, I'm sure it's lovely. Everything you give me. . . ."

Well, it hadn't been true before, but it was this time, he said to himself, watching her as she undid the little package. When the tissue paper parted with a soft rustle, and Louise saw the word TIFFANY peeping out from between the folds, she looked up at him questioningly. The first box—cardboard covered with glazed white paper—enclosed a second one, made of velvet. She pressed the spring which controlled the lid and this flew open. Inside, formed like a tiny steamboat, was a diamond brooch.

"Larry—Larry! It's perfectly beautiful! But you shouldn't have! You know we agreed—"

"Yes, I know what we agreed and I know that agreement's got to be revised now." Purposely, he had offered no explanation of Frank's visit and she had asked for none. Now the words came tumbling out of themselves. "Our luck's turned, I know it has. This is your luck piece. Let me pin it on you, darling, and see how it looks."

The shot crews, as Larry soon learned to call them, arrived a few days later—a dozen or so brisk young men in four vehicles. One of these vehicles was a truck carrying a portable drilling rig. Another truck carried a mobile darkroom, within which Larry was shown a maze of instrument panels, recording devices and tiny, winking bulbs of vari-colored lights, which meant rather less than nothing to him, apart from a general impression of bewildering intricacy. The third truck carried angry-looking red flags and startlingly lettered signs, with the single word EXPLOSIVES prominently displayed on each side. The fourth vehicle was the dust-covered, dingy Ford touring car in which the crew chief and his assistant rode.

From then on, the peace and serenity of Cindy Lou were shattered at intervals by thunderous explosions. Nuffy, who was old and irritable now, greeted each blast with an ear-piercing howl, as he scuttled for shelter. Nappy complained that he would have to send the cows away, for their milk was being soured. One of the field hands came to say that his wife insisted on being reimbursed for a setting of eggs that had been addled by a detonation close to their cabin. Tregre angrily demanded that Larry do something to prevent the explorers from jarring his sugarhouse machinery out of alignment on its massive foundations. Tudie muttered that she no sooner had the children settled for their naps than the unearthly racket woke them up and that then they were fussy for the rest of the day. It was a task to keep the peace among all these malcontents. Larry tried his best to have the crew chief explain what was being done, but that lean and bronzed individual was singularly taciturn whenever he emerged from the mysterious fastnesses of his mobile darkroom.

"I hate to disoblige, Mr. Vincent," he drawled. "I sure do hate it. But a lot of oil people would give the teeth out of their jaws to know what's in these pictures. Don't mind showing you this, though, on account of even if you did understand them, just one wouldn't be of any help." He displayed a long strip of black photographic paper, on which white intersections were ruled, and on which crazy lines seemed to dance in wild confusion over the regular spacing. "But you can tell your people to rest easy from here out," he added. "We're moving back toward the swamps tomorrow, to make another set of shots around that gravel land —the Boisblanc part, I think is the name."

The Boisblanc part! The tract that had seemed so worthless to Valois Dupré that he had sold it back to Clyde Batchelor for one dollar! But that was also the tract where, from time immemorial, the plantation Negroes had claimed there was buried treasure—where Cary Page and, later, her son Larry had dug for it, because they listened to these legends and believed them. That was where Frank Waddill's crew was going to dig for treasure now—not pirate gold, to be sure, but black gold, deposited millions of years before by the death and decay of billions upon billions of billions of minute creatures of the sea, each so small as to be invisible, yet in the aggregate so rich as to make Ali Baba's cave look like a refuse heap. But treasure just the same.

When Larry went out to the Boisblanc tract very early the next morning, the exploratory shooting had already begun. After that, every night, messengers carried sheaves of photographic records to the express office where, under heavy seal, they were dispatched to Tulsa. There, figures and other data were entered from these records upon a master chart, which claimed more and more attention from a growing number of department heads and executives as it neared completion. When Frank returned to Cindy Lou, he brought with him a thick roll of maps and a brief case bulging with blue-backed legal documents. This time, there was none of the jovial back-pounding and affectionate obscenity of their former reunion. Spreading his papers over the desk, Waddill came directly to the point.

"I'm not taking you around Robin Hood's barn," he said. "We've found a structure all right; that is to say, the geology sharps and the fossil boys and all the rest of our scientists back in the home office have come to the conclusion there's a dome somewhere under your Boisblanc acreage. Might be oil there, might not be; but it looks promising as all hell, and our geologists are excited no end. They say if it proves up, the whole industry will have to revise its concept of oil exploration and, for a starter, forget that business about no pools east of the Mississippi. Anyway, I'm ready to offer you not a dollar and a half, but two whole round iron dollars an acre to lease every inch of your land for oil drilling."

Larry started to speak, but Frank waved him off.

"Let me finish before you say anything. That's our top offer. The only reason I made it right away is for old time's sake. Naturally, I was instructed to start by offering you a dollar, even when I told the boss I had already casually mentioned a dollar and a half. And incidentally, I'm not driving such a hard bargain. Two bucks an acre makes a nice, cozy sixteen grand for a guy I knew when he was pulling down thirty plasters a month."

This time when he stopped, Larry waited before asking, "Okay if I speak my little piece now, big shot?"

Waddill looked at him with a hint of uneasiness in his glance. "Shoot," he directed. "But where's the bunting and red carpet? I figured you'd greet me with at least that much when I dumped half the mint in your lap, or anyways offered to. What's itching you?"

"Nothing. Only you'd better sit down and hang onto something before I let you in on what I got figured out. I don't want you passing out in the middle of the floor."

"I already told you I'd made you our top offer right off. Remember?"

"Surest thing you know. And instead of two dollars an acre, I want you to go back down to a dollar and a half."

"WHATTT!"

"You heard me. You aren't all that sunburned. A dollar and a half is the figure—*provided*. . . ."

"Provided what?"

"Provided you also put into the contract that if you find oil the C. & L. Navigation Company, which is Louise and I, gets to transport it."

Waddill looked doubtful.

"That's out of my line," he said, hesitantly. "I'm in exploration and drilling. The transportation department. . . ."

"Don't give me that applesauce, Frank!" Larry chuckled. "Sure, there's a transportation department. But here's the deal. If you hit oil, you'll have to put a pipe line to either the Valley or the Edenborn, or the I. C., and they'll have to build a loading spur for you. The most cars you can get on there at a time is eight—and think of all the time you'll lose loading your oil in tank car lots. Whereas you can build a pipe line straight across my land, on high ground—I'll give you the right of way for a canceled two-cent stamp paid in advance—to the river, where you can run it into my barges in a fiftieth of the time and at a fiftieth of the cost, and I can move it, either to tidewater in New Orleans or to any riverside refinery you want. You folks have one of those refineries in West Virginia, haven't you? See what I mean?"

"Yes, of course. That's how Standard does it with the Chotins, from Baton Rouge, only they ship refinery products like Diesel oil and gasoline."

"'But they haven't got an oil well right alongside the river."

"No, and for that matter neither have we—though it looks good. Tell you what I'll do. Hold the offer open while I drive to Lutcher and make a phone call to Tulsa. Better yet, hold it open until tomorrow, in case it takes me longer than it should to get a call through. Incidentally, can you lay your hands on the equipment if they want to make the deal?"

"I already have a Diesel-powered, all-steel towboat, the *Clyde Batchelor*. She's under charter to the Vicksburg and Bayou Sara people, but the charter can be canceled, by either side, on thirty days' notice. The barges—and I'd need three of those. . . ."

"How come you know all that—and the time-cost differential between barge and rail shipments so pat, anyway?"

"I learned it all from my grandfather, who knew more about the river than I'll ever find out." Larry paused. For the first time, the awareness of Clyde brought with it no grief. It was poignant still; but this was the poignancy of triumph, the exaltation of long-delayed fulfillment. As clearly as though they had been spoken only the day before, his grandfather's words came ringing out to him: "There's one commodity—oil, that is—where the railroads, damn them, can never compete with the river. A tow of three barges, say, could carry as much oil

542

as seven trains of sixty tank cars each, and think of the time to be saved in loading those barges! Only three couplings to make. One man could do the whole thing in twelve hours. On those seven trains more than four hundred couplings would have to be made and unmade, and you couldn't load more than a dozen cars at a time on any single spur, anyway. So it would take a week just to fill the tank cars and another week to empty them when they got to their destination. Yes, indeed! *Oil!* That's the thing to bring the river back to its glory! . . ."

"I wish he could know what's cooking here, today," Larry said to himself. "Well—perhaps he does." Larry looked across the desk at Frank. "About those barges," he said steadily. "I can get the mint to finance me on buying them if I have a contract with you and a producing oil well in my back yard. There's a friend of mine, incidentally, a salty old steamboat captain named Bourgeois, you'll want to meet one of these days. He's in command of the *Clyde Batchelor* now. My grandfather trained him . . . but never mind about that. Sure. Go make your phone call. I think we both know what the answer's going to be."

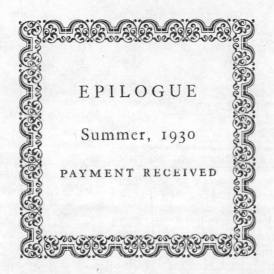

EPILOGUE

Summer, 1930

PAYMENT RECEIVED

Everything connected with the preparations for dedicating the Clyde Batchelor Community Center seemed propitious.

In the first place, the Big House at Cindy Lou lent itself far more easily than had been expected to adaptation for the purposes planned. On the ground floor, the gaming room and Clyde's office remained unchanged. The gaming room, it was agreed, should be used exactly as it had been throughout Cary Page's girlhood, for almost any sort of recreational purpose; if more persons wished to play cards, dominoes, checkers or chess than could be readily accommodated at one time, it was understood that they might set up folding tables in the adjoining office. Larry's schoolroom underwent only such minor alterations as would make it suitable for night classes in handicrafts, bookkeeping and English composition, with special emphasis on letter writing. These would be open to anyone who wished to take advantage of such instruction, not only at the terminal, the oil field and on the plantations, but in the general locality. The office which Louise had helped Larry equip was kept almost exactly as they had arranged it on his return from war and as he had used it in his capacity of terminal superintendent. The head stenographer, who also acted as his private secretary, was installed in the next room; and this still left plenty of space for the other clerical employees, after providing offices for the harbor master and the engineer. The huge antiquated bathroom had been divided into separate washrooms, complete with showers, for men and women. The old racks in the wine closet were not removed; but coolers for Coca-Cola and cigarette and candy vending machines were set up beside them and supplemented by general utility cupboards, a porcelain sink and a small gas range, where coffee could be dripped continuously. It was easy to visualize the adjoining room, where business visitors had formerly been given their meals, as an attractive setting for self-service snacks.

The main floor had required even less adjustment for the needs it was now intended to meet. True, the books which had originally belonged to Alexander Peyton, and other volumes of special significance and value had been removed to Victoria; so had the more precious silverware, porcelain and ornaments. But to the casual observer, the dining room and the drawing room looked much as they had in their best days. However, a trained librarian had been installed, subscriptions entered to leading magazines and newspapers and numerous weighty books of reference purchased; nor had the wider appeal of light reading gone unconsidered; books of fiction could be borrowed, or they could be read on the premises. In the drawing room and dining room, meetings could be held or parties given after reasonable notice to the capable manageress, who was another recent addition. She and the librarian were friends and were already sharing the chamber with the convent beds. It was understood that Bushrod's old room and Cary's old room were generally to be used for such guests as wished to "rest their wraps," but that occasionally some especially favored visitor might spend the night there. Nothing had been said, as yet, about Clyde's old room; but it was also understood that, for the time being, it would continue to remain closed. The ballroom was to be used again for small dances, though large ones would continue to be held, as such functions had been for some time now, in the pavilion at the real estate development known as Batchelor's Village.

It was astonishing how rapidly this had come into being. The Old Hickory Petroleum Company had hastily run up a few temporary buildings, near the Boisblanc tract, to shelter the first few men they sent to Cindy Lou. Then, as soon as it became evident that an oil field of considerable extent—and not merely an isolated pool—had been tapped, the personnel was enlarged to include a field superintendent, a drilling superintendent, an engineer and assistant engineer, a driller and assistant driller and a crew of twenty-four "roughnecks," who worked in two twelve-hour shifts. Very shortly thereafter, the advisability of further expansion was indicated; and more or less simultaneously, Larry found that the dock, pipe line and railroad spur of which his terminal had originally consisted now needed a machine shop, a general power plant and a tank farm; also that a correspondingly increased number of employees was required for effective operation. At this point, he was approached by a realty corporation, first with tentative suggestions and then with definite plans for a settlement where executives and employees of both the field and the terminal could be permanently domiciled: individual houses for the married men, a large boardinghouse for the bachelors, some kind of a commissary. Possibly the lane which had once divided Cindy Lou from Victoria might be made into a good road, leading to such a development, the realtor said persuasively; and there could not be a better location for the development itself than one close to that old Indian mound. . . .

Larry consulted Louise and neither was hard to convince that such a settlement would prove a great advantage to all concerned. So presently, the place was swarming with carpenters, masons, plumbers and painters; and little by little, the neat bungalows with their well-tended lawns; the big, bare-looking boardinghouse which was so surprisingly comfortable inside; and the commissary, which provided everything from needles to lawn mowers, were supplemented by other buildings to meet the requirements of a community which numbered nearly five hundred persons: a small school and a small bank; a doctor's office, where a young physician began a promising practice; a newspaper office, where an elderly reporter, tired of taking orders, became his own boss; even a beauty parlor, where an operator who had never found success in a competitive city environment discovered it in this receptive rural atmosphere. The beauty parlor opened its doors at about the same time the dance pavilion was finished and, from the first, its business was brisk. As to the pavilion itself, that was also well patronized; and the older men, some of whom had daughters of marriageable age, were not displeased to see that the bachelors were less prone to wander off on Saturday nights to distant dances, where they frequently met girls who caught their fancy, than before this attraction was so accessible. Weddings occurred more and more often and a new crop of babies came along in their wake. The young doctor began to talk about an office nurse, the schoolteacher said she needed an assistant and the elderly reporter who had turned editor said he would have to get himself a leg man. As to the beautician, she married, became a mother and advertised in the paper for a helper!

Gradually, the incredulous amazement with which Larry and Louise at first viewed the sudden improvement in their fortunes changed to a sense of security, and with this came also an increasing awareness of responsibility. Larry had been brought up in the tradition of a planter's accountability to his "people" and Louise had received somewhat the same training in respect to the peasants at Monteregard; but the present situation was different. There was no question, here and now, of dealing with individuals or groups who were ignorant or dependent; not a few of the men at both the oil field and the terminal were college graduates or had gone to good technical schools; their wives, in some cases, had benefited by similar educational advantages. But there were many instances where the persons were city bred, to whom life in the country was admittedly monotonous. Several who had come from cooler climates suffered in the torrid summers to the point of actual disability, and several others found the change from the surroundings to which they had been accustomed a real deprivation. Louise knew there was nothing she could do, she told Larry regretfully, for the man from Montana whose prickly heat had become a real problem, for the boy from the Bronx who did not "feel natural" where there were no sidewalks, or for the woman from Colorado who was pining for her mountains. But she could not get away from the conviction that there should be some way in which she could help the girl from New Hampshire who had assumed that of course there would be a local library, because she had never heard of a village without one. . . .

"I told her she was welcome to come here whenever she wanted to," Louise went on, glancing toward the well-filled shelves behind her chair. Like Lucy, she preferred the library to any room in the house, and she and Larry frequently sat there now, after supper. "But this girl —Myra Dale, her name is—said no, she'd always be afraid of intruding. It wouldn't be like going to a public library; and anyway, she couldn't get any satisfaction out of a book that she couldn't read at her leisure— especially at night, after she'd gone to bed. I told her she was welcome to borrow our books and she said no again—she wouldn't like the responsibility of doing that, even if we were willing she should. She was brought up on the theory that one book should never be taken away from the place where an entire set is kept, because if anything happened to that one book, then the whole set was spoiled."

"We've got plenty of books that aren't in sets. We could lend her those."

"Ye-e-s. But I see what she means. She wants to feel free to go into a little library and browse around for a while. Next she wants to leaf through several books whose looks she likes, and finally she wants to take one home with her. She doesn't earn enough to buy all the books she wants and she's hungry for them. There are some people to whom books come next to bread. She's one of them."

"Is she terribly plain?"

"No, she's quite pretty—in an earnest sort of way, if you know what I mean."

"Yes, I know what you mean. Well, there's a young engineer, graduate of Massachusetts Tech, who's just come on the field, and I think we'd better ask him and this girl—what did you say her name was?— to supper some night. I hear he's homesick, too. It's the food he can't take, of all things—probably hungry for baked beans! I have a hunch they'd like each other. Then maybe she'd forget about being hungry for books."

"No, she wouldn't, not even if they fell in love. She'd want him to read aloud to her while she knitted, after they finished supper."

Larry did not answer immediately. He was thinking how Clyde had told him about reading aloud to Lucy, evenings after supper; how after she died, Clyde's book and her workbasket had been found in this very room, just as they had been left the last time. Probably Louise was right —she usually was. . . . And now all this talk about reading aloud likewise brought back the times his grandfather had read aloud to *him,* out of Grimm's *Fairy Tales,* also in this very room—not because he especially enjoyed doing it, but because he believed that was the right thing to do, after supper, when you had a wife or a child to consider. Hang it all, Larry said to himself, wasn't the time ever going to come when he stopped thinking of this house in terms of his grandfather, and started thinking about it in terms of Louise and himself?

"You can't dry-nurse every discontented New Englander who comes to Louisiana, you know, honey," he said at last. "After all, they don't have to come."

"No, but their work brought them here—work that was important to them and that's important to us. I don't know about this young engineer, but the girl is doing a fine job as Dr. Taylor's office nurse. It would be a real loss, if she left."

"You don't think she's going to leave a good job just because there's no public library in the settlement, do you?"

"No, not right away. I think she'd be very conscientious about staying as long as she'd agreed to. But I think she might leave, after that. And meanwhile, I don't think she'll be altogether happy in her work. Which means she might not do it as well as if she were."

"Louise, we can't operate this big outfit just so one girl from New Hampshire will be happy. We're running it as well as we know how and there isn't a plant anywhere around that's doing as much as we are for our employees. Can't we let it go at that?"

"I don't think we should. I realize we're running it as well as we know how, but I think we ought to make an effort to find ways of running it better and better all the time."

"All right. When you think of some of those ways, tell me about them. But not tonight, if you don't mind. I've had a pretty rugged day; we've added another pipe line to the tank farm, and you know those aren't just clipped out of cardboard with scissors."

"Of course I don't mind, of course I know, and I'm sorry you're so tired. What would you like to talk about—or would you rather not talk about anything at all?"

"That's it exactly."

Of course it would have been ridiculous to suggest that the idea for the Clyde Batchelor Community Center was conceived during the course of this conversation and Louise never did suggest it. But a few evenings later she broached another subject, of infinitely more interest to Larry than Myra Dale's book hunger; and since he failed to see the slightest connection between the two, Louise did not call his attention to that, either.

"This looks like a big house, doesn't it?" she remarked, apropos of nothing in particular. "I've never quite recovered from the surprise of discovering that actually there's so little space in it."

"What do you mean, so little space?"

"I should have said, so few family bedrooms. We do need one guest chamber, at least. That's why we've still got both little girls in one room. Sometimes I think they'd be better apart."

"You're not going to suggest next that you and I would be better apart, are you?" Larry asked, grinning.

"No. Not for a minute. But I am going to suggest that as long as we stay together, we'd better face the fact that sooner or later we're going to need more space for our family."

"Well, when we do, we'll have to manage it, I suppose."

He had never told her that he did not want to use Clyde's room, but though she had never proposed doing so, he had always thought that she understood how he felt about it and had deeply appreciated her forbearance. It was quite true that they needed at least one guest room —as a matter of fact, they often needed two. And he knew that the little girls frequently disturbed each other; they were just far enough apart, in age, so that their needs and their habits were not the same; and since Tudie still slept between them, they were crowded besides. Just the same, he hoped Louise was not going to say now that this arrangement simply would not work any longer. Instead, she said something quite different.

"Then maybe we'd better begin to plan about management. Because I think that in six or seven months—"

He leaped up and pulled her to her feet. "You're sure? You're not just kidding?" he exclaimed joyously.

"Of course I'm not just kidding. I suppose it's too soon to be *really* sure. But I'm as sure as I can be at this stage. And I've been wondering —just wondering, of course—what you'd think of moving over to Victoria. Because all kinds of rooms are going to waste there, and perhaps, until the children are older—and if we keep on having them—besides, it's such a *beautiful* house!"

Move to Victoria! The idea had never crossed his mind. And what a fool, what a consummate fool he was, that it hadn't! There *were* all kinds of rooms going to waste at Victoria. Enough for as many guests and as many children as they would ever have. And it *was* a beautiful house! Suddenly he realized that the classic simplicity of its chaste columns and wide wings must be far more appealing to Louise than the manifold embellishment of Cindy Lou, that it must always have been, though she had never said so, for fear of hurting his feelings. But he remembered now that once he had seen her looking at the cast-iron fountain of the little girl with the umbrella, and he realized she had done so in a rather strange way. If anyone had asked him, he would have been obliged to admit that he did not especially admire that statue himself—that or much of the other garniture about the place. He knew, he must have known for a long time, even if he had not admitted it to himself, that the architectural pattern of Cindy Lou was not ageless and enduring, like that of Victoria; it was the transient expression of a period which did not recognize the loveliness of the unadorned, but delighted in the intricate and the ornate. Now that its flamboyancy was faded, it lacked the resplendence which had once given it glory; and since the floating palaces had ceased to glide up and down the great river, the Steamboat Gothic style inspired by them had lost its meaning, except as a memorial to the men who belonged to their era and who had contributed to its greatness. *Except as a memorial to the men who belonged to their era and who had contributed to its greatness! Men like Clyde Batchelor!* And, as these thoughts flashed through his mind, another suddenly struck him: *there would be no memories to haunt him at Victoria!* And there would be no feeling that it really belonged to someone else. It was his own house, his and his wife's, and their children's, not Clyde Batchelor's. . . .

"Darling, I think your idea is the best ever!" he said, putting his arm around her. "And, if we moved to Victoria, Cindy Lou would become—"

"Why, it would become the Clyde Batchelor Community Center, of course!" Louise answered promptly.

"Of course it would!" Larry echoed, in a tone of triumph.

And neither of them, at that moment, gave a passing thought to Myra Dale.

They did not think, either, of Michael Cobb and Daniel Keefe, two of the older engineers, who had been yearning for a quiet place where they could play interminable games of chess; or of Betty Ellsworth, one of the younger stenographers, who had formerly been a teacher in an Arthur Murray Dancing Studio, and who had been urged to start some classes of her own, with special attention to a certain group of little girls, primarily interested. Larry and Louise knew nothing of these hitherto unsatisfied yearnings, so naturally they could not consider them at the time of that significant conversation. But Cobb and Keefe and Betty all came to them, spontaneously, as soon as the plans for the Clyde Batchelor Community Center were announced, to express their gratitude and pleasure—Cobb and Keefe rather diffidently, almost apologetically, and Betty with great exuberance. Mrs. Lapham, the wife of the oil field superintendent, also came, to say how much the ladies who did Red Cross work were looking forward to using the new center for this purpose; and Mrs. Phippen, the harbor master's wife, arrived to inquire about the feasibility of holding Eastern Star meetings there. She had been afraid that Mrs. Mattina, whose husband had charge of the machine shop, and who was herself an officer in the Catholic Daughters of America, might raise some objections; but she had consulted Mrs. Mattina, who had been lovely about it, who had even gone so far as to say that turnabout was fair play. So, if Mr. and Mrs. Vincent had no objection. . . .

Mr. and Mrs. Vincent had not the slightest objection. To be sure, they were somewhat preoccupied with their own affairs, in those days, and therefore did not give undivided attention to the plans other persons were making. Even so, they were taking such general satisfaction in the turn of events that it is doubtful whether they would have raised any objections in any case. The transfer to Victoria of their personal belongings and the other possessions which they wished to retain progressed in a gradual and surprisingly effortless fashion; and the installation of the family there was also a comparatively painless process, though Louise remarked once, in passing, she had always been told that next to having a baby, the experience of moving was traditionally the most trying which a woman could be called upon to undergo! Victoria soon regained the inhabited atmosphere which had so long been lacking: the front door stood open, the sunlight poured in through the windows, busy footsteps and alert voices sounded through the hallways. The library and the gun room, which led out of each other, both seemed to gain in virility of character because of this proximity; the formality of the drawing room was tempered by the coziness of the morning room. Lucy was old enough to take great pride in the fact that she now had a room of her own, and Amy could talk well enough to echo her sister's expressions of pleasure. Larry did not voice his enjoyment of a dressing room, almost as masculine in character as the gun room; but Louise did not fail to note how readily he fell into the habit of using it; and he needed no prompting from her to admire the new nursery. Now that the household staffs in the two places were combined, there was not overmuch work for anyone, especially with the labor-saving devices unheard of only a short time before; and the servants, like their master and their mistress, were pleased over the change and excited over the prospect of the new baby.

After the baby came, Louise said laughingly she had always known there was not much truth in that old saying about trying experiences: she had really enjoyed the moving; and as to the feat of bringing Clyde Batchelor Vincent into the world, that had been done so quickly and easily that everything was all over before Dr. Mitchell and his starchy nurse had time to clutter up the scene—and meanwhile, Tudie had achieved new stature as a midwife. Larry accused Louise of having tampered with the calendar, so that there would be no question of rushing her off to Touro this time; and though she did not deny the accusation, neither was he able to speak with much severity, since it was true that both his wife and his son were pronounced, by the tardy doctor, to be in excellent condition. Besides, Larry suspected that if some tampering had been done, it was because Louise knew it would mean a great deal to him, from the viewpoint of sentiment, to have his heir born at Victoria; under those circumstances, how could he do otherwise than voice, to the exclusion of all other speech, his joy and pride?

The baby was nearly four months old before Cindy Lou was ready for dedication as a community center—big enough, Louise said, to take there with them, if they could arrange in some way for his nap; and she thought he might like to be able to say, when he grew up, that he had been present on such an occasion, even though he would have to confess that he could not remember it! Having said this much, she waited, with no appearance of impatience or aggression, for Larry to make a certain suggestion. He did not disappoint her.

"Well . . . why not put him in my grandfather's room, on the big bed? There's no danger of his being able to move around enough to fall off, is there?"

"No, not yet, if you put him in the middle. But at the rate he's developing there might be, pretty soon."

"Well," Larry said again and then hesitated. "The youth bed used to have sides, when I first slept in it," he went on. "I haven't thought about them for years—I don't even remember when they were taken off. You didn't happen to see them, did you, when you went through the store closets?"

"Of course I did. I know exactly where they are, too. Would you like to have them put back on the youth bed?"

"It wouldn't be a bad idea. We might want to take Batch over again for the day sometime—after it wasn't best to put him down in the middle of the big bed any more."

Nothing further was said on the subject. But when the day of the dedication came, and Louise and Larry and their children arrived at Cindy Lou, Larry took the baby in his arms and went straight upstairs with him. Like most men, he was rather inept at carrying babies; no matter how carefully their clothes had been smoothed down before they were handed to him, he generally had everything hunched up around their little bodies by the time he had been holding them two minutes. On this occasion, however, he kept the baby's fine lawn dress carefully in place; and when he laid Batch in the middle of the big bed, even Louise could not have done so more expertly.

"There!" he said, looking down at the baby. "There you are, son! Just the right place for you, too, if you ask me."

Nobody asked him; but Batch looked up at him, gurgling and grinning and kicking. Larry snatched at one of the small pink fists and held it fast for a moment, before he went downstairs and took his appointed place as chairman. . . .

The yard was already full of people, and he was just in time to greet the dignitaries who had come from far and wide for the occasion and who were to be seated on the gallery, at the head of the grand staircase. The chief justice of the state Charles O'Niell, a witty, pleasant-spoken man who was to make the principal address, came promptly at the appointed hour, with the congressman of the district Paul Maloney. Shortly thereafter a vice president of the Old Hickory Petroleum Company arrived, along with a member of the River Commission, the mayors of several neighboring towns, Frank Waddill and his wife, the superintendent of the oil field Captain Clovis Bourgeois, Valois Dupré, Father Le Grand, Blaise Bergeron—now chairman of the Levee Board— and Henri Laburre, who had realized his ambition of becoming a motor magnate.

The orchestra, organized at the time the pavilion was built and now stationed under the grand staircase, had played several lively airs by the time all these personages were assembled; from the rear of the yard, savory smells were already wafting—gumbo and barbecue were to be served as soon as the exercises were over and preparations for these were well under way. The crowd now filled the grounds to overflowing; there was no reason to delay the proceedings any longer.

Larry rose and, after calling for order, asked Father Le Grand to pronounce the invocation. There was a flutter of hands as most of those in the gathering crossed themselves, then a general lifting of heads as the prayer came to a close.

"You all know why we are gathered here," Larry began rather diffidently. "And those of you who know me—and that's most of you—know well and good that I'm no speaker. I'm proud to be here and prouder still to be chairman. But you realize, and so do I, that I'm acting in that capacity, not because I'm good at this kind of a job, but because I'm Clyde Batchelor's grandson. He isn't here with us in the flesh. But what he stood for, what he meant in this community, is everywhere you'd care to look."

It was true that Larry was not an easy or natural speaker. He knew what it was in his heart to say, but he still felt doubtful as how best to say it. He glanced toward Louise, who was seated in the chair next to his, with Lucy standing on one side of her and Amy on the other, and she looked quickly back at him with a reassuring smile. In her face he read complete confidence that he would do justice to his grandfather's memory, and through long and joyful experience, he had learned that the candor of her countenance reflected the candor of her thoughts. Therefore no shadow of suspicion crossed his mind that he was not reading these correctly, too. Mercifully, he did not know that Louise was saying to herself at that moment: *He's never guessed, I must never let him guess that I lied to him. Just once. But it was a terrible lie. I told him I burnt that diary because I felt no one had a right to read it. That was true enough. But I didn't tell him I'd read part of it before I burnt it—enough so that I knew I mustn't read any more, that no one must ever have a chance to read any of it.*

"One of the first things I can remember having my grandfather tell me," Larry went on, greatly encouraged by the look in Louise's face, "was the story of the hidden treasure, and of how my mother used to dig for it. Lots of people besides her believed the treasure was there, but they believed it was gold, pirate gold, just as she did. Then when oil was brought in, those same people said that must be the treasure, for true—black gold instead of pirate gold, but treasure just the same. I said so myself. Now I know better. I know that the real treasure of Cindy Lou is the memory of what my grandfather said and did in the fifty years and more that he lived here."

In the fifty years and more that he lived here! Yes, it was before he lived at Cindy Lou that he had been a gambler, true enough, Louise was thinking; and the knowledge of his devious way of life had not come as too much of a shock to his bride. Lucy had known from the beginning that there was something he was hiding from her, something of which he was ashamed. He had told her, when he first asked her to marry him, that she had a right to know about his past life, and she had said there would be time enough for that, if and when she definitely accepted his proposal. Later she had sensed his fear that though their marriage would survive his confession, because marriage to her was an irrevocable sacrament, her love for him would not; and though she could have stilled that fear, this would have meant that she must, necessarily, be the first to speak of the possible causes for it. It was not until she and Clyde had been married more than twenty-five years that, in a moment of desperation, he had poured out his heart to her. A brief notation in her diary, dated April 10, 1896, had told Louise this: "Today my dear, dear husband, of his own accord, told me that he had been a gambler, and I am thankful that he will no longer bear the burden of silence which has lain so heavily upon him all these years." The notation was written in the form of a post-script to a much longer entry, penned years before on the *Richmond*: "I felt sure, from the moment of our meeting with Mr. Pettigrew, who called himself Major Fanchon, that the secret of my dear husband's past life had been disclosed. Now the gossip which I have overheard in the observatory, when I have gone there to drink afternoon choco-late—gossip hushed as soon as the scandalmongers noticed my presence —has confirmed my belief. But I shall never let Clyde know that I have learned the truth. Why should I sadden him when he is so happy? And why should I give even a passing thought to what he was in the past, when he is no longer the same man? Truly, he must have been born again, as the Bible tells us we may be; for I am sure that in all the world there is not another being so upright, so wise and so kind."

I should have burned the diary when I read that far, Louise said to herself, as Larry went on with greater and greater assurance and ease. *I'm not sorry I burned it, I'm not even sorry I lied to Larry and told him I burned it without reading it. It is a terrible thing for a woman to lie to her husband, even once. Just the same, I believe I did right in lying, that time. I didn't do right in reading the diary though, in reading any of it. . . .*

"As I've said, I'm no speaker," Larry was telling his attentive audi-ence. "But we have someone with us today who is one of the greatest orators in the state. He can do justice to the memory of my grand-father, even if I can't, so I'm going to let him carry on from here. He doesn't need any introduction. Lots of you know him as Uncle Charlie. All of you claim him as your neighbor Charles O'Niell, of St. Mary Parish. But since we want to show how proud we are to have him here with us today, I'm going to present him by his full title—Chief Justice of the Supreme Court of Louisiana."

Genial laughter mingled with the hand clapping which greeted the Chief Justice's approach to the railing between the two wings of the grand staircase. His figure was slight, but wiry, and he carried off the impediment in his gait without self-consciousness. The people who watched him were not conscious of it, either. Instead, they were noticing, with admiration and affection, that his snowy hair was as abundant as ever, that his keen blue eyes seemed to twinkle more and more blithely with advancing years and that there was something actually impish in his grin.

"Mr. Chairman, distinguished guests, ladies and gentlemen," he began formally. Then the grin became wider. "Ah, let's cut all that sort of thing short. Let me just say, 'Friends,' and then get right on to the rest. Because that's how I think of the people in a gathering like this, anywhere in the state of Louisiana, but especially in that part of the state where Clyde Batchelor left such a lasting mark. Yes, I'm from St. Mary Parish, and it was just a few miles from my home that Clyde Batchelor launched what proved to be the revival of the Mississippi River's golden age. It was in St. Mary that he raised an old towboat from the bottom of Lake Verret and negotiated his first barge line charter and built the first new towboat for his new company. Did I hear your chairman say something about being proud? Let me tell every one of you within sound of my voice that the proudest man here today isn't anyone who's listening to me. It's the man who's talking to you. As your Uncle Charlie, as your neighbor Charles O'Niell, as the Chief Justice of your state and mine, I'm proud and honored that I've been chosen to dedicate this great memorial to a man like Clyde Batchelor."

A man like Clyde Batchelor! A man who had come to Louisiana to buy the house of his dreams for his betrothed bride, and who had fallen a willing victim there to the wiles of an adventuress! That shameful episode could not be excused on the ground that it was part of the life he had led before he was "born again"; he not only knew and loved Lucy, when it had occurred; he had already sworn to himself and to her that from thenceforth her standards should be his, and that his love for her and his loyalty to her were so intermingled as to be inseparable. The very fact that he had fervently hoped and prayed she might never learn of his unfaithfulness was proof positive that he himself did not look on it in the same light as the errant ways of his youth; unquestionably, he had thanked God, over and over again, that this sad secret he had succeeded in keeping. But he had done so mistakenly. Another entry in the diary made this all too clear: Among the women who had taken chocolate every afternoon in the observatory of the *Richmond* had been a dressmaker, returning from New York with the latest models. Before hearing Lucy's name aright, this woman had complimented her on her beautiful clothes. They had come from Sophia

Diedens, Lucy told her, with pardonable pride. Ah, yes, the dressmaker said, she should have known. She did not usually deal with so expensive an establishment; but she had once bought a complete outfit from it for an actress who was the toast of her day in New Orleans. The outfit had never been worn on the stage because the actress had died suddenly just as the play was about to open. But it had been bought in its entirety by a certain Mme Labouisse, who had just sold her plantation to some wealthy stranger, for an enormous sum. And the dressmaker would never forget how Mme Labouisse had insisted that the most striking dress of all—a crimson satin, made with the new tie-back skirt —should be an inch and a half smaller around the waist and an inch and a half lower at the neckline. . . .

"And I knew she was up to no good when she made that demand," the dressmaker had added, with a sly look. "Afterward, I heard—one does hear such things, you know, madame—that this scheming woman had worn it at the farewell dinner she gave at her plantation, in honor of the new proprietor. In fact, another customer of mine, a Mrs. Vincent, was present on that occasion."

There was more to the entry, enough to show Louise how fully Lucy had understood how and when and why the crimson satin dress had been worn, and where the money had come from with which to buy it. And this time there was no mitigating postscript added many years later. The entry stood in all its starkness, just as Lucy had written it on her honeymoon. . . .

With an effort, Louise wrested her thoughts from the disclosures of the diary and focused them on the eulogy of the day. The Chief Justice was tracing the eclipse of steamboat prosperity, the darkling days of Reconstruction, the rise of the New South. . . . Then she realized that he was talking about her, that he was referring to her first as a worthy successor of the great ladies from Old France who had come to New France during the early days of the colony; then as the mother of a second Clyde Batchelor, who was to carry on the great tradition of the first.

The Chief Justice held out his hand to her and she rose, acknowledging the spontaneous applause which included them both. Again she saw that Larry's eyes were resting on her with confidence and love, and this time there were no hidden reservations in the candor with which she returned his look. Suddenly she knew that everything which had been said about Clyde Batchelor was true, after all, that he had indeed been a great man, for the handicaps he had overcome would have defeated one who was not truly great. Even his disloyalty to Lucy was revealed in a new light: Clyde's bitter memory of his one transgression against her had been a constant incentive to atonement, and his reparation had been perfect and complete. Lucy herself had understood this, and compassion for her husband had, from the beginning, been mingled with her adoration of him. As Louise looked from Larry to the Chief Justice, and then out at the throng before her, she understood it, too; she was filled with pride that her son, who bore Clyde Batchelor's name, was to carry on his tradition.

The departure of the barge tow had been delayed in order that Captain Bourgeois and his crew might share in the dedicatory ceremonies. Now men swarmed like ants over the steel deck plates, tightening or releasing cables and hawsers and uncoupling huge flexible hoses. Finally the last cable was set free, the air whistle blared and the heavy Diesel engine of the *Clyde Batchelor* took up the rhythmic drumming they would maintain without pause or interruption until the tow docked at Louisville.

Larry Vincent stood on the gallery of the Community Center, with his son in his arms and his wife and daughters beside him, watching the vessels as they passed upstream. Just beyond the barges, purple in the gathering dusk, he could see the island where once a floating palace rode at anchor. Yes, it was gone forever; but if it had not once proudly floated over the Mississippi, the barges would not be plowing through the river now. The old order had changed, yielding place to new. But it had not died of desuetude. After a period of dormancy it had roused itself and revealed greater vitality than ever, just as a field which has lain fallow teems with fresh fecundity.

Holding the baby securely in one arm, Larry slid the other over his wife's shoulder and drew her closer to him. She still had both little girls by the hand. But once again she returned his loving look, and this time the glance had in it the quality of a caress, bringing her closer still. As he looked down at her, in the fading light, it seemed to him that he and she and their children were all welded together into a single unit, and that though this unit, too, might change with time, it would remain essentially indivisible and imperishable. A deep contentment filled his being, a sense of fulfillment and completeness such as he had never known before. But he was tired. Everything that needed doing had now been done. He wanted to rest.

"Dearest, isn't it time we went home?" he asked Louise.

LOUISIANA

Louisiana, a Guide to the State. Sponsored by Louisiana Library Commission at Baton Rouge. New York: Hastings House, 1941.
My Diary North and South (2 vols.), William Howard Russell. London: Bradbury and Evans, 1863.
Catalogue of Jefferson College, 1904–1905.
Catalogue of Jefferson College, 1918–1919.

STEAMBOATS (GENERAL)

American Paddle Steamboats. Carl D. Lane. New York: Coward-McCann, Inc., 1943.
Steamboatin' Days. Mary Wheeler. Baton Rouge: Louisiana State University Press, 1944.
Steamboats on the Western Rivers. Louise C. Hunter. Cambridge: Harvard University Press, 1949.
The Pageant of the Packets. Garnett Laidlaw Eskew. New York: Henry Holt and Company, 1929.
Mississippi Steamboatin'. Herbert Quick and Edward Quick. New York: Henry Holt and Company, 1926.
Way's Directory of Western Rivers Packets (1950 ed.). Frederick Way, Jr., compiler. Sewickley, Pa.: Privately printed, 1950.
The Saga of the Delta Queen. Frederick Way, Jr. Cincinnati: Picture Marine Publishing Company, 1951.
Pilotin' Comes Natural. Frederick Way, Jr. New York: Farrar and Rinehart, Inc., 1943.
Mississippi Stern-Wheelers. Frederick Way, Jr., compiler. Milwaukee: Kalmbach Publishing Company, 1947.
The Keelboat Age on Western Waters. Leland D. Baldwin. Pittsburgh: University of Pittsburgh Press, 1941.
Paddle Wheels and Pistols. Irvin Anthony. Philadelphia: Macrae Smith Company, 1929.
The Voyage of Captain Bart. John Erskine. Philadelphia: J. B. Lippincott Company, 1943.
Towboat River. Edwin and Louise Rosskam. New York. Duell, Sloan and Pearce, 1948.
The Mississippi Valley Historical Review (Vol. VI, No. 4, March, 1920). The Mississippi Valley Historical Association.
Shantymen and Shantyboys. William Main Doerflinger, compiler. New York: The Macmillan Company, 1951.
Fifty Years on the Mississippi, or, *Gould's History of River Navigation.* E. W. Gould. Columbus, O.: Long's College Book Company, 1951.
Old Man River. Robert A. Hereford. Caldwell, Idaho: The Caxton Printers, Ltd., 1942.
Master of the Mississippi. Florence L. Dorsey. Boston: Houghton Mifflin Company, 1941.
Road to the Sea. Florence L. Dorsey. New York: Rinehart and Company, Inc., 1947.
Father Mississippi. Lyle Saxon. London: The Century Company, 1927.
Flowing South. Clark B. Firestone. New York: Robert M. McBride and Company, 1941.
Life on the Mississippi. Mark Twain. New York: Harper and Brothers, 1917.
Thrills of the Historic Ohio River. Frank M. Grayson. Cincinnati *Times-Star.*

STEAMBOATS (GAMBLING)

Gambling Unmasked! Jonathan H. Green. Philadelphia: G. B. Zieber and Company, 1847.
Forty Years a Gambler on the Mississippi. George H. Devol. New York: Henry Holt and Company, 1926.
Gambling and Gambling Devices. John Philip Quinn. Canton, O.: J. P. Quinn Company, 1912.

MISCELLANEOUS

"Fightin' Joe" Wheeler. John P. Dyer. Baton Rouge: Louisiana State University Press, 1941.

The Era of Good Feelings. George Dangerfield. New York: Harcourt, Brace and Company, 1952.

Ever After. Elswyth Thane. New York: Duell, Sloan and Pearce, 1945.

Pheasants, Their Lives and Homes (2 vols.). William Beebe. Garden City: Doubleday, Page and Company, 1926.

Adventures of a Ballad Hunter. John A. Lomax. New York: The Macmillan Company, 1947.

Henry J. Heinz. E. D. McCafferty. New York: B. Orr Press, 1923.

With Rifle and Plow, Stories of the Western Pennsylvania Frontier. J. Ernest Wright, Pittsburgh: Pittsburgh University Press, 1938.

FRENCH

La Belle-au-Bois-Dormant. Pierre Loti. Paris: C. Lévy, 1910.

La Roche-Courbon Beau Manoir de Saintonge. Pesmé.